# BARBARA CARTLAND

## Five Complete Novels

# BARBARA CARTLAND

## *Five Complete Novels*

### MOON OVER EDEN
### NO TIME FOR LOVE
### THE INCREDIBLE HONEYMOON
### KISS THE MOONLIGHT
### A KISS IN ROME

WINGS BOOKS

New York · Avenel, New Jersey

This 1993 edition is published by Wings Books,
distributed by Outlet Book Company, Inc., a Random House Company,
40 Engelhard Avenue, Avenel, New Jersey 07001,
by arrangement with the author.

Random House
New York • Toronto • London • Sydney • Auckland

Printed and bound in the United States of America

Library of Congress Cataloging-in-Publication Data

Cartland, Barbara, 1902–
  [Novels.  Selections]
  Five complete novels / Barbara Cartland.
    p.  cm.
  Contents: Moon over Eden—No time for love—The incredible
honeymoon—Kiss the moonlight—A kiss in Rome.
  ISBN 0-517-09299-9
  1. Man-woman relationships—Fiction.  2. Love stories, English.
I. Title.  II. Title: 5 complete novels.
PR6005.A765A6  1993
823'.912—dc20
                                                          93-763
                                                          CIP

8 7 6 5 4 3 2 1

# CONTENTS

# MOON OVER EDEN

To Earl Mountbatten of Burma, whose affection for Ceylon (Sri Lanka) and its delightful people is reciprocated by their love for him, and who first told me of the breathtaking beauty of this second Garden of Eden.

# *Author's Note*

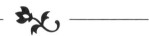

I visited Sri Lanka in 1975 and was thrilled with the exquisite, almost unbelievable beauty of the country, the charm and friendliness of its people, and I was fascinated by its history.

The background of this book is all authentic and the success of Ceylon tea after the failure of the coffee was immortalised by Sir Arthur Conan Doyle when he wrote:

"Not often is it that men have the heart, when their one great industry is withered, to rear up in a few years another as rich to take its place, and the tea fields of Ceylon are as true a monument to courage as is the lion at Waterloo."

James Taylor was not only the first man on the island to grow tea commercially but he also manufactured and sold it. His enterprise as an attempt to retrieve the tragedy of coffee which ruined thousands of people, became a sparkle of hope in Ceylon's economy. When he died his labourers called him *Sami Durai*—'the master who is god'.

In 1873 the export of tea from Ceylon was 28 lbs; a hundred years later it was 445,873,314 lbs.

# CHAPTER ONE

## 1888

Lord Hawkston drew in a deep breath of the warm, moist air.

He looked up at the starlit sky and knew how much he had missed in the cold of England, this warmth which seemed to percolate his whole body, making him feel as if every muscle had become loose and supple.

He walked slowly across the grass, conscious of the fragrance of the magnolias—the lovely moonflower—of the jasmines and the oleanders; their branches in the daytime providing a welcome shelter from the heat of the sun.

During the twenty-six days of the voyage from England he had looked forward to seeing Ceylon again almost like a small boy going home for the holidays.

It was not surprising, seeing that he had spent sixteen years of his life in what was called an 'Island Paradise', where, according to the Mohammedans, Adam and Eve had sought refuge after they were driven away from the Garden of Eden.

In England it has been easy to laugh at such descriptions

as that of the Brahmins—'Lanka, the resplendent'; or the Buddhists—'the pearl drop on the brow of India'; or the Greeks—'the land of lotus flowers'.

But back in Ceylon the mystique of the climate and the beauty of the country made Lord Hawkston feel they did not exaggerate.

Not that he was a romantic person. He was known for being ultra-reserved, a hard task-master, and ruthless when it suited him.

He had had to be because his life had not been easy! In fact he had succeeded only by fighting every inch of the way for what he wanted and by being absolutely certain of what he did want.

As he strolled further into the magnificent garden of the Queen's House, as the Governor-General's residence in Colombo was known, he thought that when he went north to his tea-plantation it would be like a Royal progress to see his friends again, his coolies, and the fine house he had built himself on the site of the small cottage which had originally been his home when he first bought the plantation.

Deep in his thoughts, it was with a sense of irritation that Lord Hawkston suddenly realised he was no longer alone in the garden.

He had waited until the Governor and his other guests had retired to their rooms before he walked out into the moonlit night, having an irresistible urge to be alone with his memories and his emotions at coming back.

Now someone else was coming across the lawn.

Instinctively, because he had no wish for conversation, Lord Hawkston stood still in the shadow of a large bamboo knowing that he was half-concealed by its feathery branches and that unless someone was deliberately seeking him out he was unlikely to be aware of his presence.

The man came nearer, and now because the moonlight was full on his face Lord Hawkston was aware that it was a young soldier who had travelled out to Ceylon with him on the same ship.

Captain Patrick O'Neill had been one of several officers returning from furlough to their military duties.

Lord Hawkston had conversed with them at meals because they were seated, as he was, at the Captain's table, but otherwise he had associated as little as possible with the younger passengers who, he felt, would think him too old to take part in their spirited chatter and incessant teasing of one another.

At the same time Patrick O'Neill, Lord Hawkston remembered, had seem a trifle more responsible than the rest and he imagined that he would in fact be an able officer in his Regiment.

Still the Captain advanced and Lord Hawkston, waiting in the shadows, thought that perhaps he was in charge of the sentries guarding the Governor and was intent at this hour of the night on seeing that they were doing their duty.

Then to his surprise, just before he reached the tree where Lord Hawkston was concealed, Captain O'Neill turned and walked across the grass directly towards the house.

Like most Colonial houses the Queen's House was extremely impressive in the front but the back rambled away into long verandahs on two floors where, in the heat of the summer months, the inhabitants slept, but which in February were unscreened and open to the night air.

It was with a sense of relief that Lord Hawkston realised he was not in danger of being discovered.

Then as he watched Captain O'Neill reach the back of the house he saw him look up at the verandah above him and heard him give a soft, low whistle.

Surprised, Lord Hawkston waited, and saw someone in white come from the bedroom and on to the verandah below which Captain O'Neill was standing.

It was a woman! Her hair was loose and it fell forward in a fair cloud as she reached the rail of the verandah and bent over it.

If she spoke Lord Hawkston could not hear what she said, but to his astonishment, Captain O'Neill, who had been standing looking up at her, started to climb up from the ground to the verandah above him.

It was not a difficult task for the supporting pillars were made of open wrought-iron work, affording an excellent foot-hold for even the most clumsy of mountaineers.

It was only a matter of seconds before the Captain flung his leg over the railing and stepped on to the verandah.

Then as Lord Hawkston watched, he saw him take the woman in his arms and they clung together in a passionate embrace.

For a moment they stood in the moonlight, embodying the eternal figure of love, their arms around each other, their lips joined, the woman's hair pale against the Captain's broad shoulder. Then they moved away and disappeared into the darkness of the bedroom behind them.

Lord Hawkston drew in his breath.

He was well aware who it was Captain O'Neill was visiting in this clandestine way and for a moment he felt not anger but sheer astonishment at the audacity of it.

For the woman whom Captain O'Neill had kissed so passionately and with whom he had vanished was the Honourable Emily Ludgrove, whom Lord Hawkston had brought out with him to Ceylon to marry his nephew, Gerald Warren!

When, eighteen years earlier, Lord Hawkston, then Chilton Hawk, had decided to go to Ceylon he had been twenty-one, and the younger son of a younger son.

There had been no prospect of his ever inheriting the family title and Estates and his father, who had very little money, could offer no inducements for a comfortable life in England.

He had however, inherited two thousand pounds when he attained his majority, and inspired by a report he had read of the success of the coffee-plantations in Ceylon, he decided to visit the country and try to make his fortune.

Ceylon in those days seemed very far away and people spoke of it in England as if it was the other end of the world.

Ten years earlier in 1860 there had been a boom in coffee after the British planters had brought with them a spirit of enterprise as well as capital to invest in the plantations.

Chilton Hawk had been at Oxford with a Scot who had gone to Ceylon three years earlier and wrote him enthusiastic letters of the opportunities which existed there for young men with energy and ambition.

On making enquiries Chilton Hawk found that in 1870, the year he came of age, Ceylon had shipped over a million cwt. of coffee.

His father was surprised at his decision to be a coffee-planter although he had expected him to travel on the legacy he had inherited from his grandmother.

"Do not commit yourself, my boy," he said. "Have a good look round first. You might do better in Singapore or India."

But the moment Chilton Hawk had reached Ceylon he realised this was where he wished to live and work.

And work he did!

He had not realised how hard it would be until he had bought 560 acres of land at £1 an acre and found he had to clear away the jungle from it.

This meant he had to employ eighty men and always there was the fear at the back of his mind that his money would run out.

He started the day with the click-clack of the axes, the crash of falling trees and the noise of saws and hammers. Then everything had to be carted away and burnt.

It was not a question of merely felling the trees but of digging out every root before the land was ready for planting.

He had the luck almost as soon as he arrived of being introduced by his Oxford friends to an experienced, thirty-five-year-old Scottish planter named James Taylor.

He was one of the planters who was to be part of the history of Ceylon, and already he had an importance which made him respected by other planters.

At the age of eighteen, James Taylor, a vigorous young giant of a man, had signed a three-year contract with the London Agents of the Loolecondera Estate which was situated some seventy miles south-east of Kandy.

The advantage of being near Kandy was that the railway to Colombo had been completed in 1867.

It afforded the planters a much more rapid form of transportation for their coffee than they could obtain with the slow bullock-carts which took weeks to move slowly down the military road to the Port.

James Taylor took a fancy to the young man who had just

come out from England and advised him to buy land near the Loolecondera Estate which was in the central mountain region.

Like Taylor, Chilton Hawk had been enchanted by the scenic beauty of the hill country, and he soon adapted himself to his strange environment.

James Taylor showed him how to obtain a labour-force of Tamil coolies and advised him where to build his first small cottage.

He encouraged him and helped him through the first years of clearing and planting when Chilton Hawk worked as hard, if not harder, than any of the men he employed.

Yet, looking back, he had often thought that that was the happiest time in his life. He was achieving something; he was his own master, and if he lost everything he possessed he had no-one to blame but himself.

And he would have lost everything if he had not been a friend of James Taylor.

For ten years the coffee boom had made Chilton Hawk believe that he was on the verge of becoming rich. Land rose to £28 an acre, cultivations extended along new roads which had been only the pilgrim paths to Adam's Peak.

Suddenly the halcyon days of coffee were numbered.

A dreaded leaf disease peculiar to coffee, known as *Hemileia Vastatrix* or 'coffee rust', threatened the whole industry.

Even now Lord Hawkston could remember the feeling of sick horror he had felt when he first saw the fungus on his own coffee-plants.

The fungus was a microscopic one, the spore of which was carried by the wind, to settle and germinate on the leaves of the plants.

It was catastrophic for every coffee-planter.

There was nothing they could do except clear an infected plantation, powder the remaining trees with a mixture of lime and sulphur and pray they would not be re-infected when the next batch of spore was brought in on the wind.

It was a hope that did not materialise.

The coffee disease wrecked the hopes of most European planters and all the Ceylonese.

There was nothing they could salvage from their ruined plantations except that some diseased coffee stumps were shipped to England to serve as legs for tea-tables.

But for Chilton Hawk his friendship with James Taylor proved a life-line.

Taylor had in 1866 been given by the Superintendent of the Royal Botanical Gardens at Peradeniya, some tea-seedlings.

Nineteen acres of Loolecondera were planted with 200 pounds of tea-seedlings and James Taylor, when he helped Chilton Hawk with his neighbouring land, persuaded him to plant the same number of acres of his precious soil with tea.

Those nineteen acres saved the estate from utter ruin.

It meant that on the rest of the plantation Chilton Hawk had to start again from scratch. He rolled up his sleeves and planted tea.

Meanwhile his friend, Taylor, was busy on a new project, a fully equipped tea-house fitted with a rolling-machine, the first even made in Ceylon.

Following the financial instability caused by the catastrophic crash of coffee, hopes rose when it became known that on Taylor's Estate and the one adjoining his, tea was proving profitable.

Disillusioned coffee-planters went along to learn how to cultivate the new crop, and all over Ceylon tea-bushes began to thrive between the stumps of dead coffee-trees. Chilton Hawk, working twenty-four hours a day, began to build up once again the fortune he had lost.

He had never in his wildest moments thought there was any chance of his inheriting the family Estates in England.

There were six lives between him and the chance of being his Uncle's heir when he had left England, but through death in battle, accident and the inescapability of old age, gradually those who preceded him were eliminated one by one.

Nevertheless in 1886 it came as an incredible shock to learn that his Uncle was dead and he was the new Lord Hawkston.

There was nothing he could do but go home, but it had been like amputating an arm or a leg to leave behind him his plantation which had now expanded to 1,200 acres, and his friends, like James Taylor.

At the same time he had grown very self-sufficient—he had to be!

Sometimes three or four weeks would pass without his seeing anybody except for his coolies.

He would sit alone in the big house he had now built for himself on the top of a hill so that it caught all the breezes during the hot weather.

It could also be cold in winter and in English fashion it had large open fireplaces where logs could be burnt.

Chilton Hawk grew used to being by himself. He liked reading but more often than not, after he had enjoyed a well-cooked and well-served meal, he went to bed, so as to rise with the dawn and return to the work which absorbed him.

He had forgotten when he returned to England what an elegant, leisurely life a gentleman could live, without pressures, without haste, and without any ambition except to fill the leisure hours with enjoyment.

He had, however, found a great deal to do on the family Estate.

His Uncle had been ill for the last years of his life and many things had been neglected. There were new farming methods to be introduced, machinery to be bought, buildings to be repaired and above all relations to meet.

While in Ceylon Chilton Hawk had been a leader and organiser of a labour force, but in England as Lord Hawkston he was now expected to be the head of a large family of relations, most of them impecunious, all of them, he thought dryly, grasping and avaricious.

His first task on returning home was to find someone who could take his place on the plantation in Ceylon.

This, he determined, would be a family possession in the future and be looked on as part of the inheritance of future owners of the title.

He thought he had found the ideal person in his nephew, Gerald Warren, the only son of his elder sister, an intelligent young man of twenty-four.

Because he was so worried about the plantation being left

with only his Ceylonese Head-man in charge, Lord Hawk-ston had sent Gerald Warren out in a precipitate manner that he would not have considered had the matter not been urgent.

He felt that Gerald, at twenty-four, should be quite ca-pable of coping with an Estate which was running smoothly and making a profit, and where there was no longer the heavy manual fundamental work to do which had been his task sixteen years earlier.

Gerald had been only too willing to acquiesce to every-thing his Uncle suggested.

Lord Hawkston was to learn later that he was not partic-ularly happy at home and had in fact fallen out with most of his other relatives.

He had however, just before he sailed, declared himself engaged to the daughter of a neighbouring nobleman, the Honourable Emily Ludgrove, but her family had dissuaded them from getting married before Gerald left.

They had for some time discouraged any talk of a be-trothal for the simple reason that Gerald had few prospects and showed no inclination to obtain any more money than the small allowance that his widowed mother was prepared to give him.

His Uncle's interest in him opened up new vistas and although the engagement was not announced it was agreed that Gerald and Emily should marry in a year's time.

"I will bring her out to Ceylon myself," Lord Hawkston had promised.

"Must we wait a year for you to do that?" Gerald asked.

"I am afraid so," his Uncle replied. "There is so much for me to do here that I think it unlikely I will get away in under twelve months."

As a matter of fact it was eighteen months before there was a chance of his leaving England and Emily seemed quite content to wait until an opportune moment presented itself.

Her family was adamant that there was no need for a hurried marriage and even after Lord Hawkston was ready to leave, small details of Emily's trousseau held them up for a further two months.

Finally they set sail from Southampton and Lord Hawkston cabled his nephew to meet them in Colombo.

He had noticed that Gerald's letters had been falling off during the past nine months.

At first he had written regularly; every fortnight a letter would arrive full of details about the plantation.

It was only lately that Lord Hawkston had begun to wonder if Gerald wrote what he thought his Uncle would like to hear rather than what was actually occurring.

Then his letters arrived once a month and finally had tailed off into quick scribbles at intervals of two, or even three months.

"The boy is busy," Lord Hawkston told himself. "I expect Emily hears from him regularly."

He saw very little of Gerald's future wife. He found her father an extremely boring man with whom he had little in common, and in any case there was too much for him to do on the Estate for him to have much time for social engagements.

In any case he found them irksome.

He had grown so used to being alone that social chit-chat and petty gossip bored him.

He was well aware that his relations not only found him difficult but were in awe of him. He did not mind that being their attitude; on the whole he preferred it.

"He is a difficult man," he had heard one of his cousins say just as he was entering the drawing-room. "I never have any idea what he is thinking and quite frankly I am not really interested to find out."

There had been the sound of laughter as the lady finished speaking but Lord Hawkston, waiting to make his entrance, had merely been amused.

On the ship he had gone out of his way to be as uncommunicative as possible.

He knew only too well that the gushing friendships of shipboard acquaintances seldom lasted once the passengers had reached dry land.

He was aware that Emily, who was chaperoned by a Colonel and his wife returning to duty in Colombo, was receiving plenty of attention from the young Army officers on board.

She was obviously amused by the dancing and charades, the fancy-dress parties and the ship's concerts which were arranged in the evenings.

He had not noticed, Lord Hawkston thought, that Captain Patrick O'Neill was more attentive to Emily than anyone else.

Now, standing in the garden of Queen's House, he blamed himself for not being more perceptive; for not having realised that the girl had lost her heart, and certainly her head, on the journey to Ceylon.

Lord Hawkston came from the shadow of the bamboo and walked across the lawn.

This was a situation he had not anticipated and he wondered what the devil he should do about it.

Of one thing he was certain. He had no intention of allowing Emily to marry his nephew.

Perhaps, he told himself, it was a good thing that Gerald had not been able to meet them in Colombo as he had expected.

The letter which had been waiting for him at Queen's House when they arrived told him that Gerald was too ill to travel, but hoped to be well enough to receive his Uncle and Emily when they arrived in Kandy.

When he had first read the letter Lord Hawkston had been annoyed.

He had already planned that Emily and Gerald should be married in Colombo immediately on his arrival.

He had thought he would send them off on a honeymoon and go up to the plantation alone.

He had looked forward to seeing what had been done, to discussing innovations with his Head-man, and greeting the coolies, some of whom had been with him since the very first day he had started to clear the jungle.

But his arrangements had been upset and he supposed the ceremony would have to take place in Kandy.

At this moment, it was almost like a blow to realise there would now be no wedding and he would have to break the news to Gerald that he must look elsewhere for a wife.

"Damn the girl!" Lord Hawkston said to himself. "Why the hell could she not behave herself?"

Even as he swore he realised that he himself was in part to blame for not having gone out to Ceylon sooner.

Eighteen months was a long time in two young people's lives! Years ago it had seemed a long time to him.

At the same time, if Emily was flighty enough to be beguiled away from Gerald by the first handsome young man who sought her favours it was better for it to happen before marriage than after.

"I will send her home on the next ship," Lord Hawkston decided.

The beauty of the night was spoilt for him and he turned and walked back to the front of the house, trying not to think of those two young people clasped in each other's arms in an upstairs bedroom.


The next morning Lord Hawkston breakfasted early. As he finished and was about to rise from the table he was told there was someone to see him.

Surprised at so early a visitor he followed the servant, resplendent in his red and white uniform, down the wide corridors to a sitting-room where to his delight he found James Taylor waiting for him.

At fifty, Taylor was a very big man with a long beard. He weighed 246 pounds and one of his fingers was as thick as three fingers of an ordinary man's put together.

When he smiled it gave his face with its deep-set eyes and long nose a strange charm.

"I heard you arrived yesterday, Chilton," he said, holding out his hand.

"James! By all that is Holy! I was hoping to see you—but not so soon! How are you? It seems a century since we last met."

"I have missed you, Chilton," James Taylor said. "I began to be afraid that you had become too grand to come back to us."

"If only you knew how much I have longed to return before now!" Lord Hawkston replied. "But I have been working almost as hard at home as I did here, only in a different way. It has not been easy."

James Taylor smiled.

"Nothing you and I have done has ever been easy, Chilton, but I expect you have managed to win through!"

"I hope so," Lord Hawkston replied.

Then he thought of Emily and his expression darkened.

"Tell me about my nephew."

"That is one of the reasons why I came here to see you," James Taylor replied.

There was something in the way he spoke which made Lord Hawkston look at him sharply.

"Has the boy settled down and done a good job?" he asked. "I want the truth."

"The whole truth?" James Taylor enquired.

"You know I would not be satisfied with anything less."

"Very well," James Taylor said. "We are old friends, Chilton, and because you and I have always been frank with each other I had to come to tell you that you will have to do something about that young man."

"What do you mean?" Lord Hawkston asked.

James Taylor hesitated for a moment before he said:

"I think, unlike you and me, he cannot adjust himself to the solitude. It is hard, as we both know, to live alone; to face long evenings with no-one to talk to, to realise one has to ride perhaps miles to find a friendly face."

James Taylor spoke quietly and there was a note of sympathy in his voice, but Lord Hawkston's tone was hard as he asked:

"What is he doing—drinking?"

James Taylor nodded.

"What else?"

"He is messing things up rather badly."

"In what way?"

For a moment there was no answer and Lord Hawkston said:

"Tell me the truth, James, and I do not want it tied up with blue ribbon."

"Very well, then," James Taylor said. "Speaking frankly, he has broken the rules where a native girl is concerned."

Lord Hawkston stiffened.

"How can he have done that?"

"We both know," James Taylor replied, "that it is quite usual and in no way reprehensible for a young man to take a mistress from a nearby village or another plantation."

Lord Hawkston nodded. What was forbidden was for a planter to approach or be involved with one of his own employees.

"Your nephew made a Ceylonese girl his mistress a month after he arrived. Now he has kicked her out and refused to pay."

Lord Hawkston rose to his feet.

"I can hardly believe that!"

"It is true nevertheless, and as you can imagine, it has caused quite an upset."

Lord Hawkston was silent for a moment, then he said:

"Tell me every detail. I want to know."

He was well aware as he spoke that the rules of cohabitation between white men who were owners or managers of plantations with a native girl was an age-old custom and as such accepted by both the planters and the natives themselves.

The Portuguese and Dutch who preceded the English in Ceylon had taken women to live with them and in many cases married them.

The English had quite a different arrangement.

A planter living alone would take a mistress on the terms usually arranged by her father. He would invite her to his house when he needed her but she lived in a nearby village or even on the compound, but not openly with him.

The girls were highly attractive, gentle and loving, and a young planter could often find real happiness with one of them.

It was considered by the Ceylonese an honour that one of their women should be the mistress of the *Durai* or master of a plantation and if a man tired of a woman there was no stigma attached to her.

She went back to her own people with a dowry that ensured she could marry one of her own kind, because in their eyes she was rich.

The number of rupees that should be given in compensation was more or less an unwritten law and accepted by both parties.

If there were children from the association they lived with their mother, and many of them moved to a certain village in the hills which was known among the natives as 'New England'.

These children were surprisingly beautiful with dark skins and blue eyes, and sometimes even fair hair.

They could, of course, cause trouble in that the parents of the girl realised a child was an excuse to extort money from the father.

The reckoning was always high, sometimes crippling. An astute peasant would have a settlement drawn up by a properly qualified proctor—a solicitor—in the bazaar and an unfortunate young planter could find he was saddled with a form of alimony for the rest of his life in Ceylon.

But in the majority of cases such unions were pleasant and as long as justice was done were without repercussions!

That Gerald should have been so stupid and obtuse as to have broken the rules which governed such arrangements was almost beyond Lord Hawkston's comprehension.

The planters in Ceylon were noted as being among the most intelligent, gentlemanly and trustworthy of any colonists in British dependences.

A microcosm of the population of Great Britain: elementary, grammar and public-school boys, University graduates, businessmen, lawyers, officers of the Armed Services, Conservatives, Liberals, English, Scots, Welsh and Irish—was the wide ranging spectrum to be found on the coffee, tea and rubber estates.

They worked hard, but they also played hard, and once acclimatised enjoyed life immensely.

Few had had to pioneer their way as James Taylor and Chilton Hawk had been forced to do.

But it was still a rough life and to rise from a novice or 'creeper' to a *Perya Durai* or Big Master, as the coolies called them, entailed working from six in the morning to six or seven in the evening.

But a *Perya Durai* lived in a spacious bungalow or house

set on a hill-top with large gardens. He did his round of the 'field' on horseback.

When he had leave he could shoot wild elephants, elk, buffalo, bear and leopards; fish, swim, play cricket, hunt, take part in gymkhanas or polo tournaments, and join the British Clubs which were within a day's journey of most plantations.

James Taylor explained very carefully what had happened.

Gerald had been drinking ever since he arrived. He had soon become bored with the plantation and everything had been left to the Head-man.

Gerald had at first gone down to Kandy where there was a certain amount of amusement to be found, then he had joined the less reputable planters who enjoyed themselves in Colombo and paid little or no attention to their plantations.

This had kept him occupied for some time but soon he found his money was running out and he could not afford the visits which always proved expensive.

Finally, because he was hard-up, Gerald was forced to sit in his house and drink; his only amusement being Sēētha, the native girl who had taken his fancy soon after he arrived.

"What happened then?" Lord Hawkston asked.

"I gather there was a scene a month ago, when Gerald had been drinking very heavily," James Taylor answered. "He accused the girl of stealing a signet ring which he always wore. Afterwards, I believe, it was discovered under a piece of furniture in the room."

He paused and his voice was scathing as he went on:

"At the time he was quite adamant that Sēētha had stolen it, and she was extremely angry and distressed knowing she had done nothing of the sort."

Lord Hawkston could imagine how indignant the girl would be. The Ceylonese employed on the plantation were usually scrupulously honest and anyway were far too frightened to take anything which did not belong to them from their Master's house.

He himself had never missed anything all the years he had lived in the hills.

"Gerald told the girl to clear out," James Taylor said,

"and because he alleged she was a thief he refused to give her the money as is usual upon dismissal."

Lord Hawkston rose to walk across the room.

"The fool!" he exclaimed. "The damned fool!"

"I agree with you," James Taylor said. "When I heard what had happened I rode over to see the boy, but he was at that moment quite incapable of understanding anything I had to say. However I saw your cable to him lying on his desk! I read it, learnt you were arriving and came here to tell you what was happening."

"That was kind of you, James."

"In the cable," James Taylor went on, "you put—'Emily and I arriving on Friday'. Does that mean you have brought Gerald a wife? I heard rumours that you were to do so. As you know, everything is known in such a small community."

"I brought with me a young woman who was engaged to Gerald before he left England," Lord Hawkston replied in a hard voice. "Unfortunately, I have discovered that her interests lie elsewhere and I shall not permit the marriage."

James Taylor gave a low whistle.

"More problems," he said. "Well, I must say, Chilton, I think it is a pity. I am sure if there is one thing that could save young Gerald it would be for him to have a sensible wife who would stop him drinking and disperse the loneliness and isolation which he obviously cannot endure alone."

"I will try to find him a wife," Lord Hawkston said, but he added beneath his breath: "It will not be Emily Ludgrove."

James Taylor looked at his watch.

"I must get back," he said. "I intend to catch the morning train to Kandy, but I wanted to prepare you for what lay ahead. I hope you will be able to sort everything out, Chilton. Then come and see me. I have some interesting new experiments to show you."

"You know perfectly well there is nothing I would enjoy more," Lord Hawkston replied. "Thank you, James, for proving yourself once again a true friend."

"I wish I had better news to bring you," James Taylor remarked. "But I will tell you one thing which will please you: the export of tea will reach over five million cwts. this year."

Lord Hawkston smiled.

"That is the sort of information I hoped to hear."

"My plantation is booming," James Taylor said, "and yours should do so if once again it has your magic touch. We need you back, Chilton. We all need you, and so does Ceylon."

"Do not tempt me!" Lord Hawkston said. "You know I would rather be here than anywhere else in the world."

There was a ring of truth in his voice that was unmistakable.

James Taylor put his hand on his friend's shoulder.

"I will be seeing you later, Chilton," he said. "We will talk about it then."

Lord Hawkston saw him to the door, then turned back with a frown between his eyes.

He knew now he had to see Emily Ludgrove. Then he had to decide what he would say to his nephew.

It was not a pleasant prospect, and yet those who knew him well, had they seen the sudden tightening of his jaw, would have been aware that Chilton Hawk was about to go into battle and, as always, emerge victorious.

Twenty minutes later Emily Ludgrove came into the sitting-room where Lord Hawkston waited for her. She was looking, he had to admit, extremely pretty.

The gown she had bought in London was in the very latest fashion and revealed the perfection of her slim figure, while the colour accentuated the blue of her eyes and the almost dazzling gold of her hair.

For almost the first time Lord Hawkston realised she was in fact lovely and he thought perhaps it had been an absurd idea that she should incarcerate herself on a tea-plantation miles away from the many admirers her beauty would attract.

"Good morning, My Lord!" Emily said in a coquettish way with the look in her eyes that she accorded any man, young or old, when she was alone with him.

"Good morning, Emily!" Lord Hawkston replied. "Will you please sit down? I wish to talk to you."

"That sounds ominous!" Emily exclaimed. "Is anything wrong?"

"I wish to inform you," Lord Hawkston said, "that I am arranging for your passage back to England on the first available ship."

He saw Emily's eyes widen in an incredulous look of surprise and went on before she could speak:

"I happened to be in the garden last night when Captain O'Neill visited you in a somewhat irregular manner."

For a moment Emily was still, then she said:

"Captain O'Neill has asked me to marry him."

"I should imagine that is the least he could do," Lord Hawkston remarked dryly.

"And I was just debating," Emily Ludgrove went on, "as to whether I should accept his offer."

"The choice is quite simple," Lord Hawkston said. "Either you accept Captain O'Neill, or I send you back to England."

"Then I think you know, My Lord, what my answer will be," Emily Ludgrove said with a smile. "You will, I am sure, make my apologies to Gerald, but I doubt if we should have found much happiness together after being so long apart."

She rose from the sofa as she spoke and Lord Hawkston could not help thinking that she had accepted the situation with a poise he would not have expected of her.

"If you have nothing more to say to me, My Lord," she went on, "I will retire and write a letter to Captain O'Neill, making him, he assures me, the happiest man in the world!"

"I have nothing more to say," Lord Hawkston said. "I feel you would not be interested in hearing my opinion of your behaviour."

"Why should I be?" Emily replied. "You do not understand, or else you have forgotten, what it is like to be young! One is old a long time, so I intend to enjoy myself while I can, and there are men who are only too anxious to help me."

There was nothing Lord Hawkston felt he could answer to this and he bowed rather ironically as Emily swept away from him towards the door.

She turned back as she reached it.

"Please tell Gerald," she said in dulcet tones, "how very much I regret making him miserable and say that I hope we shall always be friends."

She went from the room before Lord Hawkston could think of a suitable retort. Then despite his anger at her behaviour he could not help laughing.

She certainly had a nerve that he would not have anticipated and he felt that if anyone might have kept Gerald in order it would have been Emily Ludgrove.

At the same time he was quite sure she was right. She would never have stood the loneliness of a plantation in the hill country, and even if they had come to Colombo, or returned to England, he was certain that Emily would not have been content with Gerald.

Somehow she would have contrived that a number of other men were available to lay their hearts at her feet, and if meanwhile she hurt her husband's feelings, it would be something he would have to put up with.

Lord Hawkston sighed. That was one chapter closed.

Now there was Gerald to contend with and he was quite certain that James Taylor was right when he had said that what the boy needed was a sensible wife.

The trouble was where to fine one?

He stood looking out at the garden. The flowers were a blaze of colour; there were purple orchids, the crimson hibiscus, and the white trumpet-like flowers of the frangipani—or Temple trees.

It looked a perfect setting for love but Lord Hawkston told himself that he was the last person capable of choosing a wife for his nephew.

After all, he had been unable to choose one for himself and at thirty-seven he had come to the conclusion that he would remain a bachelor.

He was well aware when he returned to England that his relatives thought he should marry and he found himself being invited to meet innumerable attractive widows or girls who for some reason or another had not 'got off' in the first flush of their youth.

The family had waited expectantly for him to fall in love and were quite unreasonably disappointed when he did not.

His Aunt even tackled him on the subject.

"After all, Chilton," she said, "you know as well as I do that you should now settle down and produce an heir. I always think it so much better when the title goes in a direct line."

"You can hardly say it has come in a direct line as far as I am concerned," Lord Hawkston replied with a smile.

"I am well aware of that," his Aunt answered, "and that is why I think you should produce a son as quickly as possible."

"I have first to find a wife."

"I have been looking around for you," his Aunt said, "and there are several ladies whom I consider suitable."

"I have an uncomfortable feeling that your plans will go awry," Lord Hawkston replied. "I have no intention, Aunt Alice, and let me make this quite clear, of marrying anyone for the sake of the title, the Estate, or the family-tree."

"Now, Chilton," his Aunt said sharply, "do not be so difficult. I am not suggesting that you should marry someone without affection but you are getting a little old to be knocked head-over-heels at the sight of a pretty face."

"You are right there," Lord Hawkston smiled.

"Therefore, if I find you a charming woman, between twenty-five to thirty, or perhaps even a little older, experienced and sophisticated, who will amuse and entertain you, then doubtless in time she will arouse a response in your heart!"

The problem was, Lord Hawkston found, that the women his Aunt produced aroused no response either in his heart or his mind.

He told himself that perhaps he was expecting too much, and yet although he appeared to be reserved and ruthless, there was deep inside him a longing for a love that might mean as much to him as the beauty of Ceylon.

Often, when he had stood on the verandah of his house and looked at the green mountains peaking round it towards the sky, at the torrent of crystal water rushing below him in the valley, he had felt that the sheer beauty of it evoked a response in him that was almost like the first rising of desire for a very beautiful woman.

"It is absurd to be in love with a country!" he told himself.

And yet he knew he had grown to love Ceylon as a man might love his wife.

The loveliness, the softness, the gentleness of it, combined with the warm moist air, were everything that was feminine, everything that inspired a feeling that was almost spiritual in its intensity.

'That is what love should be!' he thought, and tried to laugh at his own fantasy.

# *CHAPTER TWO*

Lord Hawkston decided that he would speak to the Governor about his problem of finding a wife for his nephew, Gerald.

He was wondering what he would tell Sir Arthur about Emily Ludgrove, only to find the moment he opened the conversation that she had forestalled him.

Sir Arthur Gordon, a grandson of the Earl of Aberdeen, whom Lord Hawkston had known slightly before he left for England, was a man of austere dignity who inspired his subordinates with awe as well as respect.

When he had assumed charge in Ceylon in 1883 the island was still racked by the economic crisis of the coffee slump, but the tide was turning slowly and the plantations were exploring the possibilities not only of tea but also of cinchong.

Sir Arthur took a personal interest in these developments especially the establishment of the tea industry. He had sent inspectors to Loolecondera and Lord Hawkston's plantation and had been extremely impressed by their reports. He was later to visit several tea-plantations himself.

Both James Taylor and Lord Hawkston liked him and found it easy to convince him that tea would bring prosperity back to Ceylon.

What Lord Hawkston particularly liked about Sir Arthur was his determination to demonstrate his impartiality to all races.

In fact just before Lord Hawkston left for England, the Governor had threatened to withdraw his patronage from a European-Colombo Club which tried to exclude certain Ceylonese from its membership.

What endeared him even further was that he protected the interests of the village Head-men and the property rights of Buddhist Temples.

He was the most enlightened and progressive Governor Ceylon had had for many years.

He carried out the restoration of many irrigation tanks and canals, completed the Colombo Port's breakwater, the foundation stone of which had been laid by the Prince of Wales in 1875, extended the railway, and began to build an estimated 260 miles of new roadways.

It would have been difficult for people in England, Lord Hawkston thought as he looked at him, to realise the power of a Governor of Ceylon. He not only reigned but ruled, surrounded by all the trappings of Royalty.

He had residences in Colombo, Nuwara, Sliya, Kandy and Jaffma; he had a Ceylonese bodyguard more imposing than the Beefeaters in England, and a troop of Sikh cavalry to precede and follow him on visits of State.

A line Regiment furnished him with a guard; he had a special train for his travels.

All memoranda to the Queen passed through his hands. He had the last word, and what his last word was none knew but himself.

It was impossible not to remember that Sir Arthur was an aristocrat and very conscious of his authority, so that Lord Hawkston wondered how much it would be wise to tell him about Emily Ludgrove.

He decided that he would not mention her behaviour

with Captain O'Neill, not because he was particularly concerned with protecting Emily's reputation, but because he
liked Patrick O'Neill and felt that in choosing such a wife he
would certainly have enough problems on his hands.

However when Lord Hawkston entered the Governor's
study they were alone, the secretary having been dismissed,
and Sir Arthur said with a smile:

"I know what you have come to tell me, Hawkston. Miss
Ludgrove has already informed me that she wishes to marry
Captain O'Neill."

Lord Hawkston did not reply and Sir Arthur went on:

"I feel this will be annoying for you, considering that you
brought her out especially to marry your nephew. From all I
hear the young man needs the steadying influence of a wife."

Lord Hawkston was not surprised that the Governor had
so intimate knowledge of Gerald's behaviour.

He was far more astute than people realised and although
in the grandeur and splendour of the Queen's House he
seemed immune from the commonplaces of everyday life,
there was in fact little that went on not only in Colombo, but
also in other parts of the country, of which he was not aware.

"I am afraid, Your Excellency, that my nephew has been
making a fool of himself," Lord Hawkston admitted.

"It happens to a great number of young men when they
first come out here," Sir Arthur answered, "and as you and I
well know, Hawkston, there are plenty of people who are
only too willing to help a man sow his wild oats, especially if
he has money to pay for them."

"That is true," Lord Hawkston agreed somewhat grudgingly.

He remembered certain wild nights he had experienced
when he first arrived in Colombo, but he had been far too
careful of his precious money to expend much of it on taw-
dry women and the dubious entertainments which were provided for greenhorns who had just arrived from England.

He had later, however, enjoyed a pleasant liaison with a
very pretty Portuguese in Kandy whom he visited whenever
he could spare the time from running his plantation. It had
lasted for years but he had been very discreet about it.

It hurt his pride now to realise that Gerald's misdemeanours were known even to the Governor.

"I wish we could have taken better care of your nephew when he first came out," Sir Arthur was saying thoughtfully. "He had several meals here but, as you well know, hospitality in Governor House is inevitably formal and must seem tedious to the young. I have learnt from my Secretary that we invited him to a Ball I gave at Christmas, but he did not reply to the invitation."

Lord Hawkston's lips tightened.

If there was one thing he disliked more than anything else it was bad manners. He had thought in the short time he had known Gerald when he was in England that he at least knew how to behave like a gentleman in public.

"Anyway the question now is," the Governor went on, "what are you going to do about him?"

"I intend, Your Excellency, to provide him with a wife," Lord Hawkston replied in a hard voice. "I came out here with the girl he had chosen for himself, but as those plans have gone awry I must make good the deficiency by finding him someone else."

Sir Arthur laughed.

"Is not that just like you, Hawkston? You have a reputation for being undefeatable, and all I can say is that Gerald Warren is a lucky young man to have you as an Uncle."

"Naturally I shall need your help."

The Governor laughed again.

"I cannot believe that I can be of any real assistance. I assure you there is a scarcity of charming unattached young ladies in this establishment! Nevertheless, it should not be difficult to find someone suitable amongst the many English families living in Colombo."

He sat down at his desk and put his hand to his forehead.

"Let me think about it. I have not really taken very much notice of the military families, but I dare say there are one or two daughters of officers not yet snapped up by some eager Subaltern."

"I should prefer a girl who has lived in Colombo for some time," Lord Hawkston said. "I have grown so used myself to seeing all the admirable qualities of this country, that I had forgotten that people new to the rather specialised existence here might find a few snags."

"You are thinking of the loneliness of being isolated on a plantation for months on end," Sir Arthur said with a serious note in his voice. "You will have to find a very exceptional girl who will stand that sort of life, Hawkston. If you will forgive my saying so, I thought from the moment I set eyes on Miss Ludgrove that she was not the right type."

"I see that now," Lord Hawkston agreed, "but she was Gerald's choice—not mine."

"And do you think he will be prepared to accept yours without having any say in the matter?"

"He will do as he is told, unless he wishes to be sent back to England," Lord Hawkston declared. "In which case he can work his passage; for I have no intention of paying it for him!"

He spoke in the ruthless, determined manner which was familiar to those who worked with him.

The Governor gave him a speculative glance before he said quietly:

"Playing God where love and marriage are concerned is a tricky business, Hawkston. You may burn your fingers."

"I am listening to Your Excellency's warning," Lord Hawkston answered, "but I still need your assistance."

"I have just seen the list of the people who are dining here tonight," the Governor said, "and none of them will be of any use in this respect. All I can say is that you had best take a glance at the Congregation in Church tomorrow morning."

He saw the expression on Lord Hawkston's face and said with a smile:

"You know as well as I do that if you stay in the Queen's House you are expected to accompany the Governor to Morning Prayers."

"I am quite prepared to do my duty," Lord Hawkston replied.

"It will not be as hard as you think," Sir Arthur went on. "I have restricted the Vicar to a sermon not longer than fifteen minutes.

The following morning in the grey stone Church of St.

Peter's which was not far from the Queen's House, Lord Hawkston, looking round the Congregation, saw the pews were filled with elegant figures that would have surprised those who thought that Ceylon was a backwater and out of touch with the world of fashion.

Gowns of taffeta, silk, satin, bombasine, ornamented with lace, braid, buttons or ribbon were not only fashionable but luxurious!

So were the extremely fetching bonnets and hats, trimmed with flowers and feathers, that rested on the elegantly coiffeured heads of the female worshippers.

Lord Hawkston had always heard that Sunday in Colombo was a fashion parade, but as he had never himself attended a Service in the capital it surprised him to see so many European faces. He noticed that many of them were extremely attractive.

He had however a suspicion that the most elegantly garbed and certainly the most sophisticated were the wives of Army officers or Government Officials.

Behind the European Congregation with an aisle between them sat the Ceylonese, even more resplendent in their colourful saris, their silks and cottons dyed by using the wax-resistant handicraft process which was, Lord Hawkston knew, a speciality of local weavers.

The rich and exotic colours and materials, ranging from the simplest gossamer to glittering embroidery, made the Ceylonese worshippers look like a bouquet of flowers against the grey stone of the Church walls.

The Governor had been met at the Church-door by the Vicar in his surplice, and escorted in the traditional manner to his stall in the Chancel, where there were comfortable velvet cushions and prayer-books emblazoned with the British Coat-of-Arms.

Opposite the Governor's stall were the seats for the choir and behind them an organ which, Lord Hawkston noticed as the Service began, was played by a young woman wearing a white cotton dress and an ugly black bonnet tied with black ribbons.

She looked, he thought, very austere compared with the other women in the Congregation. Then he noticed with surprise that her dress was duplicated by five other figures seated at the back of the choir stalls.

All five wore identical white cotton dresses, black bonnets and black gloves and their waists were encircled with narrow black sashes.

He thought at first that it must be a special costume for choir women, but as he stared at them he heard the Governor whisper in his ear:

"The Vicar has six daughters!"

"Six?" Lord Hawkston nearly ejaculated aloud.

"His wife died two years ago," the Governor said behind his prayer-book. "It has made him even more intent on making us aware of our sins and the hell-fires which await us."

Lord Hawkston looked at the Vicar with interest. He was a thin, gaunt man who might have been good-looking in his youth. But now painfully thin and cadaverous he gave the impression of a man who had crushed out of himself all the pleasures of life.

There was a fanatical look about him, Lord Hawkston decided, and he wondered whether his daughters suffered from what, he was quite certain, was a stern rigidity and self-imposed privation.

He looked at the girls with renewed interest.

The oldest of those sitting facing him had a rather pretty face, as far as he could see under the brim of her bonnet.

The others, who were obviously not yet grown up, had pink-and-white complexions, small turned-up noses and large curious eyes which stared unblinkingly at the Congregation.

The oldest member of the family, who played the organ, seemed to have eyes in the back of her head. As her youngest sister was fidgeting she turned quickly to reprove her, at the same time handing to a small Ceylonese choir-boy an open prayer-book when he had obviously become hopelessly lost in finding the right place on his own.

When she was not playing the organ the older girl turned round so that she could watch the behavior of the choir.

'Obviously a very competent young woman,' Lord Hawkston thought to himself as he saw her once again open a prayer-book and hand it to another small boy who had no idea what responses he should be making.

When she rose from her place he could see that she had a slim, elegant figure which surprisingly was not entirely disguised by the coarse cotton of which her dress was made.

Having lived so long in Ceylon, Lord Hawkston was well aware that the gowns worn by the Vicar's daughters were made of the cheapest white material that was used only by the poorest Ceylonese.

The Governor had said that their mother had died two years ago. This meant that either the Vicar insisted on the long and tedious mourning which had become fashionable in England, or else since their bonnets were not yet worn out they would continue to wear them until it was absolutely imperative to purchase new ones.

The choir rose to sing the psalms and Lord Hawkston realised that despite the age of the organ it was being played skilfully. The Vicar's oldest daughter was definitely something of a musician.

All through the Service he found himself speculating about the family and wondering what their lives were like.

He had a better idea of the atmosphere in which they had been brought up as he listened to the Vicar's sermon.

There was no doubt the Governor was right and the man was obsessed with the idea of sin and with the punishment that would be inflicted on all sinners, from which there was no escape.

He spoke with a zeal that was unmistakable and a fire which came from the deep sincerity of conviction.

As a Priest he was undoubtedly dedicated, but as a father, Lord Hawkston thought, he must be hard to endure.

The Vicar faltered once in his sermon when he must inadvertenly have turned over two pages of his notes at the same time.

When he did so his eldest daughter turned her head quickly to look up at the pulpit and Lord Hawkston saw her face completely for the first time.

It was heart-shaped with a small straight nose and large eyes which appeared to Lord Hawkston, at the distance he was from her, to be grey.

Her eyebrows were arched almost like the wings of a bird against an oval forehead, and he guessed that beneath the black bonnet her hair, which was almost ash in colour, was drawn back tightly and unbecomingly.

The Vicar found his place and his daughter seemed to relax. She turned her head once again to see what was going on amongst the choir and bent forward to admonish a small boy who was playing with a catapult.

He had drawn it from his pocket beneath his surplice and startled by her attention dropped the catapult and the stone that he was intending to use in its sling.

It fell to the ground with a thud and the Vicar's daughter bent forward with the obvious intention of telling him to leave it where it was until after the Service was over, but she was too late.

Frightened at losing his most treasured possession, the choir-boy was crawling about amongst the legs of the two boys who sat on either side of him in an effort to retrieve his treasures.

He found them and slipped back on to the seat giving an anguished look at the Vicar's daughter as he did so.

She frowned at him. Then as he bent his head in contrition she caught the eye of her eldest sister and gave her a faintly amused smile.

It completely transformed the solemnity of her face and at that moment Lord Hawkston made up his mind.

This was the right type of wife for Gerald, he told himself; a girl who could cope with a fanatical father, a collection of naughty choir-boys and a household full of sisters, would undoubtedly be able to manage his nephew in a most competent manner.

The idea was certainly worth exploring and he could not help feeling that this was far better material on which to work for the reclamation of his nephew than the other women in the Congregation rustling self-consciously in silks and satins and obviously paying no attention to the Vicar's strictures.

"Tell me about your parson," Lord Hawkston said as he drove back at the Governor's side, towards Queen's House, in a carriage pulled by two excellent horses.

"He is a difficult chap," Sir Arthur replied. "He is always

complaining to me about the iniquities which go on round the Port and other less savoury parts of the town. I have to explain to him that it is not the Governor's job to prevent men spending their money as they wish and unless they are breaking the law I have no jurisdiction to interfere."

"What about his family?" Lord Hawkston enquired.

"I hardly know them," the Governor replied. "They are invited to various entertainments from time to time, but their father mourns his wife in a manner which precludes everything, I suspect, except prayer. So we only see the eldest girl when there are meetings regarding the Church School or at fund-raising occasions for the work the Vicar does amongst the poor."

"It sounds a gloomy existence," Lord Hawkston remarked.

"I should imagine most young women today would find it completely intolerable," the Governor agreed.

"I was reading," Lord Hawkston remarked, "that the spread of Christianity and education among the people of Ceylon is greater than in any other Eastern state."

"I think that is true," Sir Arthur replied. "On the last census we had 220,000 Roman Catholics, 50,000 Protestants and about two million Buddhists!"

He paused to add with a twinkle in his eyes:

"Other occupations of our people include 1,532 devil-dancers, 121 snake charmers, 640 tom-tom beaters and five thousand fakirs and devotee-beggars!"

Lord Hawkston laughed.

"A mixed bag!"

There was no time to say more, for the carriage had drawn up on the Queen's House.

After luncheon Lord Hawkston sought out the Governor's Secretary, an elderly man who had spent all his life in Colombo. He had served successive Governors who found his knowledge of local affairs invaluable.

"I want to know all you can tell me about the Vicar of St. Peter's," Lord Hawkston said.

"His name is Radford," the Secretary replied. "He has been in Colombo for twenty-two years. He married out here, and he is quite convinced that in the Queen's House we are a callous, un-feeling lot who have no sympathy with his violent desire to clean up the city of Colombo."

"He should compare it with other coastal cities of the same size," Lord Hawkston said dryly. "He would be surprised to find that in contrast, Colombo is, in my opinion at any rate, an exemplary example of good behaviour."

"I would not go as far as to say that, M'Lord, but there is in fact very little vice and on the whole our people are well-behaved."

"That is what I have always thought myself," Lord Hawkston said, "And now tell me about Mrs. Radford."

"She was a charming lady," the Secretary answered. "If anyone could keep the Vicar human, it was his wife. She came from a County family in England and her father was concerned with the Botanical Gardens at Kew.

"She came out with him when he was advising the Governor of the time on certain plants and trees which would do well in our particular soil. She met the Vicar—he was only a curate in those days—and fell in love with him."

The Secretary paused before adding:

"When I knew Radford first he was an attractive young man, but even then fired with a prophetic zeal which I had always thought would be extremely uncomfortable to live with."

"They had six daughters?"

"It has always been a deep sorrow to the Vicar that he had no son," the Secretary explained. "After Miss Dominica and Miss Faith were born he christened his third daughter Hope, but unfortunately she was followed by three more sisters, Miss Charity, Miss Grace and Miss Prudence!"

"Good Heavens!" Lord Hawkston ejaculated. "What names with which to saddle poor girls for the rest of their lives!"

"Dominica was lucky," the Secretary continued. "She was born on a Sunday and therefore it seemed a suitable choice, but for the others it is another cross they have to bear."

"I can well imagine that," Lord Hawkston remarked.

"They are all very pleasant girls," the Secretary said. "My wife thinks very highly of them and occasionally they are allowed to come to tea with my daughter, who is an invalid.

Otherwise they have few amusements. Their father does not approve of secular interests."

"I wish to call on the Vicar," Lord Hawkston said. "May I mention your name by way of introduction?"

The Secretary smiled.

"Mention the Governor's, M'Lord. Despite himself, the Vicar is impressed by His Excellency."

"I will take your advice," Lord Hawkston replied.

He called at the Vicarage at four o'clock in the afternoon, feeling that was not only the correct social time for calling, but it would also undoubtedly be between Services.

The door was opened by one of the sisters who looked about fourteen years old and who he suspected was Charity.

She gave him a startled glance and when he explained that he wished to see her father she ushered him in a somewhat embarrassed manner into the front room of the Vicarage, saying she would fetch him.

Lord Hawkston looked around and realised that everything was poor but at the same time tasteful.

The curtain material could not have cost more than a few pence a yard, yet they were skillfully made and in a colour which echoed the blue of the sea.

There were however no sofa cushions; the floor, scrubbed until it literally shone with cleanliness, was covered by only a few cheap native mats; the white-washed walls were bare except for one landscape in water colours.

There was a bowl of flowers on a plain table by the fireplace and the room smelt of pot-pourri, which after a moment Lord Hawkston located in a bowl set on the window ledge where ordinarily it would catch the rays of the sun.

But since it was Sunday the blinds were lowered until only a foot of light came from the bottom of each window.

Lord Hawkston knew it was customary in Scotland and in some of the country parts of England to pull down the blinds on the Sabbath, but it was something he had not expected to find in Ceylon.

He realised however when the Vicar appeared that he had in fact committed a transgression by calling on a Sunday.

"You wished to see me?" the Vicar asked coming into the

room and looking, Lord Hawkston thought, even more gaunt and austere than he had seemed in Church.

The somber black of his clothing, the sharpness of his cheekbones, the thinness of his face, and the grey of his hair which was almost white at the temples made him look like one of the ancient prophets ready to cry doom on the inhabitants of Sodom and Gomorrah.

"I am Lord Hawkston!"

The Vicar made a small inclination of his head.

"I am staying at Queen's House with the Governor," Lord Hawkston went on. "I called, Vicar, because I need your help and because I have something of importance to discuss with you."

Outside the sitting-room Charity shut the door behind her father and sped up the stairs.

Dominica was in her bedroom which she shared with Faith. She was taking off her bonnet, having just returned from the Sunday School which she held immediately after luncheon.

Charity burst into the room and she looked up in surprise.

"Dominica—what do you think? What do you think?"

"What has happened? Why are you so excited?" Dominica asked.

"A gentleman has called to see Papa and he has come in one of the Governor's carriages. It is the same gentleman who was in Church today. You must have seen him—he was sitting next to the Governor, and I saw him look amused when Ranil dropped his catapult."

"It was not at all amusing," Dominica said. "Papa heard the noise and was very angry about it. It is difficult to make him understand that the choir-boys never listen to his sermons."

"Why should they?" Charity asked lightly. "I bet the Governor does not listen either."

"I wonder what his guest wants with Papa?" Dominica said.

"He is very distinguished-looking," Charity told her, "but I do not suppose he has come to invite us to a Ball."

"Charity!" Dominica exclaimed, and then laughed. "You know that is as unlikely as if we had all been invited to stay on the moon! Anyway, Papa would not allow us to go."

"When I am grown up like you and Faith," Charity said, "I shall dance whatever Papa says."

"Then you had better not let him hear you saying it now," a voice said from the doorway, "or he will give you a good whipping!"

Faith came into the bedroom as she spoke and Lord Hawkston had been right in thinking she was a very pretty girl.

Without the ugly black bonnet which had overshadowed her face she had fair hair, blue eyes and an almost angelic expression, but she also, although it did not show in her face, had a mischievous wit and was, like Charity, ready to rebel against the restrictions imposed upon them by their father.

"What is all this?" Faith asked now. "Is it true there is a young man in the house?"

"He is not particularly young," Charity answered, "but he is smart and very impressive, and he is staying at Queen's House."

"Is he the one who was in Church today?" Faith asked.

Charity nodded.

"I had a good look at him," Faith said, "and thought he was rather attractive."

Dominica laughed.

"You would find any man attractive, Faith, as well you know!"

"I do not have the chance to see many except in Church," Faith retorted. "I hoped that Lieutenant who made eyes at me last Sunday would be there today, but he must be on duty. There was no sign of him."

Dominica glanced towards the door.

"Do be careful, Faith," she begged. "I am always afraid that Papa will hear you talking like that."

"Papa is far too busy looking for sin down the town to ferret it out in his own household," Faith replied lightly.

"I should not be too sure of that!" Dominica warned.

"What do you think the gentleman downstairs is talking about to Papa?" Charity said. "Shall I listen at the door? If Papa found me in the hall I could say I was waiting to show his guest out."

"Yes, do that," Faith said quickly.

But Dominica interposed:

"You will do nothing of the sort, Charity! It is vulgar and ill-bred to listen at key-holes, as well you know!"

"But why do you think he wishes to see Papa?" Charity asked.

"We shall know in good time," Dominica answered calmly.

Then she gave a little cry.

"Heavens, do you think he will stay to tea? I meant to make a cake yesterday, but there was no time, and also, to tell the truth, I had run out of house-keeping money, and did not dare to ask Papa for any more."

"Never mind," Faith said, "we can cut him some sand-wiches and Charity can collect some fruit from the garden. I expect he has stuffed himself with exotic luxuries at Queen's House and will not care for the peasant-fare we have in this house."

"Faith, please do not talk like that in front of the younger ones," Dominica said almost pleadingly. "You know as well as I do that Papa thinks too much luxury incites sinful thoughts."

"Judging by what we eat," Faith replied, "it is a wonder we can think at all! I am quite certain I am suffering from malnutrition!"

Dominica laughed.

"You do not look like it! The last dress I made you had to have another inch in the waist."

"That," Faith said with dignity, "was only natural growth!"

Dominica was about to reply when she heard a voice call-ing to her.

"Dominica—come here! I want you!"

It was her father and she looked at her sisters in conster-nation.

"For goodness sake cut some sandwiches!" she said

quickly to Faith. "And you, Charity, find fruit of some sort. Fill the wicker bowl with it. It looks nice, even if the fruit is not very exciting. We finished the only ripe pawpaw yesterday."

She was still giving instructions as she opened the bedroom door and ran down the stairs.

"You are keeping me waiting, Dominica!" her father said reprovingly.

"I am sorry, Papa, I was just telling Faith and Charity what to do in case your visitor stays to tea."

"To tea?" the Vicar repeated, looking as if he had never heard of such a meal. "Yes, yes, of course. Perhaps it would be polite to offer him a cup."

"Shall I go and get it ready, Papa?"

"No, the others can do that. Lord Hawkston wishes to speak to you."

Dominica looked surprised, but before she could say anything her father had opened the sitting-room door and she walked into the room.

She had of course noticed the stranger in the Governor's pew but she had reproved her sisters so often for looking about them curiously that she had trained herself not to look at the Congregation and most of all not to stare at the worshippers from Queen's House.

Nevertheless she recognized the man she had seen opposite her in the Chancel and thought that he was in fact better-looking than he had appeared in Church.

He was also in Dominica's eyes extremely elegant.

She never met the young Army officers on whom Faith cast longing eyes but occasionally she came in contact with the sons of the Civil Servants and other English dignitaries who resided in Ceylon.

When she did they always seemed to her to be somewhat self-conscious in their best clothing and high white collars, almost as if they were wearing fancy-dress to which they were not accustomed.

But she noticed that Lord Hawkston's clothes, smart though they were, seemed to be a part of him.

He wore them casually and yet she was well aware they

had an elegance which proclaimed all too clearly that they had been tailored in London.

He was standing at the far end of the room as she entered and she was conscious that as she entered the room he watched her from under his eyebrows as she walked across towards him.

The Vicar accompanied her.

"This, My Lord, is my daughter, Dominica!"

Lord Hawkston bowed and Dominica swept a low curtsey.

There was a moment's silence and Dominica wondered why neither of the men spoke. She had the feeling, perhaps erroneously, that they were feeling for words.

At last her father, clearing his throat began:

"Lord Hawkston, Dominica, has brought me an unexpected and rather strange proposition, and he has asked that you too should listen to what he has to say."

Dominica raised her grey eyes to her father's face.

"Yes, Papa?"

Again there was a pause. Then almost as if he found the situation uncomfortable Lord Hawkston said:

"I wonder, Vicar, if you would think it very unconventional if I talk with your daughter alone? I feel I would like to make my proposition, as you call it, to her myself."

There was an expression of relief on the Vicar's face as he replied:

"Of course, My Lord. Perhaps that would be best, I will go and tell my other daughters to prepare tea."

"Thank you," Lord Hawkston said.

The Vicar went from the room closing the door behind him, and Dominica looked at Lord Hawkston apprehensively.

She could not imagine what he wished to say to her, or what he could possibly have to propose.

"Suppose we sit down?" Lord Hawkston suggested and the words brought a flush to Dominica's cheeks.

"I . . . I am sorry, My Lord," she said quickly. "I should have invited you to do so, but I was so surprised to see you that I am afraid I forgot my manners."

"I think what I have to say to you will come as an even

greater surprise," Lord Hawkston replied, "but I want you to listen to me and not make up your mind too quickly."

He seated himself as he spoke on the hard sofa that stood against the wall, and he made a little gesture with his hand and after a second's hesitation Dominica seated herself beside him.

He turned a little sideways to look at her and she felt uncomfortably that he was looking her over in a scrutinising manner which she did not understand.

She had, as Lord Hawkston had suspected, ash-cloured hair with faint silver lights in it. Drawn back from her forehead it was pinned tight into a large bum which covered the whole back of her head, making him realise that her hair was long and thick.

Her eyes were grey and fringed with dark lashes, and the winged eye-brows he had noticed in Church were dark too.

But her skin was translucently fair and very pale so that when she flushed it brought a sudden beauty to her face, almost like the dawn creeping up the morning sky.

She was very thin, but despite the coarse cotton of her gown it was moulded so tightly to her figure that the soft, mature swellings of her breasts were easy to discern and her waist was very small and could in fact, Lord Hawkston thought, be spanned by a man's two hands.

Her fingers, which had played the ancient organ so skillfully, were long and elegant and she placed them now in her lap, almost like a child in school waiting to recite a poem.

"I expect," Lord Hawkston said at length in his deep voice, "you are wondering why I have called on your father?"

"We seldom have visitors on a Sunday."

"I apologise for desecrating the Sabbath!" Lord Hawkston replied with a hint of amusement in his voice. "But my excuse is a feeling of urgency to meet you and explain to your father what I require of you."

"Of me?" Dominica asked.

"This may sound very blunt," Lord Hawkston said with his eyes on her face, "but I came here to ask your father whether you would consider marring my nephew, Gerald Warren!"

Dominica made no movement. Only her eyes widened a little as she stared at Lord Hawkston incredulously.

After a moment she said in a voice which seemed to him to be deliberately controlled:

"Is Your Lordship . . . serious?"

"Completely!" he replied. "But let me make myself a little more explicit. My nephew, who has been working on my plantation near Kandy, has been in this country for two years. I arrived the day before yesterday with a young lady from England to whom he has been secretly engaged.

"They were to be married on arrival, but unfortunately when we reached Colombo I learnt that the young lady in question had changed her mind."

"Why did she now not wish to marry him?" Dominica enquired.

"She met someone she preferred on board the ship," Lord Hawkston explained, "but anyway I am quite certain she would not have made my nephew a commendable wife."

Dominica did not speak and after a moment he continued:

"My nephew needs someone to look after him, to give him companionship and relieve the tedium and loneliness which I am sure you will realise is experienced by planters when they are up-country for months on end."

He paused and then added:

"When I saw you in Church playing the organ so well, coping with the misdemeanours of the choir-boys, and at the same time giving your father your attention, I felt sure you were the person for whom I was looking."

Dominica drew in her breath.

"How can you be sure of that, My Lord?"

Lord Hawkston smiled.

"Shall I say I have an instinct for doing the right thing? I survived the coffee slump because I had been fortunate enough to plant some acres of tea on my plantation. It is now a flourishing and lucrative concern. But should my nephew not wish to make his home in Ceylon, I am sure that in a few years it would be possible for you to return to England."

There was a pause, then Dominica said:

"You said just now that you arrived on Friday and that

you had expected your nephew to marry the young lady you brought from England as soon as you reached here. Was he not very upset that his intended bride had changed her mind?"

Lord Hawkston liked the way she had worked out for herself the significance of what had occurred and was certain he had been right in thinking her intelligent—this was the proof of it.

"You are quite right to ask that question, Miss Radford," he said. "I will be frank with you and say that my nephew has as yet no idea there has been a change of plan. As it happens he is ill and was unable to meet us in Colombo. I received a letter from him saying that he hopes in a few days to meet me in Kandy."

"And will you tell him then that as he cannot have the bride he wanted you have chosen someone else for him?"

The question was spoken softly, but Lord Hawkston could not help thinking that spoken in another tone it would have sounded sarcastic.

"I think when Gerald realises he has escaped a very unhappy marriage and meets you he will be quite satisfied with the arrangements I wish to make for you both."

Dominica turned her face away to look towards the light coming in through the half-closed blinds.

Lord Hawkston could see her in profile and realised that her bone-structure was good.

Attractively dressed and with a less austere hair-style, he told himself she would be pretty.

"Are you seriously expecting me, My Lord, to say that I will marry a man I have never met?" Dominica asked after a moment.

"I am asking you to trust me," Lord Hawkston answered, "when I tell you that my nephew is a good-looking young man, in fact I have been told that some women find him handsome. He is nearly six feet tall, a hard rider to hounds when in England, and is, I believe, equally at home on the dance-floor."

"Supposing he . . . dislikes me?" Dominica asked in a low voice.

"I think in the circumstances he is living now he will

welcome with open arms the companionship of an attractive
girl who will have his interests at heart and who will make his
life comfortable and pleasant."

Lord Hawkston paused for a moment to continue:

"After all, supposing you had met him two or three times?
Supposing you had danced with him? That would constitute
enough acquaintanceship for him to ask you to marry him
and for you to accept. All I am asking is for you to dispense
with such trivial formalities and agree to be his wife, trusting
me to have described him fairly."

Dominica did not reply and after a moment Lord Hawkston went on:

"I am sure it has not escaped your notice that your father,
having six daughters, may find if difficult to provide suitable
husbands for them all. If you marry my nephew I intend to
settle an adequate amount of money for your comfort and
there will be more when I die."

Dominica glanced at him swiftly.

"That will surely not be for a long time, My Lord."

Lord Hawkston smiled.

"I am approaching middle-age and let me assure you I
have no intention of marrying. I have lived alone for so long
and have become so used to my own company, that I am
content to remain a bachelor. In which case Gerald will eventually inherit the title and the family Estates in England which
are considerable."

Dominica looked away from him again.

After a moment she said:

"Mama always said it was . . . unlucky to wait for dead
men's shoes."

"But I have promised that you will be comfortable before
I am dead."

She did not turn to look at him and after a moment he
went on:

"I have chosen you, Dominica—and I hope you will allow
me to call you by your Christian name—because when I
watched you in Church I felt you were sensible. I hope you
will apply that good sense to this proposition."

He watched her face as he spoke, liking the sensitiveness
and the true calmness of her expression.

"I know it is unusual," he went on, "unconventional, if you like—but I see no reason why you should refuse it on that account. Let me take you to Kandy and up to my plantation. When you meet my nephew I am sure you will find you have a great deal in common with each other."

His voice ceased. Dominica rose from the sofa and walked very slowly cross the room.

She pulled up the blind on one of the windows and looked out into the garden.

Sunshine flooded in and Lord Hawkston saw her silhouetted against the golden splendour of it.

She stared out with what he guessed were un-seeing eyes.

"What is worrying you?" he asked at length.

"I was thinking about Mama," Dominica answered, "and wondering what she would advise me to say."

"I think your mother would wish you to marry," Lord Hawkston said. "Your father tells me you are over twenty and most girls of that age are already thinking of a bridal veil."

"Mama was only eighteen when she married," Dominica replied, "but she fell very much in love with Papa as soon as she saw him."

"As I am certain you will fall in love with my nephew," Lord Hawkston said.

Dominica made no response and after a moment he went on:

"Let me ask you once again to be sensible about this. I have heard that your father does not allow you and your sisters to attend many social functions. How do you suppose any of you will get married if you never meet men, if you are not allowed to go to dances and parties?"

He paused.

"Do you really envisage living on indefinitely in this house in the years ahead, looking after your sisters and your father, controlling the choir-boys, and teaching, as I hear you have been doing this afternoon, in Sunday School? What sort of life is that?"

"I think Mama would have wanted us to have some gaiety," Dominica said slowly, "and to meet many more people than we do now, but it angers and upsets Papa when I suggest it."

Suddenly she turned round to face Lord Hawkston.

"You would not like Faith to marry your nephew?" She asked. "Faith is longing to be married. She wants to meet men. I am sure she would be very happy to agree to your proposition."

Lord Hawkston shook his head.

"Faith, as your father told me, is only just eighteen," he said, "and I have a feeling she has not your good sense, nor your intelligence. Anyway, I have made up my mind. I want you, Dominica. I want you to agree to travel with me to Kandy as soon as we have bought your trousseau."

"Trousseau!" The exclamation came from Dominica's lips sharply.

Then before Lord Hawkston could speak she said quickly:

"You must understand, My Lord, it would be impossible for me to have many more gowns than I already possess, or to expend much money on buying new things. Papa would never allow it and besides the money is not there. You must realise that we are very poor."

"I am well aware of that," Lord Hawkston replied, "and I promise you, Dominica, that you shall have a delightful trousseau, the best that Colombo can provide, and it will not cost your father a penny!"

"Do you mean that you will pay for it?"

"Most certainly!"

"But I do not think Papa . . ." Dominica began hesitatingly.

"Leave you father to me," Lord Hawkston said. "As I have already told you, Dominica, I always get my own way. I can easily persuade your father that as far as a trousseau is concerned my way is the best."

His eyes were on her face as he went on:

"My way is also best where you are concerned. Will you not be content, Dominica, to leave everything in my hands, to let me make the arrangements I think fit? I am quite certain you will never regret it."

"How can you be certain of that?"

"I have pointed out the alternative," Lord Hawkston replied. "Would it not be better to be the wife of a charming, pleasant young man with a certain amount of money and the prospect of a great deal more, than a future in which you will become a frustrated old maid slaving to make ends meet, and finding that your efforts seldom evoke much appreciation?"

This was a shrewd thrust which he knew went home.

He had already realised from the talk he had had with the Vicar that he had very little idea of how much his daughter did and was not in the least grateful for her efforts to keep the house going now that his wife was dead.

Lord Hawkston's eyes took in all the indecision he could see in Dominica's face and he knew that his arguments were, although she made little sign of it, causing a sense of chaos within her mind so that it was hard for her to think clearly.

Because he was used to leading men and getting from them exactly what he wanted Lord Hawkston applied the same technique to Dominica.

"Come," he said, in a kindly tone. "You have everything to gain and nothing to lose. Give me your hand and tell me that your answer is yes."

He held out his own hand as he spoke and hesitatingly, because he expected it of her, Dominica laid her fingers on his.

He could feel they were very cold and they trembled a little.

"Your answer is yes, is it not?" Lord Hawkston insisted.

"Yes . . . My Lord," Dominica answered, but her voice was hardly above a whisper.

# CHAPTER THREE

Lord Hawkston did not wait for the tea which had been prepared for him with so much trouble.

He had learnt in the business world that having concluded a difficult negotiation it was always wise to leave before the other party began to regret that he had accepted the proposition and wished to change his mind.

"Do not disturb your father," he said to Dominica. "I will leave now, but I will return tomorrow morning and arrange to take you shopping for your trousseau."

Dominica did not answer and he knew that she felt as if her voice had died in her throat.

"I am very grateful to you," Lord Hawkston said, "for agreeing to marry my nephew."

He bowed, Dominica curtseyed and opened the front door for him.

The Governor's carriage, emblazoned with the British Coat-of-Arms, its fine horses and silver accoutrements, was looking very resplendent outside the shabby Vicarage.

Dominica could not help feeling that the servants in their elaborate livery looked disdainfully at their surroundings.

A footman opened the door of the open carriage for Lord Hawkston and he stepped into it. Having put a light rug over His Lordship's knees to keep off the dust, the footman sprang up on to the box and the horses started off.

Lord Hawkston raised his high hat and Dominica curtseyed again.

She stood watching the carriage until it was out of sight and did not know that Lord Hawkston had liked the way she stood quite still, her head held a little defiantly as if she summoned some inner courage to her aid.

"A very sensible girl!" he told himself as he drove away. "She will be the saving of Gerald and undoubtedly they will deal very well together."

When there was no longer any sign of the carriage on the unkept Vicarage drive, Dominica walked back into the house, shut the door and stood for a moment leaning against it as if she needed to support herself against a sudden weakness.

Then she ran into the kitchen at the back of the house where she knew she would find her sisters.

They were all there: Faith was cutting sandwiches and Charity and Hope were arranging the fruit in a wicker basket.

They had been chattering as Dominica entered the room, but immediately they fell silent as they all turned their faces towards her, a question in their eyes.

"What did he want?" Charity asked.

Faith, throwing down the butter-knife, exclaimed:

"You do not mean to say he has gone without the tea we are taking so much trouble over! How could you let him go, Dominica, when we all wanted to see him?"

"He has gone," Dominica answered in a strange voice, and walking to the table she sat down on one of the hard chairs.

"What did he come about?" Hope enquired.

She was not as pretty as Faith, but she had the same blue eyes and golden hair. She was, however, at sixteen, going through a tom-boy stage and her hair was invariably untidy and her finger-nails dirty.

"Yes, what did he want?" Charity repeated impatiently.

"He has asked me to marry his nephew!"

Dominica knew that at first they did not believe her. Then as if the quiet seriousness of her voice convinced them, they stared at her wide-eyed and astonished to the point of what might have seemed ludicrous were Dominica not experiencing the same feeling herself.

"He has asked you to do what?" Faith said at last.

"To marry his nephew," Dominica replied. "He is a tea-planter and the girl whom Lord Hawkston brought out to marry him . . ."

She got no further.

"Lord Hawkston?" Charity exclaimed. "Do you mean to say that he is a Lord?"

"A Lord!" Faith interposed. "And he actually came here to the house! Oh, Dominica, how could you have let him go?"

"He is coming back tomorrow to buy my trousseau for me."

There was a babble which made it impossible to distinguish anything anyone was saying. The words 'trousseau', 'Lord', 'marriage', seemed to be repeated over and over again and jumbled into a roar of sound which made Dominica finally put her hands over her ears and cry:

"Stop! I must think! I must be certain I have done the . . . right thing!"

"If you really mean you are going to marry the nephew of a Lord, I cannot imagine you have anything to think about," Faith said. "It is the most exciting, thrilling thing I have ever heard!"

"Of course it is!" Hope exclaimed. "We can all come and stay with you. Do you think he would lend me a horse to ride? And there is fishing up in the mountains where the tea grows. I would not be any trouble! You will ask me, Dominica?"

"She will have us all to stay," Faith answered as Dominica did not speak, "but leave her alone now. Give her a cup of tea, Charity. Dominica, eat one of these sandwiches. They are quite nice and you ate practically nothing at luncheon."

"There wasn't much to eat!" Grace said.

She was small, fat and greedy and was always complaining she did not have enough food.

"Well, you don't go hungry at any rate," Hope said sharply. "You never do."

"Stop squabbling, you two," Faith commanded. "Can't you see that Dominica is upset?"

She put two sandwiches on a plate as she spoke and put them down in front of Dominica.

Charity set a cup of tea beside her.

"Drink it up," she said encouragingly, "and then you can tell us all about it."

Prudence, the youngest, who was only nine, went to stand beside her oldest sister.

"Don't leave us, Dominica," she said in a pleading voice. "We'll never be able to manage without you."

Dominica put her arm round the child and drew her close.

"That is what I am afraid of!" she exclaimed. "Oh girls, have I made the right decision? When I said I would do as Lord Hawkston proposed, I thought I would be able to help all of you."

"We can come to stay," Hope said irrepressibly.

"And you can give us all your cast-off clothes," Faith said.

"I expect he has lots of money," Charity remarked. "Lords are very rich."

Dominica took a sip of the tea, then, as if it sustained her, she went on:

"Lord Hawkston said that if I would marry his nephew he would give us enough money to be comfortable. I will be able to help you and I must somehow persuade Papa that you will need Mallika to come in every day to do the housework and not just once a week as she does now."

"She will have to help with the cooking," Faith said quickly. "You know how bad I am at it. The stove will never work for me."

"But will Papa agree?" Dominica asked. "I am sure I ought to have said no! Besides it must be wrong to marry a man you have never seen."

"I expect he is tall and handsome like his Uncle," Charity

said, "and when he sees you, Dominica, he will fall madly in love with you and you with him. It will be just like a fairy-story!"

Dominica put down her cup and rose from the table.

"I do not believe it is true!" she cried. "Did Lord Hawkston really come to the house, or have I dreamt it all?"

"It is true! It is true!" Charity replied. "I let him in! I fetched Papa, and think, Dominica, how exciting it will be to have a wedding in the family! Is Papa going to marry you?"

Dominica looked at her sister with troubled eyes.

"I do not think so," she said. "I believe Lord Hawkston means to take me up to Kandy and I shall be married there."

"Then we cannot be bridesmaids," Faith exclaimed in a tone of disappointment. "Oh, Dominica, I did want to be your bridesmaid!"

"Why has the young man, whatever his name is, not come to Colombo to meet his Uncle?" Hope asked.

"He is ill," Dominica answered, "and his name is Gerald Warren."

"I think Gerald is quite a romantic name," Charity murmured.

"Warren is rather dull," Faith said, "Mrs. Warren . . . well, I suppose it sounds all right! It is a pity he is not a Lord."

"He will be one day, if his Uncle does not marry, and he says he intends to remain a bachelor," Dominica said in a low voice.

All three older girls gave a cry of sheer excitement and Charity exclaimed:

"You will be a Lady! Think of it, Dominica! You will be a Lady and sit on the right of the Governor when you dine at Queen's House."

For the first time since she had come into the kitchen Dominica smiled.

"That possibility is a long way ahead. After all, Lord Hawkston is not old."

"I thought in Church that he looked about thirty-five or thirty-six," Faith said. "I am rather good at guessing ages."

"I thought he was much older than that," Charity contradicted. "But he looks distinguished. I would like to see him with a coronet on his head."

"I do not suppose he travels with it," Dominica said with a smile.

"What else did he. . . ?" Faith began, then the bell on the wall pealed and there was a sudden silence.

"Papa!" Faith exclaimed. "Charity, go and see what he wants!"

"No, I will go," Dominica interposed. "I am sure he wants me."

There was no protest against her answering her father's summons. All the girls, with the exception of Dominica, were afraid of their father and even the thought of him was enough to change the subject of their conversation and the tone of their voices.

Dominica walked to the kitchen table and picking up her cup of tea drank from it. Then, as if it made her feel stronger, she went from the kitchen without another word.

She walked along the narrow, rambling passage which led to the front of the house.

The Vicarage had been built fifty years earlier in the grandiose Colonial manner which had given the first Vicar who had lived in it a background of pomp and importance.

He had however been a rich man while the incumbents of St. Peter's who followed him were poor and without private means to supplement the very modest stipend they were allowed by the Church Commissioners in England.

Only Dominica and her mother before her knew how hard it was to keep such a big building clean, but she accepted the work it entailed as part of her daily life and made no complaints.

The Vicar's Study was an enormous room overlooking the garden and while the best pieces of furniture they possessed were arranged there, they still seemed sparse and miserably inadequate.

The Vicar was sitting at his desk and when Dominica entered, closing the door behind her, he said sharply:

"Why did you not fetch me to say goodbye to Lord Hawkston?"

"He did not wish to stay to tea, Papa," Dominica answered, "and he will be calling again tomorrow."

"He told you what he proposed?"

"Yes, Papa."

"I accepted his proposition because I thought it was best for you, Dominica. After all, as His Lordship pointed out to me, I have six daughters who will all doubtless require husbands in the future."

"Yes, Papa."

"I would have wished to see the young man for myself," the Vicar said, "but Lord Hawkston speaks well of his nephew and I know your mother, Dominica, would have been glad for you to marry an Englishman who has not been corrupted by the sin and depravity which I find so prevalent in this country."

"Yes, Papa."

"Lord Hawkston has told you of his plans? That he should take you to Kandy and that you should be married there?"

"I would have wished you to marry me, Papa."

"It is what I had always hoped to do," the Vicar said. "But you know as well as I do, Dominica, that I cannot spare the time, and what is more, I could not contemplate the expense."

"No, of course not, Papa."

"I will give you my blessing before you leave," the Vicar said. "And now, Dominica, I think we should both pray that you will have God's help to sustain you in your new life, and that you will not fall short of the ideals and standards that I have instilled in you since you were a child."

As he spoke, the Vicar dropped to his knees beside his desk.

Dominica knelt down on the floor in front of it.

They were all used to their father praying at any time of the day that occurred to him besides taking part in the long Service of prayers he conducted every morning and every evening.

Dominica was not the least self-conscious and, kneeling on the floor without any support, she clasped her hands together and closed her eyes.

As her father burst into a long exhortation to the Almighty to preserve her from sin and temptation, Dominica said her own prayers, which were far simpler and indeed more comforting.

"Help me, God! to be sure I have done the right thing," she prayed, "and that Mama would have approved. It seems strange and somehow wrong to marry a man one has never seen, but I shall be able to do things for the girls! Please make Papa understand that they cannot manage without Mallika coming in every day, and make Faith able to look after Grace and Prudence."

She was so concentrated on what she was saying that she did not realise for a second that her father had come to the end of one of his lengthy exhortations and was waiting for her response.

"Amen!" she said quickly.

"The response should be, 'Good Lord, Deliver us from Evil'," her father said in an irritated tone.

"I am sorry, Papa—Good Lord, deliver us from evil."

"Amen!"

The Vicar rose to his feet.

"We will pray a little longer when we are gathered together this evening, Dominica," he said. "I feel that our prayers will be like an armour to protect you from the difficulties and temptations which may lie ahead."

"Thank you, Papa."

Dominica went from the Study leaving her father alone. She did not go back to the kitchen. Instead she went up to her bedroom.

Over the mantelpiece there was a sketch of her mother.

It had been roughly drawn by an amateur artist who had insisted on drawing Mrs. Radford soon after she was married.

He had actually excelled only in water-colour, but he had been an efficient enough draughtsman to put some of his subject's beauty down on paper and Dominica could fill in from memory all that he had left out.

Mrs. Radford had been a very pretty woman. She had the same blue eyes as Faith and her hair was fair, but Dominica had inherited her small straight nose and the soft curve of her lips.

The heart-shaped face was the same too, and the winged eyebrows, which gave her a balanced look, or what Lord Hawkston thought of as 'sensible'.

Dominica looked up at the picture.

"What would you have told me to do, Mama?" she asked.

She waited almost expecting to hear an answer, but there was only the buzz of the bees as they sipped the nectar from the climbing rose-tree whose blossoms reached the window-sill of her bedroom.

"Suppose when we meet I hate him?" Dominica whispered. "Suppose he dislikes me?"

Then, as if she received an answer to her question, she told herself she could return home.

She would go up to Kandy unmarried, and if Lord Hawkston was mistaken and she and his nephew took an immediate dislike to each other, then she was quite certain he would realise his proposal was insupportable and would pay her fare back to Colombo.

"In which case," Dominica told herself practically, "I have nothing to lose, and if I should like him, then things could be very different."

What was important was that she would be able to help the girls.

She knew that her father was growing more and more difficult to live with, and he had in fact made things very hard for all of them since her mother's death.

For one thing he grudged every penny that was spent on food. Next month would be Lent and Dominica knew he would try to insist on two fast-days a week.

Even out of Lent they regularly had one fast-day and the money saved was given to the poor of Colombo, many of whom, Dominica could not help thinking, ate a great deal better than they did.

Grace was always hungry and Prudence at all times had to be tempted to eat. Dominica was sure that it weakened her strength if she went for a whole day with nothing inside her but water.

Actually she cheated where the youngest was concerned.

"Why is Prudence having an egg?" Grace would enquire. "I thought this was a day of abstinence."

"It is medicine where Prudence is concerned," was Dominica's invariable reply. "It would cost Papa a great deal more if we had to send for the Doctor. I am sure she is anaemic."

"I'm anaemic too."

"You are just greedy!" Faith interposed disparagingly.

"I do not see why we should have to go without food just to please Papa."

"It is not to please Papa, but to discipline ourselves like good Christians," Dominica would say automatically.

"Well, I would rather be a bad Christian and not feel so hungry!" Faith said sharply, "Anyway, there are some bananas in the garden and if there are half-a-dozen angels with flaming swords protecting them I still intend to eat one. It will at least stop my tummy rumbling!"

Dominica often wondered what they would do without the garden where fruit grew wild and there were bananas, pawpaws, mangoes and many other fruits and vegetables indigenous to Ceylon.

Her father of course stuck strictly to his fast and always emerged from a day of abstinence a little more harsh and, Dominica would think, more aggressive in his condemnation of evil and the sins of society.

"When I am married," she told herself now, "the girls shall stay with me and I must find Faith a nice husband. The others shall lead an ordinary existence in a household where one need not have to pray over every crumb of bread and be eternally conscious of the sins of humanity."

She felt guilty at such revolutionary thoughts, but she knew how impatient the older girls were with their father's fanatical asceticism and she knew that none of them had any real affection for him.

"I have tried to look after them as you did, Mama," she said, looking up again at her mother's picture, "but it has been difficult . . . very, very difficult!"

She knew it would be worse for the others once she had left, but at the same time she would be able to ensure that

sooner or later they could escape from the restrictions imposed on them by their father.

'What a pity,' she thought, 'that Lord Hawkston would
not consider Faith as his nephew's wife. She would make a
much more willing bride than I shall be.'

A bride!

It gave her a strange, frightening feeling inside to think
that she was to be the bride of a man she had never seen and
had never heard of until an hour ago.


Lord Hawkston arrived the following morning before
Dominica expected him.

She thought it very unlikely that he would appear before
half past ten or eleven o'clock, but he must have let himself
into the house because Dominica was down on her knees
scrubbing the kitchen-floor when he walked in.

She gave a startled exclamation as she saw his highly
polished feet advancing towards her. Then she sat back on
her heels and looked up at him, the blood suddenly rising in
her cheeks in her embarrassment.

"You were not expecting me?" Lord Hawkston asked in
his deep voice.

"N . . . no, My Lord. It cannot be much after half past
nine, and I thought you would not be here until later."

"I am an early riser," Lord Hawkston said, "and we have
a great deal to do, Dominica. I think the sooner we start, the
better."

"I will get ready, My Lord," Dominica said in a low voice.

She was very conscious of the large scrubbing-brush in
her hands, of the piece of coarse soap on the floor, the bucket
of warm water beside her and the brown sacking apron she
wore over her cotton dress.

She collected the soap and started to rise to her feet as
Lord Hawkston asked:

"Do you have to do this?"

"Papa can only afford to pay a woman to come in once a
week," Dominica answered, "and the kitchen-floor gets dirty
very quickly."

"I can understand that," Lord Hawkston said gravely. "What will happen when you are no longer here?"

Dominica was now standing up, but before she replied she put the soap down on the edge of the table.

"I promised Faith, who hates domestic work, that I will try to persuade father to have Mallika, who is an excellent worker, every day once I have gone, but I am not certain he will agree."

Dominica spoke in a worried voice and now she started to take off the rough apron, the bib of which reached nearly to her neck.

"I can see, Dominica," Lord Hawkston said, "that your leaving home will present a number of problems I had not anticipated. Would it make things any easier if I promise to pay Mallika's wages myself? After all, I owe your father something for the inconvenience caused by taking away not only his daughter but apparently his 'maid-of-all-work'!"

He spoke a little quizzically. He knew that in no other house in Colombo would the lady of the house scrub her own floor. The colour rose once again in Dominica's face.

"I think Papa might be too proud to allow you to pay the wages for what ostensibly would be his own servant," she said hesitatingly.

Then she added:

"No . . . that is not true. I think really that if you gave Papa the money for Mallika he would be sure to divert it to some family whom he considered to be more deserving than his own. In which case, Faith would still have to clean the house, or leave it dirty."

There was a faint smile on Lord Hawkston's lips as he said:

"I see I must find another solution. You shall pay Mallika with the money I give you for the purpose. Will that be more satisfactory?"

"It would indeed!" Dominica said with a little lilt in her voice. "But you are . . . sure you can . . . afford it?"

"Quite sure!" Lord Hawkston said. "As it happens, Dominica, I am what you would consider a rich man, so you need have no qualms about accepting from me not only the money for Mallika's wages, but also for the trousseau we are now going to buy."

Dominica drew in her breath.

She seemed about to say something, then changed her mind.

"I will go and change," she said. "I would not wish to keep Your Lordship waiting."

She went from the kitchen before he could reply.

Lord Hawkston looked round him, noting the primitive stove, the bare floor, the hard chairs and the cheap china stacked on the dresser. Then he went from the kitchen into the sitting-room where he had interviewed the Vicar and Dominica the previous day.

He had not to wait long.

He heard Dominica's footsteps hurrying down the uncarpeted stairway and she came into the room less than five minutes after leaving him.

She had changed into the dress she had worn in Church, the same ugly black bonnet covered her hair, and there were black cotton gloves on her hands.

"I am sorry I was not ready when you arrived, My Lord," she said in a tone as if she was still reproaching herself for being so tardy.

"Where are the rest of the family?" Lord Hawkston enquired.

"They are all with their teachers, with the exception of Faith who has accompanied Papa because I was coming out with you. It meant that she could not have her French lesson."

She thought Lord Hawkston looked faintly surprised and added by way of explanation:

"Mama insisted that however poor we were we should all have a good education. Sometimes Papa resents how much he has to pay, and he wanted to stop Faith's lessons as soon as she reached eighteen. But I persuaded him to let her continue for the rest of this year."

"You sound as if you missed your lessons," Lord Hawkston said.

"More than I can ever say," Dominica answered. "It was like stepping into another world."

She gave a little sigh.

"If only I could get some more books!"

A thought struck her and there was a sudden light in her eyes as she asked:

"Will there be books at your plantation?"

"There were quite a number of them when I left," Lord Hawkston answered, "but what you cannot find on my bookshelves can easily be supplied. There is, I well know, a bookshop in Kandy and several in Colombo. You must tell me what your interests are, Dominica. I would like to hear about them."

As he spoke he walked towards the front door which was open and she could see the carriage waiting outside.

Dominica could not help a little thrill of excitement as she stepped into the Governor's well-padded victoria and the footman put a light rug over her knees.

Lord Hawkston seated himself beside her.

"What do you like reading?" he asked.

"Everything," Dominica said, "but especially the histories of other countries—and most especially about England."

"You have never been there?"

"No. Mama used to tell us what she did as a girl and of the Manor House in which she lived in Gloucester. It all sounded fascinating!"

"Do you like Ceylon?"

"Of course," Dominica replied. "It has always been my home and I love Colombo, the people, the flowers, and the sea. Mama always said that if we went to England we would miss the sunshine but there were many compensations."

"And what did she think those were?" Lord Hawkston asked in a slightly sceptical voice.

"I think Mama felt her roots were in England, and that therefore the country was a part of herself. I am sure she was right and Nationality is something far deeper and more fundamental than merely having a certain type of passport."

Lord Hawkston glanced at Dominica in surprise.

This was not the sort of remark he had expected from a young girl.

"So you want to travel?" he remarked.

"With my body, as I have travelled with my mind," Dominica replied. "But of course, the latter is the far cheaper method!"

She laughed as she spoke and Lord Hawkston noticed how it changed and illuminated her face.

They drove past the race course on the sea front in silence and then Dominica said:

"Having lived so long in Ceylon, where do you feel that you belong?"

"That is a question I have often asked myself," Lord Hawkston said. "When I had to leave Ceylon two years ago I felt I was leaving everything that was familiar; everything I thought of as home. And yet, once back in England, I found so much that mattered to me because it was a part of my childhood, my adolescence, and the time when I first thought of myself as a man."

"And so you loved it just as you loved Ceylon!" Dominica said.

"I suppose that is true," Lord Hawkston agreed but almost in surprise, as if he had not thought of it that way before.

They had reached the more crowded streets teeming with every variety of oriental race and costume.

There were the Ceylonese, the men as well as the women wearing their hair tied behind in knots, the latter adding elaborate hairpins, and there were the darker-skinned Tamils who came from India.

Hindus of every caste jostled Moormen of Arab blood who introduced coffee to Ceylon. Afghan traders, Malay policemen, Parsees, Chinese—and there were Eurasians of Dutch or Portuguese or English descent.

It was all a kaleidoscope of movement, colour, noise and confusion.

"Where are you taking me?" Dominica asked.

"I have learnt from the Governor's most able and efficient Secretary," Lord Hawkston replied, "that the smartest and most important dressmaker in Ceylon is Madame Fernando."

Dominica turned to look at him with large eyes.

"So she is," she said, "but I must warn Your Lordship that she is also very expensive."

"I have already assured you, Dominica, that you shall have the best and most beguiling trousseau that any girl could wish for. I therefore intend to introduce you to Madame Fernando, explain that the bills are to come to me, then leave you to explain what you and she think most suitable."

Dominica drew in her breath and turned her head to look straight in front of her.

Lord Hawkston was sure that she was thinking excitedly of what she would purchase.

What girl dressed as she was, in the cheapest material the market-place could supply and made, he was quite certain, by her own hands, could resist the lure of clothes which, if the Governor's Secretary was to be believed, were worn by all the smartest and most fashionable ladies in Colombo?

They reached Madame Fernando's shop which displayed nothing in the window except an exceedingly smart bonnet trimmed with large ostrich plumes of crimson and blue.

It was obviously just decorative rather than anything that a lady would wish to wear, but Dominica looked at it with what Lord Hawkston thought were appreciative eyes and he wondered for the first time if he was wise to trust her taste.

Then as the footman got down from the box of the carriage to open the door for them, Dominica turned impulsively.

"Please," she said to Lord Hawkston in a low voice, "will you choose what I should wear? I am sure I will make mistakes and you will be ashamed of me."

Lord Hawkston was surprised.

He had planned exactly what he would do after he had left Dominica at the shop and where he would go before he returned to collect her.

He had never envisaged for a moment that he would be called upon to sit in a dressmaker's choosing gowns for a young woman, or to take an active part in providing her with a trousseau other than writing a cheque in payment for it.

Then with a faint smile on his lips he made up his mind.

"Why not?" he asked more to himself than to Dominica.

"After all, I have always believed that if one wants a thing done well, one should do it one's self. I will, as you suggest, stay with you, Dominica, but do not blame me if we have conflicting ideas as to how you should appear."

He saw the gratitude in her eyes and knew she had not only been worried about making mistakes, but also felt shy at being in such a grand shop by herself.

Madame Fernando was, Lord Hawkston was prepared to admit, somewhat over-powering and he soon realised that, if he had not stayed with Dominica at her request, she would have had little say in the choosing of her trousseau.

French by birth, Madame Fernando had come to Colombo as the young bride of a Portuguese planter.

She had however soon grown tired of life on a plantation and had come to Colombo to get orders for under-clothes which she embroidered skilfully for any lady who required them.

She was fortunate in securing the patronage of the Governor's wife and from that moment her success was ensured.

At first she worked night and day to complete the orders she received, then she engaged the help of Ceylonese girls whom she taught to embroider as well as she could herself.

In ten years she was established as a dressmaker with a shop, a large staff and a bank balance which increased year by year.

It was fortunate for her husband that the bank balance was there when the coffee disease destroyed his plantation overnight.

Disgusted and disillusioned with Ceylon, he wished to return to Europe. His wife however refused point blank to go with him.

She was happy in Colombo and she had also several attentive admirers she had no intention of leaving.

In the end Mr. Fernando went home without her.

There was no question of a divorce as both of them were Catholics, and Madame Fernando was quite certain that he would find plenty of charming ladies to console him in Lisbon.

Now Madame Fernando with shrewd eyes took in every detail of Lord Hawkston's appearance and she had already been informed by one of her receptionists in awe-struck tones that he had arrived in the Governor's carriage.

"May I be of assistance, *Monsieur*?" she asked in an ingratiating voice which had never lost its broken accent.

"I am Lord Hawkston and I need your help, Madame."

Madame Fernando dropped a curtsey.

"I am yours to command, Milord."

"This young lady, Miss Dominica Radford, is to marry my nephew, Mr. Gerald Warren. She needs an entire trousseau."

There was a decided glitter of excitement in Madame Fernando's eyes as she replied:

"It will be a pleasure to dress anyone so charming as *Mademoiselle*!"

She glanced however as she spoke at Dominica's gown, then looked away as if its material and shape made her shudder.

"There is one difficulty," Lord Hawkston explained.

Madame waited a little apprehensively.

"It is that we wish to leave no later than early on Thursday for Kandy, which means that Miss Radford must have enough gowns ready by then, in which to travel. The rest can be sent after her."

Madame Fernando drew in a deep breath of relief.

She had been half-expecting that Lord Hawkston was going to stay that he could not afford to pay at once for all the things he desired. To hurry, however, would cost him more as the seamstresses would have to work late into the night to finish the orders.

But that was of little consequence.

"I have some dresses ready or half-finished which I am sure would suit *Mademoiselle* to perfection," Madame Fernando said. "May she put them on for Your Lordship's approval?"

"We are in your hands, Madame," His Lordship replied with an air which Madame Fernando could not help thinking was extremely attractive.

She said as much to Dominica as she took her to a dressing-room, after she had given a dozen orders to the young Ceylonese girls to bring her what was required.

"Milord, your Uncle-in-law to be, *Mademoiselle*, has an air *très distingué*. He is obviously, how you say in England, a great gentleman!"

"He is very kind," Dominica answered, "but I would not wish to choose, Madame, always the most expensive."

"Do not worry your head over such things," Madame Fernando said soothingly, "the cost is between *Monsieur* and myself. But first for you to show my gowns to perfection we must start with the right foundation."

She helped Dominica out of her dress and gave an exclamation of horror as she saw the plain calico under-clothes beneath it.

For the first time in her life Dominica was laced into a corset which gave her figure an elegance she had not thought possible.

"You are thin, *Mademoiselle*," Madame Fernando said. "That is good, but the shape must be right—a very small waist, the suspicion of a bosom, and well-moulded hips."

She attended to Dominica as she spoke, and when finally what she called the foundation of her gowns was achieved, Dominica could hardly believe that silk could feel so soft against her skin or that silk stockings could make such a difference to her legs.

Finally a gown was put over her head which made her gasp with astonishment.

Of soft pink silk it seemed to accentuate the lights in her hair and the purity of her skin.

"It is too rich . . . too grand!" Dominica protested, overawed by the frills and flounces, the small bustle and the little train that swept out behind her.

"I shall never have an occasion to wear anything so elaborate!" she gasped.

"Let us show you to Milord," Madame Fernando suggested. "There are a number of others for him to see if he does not like this one."

Dominica went out into the Salon very shyly.

As she saw Lord Hawkston sitting at his ease in a damask-covered arm-chair she felt that it had been audacious to ask him to stay with her, and yet she doubted she could ever in fact have faced being left on her own.

Madame Fernando was to her mind terrifying, and she

was certain that Lord Hawkston would never have understood what gowns she had been compelled to buy unless he had actually been present at the transaction.

She waited his verdict, her eyes on his face.

"Charming!" he said, "It suits you, Dominica. Do you like it yourself?"

"I shall never have occasion to wear such a gown," Dominica protested.

"I told you that my nephew was a gay young man. I am certain he will want to take you into Kandy and you will find he has friends you will visit in the neighborhood."

He turned towards Madame Fernando.

"That must certainly be included in the trousseau, Madame. What else have you for me to see?"

Dominica tried on six other gowns all of which Lord Hawkston insisted on buying; then a number of others were held up for his inspection, the majority of which he approved.

Finally, Madame produced her *pièce de resistance*—a wedding-gown of white lace so beautiful, so alluring, that when Dominica looked at herself in the mirror she could hardly believe it was her own reflection.

There was a veil and wreath of orange-blossom.

"We shall have to alter your hair-style, *Mademoiselle*," Madame Fernando admonished her. "It is too severe, too harsh for a young lady of your age. I will send you a hairdresser. He will show you what is a more fashionable style."

"N . . . no, do not engage him until I am ready to receive him," Dominica said hastily.

She could not help thinking how horrified her father would be if he found a hairdresser in the Vicarage.

At the same time she knew that Madame Fernando was speaking the truth in saying that the style in which she did her hair was not in keeping with the elegance of her new gowns.

To please Madame, who was very insistent, Dominica loosened the hair over her ears, made it fall from a parting in the middle in a soft wave on either side of her forehead and pinned at the back into a chignon.

"That is better!" Madame approved. "But you need curls

on the top, *Mademoiselle*, especially in the evening. They are very becoming."

"I will think about it," Dominica faltered.

But somehow she felt that Lord Hawkston would agree with Madame Fernando.

She was well aware that he was not buying such delectable gowns entirely for her own satisfaction. She knew that he wished to make her look as attractive as the girl who had jilted his nephew and whom he therefore could not take with him to Kandy.

'I expect she was very pretty,' Dominica thought.

She wished she could have seen the lady who had transferred her affections elsewhere as that she would have some idea on what to model herself.

Then she decided that to be a mere copy of another woman who had not honoured her word and had failed not only Gerald Warren, but also his Uncle, would be a mistake.

For one thing it might annoy Lord Hawkston if he thought that she was equally frivolous and untrustworthy.

"I will be myself," Dominica decided. "I am Mama's daughter and Mama always said that we each of us have our own personalities, our own characters and our own standards. I will try to make the best of myself, but I will not try to imitate anyone else."

The thought made her walk into the Salon wearing the wedding-gown and made her appear as if she had stepped out of a fairy-story.

Lord Hawkston looked up at her for a long moment before he said quietly:

"It might have been designed for you!"

"You approve, Milord?" Madame Fernando enquired.

"I will take it with the rest of the gowns."

"Thank you, Milord! Thank you!"

Madame Fernando turned away to give some instructions and Dominica moved nearer to Lord Hawkston.

"Are you sure we should buy this gown?" she asked. "You do not think it . . . unlucky to anticipate that your nephew will accept me as his . . . wife?"

"I cannot think of any young man who would not eagerly accept you at this moment," Lord Hawkston replied. "Look in the mirror, Dominica. You will see for yourself how charming and attractive you look."

She gave him a faint smile but at the same time her eyes were worried.

"You have done enough for one morning," he said. "Change into one of your new dresses and I will take you out to luncheon at the Galle-face Hotel."

Dominica looked surprised, but when she told Madame Fernando what was required she dressed her in a simple but exceedingly attractive gown of flowered muslin trimmed with pink ribbons.

There were new shoes to match the dresses, there were gloves and reticules to match most of them.

What was more, to go with the gown that Dominica was wearing there was a little bonnet trimmed with a wreath of exquisite silk roses and ribbons of a soft pink to tie under her chin.

"Shall I throw away the clothes in which you arrived?" Madame Fernando enquired.

Dominica gave an exclamation of horror.

"No, of course not! There is a lot of wear in them still and I have five sisters younger than I am."

"You will no doubt have far more attractive clothes to hand down in future," Madame Fernando said with a smile.

"That is what I think myself," Dominica replied, "but in the meantime . . ."

Her voice died away.

She could not explain to Madame Fernando that her father would be horrified at the clothes she was wearing now and she was already worrying how, when she returned home, she could change quickly into one of her ordinary dresses before he saw her.

He had so often denounced as sinful the women in his Congregation who dressed extravagantly. He was quite certain that frivolity was a sin and that beautiful clothes corrupted those who wore them.

"Please pack everything in which I came," Dominica said, "and I will take them with me in the carriage."

"The gowns which are ready will be sent to the Vicarage this evening, *Mademoiselle*," Madame Fernando said. "The others will follow just as soon as they are finished until Thursday morning. After that the clothes will be sent by train to Kandy. I will speak about it with Milord."

When Dominica came from the dressing-room it was to find Lord Hawkston writing a cheque.

She knew it must be for an enormous sum and she felt exceedingly guilty that so much money had been spent on clothes which could have fed those who were hungry.

But it was impossible not to be thrilled with her appearance and the fact that she possessed so many delectable things—so many she could hardly remember how many there were.

She reached Lord Hawkston's side as he was handing the cheque to Madame Fernando and he turned to smile at her.

Her eyes were on his face and he saw there was a pleading expression in them.

"What is it?" he asked.

"I want to ask you something," Dominica said. "You may refuse, but I must . . . ask you."

"Tell me," he said quietly.

She drew him a little to one side out of earshot of Madame.

"It is just that you have given me so much—so much more than I expected or even dreamt of," she said. "Could we possibly give back one dress and buy new bonnets for my sisters? We have worn the black ones ever since Mama died, and they will have to go on wearing them for years and years! We all hate black!"

There was a little throb in her voice and her eyes pleaded with him to understand.

"Just one dress less?" Dominica pleaded, "It would cost you no more."

Lord Hawkston smiled at her, then turned towards Madame Fernando.

"Madame," he said. "I have another commission for you."

"But of course, Milord," she smiled.

"There are," Lord Hawkston said slowly, "five more Miss Radfords of varying ages. I would like you to make a simple Sunday dress such as Miss Dominica is wearing now for each of them. They will also require bonnets to match, each one to be different and suitable to their particular age and individuality. I think it would be wisest if you send someone to the Vicarage, perhaps this evening, to measure them."

"It will be a pleasure, Milord!" Madame Fernando said in a gratified voice.

She bowed Lord Hawkston and Dominica out of the shop with many expressions of gratitude.

When finally they drove away in the carriage Dominica turned towards Lord Hawkston.

"I did not know anyone could be so marvellously and wonderfully kind!" she exclaimed. "Thank you, My Lord! Thank you with all my heart!"

"It has been a pleasure, Dominica," he replied—and meant it!

# CHAPTER FOUR

The train was moving at what seemed to Dominica to be great speed through a succession of rice fields and swamps.

She sat looking out, feeling as she had felt from the moment Lord Hawkston came into her life that everything was happening in a dream and there was no reality or substance about it.

Up to the very last moment she could hardly believe that she was really leaving the Vicarage for good and saying good-bye to her sisters.

They had been almost too excited about the new dresses and bonnets Lord Hawkston was giving them from Madame Fernando's to be upset at the thought of Dominica leaving them.

When she first told them what he had ordered they could hardly believe it was true.

"Will Papa let us wear them?" Faith asked at last. "What will he say when he sees us in such grand clothes?"

"He will say," Charity remarked, mimicking her father's

voice: " 'A woman's conceit and her lust for rich attire is an abomination in the eyes of the Lord'!"

"I am quite certain he will make us go on wearing our old dresses and those hateful, hideous bonnets!" Faith said despairingly.

"I thought about that coming home," Dominica said. "Although perhaps it is wrong of me, I can tell you what you must do."

"What is that?" the older girls asked in unison.

"When your new bonnets arrive," Dominica said, "burn your old ones!"

"Burn them?"

The words were almost a shriek.

"You know as well as I do," Dominica went on, "that Papa would never let you spend money on buying a new bonnet if you had one that was still wearable. And you could not go to Church bare-headed!"

Faith put her arms around Dominica and hugged her.

"You are a genius!" she exclaimed. "That is exactly what we will do."

"Perhaps it is a little deceitful," Dominica said hesitatingly, "but I am sure the gowns will be lovely . . . as lovely as mine . . . and Lord Hawkston told Madame Fernando they were all to be different."

"He is the most wonderful man in the world!" Faith cried exultantly.

"Be careful not to thank him in front of Papa," Dominica said admonishingly.

They remembered her warning although it was difficult to say nothing until the moment came when they were alone with him.

Then their gratitude burst forth.

"How can you be so kind?" "It is so exciting!" "We can hardly believe that you are giving us such a wonderful present!"

"I shall look forward to seeing you dressed as you should be," Lord Hawkston said, and Dominica fancied there was a twinkle in his eyes.

Prudence, who had said little, came to stand beside him.

"I think you're very kind," she said with a slight lisp. "I'll marry you when I'm grown up!"

Lord Hawkston looked somewhat startled, but he said:

"I am very honoured at receiving the first proposal of marriage any lady has ever made to me!"

"You'll wait for me?" Prudence enquired.

He looked down at her and realised she was a small replica of Dominica. She had the same ash-blond hair, grey eyes and small straight nose.

She looked fragile and he guessed she was the weakest member of the family.

"Will you wait?" Prudence asked earnestly.

"I'll tell you what I will promise you," Lord Hawkston said after a moment's pause. "When you are eighteen I will give a grand Ball at which you shall meet all the most handsome, eligible and charming young men of my acquaintance."

Prudence's eyes lit up.

"I must learn to dance!"

"You must also be strong and eat up all your food," Dominica interposed, "otherwise you will not be strong enough to dance all night. Is that not true, My Lord?"

She glanced at Lord Hawkston meaningfully as she spoke.

"It is indeed," he said gravely. "Dancing can be very strenuous. It would be extremely disappointing if, like Cinderella, you had to leave your own Ball at twelve o'clock!"

"I'll eat," Prudence promised.

It was clever of him, Dominica thought now as she looked out of the train, to give the child an inducement. There had been so many struggles in the past because Prudence was fastidious and found the very limited fare their father would permit unpalatable.

The rice fields alternated with jungle-covered knolls which seemed like small islands surrounded by the emerald green of the young rice. Dominica could see the splay-footed buffalo hitched on to wooden ploughs floundering up to their knees where the wet ground was being prepared for a new crop.

From Rambukana it was a steady climb and another engine was hitched to the first.

At one point, which Dominica knew was called 'Sensation Rock' the line was cut into the steep side of the mountain and the view was fantastic.

There was a precipice of 700 feet below them and below that another descent of more than 1,000 feet to the paddy-fields.

The hills near the railway were covered with young tea-plants growing between the stumps of dead coffee trees, but most of the time they were passing through forest.

Lord Hawkston sat opposite Dominica, but feeling that he would not wish to talk above the noise of the engine, she looked out at the scenery, deep in her own thoughts.

She was conscious that her traveling dress was very elegant and the small jacket which lay beside her on another seat was beautifully cut.

When her sisters had seen her wearing the new bonnet trimmed with flowers they were awe-struck into silence, until Faith, breaking the tension, asked:

"How many years will you have to wear that gown before I can have it?"

"I will send it to you as soon as I am given another," Dominica promised.

There were so many things to do at the last moment, so many instructions to give to Mallika that Dominica had little time to think about her own feelings or to worry about what lay ahead.

Only in the darkness of the night had she felt a little tremor of fear when she thought of Gerald Warren waiting for her, and wondered if he was feeling as apprehensive about her as she was about him.

She at least could picture him as being very like his Uncle, and that was a consolation in itself.

But he had no yard-stick by which to measure her, and she wondered if perhaps he was feeling angry and rebellious at the idea of being married off to a stranger.

She knew that Lord Hawkston had written to his nephew on Monday, and to make quite certain he received the letter and that it was not delayed he had sent it by a bearer, paying the fare of the man from Colombo to the plantation and back again.

Lord Hawkston did not tell Dominica whether he had told the bearer to wait for an answer. She fancied that he had not expected one, being quite certain that his nephew would obey his wishes without argument.

All the same it was impossible not to feel extremely apprehensive as the train, after a four-hour journey, steamed into Kandy and Dominica knew they were to change trains for the last part of their journey.

She had always been told that Kandy was beautiful and that it was the last stronghold of the Ceylonese Kings with its Sacred Temple of the Tooth overlooking an artificial lake.

But she had not expected it to be so beautiful.

There were over two hours to wait before their connecting train went on into the Central Province, which would take them, Lord Hawkston said, within five miles of his plantation.

Because he knew it would interest her he hired a carriage and they drove through the town and along the side of the lake.

Everywhere there were orchids, jasmines, magnolias, the orange and crimson flowers of the asocas and the delicate white blossoms of the champee which had a strong and lovely scent.

"Did you know that Krishna, the Hindu God of Love, tips his arrows with the champee flowers?" Dominica asked.

"Does that make them more effective?" Lord Hawkston enquired with a smile.

"The Brahmins think so."

Then daringly she asked:

"Have you ever been in love, My Lord?"

"Not enough to wish to sacrifice my freedom," he replied.

"That means your answer is 'no'," Dominica said. "I am sure if one is really in love there is no sacrifice one would not make; nothing one would not relinquish!"

"You sound as if you have been reading some very romantic novels," he said accusingly.

"Papa would not allow a novel in the house," Dominica said, "but I know love . . . real love, if we find it, would be too strong for us to . . . resist it."

Even as she spoke she knew she was being indiscreet to

talk in such a manner with Lord Hawkston, seeing that he had persuaded her to marry his nephew without love, without even affection. But the beauty all around her made her almost irresistibly think of love.

As if he wished to change the subject Lord Hawkston told Dominica how brave the Kandyans had been and how they were the last inhabitants of Ceylon to hold out against the conquest of the country by the British.

He told her too about Asia's most spectacular pageant, the Esala Perahera, which had been held at Kandy for the last two thousand years.

"You will enjoy it," he said. "The gaily caparisoned elephants, the drummers and dancers, the Chieftains in jewelled costumes, the whip-crackers, all combine to make it the most impressive spectacle I have ever seen."

"I have often wondered how, or why, Ceylon possessed the tooth of Buddha," Dominica said.

As she spoke she was watching the women in their brilliant saris climbing the steps into the Temple. In their hands they carried the flowers of the champee tree to lay like prayers before the shrine.

"The famous relic is said by legend to have come here concealed in the hair of a Princess fleeing from India during the war," Lord Hawkston replied.

He paused to add with a smile:

"I suspect her hair was as long and luxuriant as yours."

Dominica blushed.

"How do you know . . . my hair is . . . like that?"

"I guessed that you have difficulty in arranging it."

Dominica looked worried.

"Perhaps I could be more fashionable if I cut some of it off."

"You are to do nothing of the kind," Lord Hawkston said positively. "A woman should have long hair, it is part of her femininity and undoubtedly your crowning glory."

Dominica blushed again; at the same time she felt a little glow of delight at his words. They were a compliment!

There were so many things she wanted to ask him and so much she wanted to learn that all too quickly it was time to return to the station and once again they were travelling northward.

"This is very different," he said as the train moved out of the station, "from the days when I first bought my plantation, when I used to have to ride down to Kandy. There was only a dusty track on which we conveyed the coffee by bullock cart."

He smiled and added:

"Now we can hardly visualise the days when Governor North made a tour of the island with 160 palanquin-bearers, 400 coolies, two elephants and fifty lascoreens!"

"It must have given them many a headache to try to accommodate such a large party," Dominica exclaimed.

She tried to talk naturally but every mile they progressed made her feel more nervous and more afraid.

She knew only too well that Lord Hawkston expected her to be calm and sensible. That, after all, was the reason he had chosen her to be the wife of his nephew, and if she appeared at all hysterical he would despise her.

Accordingly she forced herself to speak naturally and she was aware that he was trying to put her at her ease and make everything seem quite commonplace.

"I told Gerald in my letter not, after all, to meet us at Kandy," he said. "I thought it would be difficult for you to converse together for the first time in a rattling train. You will meet him at the house I built myself and of which I am very proud."

"Was it a difficult task?" Dominica asked.

"It was one I greatly enjoyed," Lord Hawkston replied. "At first the building was much smaller than it is now and my plans received a set-back when the coffee failed. Then when tea began to come into its own I resumed the work and the house and garden were actually completed only a year before I had to return to England."

There was a note in his voice which told Dominica all too clearly that this was another reason why he hated to leave Ceylon.

"Perhaps as a woman you will find a lot of things that I have omitted," he said with a smile, "but to me my house seemed nearly perfect and its position could not be improved on anywhere else in Ceylon!"

"I am sure I shall admire it very much," Dominica said in a low voice.

She hoped as she spoke that she would also admire its present occupant.

Supposing Gerald Warren had a broken heart for the girl he had lost and could not bear the thought of another woman taking her place?

"I must be very kind and understanding." Dominica told herself.

She was used to being gentle and compassionate.

After her mother had died her father often insisted that she went with him when he visited the families in the native quarters whom he considered his special charges.

Many of them were old, ill or dying. Some of them were deformed. A number of children were sick.

As if he read her thoughts, Lord Hawkston asked unexpectedly:

"What did you do when you accompanied your father on his visiting?"

"Papa is always trying to convert the Ceylonese to Christianity," Dominica answered. "Mama used to say he should have been a Missionary. There are many families who have been baptised by Papa, and he never allows them to become indifferent to their promises."

She gave a little smile.

"Sometimes I think he bullies them into being Christians whether they like it or not. He is certainly very severe if they miss Church on Sunday without a really valid excuse."

Lord Hawkston was quite certain that the Ceylonese, who were an easy-going, friendly people, were easily pressured by the Vicar into doing what he wished, but aloud he said:

"You have not told me what you did."

"I looked after the children while Papa remonstrated with their parents, or I would try to make the elderly and the sick comfortable. I think many of them just enjoyed seeing me because I was someone to talk to."

"I can believe that," Lord Hawkston said.

Dominica looked out of the train.

Walking along the roadway which ran beside the railway line she could see a Buddhist Priest in the bright saffron yellow robe which proclaimed his calling.

"I can never understand," she said speaking her thoughts aloud, "why any Buddhist should ever be willing to change his religion to Christianity. Buddhism is such a happy religion."

"You have read about it?" Lord Hawkston enquired.

"And talked with many Buddhists," Dominica replied, then added hastily: "Not that Papa would have approved, but I was so interested in their beliefs, in fact I have often wished I were a Buddhist."

"Perhaps you were in a previous incarnation," Lord Hawkston said.

She smiled at him.

"Do you, like them, believe in reincarnation?"

"Shall I say I consider it a possibility," he replied.

Dominica's eyes were alight with interest.

"It seems the only just . . . the only right explanation of all the troubles and ills of the world," she said. "The Priests are so dedicated, yet quiet and unobtrusive. They never force their convictions on anyone."

Lord Hawkston knew she was thinking what a contrast they were to her father.

He had begun in the last few days to realise that Dominica was extremely intelligent and thought far more seriously than he would have expected any other girl of her age to do.

He supposed in a way it was part of her unusual upbringing, and yet despite her ignorance of the social world he could not help realising she had a mind that could not be confined and would touch heights that other people would never reach.

"I will tell you something that will please you," he said unexpectedly.

"What is that?" Dominica enquired.

"I have already written to the book-shop in Kandy to despatch a consignment of their very latest volumes to the plantation."

The way Dominica's face lit up told him how pleased she was even before the words came to her lips.

"You will have plenty of time for reading," Lord Hawkston said, "when Gerald is out in the fields, but there is one thing I must say to you."

"What is that?" Dominica asked a little nervously.

"You must not do any work in the house yourself."

"Why not?" she enquired.

"Because you will have an adequate supply of servants, and to take over what is their work, would be to insult them and suggest you do not think they are competent."

"And if they do things wrong?" Dominica enquired.

"Then of course you can explain exactly what you require," Lord Hawkston replied. "But no scrubbing, no washing or dusting!"

"What about cooking?" Dominica asked faintly.

"The cook I have in my house is extremely proficient," Lord Hawkston replied. "If by chance he has left, which I think is highly unlikely, then of course you can teach whoever takes his place; but you are not, and let me make this quite clear, Dominica, you are not to cook yourself."

She gave a little sigh, then she said:

"I can see you are turning me into a grand lady. No wonder you have ordered a number of books for me to read. What *may* I do?"

"You can ride for one thing," Lord Hawkston answered. "I have a feeling you would look well on a horse."

"We used to ride a pony when we were children," Dominica said, "but when he died we could not afford another one."

"I will teach you to ride," Lord Hawkston said, then added as if it was an afterthought, "unless Gerald wishes to do so himself."

The train drew up at the station where they were to disembark at about three-thirty in the afternoon.

Before they reached Kandy they had eaten at mid-day out of a delicious luncheon basket which Lord Hawkston had brought with him from the Queen's House.

There had been delectable and exciting dishes such as Dominica had never tasted before and there was a golden wine to drink which she felt was bottled sunshine.

Now as they stepped out of the station she felt a little sick and wondered if it was from an inner fear or whether she had eaten too much at luncheon.

There was a carriage waiting for them, and as Lord Hawkston directed the porter who was collecting the luggage from the van, a Ceylonese man came towards him.

"Ranjan!" Lord Hawkston exclaimed. "How nice of you to meet me."

He shook the man by the hand then turned to Dominica.

"This is Ranjan, Dominica," he said, "my Overseer, whom I left in charge when I went to England. It is good to see you, Ranjan."

"You too, *Durai*," Ranjan replied. "We are hoping you come back."

"Is everything all right?" Lord Hawkston asked.

"No, *Durai*. Plenty trouble," Ranjan replied.

"I heard there were some difficulties," Lord Hawkston said, "but it is something, I promise you, I will put right."

"What happen now no-one put right," Ranjan said in a low voice.

Tactfully Dominica turned aside but she could still hear what the two men were saying.

"What has happened?" Lord Hawkston asked sharply.

"Sēētha, girl *Sinna Durai* turn away, dead. We find body bottom of torrent this morning."

Dominica was aware that Lord Hawkston was suddenly rigid.

He had stopped moving and was standing in the sunshine facing the Overseer whose sarong was a patch of colour against the wooden walls of the station buildings.

"She killed herself!" Lord Hawkston said almost beneath his breath.

"Yes, *Durai*. Lakshman, Sēētha's father, swear revenge!"

"You must find him, Ranjan," Lord Hawkston said firmly. "Find him immediately. Tell him how I will give him full compensation and more, for what he has suffered."

"I try, *Durai*," Ranjan answered, "but he plenty mad. Too late for money."

"You must try, Ranjan! Say I have just arrived. Say I am extremely upset at what has occurred and ask him to come and see me immediately."

"I do that, *Durai*," Ranjan answered, but Dominica thought his tone was doubtful.

"I will see you later," Lord Hawkston said.

Then in another tone of voice to Dominica:

"Come Dominica, you should not stand in the sunshine without your sunshade to protect you."

"No, of course not," Dominica replied.

Obediently she opened her sunshade and held it over her head.

Some of the luggage was piled on to the carriage in which they were to travel, the rest Ranjan took with him in a rather curiously shaped cart, made of halmila wood, which Dominica guessed was used for carrying vegetables or bamboo about the plantation.

The carriage which drew Lord Hawkston and Dominica set off at a good pace, but once they had left the station the way was uphill and they soon slowed down.

Lord Hawkston did not speak and after a moment Dominica asked a little nervously:

"Who is . . . Sēētha?"

"You heard what my Head-man said to me?"

"I could not help it."

"He should have been more discreet," Lord Hawkston said sharply.

"You said the girl had . . . killed herself. Why?"

She knew that her question was unwelcome and yet at the same time some instinct told her that what had been said was of importance to her.

After a distinct pause Lord Hawkston answered:

"You have lived in Ceylon all your life, Dominica, and you must have been aware what a lonely, isolated life the average planter lives in the hills. He is alone with only his coolies. That is why I was so anxious to find a suitable wife for my nephew."

"Sēētha is Ceylonese," Dominica said, her eyes on Lord Hawkston's face.

"Her name makes it obvious," he said abruptly. "She must have been mentally deranged to throw herself down the torrent. It is a drop of hundreds of feet, and if she fell on the rocks she would be rendered unconscious and therefore would be easily drowned by the falling water."

"Why did she kill herself?" Dominica persisted.

Lord Hawkston did not answer and after a moment she said in a very small voice:

"Was it . . . anything to do with . . . Mr. Warren turning her away? That is whom your Overseer meant by *Sinna Durai*, was it not?"

Lord Hawkston had contemplated lying, then he knew it would be an insult to Dominica's intelligence.

It was unfortunate that Ranjan had blurted out in front of her the news of Sēētha's death, but he was not to know that Lord Hawkston had with him a wife for the *Sinna Durai*.

Ranjan in fact, as Lord Hawkston was well aware, was so worried and distraught by what had occurred that it had never entered his mind to be discreet in front of a stranger.

Choosing his words carefully Lord Hawkston said slowly:

"There are always women, Dominica, who are ready to supply the female companionship that young planters find essential when they are alone."

Although she made no movement, he felt that Dominica winced. He had the feeling that she had half expected it, and yet it was a shock when it was put into words.

"You mean that Mr. Warren and Sēētha were in . . . love with each other?" she asked in a hesitating voice.

"I mean nothing of the sort," Lord Hawkston replied. "It is not a question of love as you and I think of it, Dominica. It is just that a man has a physical need for a woman, and when a woman is ready to supply that need it can become an amicable, business-like arrangement."

Dominica was silent for some moments. Then at length she said:

"I think this must be one of the . . . temptations against which Papa preaches so fervently. He tried to have the places closed in Colombo where the planters met Ceylonese women because he thought such . . . associations were . . . wicked."

"Your father has, understandably, rather extreme views on the matter," Lord Hawkston said coldly. "But after all, until your mother died he was a married man, and therefore not subject to loneliness or to the temptations which, may I say quite frankly, are recognised by most people in this part of the world."

"The girl killed . . . herself," Dominica said. "Why did your nephew send her away?"

"Let me tell you at once," Lord Hawkston answered, "that this has nothing to do with your coming here and the letter I sent to my nephew announcing our arrival. It actually happened before I had even arrived back in Colombo."

He felt his explanation might make things better. At the same time he knew that Dominica was very pale and there was an expression in her grey eyes which he could not understand.

That she was shocked at what had occurred was predictable, but he could only hope that if she understood that the situation had nothing to do with her personally, it would not disturb her unduly.

They drove in silence for a little while. Then Lord Hawkston said:

"I want you to promise me something, Dominica."

"What is it?" she asked in a low voice.

"You and I have become friends these last few days," Lord Hawkston said, "and I like to think that you trust my judgement. Will you trust me a little further when I tell you to forget what you overheard just now and put the whole incident out of your mind? Leave me to arrange matters as I think best."

There was a little pause before Dominica said:

"I will . . . try."

"You must remember we have only heard one side of the story," Lord Hawkston said. "I was told when I first arrived in Colombo that there was some difficulty over this woman, but I have not yet heard what Gerald has to say about it. I know you will agree we must be fair and hear his explanation before we blame him in any way for what may just have been an unfortunate accident."

Dominica could not answer and Lord Hawkston went on:

"As you can imagine, the coolies on the plantation who have little to think about exaggerate everything dramatically. They make a drama out of every small occurrence! I am confident that when I get to the bottom of things I will find it quite different from what we at present suspect."

As he spoke Lord Hawkston only wished he could feel as optimistic as he sounded.

James Taylor had told him that Gerald was making a mess of things, but it was now very much worse than when James had come to see him in Colombo and warn him of what he might expect.

'Damn the young fool!' Lord Hawkston thought to himself.

He was well aware that what had occurred would travel like lightning round the neighbourhood.

What was more it would unsettle the work-people and do harm to the plantation. That, he thought, he could never forgive.

He himself had the reputation of being a hard task-master, but a completely just one.

He had also paid his workers generously. Despite the fact that he worked them hard, his coolies had all respected and been loyal to him.

He could never remember a man leaving because he thought he would find a better job elsewhere, or being disgruntled at the treatment he received.

What could Gerald have been doing during the past two years? And how could he have destroyed the goodwill and the confidence of an estimable man like Ranjan?

The only redeeming feature, Lord Hawkston told himself, was that neither Sēētha nor her father were employed on the plantation.

That would have been the worst mistake of all, and he could only be thankful that Gerald had not committed the unforgivable mistake of tampering with one of his own employees.

If Lakshman, Sēētha's father, would not come to see him, Lord Hawkston decided that he must seek him out.

He had an idea that he belonged to a small village in the hills which was not far from the house.

"It will be a question of money," he said to himself, and hoped it would prove to be the matter.

The Ceylonese were a quiet, gentle people but what worried Lord Hawkston was that Lakshman might, in his grief and anger, have gone mad. He had known it happen before and the consequence could be very unpleasant.

In the meantime, he had two problems: to find Lakshman and to allay Dominica's anxiety.

Lord Hawkston was not insensitive.

He knew that to any girl, especially one with as much character and personality as Dominica, it would be a shock to learn that the man she was about to marry had not only had a mistress, but had also driven her to her death.

Too late he realised that the moment Ranjan began to speak of trouble he should have guessed it concerned Gerald and should have taken him out of earshot.

But he had in fact supposed that the man was referring to something that had happened to the crops. It was always prevalent in his mind because of the coffee disaster!

Even now he would sometimes wake in the night to find himself sweating with horror as he recalled how he had put out his hands to pluck the leaves; rubbing the diseased patches, trying to tell himself that it was not the fungoid that he suspected, and yet even as he did so knowing there was no hope.

It was with a tremendous effort that Lord Hawkston managed to speak lightly and, he hoped, normally as he said aloud:

"When we round the next turn to the road you will see my house."

They had been climbing all the time and the air, though still warm, had a freshness about it that Dominica had not known in Kandy.

As they reached the corner Lord Hawkston said:

"Shut your eyes!"

Dominica obeyed him, then heard him order the carriage to draw to a standstill. There was a moment's pause before he said:

"Look now!"

Below them was a deep valley surrounded by hills and behind them again there was a range of high peaking green mountains. Directly ahead of them there was a cascade pouring downwards into a lake, and descending again hundreds of feet in a torrent of silver.

Almost blinding in the sunshine Dominica could see beside it a long, low, white house with wide verandahs on two floors.

The gardens surrounding it were a mosaic of colour, a blaze of jungle flame: yellow, gold, white-pink, purple and even blue, which she knew belonged to the nelu, which could carpet the ground with its rare blooms.

Below the house, rising from the depths of the valley to the edge of the garden, were the dark green tea-plants luxuriantly filling their terraces which were like steps rising towards a Temple.

Dominica drew in her breath. She knew Lord Hawkston was waiting for her to speak and at last she said:

"Now I know why Adam and Eve came to Ceylon!"

"You think this is another Eden?"

"The original could not have been more exquisitely, breathtakingly beautiful!"

She knew he was pleased not merely at her words but by the sincerity with which she spoke them.

"That was what I thought," he said quietly, "when I first saw the valley!"

The view was so lovely and in a way so unexpected that Dominica sat staring at it spellbound.

"Do you like the house I built?" Lord Hawkston asked.

"It is lovely—very lovely!"

"Do you really think so?"

"It looks like something from a fairy-tale," she answered. "I am sure the lake is enchanted."

"You must learn to swim."

"I have always wanted to, but Papa would not let us go into the sea. He said it was immodest."

"No-one will see you here," Lord Hawkston assured her, "especially if you bathe when everyone else is at work."

"I will do that."

Then he saw Dominica glance at the torrent below the lake and he knew she was remembering that Sēētha had met her death by throwing herself down it.

His lips tightened in a hard line and he knew that whatever he might say, however hard he might try to prevent it, the tragedy of Sēētha's death would overshadow Dominica's arrival.

He signalled to the coachman and the carriage began to move more swiftly as the road went straight along the side of the hill towards the house.

It was the road he had built himself and he thought it was a considerable achievement of which he could be well proud.

The house drew nearer and as it did so he felt that Dominica was pressing herself back against the cushions of the carriage as if in a sudden weakness.

He smiled at her.

"Do not be nervous," he said. "There are so many interesting things to see and so much I want to show you that I know you are going to enjoy yourself."

Dominica turned to look at him and he saw the anxiety in her eyes.

"It is all right," he said quietly. "Just trust me as I have asked you to do."

"I will . . . try," she murmured.


It was not until Dominica had gone to bed that Lord Hawkston had a chance to speak to his nephew.

Gerald Warren had met them in the Hall as the carriage drew up at the front door of the house, and as he had stepped forward with what his Uncle thought was a somewhat forced smile on his face Lord Hawkston received his second shock of the day.

In two years Gerald Warren had altered almost out of recognition.

He had put on at least three stones in weight, his face was red and puffy, and even before he smelt the spirit on his breath Lord Hawkston knew the cause of such a change.

When he had last seen him Gerald had been slim, smart, and had an undoubted charm which made women like Emily Ludgrove find him easy to love.

Life in Ceylon had swept away his elegance and changed him to a point where his Uncle could hardly believe he was the same person.

He had obviously been drinking before they arrived although he was, Lord Hawkston noticed, formally attired and had made himself as presentable as possible.

He was quite obviously on edge at meeting both his Uncle and Dominica, but as the evening progressed and he had consumed a considerable amount of whisky he grew more relaxed.

His raucous laugh rang out, interspersed with long grumbles about the difficulties of tea-planting and the boredom of being so far from civilisation.

Lord Hawkston had been sure Gerald would make an effort, but if this was the best he could do it was not very impressive.

He hoped however that Dominica, not having known him before, would not be as surprised at his appearance as he was and would find him, because he was young and near her age, at least pleasant.

He himself found as the hours passed a cold fury growing inside him at the idea that any young man could have failed so completely in a position of trust and had not even appreciated the opportunity he had been offered.

"It is my fault. I should never had sent him here," Lord Hawkston told himself.

But the fact that he had been in the wrong did not make him any the less angry.

He managed, during dinner, to keep the conversation at least tolerably interesting and he only hoped that Dominica was not aware of the amount of whisky, or its strength, Gerald was consuming.

He thought she was tired and she confirmed this when she rose to her feet soon after they had finished coffee in the sitting-room whose long high windows overlooked the valley.

"I think, if you will excuse me, My Lord, I will retire," she said to Lord Hawkston. "It has been a long day."

"It has indeed," he replied. "Good-night, Dominica, and I hope you sleep well."

"I am sure I shall," Dominica replied. "Good-night, My Lord. Good-night, Mr. Warren."

She curtseyed to both gentlemen and went from the room.

Lord Hawkston had already been annoyed on arrival to find that Gerald had shut up the top of the house where he had always slept and they were all using the bedrooms on the ground floor.

"Why have you done that?" he enquired.

"I couldn't afford so many servants," his nephew replied with a truculent note in his voice. "There was no point in having them sitting about doing nothing."

Because Dominica was there, Lord Hawkston checked the words which came to his lips.

He was well aware that on the generous allowance he had made to Gerald before he left for England he could have afforded as many servants as were necessary.

He guessed from what James Taylor had told him that Gerald's allowance had been frittered away on riotous living and whisky.

He was careful, however, not to show his anger until the door closed behind Dominica and he was alone with his nephew.

It was then that he spoke in a controlled, quiet voice, but with every word as effective as a whiplash.

"I have heard about Sēētha's death," he said. "How could you have been such a fool—such a damned fool as to dismiss her without the usual payment? Anyone round here could have told you to how much she was entitled."

"I was well aware of how much she expected," Gerald said surlily, "but I hadn't got it. Do you understand? I hadn't got the money!"

"You could have at least promised that you would give it to her on my arrival," Lord Hawkston said, "or the Bank would have advanced you a loan."

"I've already had a loan."

"How much?"

"A thousand pounds, and they would not give me any more."

"You have spent a thousand pounds over and above what I sent you?" Lord Hawkston asked incredulously.

"There are also some debts," his nephew said defiantly.

Lord Hawkston walked across the room trying to control his temper.

"I see now that you were too stupid and too idle to take on a job of this sort," he said. "But I believed in you and thought you had the qualities required to carry on my work here. I was mistaken!"

"I would like to go back to England."

"And when you get there what do you intend to do? Live on your mother? She has very little money, as you well know, and you have spent most of it already."

"At least I shall be with civilised people."

"Now listen, Gerald," Lord Hawkston said. "I am not going to permit you to behave like a spoilt child and go running back to your mother just because you have made a mess of everything here."

His tone sharpened as he continued:

"It is unfortunate that Emily Ludgrove changed her mind about marrying you, but I think if you had come to Colombo to see her she would have been so shocked by your appearance that she would have broken off the engagement anyway."

"I never really thought Emily would marry me," Gerald Warren said, "not if she had known she had to live in this dead-and-alive hole."

"Well, this is where you are going to live," Lord Hawkston announced angrily. "I have brought you a wife who will look after you and, I hope, keep you in order. I will get the plantation back into working order and then when I return to England you will carry on until I can find someone more adequate to take your place. Is that clear?"

"What is the alternative?" Gerald enquired.

"The alternative," Lord Hawkston said slowly, and his voice was harsh, "is that you work your passage home steerage! You will never have another penny-piece of my money, and I shall make sure on my return to England that you have none of your mother's!"

There was a silence, then Gerald Warren threw back his head and laughed. It was an ugly, jeering sound.

"You've got it all nicely tied up, haven't you, Uncle Chilton? You have me in chains and there is nothing I can do about it. Very well, I'll marry the wife you have chosen for me. She's quite a pretty little thing and perhaps she'll contrive to make this place seem less like a mausoleum. I imagine you'll give us enough to live on?"

"I will pay your debts," Lord Hawkston said, "and I will give you an allowance which in Ceylon will make you seem comparatively rich as long as you stop drinking."

"Entirely?"

"You will sign the pledge!"

"Now really, Uncle . . ." Gerald began in a conciliatory tone.

"Those are may conditions!" Lord Hawkston interrupted. "Take them or leave them."

There was a pause.

"Very well, blast it, I'll take them!" Gerald exclaimed.

He stared at his Uncle with undeniable animosity in his eyes, then he picked up the whisky bottle.

"If I've to sign the pledge tomorrow," he said, "I might as well enjoy myself tonight. Thank you, Uncle Chilton, for your generosity. I am sure you expect me to be deeply and humbly grateful."

His voice was sarcastic.

It would have been a more dignified exit had he not staggered against the side of the door as he left the room.

# CHAPTER FIVE

Dominica lay awake thinking over what had happened during the day.

She had been tired when she came to bed, but she had been unable to sleep.

She found herself shrinking from the thought of Gerald Warren and while she knew in her heart that she could never marry him, she dared not express such a decision in words.

The difficulty would be how to explain it to Lord Hawkston.

She had quite confidently believed that Gerald would look very like his Uncle and she had repeated to herself over and over again Lord Hawkston's description of him as 'tall and good-looking'.

When she had seen the fat, red-faced man waiting for them in the Hall she had not at first realised that this was in fact the man she had come to meet; the man she had promised to marry without having seen him.

She had been far too astute not to notice the amount of whisky that Gerald consumed during the evening.

She told herself that her father's denunciation of alcohol of all sorts was one of his obsessions and that gentlemen like Lord Hawkston drank wine with their meals as a matter of course.

But Gerald Warren smelt of spirits and as she saw the tumbler at his right hand being filled again and again by the servants, she knew without being told that he was drinking too much, and that this must account for his appearance.

Besides this, when she was alone in the darkness of her room, the horror of Sēētha's death swept over her so that it was difficult to think of anything else.

Dominica loved the Ceylonese women for their gentleness, their sweet natures, their friendliness and the loving, childlike trust they had in those whom they served.

She had real friends amongst those women who attended her father's Church, many of whom came to her with their problems, and she knew them intimately.

She could imagine all too vividly Sēētha being impressed by Gerald Warren because of his position, because of the fine house in which he lived and which must have seemed to her to be luxurious beyond her wildest dreams.

Perhaps, Dominica told herself, she had loved him also with her heart whatever Lord Hawkston might say to the contrary.

Because she knew the people so well she was aware that a Ceylonese peasant who lived in the hill-country was a gentleman with a philosophy of life which he was not prepared to barter for material prosperity.

If hunger made it imperative for him to work, he did so and he did it well since he was both skilled and intelligent.

But he preferred to be poor and his own master rather than rich and at the beck and call of someone else.

Dominica had talked with the women who had come with their husbands into Colombo from many of the outlying provinces, so she knew that the Ceylonese had never become reconciled to the subjugation of their beautiful mountains to the needs of an alien agriculture.

They tried to stand aloof from both the coffee and the

tea-plantations and Kayons especially, except when they were really hungry, seldom worked on the tea Estates in a regular capacity.

This was the reason why the planters had found from the very beginning that it was essential to rely on the importation of Tamil labour who came mostly from the Coramandel coast of Southern India.

It was the Tamils who cleared the jungle and dug the terraces first for coffee, then for the tea which followed it.

Employing Tamil labour made the planters' lives more difficult because they had to learn a new language with which to converse with their labourers, who were not as quick at learning English as were the Ceylonese.

They were happy, easy-going, courteous people as a rule and Dominica wondered what agony of mind had forced Sēētha into taking their own life.

Could she really have been so unhappy at being turned away by Gerald Warren?

Why did she not seek the comfort of her own people? And why indeed did her father, if he was so fond of her, not prevent her from committing suicide?

There were so many questions that puzzled Dominica and yet she had the feeling that she would never learn the answer because it was a matter that neither Lord Hawkston nor Gerald Warren would ever discuss with her.

Restlessly she rose from the bed on which she was lying, knowing that the dawn must have broken because there was a faint light beneath the curtains.

She drew them back from the window to look out on the view which had held her spellbound the day before.

Her bedroom was at the end of the house and had one long window looking over the valley and another onto the garden and the lake.

The morning mists still shrouded the bottom of the valley, but already there was a faint light glowing behind the mountains in the distance, and the stars, which had illuminated the sky the night before, were fading into insignificance.

She turned to the outer window and as she watched, the first golden ray of the sun glittered on the cascade as it fell

from the hill above down into the lake. She could hear the
roar of the torrent as it descended hundreds of feet into the
valley shrouded with mist.

It was incredibly lovely and the beauty of the flowers in
the garden was breathtaking.

As the light grew stronger, she could see them more
clearly, the guelder roses, geraniums and campanulas, interspersed with magnolias and oleanders.

There were also feathery bamboo, orchids and mosses,
and a number of flowers which she recognised as English
such as foxgloves and lobelias, arum lilies and many different
species of rose.

With the increasing light Dominica realised that the garden, which must have been laid out with great care by Lord
Hawkston, had been allowed to grow wild. Already the jungle of convolvuli, vines and rattans were encroaching upon it,
and the undergrowth was throttling many of the plants.

She found herself thinking how upset she herself would
be if a garden over which she had expended so much love
and care should have become neglected during her absence.

She had known without his saying anything the night
before that Lord Hawkston had been angry and she was
aware that it was only his good manners and self-control
which had prevented him from speaking about it at dinner.

It had been bad enough, Dominica thought, that she
should feel awkward and shy at meeting Gerald Warren, but
what must Lord Hawkston have felt also to find his household reorganised, his servants dispersed, and his garden neglected?

"He was very brave about it," she told herself, and she
wondered if when she had gone to bed he had spoken to his
nephew with the anger he had felt inside him.

'He loves this house and everything in it,' Dominica
thought.

Then almost as if he were a part of her thoughts she saw
Lord Hawkston.

He came from the back of the house and was riding along
the further side of the lake where the torrent passed under
a small bridge.

He was on horse-back and she saw that he was wearing a

white open-neck shirt with the sleeves rolled up above his elbows.

He was bare-headed, and in his riding-breeches he looked young, slim and athletic—very different indeed from his nephew.

Dominica knew that he too must have found it impossible to sleep and so he was riding alone, perhaps to inspect his tea-plants or perhaps in search of Lakshman.

At the thought of Sēētha and her tragedy Dominica shuddered.

It was hard to think of what she must have suffered before she had thrown herself down the raging torrent to die, on the stones which must have been hidden in the mist, even as they were now.

Because she felt her thoughts were morbid Dominica picked up the wrapper which Madame Fernando had included in her trousseau, put it on over the nightgown and tied the sash of it round her waist.

Made of muslin, it was inset with lace and decorated with bows of turquoise-blue ribbon.

It was so attractive and so feminine with lace frills frothing around the hem that Dominica felt it was almost too grand to be worn in a bedroom.

Then as she looked around her she realised that it was in fact in perfect harmony with her surroundings.

It had been difficult last night because she was so confused and shy at meeting Gerald Warren to notice the house properly, and yet she had been aware that it was all in exquisite taste such as she had not expected a man might show in furnishings, even if he was proficient at building.

Now she had a confused remembrance of furniture made of the dark ebony which was one of the most prized woods of the Ceylonese cabinet-makers, and there had also been furniture in satin-wood from the magnificent trees which were found all over the island.

In her bedroom now she saw a chest of calamanda which was stronger and finer than rosewood, and another of nedun which was highly prized by craftsmen.

The bedroom was lovely and she had learnt when she

arrived that all the rooms were known by the names of flowers.

"Where is Dominica sleeping?" Lord Hawkston had enquired of his nephew.

"I told the servants to put her in the 'White Lotus Room'," Gerald replied, "and you are in the one nearby, which I believe you call the 'Red Lotus'."

He spoke in a somewhat contemptuous manner as if he thought such ideas were ridiculous. But Dominica could understand.

The giant lotus which was red or white was so supremely magnificent that it was easy to understand the reverence the people of the East had for this superlative flower.

A Botanist had told Dominica that the Hindus believed that the lotus was there before Creation itself and that from its serene perfection all things sprang.

He had shown her the giant lotus and Dominica had seen that the red variety was like a deep red rose reclining on a platform of green floating leaves.

"I have seen vast lakes in the Plains," the Botanist had said, "where no man has ever been, and they have been covered with the lotus, both red and white, which is the flower of Buddha, and on which so many of his statues rest."

Dominica was sure now that Lord Hawkston had known this when he designed her bedroom.

The carpet was of deep green like the flat leaves, and the back of the bed was carved like the petals of a lotus and painted white just faintly tinged with pink.

The walls were white tinged with pink where they met the ceiling. The curtains, of textiles blocked and hand-woven by native craftsmen, had the pattern of the lotus woven into them.

They were very lovely, as was the one picture on a wall which depicted the Buddha surrounded by lotus-buds just bursting into flower.

It was exquisitely painted and as Dominica looked at it she felt that its beauty vibrated within herself and aroused in her the same feelings that were evoked when she listened to music.

Because she felt unaccountably moved she walked again

to the window to look out over the garden wondering if she would see Lord Hawkston again.

But there was only the sunshine now shimmering on the lake and on the cascade and making the brilliance of the flowers in the garden seem even more vivid.

"It is as if one could see them actually growing in the sunshine," Dominica said to herself.

She looked at the flowers and then again at the valley where the mists were dispersing, for so long that she realised time was getting on and she should dress.

There was a bathroom opening out of her bedroom and after she had washed she put on one of the attractive thin muslin gowns that Madame Fernando had called 'her simple dresses'.

They were not simple in Dominica's eyes but she knew they were becoming, and because she wanted to look her best she dressed her hair in a new way, letting it wave softly round her cheeks, then sweeping it backwards in a thick plait that reached from her neck up the very centre of her head.

It was an easy method with which to dispose of so much hair. At the same time she knew it gave her extra height and was becoming.

She had just finished dressing when there came a knock at the door.

"Come in!" she said.

A servant entered, carrying a tray on which reposed a small pot of tea, a cup and a jug of milk.

"Good-morning, *Nona*," the servant said, using what Dominica knew was the Portuguese word for 'Madam'.

"Good-morning," she replied.

"You early, *Nona*," the servant remarked with a smile. "I bring tea, but breakfast ready on verandah."

"Then I will have my tea there," Dominica said with a smile.

She allowed the servant to show her the way to the broad verandah outside the dining-room where breakfast was laid on a table covered with a white linen cloth.

There was no sign of Lord Hawkston or Gerald and Dominica wondered if she should wait for them.

But the servants had other ideas. They poured out her

tea and brought her a slice of pawpaw with which to start the meal.

Because they obviously expected it Dominica began to eat, but slowly, hoping Lord Hawkston would appear.

She had not taken more than a few mouthfuls when round the house from the direction of the lake Gerald appeared. He had been swimming and was wearing only shorts and was bare above the waist.

Dominica blushed.

She had never before seen a white man half naked and she could not help thinking that Gerald looked extremely unprepossessing.

His wet hair was falling over his forehead, his body, fat, hairy and with a decided paunch, was sunburnt in red patches.

He carried a large white towel in his hand and Dominica wondered why he did not cover himself with it.

"Good-morning, Dominica," he said in a loud voice as he drew nearer. "You're early! I expected that you would be tired this morning."

Dominica rose to her feet a little nervously at his approach.

"I am used to rising early."

"Sit down and get on with your breakfast," Gerald said. "I'll put on a robe and join you in a second."

He walked into the house through an open window and Dominica sat down again.

She could not help noting that his eyes were bloodshot and his face appeared even more puffy than it had the night before.

She sipped her tea, but somehow she no longer felt hungry.

He returned within a few minutes wearing a long white towelling gown which fastened across his chest, but his neck was bare, and although he had brushed back his hair from his forehead, he still looked unpleasant in Dominica's eyes.

She had a feeling that her father would be shocked at the thought of her sitting down to breakfast with a man wearing nothing but a robe, and yet she could not deny that it covered him, and she told herself it was wrong to criticise or expect those who lived in the wilds of the country to be anything but free and easy.

"Coffee, *Sinna Durai*?" a servant asked at Gerald's elbow.

He hesitated, then enquired:

"Where's the Juggernaut?"

Dominica looked at him in surprise.

"That's a good description of my Uncle," he explained as she did not understand. "But if you prefer it, where is the Boss?"

"I saw him go riding some time ago," Dominica answered.

She thought it was extremely bad taste for Gerald to refer to his Uncle in such a manner in front of the servants.

"In which case," Gerald said to the servant, "I'll have a whisky—and bring it quickly!"

Dominica could not help staring at him in surprise. She had never imagined that anyone would want to drink whisky at breakfast.

As if he was aware of her astonishment Gerald said:

"Might as well indulge myself while I can. Do you know what His Lordship proposed last night?"

"I have no . . . idea," Dominica said faintly.

"He told me I had to sign the pledge! Well, I can tell you that if I do, it will be with my fingers crossed and so my oath, or vow, or whatever it is I take, will mean nothing!"

"You mean you will . . . lie to him?" Dominica enquired.

"Now don't you start!" Gerald exclaimed. "I've had enough preaching for the moment."

The whisky was put down at his side and he drank half the tumbler off in one gulp.

"That's better!" he said with a sigh. "Now it'll be easier for you and me to have a talk."

Dominica looked at him apprehensively.

She felt it was hardly the moment for them to talk with two servants in attendance.

But Gerald ignored them as if they were not there, only waving away with a disdainful hand the pawpaw when it was offered to him and looking with a jaundiced eye at a plate of bacon and eggs which was set down in its place.

"If we have to live in this dead-and-alive hole," he said after a moment, "you and I might as well enjoy ourselves. If my skinflint Uncle gives us enough money, it's easy to have a bit of fun in Kandy. It's not as good as Colombo, mind you, but they've opened up a decent Club this last year, and there are a few convivial people."

"Will you not have to . . . work on the plantation?" Dominica asked tentatively.

"Not if I can help it!" Gerald answered with one of his raucous laughs. "Of course I shall put on a good show of being interested until the Boss returns to England. I don't suppose he'll stay long anyway after we are married. At least, I hope not!"

Dominica gripped her fingers together in her lap.

It was not only what Gerald said that was so distressing, but the way he said it. There was something rough and contemptuous in his voice; something which told her that he hated his Uncle, just as he hated this beautiful house and the exquisite valley in which it was situated.

She tried to visualise to herself what he meant by 'a bit of fun' and only knew instinctively that it was everything she would dislike.

Because she felt she must say something she asked in a low voice:

"Are there any concerts in Kandy? Is anyone interested in music?"

"I shouldn't think so," Gerald replied. "Not unless you mean the type of music one has at a dance. They have one every Saturday night and although the boys get a bit rough the girls have fun! There are plenty of opportunities for a cuddle or a kiss in the garden of the Club in the moonlight. Romantic, and all that sort of thing. You'll enjoy it."

Dominica drew in her breath.

There was really nothing she could say and she felt as if her brain had gone blank.

Gerald took another swig at his whisky, finishing the glass. He snapped his fingers and a servant replaced it with a full tumbler.

He drank and looked at Dominica as he did so.

"I dare say there are a lot of things I'll have to teach you," he said after a moment, his eyes on her face. "But you'll learn. Women learn quickly. I've a feeling we are going to enjoy ourselves—you and I!"

There was something in the way he spoke, something in the expression in his face, which made Dominica feel as if a cobra had suddenly appeared beside her.

Every nerve in her body shrank from him. Even as she longed to run away and yet was afraid to move, she heard a step on the verandah and looked up to see Lord Hawkston approaching them.

She was aware, as a wave of relief swept through her, that Gerald, finishing his whisky in one gulp, had handed the empty glass to a servant who whisked it out of sight in a surreptitious manner.

To Dominica it was degrading that they should contrive together to deceive the owner of the house.

If he noticed what occurred Lord Hawkston showed no sign of it.

He had, Dominica saw, changed his shirt since coming in from riding and wore a tie. He was without a coat but his cuffs were fastened at the wrist with gold links.

"Good-morning, Dominica!" he said in his quiet deep voice which made her sense of panic subside just because he was there. "Good-morning, Gerald! I see you have been swimming."

"Of course," Gerald replied. "It's good for the figure!"

"I think you would find it even better exercise if you rode some of the horses in the stable," Lord Hawkston said. "They are under-exercised."

Gerald did not reply. He merely looked sulky.

A servant brought Lord Hawkston tea. As he sipped it he said to Dominica:

"It always gives me a sense of satisfaction which is hard to explain in words when I drink my own tea, seated on my own verandah, overlooking my own valley."

"I can understand that," Dominica said with a smile. "And the fact that you are drinking your own tea is more important than anything else."

"It was certainly the foundation-stone," Lord Hawkston said. "Did you sleep well?"

Dominica had no wish to tell the truth, but the habit of a life-time made it impossible to lie.

"I had . . . a lot to think about," she said apologetically, "and of course I found it . . . exciting being here."

She felt this sounded rather inadequate and added:

"The garden is lovely! I have never seen such beautiful flowers!"

"It *was* lovely," Lord Hawkston said in a low voice, then looking at Gerald he went on: "Need I ask what happened to the gardeners whom I trained with such care?"

"I couldn't afford them!" Gerald replied. "And really, who wants a garden?"

"I do, for one," Lord Hawkston said firmly.

"I can see how many flowers you must have brought here from other countries," Dominica interposed quickly. "But perhaps because I have always lived in Ceylon, I like our own flowers the best."

"The orchids and magnolias," Lord Hawkston smiled.

"And of course the lotus."

"They are growing—or they were," Lord Hawkston said, "on a pool that I made on the other side of the house, I will show it to you, but it will be disappointing if the lotuses are no longer there."

"It will indeed," Dominica agreed. "And my bedroom is beautiful!"

"The 'White Lotus Room'," Lord Hawkston said as if to himself. "I was fortunate in finding craftsmen who could really carve. I must show you the bedrooms on the next floor. The 'Palm Room', where they copied the Areca Palms, is, in my opinion, unique."

"I would love to see it," Dominica exclaimed.

"I think before we do anything else," Lord Hawkston said, looking at his nephew, "we should pay a visit to the plantation. I want you to show me, Gerald, the work that has been done and any innovations that have been put in hand these last two years."

"I expect you'll find it's just as you left it," Gerald answered.

"I hope so," Lord Hawkston replied. "If you will get dressed I will order the horses. Dominica can come with us.

She has ridden in the past and will find the horse I rode this morning not too obstreperous now that I have exercised him."

Dominica looked at him anxiously.

"I do not want to be in the way."

"You will not be," Lord Hawkston replied. "Put on your habit. We ordered a light one from Madame Fernando and now is the right moment to try it out."

Dominica flashed him a smile and ran to her bedroom.

She had been afraid when she heard Lord Hawkston making his plans that she would be left behind, but now he was taking her with them and her heart was singing with excitement at the thought of seeing the plantation that meant so much to him.

It only took her a few minutes to take off her muslin gown and put on an attractive habit which Madame Fernando had made her in pink cotton decorated with white braid.

There was a straw hat to wear with it and Dominica was glad to find she was ready quicker than Gerald and that Lord Hawkston was waiting alone in the Hall when she joined him.

"You will not be afraid to ride?" he asked as she appeared. "I promise you that the horse I rode this morning is really quite a peaceful animal."

"I do not think I have forgotten how to ride, even though it was five years ago since I last did so," Dominica answered.

"I think it is something one never forgets," Lord Hawkston said reassuringly.

They walked outside the house as they were speaking to find the horses waiting for them.

Lord Hawkston lifted Dominica into the saddle.

She had a strange feeling as he put his hands on her waist that she could not explain to herself.

She only knew that it was there and that she wanted to ride well so that he would be proud of her.

She picked up the reins and he smiled encouragingly.

"I see you have not forgotten."

"I hope I shall not disgrace myself."

"You could never do that."

She was looking down at him because she was seated on the horse and he was standing beside her.

She realised perhaps for the first time that his eyes were very deep blue. It seemed to her they were even more vivid because already his skin seemed to have tanned a little.

Her eyes looked into his. Then Lord Hawkston looked away.

"Are you sure the stirrup is the right length?" he asked, and Dominica had difficulty in understanding what he said.

"Yes . . . yes . . . quite all right," she answered.

Lord Hawkston mounted the other horse.

"We may as well start. Gerald can catch us up."

"Will he know where to come?" Dominica enquired.

"I imagine so."

They rode off taking the path that wound its way down the hillside into a valley below.

Lord Hawkston set the pace and the horses moved slowly.

Dominica began to get her confidence back, but a full-grown horse was rather different from the pony she had ridden as a child.

She remembered how she had longed to enter for the Gymkhana which was one of the annual amusements of the other children in Colombo, but her father had never allowed it, even though her mother pleaded with him.

"You can attend if you have nothing better to do," he conceded grudgingly.

But he had not allowed them to compete, even though Dominica had known there were several competitions which either she or Faith could have won.

Now she wondered if such deprivations had made them better people in any way, or indeed better Christians.

Why should religion always be so gloomy, so austere?

Why must laughter and happiness always be frowned on by the God her father worshipped?

Then she forgot to be introspective because Lord Hawkston was explaining to her about the tea.

"Tea is the one crop which can be picked six days out of seven all the year round," he told her, "with the exception of two or three of the great Hindu festivals."

Before they reached the coolies working amongst the tea-plants Dominica could already hear them.

"The Tamils are noisy and very often quarrelsome," Lord Hawkston said as she looked at him as if for explanation. "But they are good workers."

They drew nearer and Dominica could see that the tea-pluckers had large round bamboo baskets slung onto their backs by means of a rope which passed around their fore-heads.

The women wore gaily coloured cloths wound Grecian fashion across their breasts, and round their heads, padded where they took the strain of the rope on their foreheads, they wore a headcloth like a turban.

In green, red, gold or white the effect of a hundred or more pluckers waist-high in greenery was, Dominica thought, very picturesque.

She was fascinated by the speed and skill with which the women picked the ripe leaves—always two and a bud—gathering them in small heaps in the hand, then throwing them with a lithe, quick jerk over their shoulders into the waiting basket.

"The supervision of the work is in the hands of the men," Lord Hawkston explained. "They are called *kanganies,* or overseers."

There was a faint smile on his lips as he looked at them and it was with difficulty that Dominica prevented herself from laughing.

The insignia of their rank was usually an ancient European-type jacket, a turban and an umbrella—a high sign of superiority—caught in the collar of the coat and hanging down their backs.

"Four times a day," Lord Hawkston went on, "the leaf is carefully weighed, each plucker's tally being entered in a small account book by the *kannackapiller.*"

He looked at the pluckers with an expression of pride in his eyes.

"There is never any cheating. If the accounts are challenged, the coolies' recording, for they know exactly how much they have picked, can be accepted as completely accurate."

Everyone seemed to be very happy and it was impossible not to notice how delighted many of the coolies were to see Lord Hawkston.

There was a note of pleasure in their voices when he talked to them and Dominica was sure that they had a genuine fondness for him.

It was very different when a little while later Gerald came trotting up to them.

He was looking hot and the perspiration was running down his face.

With what Dominica thought was an effort to impress his Uncle he dismounted and walked round to the pluckers finding fault with their work and speaking to them in a tone of voice which made her instinctively grip the reins tighter.

No-one answered back; everyone went on working; but Dominica was sure they resented Gerald's hectoring manner, the loudness with which he gave orders, and his whole attitude of arrogant superiority.

They watched the weighing of the tea outside a store which, Lord Hawkston told Dominica, had originally been built for coffee.

All too soon it seemed to Dominica time passed, and they rode back along a different route towards the house.

Gerald was blustering and making long and garbled explanations as to why the tea production had fallen in the last year.

He blamed the coolies, the overseers, the weather, the plants themselves, while in fact, Dominica was sure, it was all a cover-up for his own inadequacy.

Lord Hawkston said little but she knew that he was feeling disappointed and upset that the plantation he had left in such excellent condition, thriving and improving month by month, should have gone backwards instead of forwards and would undoubtedly show a financial deficit instead of a profit.

After a time when his words evoked no response from his Uncle, Gerald's voice ceased, and Dominica was glad to ride in silence and look at the beauty all around her.

She was fascinated to see that where the country had not

been cultivated the jungle was even more beautiful than she had imagined it could be.

There were varieties of immense feathery bamboos, and she noticed low down in the valley giant fern trees rising sometimes to a height of more than twenty feet.

Almost everywhere in the thick undergrowth there was the vivid blue of the nelu in a great sheet of colour, and besides the magnolias there were myrtles and various varieties of camellia.

When she was looking at one, entranced by the perfect wax-like blossoms, Lord Hawkston followed the direction of her eyes and said:

"You know of course that the tea-plant is a cousin of the camellia?"

"No, I did not know that," Dominica answered, "but now that you mention it, they do look rather similar."

"Let me show you something even more beautiful," he said.

They rode on for a little distance and then he pointed to the *katu-imbul* or silk-cotton tree.

Dominica had seen one in the gardens in Colombo, but here there were a dozen of them growing wild and the glorious trumpet-like petals were in an almost crazy profusion.

The ground beneath the trees was carpeted thick with petals like a crimson rug, and the branches of the tree grew out at right angles from the bore like the yards of a ship.

It was so lovely that she could hardly bear to leave it behind and ride on but she told herself that whatever happened she must come again before the blossom finished.

They reached the house and Lord Hawkston said as he lifted her down from the saddle:

"You may think we have returned early, but here as men breakfast soon after dawn it is usual for the midday meal to be at noon."

"Whatever the time is," Dominica said with a smile, "I am hungry!"

That was true because she had been unable to eat any breakfast as Gerald Warren had upset her.

Now she tried to tell herself she was being stupid and

ultrafastidious. He was Lord Hawkston's nephew, and she must try to understand him.

'He is feeling awkward, as I am, about . . . the arrangements that have been made for us,' she thought.

It sounded reassuring and sensible, but she knew that inside she shrank with every nerve in her body from the idea that she should mean anything to this hard-drinking young man, or he to her.

After luncheon Lord Hawkston insisted that Dominica should rest.

"It is always a mistake to do too much on the first day," he said. "The height, although one does not realise it, affects one after coming up from sea-level. Besides, Gerald and I are going for a long ride which will be too much for you."

She was disappointed, but she could not help knowing he was being wise. In fact when she went to her room she lay down on the bed meaning to read one of the many books she had found waiting for her, but fell asleep.

She had not slept the night before, and now she slept peacefully to find when she awoke that it was six o'clock in the evening.

"You should have wakened me," she told the servant when she rang for him to find out the exact time.

"*Durai* say you should sleep, *Nona,*" he replied. "You like bath?"

"Thank you," Dominica said.

By the time she had had her bath it was getting on for seven o'clock and she put on one of the pretty evening gowns which Madame Fernando had included in her trousseau.

Pale yellow, it was the color of syringa, the bodice fitted her closely and was cut low at the front and at the back. There were tiny puff sleeves fashioned of yellow tulle which was also draped round the full skirt.

It seemed very grand and very décolletée for a quiet evening in the hills, but Dominica hoped Lord Hawkston would admire her in it.

Feeling a little shy she went into the sitting-room.

It was a long and very beautiful room filled with treasures of native craftsmanship which Dominica was longing to inspect.

To her disappointment she found not Lord Hawkston but Gerald, and he was alone.

He had a glass of whisky in his hand and looked up apprehensively when she entered as if he thought it might be his Uncle.

"Oh, it's you, Dominica!" he exclaimed. "You're early! I've not yet changed for dinner."

"Did you enjoy your ride?" Dominica asked, crossing the room towards him.

"Not much," he said. "I felt like a small boy who had forgotten to do his homework!"

For the first time Dominica felt rather sympathetic towards him.

"Was His Lordship very angry?" she asked.

"I'm in disgrace—you know that!" he replied. "But don't let's worry our heads about it. There are other things we can do besides sit in sack-cloth and ashes."

He put down his glass and said unexpectedly:

"For instance, you could start by giving me a kiss. We're going to be married, Dominica, but so far we have not had a chance of getting to know each other."

He put out his arms as he spoke and pulled her roughly towards him.

Instinctively and without conscious thought she struggled and fought herself free.

"No!" she said. "No!"

There was a tremor of fear in her voice.

"Why not?" Gerald asked. "Are you playing hard to get, Dominica? After all, you've come here to marry me."

"Yes . . . I know," Dominica said breathlessly, "but it is too . . . soon. We have only . . . just met. I . . . I have hardly spoken to you."

"That's not my fault!" he said. "And now that I've had a chance to look at you, I can say you're very pretty! What's more, you have a very white skin. I like that. It's a change!"

As he spoke he put his arms round Dominica again and kissed her bare shoulder.

It happened so swiftly that she was unable to move away or prevent it. Then, as she felt the touch of his lips, she realised what he had said.

"It's a change!"

A change from Sēētha . . . a change from the girl who had killed herself because of him.

Even as her whole being was revolted at the thought, Dominica felt his lips hot and greedy on her bare skin.

"No! No!" she cried again and parted her lips to scream.

As she did so the door opened and Lord Hawkston entered the room.

He had changed for dinner and, although he must have seen what was happening as he came towards them, his voice was completely expressionless.

"You will be late, Gerald, if you do not hurry."

Gerald took his arms from Dominica and she felt for one moment that she was going to faint.

She put out her hands. Just beside her there was the back of a chair and she held on to it.

"I won't be long," Gerald said and walked away.

Dominica fought for breath.

She had her back to Lord Hawkston and did not turn round.

She only knew she felt an intolerable relief because he was there and at the same time a sense of acute embarrassment because he had seen Gerald kissing her bare shoulder.

What did he think? How could he credit that she would permit such a thing?

Then she told herself it was what he would expect! He had brought her here to marry his nephew, and he would be glad that they were getting to know each other and that Gerald was attracted to her.

Even as she thought of him she could feel the heat of his lips; could smell his spirit-laden breath; could feel the roughness of his arms as he pulled her against him.

"I cannot . . . do it!" she told herself. "I must . . . tell Lord Hawkston that I . . . cannot do it!"

She heard him walk across the room to the window.

"Have you seen the sunset?" he asked in a quiet voice.

It checked the words that would have sprung to Dominica's lips, words in which she would have explained how Gerald revolted her; how she could never let him touch her again; how she could not stay here.

Then as if someone was pointing an accusing finger at her she remembered all that she owed Lord Hawkston!

Her whole trousseau which had cost an astronomical sum, gowns and bonnets for the girls, the kindness he had shown to her as they travelled here, and how he was doing everything to make her feel at home.

"How can I be so . . . ungrateful? How can I explain that I must break my word . . . go back on my . . . promise?" Dominica asked herself.

She felt the faintness that had come over her when Gerald released her was now passing, but she was still conscious of his lips on her shoulder where he had kissed her.

She still felt a kind of sick depression inside but she told herself that she had to be brave.

What else could she do, owing Lord Hawkston so much? Being so desperately and hopelessly in his debt?

'If I worked for a hundred years I could never pay him back for all he has spent on me,' she thought.

With an effort that was superhuman she walked towards him.

As she reached his side he stepped forward through the open window and out on to the verandah.

"Sometimes I think this is the loveliest part of the day," he said. "When I lived here alone I always used to try to be back in time to watch the sun go down and the stars come out. It is more beautiful and more moving than any play in a theatre could be, and the sounds of the night have a music that to me are finer than the greatest opera."

Dominica knew he was trying to soothe and reassure her! He was attempting, she was sure, to tell her that if she did not panic, if she used her common-sense, everything would be all right.

But would it?

Would she ever be able to endure Gerald near her; to feel him touching her; to let him kiss her?

She reached out her hand to hold on to one of the pillars of the verandah and saw it was trembling.

"How can I tell him the . . . truth?" she asked herself, and knew it was impossible.

# CHAPTER SIX

It was another uncomfortable evening, with Lord Hawkston trying to make conversation and getting little response from either Dominica or his nephew.

Dominica did make an effort, but at the same time she found it was hard to chatter and smile and impossible to prevent herself from shuddering when she looked at Gerald.

It seemed to her however that Lord Hawkston was quite unaware that there was an undercurrent to the conversation, nor did he seem to notice that Gerald had imbibed a great deal of whisky before he came back to the sitting-room dressed for dinner.

During the meal he ostentatiously drank the fresh lime juice that had been prepared for Dominica, but after dinner when he left the room for a few minutes, she was sure it was because he was seeking another drink.

They had coffee on the verandah and by now the sky was darkening and the stars were coming out one by one.

There was a faint glow over the valley and she knew that

in the depths of it the mists would be rising to cast a gossamer film over the tea-plants.

There was the sound of the torrent and the cry of the night-birds besides the shrill note of the 'flying foxes'.

These tiny bats, hardly larger than a thumb-nail, swooped around the verandah as if they were inquisitive. Whenever the lights came on in a Ceylonese house they appeared in a flock, lured by some mysterious attraction.

The moths however were too numerous for the party to linger long on the verandah, and soon they returned to the sitting-room.

Lord Hawkston talked to Dominica for some time about the furniture that he had had made in different parts of the country and which had been brought to his house by various different means. One piece had been carried on the back of an elephant!

All the time he was talking Dominica was conscious of Gerald sprawled in an arm-chair, doubtless wondering how soon he could obtain another drink without his Uncle being aware of it.

It was not yet ten o'clock when she decided she would go to bed.

She bade both gentlemen good night, curtseying as she did so, then went to her room feeling it was a relief to be alone.

At the same time she would have liked to go on talking to Lord Hawkston.

She undressed and was ready for bed. Then having blown out the light she pulled back the curtains and opened the long windows on to the verandah which overlooked the lake.

The garden was very quiet and peaceful. In the light from the starlit sky the water of the lake was luminous and the fragrance of the flowers almost overpowering.

"It is lovely . . . so incredibly lovely!" Dominica told herself. "If only one could be here with someone . . ."

She checked the thought before it went any further.

What was the point of wishing for the impossible?

If she stayed she must stay with Gerald as his wife.

She turned back into the bedroom as if the beauty outside hurt her. She crept into bed closing her eyes to try not to remember what she had felt when he had touched her; when he had kissed the whiteness of her skin and said with incredible insensitivity:

"It's a change!"

How was it possible, she asked herself, for her ever to forget Sēētha and that she had killed herself because this man had turned her away?

"I will not think of it . . . I will not!" Dominica told herself.

And yet she felt almost as if Sēētha was beside her, talking to her, telling her how much she had suffered.

Suddenly Dominica knew the reason why Sēētha had killed herself!

It was because she was too ashamed at being turned away without money, to return to her village!

It would mean that no man would marry her without a dowry. She could not face the scorn of her friends and relations and knew herself to be a failure.

Death was preferable to disgrace and the torrent made death easy!

"How could Gerald have done that to her?" Dominica asked the darkness.


As Dominica went from the sitting-room Lord Hawkston said to his nephew:

"I have something to tell you, Gerald."

"What is it?"

"I got up early this morning," Lord Hawkston answered, "and I rode over to the village where Lakshman lives. I hoped to see him but he was not there. However I discovered some important facts about him."

Gerald did not answer. He only looked at his Uncle with a surly expression on his face as if he resented his intrusion into what he felt were his own private affairs.

"The villagers told me that Lakshman has been struck by the Rakshyos with madness."

"What the devil does that mean?" Gerald enquired.

Lord Hawkston made an impatient gesture.

"You have been in this country for two years," he said.

"Surely you have tried to understand something about these people? Especially those in the hill-country with whom you are dealing."

"If you're referring to their religious beliefs, I can't make head or tail of such rigmarole!"

The tone in which he spoke made Lord Hawkston tighten his lips, but in a quiet voice he answered:

"You must be aware that although the Ceylonese are Buddhists, the villagers still depend in many ways on the Hindu Gods. They believe in good and bad omens and in evil spirits and demons, which were the beliefs of their Yakkho forebears."

Looking at his nephew Lord Hawkston realised he was not particularly interested, but he continued:

"They are in fact still devil-worshippers and even their worship of a peaceful, gentle Buddha does not prevent this. Cruelty and death, sickness and pain are all in the hands of legions of devils and spirits with which the unseen world teems."

Lord Hawkston paused and there was a smile on his lips as he said:

"There is, in fact, in my opinion, very little difference between the spirits and devils of the Ceylonese and the doctrine of Satan and Hell which is preached so fervently in Colombo by Dominica's father."

"You told me he was a Parson," Gerald said. "Why, in Heaven's name, did you choose me a Parson's brat for a wife?"

"I chose Dominica," Lord Hawkston said, and now his voice was cold, "because she has both personality and character, something which I am sorry to see is singularly lacking where you are concerned."

"You have made that obvious," Gerald said with a snarl in his voice. "Go on with your lecture."

Lord Hawkston ignored the rudeness in his tone.

"The good spirits of the villagers," he continued, "are the Yakshyos, who are kind and gentle with a veneration for the Lord Buddha.

"On the other hand the Rakshyos are fierce, malevolent and evil. They inhabit the places of the dead and forests, where each has his own particular tree from which he will strike a passer-by with madness!"

Lord Hawkston walked across the room before he continued:

"This may seem strange and far-fetched to you and me, but the people here believe it, and they told me with all sincerity that Lakshman had been driven mad by a Rakshyo."

"Then bad luck to him!" Gerald said lightly. "I cannot see that I can do anything about it."

"It is more serious than you seem to imagine," Lord Hawkston said sharply.

"Why?" his nephew enquired.

"You have been here during the Ceylonese New Year," Lord Hawkston replied. "You must know, if you have taken the slightest interest in our people, that the long anticipated festival, which is a time of family reunion all over the island, brings in its train a great number of evils—particularly gambling and drinking."

Lord Hawkston glanced at his nephew as he spoke and continued evenly:

"Under the stress of such excitement the excitable side of the Ceylonese nature overcomes their habitual gentleness and passivity. Quarrels flare up suddenly, stabbings are frequent and, as you may not be aware, the murder rate in Ceylon is very high."

"Are you suggesting," Gerald asked, "that Lakshman will murder me?"

"I consider it quite a possibility," Lord Hawkston answered. "The *Kappurala*, or the Devil-Dancer, in the village whose job it is to cast out or placate evil spirits spoke very seriously of Lakshman. He knows his own people and I am prepared to listen to his warnings."

"Well, I'm not!" Gerald exclaimed positively. "If you ask me, the whole thing is a lot of nauseating rubbish thought up by the priests to extort money from the fools who listen to them. I know Lakshman. I met him when he came to offer me his daughter. He's a quiet, inoffensive chap about half my size. I'm no more afraid of him than I would be of a strutting bantam-cock!"

"Very well," Lord Hawkston said, "I have now arranged for a thorough search to be made for Lakshman so that I can pay him the money you owe him and try in some fashion to compensate him for the loss of his daughter. All I can say is that your behaviour in the matter and your callous indifference to the death of this wretched girl appals me!"

As if he was afraid he might say any more Lord Hawkston went from the sitting-room closing the door behind him.

His nephew sat still for a few seconds, then clapped his hands to summon a servant to bring him a whisky of which he felt in vital need.

Dominica was dreaming.

In her dream she heard Prudence crying.

Sometimes, after their mother had died, Prudence had suffered from nightmares from which she had awoken calling for her mother, only to burst into floods of tears when she found she was not there.

Dominica had always left the door of her and Faith's room open, so that they would hear Prudence if she cried out since she slept on the other side of the passage.

It had been a desperate loss for all the sisters when Mrs. Radford had died, but Prudence had only been seven and she had missed her mother with an intensity that made Dominica fear at times that her sorrow would undermine her health.

It is true she had never been very strong. She had been born prematurely and from the time she was a baby, she had been small, pale and more prone to sickness than the others.

Perhaps because she was the weakest one of the family Mrs. Radford had seemed to love her the most, and yet none of her other children had been jealous.

Prudence, they felt, was someone special and Dominica had decided when she left Colombo that the first person she would have to stay with her in her new home would be not Hope, but Prudence.

She was well aware that Prudence's sensitive nature found it hard to endure the harshness of her father's religion and his attitude towards them.

He disciplined them all as if he felt they were sinners who must be purged of evil, and for Prudence to be included in this general condemnation was, Dominica knew, bad for her not only mentally but also physically.

She had been thinking of Prudence before she fell asleep tonight, and wondering how she, or her other sisters, would fit into the household.

She had fondly imagined before she arrived that Gerald Warren would both look like his Uncle and also be kind and understanding as Lord Hawkston had been ever since she knew him.

But now not only her own dreams of the life she might lead were fading but also her plans for her sisters were evaporating like the mists over the valley.

What would Faith think of Gerald's drinking?

She was certain that Charity with her sharp intelligence would see at once that he treated the workers in the wrong way and might even find out the truth about Sēētha.

That was an episode, Dominica told herself, about which the girls must never learn.

She knew only too well how shocked and horrified they would be, because like her they loved the gentle, attractive Ceylonese women.

At the same time Dominica was aware that the air here in the mountains would suit Prudence and perhaps bring some colour into her pale cheeks.

She would enjoy the meals, because whomever else he dismissed Gerald had kept his Uncle's superlative cook and Dominica found every dish a delight she had never before experienced.

Now half asleep she sat up in bed thinking that she must go to Prudence and comfort her. Then she realised where she was.

She was not in the Vicarage but miles away from her family, and the cry she thought had come from Prudence was obviously from some animal out in the garden.

It came very clearly through the window she had opened on to the verandah, and now more fully awake she realised it was not a cry but a whimper or whine that a very small animal might make.

She was well aware that many animals in the jungle made strange sounds. She had read books on how travellers had been frightened almost out of their wits by jackals whose cries are so blood-curdling they strike a chill to the heart.

There was no reason to be afraid or upset by the little whimper she heard, and yet somehow as it continued, it was rather sinister and she was sure the animal, whatever it was, was just outside the window.

"It will move away in a moment," Dominica told herself and lay down again.

But it was impossible not to hear the continuous sound. It was piteous, so that Dominica knew it would be impossible to sleep again as long as it continued.

"It will go away in a moment," she told herself again. "It would be ridiculous for me to try to help the animal."

Perhaps it was in pain, but it was very unlikely, even if it was, that it would allow her to go near it.

"I will not listen," Dominica determined.

She turned her head sideways on to the pillow. Nevertheless she knew she was still tense as the whining continued.

She wished now she had not left her bedroom window open.

Supposing it came into the room? Supposing, worse than the plaintive animal, a snake came in from the verandah?

She felt her heart begin to thump in fright. Then suddenly, there was a snarling noise that made her leap with fear.

There could be no pretending that this was not a savage animal, and one that was definitely dangerous! The snarling became a roar and the sound seemed duplicated and the intensity of it was deafening.

For a moment Dominica was paralysed with fear. Then in a panic which swept away every thought, every feeling except that of a terror which shot through her like the sharpness of steel, she sprang from her bed and running across the room pulled open the door.

She had no idea where she was going; she was past thought, past everything but a horror which drove her instinctively with a sense of self-preservation to run away.

She opened another door and ran quickly, wildly, frantically, to where she knew she would be safe.


Lord Hawkston had also been awakened by the noise and he knew at once that it was two leopards fighting. As he awoke he cursed his nephew once again for his indolence and indifference to what was the ordinary duty of a planter.

The leopards had at one time been so prolific in the jungles of Ceylon that they had proved a real menace to the tea-planters.

With their numbers kept under control, they had become more rare and were not dangerous to man under normal circumstances.

They brought down deer and cattle and exercised mesmeric power on the monkeys whom they seemed to regard as their natural enemies.

But if a planter allowed the wild beasts of the jungle to encroach upon his plantation and become a menace, not so much to the workers, as to their animals, like pigs and dogs, he had no-one to blame but himself.

As Lord Hawkston sat up, he wondered if the leopards would remain in the garden long enough for him to find a gun and shoot them.

Then, even as he thought about it someone small and terrified came through the door of his room and running towards the bed flung herself upon him.

His arms went round Dominica and he knew as she pressed herself against him that she was trembling all over and he realised how frightened she must be.

"It is all right," he said quietly. "They will not harm you."

Her hands clutching at his night shirt were convulsive and he felt her press herself even closer as if she sought sanctuary from the fears which beset her.

"It sounds very terrifying," Lord Hawkston said in his calm, deep voice, "but at this time of the year, when the animals are mating, there are frequently fights in the jungle and the wild elephants make the most noise of them all!"

He realised as he spoke that his words were having little effect upon Dominica.

She was still trembling convulsively and her face was hidden against his shoulder.

"The leopards are still there. Let me go and find a gun, Dominica. I will shoot them and they will never worry you again."

"No . . . no! Do not . . . leave me!"

Her voice was low but he heard the panic in it.

"I will not do anything which will upset you further," he said, "but you must be sensible about this."

He got no further.

"I am not . . . sensible! I never . . . have been . . . sensible!" Dominica cried. "I have . . . tried to be what you . . . wanted . . . but it is . . . impossible! I am . . . frightened of . . . everything. I have tried to . . . hide it but it is no . . . good."

"That is not true," Lord Hawkston said. "I think you have been very brave about many things."

"I am . . . not, I am . . . not!" Dominica said. "I have been . . . acting a . . . lie . . . but you have not . . . realised it. I have been . . . afraid ever since I was a child. I was afraid of . . . angels; so Papa made me stay all . . . night in the . . . Church alone and now I am . . . afraid of the . . . dark! I am afraid of . . . snakes and of . . . leopards! I am afraid of . . . Mr. Warren, and of having to . . . marry him!"

The words were said in a passionate whisper, but they were said and Lord Hawkston knew as he listened that he might have expected them.

"You will despise me . . . I know you will," Dominica went on, "and I am . . . afraid of making you . . . angry. But you have to . . . know the . . . truth and I am . . . ashamed I have . . . deceived you."

She burst into tears as she spoke and Lord Hawkston felt the tempest which racked her thin body. It made him feel as if he held a very young and very unhappy child in his arms.

For a moment there was nothing he could say. He could only hold her close as she wept despairingly, hopelessly, as if she no longer had any control over her emotions.

She must have bottled up her feelings for so long, Lord Hawkston thought, that now it was like a dam that had broken and her pent-up emotions were sweeping everything away in a flood, leaving her nothing but her sense of insecurity.

"Do not cry, Dominica," he said gently at last. "I will put everything right for you. It is not as bad as you think."

"It . . . is! It . . . is!" Dominica murmured in between her tears. "I have . . . let you . . . down. I have broken my . . . promise, but I cannot . . . help it. I am such a . . . coward . . . such a . . . hopeless and . . . despicable coward!"

"You are nothing of the sort!" Lord Hawkston said.

His nightshirt now soaked with her tears, but he was aware that she was not trembling so violently in his arms.

Then suddenly he realised there was no longer any sound from outside.

"The leopards have gone!" he said. "I am sorry in a way you could not have seen them because the Ceylon leopard is a very fine and impressive creature. There are black rings round his body rather like a tiger, but much less clearly marked. He has spots only upon his legs, and his spring, which is enormous, is one of the most graceful movements in the whole animal world."

He was talking deliberately to divert Dominica's mind from her misery, and as he went on he knew that she was listening to him.

"There is also a pure black leopard on the island. He is very beautiful, but I have seen only three of them all the years I have been in Ceylon."

Dominica gave a little sigh.

Her tears ceased, but she did not move her face away from Lord Hawkston's shoulder.

He knew she had turned to him in her terror entirely for protection.

She had forgotten she was wearing only a thin muslin nightgown, one of the beautifully embroidered ones that Madame Fernando had included in her trousseau.

She was not even aware that Lord Hawkston was in fact a man.

He was everything that was safe; a stronghold against terror; a sanctuary against fear; a protection against anything that might hurt her.

He was in fact, quite impersonal and yet she had turned to him because he was the one man whom she knew she needed at this particular moment.

"Everything is quiet," Lord Hawkston said softly.

Dominica raised her head.

He could not see her in the darkness, but he could feel her long hair trailing over her shoulders and falling well below her waist.

She smelt of a flower which for a moment he could not identify. Then he realised it was in fact the sweet fragrance of lavender.

It was a strangely English scent amongst all the exotic perfumes of the East, and somehow it made him think of all he loved in England and of his mother.

"You need no longer be afraid, Dominica," he said gently.

"I am . . . not," she replied, but her voice caught in her throat as she spoke and sounded somehow infinitely pathetic like a very young child's.

"Tomorrow I will make certain that the leopards do not disturb you again," Lord Hawkston promised. "I will have the bedrooms opened up on the next floor. I should have insisted on it as soon as I arrived."

"I would feel . . . safer up . . . there," Dominica said, "but not if I was . . . alone."

"My bedroom is there," Lord Hawkston answered. "The one I built for myself. The 'Palm Room', but you know, wherever you might be, that I would protect you."

"That is . . . why I came to . . . find you," Dominica whispered.

Her face was no longer hidden against his shoulder, but she made no effort to move from the protection of his arms.

He was aware that even while she tried to speak naturally she was still tense, still listening, a if she feared the savage sounds of the leopards might break out again.

"I wanted you to have a good night," he said. "You have been tired and perhaps upset by many things since we left Colombo."

"I . . . could not go . . . back to . . . that room."

"No, of course not," he agreed. "We will change places.

You can sleep here and I will keep a watch for the leopards. But I promise you, they will not return."

"Do not . . . leave me yet," Dominica begged. "Not for a . . . moment."

He felt her hand tighten once again on his nightshirt.

"I will not leave you until you tell me to do so," Lord Hawkston said, "but I think you ought to try to sleep. So what I am going to suggest is that you get into bed and I will stay beside you until it is dawn, or until you are asleep."

"You must . . . think I am very . . . foolish," Dominica said with a little sob.

"I think you did exactly the right thing in coming to find me when you were frightened."

Very gently he took his arms from her. Then as she sat up on the bed on which she had been lying against him he stepped out on to the floor and put out his hands to find his dressing-gown which was lying over an adjacent chair.

He put it on and as he did so Dominica got into bed and pulled the sheet over her.

"You will . . . not go . . . away yet . . . will you?" she asked.

Lord Hawkston sat down on the bed and putting out his hands found hers.

"I promise you I will stay."

She gave a little sigh as if of relief. Then her fingers tightened on his.

"Are you . . . very angry with . . . me?"

"I am not angry, I do not despise you, and I do not think you in the least foolish," he answered. "I think, as I have always thought, that you are a very exceptional and very brave person."

"I am not . . . you know I am not!" Dominica said. "But I like you to . . . think so."

"I promise you I am speaking the truth."

There was a silence and then he said:

"Shut your eyes, Dominica. I think you will find it easier to fall asleep and actually there is very little of the night left. I do not need to look at my watch to tell you that in under half an hour the dawn will be breaking over the mountains, bringing us another golden day of sunshine."

He felt her fingers relax beneath his. She did not move and after a short while he heard her breathing evenly.

He had known that she had exhausted herself both by fear and with her tears, and he had been certain that once she relaxed she would sleep quickly and deeply as he had seen men sleep after some abnormal exertion or emotional stress.

He did not move but sat very still, his hands still on Dominica's until, as he had expected, there was a faint light between the curtains as they stirred with the dawn breeze.

Still Lord Hawkston waited. Then as it grew lighter he could see first the outline of the furniture in the room, then Dominica's face against the pillows.

Her hair covered her shoulders and he could see that her eyelashes were still wet as they lay dark against the pale cheeks of her little heart-shaped face.

She looked very young and very defenceless and Lord Hawkston looked at her for a long time. Then gently he disengaged his hands from hers and, rising, moved silently across the room to the half-open door.

He passed through it and closed it very quietly behind him.

He walked along the passage and entered Dominica's room. He saw the bedclothes thrown back as she had left them when she ran away and the window open on the verandah.

He walked through it. The lawn where the leopards had fought was scratched up, flowers were broken and plants were lying with their roots in the air.

Lord Hawkston stood looking at the damage then his eyes dropped to the edge of the verandah.

Attached to one of the supporting pillars was a piece of broken string which would have held captive a small animal—such as the kid of a spotted deer!

Lord Hawkston stared at the thickly covered hills. Somewhere hidden in them Lakshman was waiting to avenge his daughter's death.

If Dominica had gone to the assistance of the frightened kid last night, the leopards would have attacked her!

He knew that he must find Lakshman and quickly.

\* \* \*

When Dominica awoke and found herself in a strange room and in another bed, the events of the night before came flooding back to her.

She glanced at the clock which stood beside the bed and realised that it was late and she had slept well into the morning.

It was not surprising. At the same time she felt ashamed of her own weakness and shy when she remembered that she had driven Lord Hawkston from his bed because she had been so afraid.

"How could I have been so stupid?" she asked herself.

At the same time even to think of the terrible noise of the leopards in the darkness was to feel a renewed tremor of fear.

She had been truthful when she told Lord Hawkston she had always been timid. She had forced herself not to show it, because she knew she must set an example to her younger sisters, but she had never forgotten the terrible experience her father had made her undergo when she was only seven years old.

Her mother being ill at the time had not realised what was happening, although afterwards she had in fact been very angry.

Her father had been giving her a Scripture lesson on which he had talked of angels guarding people and saving them from the devils which existed in Hell.

He made it all seem very vivid and very real to the child he was teaching, and as usual he was carried away by his own oratory and described Hell in such vivid terms that Dominica had cried:

"I am frightened of devils, Papa. I am frightened they will catch hold of me."

"You will be safe as long as you are good," her father replied. "God sends his angels to protect you, and angels are always around you, Dominica, saving you from sin."

"I am frightened of angels too," Dominica said. "I do not want anything around me . . . I want to be alone!"

The Vicar had looked on this as sacrilege and had rebuked Dominica. Because even at seven years old she had a great deal of spirit and she had defied him.

"I *am* afraid of angels, Papa, whatever you may say about them . . . I am, I am!"

It ended in her being shut in the Church all night so that she could meditate on the angels and realise she was safe in God's hands.

Dominica remembered it all vividly, how the darkness had seemed peopled not with angels, but with devils.

Finally in her terror she had crouched down on the floor in the Governor's pew, making herself as small as possible, and put her hand over her ears in case she should hear the angels talking to her.

They found her in the morning asleep from sheer exhaustion with her head on one of the crimson hassocks.

The Vicar had never inflicted such a punishment on any of his other children. He had been far too afraid of his wife's anger.

But it had given Dominica a sense of insecurity that she had never lost. It had made her afraid of the dark, so that it had always been a comfort to have Faith sharing a room with her.

She had, however, as she was the eldest, forced herself to assume authority, and when her mother died she tried to take her place not only with her sisters, but also with her father.

It was not always easy where he was concerned, but she could sometimes soften the strictness of his orders or divert him from his most austere demands on them.

Only when it came to obtaining money from him for payment for food and other necessities did she admit to herself that she was a hopeless failure.

At the same time she had never in her life behaved quite so weakly or, she thought, so humiliatingly as she had last night.

She was aware that it must have been the culmination of many things—shock at Lord Hawkston's proposition; unhappiness at leaving home; the revulsion she had felt when she met Gerald, most of all the horror of his lips when he had kissed her shoulder and the terror she felt for the future.

She wondered what Lord Hawkston was thinking about her this morning and whether he regretted having brought her with him to the house he had built himself.

If he had thought her worthy of living here, if he had imagined her as its hostess and chatelaine, surely now he would be terribly disillusioned at finding her so timid and so dishonest in not being prepared to fulfil her part of the bargain.

"He has given me so much," Dominica told herself miserably, "and now I am failing him when he relied on me."

The idea brought the tears once again to her eyes and she realised she felt tired and limp after her experience of the night before.

"I must get up," she told herself.

But she lay watching the sunshine creeping into the room through the sides of the curtains and illuminating the decorations which depicted the red lotus.

The bed had been carved in the same style as the one in her room, with petals painted the deep rose red of the King of flowers. The curtains had a symbolic motif of lotuses, but the picture on the wall was different.

This was not of the Buddha. It was a beautifully painted picture of the lake in Kandy with the red lotus growing on it.

In the distance on the other side of the lake there was a glimpse of the Temple of the Sacred Tooth and hanging over the water were the Temple flower-trees in bloom as Dominica had seen them when she had driven there with Lord Hawkston.

It seemed to her in retrospect that it had been a day of inescapable magic.

She had never known such beauty existed! She could still feel the intensity of it.

Then as she lay there looking at the picture and remembering the scene she suddenly understood why Kandy had seemed so beautiful; why the lake had shone with a strange mystical brilliance; why the beauty and colour of the flowers had seemed more vivid than she had ever known them.

It was because she had been with Lord Hawkston; because he was beside her; because she was acutely conscious of him and she was happy—happier than she had ever been in her whole life.

And the reason for her happiness came to her in a blinding light.

It was all so simple, and yet she had not understood until now that what she felt had been love.

Love for Lord Hawkston!

The man who had brought her up into the hills to marry his nephew!

# CHAPTER SEVEN

It was nearly noon before Dominica arose. But when she was dressed and went from her room it was to find the house was empty: neither Lord Hawkston nor Gerald were anywhere to be seen.

She picked up her sunshade thinking she would go into the garden.

The new way in which she had arranged her hair in a corolla on top of her head was, she thought, becoming, so that she decided she would not spoil it by wearing a bonnet.

Anyway there was no-one to see her.

She had however just reached the front door when she heard the sound of a horse's hoofs and saw Lord Hawkston come riding down the path which led up the mountain.

He dismounted and she thought his horse looked as if he had ridden it hard.

She also noticed that he wore a pistol in the belt that encircled his waist.

She supposed he had been out looking for the leopards,

but it was difficult to think of anything except that her heart leapt at his appearance. At the same time she felt overwhelmingly shy.

His white shirt was open at the neck as it had been when she had seen him riding the previous morning, and his sleeves were rolled up above his sun-burnt arms.

"Where are you going?" he asked with a smile.

She thought his eyes rested appreciatively on the colourful muslin gown she wore with its full skirts and ribbons at the neck.

"I was just . . . going for a walk in the . . . garden before . . . luncheon," she replied wondering why it was hard to speak and the words seemed somehow constricted in her throat.

A servant led Lord Hawkston's horse away and he said:

"We have time, if it will please you, to look at the giant lotus."

"I would . . . like it . . . very much," Dominica exclaimed breathlessly.

He turned to walk beside her across the lawn, and she thought as she had done before how young and athletic he looked when he was dressed unconventionally.

At the same time, because she loved him and was receptive to his moods, she had the feeling he was worried about something and she hoped he would tell her what it was.

But instead he talked of the garden, showing her the different flowers he had planted and pointing out the rare trees and shrubs, some of which Dominica had never even heard of before.

"In two months' time," he said, "the rhododendrons will be in flower. They blossom later in these high altitudes, but their colours are indescribable."

Dominica longed to ask if he thought she would be there in two months' time, then even as the words trembled on her lips she knew she could not say them.

He trusted her; he believed in her and she remembered how, when they were in Kandy, she had told him that if one was really in love there was no sacrifice one would not make.

Well, she was in love, and the sacrifice required of her

was that she should do what Lord Hawkston wished and marry his nephew.

Even to think of it made her want to cry as she had cried last night on his shoulder, but she knew that to do so would make him despise her even more than he must do already.

He was being courteous and charming, because he wished to make it easy for both to forget the way she had run to him for protection and lain in his arms to cry against his shoulder.

At the time it had seemed the only thing she could do; but now that she was with him again, Dominica could not help blushing at the thought of how she had behaved.

It was true that at that moment she had not thought of him as a man, but rather as a tower of strength, a comfort and a protector.

But he was a man, and she had known it when she had awoken in his bed to look at the picture on the wall in his room.

"I love him! I love him!" she told herself.

But she knew she must never let him know of her feelings for him. Instead she must sacrifice her whole life to doing what he wished.

She tried to concentrate on what Lord Hawkston was saying, and yet she could only think how thrilling it was to be beside him and how if he touched her arm accidentally or drew close to her as they inspected a flower or a bush, it sent a little tremor of excitement all through her body.

She wondered why she had not realised last night when she had wept against him and felt his arms holding her so securely that this was what she had wanted more than anything in the whole world.

She wondered now what he would think if she asked him to hold her once again; to give her that sense of security and protection which had finally swept away her fears, so that she had fallen asleep holding his hand.

"Could any man," she asked herself, "have been kinder, more understanding than he was?"

She knew how angry her father would have been at her behaviour; she knew that everyone, if they learnt of it, would be shocked at the thought of her clinging to Lord Hawkston, wearing nothing but the thin, laced-trimmed nightgown which had been part of her trousseau.

Had he thought her fast and brazen because of her behaviour?

She was certain that he thought of her merely as a rather tiresome child; a foolish girl who was afraid of the dark, and who, though having lived all her life in Ceylon, was yet scared of two leopards fighting each other and being of no danger to her personally.

"I may seem a child to him," Dominica told herself, "but I love him as a woman. I love him with my whole being, and I know this is love as it was meant to be; love which has existed since the beginning of time."

She knew that what she felt for Lord Hawkston was a spiritual yearning which was in fact part of the Divine.

It was something, she told herself, that Gerald would never understand.

How could she stay with a man year after year who was coarse and materialistic and without any sensitivity whatsoever?

How could she endure his whole attitude to life and, worst of all, how could she contemplate the moment when he would not only kiss her, but they would be united as man and wife?

Instinctively, because she was once more afraid, she moved a little closer to Lord Hawkston.

As if he realised that something perturbed her he said:

"Perhaps we are lingering too long. Come, I promised to show you the giant lotus before we return to the house for luncheon."

He led her from the garden down a path which had obviously been cut through the jungle.

On either side there were trees in bloom, but Dominica realised that the original path had narrowed because it had been left unattended and the undergrowth on either side of it had encroached so that in some places they had to walk singly.

At the same time it was very beautiful and the scent of the magnolias, the jasmines and the champees made her feel as if she was really in the Garden of Eden.

Then, almost unexpectedly, they came upon the pool they were seeking.

It was surrounded by trees and not very large. It was shaded from the sun which filtered through the branches, throwing a variegated pattern of gold and giving the clearing a strange mysticism that was difficult to describe.

The pool itself was breathtaking. Covered by the giant lotus, some of which were open and some in bud, it was a picture of colour and beauty which made Dominica draw in her breath because it was so lovely.

On the other side of the pool stood a pedestal on which there was a statue of Buddha.

Lord Hawkston, following the direction of her eyes, said:

"Here is one of my special treasures that I particularly wanted to show you. I think it originally came from Anuradhapura, but I found it neglected and forgotten amongst some ruins in the jungle and I brought it here, so that at least it has a reverent and appropriate setting."

"It has indeed!" Dominica said, speaking for the first time since she had seen the pool.

"Come and look at the carving on it," Lord Hawkston suggested.

They encircled the pool, having a little difficulty in pushing through the ferns and plants which had forced their way between the trees when there had been no gardeners to keep them under control.

They reached the statue of Buddha and Dominica realised that Lord Hawkston had placed it against a background of Temple-trees and champees which were to be found near every Buddhist *wihara* on the island.

Buddhism, she knew, was the religion of flowers and she thought that Lord Hawkston was one of the few Englishmen who would have treated the sacred emblem of a religion other than his own with such reverence.

She thought as they reached the statue, which on its pedestal stood a little above them, that he looked annoyed to find the fig-ivy which climbs all over rocks and buildings was curling itself round the ancient grey stone.

He put out his hand to start pulling it away from where

it was encroaching on the stone lotus on which the Buddha was seated.

"It must be very old . . ." Dominica began when something, she was not certain what it was, made a movement that attracted her attention.

She turned her head and screamed.

Just behind them, having come silently through the undergrowth, was standing a man!

His face was contorted into a mask of demoniacal hatred, his arm was raised and in his hand was a wooden-handled, sharp-pointed *kris*.

Without thinking, just acting as her instinct told her to save the man she loved, Dominica threw herself against Lord Hawkston as he bent over the stone lotus.

He staggered and the knife which would have struck him in the base of the neck, missed.

Instead the sharp-pointed blade passed through the thick corolla of plaited hair which Dominica wore on top of her head, and the force of it threw her backwards so that she was impaled against the trunk of a tree.

It all happened so quickly that Dominica's scream of fear had hardly died away before Lord Hawkston, regaining his balance, had drawn his pistol and shot the madman who menaced them.

Even as he fired, Lord Hawkston realised that it was Lakshman, whom he had been seeking all the morning.

Lakshman threw up his hands as the bullet hit him in the chest and he fell backwards into the pool, his body splashing through the giant lotus.

Lord Hawkston turned to Dominica and realised that after the shock of what had happened she had fainted and was held upright only by the *kris* which pinioned her through her hair to the tree.

Hastily he put his arm around her and drew out the knife, feeling a sudden fear because it was covered in blood.

Then as he threw it to the ground and examined Dominica's head he saw with relief it was not her blood which stained it.

She was still unconscious and he picked her up in his arms and carried her round the side of the pool.

Only as he reached the path which led back to the house did he look down at the water and realise there was no sign of Lakshman.

The lotus blossoms had closed again over the spot where he had fallen through them.

Except for the blood-stained *kris* lying at the foot of the statue of Buddha, there was nothing to show that murder had been attempted in that quiet spot and that two people had been saved from being massacred by only a hair's breadth and a frightened scream.

Holding Dominica closely in his arms Lord Hawkston walked quickly down the path which led back to the house.

Only when he reached the cultivated part of the garden did he find Gerald.

His body was lying face downwards on the grass, his white shirt stained crimson where Lakshman had struck him in the back as he was walking home for luncheon.


Dominica stirred.

Vaguely she remembered coming back to consciousness more than once, but what she thought or felt had been very hazy.

Someone had given her something to drink and she had fallen asleep again—the deep, dreamless sleep of complete oblivion.

Now she felt different. It was almost as if she could feel herself coming alive: her brain began to work and she was no longer sleepy.

Slowly she opened her eyes and for a moment it was difficult to imagine where she could be.

It was a room she had never seen before and the bed in which she was lying was very large. There were two posts at the end of it reaching right to the ceiling.

The sunshine was coming through the curtains which were only half-closed and the windows were open on to the verandah.

Suddenly Dominica was aware that she was in the room about which Lord Hawkston had spoken, the 'Palm Room' which he had built for himself and which Gerald had closed.

At the thought of Lord Hawkston a little tremor went through her. Now she remembered!

Slowly she recalled the contorted face of Lakshman when he had tried to kill him.

She had known without being told who the madman was, known that he was Sēētha's father desiring revenge for the way in which his daughter had been treated. He must have wished to kill not only Gerald Warren, who was responsible for her death, but also any white man connected with him.

Before she had fainted with the horror of what had occurred, she had heard the report of Lord Hawkston's pistol and seen Lakshman fall into the pool.

It was then a merciful darkness had covered her so she had known nothing more.

"I wonder how long ago it happened?" Dominica asked herself.

She had the feeling that some time had elapsed and yet she could be sure of nothing.

Surprisingly, she told herself, she was no longer afraid.

Perhaps it was because she was in Lord Hawkston's room, and although she was alone it was as if the sense of protection he gave her lingered there in the atmosphere.

She looked up and was spell-bound by what she saw.

The posts she had noticed at the end of the bed were carved like palm-trees; the ceiling was arched and palm branches were painted on it.

Now she looked around the room and realised that every six feet or so there were carved trunks of palm-trees rising from the floor to the ceiling and between them, vividly and skilfully executed, were murals of the jungle.

There were trees, ferns and convolvuli, vines and rattans. There was the weaving plant, known as the *kudumirris,* which weaves itself from tree to tree.

There were lianas which wove fantastic patterns in the tree-tops, falling to the earth in marvellous festoons. And of course there were the flowers. Orchids of every shape, size and colour, magnolias and camellias, rhododendrons and roses.

It was all so beautiful and unexpected that Dominica

could only lie against her pillows looking around her with delight.

There were the birds which she had known all her life: the crested eagle, the hawk, the martin and the swift.

There were also halcyons, or kingfishers, small, red-billed and resplendent, their bodies sapphire-blue—the bluest blue it was possible to imagine.

She could also see the green bee-eaters and the paradise fly-catchers with their rich chestnut plumage, orioles black-headed and golden, the blue-tailed pittas and green pigeons.

How could Lord Hawkston have thought of having a bedroom so exciting, she thought in delight, and so incredibly lovely?

She remembered he had told her that it was unique and she knew there could not be a room in the whole world that was so different from everyone else's.

She raised herself a little higher on the pillows so that she could go on looking at it.

Now she could see little monkeys had been painted in the trees and in one corner of the room there was the 'walura' or boar, which Dominica knew was happy, grubbing and greedy, unless he was cornered, when he could become extremely vicious.

There were also glimpses through the exquisite foliage of a bear, a sambhur and a leopard.

But what were much more beautiful were the butterflies of every size and colour and the lizards, which Dominica had tried to tame ever since she had been as small as Prudence.

It was all like watching a fairy-story being projected before her, and she lay for a long time looking at it with fascinated eyes until she found herself wondering how many of Lord Hawkston's friends, especially those in England, would think him capable of creating such an imaginative fantasy.

"It is because he loves the country so much," Dominica told herself, "that he wants to keep it around him even when he is asleep."

And she knew that just as Lord Hawkston loved Ceylon Gerald hated it.

The thought of Gerald made even the sunshine seem

dark for a moment. Then the door opened and a woman came in.

Dominica had never seen her before, and yet she knew she must have been aware of her even while she had been unconscious.

She was a smiling, pleasant-faced Englishwoman, wearing a badly-fitting white blouse and skirt, and her mousy hair had escaped untidily from a bun pinned at the back of her head.

"You're awake!" she said with a smile. "I thought you would be."

"How long have I been asleep?" Dominica enquired.

"For three days!" the woman replied and as Dominica looked incredulous she said:

"I'd better introduce myself. I am Mrs. Smithson and I have been looking after you."

"Thank you," Dominica said. "Are you a Nurse?"

The woman crossed the room to draw back the curtains a little further and let in more sunshine.

"I'm what they call a Medical Missionary," she replied. "But Nurse is a better word, for if anyone is ill in this district I am the only person they can ask for unless they are prepared to travel all the way to Kandy."

She turned from the window towards the bed.

"I'm glad you are awake, Miss Radford," she said, "because, as a matter of fact, I've come to tell you that I must leave."

"Have . . . have you told . . . Lord Hawkston?" Dominica stammered, a little bewildered.

"Lord Hawkston will be returning on the afternoon train from Kandy," Mrs. Smithson said. "He has been at the funeral."

"The funeral?"

"Of his nephew, Mr. Warren," Mrs. Smithson said quietly.

She saw Dominica stiffen and the surprise in her eyes.

"Lakshman killed him before he attempted to take Lord Hawkston's life," she explained. "His Lordship told me that you saved him!"

"Lakshman killed . . . Gerald?" Dominica repeated almost beneath her breath.

"He died instantly," Mrs. Smithson said. "A native *kris* is a very lethal weapon!"

Dominica said nothing and after a moment Mrs. Smithson went on:

"I'm sorry about this. Everything that happened must have been a terrible shock for you. But I know you'll realise there's nothing you can do about it, except forget it. Such tragedies occur, but not often, I'm glad to say."

"And . . . Lord Hawkston shot . . . Lakshman?" Dominica asked hesitatingly.

"He was quite mad, poor man!" Mrs. Smithson replied. "As a matter of fact, when I treated him for an affliction in one of his eyes a few months ago, I thought he was decidedly unhinged. He was a difficult man and no-one would employ him."

She leant against the carved post of the bed and looked at Dominica.

"Forget it all, child," she said, "and if you take my advice you'll get up, go downstairs and be ready to greet Lord Hawkston when he arrives."

"How did you keep me asleep for so long?" Dominica enquired.

"It was His Lordship's idea," Mrs. Smithson said, "and, as it happens, I agreed with him. It wasn't anything drastic, just a few herbs that I give to women who are in pain to make them feel a bit 'muzzy'. You'll be quite all right when you've had a cup of tea."

She gave a little laugh.

"I always say there's nothing like a good strong cup of our own tea to sweep away the cobwebs!"

She glanced at the clock.

"I'll tell the servants to bring you up some and prepare your bath. I'm sorry I can't stay so that we can get to know each other, but doubtless we'll meet again."

"Why are you leaving?" Dominica asked.

"That's what I came to explain," Mrs. Smithson replied. "Will you tell His Lordship that Mrs. Davison, whose husband is a planter on the other side of the hill, has started her first baby and they've sent for me? I know he'll understand."

"I am sure he will," Dominica said, "and thank you very much for looking after me."

"It's been a pleasure!" Mrs. Smithson smiled. "And between ourselves, I'd do anything for Chilton Hawk—I beg his pardon—Lord Hawkston! And you tell him for me, the longer he stays, the better! We need him here!"

"I will give him your message," Dominica said.

Mrs. Smithson held out her hand.

"Goodbye, Miss Radford! And try not to worry about what's happened. There's always tomorrow. That's what I always say!"

"I will try to do as you suggest," Dominica smiled.

Mrs. Smithson shook her hand heartily.

"Goodbye!" she said again. "Take care of yourself. I'll be popping in to see you one of these days!"

When she had gone Dominica lay back against the pillows.

So Gerald was dead!

It might be wrong—it might indeed be wicked—but she could not help feeling a sense of unutterable relief.

Now she would not have to marry him! Now she would be free of the promise she had given Lord Hawkston.

Then suddenly another problem presented itself.

Would this mean that she must go home immediately? That she could no longer stay here in the hills? That she must return to the life she had lived before Lord Hawkston had taken her into a world she had never known?

It was a world that contained drama and danger and strange passions—at the same time a world so beautiful, so wonderful, that she knew it had changed her whole being.

Then with a sudden urgency which revived her like a glass of wine she knew that she wanted to see Lord Hawkston again; she wanted to talk to him, to be with him; and for the moment she could think of nothing else!

Dominica was downstairs waiting in the sitting-room when she heard the carriage which had met Lord Hawkston at the station driving up to the front door.

The big doors of the house were always left open so that the cool air could blow through, and now she was suddenly tense as she heard the servants greeting their master and heard Lord Hawkston reply:

"I want to wash and put on something comfortable."

"Your bath is ready, *Durai.*"

Dominica heard Lord Hawkston go upstairs. She knew that while he had given up his room to her he had slept in another which was on the same floor.

Already she had discovered that even in the three days she had been ill things had changed about the house.

There were many more servants and the place seemed to shine with a new cleanliness and brightness as she came down the stairs.

She had looked out into the garden and seen no fewer than five men working to cut back the encroaching jungle, replace the flowers that had been rooted up by the leopards, and water the green lawns.

She thought too that some pieces of the furniture had been moved, and she guessed that they had been put back in the places which Lord Hawkston had originally planned for them.

The sitting-room was filled with flowers and there had been big bowls of flowers in her bedroom. They had seemed almost a part of the murals on the walls.

But in the sitting-room they now stood on every chest and table, and in the hall there were great vases of lilies which scented the whole house with their sweet fragrance.

Dominica had spent much longer than usual after she had had her bath in making herself look as attractive as possible.

She seemed thinner since her long sleep and her eyes seemed to fill the whole of her small heart-shaped face.

She could not bear to plait her hair and dress it as it had been before. Even to think of the corolla on her head was to remember the impact of Lakshman's *kris* as it had passed through it and pinioned her to the tree.

Instead she coiled it into a chignon at the back of her head and hoped that Lord Hawkston would not think it looked too old-fashioned.

She chose her prettiest gown; then when she had it on, wondered if she should change into another.

She had the feeing that it was important to look her best because, although she would hardly face the fact, she knew that her whole future depended on what he was about to decide for her.

As she sat waiting in the sitting-room, forcing herself to sit still with her heart thumping tumultuously in her breast, she knew that her lips were dry with fear.

While she longed irrepressibly to see him again, she was afraid that when she did so, he would tell her that he expected her to go home at once, perhaps tomorrow.

"How can I bear it? How can I face it?" Dominica asked herself.

She thought how humiliating it would be if she burst into tears and cried against him as she had done when she had been so frightened by the leopards.

Yet when he came into the room she felt her heart leap and it was impossible to speak; impossible to do anything but rise to her feet to stand looking at him, conscious that her knees were trembling.

"Dominica!" Lord Hawkston exclaimed, and she thought he looked happy. "I was hoping you would be well enough to get up. But where is Mrs. Smithson? The servants tell me she has gone away."

With a tremendous effort as if her voice came from very far away, Dominica replied:

"She asked me to . . . tell you she had to go . . . Mrs. Davison who is having . . . a baby. She knew you would . . . understand."

Lord Hawkston walked nearer.

"I do understand," he said. "At the same time it is inconvenient."

Dominica felt her spirits drop.

He obviously did not want to be alone with her. He wanted Mrs. Smithson to be there, perhaps because it would prevent them from talking intimately.

The servants came in with cool drinks and some sandwiches.

Lord Hawkston took a glass in his hand and walked towards the window.

"It was very hot in Kandy," he said in a conversational tone. "I was looking forward to being back."

The servants left the room but Dominica could find nothing to say. She could only stand looking at him, thinking how handsome he was, how at ease he appeared in his white suit, and yet how elegant!

He turned and looked at her.

"How do you feel?"

There was a note of anxiety in his voice that had not been there before.

"I . . . I am . . . all right," Dominica answered.

"That is what I hoped you would say."

He put down his glass.

"It is however annoying," he went on, "that Mrs. Smithson has had to leave so quickly. I had hoped she would be able to stay while we talked about your future, and now you have no chaperon!"

"Is it so . . . important for me to have . . . one?" Dominica asked.

"It is conventionally correct, as you well know."

He stood with his back to the fireplace and after a moment Dominica said in a very small voice:

"Are you . . . sending me . . . away?"

He did not look at her but stared towards the window as he replied:

"I have been thinking about that, Dominica, in fact I have thought of little else these past few days. It seems to me there are two alternatives."

"What are . . . they?"

"The first, of course, is that you might return to your family," Lord Hawkston said. "And considering that you were so nearly married to my nephew, I think it only fair that I should settle a certain amount of money on you."

"That is unnecessary!" Dominica said quickly.

"On the contrary, I think it very necessary," Lord Hawkston contradicted. "At the same time, I have a feeling that you might see very little of it and that your father would spend it on those he thought more needy than you."

This was so true that Dominica felt it did not need an answer.

"On the other hand," Lord Hawkston went on, "I can take you with me to England."

He looked at her as he spoke and saw the sudden gladness in her face which was like a light.

"Once we are there," he went on. "I can quite easily find you a suitable husband."

The light faded.

Dominica's eyes met his and it seemed as if neither of them could look away.

It was impossible to move, impossible to breathe. Then she said in a voice he could hardly hear:

"Let me . . . stay with . . . you."

"Do you know what you are asking? I am too old for you, Dominica."

Just for a moment it seemed as if she did not understand. Then she moved towards him swiftly and instinctively, seeking him as she had done the night she had been so frightened.

His arms went round her and it was like reaching Heaven to feel them holding her as she wanted to be held.

"I said I am too old," he said in a strange voice that she had never heard from him before.

"I love . . . you!"

She whispered the words, and yet they were quite clear.

"Are you sure? Oh, my darling, are you sure?"

She lifted her face to his.

For a moment he looked down into her eyes, then he pulled her against him and his lips were on hers.

It seemed to Dominica as if the whole world were illuminated with a golden radiance that was blinding.

She felt that his lips possessed her, and yet gave her everything that had ever been beautiful and moving, exquisite and lovely! It was what she had sought in the music she had played and listened to on the breeze of the wind.

It was also what she had found in the brilliance of the flowers in Kandy, and in the enchantment of the jungle.

"I love you! I love you!"

She was not certain if she said it aloud or with the feelings he evoked in her which seemed to pass from her lips to his.

She loved him so intensely that she felt already that she was a part of him; they belonged to each other; they were indivisible and no longer two people but one.

Finally Lord Hawkston raised his head.

"My precious, my darling!" he exclaimed unsteadily. "This is wrong! You should find someone of your own age."

"There is only . . . you in the . . . whole world."

"Do you really mean that?"

"I think I knew it from the very first . . . moment I met . . . you," she whispered. "But I was not . . . aware that it was . . . love."

He kissed her again and she felt herself thrill and come alive with sensations such as she had never known existed.

Looking down at her face radiant with happiness he asked masterfully:

"When did you first know you loved me? Tell me—I want to hear."

"I think I . . . loved you first when you were so . . . kind in giving each of the girls a new gown and bonnet," she answered, "and when you told Madame Fernando that they were all to be different. I thought you were more under-standing than I could have expected any man to be."

She gave a little sigh of sheer happiness and continued:

"And when you were so clever with Prudence, telling her she must eat her food so that she could go to her Ball you would give for her, I knew . . ."

Dominica's voice faltered for a moment and a blush arose in her cheeks.

"What did you know, my sweet?"

"I . . . knew that was how I would like the . . . father of my . . . children to . . . behave with them," she murmured, and hid her face against his neck.

He held her so tightly that it was impossible to breathe.

"And when did you first admit to yourself that you loved me?"

"When we were at Kandy," she answered. "It was so beautiful that I could think of nothing but . . . love. Then afterwards, when I saw the picture of your bedroom I knew why. It was because I . . . loved you. I loved you with all of me . . . but I thought you would . . . despise me."

"I loved you from the very first moment," Lord Hawkston said. "I realised what a hard life you were living and I wanted to take you out of it, to protect you!"

He paused before he said:

"I have never before in my whole life wanted to protect and take care of a woman, not for my own pleasure but for hers. I wanted to shelter you from harm, to stand between you and anything which could hurt or distress you."

"That is why I . . . ran to you when I was . . . frightened," Dominica told him. "I knew I would be safe with you."

"As you always will be," Lord Hawkston said, "And when I saw you in your wedding gown, I knew you were the embodiment of everything a man could desire and long for in a bride. You were beautiful, exquisitely beautiful and yet at the same time I had already learnt how much character and personality you had."

He kissed her forehead.

"Will you wear that gown tomorrow for me, my darling, when we go to Kandy to be married?"

She turned her face up to his and her eyes seemed full of stars.

Then he felt her stiffen and she dropped her head.

"What is it?" he asked.

"I had forgotten," she said in a low voice, "that in England you are very . . . important. I have been thinking about you only as living here . . . a planter. Perhaps you will be . . . ashamed of me amongst your smart friends."

Lord Hawkston put his hand under her chin and turned her face up to his again.

"I have no friends amongst whom you would not shine more brilliantly than the sun itself!" he said. "You are mine, Dominica, mine, as you were always meant to be, and perhaps you have been in the past! Now that you have said that you love me, I will never let you go!"

"That is all I want," Dominica cried, "to be . . . yours for all eternity."

"That is what you will be," he said, "and because I think

it will please you, and because too I want it myself, I intend that we shall live here for six months of each year. It does not take long to travel to England. We will go back in the summer and do our duty for the family and the estate but for the winter we will return here. Will that make you happy?"

"You know it will!" Dominica answered, "and you know too that I will be happy anywhere . . . anywhere in the world . . . as long as I can be with you!"

There was a note in her voice that brought the fire into Lord Hawkston's eyes. Then his lips were on hers and he was kissing her until she could no longer think, but only feel her heart and soul were both his.

The stars were very brilliant in the sky as Dominica and Lord Hawkston came from the Palm Room onto the verandah.

Dominica was wearing the white gown in which she had been married earlier in the day.

She had changed for the train journey, but when she had come home she had put on her wedding-gown again because she knew that Lord Hawkston liked to look at her in it.

It had been a very simple and quiet wedding with only James Taylor as their best man, but to Dominica it had been a service of dedication and she had known that Lord Hawkston felt the same.

She had heard James Taylor say when the service was over:

"I am happy for you, Chilton, you always needed a wife."

"To keep me in order?" Lord Hawkston answered with a smile.

"To complete the story of your success!" James Taylor had replied. "When you have finished honeymooning come and see me. I have not only new methods of tea dyeing to show you, but I have also a young man who is just the sort of manager you need. He has been out here for two years and you can trust him."

"Thank you, James," Lord Hawkston said.

It had been very moving for Dominica to arrive back at

the house and know it was to be her home with the man she loved.

As she saw it standing over the valley like a precious jewel encircled by the gardens and the silver lake her fingers had tightened on her husband's hand.

"We will be happy!" she said.

"I know now that I built it for you," he answered, "and there was always something missing when I was in the Palm Room."

Dominica blushed and he kissed her hand.

"You need never be afraid of being alone in the darkness again, my lovely one."

They had so much to say to each other, so much to talk about, that they had lingered long over the superlative dinner which the Cook had provided for them. Now as they stepped onto the verandah it was too late to see the sunset.

Dominica looked up.

There was a half-crescent moon moving up the sky and as Lord Hawkston followed her eyes he said quietly:

"Do you know what the crescent moon is called by our people?"

"No . . . tell me."

She knew that even the sound of his voice made little tremors of excitement run through her and the fact that his arm was around her made her quiver and long for the touch of his lips.

"It is called 'a lovers' moon,'" Lord Hawkston said, "and that, my precious, wonderful wife, is what it means to us."

"A lovers' moon over the Garden of Eden!" Dominica said softly. "What lovers could ask for more?"

"What indeed?" Lord Hawkston agreed, "and no man could ask more than to have you as his wife!"

She raised her face to his and in the light from the sky he could see her expression of happiness very clearly.

"You are so beautiful," he said, "so exquisitely perfect! I want to tell you something."

"What is it?" Dominica asked.

"When I first came to Ceylon," he said, "and I was only twenty-one, I thought, as I suppose all young men do, that sooner or later I would find someone I would love and we would get married. But what happened was very different."

Dominica looked at him a little apprehensively as he went on:

"I fell in love—not with a woman, my darling, but with a country. I loved Ceylon! It seemed to me everything that a man could wish to find in the woman he would love. It was soft and warm, sweet and friendly, and besides giving a man so much materially, it also had a spiritual message for those who would listen to it."

"I can understand that," Dominica whispered.

Lord Hawkston kissed her hair and it smelt of the fragrance of the jasmine buds she had entwined amongst the orange blossom wreath which Madame Fernando had made for her.

It was the fragrance of Ceylon, he thought, a fragrance which was irresistible and wholly feminine.

"Sometimes," he went on, "when I stood on this verandah I used to think that I would be alone for the rest of my life. No-one, I thought, could ever mean to me what this country had come to mean. No woman could ever be so beautiful or so utterly and completely desirable."

His arms tightened around her.

"Then I found you!" he said. "And I knew that you were all that I wanted; all that I had dreamt of; all that I had thought of as the utter and complete perfection that any woman could attain."

"Suppose I . . . fail you?" Dominica asked in a breathless little voice.

"You could never do that!" he answered. "We shall doubtless have our difficulties, set-backs, perhaps even storms, like the rains that fall on the valley, but fundamentally, we are one, we belong to each other, Dominica, and nothing can change or alter that!"

"Another Adam and Eve!"

She felt his lips against the softness of her skin.

"You are my Eve," he said. "I love you with all the love that exists in the whole world, and I will spend my life making you sure of it."

He drew her closer as he spoke and now their lips met

and Dominica put her arms round his neck to draw him closer still.

"I love . . . you! I love . . . you!"

She felt his hands on her hair drawing the pins from it so that it fell in a silken wave over her shoulders.

He kissed it, then sweeping it aside he kissed her neck, her shoulders, and as he unfastened her gown and it slipped lower, her rose-tipped breasts.

"You are like a lotus flower," he said passionately. "I worship you."

Then he drew her gently, his lips holding her captive, back into the Palm Room and the curtains closed behind them.

Outside the lovers' moon rose slowly up the starlit sky throwing its mystical silver light over the sleeping valley.

# NO TIME FOR LOVE

# CHAPTER ONE

———— ❧ ————

# 1904

Larina Milton, walking up Wimpole Street, remembered that the Barretts had lived there.

Instantly her imagination carried her into the sick-room where Elizabeth Barrett had lain year after year thinking she was an incurable invalid.

Then suddenly Robert Browning had come into her life and everything was changed.

> *"How do I love thee? Let me count the ways,*
> *I love thee to the depth and breadth and heighth*
> *My soul can reach."*

Larina quoted the lovely words and wondered if she would ever feel like that about a man.

'Supposing,' she thought, 'a man like Robert Browning appeared now at this moment and asked me to go away with him to Italy? Would I accept?'

The idea made her laugh, then she thought she would never have the courage that Elizabeth Barrett had shown.

She gave a little sigh.

"There are no Robert Brownings for me," she told herself. "I have to be practical. I have to find work."

Her mother had so often chided her for day-dreaming, for letting her imagination carry her away from the mundane affairs of everyday life into a fantasy world where she could forget everything else.

Work! Work!

The word seemed to repeat itself over and over again in her mind and she knew it was going to be difficult.

Women of her social position did not work; they sat at home with their parents until they got married; then they kept house having plenty of servants to do the menial tasks.

But those were women, or rather ladies, who had money, and a sudden fear of the future made Larina tremble.

She had known they were spending their last penny on her mother, but nothing had mattered except that she should get well.

But even money had failed to save Mrs. Milton, and when she died Larina's whole world crashed around her.

She had not even contemplated during those long months in the Sanatorium what it would be like when she was alone.

She had been buoyed up with the hope that her mother would live, convinced that her prayers would be answered, optimistically confident about the future.

It had been a Fool's Paradise, another fantasy from which she had been brought back to earth with a bang.

Deep in her thoughts Larina realised that she had walked past the number she was seeking, 55, and she had already reached 73.

She turned back to retrace her steps, and once again almost irresistibly she thought of Robert Browning walking as she was, up Wimpole Street, towards the Barretts' house.

There would have been a look of excitement on his face and he would have walked quickly because he was so anxious to be with Elizabeth again.

> '—*I love thee with the breath,*
> *Smiles, tears, of all my life!—and, if God choose,*
> *I shall but love thee better after death.*'

Elizabeth must have written that, Larina thought, because death was always very near her and therefore inevitably in her thoughts.

How could she be so sure that she would survive death? How could she know that wherever she might be she would still be thinking of Robert and loving him?

There was no answer to this question and now Larina had found number 55 and was walking up the steps with their iron railings on either side of them.

She stood looking at the door in an ugly shade of dark green, with its heavy brass knocker and wide-mouthed letter-box.

'It is a waste of money for me to come here,' she thought. 'It is sure to cost a guinea, perhaps two, and I can ill afford it.'

She hesitated.

Should she go away?

She felt so well, there could be nothing wrong with her. But Dr. Heinrich had made her promise that when she had been home for a month she would have herself examined by Sir John Coleridge, physician to the Royal Family.

"There is, I believe, absolutely no danger that you might have contracted tuberculosis from your mother," he had said in his broken English.

"I kept to all the precautions which you insisted upon," Larina replied. "I have never been with the other patients, except out of doors."

"You have been very good, Miss Milton," Dr. Heinrich approved, "an exemplary visitor, if I may say so. Very unlike some of the relatives who often make my work very difficult for me."

"I shall always be grateful for your kindness to Mama." Larina told him.

"If only she had come to me sooner," Dr. Heinrich said with a sigh. "It upsets me, Miss Milton, more than I can ever tell you when I lose a patient. But in your mother's case, her lungs were far too infected when she arrived here for my treatment or for even the magnificent air of Switzerland to effect a cure."

"Mama was quite young," Larina said almost as if she spoke to herself. "I thought that would tell in her favour."

"It would have," Dr. Heinrich replied, "if she had come to me at least a year sooner. Then I should have had a hope of keeping her alive."

He paused and then he said:

"I am going to be frank with you, Miss Milton, and tell you that your mother did not help me as she should have done. If a patient has the will to live, if he or she stubbornly clings to life, then that is often far more effective medicine than anything a Doctor can prescribe."

"Mama missed my father so desperately," Larina answered. "They were so happy together. She told me once that losing him was like losing half of herself. She felt she had nothing left to live for."

There was a little throb in her voice which made the Doctor say in a different tone:

"Now we have to think about you. Have you any idea what you are going to do?"

"I will go back to London," Larina replied. "After my father died my mother leased a small house in Belgravia. It has been let, but it is actually free at the moment."

"I am glad to hear that," Dr. Heinrich said. "We have all grown very fond of you, Miss Milton, and I did not like to think about you alone with nowhere to go."

"There is no need to worry about me," Larina answered with an optimism which she did not in fact feel.

At that moment however she had no idea that all the money her father had left had been spent. That was a shock waiting for her when she arrived back in England.

"There is one thing I want you to promise me," Doctor Heinrich said.

"What is that?" Larina enquired.

"A month after you have been home in London you will consult my friend, Sir John Coleridge, and get him to give you a check-up. I shall take every possible test before you leave. At the same time, let us be frank, you have been living for nearly twelve months with people who are all infected with what we have to admit has been an almost incurable disease."

"Surely they will find a cure one day for consumption?" Larina cried.

"There are experiments taking place all the time," Dr. Heinrich replied. "I may say without conceit that the most successful treatment up to now has been my own. It is not always looked on with favour by my more orthodox colleagues but a number of my patients leave here with improved health."

"Everyone speaks of you in the most glowing terms."

"At the same time I have my failures and your mother unfortunately was one of them. That is why you must promise me that you will be overhauled not only in a month's time, but again in perhaps six months."

He saw Larina's expression and added:

"I do not want to frighten you. There is, I am absolutely convinced, virtually no chance that you could have caught consumption from your mother or anyone else, but in my experience precaution is far better than cure."

"I promise!" Larina said.

"Sir John will tell you after his examination when he wants to see you again and you must do as he tells you."

Larina nodded.

It would, she thought at the time, be very ungracious and ungrateful of her to argue with Dr. Heinrich after he had been so kind.

Because her father had been a Doctor, Dr. Heinrich had taken her mother and also herself at very cheap and generous terms which the other patients in his expensive Sanatorium might well have envied.

Little though it was, it was more than they could afford; but whatever it cost, it had been the only chance Mrs. Milton had of survival.

With an effort Larina put out her hand now towards the bell on the right hand side of the door. As she did so she saw there was a notice above it which read:

*'Bell out of order—please knock.'*

So instead she lifted up the heavy brass knocker and gave two rat-tats on the door.

For a moment there was no sound. Then she heard footsteps on what she guessed was a marble floor and a moment later the door opened.

She had expected to see a servant, but instead a man wearing a conventional black frock coat stood there. He had a high stiff collar and a well-tied black cravat in which there was a tie-pin consisting of a large pearl.

"I have an appointment with Sir John Coleridge," Larina said nervously.

"You are Miss Milton? I was expecting you. Come in."

"Are you Sir John!"

"I am!"

Larina entered and closed the door behind her.

"My secretary has gone out for her luncheon," he said, knowing she must think it strange that he should open the door himself, "and the servants are ill with influenza, a fashionable complaint at this time of the year!"

"Yes, yes, of course," Larina said apprehensively.

Sir John led the way across the Hall into a room which looked out onto the back of the house.

It was a typical Doctor's consulting-room and all too familiar to Larina.

There was a big, impressive, leather-topped desk, with a hard, upright chair in front of it. A couch against one wall was half-concealed by a screen, and a book-case was stacked with medical tomes.

There was a table with a number of unidentifiable instruments on a clean white cloth.

"Sit down, Miss Milton," Sir John said, seating himself behind the desk and opening a folder which contained, she saw, a letter from Dr. Heinrich.

Sir John picked up a pair of spectacles and placed them on his nose, then lifting the letter read it carefully.

"Dr. Heinrich informs me that your mother has died of tuberculosis," he said. "He has asked me to examine you to make sure there is no chance that you have contracted the disease."

"Dr. Heinrich examined me before I left the Sanatorium," Larina said, "and every test was absolutely clear."

"That is what he says in the letter," Sir John said with just a note of reproof in his voice as if she had anticipated what he was about to tell her.

"I am sorry to hear that Dr. Heinrich could not save your mother," he remarked after a moment.

"He did everything that was humanly possible," Larina replied.

"And who should ask for more, even from a Doctor?" Sir John remarked. "Very well, young lady, undress behind the screen. You will find a garment you can put on. Then lie down on the couch and let me know when you are ready."

Larina did as she was told.

She took off the plain, inexpensive gown she had bought before she went out to Switzerland and laid it over the chair which stood beside the couch.

Her petticoats and underclothes followed.

It did not take long, and she slipped her arms into the shapeless white linen hospital-gown which was lying at the end of the couch.

"I am ready!" she said as she lay down, her head on the small hard pillow.

Sir John walked with heavy footsteps across the room and pushed the screen aside so that there was more light from the big window.

"You are nineteen, I believe, Miss Milton?"

"Nearly twenty," Larina answered.

Sir John had already inserted the ends of his stethoscope in his ears, so it was doubtful if he heard her.

'Nearly twenty!' Larina thought to herself. 'I have done so little in my life and I have so few qualifications.'

The only thing she could really say in her favour was that she read a lot.

Her father had encouraged her to read the books which interested him and were mostly on ancient civilisations and, as her mother often pointed out, not much use when it came to living in the world today.

"Instead of learning about the ancient Greeks and Romans," Larina told herself, "I ought to have been studying shorthand and learning how to type."

The large, noisy typewriters she had seen in offices and

which had been used by her father's secretary were a complete mystery to her.

Now she thought how foolish she had been not to take the opportunity of at least trying to understand how it worked.

She had been just seventeen when her father died and was still having lessons with teachers who came to the house.

"I am not going to have a Governess living with us," her father had said firmly. "And I do not approve of girls going to school and getting independent ideas. A woman's place is in the home!"

It would have been a very nice idea, Larina thought to herself, if she had a home to be in.

"Turn over, I want to listen to your back," Sir John's voice said.

She did as she was told and felt the stethoscope against her skin.

'I wonder what this is going to cost me,' she thought. 'It is just a waste of time and money!'

"You can dress now, Miss Milton."

Sir John moved away from her pulling the screen back into position as he did so. Larina got down from the couch and started to put on her clothes.

She wore a very light corset. There was no need for her to have tight laces with which to pull in her waist. It was in fact less than the standard eighteen inches.

But she was well aware that the rest of her figure from a fashionable point of view was much too thin.

"You must eat more, darling," her mother had said to her in Switzerland. "Do you really think such long walks are good for you?"

"I cannot just sit about doing nothing, Mama," Larina answered, "and I love walking. The mountains are so beautiful and I only wish you could come with me along the paths through the woods. They have so much mystery about them. They make me think of all the fairy-tales I have ever heard."

"How you used to love them when you were a child!" Mrs. Milton had replied with a smile.

"I remember you reading me a story about the dragons

who lived in the very depths of a pine-wood," Larina answered, "and I still believe it!"

Her mother had laughed.

"You belong to the sea," she said. "That is why I called you Larina."

" 'Girl of the Sea'," Larina had exclaimed. "Perhaps I have an affinity with it, I am not sure. We have never been to the sea long enough for me to find out. Here I feel I belong to the mountains."

"As long as it is not too boring for you, my dearest," Mrs. Milton had murmured.

"I am never bored," Larina had answered and it was the truth.

She put her hat on her head and fastening it securely with two long hat-pins she pushed back the screen and walked across the room to where Sir John was sitting at the desk.

He was writing on a piece of foolscap and she saw her name at the top of it.

"I have something to tell you," he said, "which I am afraid you will find very distressing."

"What is it?" Larina asked.

She felt as if her heart had stopped beating and that every nerve in her body was suddenly tense.

"You have not contracted the disease which killed your mother," he said, "but you have in fact only three weeks to live!"


Going back to the little house in Eaton Terrace, Larina could not believe that she had actually heard Sir John say the words.

It seemed as if her mind had ceased to function and she told herself that what he had told her was impossible to believe as the truth.

As she journeyed part of the way in the horse-drawn omnibus, she found herself looking at the passengers and wondering what they would say if she told them that a sentence of death had just been passed upon her.

After Sir John had spoken she had stared at him with

wide eyes, shocked to the point when her voice seemed strangled in her throat.

"I am sorry to have to tell you this," Sir John said, "but I can assure you that I am absolutely certain of my facts. You have a heart complaint which is very rare, but it is in fact a disease I have been studying for many years."

He cleared his throat and went on:

"Every Doctor who suspects it sends his patients to me for a final diagnosis, so I cannot suggest that you have a second opinion."

"Is it . . . painful?" Larina managed to gasp.

"In most cases there is no pain whatsoever," Sir John said reassuringly. "I will not burden you with the medical details, but what happens in fact is that your heart suddenly ceases to beat. It may happen when you are asleep, it may occur when you are walking, sitting, even dancing."

"And . . . there is no . . . cure?" Larina asked in a shocked tone.

"None that is known at the moment to the medical profession," Sir John replied. "What I can tell you, as an authority, is that it happens instantly, and when it is diagnosed the patient usually has exactly twenty-one days before the end comes."

"Twenty-one days!" Larina echoed faintly.

As she walked through Sloane Square towards Eaton Terrace she felt that her footsteps echoed the number on the pavement. Twenty-one! Twenty-one! Twenty-one!

That meant, she told herself, that she would die on the 15th of April.

It was a time of year, she thought inconsequentially, she had always loved. The daffodils would be out, there would be blossoms on the trees, the chestnuts would be coming into bloom and the sunshine would be particularly welcome because one had missed it during the winter.

On the 16th of April she would no longer be here to enjoy it!

She took her key out of her hand-bag and opened the door of number 68 Eaton Terrace.

As she let herself into the narrow Hall, off which opened a small Dining-Room with a tiny Study behind it, she was conscious of the silence and the loneliness of the empty house.

If only her mother were in the Drawing-Room she could run to her to tell her what had happened!

Her mother would have put out her arms and held her close.

But there was no-one to help her now and taking off her hat, Larina walked slowly up the stairs.

Some detached part of her mind noted that the stair-carpet was very worn: it must have been given hard wear while they were away in Switzerland. Then almost sharply she told herself it was of no consequence.

In twenty-one days she would not be in the house to notice that the carpet was threadbare, that the curtains had faded in the Drawing-Room or the brass bedstead in her room had lost a knob.

Twenty-one days!

She went up another flight of stairs to her bed-room.

There were only two bed-rooms in the house, unless one counted a dark airless place in the basement which had been intended for a maid they could not afford.

Her mother had occupied the front room on the second floor and she had a small slip of a room behind it.

She went into it now and looked round her. All her possessions were here, all the small treasures she had accumulated since childhood.

There was even a Teddy Bear she had loved and taken to bed with her for many years, a doll which opened and shut its eyes, and in the book-case, beside the volumes she had acquired as she grew older, were the first books she had ever owned.

"Not much to show for a life-time!" Larina told herself.

Then as if the horror of what she had heard swept over her like a flood-tide, she moved to the window to stand looking out over the grey roofs and the back-yards of the houses behind them.

"What can I do? What can I do about it?" Larina asked herself.

Then almost as if the thought came like a life-line to a drowning man she remembered Elvin.

She wondered as she thought of him why he had not come into her thoughts from the very moment Sir John had pronounced the death sentence.

She supposed it must be because she had been shocked into a kind of numbness which had made it impossible for her to think of anything except the twenty-one days which were left to her.

Elvin would have understood exactly what she was feeling; Elvin in his inimitable manner would have made everything seem different.

They had talked of death the very first time they had met.

It had been a day when Mrs. Milton had been very ill and Larina had known by the expression on Dr. Heinrich's face that he was worried.

"There is nothing you can do," he said to Larina. "Go and sit in the garden, I will call you if she needs you."

Larina had known if she was called it would not be a case of her mother needing her, but because Dr. Heinrich thought she was dying.

She had turned and gone blindly out into the garden of the Sanatorium.

For the first time she did not see the brilliance of the flowers or the beauty of the snow-capped mountains which had never failed to make her heart leap whenever she looked at them.

She moved out of sight of the buildings to a place among the pine-trees where there was a seat that had been specially put there for patients who could not walk far.

It was very quiet. There was only the sound of the cascade pouring down the side of the mountain into the valley below and the buzz of the bees as they sucked the nectar from the mountain-plants that grew among the rocks.

It was then, because she thought no-one could see her, that Larina had put her hands over her face and begun to cry.

She must have cried for a long time before she heard a movement beside her, and a man's voice said gently:

"Are you crying for your mother?"

Larina with tears still running down her cheeks had turned to see who was there.

A man seated himself beside her and she saw that it was Elvin Farren, an American she had not spoken to before because he slept in a hut by himself in the gardens of the Sanatorium and never came to the Dining-Room for meals.

"Mama is not dead," Larina said quickly as if in answer to a question he had not put into words, "but I know that Dr. Heinrich thinks she may be dying!"

She drew her handkerchief from her belt as she spoke and wiped the tears from her eyes almost fiercely. She was ashamed of having given way so completely.

"You must go on hoping that she will recover," Elvin Farren said.

Larina did not speak for a moment, then she answered:

"I am frightened, but then I suppose everyone is frightened of death."

"Perhaps for other people," Elvin Farren replied, "but not for one's self."

Larina looked at him and knew that he was very ill. He was extremely thin: there was something almost transparent about his skin and the tell-tale patches of bright colour on his cheek-bones were all too obvious.

"You are not afraid?" she asked.

He smiled at her and it seemed to transform his face.

"No."

"Why not?"

He looked away from her towards the panorama of mountains where the sun shining on the snows remaining after the winter was almost blinding.

After a moment he said:

"Do you want the true answer to your question, or the conventional one?"

"I want the true answer," Larina replied. "I am afraid of death because it must be so lonely."

She was thinking of herself as she added:

"Not only for those who die, but also for those who are left behind."

"For those who die," Elvin Farren said, "it is an adventure, a release of the mind, and that in itself is something exciting to look forward to!"

He glanced at her to see if she was following him. Then he went on:

"Have you never thought what an encumbrance one's body is? If it were not hampering us, keeping our feet on the ground, so to speak, we could fly wherever we wished to go! To other parts of the earth, to the moon or, more especially, to the Fourth Dimension."

"I think . . . I understand what you are . . . saying to me," Larina said hesitatingly.

Her grey eyes were wide in her oval face.

This was not the sort of conversation she had ever had with anyone before.

"And as for being alone while we are on earth," Elvin Farren said, "why that is actually impossible!"

"Why?" she asked.

"Because you are a part of everything that is living," he replied. "Look at these flowers."

He pointed as he spoke to a little bunch of blue gentians on the rocks in front of them.

"They are alive," he said, "as much alive as you and I are. They are living, and what is more, they feel even as we feel."

"How do you know that?" Larina asked.

"I have a friend who has been working on the reactions of plant-life for some years," he replied. "He believes, and I believe with him, that a plant has feelings because it contains, as we do . . . the cosmic force which we call life."

"Explain . . . explain it to me," Larina begged.

She was fascinated by what this stranger was telling her, and she turned towards him feeling in some inexplicable manner that she must get closer to him.

"The Buddhists never pick flowers," Elvin began. "They believe by touching one and loving it they share its life and it becomes a part of themselves."

He smiled as he said:

"In my country, the American Indians when they are in need of energy will go into a wood such as this. With their arms extended they will place their backs to a pine-tree and they replenish themselves with its power."

"I can understand that," Larina said, "and I am sure it is true. I have often thought when I have been walking alone in the woods that the trees were pulsatingly alive and that there was a kind of vibration coming from them."

"So when there is life all around you, how could you ever be alone?"

It had been easy to understand what he was saying to her when they were sitting in the pine-woods and looking at the flowers, Larina thought. But in the confines of her little bed-room in Eaton Terrace she felt that she needed help desperately.

If only she could talk to Elvin, she wished, as they had talked together so often after that first meeting.

Mrs. Milton's health had improved and Dr. Heinrich said she was out of danger for the moment. Larina had gone to find Elvin on the balcony of his isolated châlet because she wanted to share her joy with someone.

He invited her to sit down and she realised that from his balcony there was an even more marvellous view of the valley beneath them and the mountains in the distance.

While at first she had been afraid of imposing herself on him, she had soon learnt that he enjoyed seeing her, and whenever she was not with her mother she found her way to his balcony and they would sit talking in the crisp clear air.

Nearly always they spoke of the mystical things that Elvin believed existed in other dimensions.

"This is a material world," he said. "It is merely a shadow of the next which is non-material and very much more advanced mentally and spiritually."

"But suppose someone like myself is not clever enough to understand it?" Larina asked.

"Then you will have to stay here," he replied, "and go on learning and developing until you can."

He had so much to tell her that Larina had begun to count the hours to when she could be with him.

Yet sometimes when he was too ill to walk even as far as his balcony, she would have to wait impatiently until he was better and she could see him again.

She had known without his having to tell her that he had not long to live.

"I am almost looking forward to dying," he asid. "There is so much I want to know, so much I want to find out."

Larina gave a little cry of protest.

"Do not talk like that," she begged.

"Why not?" he enquired.

"Because if you go away I shall have no-one to explain such things to me; and when I come to die I shall be afraid . . . very afraid!"

"I have told you there is no reason."

"That is because you are so sure, so certain of what you will find after you are dead," Larina said. "I am not sure, I only want to believe what you tell me, and while I do believe it while I am with you, when you are not there I lose faith."

He had smiled at her as if she were a child.

"When the time comes for you to die," he said, "which will not be for many, many years, call me and I will come to you."

Larina had looked at him wide-eyed.

"You mean . . . ?" she began.

"Wherever I am, whatever I am doing, if you want me, if you call for me, I will hear you."

He put his hand over hers.

"We will make a pact, Larina. When I am dying I will call for you, and when you die, you will call for me."

"There is no reason why I should not die before you," Larina replied. "I might fall down a mountain or have a train accident."

"And if that happens," Elvin said gravely, "send for me and I will come to you."

"You promise?"

"I promise!" he answered. "Just as you must come to me."

His fingers tightened for a moment on hers.

"I know of no-one I would rather be with when my spirit takes wings."

There was something in the way he said the words which told Larina it was in fact not only the highest compliment he could pay her, but also, in his own way, an expression of love.

She was very inexperienced where men were concerned, having known so few in her life; but she was woman enough to realise that Elvin's thin face lit up when she appeared and there was a look in his eyes that was unmistakable.

If he had not been so emaciated with the disease which

often made him start coughing so convulsively that each spasm left him breathless and exhausted, he would, Larina thought, have been very handsome.

But the disease was eating his life away and she knew even though he was only twenty-five years of age, there was no hope of his survival.

Sometimes when she thought about Elvin in the darkness of the night she wondered whether, if they had met before he fell ill, they would have fallen in love with each other.

She loved him as he was, but as if he were a brother.

She wanted to be with him, she loved talking to him; but because of the way he was suffering she could not think of him as an attractive man, a man to whom she could give her heart.

Nevertheless when one day Elvin told her he was going back to America, she had felt an almost incalculable sense of loss.

"But why? Why?" she asked.

"I want to see my mother," he said. "She is ill, and as I am the youngest member of the family I perhaps mean more to her than my brothers."

"How many brothers have you?" Larina asked.

"Three," he replied. "They are all very clever, very busy with their careers and their families. We have also a sister who is married. I am my mother's baby, and I know at this moment she needs me and therefore I must go to her."

"Will the journey not be too much for you?" Larina asked.

"Does it matter if it is?" he answered again with one of his beguiling smiles.

"It matters to me!" Larina cried. "Oh, Elvin, I shall miss you so much! It will be horrible here without you!"

She paused and then added:

"I could bear it before you came, although sometimes I was the only healthy person in the whole place. But now that I have been with you I cannot imagine how I will fill the days without seeing you, without talking to you. It will be unutterably lonely."

"I have told you that you are never alone," Elvin replied. "When you sit in the garden or on the seat in the pine-woods where we first met, imagine I am there, because in fact I shall be. I shall be thinking of you, and all of me that matters will come to you from America or whatever part of this world or the next I may be in at that particular moment."

"Do you really believe you can get in touch with people by thought?" Larina asked.

"I am completely and utterly convinced of it," Elvin replied. "Thought is stronger than anything else. Thought moves quicker and far more efficiently than anything man can devise, and thought can bring us anything we want—if we want it enough."

"I will think of you," Larina promised.

"Believe that I am near you," Elvin told her, "and I will be!"

Nevertheless once he had gone and the châlet where they had sat together was empty, it was not the same.

Obediently Larina had sat in the garden thinking of him, or had walked, sometimes twice a day, to the seat near the pine-trees.

Then two weeks after he had left her mother became really ill and Larina could think of nothing but her.

Her grief, the tears she shed every night when she was alone, the long journey home alone, the empty house to which she had returned, made it difficult to talk to Elvin in her thoughts, as she had meant to do.

And yet his letters were a source of joy so that she watched for the post and was quite unreasonably disappointed when she did not hear from him.

He had written his first letter to her before he left the Sanatorium and she had received it after he had gone.

It was not a long letter because writing tired him, and she knew he was summoning all his strength for the journey.

He thanked her for all she had meant to him, for the happiness they had shared together, and he finished with the words:

'Never forget that I shall be thinking of you, Larina, that I am near you and if you want me you have only to call and I shall be at your side. Perhaps I shall come back to the Sanatorium when my mother no longer needs me and then we can be together again. You have meant more than I can ever say. God bless you and keep you.'

The next letter was only a few scribbled lines written in the train. Then there had been several after he had reached New York.

He told her that his mother was thrilled to see him and that he was glad that he could be with her because she needed him so badly.

Elvin's letters gave Larina courage even while every day that she was alone in London made her feel more helpless and more lonely.

It had taken her some time to clean up the house after the tenants had left it. She had found it both dirty and untidy.

She was glad in a way that her mother could not see how badly they had treated the things she treasured, how shabby the curtains, carpets and cushions had become in a year.

Larina began to think that one way she could help keep herself would be to take a lodger. It would be easy to rent to someone her mother's bed-room and perhaps the Drawing-Room.

She even began to consider whether two lodgers would not be feasible, if she slept in the Study behind the Dining-Room.

Every time she wrote a cheque for the rent or for her food, she realised how very little there was left in the Bank until she knew she could no longer procrastinate and that it was absolutely essential that she should do something practical about her future.

Sir John had charged her two guineas and she thought as she put the gold sovereigns on his desk that it was a big price to pay for what he had to tell her.

But now that she had reached home she thought that in one way her troubles were over. There would be no need now to find employment, no need to let the rooms, no need to accept strange lodgers.

What was left in the Bank would provide her with enough food for the twenty-one days that remained of her life.

Even to think of it made a quiver of fear run through her.

'Elvin would despise me for being afraid,' she thought, 'but I am, I know I am! I do not want to die! I do not want to find out about the unknown! I want to stay here on earth!'

Suddenly she picked up her hat from where she had laid it down and put it back on her head.

She knew what she was going to do. She was going to tell Elvin what had happened. She was going to send him a cable. It would be expensive, but did money matter at the moment?

Only Elvin would understand—only Elvin could comfort her.

She turned from the mirror and as she did so a sudden thought came to her.

Elvin had said that if she called for him he would come to her.

She would ask him to come, and she was quite sure that he would keep his promise.

Larina ran down the stairs. There was a light in her eyes that had not been there before.

"I will ask Elvin to come to me," she said aloud.

Slamming the front door behind her she began to run down the street towards the Post Office in Sloane Square.

# CHAPTER TWO

The funeral cortège drew up outside the brown stone building in Fifth Avenue.

The first carriage contained the three Vanderfeld brothers.

The horses wore black crêpe on their head bands and the coachman a wide crêpe band around his tall hat.

The three Vanderfeld brothers led by the oldest, Harvey, started climbing the long flight of steps to the front door.

On every third step a footman in knee breeches and with powdered hair stood shivering in the pouring rain, a black armband on his crimson livery coat.

Harvey Vanderfeld walked into the large marble Hall where the chandeliers were made of Venetian glass, the Gobelin tapestries came from France, the heavily carved gilt chairs from Italy, and the rugs from Persia.

He walked in his quick characteristic way, passing the waiting flunkeys into the great Drawing-Room, where more footmen were waiting to serve drinks. The Company were to assemble there before they proceeded to luncheon served on gold plates, in the Mediaeval Dining-Room.

The Drawing-Room was furnished with Louis XIV cabinets, Italian and Dutch pictures and Aubusson carpets. The walls were white, picked out in gleaming gold and the Genoese velvet curtains were decorated with a profusion of tassels and silk fringes.

"Champagne or Bourbon, Mr. Harvey?" the Butler asked.

"Bourbon!" Harvey Vanderfeld replied and immediately lifted a glass to his lips.

His relatives started to file into the room, the women in gowns heavily embellished with crêpe; black veils which they had now pushed back from their faces fell over their shoulders and down their backs.

"It was a beautiful funeral!" a middle-aged woman gushed at Harvey Vanderfeld.

"I am glad you thought so, Cousin Alice."

"And your address, it is magnificent! You were more eloquent than I have ever heard you. There was not a dry eye in the Chapel of the Crematorium."

Harvey Vanderfeld preened himself a little. Then as more relatives of every age came pouring through the double mahogany doors, he said to his brother Gary who was standing beside him:

"I want to speak to you. Come into the Study."

They left the Drawing-Room and walked past several other large Salons to the Study where the walls were covered with leather-bound books which no-one opened. There was large, rather consciously masculine leather furniture and the pictures of horses were by Stubbs.

The brothers had left the Drawing-Room each with a glass of Bourbon in his hand, and finishing his, Harvey Vanderfeld walked to a side-table in the corner of the room to replenish his glass from a decanter.

"It went off well, Gary!" he said.

"Very well, Harvey. I have never heard you speak better!"

"I hope the Press got it all down."

"I am sure they did, and anyway there were copies at the door for those who wanted them."

"Good! I thought the Stars and Stripes draped over the coffin was a pleasant touch, and Mama's long cross of lilies was most touching!"

"You must tell her so," Gary suggested.

"I am quite sure that Wynstan has gone upstairs to do that. I am sorry she could not have been present."

"It would have been too much of an ordeal for her even though she is better."

"I am aware of that, but there is always something especially poignant in a mother's grief."

"I think the whole country will be grieving with you tomorrow, Harvey, when they read the newspapers."

"If Elvin had to die it could not have been at a better moment than now," Harvey Vanderfeld said, "on the eve of an election when a great number of people have no wish to see Theodore Roosevelt elected for a second term in the White House."

"There are however a large number who admire the strong hand he is taking over the disorders in the Caribbean countries. His policy of extending American power is popular."

"Yankee Imperialism!" Harvey sneered. "If I am elected as President I shall stop all that nonsense! What we should do is look after ourselves at home, not poke our noses into foreign countries which are of no importance to us."

"No need to canvass me, Harvey," Gary replied with a smile. "I have heard you too often on a platform."

"Yes, yes, of course," Harvey agreed.

He was outstandingly handsome but he was thickening about his body and walked like a man older than his thirty-six years. He had however a smile which proved an invaluable vote-catcher.

Gary at thirty-three had already begun to grow fat with too much luxurious living. He also however, had a charm which was inescapable and which was so characteristic of all the Vanderfeld brothers that they had been nick-named by the press, 'The Princes Charming'.

Harvey was the most ambitious and most ruthless. He

had fought his way to power, and his stupendous fortune was at the moment being utilised in the most extravagant and most expensive election campaign the United States had ever seen.

He was completely confident that he would beat Theodore Roosevelt and the whole Vanderfeld clan had rallied behind him, eager to find themselves in the White House.

The Vanderfelds were of Dutch origin, and the first member of the family had come to America in the 17th century to live in New Amsterdam, as New York City was then known.

In the following centuries the family fortune was founded to increase with every succeeding generation until the 'House of Vanderfeld' was looked on in America almost as if it were Royalty.

The huge mansion on Fifth Avenue was only one of their properties. They had a house at Hyde Park on the Hudson River, Gary had recently built himself a marble palace at Newport, and there were ranches, plantations and Estates scattered all over America.

Their mother, Mrs. Chigwell Vanderfeld, had lived in the house on Fifth Avenue ever since she had been widowed, and Harvey's wife, a quiet, unassuming woman, had not attempted to take her place.

It was Mrs. Vanderfeld who decided what should or should not be done by her children, and who was undoubtedly responsible for the good looks of her family as well as their ambition.

She had been a Hamilton and her ancestors had come out from England, but not, as the Vanderfelds always said scornfully, in the overcrowded 'Mayflower' which must have been as large as Noah's Ark.

The ship which had brought their great-great-grandfather from his native Scotland was his own, and he had filled it with a crowd of retainers, their families and their children, so that there was no room for anyone else.

Mrs. Vanderfeld was proud of her Scottish descent, but even more proud of the fact that she came from Virginia, and had been brought up in the middle of the peach country among the foothills of the Blue Ridge Mountains.

Like the Vanderfelds, the Hamiltons had made a fortune, but then they had been only too willing to give up their railway contracting and gold-mining so as to have time to spend their money.

Mrs. Vanderfeld's father had never worked. All his life he enjoyed the life of a country gentleman, administrating his Estate, which was centred round a large roomy house, its pillars, porch, marble Hall and curling staircase an adaptation of English Georgian.

When his daughter said she wished to marry Chigwell Vanderfeld he had not been overpleased. He had hoped that she would find a husband among what had been left by the Civil War of the gentlemen of Virginia.

He had however little say in the matter. Sally Hamilton was far too self-willed and head-strong to listen to any opposition where her heart was concerned, and she had in fact been extremely happy with her multi-millionaire husband who never stopped working.

Money however was not what she required for her sons: she wanted power, and she made up her mind with a cast-iron determination that Harvey would be the next President of the United States.

It was a determination with which he readily concurred.

"As I have just said," he remarked to his brother, "this funeral could not have come at a better time. Elvin was of course practically unknown to the public or the Press, but I think now he will be fixed in their memory as someone very exceptional, a brother of whom any man could be proud."

Gary did not reply. He had already heard Harvey say almost the identical words in the carriage when they had left the cemetery.

He walked across the room to pour himself another drink, and as he did so the door opened and the Butler came in carrying a silver salver.

"A cable has just come addressed to Mr. Elvin," he said. "I thought, Mr. Harvey, I should bring it to you. It might upset Mrs. Vanderfeld if she saw it."

"Of course," Harvey replied. "Do not take her anything that might be distressing. I have already told one of the secretaries to collect the names of everyone who sent wreaths. I will deal with the letters to express our appreciation. It would be too much for Mrs. Vanderfeld."

"Much too much, Mr. Harvey!" the Butler agreed.

He held out the salver as he spoke and Harvey picked up the cable which lay on it.

He looked at it for a moment, then remarked:

"Mr. Elvin Farren?"

"That was the name Elvin used when he was abroad," Gary explained from the side of the room. "You know we decided that he should not use the family name, since you did not wish the Press to know that he was in a Sanatorium."

"Yes, yes, of course I remember now," Harvey said. "And they never did discover where he was."

"He was of no particular interest to them until he died," Gary said.

There was no sarcasm in his voice. Gary was far too easy-going and good-humoured to be sarcastic.

Harvey opened the cable as the Butler went from the room.

"I see this comes from England," he remarked. "I thought Elvin had been in Switzerland."

"He was," Gary replied.

There was silence then suddenly Harvey ejaculated:

"My God! This cannot be true! There must be some mistake!"

"What is the matter?" Gary asked.

"Listen to this," Harvey said in a sharp voice and read aloud:

"It has happened to me—Stop—I am frightened—
Stop—Please keep your promise and come to me—
Stop—Your letters my only comfort.
Larina"

Harvey's voice ceased and he stood staring at the paper as if he doubted the sight of his own eyes.

Gary reached his side and looked down at the cable.

"What does it mean?" he asked.

"What does it mean?" Harvey shouted. "Are you crazy? Can't you understand what I have just read out to you? It is perfectly clear to me!"

"What is?" Gary asked.

Harvey walked across the room in an agitated manner as if he could not keep still.

"That this should happen at this moment! Just now! It would have been bad enough at any time, but on the eve of the election—!"

"I do not know what you are talking about," Gary said. "Who is this woman? I have never heard of her."

"Does it matter whether we have heard of her or not?" Harvey asked. "She has heard of Elvin all right, and I suspect she has heard of me too. It is blackmail, dear boy! Black-mail—and we will have to pay it!"

"For what?" Gary asked.

"For her silence—for those letters. Do not be half-witted, Gary! It is obvious that Elvin has put her in the family way and she is having a baby."

"Elvin?" Gary exclaimed. "He has been ill—desperately ill—for years!"

"With consumption, Gary! We all know what consumptives are like sexually, although I did not think it of Elvin."

He put up both his arms towards the ceiling and cried:

"How could he have done this to me at this moment?"

Gary bent to the floor to pick up the envelope in which the cable had arrived.

After a moment he said a little tentatively:

"Whatever Elvin may or may not have done, it appears to me that she does not know who he is. Otherwise why should she address him as Farren rather than Vanderfeld?"

Harvey was still for a moment.

"There is some point in that," he said slowly. "If she does not know, there is hope!"

He appeared suddenly to make up his mind and walked across the room to tug at the bell-pull.

The door opened almost instantly.

"Yes, Mr. Harvey?" the Butler enquired.

"Ask Mr. Wynstan to come here immediately!" Harvey

said. "If he is not in the Drawing-Room he will be with Mrs. Vanderfeld."

"I'll tell him you want him, Mr. Harvey," the Butler replied in his grave voice.

He closed the door and Harvey once again walked agitatedly across the thick carpet towards the Regency desk and back again.

"I cannot believe it!" he said. "I cannot credit my brother, my own brother, could treat me in such a manner!"

"Elvin cannot have intended to involve you personally in this," Gary said, with just a hint of a smile on his lips.

"But I am involved!" Harvey replied. "You know that as well as I do! Can you imagine what the papers will make of it? It will be a front-page scandal, and how the Republicans will love it! I can just imagine Theodore Roosevelt enjoying every word and making full use of it in his campaign."

"There must be something we can do," Gary said feebly.

As if it might give him inspiration he finished off his drink in one gulp and went to the side-table to pour himself another.

The two brothers were silent until a few moments later the door opened and Wynstan Vanderfeld came in.

At twenty-eight Wynstan was so good-looking that, as his sister Tracy had told him often enough, it was 'unfair on women'!

Tall, broad-shouldered and with square-cut features, he was the Cosmopolitan of the family and had spent in the last seven years of his life more time abroad than he had in America.

"Wynstan," someone once said, "is traditionally American, overlaid with English and under-sprung with French!"

But Tracy had summed it up more aptly when she said:

"Wynstan is the entire creation of Mama without any help from Papa!"

He certainly was unlike his brothers, Harvey and Gary, in that his body was slim and he had the look of an athlete.

He was in fact an outstanding Polo player, had won many horse races, and at College had made his name on the baseball field.

As he came into the room now it was noticeable that he

had a twinkle in his eye as if his brothers, like all his other relatives amused him and he found it difficult to take them seriously.

"Hudson tells me you need me urgently," he said. "What has happened?"

In answer Harvey held out the cable. Wynstan took it from him and noticed in surprise that his brother's hand was trembling.

He read it carefully and then the twinkle in his eye was even more pronounced as he said:

"If it means what I think it means—good for Elvin! I am glad he had a little fun before he died."

Harvey let out a sound that was like the roar of a lion.

"Is that all you have to say?" he stormed. "Do you not understand what this will mean to me? This is dynamite, Wynstan! Dynamite to my cause and to the election!"

His voice seemed to ring round the room as he continued:

"You know as well as I do that my whole campaign is based on the cries: 'Clean up America!' 'Keep out of Foreign Affairs!' 'Strengthen and support family life which is the foundation of our great Nation!' "

Carried away Harvey declaimed the words and Wynstan gave a little laugh.

"Stop tub-thumping, Harvey!" Wynstan said. "Let us talk sensibly!"

"That is just what I am trying to do," Harvey replied.

"It does not sound to me as if this girl, whoever she may be, is trying to threaten your position. She addresses herself to Elvin and pleads with him to come to her."

"Well, he cannot do that!" Harvey snapped. "And what do you think she wants from him except money?"

Wynstan looked at the telegram again.

"Perhaps you have missed that sentence about the letters," Harvey suggested. " 'My only comfort your letters.' What does that mean except that she damned-well thinks she can put a big price on them!"

"It is possible that that is what she intended," Wynstan admitted. "At the same time she says: 'Please keep your promise'. Now what promise could Elvin have made to her?"

"I suppose that he would marry her if she had a child," Gary interposed.

"He cannot do that either!" Harvey said harshly.

"That is true!" Wynstan agreed. "But if she is having Elvin's child, she may have some claim on his Estate."

"My God!" Harvey ejaculated. "I had not thought of that! Do you know what Elvin is worth?"

"I have a vague idea," Wynstan replied. "Father left his fortune, which we all know was considerable, divided between the four of us, after Tracy had been provided for."

"The money does not really matter," Harvey said quickly with an effort. "What is absolutely essential is that there should be no scandal, such as would be inevitable if Elvin's illegitimate child pops up from nowhere and asks to be taken into the bosom of the family!"

"I can see the complications," Wynstan said quietly.

"Well, if you can see that, do something about it!" Harvey shouted.

Wynstan looked at him in surprise.

"Why me?"

"Because this blasted woman is English and you are always messing about in that country. You ought to know how to keep her quiet."

Harvey stopped speaking and gave an exclamation.

"That's it! That's it exactly!" he said. "You must keep her quiet at any rate until the election is over. Then we can fight her every inch of the way."

"A very noble sentiment," Wynstan remarked.

"Now don't come the gentleman over me!" Harvey said angrily. "This is a situation where we have to take off our kid-gloves to fight a blackmailer."

"Who said she was a blackmailer?" Wynstan enquired.

"I say she is one, and that is what she damned-well is!" Harvey answered.

"I did point out," Gary said, "that she addresses the cable to Mr. Farren. If she had known Elvin's real name, do you not think she would have used it?"

"That is a very good point, Gary," Wynstan said.

"It does not matter what she calls him," Harvey said impatiently. "If she is having Elvin's child, or pretends she is—

for personally I do not believe he was capable of producing one—then she will fleece us down to the last cent. You can be certain of that!"

"I think you have overlooked one thing," Wynstan said in a quiet voice.

"What?" his brother asked.

"Knowing Elvin as I did, and perhaps I knew him better than either of you, I do not believe he would have been interested in the type of woman you are describing."

There was silence for a moment then Harvey said:

"That's all very well. We know what women are like when they get their hands on a rich man. Elvin was a child in many ways. Against a woman who had deliberately set out to get him he would not have stood a chance."

"Perhaps you are right," Wynstan said reluctantly. "What do you want me to do?"

"I want you to go over to England just as quickly as you can and shut this woman's mouth!" Harvey said. "Strangle her, suffocate her, kidnap her and keep her silent until the election is over. Do anything as long as she does not go near a newspaper reporter or realise how much she can damage me."

Wynstan looked amused as he turned round to put his hand out towards the bell-pull.

"What are you doing? Who are you ringing for?" Harvey enquired.

"I have to find out something about Larina or whatever her name is," he said. "She has signed only her Christian name, and there is no address."

"No-one must know about this," Harvey said quickly. "If the newshawks get even a smell of it, I am finished!"

"I am going to speak to Prudence," Wynstan said soothingly as if speaking to a child. "Prudence has been with Elvin ever since he came back from Europe, she has also been with us since before I was born. I imagine we can trust her after all these years."

"Yes, of course," Harvey agreed in a somewhat shamefaced manner.

The Butler opened the door.

"Ask Prudence to come downstairs for a moment, Hudson," Wynstan said to him. "I imagine she is back by now from the funeral."

"Yes, Mr. Wynstan, she is upstairs."

"We would like to speak to her."

"Of course, Mr. Wynstan."

The door closed and Wynstan stood in front of the fireplace.

"Stop being so agitated, Harvey!" he said after a moment. "You are sweating, and anyone who knew you would know that you are frightened!"

"I am frightened!" Harvey said. "I do not mind telling you, Wynstan, this is a stab in the back which I had not anticipated, and certainly not from one of my own brothers!"

"I think you are being unnecessarily apprehensive," Wynstan said, "but because I am fond of you, Harvey, and Elvin meant a great deal to me, I will certainly try and see if I can solve this problem."

"Pay anything—anything." Harvey said, "but keep her quiet, that is all I ask. Keep her quiet!"

When Prudence came into the room she looked surprised to see all three brothers together in the Study while, as she knew, the big Drawing-Room was filled with their relatives and friends.

She was an elderly woman with a kind, open face which made adults and children alike trust her instinctively. Her eyes were red and a little swollen from weeping.

She was dressed, as she always had been ever since the brothers could remember, in a dress of grey cotton with stiff white collar and cuffs that were always spotlessly clean.

She had grown stouter and heavier over the years, Wynstan thought as she walked towards them, but otherwise she had changed very little from when as a child he had said his first prayers at her knee and she had taught him his alphabet.

"Come in, Prudence," he said. "We want your help, which is nothing unusual!"

"What happened?" Prudence asked looking from Wynstan to Harvey and then at Gary.

"We want you to tell us what you know about a woman called Larina," Wynstan replied.

Prudence did not hesitate.

"She was a friend of Mr. Elvin's."

"What sort of friend?" Harvey questioned quickly.

"I think it was someone he met while he was in Switzer-land," Prudence answered. "He had several letters from her after he returned and I know that he wrote to her."

"Where are they? Where are the letters?" Harvey asked. "Fetch them at once."

"I can't do that, Mr. Harvey," Prudence said.

"Why not?"

"Because Mr. Elvin burnt them."

"Burnt them?" Harvey exclaimed.

"Yes, a few days before he died he said to me: 'Prudence, I think I had better tidy up my possessions. Bring me my special box.' "

"What box was that?"

Prudence looked at Wynstan.

"You remember it, Mr. Wynstan."

"Yes, I gave it to him," Wynstan said. "He must have been fifteen at the time. I remember saying that every man should have a place where he could lock away papers he did not want everyone else to read."

Wynstan paused and smiled as he added:

"That was after I found Mama reading letters I had received from a girl-friend of whom she did not approve."

"She must have been kept busy if she read all your love-letters!" Gary teased.

"Go on, Prudence." Wynstan said quietly.

"I fetched the box to his bed and he took out some poems he had been writing from time to time. Sometimes he would read them to me and sometimes he would not. He looked at them and said:

" 'Burn these, Prudence!' "

" 'Why?' I asked. 'They're beautiful, Mr. Elvin! Let's keep them. Someone might publish them one day.' "

" 'That is what I am afraid of and it would not be because they wanted to understand what I was trying to say,' he answered. 'Burn them, Prudence!' "

Prudence made a little gesture with her hands.

"So I burnt them."

"And what else?" Wynstan asked.

"The letters he had kept over the years, one or two from you, Mr. Wynstan, some from his mother, and those he had received from the young lady."

"How do you know they were from her?" Wynstan asked.

"They were the only letters he received after he returned home," Prudence answered, "and he seemed happy to have them. He also said to me: 'Don't you think Larina is a pretty name, Prudence? I think it is lovely!' "

Harvey's eyes met his brother Gary's.

"What was her surname, Prudence?" he asked.

"I don't know, Mr. Harvey!"

"But you must have some idea."

"No, Mr. Elvin never told me anything about her."

There was silence, then as if she knew the brothers were perturbed. Prudence said:

"But Mr. Renour will know it."

"Renour? Why should he know it?" Harvey asked in surprise.

"Because Mr. Elvin wrote to her and it would be entered in the post-book."

"Of course!" Wynstan exclaimed. "I had forgotten that we kept a post-book in the house! He will also have her address."

"Of course," Prudence agreed.

"Then would you be kind enough to ask him to bring the post-book here to us?" Wynstan said. "And thank you, Prudence, for your help."

"I hope I have been able to assist you," Prudence said looking from one to the other.

She waited for a second then she said:

"Thank you, Mr. Harvey, for the beautiful things you said at the Service. I'm sure Mr. Elvin would have been pleased."

Tears came into her eyes as she spoke and she turned quickly and went from the room.

"Beautiful things!" Harvey said scornfully. "I wonder what Prudence would say if she knew the truth."

"You certainly made Elvin a cross between the Archangel Gabriel and St. Sebastian," Wynstan remarked.

"All the more reason why he should not get knocked off his pedestal!" Harvey snapped.

"Now stop agitating yourself!" Gary pleaded. "Wynstan said he will help and he is pretty efficient when he makes up his mind to do something."

"Thank you!" Wynstan said with an amused smile.

The door opened and Hudson came in.

"Prudence said you wanted the post-book, Mr. Harvey," he said, "but Mr. Renour is not yet back from the funeral so I have brought it myself."

"Thank you very much, Hudson."

Harvey took it from him and turned the pages quickly.

"I had no idea we sent out so many letters from this house!" he remarked. "With what we contribute the Post Office should pay a dividend!"

Neither of his brothers answered and he knew they were waiting impatiently to see what he would find.

"Here it is!" he said at length. "Miss Larina Milton, 68 Eaton Terrace, London, England."

"Well, at least we know where she is!" Gary said.

"I suppose you want me to see her as soon as possible?" Wynstan said in a resigned voice. "I will do it, but I would like to point out that it is extremely inconvenient. I have a new car being delivered tomorrow and there are two polo ponies I wish to train before the games start in May."

"Polo ponies!" Harvey said with a groan which was also a sound of contempt.

"I have an idea!" Gary said suddenly.

Both brothers turned to look at him.

"What is it?" Wynstan enquired.

"I have just thought that the election will be reported in the English newspapers. Even if this girl had no idea who Elvin was when he was in Switzerland, she will read about Harvey and they may easily mention Elvin's death. Then she will know—"

"Just how much money she can get out of us!" Harvey interjected. "She would up her price every day of the campaign."

Wynstan did not speak and Harvey went on:

"Gary is right—of course he is right! It is no use your

seeing her in London and trying to keep her quiet. You have got to get her away. Take her to France—Spain—Italy—anywhere so long as the newspapers are not delivered regularly every morning."

"We have no reason to suppose that she already knows that Elvin was a Vanderfeld," Wynstan said.

"We have no reason to be sure she does not!" Harvey retorted. "It would be a mistake to take a risk. Besides although Elvin became pathetically thin after he got so ill, there is a likeness about us all. Mama has often remarked on it."

"And added that Wynstan is much the best-looking!" Gary said.

"Do not let it make you jealous!" Wynstan remarked. "It is often a liability!"

"You can hardly expect us to believe that!" Gary laughed. "You know as well as I do, Wynstan, that the girls fall down like a set of ninepins whenever you appear."

"I tell you it is often a liability!" Wynstan insisted.

"Oh, keep to the point!" Harvey said irritably. "Gary has had a good idea. We must consider it. Where can you take her, Wynstan?"

"Presuming of course that she will go with me," Wynstan replied. "I presume also that you want me to tell her that Elvin is dead?"

"No, I have a better idea," Harvey said.

"What is it?"

"In this cable she has sent to Elvin she has begged him to come to her, and it is obvious that he promised her he would. Well then, he must keep his promise."

"What do you mean by that?" Wynstan asked.

Harvey's eyes narrowed a little, as those who did business with him on Wall Street knew always happened when he was doing a big deal.

"We will send her a cable from Elvin saying that he will meet her at the Villa. That ought to get her away from London."

"The Villa in Sorrento?" Wynstan asked. "Good Lord, I have not been there for years!"

"Grace and I spent a fortnight there in 1900." Gary said. "It is being kept up in just the same way as when grandfather built it, or rather restored it to its Roman glory, and spent a fortune in the process!"

"As a matter of fact I would rather like to see it again," Wynstan said. "I remember as a child thinking it was the most beautiful place in the world."

"Then that is settled," Harvey said briskly determined to get back to business. "We will send her a telegram and sign it with Elvin's name."

"You had better take it to the Post Office yourself. It cannot be sent from here. Renour must not know about this."

"Supposing she refuses to go?" Gary said. "Besides, you cannot expect a woman to travel all that way alone."

"No, of course not," Harvey said impatiently. "Why do we keep that large, expensive office in London except to do what they are told in a situation like this?"

His lips tightened, then he went on:

"On second thought, we will cable Donaldson to see this woman and persuade her to go to Italy."

He paused to explain:

"No point in her receiving anything else signed by Elvin—it might strengthen her case against us."

"I can see that," Gary remarked.

"Then we tell Donaldson," Harvey went on, "to arrange for the Villa to be got ready for Wynstan, and to get Larina, or whatever her name is, there as soon as possible. If he cannot take her himself, he can send a competent Courier with her. It is only a question of organisation."

Harvey paused to look at his brothers for their approval.

"It is certainly an idea," Wynstan said slowly.

"Have you a better one?"

"No, and I would much prefer to argue this thing out in Sorrento rather than in London."

"I am glad somebody is pleased about it!" Harvey said in an exasperated voice. "I shall not have a moment's peace or a good night's sleep until I know you have settled this matter, Wynstan. I am relying on you to save the people who have given me their faith and trust."

There was almost a sob in his voice.

His brother laughed.

"Spare me the dramatics, Harvey! I will do my best, although I do not mind telling you I find it an intolerable nuisance to have to go traipsing off to Europe just when I want to be at home."

A sudden thought struck him.

"What are we going to tell Mama?"

"Oh, God!" Harvey ejaculated, then quickly he added:

"We will just have to pretend that you have had an urgent message from one of your lady-friends."

"She is not going to be pleased about that!" Wynstan said. "And she particularly wants me here now when she is so upset about Elvin."

"Mama will always accept that affairs of the heart—yours at any rate—come first!" Harvey said with an almost spiteful note in his voice.

"And I think," Gary interrupted, "she is secretly rather proud of your success. She thinks you are a chip off the old Hamilton block, who from what Mama tells us behaved in a very reprehensible manner with the lassies in the heather before they were told to get out of Scotland!"

"I will think of something to tell her," Wynstan said in a weary voice, "but if I find that you, Harvey, have been de-crying me behind my back or saying any unpleasant things such as you have said in the past, I swear I will tell her the truth."

"I promise you I will support you in every possible way," Harvey replied. "And another reason why it is so important for you not to go to London is that Tracy might ask questions. We do not want that supercilious Duke of hers looking down his aristocratic nose and saying that the English do not get into this sort of jam!"

"Personally, I like Osmund," Wynstan said. "He is not supercilious to me. At the same time it is important that Tracy should not learn about this, if indeed there is anything to learn."

He walked towards the door.

"Personally, I think I shall find that the whole drama is a figment of Harvey's fertile imagination."

"Where are you going?" Harvey asked hastily. "We have to compile a cablegram."

"You can do that without me," Wynstan answered. "If I

have to sail across the Atlantic, which let me say is the last thing I want to do at this moment, I might as well do it in comfort. The 'Kaiser Wilhelm der Grosse' sails tomorrow morning, and I will be on her."

He left the room and closed the door behind him.

Gary and Harvey looked at each other.

"I congratulate you, Harvey," Gary said. "I never thought for one moment that Wynstan would agree to what you suggested."

"Frankly neither did I," Harvey replied.

Wynstan boarded the 'Kaiser Wilhelm der Grosse' just before she was ready to leave New York harbour on the morning tide. She was noted as being fitted out with every comfort and also providing the maximum amount of entertainment with which to while away the passage across the ocean.

Wynstan was however more interested in the passenger-list of which he had taken a copy from the Purser's office.

Although his booking had been made at the last moment, the magic name of Vanderfeld had secured for him one of the best suites and only the Purser was aware of how difficult it had been to re-allot the other passengers without causing offence.

However as an experienced traveller, Wynstan approved his cabins, tipped his stewards, which he always did at the beginning of the voyage, and left his valet to arrange things in the manner he found most comfortable.

He settled himself down in an arm-chair, ordered a drink, and studied the passenger-list.

There had been no-one to wave him good-bye on the Quay, a custom he always detested. It suited him that Harvey had been insistent that he should creep out of America as quietly as possible, so that no-one, except his immediate family should be aware that he was leaving.

"For God's sake, Wynstan, do not get involved with the Press," he said. "You know what they are like if they suspect that anything unusual is occurring."

Wynstan however had been concerned less about the Press than about his mother.

"I thought you would stay with me, darling," Mrs. Vanderfeld said tearfully when he told her he had to sail to Europe immediately.

"I know, Mama, and I wished to be with you now," Wynstan replied, "but I have unfortunately promised to help this friend of mine if he was ever in trouble, and now he is keeping me to my promise."

"He?" Mrs. Vanderfeld asked suspiciously. "You do not expect me to believe, Wynstan, that there is not a woman at the bottom of it?"

"Your mind invariably works in the same direction, Mama," Wynstan replied with a smile. "There must be some French blood in you because your maxim is always '*cherchez la femme*'!"

"With reason!" Mrs. Vanderfeld replied. "I thought you had finished your affair with that French actress, what was her name?"

"Gaby Deslys," Wynstan answered. "How did you know about her?"

"I hear about everything," Mrs. Vanderfeld said with satisfaction, "and although you are determined not to tell me the truth about this hasty journey of yours, you can be sure I will learn every detail about it sooner or later!"

"I am sure you will, Mama," Wynstan agreed.

His mother looked at him as he sat on the end of her enormous bed, an imitation of the elaborate blue and silver one used by King Ludwig of Bavaria.

The curtains, dressing-table cover, pillow cases and the edges of the sheets were all edged with real Venetian lace, and there was a balustrade separating the bed from the rest of the room as in most Royal State bed-rooms in France and Bavaria.

"I suppose," Wynstan had said when he first saw it, "that only princes of the blood are allowed behind the balustrade."

"Really, Wynstan, you are not to say such things!" his mother had replied.

At the same time she loved it when he teased her, especially about her admirers of whom she had quite a number even in her old age.

"You know, Wynstan," she said now looking at his handsome face appreciatively. "I think you are a throw-back to one of my forbears who was a pirate and buccaneer at the time of Queen Elizabeth. He had a way with women. Otherwise, the Queen would have had little use for him."

"And yet she remained a virgin," Wynstan said.

"I have often had my doubts about that!" Mrs. Vanderfeld remarked, and her son laughed.

"If you talk like that in front of Harvey, Mama, he will have a stroke! He is running his whole campaign on purity and insists that we must all be Puritans!"

"It is the last thing I have ever wanted to be," Mrs. Vanderfeld said sharply. "Harvey is an old woman—he always has been! At the same time I would like to see him at the White House."

"And so would I," Wynstan said. "It would make him so happy, and at least he is a great deal better-looking than Theodore Roosevelt!"

"That would not be difficult!" Mrs. Vanderfeld snapped, "but I am not certain you would not make a more effective President!"

Wynstan put up his hands in horror.

"Have you forgotten I am the play-boy of the family?"

"Is it not time you began to think about settling down?" Mrs. Vanderfeld asked. "You have had a great deal of fun in the past few years, and I do not blame you. But I would like to see your son before I die."

Wynstan laughed.

"That is a very good line, Mama, but you are not really thinking of dying, although you give us a fright occasionally, as you did last month. You know really you are as tough as your pioneering ancestors and you will easily live to be a hundred!"

"I might do that just to spite you all!" Mrs. Vanderfeld said. "As long as I am alive I can keep the family under control, at least where the others are concerned!"

"And I am the exception?" Wynstan asked.

"You always were an obstinate, uppity little boy," Mrs. Vanderfeld said, "but you managed, even when you were very young, to charm a bird off a tree if it suited you."

"It always suited me where you were concerned, Mama,"

Wynstan said, "and I think the reason I have never married is that I have never found anyone half as amusing, as witty, or as attractive as you."

"There you go!" Mrs. Vanderfeld exclaimed. "Now I am quite certain that you have something to hide from me, or you would not be going out of your way to flatter me."

She looked at her son and her eyes twinkled rather like his.

"Do what you have to do," she said, "then come back and tell me all about it. I get a vicarious excitement at my age hearing about your love-affairs."

"As a change from your own, Mama?" Wynstan asked and again she laughed.

She had however kissed him very tenderly when he said good-bye to her.

"Take care of yourself, my darling," she said softly. "You are my baby now that Elvin is gone and I shall be thinking about you and praying that you will come back safely."

"I will be back, Mama," Wynstan replied, "and just as quickly as I can manage it."

"And remember what I have said about that son of yours," Mrs. Vanderfeld cried as he reached the door.

"You have enough men loving you already," Wynstan replied and they were both laughing as he shut the door of her bed-room.

Looking down at the list of 332 first class passengers Wynstan found a name that held his attention.

The Earl and Countess of Glencairn were on 'B' deck.

He had known the Earl for some years, an elderly Peer, who had once been an outstanding rider to hounds. He had broken his leg when he was over seventy and now had to spend his time in a wheel-chair.

He had, however, a few years before this happened taken as his second wife an extremely attractive dark-eyed French-woman.

She had had a somewhat chequered career in Paris, and it had undoubtedly been an achievement on her part to confound those who criticised her by stepping into the English Peerage.

Wynstan had met her six months before when she had

dined with his sister at the Duke's magnificent house near Oxford. He had sat next to her at dinner, and she had flirted with him in a manner which had told him they were both masters of the ancient art.

There was a slightly cynical smile on Wynstan Vander-feld's lips as he put down the passenger-list.

The voyage would not be as boring as he had anticipated.

# CHAPTER THREE

Larina felt as if her heart had already stopped beating.

She could think of nothing except that the days, hours and minutes were passing and while she felt she ought to do something special, something important before she died, she had no idea how to set about it.

She felt as if her will-power had dissolved and she needed, more than she had ever needed in her life before, someone to take control of the situation and tell her what to do.

She could only wait with a kind of hopelessness for Elvin's reply to her cable.

Supposing, she thought, he was too ill to answer her cry for help?

Because the idea made her frantic she would take out his letters every hour and read the last one she had received from him from America.

He told her how pleased his mother had been to see him

and also that he had in fact stood the journey far better than he expected.

"I think the sea air did me good," he wrote. "It made me think of you and a grey day reminded me of your eyes."

His letters were not long and Larina knew that even if he had wished to write more it would have been too much of an effort.

And yet he had said he felt better. That in itself was encouraging and she was sure that Elvin was alive, otherwise she would have been aware of it.

Because she had felt so terribly lonely when she first returned to London she had tried to remember all he had told her.

"How can you ever be alone," he had said, "when there is life all around you?"

Remembering his words and telling herself how much they must mean to her now that she had no one to turn to in her loneliness, she walked through the streets into Hyde Park.

It was a relief to get away from the little house which was so silent and oppressive, and there was a sharpness in the wind which made her think of the clear, crisp air of Switzerland.

She walked across the green grass until she reached the Serpentine and although it had been a dull day until then, a pale sun came out and she sat down on a bench near the water.

She looked around and realised that the daffodils were in bloom and the red tulips stood in the flower-beds like Guardsmen.

She had been so intent on her worries which encompassed her like a fog, that walking through the Park she had seen nothing and been aware of nothing except her fear of the future and the difficulties of getting a job.

She pretended that Elvin was there beside her, telling her that there was life everywhere and that she was a part of it.

"Oh, Elvin, Elvin!" she whispered. "Help me! Help me!"

She felt as if she shouted the words aloud. But there was no reply, only the rustle of the wind blowing the dead leaves which still lay beneath the trees and the movement of the branches overhead which were just beginning to show the first green buds of spring.

The wind rippled the water of the Serpentine and the daffodils bent their heads as the breeze touched them.

"I am a part of it, and it is a part of me," Larina told herself, but she felt they were only words and she could not really understand them.

Then suddenly there was a light on the water that was almost blinding, the daffodils were as golden as the sun itself and she could almost see the grass growing beneath her feet.

It was intense, magic, divine, a glory which lighted the sky and her soul.

She was one with it and it was part of her!

Then as she longed to cling to the vividness and the beauty of it, to hold it close, to be sure it was really happening, it was gone!

It was so momentary, such a transitory experience, that when it was past she thought it must have been an illusion. Yet at the same time she knew it had happened!

"Now I understand what Elvin was saying," she told herself.

She tried to recapture the radiance, but while the sun was still on the water, it had not the light that she had seen for that one incredible moment.

"Perhaps it will grow easier with practice," Larina hoped.

The moment of magic glowed like a jewel in her mind as she walked homewards.

It had uplifted and elated her, but it was not exactly comforting. It just made her long more desperately for Elvin to tell her more, to be with her.

She did not forget it as the days passed; she kept trying to make it happen again; but the ecstasy and the wonder eluded her.

Now she could think of nothing but the moment when her heart beating in her breast would stop; when the breath moving in and out of her lungs would cease.

She could only call out to Elvin, as he had told her to do, in her mind and pray that he would answer her cable.

Only Elvin could keep her from being terrified as she knew she would be when the twenty-first day arrived.

If Elvin could not leave at once, it would be too late, and even if he did they would only have a very short time to-gether!

It seemed impossible that what she had said to him in Switzerland had come true.

"I might easily die before you," she had told him, but she had not meant it.

It had just been a way of talking, but now she knew she would not outlive Elvin, and she was not prepared, as he was, to face the inevitability of death.

'Help me, help me!' she cried in her heart as she walked home.

She felt there was something almost menacing about the empty house as she entered the door which needed painting, saw the shabby stair-carpet and felt the silence.

Neither she nor her mother had cared much for 68 Eaton Terrace.

They had in fact both hated leaving their big comfortable home in Sussex Gardens on the other side of the Park.

When Dr. Milton had died unexpectedly from a virus he had caught from one of his patients, his wife found the house belonged to his partners in the practice.

Larina and her mother had also discovered in consterna-tion that he had left very little money.

Dr. Milton had a fairly lucrative practice amongst well-to-do people who lived in that part of London.

But being a man of deep compassion and sympathy, he treated a great number of the poor in the slums around Paddington without charging them a fee, and moreover out of his own pocket, he often provided them with medicines and small luxuries they could not afford for themselves.

Many of his poorer patients carrying pathetic little bunches of flowers attended his funeral, all of them ready to talk of the 'good doctor' and his kindness.

At the same time it was depressing to realise how little money he had left his wife and daughter.

Because her mother was so unhappy and in a state of collapse after her father's death it had been left to Larina to find them a place to live.

Because she thought it was a good idea for her mother's

sake to get away from the neighbourhood where she had been so happy, Larina had gone south of the Park and searched round Belgravia for a cheap house to rent.

The one she had found in Eaton Terrace was certainly cheap, but it seemed small, stuffy and unattractive even after it had been furnished with the things they brought with them.

"It is stupid of me, I know," Mrs. Milton had said after they had been in it a few weeks, "but I find it difficult to think of this house as home."

She was finding it, Larina knew, far more difficult to adjust herself to being a widow with no husband to take care of her.

Mrs. Milton had always been cosseted and loved all her life. She had no desire for independence nor was she interested in the much talked of emancipation of women.

"I do not want to vote, darling," she said to her husband once in Larina's hearing. "I am quite content for you to explain the political situation to me if I have to hear about it, and, quite frankly, I would rather talk of something else."

"I am afraid you will never make an efficient modern woman," her husband had replied with a smile.

"I just want to be your wife," Mrs. Milton had said with an adoring look in her eyes.

They had been so happy together that sometimes Larina had felt unwanted.

Yet she knew that her father loved her deeply, and when he died her mother clung to her in a manner which assured her over and over again how much she mattered.

But now she was alone and she realised how unfit she was to endure loneliness after the close companionship she had enjoyed with her parents.

"Perhaps it is a good thing to have so short a time to live," she told herself somewhat bitterly. "I have been brought up in the wrong way to cope with a world where a woman is helpless alone."

She thought of how when she was on her way to visit Sir John Coleridge she had been planning that she must get a job as a secretary.

It had been an idea, but she knew that there was a great deal of unemployment in the country at the moment and it was very unlikely that anyone would employ a woman when they could obtain the services of a man.

Restlessly she walked up to the Drawing-Room to look at her mother's special treasures: the work-box of inlaid marquetry in which she had always kept her embroidery, the little French writing-desk between the windows on which stood photographs of her father and herself.

She touched the china ornaments on the mantelpiece which had been a present one Christmas and which her mother had loved because they were so pretty.

Looking at them Larina noticed that the china shepherdess's hand was missing.

She felt angry that the tenants should have been so careless and had not even repaired the broken piece. Then she asked herself why should it matter?

Her mother would not know that the precious mementoes of her married life had been damaged, and in a few days she herself would not be there to see them either.

"What am I to do with all these things?" Larina asked herself in a sudden fright. "I cannot just die without telling someone I have no further use for them."

She tried to think of a friend in whom she could confide. But while her father and mother had many acquaintances where they had been living in Sussex Gardens, she had, by usual convention, not been allowed to take part in the social entertaining given by her parents.

Being shy, she had not made friends with the few girls she had met. But her mother had always talked as if everything would alter when she was grown up.

"We must give a Ball for Larina," she had said to her husband once. "You had better start saving, John, because when she is eighteen, I intend to be very extravagant about her clothes, especially her evening-gowns."

"You will be saying next that you want to present her at Court!" Dr. Milton replied.

"Why not?" his wife asked. "I was presented when I was eighteen!"

"Your family lived in rather different circumstances," the Doctor replied.

"All the Courtneys were presented," her mother said with

dignity, "'and I would not feel I was doing my duty by Larina unless she went to Buckingham Palace to make her curtsey."

She smiled at her daughter as she spoke and said:

"If they do not think I am important enough to present you, my darling, I shall ask your godmother, Lady Sanderson. She has always sent you a present at Christmas. Although she lives in the country and we seldom meet, I know she is still the dear friend she always was."

But Lady Sanderson had died the following year and her mother had wept at losing a friend who had meant a great deal to her, Larina gathered, in her childhood.

So there was no Lady Sanderson to whom she could turn now, and having been away for a year in Switzerland, and the year before that being in deep mourning, she found it was difficult even to remember the names of the people who had come to the house in Sussex Gardens.

"Besides," Larina asked herself, "who wants to meet someone who merely seeks comfort because they are afraid of their approaching death?"

She knew that apart from anything else she would feel shy to talk about the fate which hung over her like the sword of Damocles.

'I will keep it to myself,' she thought with sudden pride. 'I will not whine and complain as women used to do to Papa.'

She could remember her father saying once:

"I am fed up with grizzling women!"

"What do you mean, 'grizzling women'?" her mother asked with a smile.

"The ones who have more aches and pains than anyone else! Needless to say, they are always the richest! The poor are concerned with the fundamentals such as being born, keeping alive and having the bravery to die, as one man said to me, 'with his boots on'."

"They have courage," Mrs. Milton said softly.

"That is what I admire about them," the Doctor said. "Many of them are bad, the reformers call them wicked, but at least they have guts! It is the other sort I cannot stand!"

"I must not complain . . . I must be brave," Larina told herself. "I would want Papa to be proud of me."

She sat down on the sofa and wondered what she should

do. There were things that wanted mending and quite a lot of the furniture needed repairing.

But what was the point of doing it?

It was then that there came the sound of the front-door bell ringing in the basement. She could hear it quite clearly in the empty silence of the house.

'Whoever can it be?' she wondered then suddenly thought it might be a cable from Elvin.

She jumped to her feet and there was a light in her eyes that had not been there before as she ran down the stairs.

Hastily she pulled open the front-door, but it was not a telegraph-boy who stood there as she had expected, but a man, middle-aged, well-dressed and wearing a bowler hat.

He appeared to Larina to be a kind of superior clerk or perhaps someone in the Civil Service as a number of her father's patients had been.

"Does Miss Larina Milton live here?" he asked.

"I am Miss Milton!"

She saw there was a faint look of surprise in his eyes as if he had not expected her to open the door.

Then because she felt it might seem strange to admit that she was alone in the house Larina added:

"I am afraid the maid is out!"

"May I speak with you, Miss Milton?" the man asked.

He had removed his bowler hat when she had appeared and she saw his hair was grey and she told herself he looked extremely respectable.

At the same time she did not like to let him into the house.

"What is it about?" she enquired.

As she spoke she wondered if in fact he had come to sell her something.

She was well aware it was often the most unlikely looking people who hawked insurance or expensive goods for sale from door to door.

"I have had a communication from Mr. Elvin Farren," the man replied.

Her suspicions vanished.

"Oh, will you come in?" she asked quickly.

The man did as she asked, wiping his feet carefully on the

mat. IIc was rather large and it was difficult for him to squeeze past her in the narrow Hall, but he managed it and waited while she closed the door.

"Will you come upstairs to the Drawing-Room?" she asked. "It is on the first floor."

He put his hat down on a chair and waited at the bottom of the stairs for her to precede him.

Larina led the way.

As they entered the Drawing-Room, despite the faded curtains and the worn carpet it looked quite attractive in the late afternoon sunshine coming through the narrow windows.

"Will you sit down?" Larina asked politely.

"My name is Donaldson, Miss Milton," the man said as he seated himself on the edge of the sofa while Larina took an arm-chair opposite him.

"You have heard from Mr. Farren?" she asked eagerly.

"Mr. Farren asked me to call on you," Mr. Donaldson said. "I understand, Miss Milton, from what he said in his cable that you wish to see him."

"Yes, I want to see him very much," Larina answered and added, " . . . if it is possible."

"Mr. Farren has suggested that you should meet in Sorrento."

"In Sorrento?" Larina ejaculated. "In Italy?"

"Yes, Miss Milton, his family have a Villa there and Mr. Farren suggested that I arrange for you to go there immediately."

Larina looked at him in astonishment.

"Did he suggest that I should travel . . . all that . . . way to see him?"

"He will be coming a great deal further from America," Mr. Donaldson said, "and I imagine that he thought it would not be too much to ask you to make the journey from here."

"No, no, of course not!" Larina said. "It is not that it is too much to ask, it is just that it was such a surprise!"

"You know where Sorrento is, Miss Milton?"

"Yes, of course," Larina answered. "It is near Naples. My father has often spoken to me of Naples. He was very interested in Pompeii and Herculaneum."

"They have made some great discoveries there, I believe," Mr. Donaldson said.

"So I have read."

Larina was talking automatically because her brain was dazed with the idea that had been presented to her.

She had naturally supposed that if Elvin was able to keep his promise he would come to London.

He had told her once that when he stayed in London he went to a hotel called Claridges, and Larina had imagined she would be able to visit him in his Sitting-Room there and perhaps he would be well enough to come to her house.

But Sorrento!

She felt as if she could not take it in.

"Mr. Farren was not, of course, expecting you to travel alone," Mr. Donaldson was saying. "He asked that I should either escort you there myself or engage a Courier for you."

Larina did not speak and after a moment he went on:

"Perhaps I should explain, Miss Milton, that I look after Mr. Farren's interests in London where he has an office."

"An office?" Larina asked in surprise. "Why would he need an office?"

There was a pause before Mr. Donaldson answered:

"Mr. Farren has various business interests not only in his own country but also in Europe, which we look after for him."

"Oh, I see," Larina said.

She had thought that Elvin must be fairly rich, otherwise he would not have been able to afford a chalet by himself. She knew also that apart from herself and her mother, Dr. Heinrich's fees were very high.

But an office to look after his business affairs suggested considerable wealth and it did not seem like Elvin somehow to be concerned with material things.

Yet Mr. Donaldson was continuing in a brisk, businesslike way:

"What I am suggesting, Miss Milton, is that you leave everything to me. I'll make your journey as comfortable as possible. All I want to know is how soon you can leave."

"How soon?" Larina questioned in a bewildered manner.

"Mr. Farren seemed to think it was important that you

should go to Italy as soon as possible. I am not quite certain how quickly he can be there."

There was a moment's pause and then Larina said:

"H . . . have you any . . . idea how much it would . . . cost?"

She felt embarrassed as she asked the question.

"I'm afraid I'm explaining myself very clumsily," Mr. Donaldson answered. "If you go to Italy, Miss Milton, it'll be as Mr. Farren's guest. He made that very clear in the cable. I'll see to all the expenses."

"But I do not . . . think I could permit . . . " Larina began, then her voice died away.

What was the point of protesting?

If Elvin wanted her to go to Sorrento the only way it would be possible for her to get there would be at his expense.

She knew quite well that she had not enough money left in the Bank to buy her ticket.

It was ridiculous to make difficulties or to argue about anything when Elvin was being so kind, so overwhelmingly kind in responding to her cry for help.

She had wondered after sending the cable if she could have worded it better. But somehow she thought he would understand what she was trying to say, and it was quite obvious now that he had done so.

He was coming to her aid; he was helping her as he had promised he would; she must agree to anything he suggested.

Mr. Donaldson was watching her from the sofa.

"All you have to tell me, Miss Milton," he said after a moment, "is how soon you can be ready."

Larina looked rather helplessly around the room, then she answered:

"I would be ready at once, if it were not for one thing."

"And what is that, Miss Milton?"

"I shall have to sell the contents of this house," Larina replied. "I need the money . . . I must have some new clothes if I am going to Sorrento."

She felt Mr. Donaldson looked surprised and she explained:

"You see, I have been living in Switzerland, which is where I met Mr. Farren. We wore thick clothing there as it was very high up and even in the summer it could be very cold in the evenings. But Sorrento will be warm."

"It will indeed," Mr. Donaldson agreed. "In fact I should think it will be getting really hot as soon as we move into April."

"That is what I thought," Larina agreed.

"I can quite understand that you need some summer dresses," Mr. Donaldson said.

He smiled and it gave him a humanity which had been rather lacking before.

"I have a wife and three daughters who seldom talk about anything else. So I am well aware how important they are."

Larina smiled.

"Then as you understand perhaps you will help me. I have no further need for anything in this house, and so I want to sell everything it contains."

"You will be leaving this house then, when you come back from Sorrento?" Mr. Donaldson asked.

"Yes . . . I will be . . . going away."

"Well we could put the furniture up for auction, or even try to find a buyer among the dealers, but it is going to take time."

He looked around him, then said:

"I wonder if you could show me the rest of the house, Miss Milton?"

"Of course," Larina agreed.

She rose to her feet and led Mr. Donaldson over the house.

There was not a great deal to see.

The mahogany bed and the matching furniture in her mother's room, while attractive, were not valuable.

There was nothing in her own room which was worth more than a few pounds, but the Dining-Room table was good and so were the chairs which her father had said were Hepplewhite.

They were however not fashionable at the moment and there were some pictures on the walls which seemed to interest Mr. Donaldson more.

Finally they went into the tiny Study, and he glanced round quickly, apparently not interested in the books.

"I am afraid that is everything!" Larina said apologetically. "There is practically nothing downstairs in the kitchen. You see, since my father died we have not been able to afford a maid."

She blushed as she spoke, thinking he would find it strange that she had lied to him on his arrival.

"You are living here alone?" he asked.

She nodded.

"I do not like to think of your doing that Miss Milton," he said. "I should not permit it if it was one of my own daughters. It seems to me that the sooner you get to Sorrento the better!"

He paused, then added with a smile:

"Naturally you cannot go without something to wear and I think I can solve the problem."

"How can you do that?" Larina asked.

"I am going to advance you a hundred pounds, Miss Milton, and while you are away I will sell the contents of your house. It if comes to more than a hundred pounds then I will let you have the balance when you return."

"Supposing it is less?" Larina asked apprehensively.

"I do not think it will be," Mr. Donaldson replied. "It is just a question of finding the right purchasers and that takes time. Some of the things, like the desk in the Sitting-Room, are quite valuable and the sideboard in the Dining-Room is worth perhaps fifteen pounds!"

"Perhaps you should get further advice before you commit yourself," Larina suggested nervously.

"I'll take a gamble on it," Mr. Donaldson smiled.

He sat down as he spoke at the desk in the Study which Larina had used.

It was a sturdy piece of furniture and had none of the elegance of her mother's upstairs.

"If I write you a cheque," Mr. Donaldson said taking a cheque-book out of his pocket, "you'll be able to cash it tomorrow. Could you buy all the clothes you need in three days?"

"Yes, I am sure I could," Larina agreed.

"That will give me time to make the reservations on the

boat from Dover to Calais and on the trains that will take you first to Rome and then on to Naples."

"I can hardly believe it is true," Larina exclaimed.

"I'll let you know what time I shall be calling for you on Thursday morning." Mr. Donaldson said. "I have a feeling it will be early."

"I will not mind that."

Mr. Donaldson blotted the cheque.

"If there is anything you want to ask me in the meantime," he said, "you can get in touch with me at this address."

He made as if to take a card from his pocket—then changed his mind and wrote the address down on a piece of paper.

"Just call a messenger," he said, "and I'll come round as quickly as possible."

"I am sure I shall want nothing," Larina replied. "I shall be too busy shopping."

"That's right," Mr. Donaldson smiled. "You enjoy yourself, Miss Milton. I don't think you will want anything very elaborate. Since Mr. Farren has been ill I don't suppose he will be entertaining extensively."

"No, of course not," Larina answered.

"The gardens of the Villa are very beautiful," Mr. Donaldson said. "In fact people say they are the most beautiful gardens in the whole of Southern Italy, and the Villa itself is superb! It was originally the house of a famous Roman Senator, but I expect Mr. Farren will want to tell you about it himself."

"I feel I am dreaming!" Larina said. "This cannot be happening. If you only knew what it meant to me . . ."

She stopped suddenly. She had been on the verge of revealing too much of her private feelings to a stranger.

"I can understand," Mr. Donaldson said. "I often feel like that when I am dealing with Mr.—"

He checked himself and seemed to stumble over the name as he finished: "—Farren and his brothers."

He moved towards the door.

"And now, Miss Milton, if you will excuse me," he said. "I have a lot to do before I call for you on Thursday, and there is not much of today left."

Larina saw him to the door and held out her hand.

"Good-bye, Mr. Donaldson," she said. "Thank you, thank you very much indeed!"

"Good-bye, Miss Milton," he replied gravely.

As he walked away, she saw that he had a motor-car driven by a chauffeur waiting for him a little way down the street.

She stared in surprise.

A motor-car!

There were only a few of them in London and the public looked at them in surprise and even consternation.

Elvin had never mentioned anything about motor-cars when they had been talking together, and she could not imagine him driving one of those ugly vehicles which caused so much dust and frightened the horses.

"The day I have to visit my patients in a motor-car," she had heard her father say often enough. "I will give up my practice! Why, to come hooting up to the door would frighten anyone with a bad heart into having a seizure!"

"They are so nasty and smelly!" Larina's mother had complained.

"Everyone is crazy for speed," Dr. Milton had gone on, "faster trains, faster ships, motor-cars rushing along the roads, running over children and dogs—where will it all end?"

"Where indeed?" his wife echoed with a sigh. "I know of nothing more delightful than driving quietly and with dignity in a comfortable carriage."

But secretly Larina had often longed to go in a motor-car. Then peeping round the door, as she saw Mr. Donaldson drive off she half wished she could be sitting beside him.

Even the noise the car made as it journeyed down Eaton Terrace had something exciting about it.

But as she closed the door she told herself that for the moment everything seemed exciting.

How could it be possible that she was going to Italy in three days' time?

Italy which she had always longed to see, which she had learnt about, read about and talked about to her father.

And Sorrento of all places!

She had not told Mr. Donaldson because it made her feel shy. But the reason she was particularly interested was that it was near Sorrento that Ulysses was said to have resisted the call of the Sirens. He had plugged the ears of his crew with wax and made them lash him to the mast of the ship so that he should not be enslaved by their voices.

Of all the books that her father had made her read Larina had been most interested in those about Greece.

Dr. Milton had been particularly concerned with archaeological discoveries in Pompeii and Herculaneum and with the tombs that had been recently excavated in Egypt, but he had also encouraged her to study the religions and histories of all the ancient civilisations.

She knew from what she had read that Sorrento was in the Bay of Naples where the rich Romans had built their summer Villas.

But before the Romans, it had been colonised by Greek settlers who were said to have founded the Temple of Athene on the tip of the promontory.

In all her reading of history, the Greeks had thrilled Larina as no other people had been able to do.

She had tried to be enthusiastic about the other cultures and religions which absorbed her father. But the Babylonian and Assyrian gods were heavy and earthy, the Egyptian gods with their animal features grotesque.

The Greeks had no Kings as splendid as the Pharaohs, no pyramids, no Nile to bring fertility to the land.

Yet it seemed to Larina that they had discovered something which was different to all the other civilisations—it was light and was personified in their god, Apollo.

As the god of light, the god of divine radiance, every morning Apollo moved across the sky, intensely virile, flashing with a million points of light, healing everything he touched, germinating the seeds and defying the powers of darkness.

To Larina he became very real.

Even as the Greeks had seen him not only as the sun, but as a perfect man, she had visualised him too, and gradually there had grown up a picture of him in her mind.

He was not only the sun, he was the moon, the planets,

the Milky-Way and the stars. He was the sparkle of the waves, the gleam in the eyes. Of all the gods, her books had told her, he was the one who conferred the greatest blessings and was the most generous and the most far-seeing.

What she had loved was when her father had told her that Apollo's constant companion was the dolphin, the sleekest and shiniest of all creatures.

Larina had gone to the Zoo and looked at the dolphins and thought of them as attendant on Apollo, shining as he shone with a light which lit not only the world but men's minds.

She tried to tell her father what she felt and thought he understood.

"I found when I was in Greece," he said, "that at night when Apollo vanishes the Greeks are miserable. I do not believe there are any other people in the world who keep so many lights burning in their houses."

He smiled as he went on:

"Even during the brightest days they will light their lamps, when they can barely afford the oil."

He paused before he added more seriously:

"Light is their protection against the evil of darkness."

"Apollo is light," Larina told herself.

If she could not go to Greece before she died, at least in Sorrento she would actually be standing on soil where Greeks had worshipped him.

It seemed to her in the excitement of what she was planning that it would not be Elvin she was meeting in Sorrento, but Apollo, who had been part of her childhood dreams and who as she grew older had in some way been part of the mind she was developing within herself.

That, she knew, was what the Greeks had brought to the world, the development not only of a perfect body, but also of a questing mind, a mind such as she had herself where she believed there were no bounds to knowledge and to reason.

There was however little time for introspection or for thinking too long about Apollo. She had to buy clothes, and for the first time she knew that what she spent would not be extravagant because she would have no sense of guilt about it.

She rose very early the following morning and hurried to the Bank, cashing Mr. Donaldson's cheque for one hundred pounds and drawing out what remained of the small balance which had been dwindling away every week since her return to London.

"I will keep ten pounds for tips and I can spend the rest," she told herself.

There would be no chance of her returning from Sorrento, since the twenty-one days would be up very shortly after she arrived there and after that she would have no further need of money.

She wished she had asked Mr. Donaldson more about the clothes she would need in Sorrento, but told herself he was unlikely to know any more than she did.

She was aware that in the sunshine one needed white or bright colours and there was very little in her existing wardrobe which would be of any use.

Besides with her one hundred pounds she was determined to look her best for Elvin, and perhaps be a worthy visitor to the Villa of which Mr. Donaldson had spoken so warmly.

The difficulty of course was that she had no time to have anything made.

The best clothes in London from the best dressmakers were designed for each individual customer and were fitted several times and took at least two or three weeks to be completed.

Her mother's best clothes which she wore on special occasions had all been made by a dressmaker in Hanover Square, but even so they had not been very expensive because the Doctor's wife could not have afforded anything extravagant.

Larina went first to Peter Robinson in Regent Street where there were dresses ready made.

She found two light gowns which could be altered by the following day to fit her. They were pretty, light muslins that were not expensive and were in fact the only gowns in the shop that were not much too large in the bust.

"You are very slim, Miss," the fitter said as she pinned away at the superfluous folds of the material.

"I know I am not fashionable," Larina said with a smile.

"I daresay you'll put on a bit as you get older," the woman said comfortingly.

The silhouette popularised by the American Charles Dana Gibson had swept England. His magazine-drawings of lovely women standing with a pronounced forward tilt, had brought into vogue 'the Gibson S bend'!

Larina knew she would never have the ample and pro-tuberant bosom or the definitely curved behind which was accentuated by the swing of the skirt, and often by discreetly hidden little pads.

One thing she was determined not to buy were the boned, high necks which most ladies affected in the daytime and which Larina knew were very uncomfortable.

Instead she chose gowns which had a piece of soft muslin round the neck which ended as a bow in the front or alter-natively a bow at the back. It was modest, but definitely not boned.

"It would be too restrictive in the heat anyway," she told herself, feeling a little guilty that she had no desire to be fashionable.

Then as she was wondering where she should buy her evening-gowns, she remembered that she and her mother when they had been in Switzerland had been looking at the pictures in *'The Ladies Journal'* and had seen some very at-tractive designs by Paul Poiret.

Underneath them was written:

'This French designer is trying to change the trend of women's clothes to what he calls a more graceful, flowing look. His new ideas, like his new creations, are causing a sensation in Paris as well as in Lon-don.'

"There would be no harm in looking!" Larina told her-self.

She knew that Poiret's shop was in Berkeley Street, and with a feeling of being utterly reckless she took a hackney-carriage instead of trying to get there by omnibus.

Ordinarily she had been far too shy and too nervous to

enter the luxurious precincts of such a shop by herself, but now that she had no future she had developed a courage she had never had before.

If people were surprised at her behavior it did not matter; if people criticised her she would not be here long enough to hear it! Even if she did something outrageous it would be forgotten in three weeks' time when she was dead.

Quite boldly, not even worrying about her somewhat dowdy appearance, she entered the shop and asked to see some of their models.

"We have very few models to show at the moment, Madam," a very superior looking Vendeuse told her. "Monsieur Poiret's new collection from Paris will be shown next week. At the moment we really only have the garments that are in the sale."

"In the sale!" Larina exclaimed.

She realised this meant the clothes were ready and could be altered to fit her.

She would not be told, as she had half-expected, that everything would take a long time to be made for her.

She felt afterwards it had been an inspiration, a stroke of good fortune, that she had been brave enough to enter Poiret's.

She came away with two evening-gowns and two for the day besides a travelling outfit.

When she explained to the Vendeuse that she was leaving for Italy on Friday, perhaps because of the excitement in her voice or perhaps because she looked very young and, although she was not aware of it, rather helpless, the woman ceased to appear superior and became warm and friendly.

Finally dropping all barriers she asked:

"How much have you to spend?"

"I have nearly a hundred pounds for everything!" Larina said.

They made out a budget together; so much for hats; she would need only one large shady one for the sun and she could change the ribbons around to match her various gowns.

So much for shoes: she would need white ones for the

daytime and a pair of satin slippers to go with the evening-gowns.

For gloves she could manage with what she had already, and all the rest could be expended on the exciting, original, delightful gowns which, as the Vendeuse pointed out, Mr. Poiret might have designed specially for her.

Larina learnt that he did not like the Gibson S bend. He liked gowns that flowed, that had a rhythm about them, and those were the sort of gowns into which Larina was fitted.

There was one of white which was made of chiffon, another in the pale pink which made her think of almond blossom.

The evening-gowns had chiffon scarves to match, and all of them seemed to fall in a fluid line which reminded her of the movement of the wind in long grass.

"You look lovely, Madam, you do really!" the Vendeuse exclaimed when finally the last gown was fitted and she was promised they would all be delivered late on Wednesday evening.

Looking in the mirror Larina had no doubt that they did become her better than anything she had ever worn in her life before.

They brought out the lights in her very fair hair, the light in the grey of her eyes which sometimes held a touch of green in them, and they accentuated the whiteness of her skin.

"You have been so kind," she said impulsively to the Vendeuse, "I still cannot believe that I could have been so brave as to come into this shop alone."

"It has been a real pleasure!" the Vendeuse said with a note of sincerity in her voice. "I only wish I could come with you to Italy and see you wearing them."

"I wish you could too," Larina answered.

"Never mind, I know how admired you will be," the Vendeuse said, "and that is a satisfaction in itself!"

Larina smiled. She was sure that Elvin would admire her and she wanted to look nice for him.

She remembered the little compliments he had paid her. Then she remembered the biggest compliment of all, when he had said he wanted her to be with him when his 'spirit took wings'.

Now it would not be his spirit which was flying away into the unknown, but hers.

'In Sorrento I shall be flying into the light not into the darkness,' Larina thought, 'and with Elvin there I shall not be afraid.'

# CHAPTER FOUR

Wynstan had travelled from Paris to Rome and from Rome to Naples in an irritated frame of mind.

He had, as he had expected, enjoyed himself on the *'Kaiser Wilhelm der Grosse'* with the alluring Countess of Glencairn.

He had known when he went down to the big Dining-Saloon the first night that he had not been mistaken in thinking that she found him as attractive as he found her.

Her dark eyes lit up when he appeared and her lips pouted provocatively, and long before the evening was over he knew they were all set to enjoy an *affaire de coeur* in which the French could indulge with such lightness that it was in fact like a *soufflé surprise*.

Having been amused by women of many nations, Wynstan found the French more sophisticated and more civilised in their attitude to love than any others.

They approached it like an epicurean discovering a new and strange dish, savoured it carefully and without hurry so that the full flavour, the underlying succulent taste, was fully appreciated.

English women, Wynstan thought, were always so deadly serious in their love affairs. It was invariably a case of 'Will you love me for ever?' 'Is this the first time you have felt as you do now?'

There was always at the back of their minds the idea that love must be a permanency rather than just a 'will o' the wisp' which could fly away overnight but which nevertheless was an enchantment for the moment.

Yvette Glencairn was experienced in the ancient science of fascinating a man, and Wynstan, who thought he knew every move in the game, was entranced to find that there were some new moves which definitely added to his education.

Because she was French and clever at keeping not one man but many under her spell, Yvette was always charming to her husband, which so often the English forgot was important when the other man was only a case of *pour passer le temps*.

The Earl hailed Wynstan with pleasure and talked to him of horses and the days when he had been Master of Hounds.

They speculated and argued as to who was likely to win the Derby and the other classic races in England that Season.

Wynstan had sat with the Glencairns at meals, and they had often come to his cabin after luncheon or dinner was over.

But when the Earl had retired to bed and the rest of the ship's passengers were settling down for the night, it was then that Yvette, in a diaphanous and very revealing rest-gown, would open the door of Wynstan's cabin to find him waiting for her.

She was enticing, exciting and very satisfying, and when she pleaded with him to stay with them in Paris, he had been sorely tempted to postpone his journey to Sorrento for several days.

He was well aware how many friends he would find in Paris at this time of the year.

The chestnuts would be coming out in the Champs Elysées, the flower-sellers' baskets would be filled with parma violets, there would be the smell of spring in the air, and Maxim's would be gayer than ever.

As his mother had found out by some mysterious means of her own, he had when he was last in Paris, spent a considerable amount of time with the successor of the *grandes cocottes Parisiennes* of the '90s, the glamorous Gaby Deslys.

She was the theatrical figure of whom all Paris was talking and it was obvious to Wynstan, as it was to all her other admirers, that her success would be phenomenal.

She had none of the beauty which Wynstan usually sought in women. But her cherubic face, her eyes warm and enticing beneath their heavy lids, her crimson lips that were always parted in a smile which revealed sensuality, gaiety and good nature, made her somehow different from anyone else.

She was audacious, bizarre, at times vulgar, and she looked like a bird of Paradise—not only on the stage, when she wore very little except feathers and pearls but in the restaurants, and also by some mysterious chemistry of her own in bed!

She had a vitality which made everything she did seem sensual, and yet the more luxurious and the more scandalous she was the more people loved her.

From the very moment she appeared she seemed to personify Paris itself, and when she had acted in London the previous year, the newspapers wrote of her as being '*la Vie Parisienne*', and meant it!

It would be amusing to see Gaby again, Wynstan told himself, and there were a great many other friends he knew would welcome him with open arms. But he had promised Harvey he would keep Larina Milton from making trouble and already the election in America was gathering momentum.

The '*Kaiser Wilhelm der Grosse*' had not equalled her regular run from New York to Southampton which was five days, twenty-two hours and forty-five minutes. Instead owing to the weather she was forty hours late.

It had taken another day and night before he got away from Cherbourg and it was very late on the 8th of April by the time Wynstan reached Paris.

This was the quickest way he could reach Rome but he

was delighted when he found that he could stay the night in Paris before catching an express the following morning.

Unfortunately he missed the express.

It was understandable as he did not reach his Suite in the Ritz Hotel until six o'clock in the morning after what had seemed a night of laughter—sparkling and frothy as a glass of champagne!

Gaby ablaze with feathers and jewels had danced on one of the tables at Maxim's, and after Wynstan had taken her home he had known there would be no chance of his catching the express which left the Gare de l'Est at a quarter to seven.

What was more the next Rome express from Paris did not leave until the following day. The alternatives were slow trains, and frequent changes which would not get him there any quicker.

He felt guilty!

Then he told himself there would be no indiscreet American newspapers in Sorrento, and if Elvin's girl-friend had to cool her heels a little she might be all the more eager to settle for a reasonable sum.

He had thought about Larina while crossing the Atlantic, and he had come to the conclusion that Harvey was wrong and that it was impossible that she should be having Elvin's child.

Elvin had never been like that—or had he?

There had been no woman in his life—that Wynstan thought he knew—but then he told himself he had been out of touch with Elvin for long periods of time.

When they were together they had an affinity which was closer than anything he enjoyed with his two elder brothers; but after all he had been abroad so much that Elvin might have developed interests of which he had no idea.

There always seemed to Wynstan to be something of Sir Galahad about Elvin.

Because he had been weak and sickly even as a child, he read a great deal more than the rest of the family, and when he talked to Elvin it had usually been on philosophy or psychology and they seldom touched on modern or commonplace topics.

But that was not to say, Wynstan told himself, that Elvin had not developed an interest in women of which he was not aware.

It was obvious from Larina's cable that she had meant something in his life.

For instance what had he promised her and what had he said in his letters? There were no answers to his questions except those he would not accept.

When finally Wynstan set off for Naples he began to feel angry.

If this woman had hurt Elvin in any way he would strangle her!

Elvin was someone special in his life, someone whose image he could not bear to have spoiled or defamed.

It was this which had made him agree to go to Europe rather than Harvey's almost hysterical fear that his election campaign might be damaged.

Wynstan was fond of his oldest brother, but he saw quite clearly his ruthlessness, his egotism, his insatiable ambition for power and importance.

He did not criticise, he merely accepted it as being what Harvey was; but where Elvin was concerned his feelings were very different.

Elvin was a part of his heart which Wynstan never revealed to anyone else.

Everything that was idealistic in Wynstan was concealed under a cynical and detached attitude which women found irresistible.

Because they could not capture him, could not pin him down, and make him their captive, they pursued him frantically and relentlessly.

The amused twinkle which was never far from his blue eyes drove them crazy, while to Harvey and Gary he was an enigmatic figure whom they decried because they could not understand him.

"Wynstan is just a play-boy! He has not a thought in his head beyond amusing himself," Harvey said often enough, and knew even as he spoke it was untrue.

Wynstan stood apart from the family and his mother knew it, which was why she claimed in all truth that he was exceptional. The rules and regulations she insisted on for the rest of her children did not apply to him.

The train was due to arrive in Naples in the afternoon.

It had been very hot since early in the morning when they had changed trains at Rome.

Wynstan's valet had laid out for him in his sleeping-compartment a white tussore suit and a fine linen shirt which made him look even more elegant than usual.

Wynstan bought his suits in London, his shirts in Paris, his shoes in Italy, and his cuff-links at Tiffany's in New York.

However he wore his clothes with an ease and elegance which made them seem so much a part of himself that people did not notice them but only him.

It was seven years since he had been to Naples and since he had stayed in his grandfather's Villa at Sorrento.

He had forgotten, he thought, that Naples—nicknamed 'the devil's paradise'—was mysterious. And he told himself as the train steamed into the station that it was one of the few cities of ancient pre-Christian times that had not perished but had survived on the surface of the modern world.

He was met at the station by a Courier who had been notified of his arrival by Mr. Donaldson.

He led Wynstan away from the bustle and noise of the station to say apologetically:

"*Scusi Signor,* but I could not find you a car at such short notice."

He thought he saw Wynstan's expression darken and went on hastily:

"I thought a comfortable carriage, *Signor,* with fast horses was better than an uncomfortable car which undoubtedly will break down on the journey to Sorrento."

There was something so ingenuous in his explanation that Wynstan smiled.

"I am in no great hurry," he said.

As he drove off, leaving his valet to cope with the luggage and follow him in another carriage, he thought that was the truth.

He was in no hurry to reach Sorrento and the problems that awaited him there, and now as the excellent horses carried him through the beautiful city he began to relax and look at his surroundings.

The houses with their elaborate porticos, the Castel Dell'Oro, the baroque Churches, Palazzos, the Piazza Pebiscito and the splendour of Naples made him remember how it had been founded by the Greeks who settled in Cumal in 730 B.C.

But what he had forgotten besides the beauty of Naples with its narrow steps ascending towards the sky, its alleys, its subterranean dwellings, and its Port filled with ships and small boats, was the quality of the air.

Wynstan drew in his breath and thought he would have recognised it with his eyes shut.

There was something different about it, an air that could be found nowhere else. Just as when he had his first view of the sea, it had a transparent luminosity that was also different.

As soon as they were outside the city he saw Vesuvius rising immediately from the coastal plain, its wooded slopes towering high above the road down which he was travelling.

Now he leant back and forgot everything except the beauty of the flowers, the shrubs, the trees in blossom and the picturesqueness of the small villages where half the population seemed to be sitting out in the sunshine drinking wine.

And where inevitably there was the sound of music.

"How could I have been so stupid as not to come here more often?" Wynstan asked himself and he wished that when he reached the Villa he could be alone there.

Because he felt suddenly reluctant to face anything that might spoil the loveliness of the blue sea, the vivid sky and the vibrant quality of the air, he stopped the carriage at the *Castellammare di Stabia.*

There he sat outside a small Inn and ordered a bottle of the local wine.

The Italian coachman was delighted. He put hay bags over the noses of the two horses and disappeared to find friends at the back of the Inn.

Ahead, Wynstan knew, was the most beautiful drive on earth and he thought that perhaps the glass of wine would sharpen his appreciation of what he had believed as a child was the road which led to El Dorado.

He had always been surprised that his grandfather, who had seemed to most people a rather frightening, overpowering man, should have had the imagination and the vision to create anything so beautiful as the Villa where he had spent the last years of his life.

He had rebuilt it to the exact design of what it was believed to have looked like in Roman times.

There had remained some of the magnificent mosaic floors, a number of pillars, a few broken walls, and of course the foundations.

Following the lines of these and collecting everything in the neighbourhood which might at some time have been remotely connected with the Villa, old Mr. Vanderfeld had created a Palace of beauty that was unsurpassed in the whole of Italy.

What was more, and this had surprised his family more than anything, he had made the garden a dream of loveliness.

It had required vision and imagination and Wynstan had often thought as he grew older that he resembled his grandfather more than his father.

There had been a poetry in his grandfather that had been transmitted to Elvin and himself, but not to Harvey or Gary.

His wine finished, reluctantly Wynstan resumed his journey, followed by the admiring glances of the dark-eyed *Signorinas* gathered round the fountain in the village.

The water of *Castellammare di Stabia* had been famous since Roman times, and there was the Grotto in the hills which had been there long before the Romans.

They drove on and now the sea was suffused with a golden light which came with the setting of the sun.

The Villa Arcadia was at the actual point where the mountains gave way to the undoubtedly fertile *Peano di Sorrento,* a natural terrace some 300 feet high, falling in sheer cliffs to the Bay of Naples.

There were, as Wynstan knew, special steps built down to the sea where there was a private jetty and where he expected to find his motor-boat.

It had been built for him in Monte Carlo and he had cabled the ship-builders to send it to Sorrento so that it would be there by the time he arrived.

He was looking forward to seeing it. He had owned motor-boats before, but this was a very special one and built to his own design.

He hoped he would have the opportunity to get away on his own and try it out in the Bay.

The plain of Sorrento was an unbroken expanse of luxuriant green except for the white walls of an occasional villa and the Church towers and domes capped with multi-coloured majolica.

Everywhere there were orange and lemon trees, burdened with their fruit, vineyards, walnut and fig trees, cherries and pomegranates and tropical flowers.

The horses turned in at the wrought iron gates which Wynstan's grandfather had copied from the gates of one of the famous Palaces in Naples.

They were magnificent, emblazoned with gold and flanked on either side with stone griffons which had once stood in the garden of an ancient Temple before it was forgotten and allowed to fall into decay.

It was a short drive rising on either side of a stone fountain surrounded by yellow azaleas.

At the front door there was a balustraded terrace covered with climbing geraniums and roses.

'It is lovelier than I remembered!' Wynstan thought to himself and stepped out to be greeted by a number of Italian servants.

The entrance-hall was cool, the pattern on the floor was a replica of one of the mosaics discovered in Herculaneum.

The marble pillars, the painted ceilings, the view from the windows, all brought the whole enchantment of the Villa back to Wynstan's mind.

He could remember running through the house as a child and hearing his own laughter echoing and re-echoing down the marble passages. The golden sunshine outside in the garden had warmed and invigorated him so that he felt free and untrammelled as he had never been again in the whole of his life.

"You had a good journey, *Signor?*" the elderly Italian who appeared to be in charge was asking him.

"Yes, thank you, a very good journey," Wynstan replied.

"You require wine or refreshment, *Signor?*"

"Not for the moment," Wynstan answered. "Where is Miss Milton?"

"You will find her in the garden, *Signor*. The *Signorina* arrived three days ago. She has spent all her time in the garden and she finds it very beautiful—*bellissimo!* We are glad she is pleased!"

"I will find her," Wynstan said.

Bare-headed he walked out into a blaze of colour. The terraces which climbed the hill to the right of the Villa looked like the Hanging Gardens of Babylon.

The scent of tuberoses, lilacs and lilies filled the air, and under the olive trees sloping down to the plain, the grass was carpeted with hyacinths. Everywhere there was a profusion of tulips, peonies and daffodils.

The almond trees which were the first to bloom had already shed their petals, Wynstan noticed, and there was a carpet of pink and white blossoms beneath them.

The branches of the Judas tree were purple against the sky, the laburnums cascaded like golden rain, and beyond them the mimosa was a yellow cloud.

He looked around and realised that as the sun was sinking, the flame-coloured azaleas were echoed by what appeared to be flames of fire rising in the sky.

He moved forward, knowing almost instinctively where Larina Milton would be at this time of the evening.

Always at sunset anyone who stayed in the Villa climbed up the twisting stone steps of the hanging gardens to where high above the Villa on a promontory overlooking the sea there was an ancient Temple.

It had been built, Wynstan's grandfather had discovered, by Greeks, and he had restored it without knowing to which god it was dedicated.

Then in the last year of his life, when they were digging to extend the garden further, they had found a statue.

Time and weather had refined the whiteness of the marble, rain and sun had brought colour to it so that it almost resembled flesh.

It was not greatly damaged, except that it had lost its arms and the features of the face were obliterated, but it had a beauty and a grace that was breathtaking.

The legs were veiled with a loose garment which began below the hips, the exquisite curves of the breasts and the lines of the lower body were undamaged. The whole statue made anyone who looked at it draw in their breath as if they had never believed such beauty existed.

"It is Aphrodite!" Wynstan's grandfather had declared. "The goddess of beauty, love and reproduction!"

"How can you be sure of that?" Wynstan had asked.

He had been fifteen at the time and pleased because his grandfather talked to him as if he were a grown man.

"Can you not see just by looking at her, that she could be nothing else?" the old man had enquired. "She was born in the sea-foam and she stood here in her Temple overlooking the sea, bringing happiness and prosperity to those who toiled on it."

Wynstan had looked for a long time at the goddess whom his grandfather had set on a marble pedestal.

He had grown lilies on either side of her because lilies, he said, were the right flowers for Aphrodite.

"Why particularly?" Wynstan enquired.

"Because they are always the symbol of purity," his grandfather had answered. "To the Greeks the goddess of love was not a many-breasted matron, but a young virgin rising out of the waves."

He had paused to stare at the statue of Aphrodite. Her head was turned to the right of her body, and although she had no remaining features it was somehow easy to imagine them.

The little straight nose, the wide, innocent eyes, the softly curved lips!

"In a sense the Greeks invented virginity for their goddesses," old Mr. Vanderfeld went on. "To them it was fresh, clean and full of promise like the coming of each day."

He saw that Wynstan was listening intently and continued:

"Aphrodite was a grey-eyed goddess, untouched and part of every man's dreams. She brought all that was beautiful and perfect to those who worshipped her so that never again could they be content with the second-rate."

He smiled at the school-boy.

"When she went to the Assembly of the Immortals the gods were silent with admiration, and Homer wrote that each wished in his heart to take her as a wife and lead her to his abode."

Everything his grandfather had told him came back to Wynstan now, and he thought as he climbed up the stone steps that when he grew old this was where he would live out his life and where he would die.

In the meantime, although he dedicated so much of his life to the pursuit of love, he had not yet found any woman that his grandfather would have described as Aphrodite.

Those he had loved and who had loved him had never been able to touch something secret in his heart that had been engendered all those years ago when his grandfather had spoken to him of love.

He had been continually infatuated, excited and delighted by women, but always there had come a moment when he knew that he no longer needed them and they no longer meant anything to him.

They were like the butterflies still hovering over the flowers but which by the morning would no longer exist, and their place would be taken by others as colourful and as dispensable as they were themselves.

The sky was growing more brilliant every moment, the sunset so vivid, so dazzling, that it was hard to look at it.

Then as he reached the last steps which led to the Temple itself, Wynstan realised that he had been right in thinking that this was where he would find Larina Milton.

There was a woman standing against the marble balustrade looking out over the sea. It was difficult to see her distinctly because the sunset was so blinding that she was little more than a silhouette against it.

She was wearing white, and her hair was very pale gold, and yet the light from the sky made it shimmer as if with tiny tongues of flame.

She must have heard his footsteps for even as he stepped onto the mosaic floor of the Temple she turned and for one incredible moment he thought that she was Aphrodite!


Larina had been disappointed when she arrived at the Villa Arcadia to find that Elvin was not already there waiting for her, but she had been entranced by the drive from Naples and the incredible beauty of the Villa.

The Courier who had accompanied her on the journey was an elderly man who told her he had once been a schoolmaster. He had explained very clearly the history of every place they passed.

He was however more interested in Venice than in other parts of Italy and it was hard for Larina to keep him on the subjects she wished to learn about when he was longing to describe to her the glories of San Marco and the tragedy of the Venetian decline.

Nevertheless he told her many myths and legends of Southern Italy and when he said good-bye she felt sorry to lose him.

"Are you going back straight away?" she asked in surprise.

"They expect me in London, Miss Milton."

"Then thank you very much for looking after me."

"It has been a great pleasure," he answered, "and I say that in all sincerity! It is not often I take on a journey anyone who has your enquiring mind and your love of antiquities!"

"I can see already that the Villa is breathtakingly beautiful!" Larina said.

He had told her how it had been restored in what was believed to be its original design.

"Mr. er . . . er . . . Farren went to endless trouble to have the experts' opinion on every room, every floor and every ceiling."

There was a perceptible pause before the Courier pronounced Mr. Farren's name which Larina had noticed on other occasions, and she wondered why everyone seemed to find it difficult to say the word 'Farren'.

"Perhaps it is because it begins with an 'F'," she told herself. "Some people might have as much difficulty with their 'Fs' as with their 'Ths'."

But it seemed strange that both Mr. Donaldson and the Courier should have the same impediment.

However her curiosity in that respect was quickly swept away by her excitement over the Villa and its garden.

The garden particularly had been unlike anything else she had ever seen or imagined.

It was easy here to imagine Apollo as she had never been able to imagine him before, and she longed impatiently to talk about him to Elvin.

She was certain he would know more than she did about the 'far-shining one', 'the friend of Zeus', 'the giver of music and song'.

Nothing the Greeks ever created, Larina told herself, could have been more magnificent than this god who tore the darkness from the human soul and lit it with divine light.

Her first evening at the Villa she had on the servants' suggestion gone up to the Temple to see the sunset.

Watching the glory of it she had almost believed that she saw Apollo in the dazzling light which turned the sea to gold and touched every mountain and beach with a light that was indescribable.

Then, as gradually the sun vanished and the darkness was encroaching, she felt there was a strange glitter high in the air, a mysterious quivering, the beating of silver wings and the whirring of silver wheels.

That, she told herself, was how the Greeks had known Apollo was near and she was certain at that moment he was close to her.

It was not the same ecstasy that she had felt at the Serpentine when she had been aware of life; it was something outside herself, and it was so perfect, so exquisite, that she wanted to catch it and make it hers.

Then with the coming of darkness Apollo had gone, but she could think of nothing else.

She had not felt lonely the next day. She had been waited on by the warm-hearted smiling Italians who had looked at her with dark, liquid eyes and tried in their own way to make her happy.

She thought as she walked about the garden that a strange music accompanied her, not only from the buzz of the bees and the song of the birds, but also as if she heard some celestial song on the air itself.

All that evening she had dreamt of Apollo.

She found books in the Villa which were written about the myths and legends of the Greeks and Romans in which there were references to him.

But they were only words, and she had but to go into the garden to feel that his very presence overshadowed everything.

She began to be aware of an expectant quietness like the presence of an unexplained mystery which would shortly be revealed.

In one of the books she had read some verses translated from Sophocles and she found herself repeating some words of it as she walked alone:

> *"He who has won some new splendour*
> *Rides on the air,*
> *Borne upwards on the winds of his human vigour."*

'Only Apollo,' she thought, 'would ride on the air.'

She felt as if she could speak to him as the evening breeze from the sea moved her hair and touched the softness of her cheeks.

Because she did not wish to miss a moment of the sunset or the first shimmering stars that followed it, she had changed for dinner early, putting on her white gown because she had worn her pink one the night before.

Throwing the long chiffon scarf over one shoulder in an unconscious imitation of the Greeks, she walked up to the Temple to stand waiting; almost as one would wait for the curtain to rise in a theatre.

Tonight the sunset was even lovelier than it had been before: the gold was more gold, the crimson more crimson, the blue more blue; and the shining glory of it seemed to blaze as the legends said the whole island of Delos had done when the goddess Leto gave birth to her son Apollo.

Larina felt herself caught up in the ecstasy of it and the music she had heard all day was beating in her ears.

She heard a step behind her and turned her head.

Her eyes were still dazzled from the setting sun, and yet under the shadows of the Temple she could see someone standing. The light from the sky touched his face and as it did so she thought with a sudden leap of her heart that it was Apollo who stood there!

For a long, long moment there was silence, a silence that was not oppressive, merely as if nature stood still and the earth stopped moving.

Then in a voice that sounded strange to himself Wynstan said:

"You are Miss Milton?"

He knew as his voice died away that Larina had difficulty in answering him. Then she said, stammering a little over the words:

"Y . . . yes . . . who . . . are you?"

He moved closer to her and now he could see why for the moment he had thought she was Aphrodite.

She was very slim, in fact the same height as the goddess that stood beside them on a pedestal. The folds of the scarf she wore over her shoulder were Grecian, so was her gown flowing to her feet.

It was unfashionable, and yet at the same time so utterly and completely right that it was impossible to think of her wearing anything else.

He reached her side and saw that the eyes she raised to his were grey, and her hair swept back from an oval forehead was pale gold but without the tongues of fire that had been there when he first saw her.

She was not like any woman he had ever seen before. Yet there was a rightness about her he could not explain even to himself, except that she seemed part of the Temple, part of the garden, and part of the sun which was sinking into the sea.

"I am Elvin's brother—Wynstan."

"Is Elvin here?"

There was a lilt, an eagerness in her voice.

"I am afraid not. I am his advance guard, so to speak!"

There was a pause, as if neither of them could think what to say, before Wynstan asked:

"I hope you have not been very lonely? I understand you arrived three days ago."

"I have not been lonely; it is so beautiful, so unbelievably, incredibly lovely!"

"That is what I have always thought," he said. "When I was a child I spent my holidays here with my grandfather."

"I cannot understand why Elvin did not tell me about it."

"I am not sure if he ever came here."

"But why not?"

"Elvin was ill even as a child, and my mother did not wish him to travel in case it proved too much for him."

"What a pity!" Larina said. "He would have loved it! And I thought there would be so much he would be able to tell me that I want to know."

"Perhaps I can answer your questions in his place?" Wynstan suggested.

"They are not exactly questions," Larina replied.

Then as if she felt she had said too much she said quickly: "Have you come from America?"

"Yes."

"And Elvin is well enough to travel? I could hardly believe it when Mr. Donaldson told me he wanted me to meet him here."

"You were not certain he would come?" Wynstan asked.

She looked away from him out to sea, and he had the feeling she was puzzling how to answer his question.

Here was something he did not understand. She had said quite clearly in her cable: 'Come to me as you promised.' Having said that why should she be surprised that Elvin was ready to oblige her?

"You knew Elvin when he was in Switzerland?" he asked after a moment.

"Yes, we were at the Sanatorium together."

"You were a patient?"

"No, I was there with my mother."

"I hope she is better."

"She died."

"I am sorry to hear that," Wynstan said. "Was that after Elvin had left?"

"Yes, two weeks later."

"It must have been a shock for you, but perhaps you really expected it?"

"No, I hoped she could be cured. Dr. Heinrich has a great reputation for effecting cures."

"So I have heard," Wynstan agreed.

"And if Elvin is better," Larina said, "as he told me he was in a letter he wrote to me after he arrived in New York, then it is entirely due to Dr. Heinrich."

"Yes, of course."

The sun had now finally disappeared below the horizon, and it was just that moment of dusk, pale blue and purple, when the first stars are faint but twinkling, their light growing stronger as the darkness deepens.

Larina looked out to sea and Wynstan could see her small straight nose silhouetted against the sky.

Once again he wondered if she was real. There was something insubstantial and ethereal about her, something which made him think of his dreams of Aphrodite when he was a boy.

Then she looked at him and said:

"I expect you want to go back to the Villa. It will soon be time for dinner and you must be hungry after your journey."

He felt as if she was saying one thing, while at the same time her thoughts were elsewhere. They moved across the marble-floor and found the steps which led down into the garden below.

"Be careful!" Wynstan warned. "It is easy to slip, and this path is very steep."

There was still sufficient light for them to see their way.

The azaleas were already scented shadows and the cypress trees were sharp points rising above their heads.

Larina's gown gleamed white. She seemed to move instinctively without hesitation, and her footfalls were so light that Wynstan walking behind felt almost as if she floated down.

The lights from the Villa were warm, golden and welcoming as they stepped into the marble hall.

"If you will excuse me," Wynstan said formally, "I will go and change. I will not be long."

"I will wait in the Drawing-Room," Larina answered.

She moved away from him down the marble passage to the big Drawing-Room with square windows overlooking the bay on one side and the garden on the other.

It was full of exquisite pieces of furniture that had delighted her ever since she had arrived. She felt they had all been chosen not primarily because they were valuable but because each one was just right for the Villa.

They were not antiques of ancient Rome, of course, but they were classical in their taste; their beauty was something which had been handed down through the centuries and had nothing to do with what was momentarily fashionable.

In the room great pots of arum lilies scented the air and there were fragments of Greek and Roman statuary which must have been found locally.

There was the head of what Larina suspected was a Gladiator, a vase which was broken and yet was so exquisitely beautiful in its proportions that it must be unique.

There were urns and plates, and the marble hand of a child which had existed for centuries long after its owner had grown up and died of old age.

It was all fascinating to look at, but now for the first time since she came to the Villa Larina did not notice her surroundings but sat thinking of the man who must be a part-owner of it.

Mr. Donaldson had said that the Villa belonged to the family, and the family meant Elvin, his three brothers, his sister and his mother.

How strange that they so seldom came here, she thought, and that Elvin had never seen this exquisite family property which she was sure would have filled him with delight.

How could he not have felt part of the life that was pulsating in the beautiful garden? Or part of the sea and the sky that was bluer and more translucent than any sky she had ever imagined?

Then, as if all the time her thoughts had been drawing her in that direction, she thought of Elvin's brother and how for one incredible moment she had thought as she saw him that he must be Apollo.

With the light of the setting sun on his face he had looked exactly as she had always imagined Apollo would look.

There had been a strength besides beauty about him. His clear-cut features, his deep-set eyes and his fair hair brushed back from a square forehead might have served as a model for any of the statues of Apollo that Larina had seen illustrated.

When they had reached the hall she looked at him and realised he had a resemblance to Elvin, or rather, because he was the elder, Elvin resembled him.

But Elvin had been thin, emaciated by his disease, while his brother seemed to glow with health and vigour.

"I had not thought that any man could be so handsome!" Larina told herself.

As he advanced towards her in the Temple, she had had an almost irresistible impulse to kneel at his feet, to worship as the Greeks had worshipped the giver of light.

She told herself that it was going to be difficult to talk to him naturally, to discuss commonplace things, to speak of his voyage from America and her own from London.

Then she told herself he would think it very strange if instead she spoke to him of his life on Olympus, of how he ruled the world by the power of his beauty.

'He would think me mad!' Larina reflected with a smile and knew she must be very careful, very careful indeed, in what she said to him.

# CHAPTER FIVE

Wynstan came down to breakfast and entered the Dining-Room with its fine plaques decorated with the heads of Roman Emperors which had been found amongst the foundations of the Villa.

The servants hurried to bring him coffee and food, and as he looked out at the sunshine he was glad not to be in New York.

He wondered how Harvey was faring and realised that yesterday had been Election day.

He could imagine the crowds, the turmoil, the noise, the violence, the heart-ache and the bitter disappointment of the unsuccessful candidate.

He had a feeling that, however optimistic Harvey might be, Theodore Roosevelt would be re-elected.

He had his enemies—at the same time people looked to him for stability and that was something that was going to count in this particular election.

However, if Harvey did lose, he could not ascribe it to any trouble that Larina had made for him.

Thinking of her, Wynstan could not imagine her making trouble for anyone.

He had thought as they sat at dinner last night that she was different from any woman he had ever met before.

It was not only her looks, which still made him think of the statue of Aphrodite, but also the way she behaved when she was alone with him.

Wynstan had realised, after he had changed and come downstairs to find her waiting in the Drawing-Room, that she was a lady and it was therefore an insult that they should have asked her to come to the Villa un-chaperoned.

But Harvey had been so convinced that she was a gold-digger, a brazen hussy who had got her claws into Elvin because he was rich, that Wynstan had not stopped to think that she might turn out to be very different from the image his brother had created.

Yet he thought it extraordinary that she had accepted Elvin's invitation. She could have refused to set out on the journey accompanied only by a Courier, or she might have insisted on bringing a Chaperon with her.

He did not realise that when he went to change before dinner Larina had thought much the same thing.

The question of a Chaperon had simply not arisen in her mind, when she expected she was meeting Elvin at the Villa.

She longed to see him, she had a deep affection for him; but she had never thought of him as a man such as her mother had warned her about, or in whose company she was well aware she should be strictly chaperoned.

But although she had thought of Wynstan as a god, he was still a man, still disturbingly masculine, and when twenty minutes later he came into the Drawing-Room wearing his evening-clothes she thought it would be impossible for any man to look more elegant or more attractive.

"I should not be here alone," she told herself. "Mama would be shocked!"

Then she thought that perhaps as Wynstan was an American he would not realise that she was defying the conventions of society.

"And even if I am," Larina asked herself, "what does it matter?"

They sat down to a delicious meal, for as Larina had already found, the Chef in the Villa was outstanding and his dishes were so novel and unusual that they were a delight in themselves.

Before Wynstan arrived, when she had been alone she had, of course, talked to the Italians who waited on her, who had explained to her the dishes and were delighted that she appreciated them.

She had learnt that Naples was famous for its spaghetti in all forms and that *Maccheroni alla Napoletana* was spaghetti served with sauce made from a special plum-shaped tomato and grated cheese.

But what Larina had enjoyed most had been the delicious fresh fish. The Italian Butler had told her that she must visit the fish-markets where she would see every variety from the little silver-blue anchovies to a gigantic octopus.

The Chef at the Villa cooked *trigla* or red mullet, superbly and also the *spigola* or sea bass of the Mediterranean which Larina learnt had no English equivalent.

Wynstan was offered grilled *tonna* or tuna fish, for breakfast which the cook had decorated with scampi.

He had just helped himself from a silver dish when Larina came in from the garden.

She was wearing one of the thin muslins she had brought from Paul Poiret. It was of a very soft green, the colour of the first buds of spring and her hair looked like the pale morning sun.

"You are early!" he exclaimed rising to his feet.

"I have been up for a long time," she answered in her musical voice. "I could not bear to miss . . . anything."

There was something in the way she spoke which made Wynstan look at her speculatively.

Then one of the servants pulled out a chair from the table and she seated herself opposite him. As she did so, he thought of how long they had talked last night.

He had found it a new experience to have a woman listening to him wide-eyed, as if he was the source of all wisdom, and without making any attempt to draw his attention to herself.

After the flirtatious enticements of Yvette Glencairn, who could not say 'good-evening' without suggesting a *double entendre* he found that Larina's grey eyes fixed on his face spurred him to an eloquence he did not know he possessed.

They talked, as was inevitable, of the Villa, of the Greeks who had built there and the Romans who came after them.

He told her how his grandfather had found the site quite by chance when he was looking for somewhere to retire; how he had become obsessed with the idea of re-building on the old foundations; and how every expert in Italy had come to Sorrento to advise him.

Larina listened wide-eyed.

Then when Wynstan told her how his grandfather had sought all over the country for the furniture, the pictures and pieces of statuary to decorate not only the house but also the garden, she had said as if it suddenly struck her:

"It must have been very expensive!"

Her words stopped Wynstan as effectively as if she had slammed a door in his face.

'So she is thinking of money!' he thought.

Because he had been carried away by a subject which interested him, he had revealed all too clearly that expense was of little importance where the family was concerned.

Harvey would have sneered at him for being so inept and because he felt he must somehow explain away what had already been said he replied:

"Labour is very cheap in Italy. It would naturally cost a great deal more today than it did then."

"Yes, of course," Larina said. "I was really thinking how fortunate it was that your grandfather in his wide search was able to buy so many ancient treasures which would otherwise have been lost, or perhaps deliberately destroyed by those who did not understand them."

There was a cynical smile on Wynstan's lips as he said:

"We appreciate them, and there are a number of us amongst whom the house and grounds must be divided."

He realised as he spoke that Larina was not listening, but following the train of her own thoughts.

"I have always longed to own a piece of Greek sculpture," she said. "Once I saw a marble foot in a shop window in London which I was certain was Greek, but it was too expensive and I could not afford it."

"Perhaps we can find you something while you are here," Wynstan replied. "In the obscure villages and in the poorer parts of Naples there are often treasures of which their owners have no idea of their value."

For a moment he thought Larina's eyes lit up. Then she said in a tone he did not understand:

"It is too . . . late now!"

They had talked after dinner until it was nearly midnight, and only the striking of the clock made Larina realise that perhaps she was being selfish.

"You must be tired," she said in consternation. "You have been travelling for days to come here and I should have suggested that we retire early."

Wynstan did not reply. He was tired not so much from the travelling as from the two nights he had spent in Paris.

He had in fact been feeling rather guilty after meeting Larina that he had been delayed by his own desire for enjoyment and therefore she had been alone in the Villa except for the servants.

She did not appear to have minded, but he could imagine that most women of his acquaintance would have been exceedingly annoyed at such cavalier treatment, even if they had not actually been frightened.

But Larina, he thought, seemed already a part of the Villa.

"Do you think that Elvin will arrive today?" she asked.

"He might," Wynstan answered cautiously. "Are you so impatient to see him?"

"Yes, I must see him . . . I must see him quickly!"

There was something in the way she spoke which made him look at her in surprise. Then leaving her breakfast unfinished she rose from the table and walked across the room to the window.

"Harvey must be right and she is having a baby," Wynstan told himself.

And yet as he looked at her slim figure with its small waist silhouetted against the sunshine, it seemed highly improbable.

It was not only her figure which perplexed him; there was something in her eyes and in the expression on her face which made him feel it was impossible she could be anything but pure and innocent.

'I am a fool to be taken in by her!' Wynstan thought and he went on with his breakfast.

It was difficult to think that with his experience of women he could be deceived by someone as young and unsophisticated as Larina. Yet he knew, if he was honest, he would have staked a fortune that she was what she appeared to be.

There was something untouched and innocent about her which made him once again think of Aphrodite.

At the same time he had to face facts: she was certainly in a state of agitation because Elvin had not arrived as she had expected.

He could not know that Larina looking out onto the garden was telling herself there were only two days left.

Time had slipped by so quickly ever since Mr. Donaldson had called on her in London. The excitement of the journey abroad and the enchantment of the Villa when she arrived had made her almost forget that the sands of time were running out.

Today was the 13th. There was tomorrow and then . . .

She drew in her breath.

It was difficult to know how Sir John could have been so precise, but there had been something in the way he spoke and the gravity of his manner which told her he was utterly sure of his facts.

She felt her heart give a frightened leap.

Suppose it stopped now at this very moment when she was looking at the brilliance of the flowers and the butterflies hovering above them?

Then she told herself she had two days more besides the rest of today in which to enjoy all this beauty and she must not spoil it by fear.

With an effort she turned and went back to the table.

"If Elvin said he would come . . . I know he will keep his

promise," she said, more as if she was speaking to herself than to Wynstan.

"What did he promise you?" he asked in a deliberately casual tone.

There was a moment's pause before Larina answered:

"That he would come to me . . . if I wanted him."

"And why do you want him so particularly?"

Wynstan did not look at her as he spoke but seemed intent on buttering a piece of bread.

There was a silence. Then at length Larina said:

"There is . . . something I have to tell . . . him."

"Would you not like to tell me? If it is a problem of any sort, I am sure I can solve it for you."

"No . . . no!" Larina cried sharply.

As Wynstan looked at her she added:

"Only Elvin will . . . understand. That is why I am so . . . anxious to see him."

Wynstan thought there was no point in pressing her at the moment.

Perhaps he might do so, but somehow it seemed unkind.

She seemed so young, such a child in some ways, that he could not bully her as Harvey would have done. Instead he felt certain that sooner or later he could charm her into telling him her secret.

"I was wondering whether you would like to come down to the jetty with me and see my motor-boat," he said in a different tone of voice.

"A motor-boat?" Larina exclaimed. "I have never seen one!"

"They do exist!" Wynstan said with a smile, "and this is a boat I had specially made for me."

He saw she was interested and went on:

"I was friends with Captain William Newman, who two years ago crossed the Atlantic from West to East in a boat which had the unusual name of '*Abiel, Abbot Low*'."

"I have never heard of him," Larina said.

"Perhaps the Americans were more excited about his achievement than the English," Wynstan said. "But it certainly made history since the boat was powered by a paraffin engine of a mere 12 h.p.!"

"And you have a boat like it?" Larina enquired.

"Not so big," he replied. "In fact mine is much smaller. Shall we go and look at it?"

"Oh, yes, I would love that! Will you wait while I get my hat?"

"Of course," he replied.

She ran from the room eagerly.

He looked after her with a puzzled expression in his eyes.

He supposed it was because he had had so little to do with young women that he found it difficult to understand her.

All his love-affairs had been with mature, sophisticated, social personalities who had enormous confidence in themselves and their attractions.

He knew that Larina was unsure of herself, and he found the way that she looked at him to see if she had said or done anything wrong was very appealing. She was very young!

And yet, their conversation last night had told him that she not only read a great deal but she also had a good mind.

He might have expected a banal, brainless conversation with a girl who was so young, or else a flirtatious coquettishness just because he was a man and she was a woman.

But Larina's mind, he found, was focused not on him, except in so far as he could instruct her, but on the mythology of which they talked and the gods and goddesses who seemed so much more real to her than human beings.

And yet, as she came running back to him, now holding a large straw hat in her hand, she had the excited eyes of a child being taken for a special treat.

Wynstan led the way through the garden and down the narrow steps which his grandfather had made in the cliff.

As they descended Larina could see below them a small rocky bay with an artificial breakwater and a jetty.

Tied up beside it was the motor-boat!

It was smaller than she had expected, feeling that anything to do with a motor must be large, and when they reached it Wynstan looked at it appreciatively.

It had a long, pointed bow she noticed, which she felt must contain the engine.

She could see the place where the driver stood in the centre of the boat and behind it was a small cabin which

Wynstan showed her contained a table with two cushioned benches on either side of it which were large enough, if necessary, to turn into sleeping-bunks.

"This is a 'Napier Minor', if you are interested," he said, "and the firm which makes them confidently believes that it will win the first cross-channel race which will take place this year."

"It looks almost too small to cross the Channel."

"It is easy to handle."

"Will you drive it yourself?" she asked in surprise.

"I have every intention of doing so," he replied. "I like to ride my own race-horses, drive my own motor-cars and be the engine-driver of my own train!"

Larina laughed.

"I believe every small boy wants to be a train-driver!"

She did not realise that the Vanderfelds did in fact own a private train and that Wynstan often drove it.

Because he realised that once again he had made a slip of the tongue, he drew her attention to the boat, showing her it was made of seasoned cypress on white oak timbers.

"And it has a paraffin engine?" she asked hoping she was saying the right thing.

"Just like the one that crossed the Atlantic."

"Can we go to sea in it?"

"That is exactly what I was going to suggest," Wynstan replied. "Where would you like to go? Pompeii?"

The colour rose in her cheeks with excitement.

"Could we really do that?"

"There is no reason why not," he answered, "and it would be far quicker than making the journey by road."

He smiled as he added:

"I have a feeling that like all tourists you are determined to see Pompeii before you leave Italy, and so we might as well combine business with pleasure."

Then they had climbed up the cliff and taken an open carriage to Pompeii.

"I should have thought that driving the boat and seeing Pompeii were both pleasure!" Larina replied.

"I have to try her out before I pay the bill."

"Papa always said it was stupid to pay for anything unless

one had made absolutely certain it was exactly what one had ordered."

"Your father was obviously very sensible," Wynstan approved.

He had taken his place at the wheel of the boat having started up the engine and cast off the ropes which tied it to the jetty.

Larina stood beside him as slowly he began to ease the vessel into the centre of the small bay and through the opening in the breakwater.

"This is exciting—very exciting!" Larina cried. "I never thought I would travel in a motor-boat! How fast can we go?"

She thought as she spoke that this was another thing of which her father would have disapproved because it meant speed.

She was sure he would have been quite content to row a little way from the cliffs and row back again, but instead they were out in the open sea and Larina could see the Gulf of Naples from a new angle.

The white houses, the cliff hamlets, the towers of the Churches, the vine-covered hills were an enchantment it was impossible to put into words.

Then there was Mt. Vesuvius dominating the horizon, somehow sinister even though it was bathed in sunshine.

There was a small plume of smoke rising from its cone and as she looked at it apprehensively Wynstan, as if he read her thoughts, asked:

"Are you nervous of encountering the same fearful catastrophe that took place in 79 A.D.?"

"I have read about it," Larina said, "but that is very different from seeing the place where it actually happened."

She was to think this again when an hour later they had entered the Port of Torre Annunziata and moored the motor-boat.

Then they had climbed up the cliff and taken an open carriage to Pompeii.

As they reached the entrance Wynstan waved away the guides who surged eagerly towards them.

"I came here so often when I was a boy," he said. "I want

to see if I can remember everything about it. Enough at any rate, to keep you interested!"

"I do not want to miss anything!" Larina answered and Wynstan laughed.

They moved into the Forum where among the broken pillars he told her how Pompeii had been a prosperous industrial and trading centre.

It had sided with the Italic towns against the Romans and withstood a siege of nine years. But after the Pompeians had opened their gates because they could no longer go on fighting, a colony of Roman veterans had arrived in the town and it had become increasingly Romanized.

"You said it was industrial," Larina said. "What did they make?"

"It sounds amusing today," Wynstan replied, "but one particular export of the Pompeians was a popular brand of fish-sauce. Their wine trade was very important, and later of course like Herculaneum it became a resort for rich Romans."

They walked on, looking at the Temples near the Forum, at the *Building of Eumachia* who had been a priestess, and came to the Gladiators' Barracks.

"In these barracks," Wynstan said, "they found evidence of sixty-three people who had lost their lives there. One was a woman whose rich jewellery suggested that she was there on a visit to her Gladiator lover!"

"It must have been very frightening!" Larina said in a low voice.

"The earth tremors had been taking place for some time," Wynstan went on, "then on August 22nd they ceased. The sky was blue and cloudless but the air had a strange foreboding silence."

Larina shivered.

There was something eerie in thinking of the people going about their ordinary business and not realising what was going to happen to them.

"The morning of the 24th was very hot," Wynstan continued, "the sky was clear and everyone's fears had subsided."

He looked round the Amphitheatre, which could hold

twenty thousand spectators, to which they had walked while he was talking.

"Everyone was preparing for luncheon when a severe earth-tremor was followed by what seemed like a terrific clap of thunder."

He looked up.

"Everyone stopped what they were doing and turned to look at Vesuvius. The top of the mountain had literally burst open and was pouring forth a glowing fire."

Larina looked apprehensively at the thin column of smoke rising against the sky.

Wynstan's story was so dramatic that she almost felt it might change into fire at any moment.

"A huge mushroom-shaped cloud formed," he went on. "Then there was a series of explosions which hurled huge boulders high into the sky."

He paused before he continued:

"Suddenly it began to rain and mixed with the rain were cinders, pumicestones, lumps of large rock and dust which quickly turned to mud. The birds fell to the earth. In a matter of minutes the sun was obscured and the bright day had turned into the blackest night."

He looked out onto the Gulf.

"The sea was in a turmoil alternately retreating then flooding in with huge waves which pounded against the coast."

"What did the people do?" Larina enquired.

"I imagine they must have begun to run screaming from the town. There were twenty thousand of them, but more than two thousand are known to have lost their lives, under the hail of pumicestone, mud, cinders and ashes, which buried the town with such astounding rapidity."

"I cannot bear to think the people had no time to escape," Larina cried.

"I imagine that a great many more died than the archaeologists actually found inside Pompeii," Wynstan replied.

"Perhaps it was a quick way to . . . die," she said in a low voice. "After the first moments of terror they could have known . . . nothing about it."

"I think it is a horrible way to die!" Wynstan said firmly.

"When my time comes I want, like the Greeks, to die in the sun."

"That is what I want too."

There was something almost violent in her tone of voice which made him look at her sharply.

"You funny little thing! It has really upset you," he said in a kind voice. "I thought you liked excavating the past."

"It is . . . different when it concerns buildings, Temples, the statues of gods who are . . . immortal." Larina answered. "But these were ordinary people and they were not expecting death. So it seems somehow horribly intrusive to stare with curiosity at where they died.

"When one dies, can it matter where or how?" Wynstan asked.

"I do not . . . know," Larina replied. "But it is . . . frightening to think of them . . . screaming and fighting to . . . live!"

There was such genuine horror in her voice and in the expression in her eyes, that Wynstan put his arm through hers and said:

"Let us be more cheerful. It all happened a long time ago and neither you nor I are going to die for a very long time. Come and look at the Temple of Jupiter, and tell me if you can imagine it filled with spectators for the shows which were held there before the Amphitheatre was built."

He knew she made an effort to answer him as she replied:

"From what I have read about the Roman shows I should not have thought they were very suitable for a Temple!"

Wynstan laughed.

"You are right! But the Romans were a very practical people with little imagination and they developed a religion which corresponded with their needs."

"I tried . . . when I was journeying here," Larina said, "to think about the Romans. Instead I found myself so much more concerned with the Greeks."

'And one in particular,' she added secretly to herself, 'called Apollo.'

"I always find myself doing the same thing," Wynstan agreed. "The Romans felt no mystic necessity to love and worship the superhuman powers of the gods as they conceived them. At the same time Jupiter did have a certain majesty about him."

"I think he was cruel!" Larina argued. "His function was to warn men, to punish them, and for this purpose he possessed three thunder-bolts!"

"The Romans were a hard-fighting, cruel people," Wynstan replied. "Jupiter was a warrior-god and he expected to be obeyed."

Larina did not answer him. They moved away from the Temple of Jupiter and wandered down the narrow streets, which had once teemed with people but now contained only the empty shells of their houses.

They saw the House of the Lyre Player, then began to wend their way gradually towards the exit.

"I am thinking of what you said about the Romans being cruel," Larina said. "I think the reason was that they did not worship beauty and their goddesses were not like those of Greece."

"That is true!" Wynstan agreed. "And they were cruel even to their Vestal Virgins. They took vows of absolute chastity but those who broke them were punished by being whipped to death."

"Oh, no!" Larina exclaimed involuntarily.

"Later this was modified," he went on. "They were whipped and then walled-up alive in a tomb which was sealed off with a few provisions deposited in it."

"No wonder people were afraid of the Romans."

"You need not worry about the Vestal Virgins too much," Wynstan smiled. "During the course of eleven centuries only twenty broke their vows and suffered such punishment. But if a Vestal let the sacred fire go out she was whipped!"

"Let us talk instead about beautiful gods of the Greeks," Larina begged, "who Homer said 'tasted a happiness which lasted as long as their eternal lives'."

"One day you must obviously visit Greece."

Wynstan saw a strange expression come over Larina's face as he spoke and did not understand it.

He was wondering if she was thinking that she could not afford the journey, but somehow he sensed it was something more than that.

She did not answer and he did not want to question her.

They drove back to Torre Annunziata, but instead of getting into the boat Wynstan led Larina to a small restaurant at the side of the Quay.

There were tables outside in the sunshine and waiters hurried to attend to them as soon as they sat down.

"What would you like to eat?" he asked.

"Please order for me," Larina begged.

He chose *antipasto* of smoked ham with fresh figs to start with. After that they had *Zuppa de pesce* the famous fish-soup of Southern Italy which he told Larina was a kind of *bouillabaisse* with differing ingredients from season to season.

Afterwards there was *Abbacchio al torno*—a typical Roman dish of suckling lamb seasoned with rosemary and garlic and roasted in the oven.

"I cannot eat any more!" Larina protested when she was begged to try other special Neapolitan delicacies.

But the waiter insisted that she finish her meal with a peeled peach in a glass of white wine, and she was not allowed to refuse the coffee because Wynstan told her that the coffee of Naples was the best in the world!

They drank a local wine, but Larina was disappointed to hear it was not *Vesuvino* which was grown on the slopes of Vesuvius.

"I am afraid that has deteriorated with time," Wynstan explained, "like *Falerno* which is still produced in the Phlegragan Fields. It was much praised in antiquity but I have come to believe that the classic taste was different from mine!"

He filled her glass as he said:

"This is *Epomea* which comes from the Isle of Ischia."

It was, Larina thought, delicious. Bright yellow in colour, it seemed to have captured some of the sunshine all around them.

They sat talking for a long time after their luncheon was finished until they finally got back into the motor-boat and started for home.

"Tomorrow I will take you to Ischia," Wynstan said. "It is one of my favourite islands, and of course another day we must visit Capri."

"That would be lovely!" Larina answered.

At the same time she wondered if she would ever see Capri.

She had the feeling that she was on an express train and it was going faster and faster but there was nothing she could do to stop it.

"I must not think of what lies ahead," she told herself. "I must live every moment, every second. I must cram everything into what time is left to me."

She knew she was growing more and more afraid and when she returned to the Villa and found that Elvin had not arrived she felt a moment of panic and had to fight for self-control.

Because Wynstan had been so kind to her Larina considered the idea of telling him the truth. Then she knew it was impossible to speak of her death to anyone except Elvin.

No-one else would understand. Wynstan would commiserate with her. He might also say it was impossible and try to give her false hope, and that would be even worse.

She would rather face the truth and be prepared.

When she had gone to bed last night she had prayed for a long time, not that she might live, but that she might be brave.

"No-one who is a Christian should be afraid of dying," she told herself severely.

But it was hard to practise what she knew was logical when death was coming nearer and nearer.

Everything that had ever frightened her about death, like the head of a skeleton, the trappings of a funeral, the dark veils and crepe bands with which mourners paraded their grief seemed to flutter beside her as if they were birds of ill-omen.

Then she told herself there would be no-one to mourn her and no-one to assume black in her memory.

Perhaps she would die in the sun as Wynstan wished to do, and she knew that would be the perfect way for her 'spirit to take wings'.

And if Elvin was beside her, holding her hand, she would not be afraid.

Then she would imagine she was flying away into the blue of the sky and into the arms of Apollo who would hold her close. When there was no longer any life, there would be no fear either.

"What are you thinking about?" Wynstan asked suddenly, breaking in on her thoughts.

They were sitting outside the Villa on the terrace where the servants had brought them cool drinks and the fragrance of the flowers was almost overwhelming.

"I was thinking . . . of death!" Larina said without choosing her words.

"Pompeii has upset you," he said. "Forget about it. Tomorrow you will see the loveliness of Ischia. It too has a volcanic mountain, but it has never been known to erupt. Instead it has luxuriant vineyards, olive groves, pine forests and the chestnut trees are very beautiful. We will sit and drink the island's delicious wine and talk about life."

"That would be . . . lovely!" Larina said.

But he felt there was still a shadow in her grey eyes. Bending towards her he said in a voice which women always found irresistible:

"Will you not tell me what worries you?"

Larina shook her head.

"I am waiting for . . . Elvin."

"Supposing, after all, Elvin cannot come?"

He saw that she was startled and went on choosing his words with care:

"He may have been taken ill on the journey. He may have found it too much for him. It is a long way for him to travel."

"Yes, of course, I thought of that. But Mr. Donaldson said he had had a cable from him saying he would definitely meet me here."

"And the idea pleased you?"

"It was what I wanted more than anything else in the world—to be with Elvin at this moment."

"Why particularly at this moment?"

Larina did not answer and after a moment Wynstan said:

"I asked you a question, Larina. Why particularly at this moment?"

There was a pause, then she said:

"Did I say that? I was thinking of his being here . . . of our being together. That is what I meant."

Wynstan had the feeling she was not telling him the truth.

Suddenly Larina said in a voice that was tense and agitated:

"He must come! If anything had prevented him he would have sent a cable! We should have heard by now! Surely he will arrive tomorrow?"

There was a note of tension, of despair in her voice and Wynstan looked at her in a puzzled manner.

Even if she were having Elvin's child, why should there be so much urgency for her to see him?

If she meant him to marry her, there was plenty of time before there was any chance of the child being born.

And if it was not a baby which was troubling her, then what could it be?

Because he could see she was not far from tears he said soothingly:

"Perhaps we shall have news of Elvin tomorrow, but there is nothing we can do just now."

"No, of course not," Larina said with an effort. "I am being foolish! It is just that I was . . . so looking forward to seeing him . . . I felt you would understand."

Wynstan told himself he did not understand, but there was no point at the moment in saying so.

He felt he was being rather dilatory in not pressing Larina further, in not finding out about Elvin's letters, and most of all about what she wished to tell his brother.

But he found it difficult deliberately to sweep away the happiness in her face and to see it replaced by an expression to which he could not put a name, but which seemed to him to be something near terror.

As he talked quietly to her of other things, gradually he realised that Larina had recovered her composure, and when they both went to change for dinner she was laughing.

Dinner was once again a superb meal. They had finished it and moved into the Drawing-Room where Wynstan began to look for some photographs to show Larina of what the Villa had looked like before his grandfather started to rebuild it.

As he was searching for them there was suddenly the sound outside of a carriage and horses.

Wynstan went to the window which overlooked the front of the house and saw a large, private brougham had drawn up at the front door. Out of it were getting several people, among them a woman in an evening-gown.

"Who is it?" Larina asked. "Could it be Elvin?"

"No," Wynstan replied. "It is visitors. I do not think they should find you here. It would be difficult to explain why you have no Chaperon."

Larina looked at him and said quickly:

"Yes, you are right! I will go upstairs."

As she spoke Wynstan realised that the guests, whoever they might be, had already been let into the house by the servants.

He had given no instructions to turn callers away and the Italians, who were always hospitable, would show anyone who arrived into the Drawing-Room.

"You will be seen," he said to Larina. "Go by the garden—I will get rid of them quickly!"

Without a word Larina ran across the room and out of the open window into the garden.

The stars had come out while they were talking, the moon was climbing up the sky, and it was not dark.

She had only to walk along the terrace to find another door into the Villa, but she stopped and hesitated.

Then she started up the path which climbed to the Temple.

When she was free of the lights of the house she stopped again to move from the steps, to amongst the azaleas. She sat down on the ground so that the shrubs reached above her head.

Through the flowers she could see the lights pouring from the windows of the Drawing-Room onto the terrace and she wondered if she would catch a glimpse of Wynstan's guests.

She was curious—very curious!


Wynstan waiting in the Drawing-Room heard voices coming down the corridor. Then the first person to enter the room was the Contessa Spinello whom he had known in Rome and had also met in Monte Carlo the previous year.

She was dark, vivacious, very lovely, and with diamonds glittering round her neck and in her ears she seemed to sparkle as she ran across the room towards him and raised her face to his.

"Wynstan—it is true!" she cried in her fascinating broken English. "I heard you had arrived, but I did not believe it!"

"It is delightful to see you Nicole," Wynstan answered, "but who told you I was here?"

"Do you not suppose that the whole of Sorrento is talking about the Vanderfelds having opened their Villa again after so many years? And that a Vanderfeld *'molto bello'* had arrived. Who could that be but you?"

"Who indeed?" Wynstan replied with an amused smile.

He held out his hand to her brother who with two other men had followed the Contessa into the room.

"How are you, Antonio?" he asked. "It is nice to see you again."

"I did not believe it, but I hoped you were here," Antonio answered. "When we bought a Villa on the other side of Sorrento three years ago, we were told that the Vanderfelds never visited such an unfashionable neighbourhood!"

"It must be fashionable if you are living here!" Wynstan said.

"Did I not tell you that he always says the right thing?" the Contessa enquired of the two other men who were waiting to be introduced, and who were both Italians.

Wynstan shook hands with them, then the Contessa said:

"You must come and visit us immediately, Wynstan. What about dinner tomorrow? Chuck is arriving from Rome—you remember Chuck? You were at college with him."

"Chuck Kennedy? Of course I remember," Wynstan agreed. "But I will have to let you know about dinner."

"If not tomorrow—the next night," the Contessa insisted. "I will not take no for an answer! I want you to see our delightful Villa, although naturally it does not compare with yours!"

"How is your motor-boat, Antonio?" Wynstan enquired. "I have just had my new 'Napier Minor' delivered."

"What is it like?" Antonio enquired.

"I tried it out today and it seemed excellent!" Wynstan replied.

"Now stop talking about motor-boats, both of you," the Contessa ordered, "and talk about me! Wynstan is the love of my life and I cannot bear his predilection for mechanical objects!"

"Shall I tell you you are looking more beautiful than ever?" Wynstan enquired. "I expect that is what you really want to hear."

"But of course I do!" she smiled at him. "No-one can say such nice things as you, and even though they are insincere one believes them."

"Why should you doubt my sincerity?" Wynstan asked.

"Because there is a little twist to your lips, a look in your eyes, that belies everything you say," the Contessa replied. "Nevertheless I believe what I want to believe—it makes me happy!"

"That is a very good philosophy," one of the Italians remarked. "I wish I could do the same."

"Try it," the Contessa replied.

She flashed a flirtatious glance over her shoulder and walked through the open window out onto the terrace.

"Oh—your garden!" she exclaimed. "We have a dozen gardeners struggling to create one for our Villa, but it will never look like this!"

Wynstan followed her out and now Larina could see them standing in the light from the room behind them.

She could see the fashionable outline of the woman's gown, the jewels sparkling round her neck and on her wrists and it was impossible not to notice the way she turned her face enticingly towards Wynstan's.

Then the Contessa glanced back to see that her brother and his friends had not followed her, and slipping her arm through Wynstan's she drew him away from the open window along the terrace and nearer to where Larina was hiding.

"I have missed you, Wynstan," she said in a soft tone. "I had thought you might have come to Rome this winter. As you did not, I have been praying we would meet in Monte Carlo, but again you disappointed me!"

"You must forgive me," Wynstan said, "'but I have been on a visit to India and actually arrived back in America only a week or so ago."

"Then you came here. Why?"

"I had a reason," Wynstan replied evasively, "and now the Villa has been opened up again I am sorry I have not been here before."

"But you will come again—and anyway, you are here now!" the Contessa answered. "We must see a lot of each other."

"Your husband is with you?" Wynstan enquired.

"He is in Florence," the Contessa replied. "That is what makes it so perfect!"

She lifted her face to Wynstan's and Larina watching knew that she expected him to kiss her.

She was sitting amongst the azaleas spellbound by what was happening below her.

She had not imagined that two people could look so attractive, Wynstan with his broad shoulders and narrow hips like the god she thought he resembled, and the Contessa with her raven-black hair which grew in a widow's-peak on her oval forehead.

Her dark eyes seemed to flash in the darkness and Larina saw she had long, pointed fingers as she placed them on Wynstan's shoulder and pressed herself against him.

He glanced towards the Drawing-Room window.

"We must go back."

"Why?" the Contessa asked. "Antonio knows I want to be with you. I love you, Wynstan—I have never forgotten the happiness we found together! Have you?"

"No, of course not."

"You are tired of me," the Contessa said. "Is there someone else? But that is a stupid question!"

She made a sound of exasperation and went on:

"There is always somebody else where you are concerned. Always, always! And yet I believed you could come back to me because our love must have meant as much to you as it did to me."

"You are very beautiful and very attractive," Wynstan

said, "but, Nicole, you cannot expect me to believe there have not been a dozen men to take my place."

"Dozens!" the Contessa said lightly, "but none of them were you—none of them had that power to excite me in the way you did."

"You flatter me!" Wynstan said and there was a note of laughter in his voice.

Then as if she was tired of talking the Contessa put her arms round his neck and drew his head down to hers.

He kissed her. It was a long kiss.

Then firmly, with his arm around her shoulders, Wynstan drew her back towards the Drawing-Room and in through the lighted window.

Larina realised she was holding her breath.

She had never before seen two people kissing each other passionately. She had never seen a man holding a woman so that they were locked together by love.

It gave her a strange feeling within her breast—a feeling she did not understand.

Yet there had been something in the angle of Wynstan's head, the manner his lips had met the Contessa's, the closeness of their bodies against each other, which made her feel she watched something momentous taking place.

But the Contessa was married!

Then Larina told herself this was the way fashionable people behaved. She had read about it, she had heard people talk of the King's flirtations and the behaviour of the 'Marlborough House Set'.

But reading and listening were very different from seeing, and in particular from watching Wynstan, with whom she had spent the day, kiss somebody so lovely and attractive as the woman who had been with him on the terrace.

It was no concern of hers!

"No-one will ever kiss me like that!" Larina whispered and it was a cry of despair.

# CHAPTER SIX

Larina waited a moment or two and then rose from amongst the azaleas to step down the path.

Running across the terrace she entered the Villa by a garden door which led her into a passage off the Hall.

Here there was another staircase leading to the first floor. She hurried up it and into her bed-room, and closed the door.

For the first time since she had been at the Villa she did not pull back the curtains to look out over the sea at the lights of Naples twinkling in the distance or those which glowed round the bay wherever there was a fishing-village or a house.

Instead she undressed and got into bed.

Every night since she had come to the Villa she had been thrilled by the comfort and luxury of her bed-room.

It not only had a magnificent view from the balcony from where she could look out in the day-time, but it also was far more luxurious than anything she had ever known in her life before.

There was a bathroom adjoining where the bath was sunk in the floor as had been the custom in Roman times.

It was very American, she knew, to have a bathroom attached to every main bed-room in the house and when she sat in her marble bath with its colourful tiles copied from those which must have decorated the original Villa, she felt herself carried back in time.

She would pretend she was the wife of a Roman Senator, or perhaps his daughter, and that waiting outside was all the pomp and glitter which had been characteristic of the Romans wherever they were.

But tonight all Larina wanted was to creep into bed and in the darkness tell herself that the sooner she went to sleep the better!

She wanted to see Wynstan again, she wanted desperately to go on talking to him, to be with him alone as they had been before the Italian beauty with her glittering diamonds had arrived.

Yet at the same time she could not bear to see him, knowing he had just kissed the lovely Nicole and he would be thinking of her.

She could not understand her own feelings; she only knew that the strange emotion in her breast, which she had felt as she had watched him kissing Nicole, had now become a vivid pain—a pain which was so intense that she wondered for a moment if she was on the point of dying.

Even as she thought of it she longed to run downstairs, throw herself into Wynstan's arms and ask him to hold her closely.

How could she make him understand that she needed his strength and she wanted him to give her courage?

Then she told herself he would only despise her for being a coward.

He had laughed at her today when she had been upset in Pompeii. He had not understood that to think of the Pompeians choking to death under the black pall of dust and pumicestone had made her afraid that was how she would feel when she came to die.

Suppose she had to endure the horror of choking, of

suffocating as life left her body? Or feeling helpless, terror-struck, and having nowhere to turn for comfort?

How could she tell Wynstan of such things? She felt that close proximity with someone who was about to die would bore, if it did not disgust him.

Elvin was different. Elvin had lived so long with the thought of death that he would understand. He would be able to make her believe that it did not matter: that it was only the release of the spirit from the body and one was much happier once one was free.

"I want to believe . . . I want to believe!" Larina whispered in the darkness.

Then she found it difficult to keep her mind on death when all she could see was Wynstan kissing Nicole, his arms enfolding her, his head bent to hers.

"Perhaps I could ask Wynstan to kiss me once before I die," Larina said to herself and wondered if he would be shocked as well as surprised.

She had always believed that a woman did not ask a man to kiss her, and yet Nicole had put her arms around his neck and drawn his lips down to hers.

What had she felt? Had it been a sort of rapture, Larina wondered, which she herself had never experienced?

She had been in bed a long time when she heard voices outside and the sound of a carriage driving away.

They had gone! It was not very late and perhaps Wynstan would be expecting her to return to the Drawing-Room.

She could not bear to see him, not tonight with his lips still warm from Nicole's.

She found herself listening. The Villa was very quiet. She wondered where Wynstan was; whether perhaps he had left with his friends and gone to spend the rest of the evening with them.

Then as she lay there tense, her mind chaotic with feelings she did not understand but which were nevertheless very intense, she heard him coming along the passage.

His room was on the other side of the house and therefore he must be coming to her.

She held her breath.

There was a tap on the door.

"Who is . . . it?" she asked, although she knew the answer.

"Are you all right, Larina?"

"Yes . . . quite!"

"Then sleep well! Goodnight!"

"Good . . . night!"

Her voice was hardly loud enough for him to hear it. Then as she heard his footsteps going back towards his own room she started to cry.

She had not cried since her mother died. She had not shed a tear since she had known that she too must die.

Now she cried helplessly and desperately for herself, because her life was nearly at an end and because she would never know love.

She cried until her pillow was wet with tears and she felt in the darkness that everyone had forsaken her: Elvin, Wynstan and . . . Apollo.


Wynstan had been quite sure that Larina would go to her bed-room as she had said she would.

At the same time he did not wish to linger in the garden with Nicole.

They had enjoyed a wild, tempestuous, fiery affair in Rome the previous year. But before he left he had realised that the flames were dying down and as usual he was growing bored and a little impatient.

He could never explain to himself why a woman who had first seemed so desirable should suddenly begin to pall.

The little mannerisms which at first he had found fascinating became irritants; he knew what she was going to say before she said it. As always in his *affaires de coeur* he ceased to be the hunter and became the hunted.

Nicole had been no exception.

The moment she felt he was cooling off she pursued him relentlessly, and he found it more and more difficult to escape from her demands, to avoid finding himself isolated with her even in the midst of the gay, over-hospitable Roman society.

If he accepted an invitation to other friends, Nicole always managed to be there, and somehow it was inevitable, because she arranged it, that he had to take her home.

Which meant there was no escape from her clinging arms and her demanding lips.

The Count, who had interests of his own, was seldom at home. He had properties in the north of Italy where he preferred to spend most of his time.

Nicole made it very clear that the only tie which kept them together was the fact that they were Catholics and divorce was impossible.

The last person Wynstan had expected to see, or indeed wanted to see in Sorrento, was Nicole, and he had no intention of accepting her pressing invitations or of inviting her to the Villa.

That was not to ensure that she would not invite herself! He thought irritably there was nothing more tiresome than a woman who would not admit that a light-hearted affair was finished and there was no chance of resuscitating it.

Wynstan sighed as he realised he would have to be firm and make it very clear that he had no intention of being any longer at her beck and call.

There had been a few occasions in the past when he was forced to be ruthless, but usually the women he had loved became friends and he liked the sort of friendship which could mellow with the years into something very precious.

But he knew that Nicole would never come into that category, and he told himself that when he wrote her a note tomorrow saying that he could not accept her invitation to dinner, he would make her understand, once and for all, that it was the end of their association.

His thoughts sent him to Larina.

It had not been polite to ask her to leave so that she should not meet his friends, but he knew that Nicole would address him by his correct name, which would involve him in explanations that he had no wish to make at the moment.

Always at the back of his mind was Harvey's contention that Larina was out for money.

There was no doubt that she was desperate to see Elvin, and whether it was to make him marry her or to provide for her, it would be a mistake to let her know exactly how much Elvin was worth.

It seemed impossible to think of Larina as being concerned about money.

Yet from what she had told him in the course of their conversations Wynstan was aware that she and her mother had been living in poor circumstances.

She had explained that they were in Dr. Heinrich's Sanatorium, which was extremely expensive, only because he had taken them on special terms because her father had been a Doctor.

Wynstan knew London well enough to know that Eaton Terrace was a cheap neighbourhood from a residential point of view.

At the same time he had no wish to hurt Larina and he felt she might have felt insulted at being pushed out into the garden and having to go upstairs to sit in her bed-room while he entertained his friends.

When they had left he thought perhaps she might have gone to the Temple.

The moonlight was silver on the garden as Wynstan walked up the stone paths that were turned to a translucent grey.

The moon not only illuminated the world with a strange mystic beauty, but appeared to bring with it a feeling of quiet and of stillness which Wynstan felt had a message for him.

It was the same stillness he had felt the moment after Elvin had died.

It had been in the morning and he had been with his brother alone.

He had gone in to speak to Elvin. Then when he had risen to leave him, Elvin had put out his thin hand.

"Stay with me, Wynstan."

"Of course."

Wynstan sat down beside him on the side of his bed.

"I want you to be with me. You have always understood."

"I have always tried to," Wynstan answered.

The words he was saying meant nothing. He had known as he took Elvin's cold hand that he was dying and there was nothing he could do about it.

He made no attempt to call anyone. The nurses were only just outside, the Doctor could be reached in a few minutes. But he knew with a perception that was always there where Elvin was concerned that it was a waste of time.

They were together with a closeness they had known ever since they were children and as Elvin's fingers tightened on his hand, Wynstan knew that this was the end.

Elvin's eyes were closed. Then suddenly he opened them and there was a light in them.

"It is . . . wonderful . . . to be . . . free!" he said. "Tell . . . "

His voice died away, his eyes closed and his fingers relaxed.

Wynstan sat very still.

For a moment it seemed to him there was something moving in the room almost like a flutter of wings. Then there was only the stillness and a silence so absolute that he thought he could hear his own heart beating.

He had not been able to speak of those last moments with Elvin to anyone, not even to his mother.

He had sat for a long time on the bed thinking of Elvin, but knowing he was no longer there and the body he had left behind was unimportant.

It was with a superhuman effort, because he knew he had to face the world again, that he had risen to tell the nurses that their patient no longer had any need of their services.

Then he had gone out of the house to walk alone in Central Park.

He forced himself when he returned not to grieve for Elvin. No-one who loved him could want him to go on living with his illness destroying him, making every breath he drew difficult and laboured.

And Wynstan knew too although he could never speak of it to anyone, that Elvin was not dead.

Now as he reached the Temple Wynstan thought how Elvin would have loved the beauty of the moonlight and the statue of Aphrodite.

She seemed almost to be alive as she stood there on her pedestal with the lilies at her feet and her head turned to look out over the sea below.

Wynstan found himself remembering how when he had come up to the Temple on his arrival, Larina had been standing in much the same pose, her head turned away from him, her hair vivid with tongues of fire from the setting sun.

He remembered that strange feeling when for one second he had thought she must be Aphrodite herself.

He thought now it was the impression of slim, untouched virginity about both Larina and Aphrodite which made them seem alike.

He thought too, that when he had stared at the statue as a boy he had always been sure that the goddess had grey eyes, a small straight nose, and curved lips that were not sensuous but sensitive.

"The goddess of love!" Wynstan said aloud, then abruptly he turned and went back to the Villa.

He had gone to the Drawing-Room, hoping that perhaps Larina had come downstairs once she heard his friends leaving, but the room was empty!

So he went to her bed-room to make quite certain that she was there and safely in bed.

He thought her voice trembled when she answered him. Then he told himself that doubtless she had been half-asleep and he had woken her.

As he walked to his own room, Wynstan wondered, as he had wondered all day, what was the secret that Larina was hiding which she would convey only to Elvin.

Because she felt she had wasted so much of her precious time in going to bed early and in tears Larina rose very early.

The dawn was only just breaking as she drew back the curtains of her bed-room and she decided that she must see it from the Temple perhaps for the last time.

Tomorrow was the day she would die and she had no way of knowing whether it would be early in the morning or late in the evening and therefore she was determined that today must not be wasted.

She looked at herself in the mirror and realised she must wash away the traces of the tears she had shed the night before, in case Wynstan should question her.

In the morning light she faced the fact frankly that some of her unhappiness had been due to the fact that she had seen him kissing the Italian and she thought how humiliating it would be if he ever guessed what had upset her.

"He is far more perceptive," she told herself, "'than I imagined a man could ever be."

So often when they were talking he would be aware of what she was going to say almost before she said it, and when she could not put what she felt or thought into words he would do it for her. He never misunderstood what had been her intention.

As she finished dressing she felt herself longing with a physical yearning to see him again.

There was so little time left for her to be with him! Only today and perhaps part of tomorrow. Then she would be gone and he would go back to America and never think of her again.

Because she realised her tears the night before had left her pale with shadows under her eyes she chose the brightest of her summer gowns which she had bought at Peter Robinson.

It was a muslin of tiny pink and white stripes, trimmed round the neck and over the shoulders with white *broderie anglaise* which also edged the two frills of the skirt.

It made her look very young, like a rose which was not yet in bloom. But Larina had no time to spare on her reflection.

She swept her hair back from her forehead in the fashion which Charles Gibson sketched so attractively. Then she opened her bed-room door and tip-toed down the stairs so as not to wake Wynstan if he was still asleep.

She let herself out of the Villa and climbed to the Temple.

The dawn was just breaking as she reached it, and now Aphrodite's beauty was not the shimmering silver that Wynstan had seen the night before but warm, almost flesh-coloured, in the first glow of the sun.

Larina leant over the balustrade to see the sea slowly turning from grey to emerald, the sky from blue to crimson.

It was so lovely that she drew in her breath and felt for a

moment as if she had wings and could fly out to greet the sun-god when he appeared over the horizon.

She found herself repeating the last words of a poem she had read, by Pindar.

> *"We are all shadows. But when the shining*
> *comes from the hands of God,*
> *Then the heavenly light falls on man, and*
> *life is all sweetness."*

"The heavenly light!" Larina repeated to herself and wanted to hold out her arms towards it, to feel it enfolding her as if it was in fact a man and she was in Apollo's arms.

Apollo's or Wynstan's?

The question came to her and she knew for the moment it was impossible to divide them. They were one and the same and she wanted their closeness.

Larina had nearly finished her breakfast when Wynstan joined her.

"Good-morning!" he smiled. "The servants told me you were up very early. You put me to shame!"

"You slept well?"

"If I need an excuse, I read until very late," he answered. "I found a book which I think will interest you, and I will tell you about it when we are at Ischia."

"We are going there for lunch?"

"That is what I planned," Wynstan answered, "but I thought as we are early this morning, we would take the boat straight there across the open bay instead of keeping under the shelter of the coast. You wanted to see how fast she would go, and it is something I want to know myself."

"That sounds exciting!" Larina exclaimed.

Wynstan turned to the servant.

"Has the mechanic seen to the motor-boat?"

"*Si, Signor,* he is down there now."

"Good!" Wynstan answered. "I want to talk to him."

He rose to his feet saying to Larina:

"Join me when you are ready. There is no hurry; I have one or two things I want to discuss with my mechanic."

Larina fetched her hat and when she was in her bed-room she wondered if they were going out to sea whether she would need a coat. Then she told herself it was already warm and looked like being a hot day.

She put on the big straw, having changed the ribbons from the green one which had encircled the crown yesterday to a pink one which matched the dress she was wearing.

"I expect the wind will blow it away if we go very fast," she told herself practically, "but I will wear it to go down to the Quay."

She knew it was becoming, and she had thought when she wore it yesterday as they walked around Pompeii there had been a look of unmistakable admiration in Wynstan's eyes.

Then she felt with a little drop of her heart that it was unlikely he would admire her since she was fair while the woman he had kissed last night was dark.

"I am sure fair men like dark women," she told herself despondently, then shook herself mentally.

'At least I will be alone with him all day today,' she thought. 'After that will it matter to me who he is with?'

Because she had no wish to waste any time she ran down the stairs and out into the garden.

The bees were already busy amongst the flowers, the but-terflies seemed brighter than ever, as she started the descent down the cliff.

She could see Wynstan below her talking to the mechanic and the motor-boat gleaming white in the water.

As she reached them Wynstan turned to smile at her.

"Everything is ready," he said, "and now we must see what speed-records we can break!"

"Can we really break one?"

"We can try," Wynstan replied. "At the same time if we come back and say we have done a hundred miles per hour no-one will believe us!"

"I am sure that would be impossible!" Larina smiled.

They moved slowly out of the little harbour and Wynstan headed out to sea.

He stood at the wheel and Larina stood beside him rest-ing her arms on the woodwork in front of her.

When they had gone a little way she took off her hat and bending down threw it into the cabin behind her.

"You must not get sun-burnt," Wynstan said.

"Why not?" she asked.

"Because women should be white-skinned," he answered, "like goddesses who are sculpted in marble."

"I do not believe I sun-burn easily," Larina answered. "And at the moment there is no sun."

That was true.

The sun which had risen so gloriously at dawn seemed to have disappeared.

Now the sky overhead was grey and there were some ominous-looking clouds to the north.

"They will go away," Larina told herself hopefully.

She could not bear to miss the sunshine today of all days.

They drove on and now Wynstan was increasing the speed until it seemed to Larina that they almost flew over the water.

Away from the shelter of the coast the sea was rough, far rougher than it had been yesterday. Now there was the slap of the waves against the bow which with their speed seemed almost to be lifted out of the water.

Larina looked back.

Now they were a long way from the shore and the mountains in the background were rising higher and still higher.

She could see Mt. Vesuvius very clearly, its small column of smoke like a ghost in the air above it.

She could see Naples and immediately behind them the small Isle of Capri.

On they went, until soon it was difficult to distinguish anything in the distance except the outline of the mountains.

There was something exhilarating in being surrounded only by sea and almost out of sight of human habitation.

Then suddenly there was a splutter from the engine and it stopped.

"Blast!" Wynstan ejaculated.

"What has happened?" Larina enquired.

Everything seemed suddenly very silent after the noise of the engine and the boat began to rock on the waves.

"I shall have to find out," Wynstan replied.

He took off his light summer coat and, as Larina had done, threw it behind him into the cabin.

Then he rolled up the sleeves of his shirt, and opened two doors low down on the floor so that he could look at the engine.

"Do you know what has gone wrong?" Larina asked.

"I can guess," he answered. "But it could be a number of things. I suppose, if I had been sensible, I would have brought the mechanic with us."

'That would have spoilt everything!' Larina thought.

She could not say so to Wynstan, but it was very exciting for her to be alone with a man!

It was something she had never experienced before and something which she knew she ought not to be doing now.

No well-brought-up young woman would have dreamt of going off in a motor-boat, of all modern inventions, without even knowing where she was being taken.

Larina was well aware it would have shocked not only her mother but certainly all the acquaintances they had known in the days when they lived in Sussex Gardens.

Larina could remember the ladies who had called on her mother and come to her 'at home' days, and also those who came to the house for the purpose of consulting her father.

The Dining-Room was always used as a waiting-room. Larina would sometimes peep in to see the fashionably-dressed women, wearing sables and ostrich feathers in their hats, turning over the magazines which were laid on the table every morning by one of the maids.

Sometimes they left behind an expensive fragrance and when they went from the Dining-Room into her father's consulting room she would hear the rustle of their silk petticoats under their full skirts.

Yes, they would definitely be shocked at her behaviour, but as they would never know about it why should she even think of them?

Wynstan, who had been half-inside the lower-deck, pulled himself out to say:

"You will find some papers in a drawer in the cabin. Please bring them to me. There should be a plan of the boat somewhere amongst them."

Larina did as she was told.

When she had found the papers and was emerging from the cabin to hand them to Wynstan, she realised it was getting far rougher than it had been before.

Now the boat was rocking almost violently from side to side, and occasionally it pitched forward which made her stagger so that she had to hold on to something.

Wynstan sat on the floor studying the plans she had given him.

"Can I help?" she asked.

"Not unless you understand paraffin engines."

Larina looked back the way they had come.

Now it was impossible to see even the mountains.

A grey mist seemed to have descended over them and after looking at it for some time she realised it was rain.

A few seconds later she felt the first drops and heard them spatter on the foredeck. They also fell on the papers which Wynstan was studying.

"This is ridiculous!" he said angrily. "I thought I knew all about engines."

He picked up a tool and half-disappeared through the door. Only his legs remained outside and Larina knew he would get wet.

She was just wondering whether she should go and sit in the cabin, when a squall of rain so heavy it seemed almost torrential poured down on her so that in a few seconds she was soaked to the skin.

What was more the boat was rocking so dangerously from side to side that she felt frightened to move in case she should fall and hurt herself.

Thinking it was the only possible thing to do she sat down on the deck. The rain was beating on her so heavily that it was quite painful against her face and on her shoulders which were only covered with the fine muslin of her gown.

A long time later Wynstan pulled himself out of the engine-room.

"I cannot find it," he said in an exasperated tone. "I thought it must be the pistons but I have checked every one."

Larina looked at him helplessly through the rain.

"Why do you not sit in the cabin?" he asked.

"It is so rough I was afraid to move."

"I will help you."

"What is the point? I am wet now, I might as well get wetter!"

He smiled at her.

"Are you frightened?"

She shook her head.

"I am only thankful I do not feel sea-sick."

"Well, that is one blessing and we had better start counting them. It looks as if we are going to be here for a long time."

He collected some more tools and once again put his head under the floorboards.

Larina sat patiently.

The rain was now not so violent, but a strong wind made the sea even more tempestuous than it had been already.

The boat was thrown about on the waves and every so often one broke over the stern in a shower of spray.

It must have been two hours later that Wynstan stood up and steadying himself on the deck-rail, tried to start the engine.

For a moment there was nothing, then there was a splutter which quickly died.

It was, however, encouraging and Larina rose to stand beside him.

"Do you think you have found out what was wrong?" she asked.

"I hope so," he answered. "There was a wire that was broken. I have repaired it, but it may not hold."

He tried the engine again, and this time it ran for five or six seconds before once again it spluttered into silence.

Wynstan was back on the floor, then another ten minutes later he came out again.

This time the engine started and roared into life.

It seemed to Larina that they both held their breath in suspense, but there was no splutter and it appeared to be running smoothly.

"You have done it! You have done it!" she cried.

Wynstan turned to smile at her.

She was standing very close to him.

As he looked down his smile deepened. She was soaked to the skin and her muslin gown clung to her so that she might in fact have been wearing nothing.

It revealed her small breasts and clung tightly over her hips to the ground.

The wind had blown her hair loose and it fell on either side of her cheeks nearly to her waist, framing her small face and her huge grey eyes.

"You look exactly like one of the Sirens who tempted Ulysses," Wynstan exclaimed.

Then he put his arms around her and kissed her!

For a moment Larina felt her lips cold against his, then something wild and ecstatic ran through her like forked lightning.

She knew that this was what she had longed for, this was what she wanted! She felt his lips were suddenly warm and at the same time hard and demanding.

It must have been only a moment that he held her against him and his mouth possessed hers, and yet it seemed to Larina as if the whole world was hers and the stars fell from the sky around her.

It was a wonder and a rapture that she had never believed possible. Then Wynstan released her and said in a voice that was somehow strange:

"I said that you were a Siren, Larina!"

He put both his hands on the wheel and very slowly turned the boat round.

She stood beside him without moving. It was impossible to do anything but cling to the fore-deck to steady herself, and feel as if her whole body had come alive.

It was the same feeling, she thought, that she had known when she had become part of the flowers and the water.

The same, and yet in many ways even more wonderful, more ecstatic.

"We shall have to go rather slowly," Wynstan said, "or it will break down again. I am afraid it is going to take us a long time to get home."

'It does not matter—nothing matters!' Larina wanted to say, but it was impossible for her to speak.

She could only look at Wynstan's profile as he stared

ahead of them and feel that she was still quivering from the wonder of his lips.

He drove for a little way in silence, before he asked:

"What are you thinking?"

"I was thinking of a poem," Larina answered truthfully.

"Then it should be the lines written by Sophocles when he said: 'Many marvels there are, but none so marvellous as Man!'."

He gave a little laugh.

"That is me! Because I assure you it was very marvellous of me to have repaired this engine! If it gets home safe and sound, it will be a miracle!"

"And if you had not mended it?" Larina asked.

"Then we might have been drifting for hours, even days, before we were picked up—unless we had swum back to the shore."

Larina gave a little laugh and looked at the distant coast which was still shrouded in mist.

"The only possible way of doing that would be to ride on the back of a dolphin!"

"Of course, if the gods behaved properly, they would send us a dolphin each!" he answered lightly.

Larina did not answer and after a moment he said:

"I am interested to hear of which poem you were thinking."

"Yours is better!" she answered.

"I am waiting," Wynstan said.

Shyly, her voice low but just loud enough for him to hear it above the engine, she quoted the lines that seemed to have been in her mind since she came to the Villa.

> *"He who has won some new splendour*
> *Rides on the air,*
> *Borne upward on the wings of his human vigour."*

Although this came from an ode to Apollo, asking his special blessing for those who had won victory in the Pythian games, it was particularly applicable to Wynstan.

No-one could have looked more strong and vigorous than he did at this moment, his soaked shirt revealing the breadth of his shoulders, the strength of his arms and the athletic lines of his body.

His wet trousers outlined his narrow hips and Larina knew without being told that he was tremendously strong and that in a fight his adversary would come off worst.

"If you are referring to me," Wynstan said with a smile, "you have omitted two rather important lines of the poem."

"What are they?" Larina asked.

> *"For a brief space the exultant of joy,*
> *Until at last he falls to the earth,*
> *Shattered by the beckoning doom!"*

He laughed.

"In other words: 'Pride comes before a fall,' and that is something it is always wise to remember."

"Why should you fall?" Larina asked. "I am sure you never will."

"I hope you are right," he said. "But it is a mistake for one to become too conceited or to think oneself invincible."

"I have never been able to think that," Larina said, "but you are different. You would always get your own way, you would always be able to do the impossible and turn defeat into victory."

"Now again you are like the Sirens who sang to Ulysses. Perhaps the most dangerous thing a woman can do to a man," Wynstan said with a note of amusement in his voice, "is to make him believe that he is invincible and indefatigable."

He glanced for a moment at Larina's wide eyes and added:

"It is also the best thing she can do; for most men need to have someone to believe in them because they are afraid to believe in themselves."

"I believe in you," Larina said impulsively.

"In what way?" he asked.

"I think you will always get what you want in life. I think too that what you want is something which will help other people and will be of real importance."

She was not really certain of what she was saying, but the words came to her.

There was a silence after she had spoken. Then Wynstan said:

"Thank you, Larina, you have made up my mind for me on a rather important subject."

They said no more because Wynstan seemed to be concentrating on the boat, and once again there was a squall of rain which forced Larina to keep her head down.

It was late afternoon before they finally reached the private jetty of the Villa as they had been crawling along at less than three knots.

The mechanic was waiting for them and Wynstan told him what had happened. While he was exclaiming in dismay at what had occurred, Larina began to climb up the steps towards the Villa.

It was difficult to walk in her soaked skirts and Wynstan soon caught up with her.

"You need a hot bath," he said firmly, "but first a drink!"

He drew her, although she protested, into a room where there was a tray of drinks set out on a side-table.

"I am ruining the carpet!" she protested.

"Better that than having pneumonia!" he answered. "Drink this—every drop of it!"

It was cognac and Larina felt it sear its way like fire down her throat, but because Wynstan had ordered her to drink it she did so.

Then she went upstairs to where a maid was already drawing her bath, and having taken off her wet clothes she lay soaking in it for a long time.

Then there was her hair to dry, and it was hours later before she came downstairs in evening dress to find Wynstan in the room that she had learnt was usually used in the winter.

It had an open fireplace, and now there was a log-fire burning brightly and a table set in front of it.

Wynstan rose to his feet as she entered the room.

"If you are not hungry—I am!"

Larina smiled at him a little shyly.

Now that she was back in the Villa it was difficult not to think of how he had kissed her.

She thought about it while she was lying in her bath and

told herself that she must not attach too much importance to it.

It was just because he was so pleased with himself at having repaired the engine that he had to express his joy with someone, and she had been standing there beside him.

It had been a revelation to her, but she was sure that to him it had been nothing more than if he had hugged her as a man might hug a child or swing her round in his arms.

The servants appeared with delicious dishes and Larina found that she was in fact very hungry.

"Do you realise it is after seven o'clock?" Wynstan asked. "It is a long time since breakfast, and I suppose, as this must count as dinner, our luncheon is lost forever!"

"I shall not miss it," Larina smiled. "I have never eaten as much as I have done since I came here."

"I had been looking forward to giving you luncheon at Ischia," he said, "but we will go there another day. Tomorrow we will be more cautious and only go the three miles to Capri. Then if we break down again, there will be plenty of people about to rescue us."

"I am not afraid," Larina said.

"Do you want me to tell you how well you behaved?" he asked. "Any other woman would have whined and complained, and many would have been really frightened."

"I was only frightened at first because I was afraid I might be sea-sick," Larina confessed, "and that would have been undignified."

"And very unromantic!" he said.

She thought for a moment that his eyes rested on her lips and she blushed.

He insisted on her drinking wine at dinner and also having a liqueur afterwards.

Then he made her put her legs up on the big velvet sofa which stood in front of the fire and covered her with a fur rug.

"I am not cold now," Larina said.

"I am still afraid you might catch a chill," he replied. "The Mediterranean can be very treacherous at times and very misleading. It changes its moods as quickly as any woman!"

"Are we all so temperamental?" Larina enquired.

"Most woman are," he answered, "but that is what makes them so attractive. If they were always the same I have a feeling it would become very boring."

Larina smiled and snuggled back amongst the silk cushions.

"I am too tired and too contented to throw a temperament just to amuse you," she said, "but remind me tomorrow to be unpredictable about something or other."

She was speaking lightly, but as she said the word 'tomorrow' once again the question was there.

Would she be with him tomorrow to be unpredictable, or anything else?

"What is worrying you?" Wynstan asked.

"How do you know I am worried?" Larina replied evasively.

"Your eyes are very expressive. I have never known a woman whose expression changes so quickly, or whose eyes are so revealing."

He bent forward in his chair.

"Tell me what it is that frightens you, Larina," he begged. "I know there is something and I cannot bear to see the fear in your eyes."

For a moment she hesitated and then she said:

"I will tell you tomorrow night."

"Is that a promise?" Wynstan asked.

"I . . . promise!"

She thought as she spoke that by tomorrow night he would understand and there would be no need for her to tell him what was wrong—he would know!

It was very comfortable on the sofa, the fire was warm and the liqueur Wynstan had made her drink made her feel as if she were floating on a cloud.

She must have fallen asleep because she was wakened by Wynstan saying:

"You are tired. You were up very early this morning, and nothing could be more exhausting than what we went through today. It is time you went to bed."

"No . . . I want to stay . . . here," Larina protested drowsily.

I am going to have to make you do as you are told," he answered. "If you feel too tired to walk, I will carry you."

He pulled back the rug as he spoke and picked Larina up in his arms before she could protest.

"Why should you not be 'borne upward on the wings of my human vigour'?" he asked with a smile.

She gave a little chuckle and put her head against his shoulder.

It was a happiness she had never known to be held close in his arms, and she knew that she was so light that it was no effort for him to carry her across the Hall and up the broad staircase which led to her bed-room.

He pushed open the door with his foot. Then as he entered the room he saw that her eyes were closed and that she had fallen alseep against his shoulder.

Very gently he put her down on the bed.

She opened her eyes as he did so and gave a little murmur as if she minded leaving the security of his arms.

"Shall I call one of the maids?" he asked.

"No," she answered with an effort, "I . . . will manage."

"I have a feeling that as soon as my back is turned you will fall asleep again. So, because I want you to have a good night, Larina, I will turn my back while you undress; then when you are in bed, I will tuck you up."

She looked at him drowsily as he pulled her to her feet and undid the back of her gown with expert fingers.

"Hurry," he said with laughter in his voice, "otherwise I shall find you asleep on the floor!"

He walked away from her as he spoke and pulled aside one of the curtains to look out to sea.

The rain had stopped, but the clouds still hid the stars and there was no moon.

The lights of Naples were twinkling in the distance and Wynstan stood looking at them until a soft voice behind him said:

"I am in . . . bed now."

He turned and walked back to the bed which was draped in frilled muslin.

Larina's hair was golden against the white of the pillows.

He saw that she was wearing a muslin nightgown with

long sleeves trimmed with lace which fell over her hands, and with a lace-trimmed collar which fastened at the neck.

He pulled the sheet up to her chin, then he bent his head and kissed her very gently on the lips.

"Good-night, Larina," he said softly.

"Good-night . . . Apollo . . ." she murmured and her eyes closed before she had said the last word.

Wynstan stood looking at her for a long moment; then he turned out the light and went from the room.

# CHAPTER SEVEN

Larina awoke to find the maid pulling back the curtains.

"What time is it?" she asked sleepily.

"It is half past nine, *Signorina,*" the maid replied, "and I thought you would like your breakfast."

"Breakfast!" Larina exclaimed and sat up in bed.

She was dismayed to find that she had slept so long.

She had meant to get up early and see for the last time the dawn breaking, but now by sleeping she had lost some of the precious hours of her last day on earth.

She was angry with herself, and yet at the same time she felt an uncontrollable surge of excitement at the thought of seeing Wynstan again.

Now she remembered that he had carried her up to bed, and although she had been half-asleep she was quite certain that he kissed her before he left the room.

Only to think of the kiss he had given her when they were on the boat was to feel an exquisite ecstasy shoot through her body with a sensation she had never known or even imagined existed.

She had been wet and cold, and yet at that moment she felt as if she glowed like a light with the wonder of his lips.

It had no longer been a grey, wet day, the world seemed brilliant as if Apollo himself had touched it with his fingers.

"That is how I would like to die," Larina told herself and remembered how Homer had written:

*'Make the sky clear, and grant us to see with our eyes.*
*In the light be it, although thou slayest me.'*

"The light! That is what I must find even though I am slain," Larina told herself.

The maid brought her breakfast on a tray on which there rested a white rose.

It smelt delicious and as she held it to her nose Larina told herself that what was left of her life must be happy.

She must not let Wynstan be aware of her apprehension and her fear.

She would try to laugh with him, be gay; then when the moment came he would be there and perhaps she would not mind dying because she would not be alone.

She ate quickly, then walked down the marble steps into the warm bath the maid had prepared for her.

She wondered if any previous occupants of the Villa had ever faced, as she was doing, the knowledge that their life was over and their existence was coming to a full-stop.

"I must not think about it," Larina told herself, "or Wynstan will guess that something is worrying me."

She felt a sudden warmth because he was concerned for her, because last night he wanted her to tell him her secret. She had promised to do so, knowing that she would not have to say it in words, that what happened would speak for itself.

'Will he mind?' she wondered. 'Will he care?'

Then she told herself she was being ridiculous.

Why should he care for her when he had only known her for such a short time?

He had been charming and kind, but it was because he was habitually like that, and although he had kissed her he had also kissed the attractive Italian Contessa.

"Which gown will you wear, *Signorina?*" the maid enquired.

There was one gown which she had not yet worn, one she had bought at Poiret's.

It was white, trimmed with fine lace and slotted through with turquoise-blue ribbons, and a sash of the same colour encircled her waist.

She thought it was the prettiest day-gown she had ever seen in her life and almost instinctively, she thought now, she had kept it for her last day.

She brushed her hair until it shone, then swept it back from her forehead and coiled it low in the back of her neck.

"The *Signorina* is very beautiful! *Bellissima!*"

"Thank you!" Larina replied, feeling the words spoken with obvious sincerity were just what she needed.

She went downstairs and despite her eagerness to reach Wynstan, she was feeling a little shy.

She found him in the Drawing-Room, seated at the desk writing a letter.

He rose when she appeared and she was sure that he looked at her admiringly.

"I am ashamed of having slept so late," she said.

"You had every reason to be tired."

"What are we . . . going to . . . do today?"

The question was breathless simply because it was so important, and she was afraid he might have changed his plans.

"I promised I would take you to Capri," Wynstan answered, "unless you are afraid to trust yourself again in my badly behaved motor-boat? The mechanic informs me that we can go for miles, and even years, without a recurrence of what happened yesterday!"

"I am not afraid," Larina answered, "and I have wished so much to see Capri."

"Then your wish shall be granted!" Wynstan said. "If you are ready we may as well start right away."

Larina looked up at him excitedly.

She had brought her hat downstairs, and when they reached the Hall Wynstan picked up a blue sun-shade which was lying on a table.

"This belonged to my sister-in-law," he said, "and I think

it would be wise to take it with us. It can be very hot on Capri, even though we can try to find somewhere shady under the olive trees."

Larina looked at him enquiringly and he explained:

"I thought today we would have a picnic. I want to go to the south of the island where, as far as I know, there are no restaurants. So the Chef has filled the basket with what he thinks we should eat and drink on such a beautiful island!"

"Then of course it will be ambrosia and nectar!" Larina smiled.

"Naturally!" Wynstan replied. "What else would the gods consider to be palatable fare?"

They descended the cliff followed by one of the servants carrying the wicker baskets.

The mechanic was waiting for them and assured Wynstan that everything was in order and another break-down was impossible.

"I hope you are right, and thank you!" Wynstan said in fluent Italian.

The servant stowed the picnic away in the cabin.

Wynstan started up the engine and they set off moving at a very different speed from that at which they had limped home the day before.

Today the sea was calm without even a ripple of a wave, and already the sun was blindingly golden and very hot.

Capri was only three miles from the promontory of Sorrento.

As they left it behind Larina looked back and thought how right Ulysses had been to build a Temple to Athene on the outermost point.

"I know what you are thinking," Wynstan said with a smile, "but there were also many Temples on Capri when the Greeks settled there."

"Of course," Larina murmured.

"When Caesar Augustus saw Capri," Wynstan went on, "he was so struck by its beauty that he acquired it from the City of Naples in exchange for Ischia."

He saw that she was listening attentively and he said:

"Tiberius, who came after him, built twelve Villas dedicated to the twelve divinities of Olympus."

"Do any of them still exist?" Larina asked.

"One, at any rate, is in the process of being excavated," Wynstan replied, "but it is going to be too hot for us to do very much sight-seeing. I am afraid you will have to be content with the beauty of the island."

There was no doubt that it was beautiful.

As they drew nearer Larina saw that its high mountains, the highest being Mt. Salerno, seemed almost blue, a mystical, entrancing blue that she felt must somehow belong to the gods.

They passed the Marina Grande, the main harbour, and proceeded round the high sharp cliffs.

Wynstan pointed out to her various grottos that he said she must explore another day.

Then with the sea vividly blue, the dolomitic cliffs rising perpendicularly out of it, cut and tunnelled by time into fantastic shapes, they came to the south of the island.

Here there was a small harbour beside a natural formation of rock jutting into the sea.

"This is the Marina Piccola where we leave the boat and climb," Wynstan explained. "I am afraid there is no road and no carriage, so I hope you are feeling energetic?"

"I am!" Larina answered.

"High above this Marina are the gardens of Augustus," Wynstan told her. "I warn you—it is a steep climb!"

"I am not afraid."

They tied up the boat, then Wynstan carried the wicker baskets and they set out to climb from the little beach up the side of the cliffs.

There was a path, narrow and twisting, and it was not too difficult but Larina was glad of the sunshade as the sun beat down on their heads.

Finally they found at the top of the path trees, grass and a profusion of wildflowers of every colour.

"I think we have gone high enough," Wynstan said.

As he spoke Larina gave a little cry.

She could see some ruins, two arches worn by time and the weather, which had obviously at one time been part of a building.

"Is that the Villa of Augustus?" she asked.

"It is," Wynstan replied, "and you can imagine him coming here to rest, and planning where else the Romans could extend their Empire, and perhaps too deciding how he could extort more money and more slaves from the races he had conquered!"

"Do not spoil it for me," Larina begged. "I want to think of people being happy on this beautiful island."

It was, she thought, more beautiful than she could ever have imagined. The vivid blue of the Mediterranean which reflected the blue of the sky seemed to intensify the green of the grass and the flowers which filled it.

Wynstan found a comfortable place near a tree where he set down the wicker baskets.

Then he half-laid down on the ground supporting himself on his elbow.

"Come and join me," he said to Larina as she stood looking out to sea. "We can pretend we are Romans, or Greeks, if you prefer and the world, or what has been discovered of it, will be well lost in exchange for this little Paradise on its own."

'That is exactly what it is,' Larina thought.

She did as Wynstan suggested and sat down beside him, shutting her sun-shade and taking off her hat.

Wynstan watched her.

"You are Greek!" he declared and after a moment: "Pure Greek with your straight little nose and your hair which seems to hold the sunshine."

"There is no need for me to return the compliment!"

"Last night you called me Apollo!"

She felt the colour come into her face and dropped her eyes.

"I was asleep," she answered.

"I am not complaining!" he said with a smile, "and if we were Greeks, even quite ordinary Greek people, we should, if we were born at the right time, think of ourselves as creatures shining in a divine light."

"Did they really think that?" Larina asked.

"Their naval victory over the Persians off the Island of Salamis," Wynstan answered, "was so close to being a miracle that the Greeks really believed that the gods had been present, fighting on their side."

"When was that?" Larina enquired.

"On a warm sunny day rather like this," Wynstan replied, "in September, 280 B.C."

"And after that, they were free, liberated from the threat of Persian domination?" Larina enquired.

"Completely!" Wynstan replied. "And for fifty years they lived, thought, built Temples, sculpted and painted as if they were the natural children of the gods."

"Why?" Larina asked.

"I believe that their prodigious strength," Wynstan replied slowly, "came from the fact that in some way which we have forgotten or lost they linked up with a divine force which men call 'God' or 'Life'."

"Do you think it is always there if we need it?" Larina asked.

"I am sure of that," Wynstan replied, "and that is why in the space of two generations the Greeks set out to conquer the furthermost regions of the human spirit, and in doing so established an Empire over the mind which has altered the whole course of human thinking right up to the present day."

"Is that really true?" Larina asked.

"Because a divine visitation occurred in Greece," Wynstan answered, "men's minds moved faster, their eyes saw further and their bodies were equipped with unsuspected powers."

"And today?" Larina asked.

"We can still find what the Greeks found—if we try hard enough."

Larina drew in her breath.

"What you are really saying is that we ourselves can tap this power or 'Divine light', and we can not only use it in this world, so that we can become permeated with it but we are part of it when we die?"

It seemed to her as she spoke as if Wynstan had cleared away from her mind everything that had been worrying her, everything she had not understood.

There was silence, then he said:

"Blake wrote: 'Where others see but the dawn coming over the hill, I see the Sons of God shouting for joy'!"

He smiled at Larina as he went on:

"The Greeks regarded themselves as the sons of God and the echo of their joyful shouting can be heard down the ages. We can do the same!"

"That is what I want to do," Larina said. "I think it is what I have always wanted but now you have made it clear."

"It is Capri which makes it clearer than anywhere else outside Greece itself," Wynstan said.

He lay down on his back and looked at the branches of the trees above him.

"Here it is easy to believe," he said, "away from the sounds of traffic and machinery, away from the overpowering height and size of sky-scrapers! Men's buildings belittle themselves."

"I know what you mean," Larina said.

There was no need to put into words that the translucent light, the blue, limpid glow of the island, was so exquisite and so serene she felt as if she could leap either into the sky or into the sea and be no longer herself but a part of them.

Here in Capri the mind could soar free, and there were no longer any problems or fear, but only beauty.

They were silent, and yet it was a close sort of silence which made Larina feel almost as if Wynstan touched her.

Then after a long time he said:

"I do not know about you, but I am hungry! I had breakfast very early."

"That is what I meant to do," Larina said, "and I was angry with myself for over-sleeping."

"We will make it up," Wynstan said lightly. "Why not open the baskets and see if there is anything to eat?"

Larina did as she was told, then laughed.

"There is enough food here for a whole army!" she exclaimed.

"There is nothing Italians enjoy more than arranging a picnic," Wynstan replied.

He was busy as he spoke opening a bottle of golden wine.

"It should really be cooler," he said. "The one thing that is sometimes lacking on Capri is water. Yet strangely enough, or perhaps through divine influence, the vineyards, orange-groves and gardens are highly productive. I have always been told there are more variations of flowers and shrubs here than anywhere else in Italy."

He poured some of the wine into two glasses and held one out for Larina.

"Drink it slowly," he said, "and imagine it is nectar. Even if the gods have a purer taste, I think I shall find it palatable."

Larina did as she was told.

"It is delicious!" she exclaimed.

"That is what I thought," Wynstan smiled.

She spread out on the grass all that the Chef had packed for them.

There was a fish pâté so light and so smooth it seemed to melt in the mouth. There were slices of ham cut fine as a pocket handkerchief, and small *Neapolitan dolci* known as *Sfogliatelle* made of baked pastry and filled with such delicious and novel ingredients that it was difficult to guess what they contained.

There were black olives exactly ripe because Italians think those are important to any meal, and there were *Crocchette di Patate* or croquettes which Wynstan said were a favourite in Naples and consisted of potatoes and parmesan cheese rolled in fine breadcrumbs and fried in oil.

Besides these there were a number of local cheeses and one speciality *Prouola di pecora* from the Sorrentine district which was made from ewe's milk.

They were all delicious, and afterwards there were peaches which Wynstan insisted on peeling for her and putting in a glass of white wine, and there were figs and walnuts, another speciality of Sorrento.

There was coffee in a flask which had kept it warm and which Wynstan enjoyed more than Larina.

"That is better!" he exclaimed.

"Much better!" Larina agreed. "But the trouble is that now I feel lazy and not half so eager to explore the island as I was before we started luncheon!"

She packed what was left of the food, with the knives, forks and glasses back into the picnic baskets. Then she looked rather doubtfully at Wynstan who was lying back amongst the grass as he had done before the meal.

"I feel that we should start off at once and see the rest of Capri," she said tentatively.

"It is too hot," he replied. "No sensible Italian ever hurries about at this time of the day. Lie down for a few moments, Larina. A *siesta* is good for the soul as well as the body."

Because she had no wish to go off exploring alone Larina did as he suggested.

Lying full length on the soft grass she was conscious of the fragrance of the flowers, the smell of freshness, as if everything was young and untouched.

"That is better!" Wynstan said approvingly. "I do not like busy women!"

"Is that what I am?"

"No. You have a serenity about you which I like and envy."

"Just as I envy you."

"Why should you do that?"

He raised himself on his elbow as he spoke and looked down at her.

Now she could see his head silhouetted against the branches of the trees and the sunlight coming through them seeming to envelop him with an aura of light.

"I envy you," she said, "because you seem so sure of yourself and you have so much more to do in the world."

Wynstan did not answer.

Then she realised he was looking down at her and she felt shy of the expression in his eyes. Suddenly he said:

"You are lovely! Lovelier than anyone I have ever seen before!"

As he spoke his lips found hers and it seemed to her as if he swooped down from the sky and took possession of her.

For a moment his kiss was gentle and her mouth was very soft beneath his. Then as his lips grew more demanding, more insistent, she felt herself quiver with the ecstasy that she had known before, though now it was more insistent, more divine.

It was as if a light invaded her whole being, infusing it with a strange glow and a wonder that was indescribable.

She felt as if everything beautiful around them was in the

feeling Wynstan gave her. The blue of the sea and sky, the mystery of the island, the flowers and the very leaves of the trees were all part of the wonder of herself and him.

There was nothing in the whole world but Wynstan. He filled the Universe and she no longer had any identity of her own.

Finally he raised his head a little to say:

"My darling, I cannot resist you! You have enslaved me from the moment I first saw you in the Temple and thought you were Aphrodite!"

"I thought . . . you were . . . Apollo!" Larina whispered.

She could hardly speak, it was hard to do anything but thrill with a pulsating wonder because he had kissed her.

"What more could either of us ask?" Wynstan enquired.

Then he was kissing her again, kissing her mouth, her eyes, her forehead, her small straight nose, her cheeks, her ears, then her mouth again.

For Larina there was no time, there was only a glory which blinded, dazzled and bewitched her until she could no longer think.

Later Wynstan undid the muslin bow she wore round her neck so that he could kiss the rounded softness of it.

It made her quiver with a new sensation she had not felt before and now the breath came quickly between her lips and her eye-lids felt a little heavy, although she was not sleepy . . .


"How can anyone be so beautiful?" he asked a long time later, tracing the outline of her forehead with his finger down the straightness of her nose, over her lips and under her chin.

"Your face is perfect!" he went on. "I knew when I first saw you that I had seen you in my mind when I first looked at the statue of Aphrodite in the Temple."

"I had been thinking of Apollo all day," Larina said, "and I was thinking as the sun went down that it was Apollo taking the light to the other side of the world and leaving me in darkness. Then I turned and you were there!"

"If I had done what I knew instinctively I should do," Wynstan said, "I should have taken you in my arms. There would have been no need for explanations, no need to get to know each other. We knew already!"

Then he was kissing her again, kissing her until she moved nearer to stir against him, her whole body seeming to ache with a strange feeling that she could not understand.

"I love you! I love you!" he said over and over again. "I have been looking for you all my life. Every beautiful woman I have met has disappointed me because she was not you!"

He kissed her small chin and the corners of her mouth as he continued:

"There was always something missing, something I could not put into words, but which my heart missed."

"Is that why you have never married?" Larina asked.

Even as she said the word she felt as though she had thrown a stone into the water and the ripples from it spread out and multiplied.

There was silence, then Wynstan said:

"I have never asked a woman to marry me, until now. You have secrets from me, Larina—secrets you have promised to tell me tonight. I do not mind what they are. Whatever you have done or whatever you are hiding, it is of no consequence."

His arms tightened.

"Our spirits have found each other. You are everything my heart has been looking for and that is all that matters."

He bent his head again and now he was kissing her more passionately, more fiercely than he had done before.

He kissed her until she felt as if the ground was insubstantial beneath her, and the sky moved dizzily overhead.

He kissed her until it was no longer possible to breathe and she felt as if her whole body glowed with a strange light.

"I love you! I love you!" he was saying and she heard her own voice tremulous, and yet lilting with an inexplicable joy reply:

"I love . . . you! Oh, Apollo . . . I love . . . you!"

He kissed her again and again, then his lips were on her neck evoking the strange sensations he had done before.

Quite suddenly Larina thought this is how she must die, close to Wynstan when she belonged to him and she was his. There would be no fear and no suffering in his arms.

"I love you!" he said again.

"Will you not . . . love me completely," she whispered, "as a man loves a woman and makes her . . . his. I want to . . . belong to you . . . to be yours!"

Her voice died away because she realised that Wynstan was suddenly still.

He seemed to stiffen and she knew in that moment that what she had said was wrong! It had raised a barrier between them and she could have cried out at the misery of it.

Slowly he raised himself, then without speaking he rose to his feet to walk a little way from her and look down at the sea.

Larina sat up.

She had made a mistake, she had lost him and it was an inexpressible agony, like a knife turning in her heart.

He stood there for what seemed to be a long time and she watched him apprehensively also without moving.

Finally he seemed to give a deep sigh which came from the very depths of his being.

"I think we have to go back," he said. "There are a lot of things we have to talk about and I do not want to keep you out in the dark."

Larina wanted to protest! She wanted to run towards him and say she did not mean it, to ask him to kiss her again, to feel the closeness and warmth of him, but somehow the words would not come to her lips.

There was nothing she could do but pick up her hat and sun-shade.

Wynstan moved towards the picnic baskets and now she did not look at him but started the descent towards the Marina below them.

As she went she was vividly conscious of his footsteps following her.

The sun was no longer as strong as it had been during the afternoon and Larina knew it was growing late.

Everything still had that transparent luminance and once they were in the boat she could see that the mountains above the cliffs were even more blue than they had been before.

Wynstan drove the boat speedily, but while they were rounding the island Larina had plenty of time in which to wonder miserably how she could explain to him, how she could make him understand why she had said what she had.

'Perhaps I shall be dead before we reach the Villa,' she thought.

But everything within her cried out at the idea that she should die without Wynstan's lips on hers, without his arms around her.

It was impossible to speak intimately above the noise of the engine and yet every second that passed, it seemed to Larina, might make it too late to explain, too late to make him understand.

They rounded the south point and when Larina thought Wynstan would head straight for Sorrento he turned towards her with a smile and said:

"We have missed our English tea. I think perhaps before we set out on the last part of our journey we might stop at the Marina Grande and have some oysters. What do you think?"

Because he was speaking kindly to her again, because there was a smile on his face, Larina would have agreed to anything.

"That would be . . . lovely!" she cried.

"And they have clams and very large prawns which I am sure you would enjoy if you have never tried them," he said conversationally.

She felt as if he had deliberately set aside what had upset him and perhaps puzzled him.

He was being as kind and charming to her as he had been on the outward voyage.

Although she longed for the deep note in his voice when he said he loved her, although she wanted to see again the expression in his eyes which had told her he spoke the truth, she was content for the moment.

He wanted to talk to her and at any rate he seemed not actually angry.

"How could I have suggested anything so . . . immodest, so . . . wrong and . . . wicked?" Larina asked herself accusingly.

It had just been a moment of desperation because she had known there were perhaps only a few hours or a few seconds left, and she loved Wynstan with all her heart and soul and more than her hope of eternity.

Nothing mattered except him! Nothing existed in the whole world except his lips!

"He will . . . understand when I am . . . dead," she told herself miserably.

She watched him, her eyes on his profile, knowing that to her he was perfect. Even if he were angry with her it would only make her love him more.

They reached the Marina Grande. Wynstan entered the harbour and brought the motor-boat up against the jetty.

The sun was shining and now the white buildings all along the water's edge were diffused with colours—crimson and gold.

Behind them, the green mountains with their bare tops also glowed as if from a fire and the sea shimmered with it.

"I will tell you what I will do," Wynstan said. "I will go and fetch the oysters and whatever else there is for us to eat. You set the table in the cabin."

"I will do that," Larina agreed, glad to have something with which to occupy her mind.

Then as Wynstan was ready to step ashore she said:
"You will . . . not be long?"

"No," he answered, "the restaurant where one buys the oysters is quite near. I shall not be more than a few minutes."

There were a number of small boys on the Quay only too willing to help tie up the boat. They stared at it excitedly, pointing out the wheel and the engine and chattering amongst themselves.

Larina went into the cabin. She found a cloth of gay red and white checks with which she covered the table.

In the same drawer were knives, forks and glasses which she arranged while all the while her mind was on Wynstan.

Finding there was a mirror in the cabin she smoothed her hair and retied the little muslin bow at her neck which he had undone and which she had replaced hastily with trembling fingers before they had started the descent to the boat.

In the mirror Larina could see her eyes very large in her pale face.

'Oh, God . . . make him . . . understand,' she prayed. 'I

love him! I love him so desperately! Make him understand and . . . love me again before I . . . die!"

Wynstan found to his satisfaction that the restaurant he had known ever since he first came to Sorrento was still in existence.

It was famous for its fish, but most especially for its oysters, clams and mussels.

There were fish swimming in tanks of water outside the door, and as a boy he had found it amusing to choose what he wanted to eat and watch the waiter catch it in a small net.

He entered the restaurant and gave his order for an *arogosta*-lobster which already cooked was lying on a green salad garnished with prawns.

"The Signor must try our *Zuppa di cozze*," the proprietor suggested.

Wynstan knew this was a soup made from mussels which was a speciality of the restaurant.

"Will it take long?" he asked.

"Five minutes, *Signor*, and I will serve it in a covered dish so that you can take it to your boat, as long as you promise to bring back the dish!"

"I will do that," Wynstan answered. "Very well then, I will have the *Zuppa di cozze* and two dozen *Ostriche*-oysters. Open them and in the meantime, I will take the lobster and the wine back with me now."

They were being packed into an open basket and Wynstan was waiting to leave the restaurant when he heard a voice he recognised.

"Wynstan! What are you doing here?"

It was Nicole, surrounded as usual by men and looking extremely attractive.

"As you see," Wynstan answered, "I am shopping."

"It sounds very domestic," she smiled, "but I will not ask awkward questions. I am well aware that you could not eat all that yourself."

"Hello, Wynstan," the man who had joined her remarked.

"Hello, Chuck," he said. "I have not seen you in ages."

"I arrived this morning. Nicole told me you were in Sorrento and I had hoped we could get together and talk over old times."

"I hope so," Wynstan replied automatically.

"By the way," Chuck said, "I was sorry to hear about your brother, but he really had not much chance against Roosevelt."

"Roosevelt has been re-elected?" Wynstan asked. "I expected it!"

"Yes, he is back in the White House," Chuck said. "If you want to read about it I have yesterday's newspaper which I brought with me from Rome."

"Thank you," Wynstan said.

"Do come on, Chuck," Nicole interposed, "you know we have people for dinner and we shall be late if you do not hurry."

She paused to say to Wynstan:

"Join us if you feel like it. You know I want to see you."

"I am afraid I shall be too late," Wynstan replied.

She had received his note, he thought, and she was really behaving quite sensibly about it.

"Here is the newspaper," Chuck said.

He handed it to Wynstan and hurried after Nicole who, with the two other men in the party, was already walking towards the jetty.

Wynstan picked up the rest of his purchases but gave them time to move away in a motor-boat which was not as up-to-date as his own and which required two crew to run it.

He then walked back to the 'Napier Minor' and saw Larina smiling at him from the cabin as he stepped aboard.

"Here is the first course, at any rate," he said handing her the wicker basket. "I have to go back for the rest, but I have ordered something which I think you will like."

"It sounds exciting!" Larina replied.

"You will enjoy the *Zuppa di cozze*," Wynstan promised. "I will not be long."

He walked away again back towards the restaurant.

Larina carried the basket into the cabin. She put it down on one of the bunks, saw there was a newspaper on top of it, and laid it on the table.

Then she lifted out the lobster and thought how prettily arranged it was on the dish. There were also two bottles of wine, fresh rolls and a small china pot containing butter!

As Larina looked at the lobster she realised that she was in fact not hungry.

She had felt ever since she had upset Wynstan that there was a constriction in her throat, and something suspiciously like a stone heavy in her breast.

Because she could not bear for the moment to think about herself or how foolish she had been, she opened the paper.

It was an American paper, published in Rome, but printed in English.

### ROOSEVELT BACK AS PRESIDENT

Larina read the headlines and wondered if Wynstan was interested in politics. He had never mentioned them, and yet, she thought, if there had been a General Election in England, people would have talked of little else.

She looked further down the page, then suddenly she gave a shrill cry like an animal that had been wounded.

It seemed to echo round the small cabin. Then with a violent gesture, she threw the paper onto the floor and climbing out of the boat onto the jetty, started to run frantically— wildly!

Wynstan had to wait longer than he had expected for the *Zuppa di cozze*.

"It is coming. *Signor*—one little second!" the proprietor kept assuring him.

The oysters were opened and arranged neatly on a tray so that they were easy to carry.

Finally the *Zuppa di cozze* came from the kitchen and the proprietor told a waiter to carry it to the boat.

The two men set off down the jetty.

By now the sun was very low on the horizon and darkness was encroaching across the sky carrying with it the first faint twinkling stars.

Wynstan glanced up and remembered that the moon

would be full tonight, so there would be no difficulty in finding his way back to Sorrento.

There he would talk to Larina and there would be no
more secrets between them. He would no longer be apprehensive about what she had to tell him.

He knew he had hurt her, he knew he had brought her
back, from an ecstasy that had seemed to them both divine,
to the mundane and the common-place.

Yet he had not been able to prevent his feelings about
something which concerned Elvin.

He had to know! He had to hear what it was that had
worried and perturbed her ever since he had known her and
which had made her send that frantic telegram across the
Atlantic.

He and the waiter reached the boat.

There was no sign of Larina and Wynstan thought she
was perhaps lying down on one of the bunks inside.

He put the tray with the oysters on the flat roof of the
cabin and took the soup from the waiter, tipping him as he
did so.

"*Grazie, Signor,*" the waiter said and hurried back towards
the restaurant.

"Here I am, Larina?" Wynstan called out, "with our cu-
linary feast!"

He bent his head and entered the cabin as he spoke to set
the deep dish containing the soup down on the table.

To his surprise Larina was not there!

'She must have gone for a walk,' he thought.

He collected the tray from the roof of the cabin and put
that too on the table. Then he went outside again.

There was no sign of her on the jetty and it surprised him
that she could have walked towards the harbour without his
seeing her.

He swung himself out of the boat and started to walk
slowly back the way he had come from the restaurant.

'Where can she be?' he wondered.

There were no shops by the water's edge to interest a
woman and now the sun had almost vanished and the dusk
was purple in the shadows.

Wynstan reached the Quay and looked around him.

The restaurants and the cafes were already bright with light, but there were not many people about and the small boys had gone home for their supper.

A few fishermen were getting their boats ready for the morning, but otherwise it was very quiet. He thought perhaps he had made a mistake: Larina must in fact have been at the end of the jetty and he had not seen her.

He walked back to the boat.

Everything was as he had left it and there was no sign of her.

He wondered where on earth she could have gone to. In spite of what she had said to him yesterday she had never seemed to be unpredictable, but always easy and pliable, and in that aspect different from any other woman he had ever known.

He decided she would not be long and he might as well open the wine.

He found a corkscrew, drew the cork from one of the bottles and sampled it. It was good, although it did not compare with the wine they drank at the Villa, most of which had been put down in his grandfather's time and was exceptional.

He came out of the cabin and stood in the front of the boat. It was not easy to see far in the gathering dusk, but there was still no sign of Larina.

Her dress was white and he knew he would have seen it long before he would notice any other colour.

Puzzled he went back to the cabin again.

It was then his eye alighted on the newspaper lying on the floor.

The way it was unfolded and thrown down told him that Larina must have read it.

He picked it up and saw the headline.

ROOSEVELT BACK AS PRESIDENT

She could hardly be upset about that, he thought, unless there was something in the report.

He read it hastily.

It told him that Harvey had won a number of votes though not enough. There was nothing that could have dis-

— 313 —

turbed Larina or lead her to associate the election in any way with him.

Then his eye caught a paragraph low down on the page headed—London.

He read it automatically hardly realising he was doing so.

### MAD DOCTOR IMPERSONATES ROYAL CONSULTANT. ANXIETY FOR THOSE GIVEN FALSE SENTENCES OF DEATH.

George Robson, a Doctor, who last year was struck off the Medical Register for unprofessional conduct, was arrested in London today and charged with impersonating Sir John Coleridge, Consultant to the Royal family.

Sir John, who was on holiday abroad, left his house in Wimpole Street in charge of a caretaker. George Robson, who had a particular grudge against Sir John because he was on the Board of the B.M.A. who had condemned him in 1899, gained access to No. 55 Wimpole Street. He imprisoned the caretaker in a downstairs room where he subsequently strangled him, and dressed in borrowed clothes, proceeded to interview any patients who called to see Sir John or who endeavoured to make appointments.

Robson was clever enough to see only patients who had not previously been examined and would therefore not recognise Sir John. The masquerade was only discovered when Sir John returned from his holiday four days earlier than he had intended.

George Robson had in fact left 55 Wimpole Street the previous day. Sir John was confronted with an angry patient who had obtained a second opinion on his condition. It was then discovered that every patient who had been seen by George Robson in the last month had been given exactly twenty-one days to live.

He told them they had a strange and unusual condition of the heart, that he was an authority on the disease and there was no hope of their survival. Sir John is trying to contact all the patients who might have been interviewed by George Robson, but as there is no record of how many people Robson saw, it will of course take some time.

Wynstan read the report at first quickly and then slowly for the second time. He realised that here must be the explanation of everything which had puzzled him, everything which Larina had kept secret.

Now he knew he must find her quickly.

He jumped out of the boat and ran down to the jetty.

It was obvious when he reached the Quay that she would turn right because there were fewer houses that way and almost immediately there was a road rising up the hill.

He walked up it, but when it turned at a right angle it seemed to him that she would not have carried on to where there were other houses and shops, but would have taken to the mountainside.

There was a path, narrow and twisting but he knew he had to trust his instinct, and he was almost sure this was the way she would have gone.

He set off looking around him and feeling thankful, as the sun sank and the stars came out, that there was also moonlight.

It was not bright at first but it grew brighter. There was not a cloud in the sky and soon the island was bathed in a silver light, ethereal and compelling.

Soon Wynstan had climbed above the olive-trees and grotesque, twisting rocks rose abruptly in front of him.

He still climbed, looking everywhere for something white, something he knew would show even against the rocks and stones which gave back a dull reflection of the moonlight.

It must have been two hours later that he saw Larina, below him instead of above, a patch of brilliant white against the lesser white of the stone on which she sat.

He started to make his way down to her and realised she was crouched on the ground, her head bent, her face hidden in her hands.

Now there was no urgency, no hurry and he came towards her slowly and quietly so as not to frighten her.

He stood for a moment looking down at her, her attitude one of poignant despair. Then he knelt beside her and put his arms around her.

He felt her quiver convulsively.

"It is all right, my darling!" he said. "I understand."

For a moment he thought she would resist him, then she hid her head against his shoulder.

"It is all right! he said again. "There is nothing more of which you need be afraid. It is all over!"

He realised as he spoke that she was very cold with shock and also from the night air, which was chilly when one was not moving.

He pulled her to her feet and picked her up in his arms.

She made a little murmur as if of dissent, then she put one arm around his neck and hid her face again.

Afterwards Wynstan used to wonder how he had managed to carry Larina sure-footedly over the rough ground, down the steep paths—little more than sheep-tracks—that twisted and turned their way from the hill to the Quay.

But he had never slipped, and he seldom faltered.

Finally he reached the boat and carrying Larina aboard, he took her into the cabin and set her down on one of the bunks.

There was a cushion for her head but when he wanted her to lie against it she gave a little cry of dissent and her arm tightened around his neck.

"I want to give you something to drink, my sweet," he said.

It was then she began to cry: hard, broken sobs which shook her whole body.

He held her very close, cradling her against him as if she were a child, and murmuring soft endearments as she wept.

"It is all right, my sweet, my darling, my precious little Aphrodite. You are not going to die! You are going to live! There is nothing to be unhappy about—nothing to worry you any more!"

Larina's sobs began to abate and finally Wynstan took out

his handkerchief to wipe her closed eyes and the tears which had run down her cheeks.

"Why did you not tell me?" he asked at length when she had taken a few sips from the glass of wine he held to her lips.

"E . . . Elvin had said . . . he would come to me if I ever . . . needed him and if I was dying," Larina answered. "I could not . . . bear to tell . . . anyone else."

"I understand that," Wynstan said, "'but Elvin, my precious, is dead!"

"De . . . ad?"

She was very still.

"I was with him when he died," Wynstan went on, "and he said something which now I understand."

He knew she was listening and he continued speaking very quietly:

"Elvin said: 'It is wonderful to be free! Tell . . .' I am sure now he was about to say your name; but if he did, I could not hear it."

Larina drew a deep breath.

"What . . . day did he . . . die?"

"It was on the 23rd of March."

"He said he would . . . call me when he was . . . dying."

"Perhaps he was about to do so," Wynstan answered soothingly.

Larina gave a little cry.

"What is it?" he asked.

"The 23rd!" she exclaimed. "I knew . . . I did know! . . . He came to me as he . . . said he would!"

"How?" Wynstan asked.

"What time . . . did he . . . die?"

"About ten o'clock in the morning."

"Is there not . . . five hours difference between New York time and London?"

"Yes, there is."

"Then . . . that was the afternoon! I went to Hyde Park and sat near the Serpentine. Because I was so . . . lonely I called . . . Elvin and he came to me . . . in his own way . . . he came to me."

There was an elation in Larina's voice that was very moving, and as she looked up at Wynstan he saw tears in her eyes—but they were now tears of joy.

"He kept his . . . promise! Only I did not . . . realise that it was he bringing me . . . life and . . . light."

"That is what he found himself," Wynstan said in his deep voice.

"I understand now," Larina said, "and I think . . . he must have . . . sent you to me."

"I am sure he did. But why did you run away?"

She hid her face against him and whispered:

"I am . . . so ashamed . . . of what I . . . suggested."

Wynstan's arms tightened as she went on:

"I am not . . . really sure . . . about what men and women . . . do when they . . . make love . . . but it must be . . . wonderful . . . because the gods used to . . . assume human guise . . . "

Her voice died away.

"It is wonderful, my darling, when two people love each other," Wynstan said.

"I thought . . . I would . . . die . . . while you were . . . loving me."

"I will make love to you, my precious little Aphrodite, but you will not die."

It was like a pattern unfolding before his eyes, he thought. But Larina must never know what Harvey had suspected or what he himself had begun to believe on the journey from New York.

Harvey would never understand what had really happened nor would Gary. But perhaps one day he would be able to tell his mother.

In the meantime he had found Larina and she had found him which was all that mattered. They were together, just as Elvin would have wanted them to be.

His lips were on Larina's forehead as he said:

"Suddenly everything seems very simple, my precious. All the difficulties, all the complications and the secrets have gone!"

"It is like coming out into the light," Larina answered. "I have been afraid . . . so desperately afraid of . . . death and of dying . . . alone."

She gave a deep sigh.

"I shall never be afraid again . . . not even when I really come to . . . die. Elvin has taught me that."

She paused to add shyly:

"And so have . . . you!"

"There is so much for us both to do together before we die," Wynstan said. "You said yesterday that I had work to do in the future which would be of benefit to other people. I think I have found something which will certainly interest me, and I hope, you too."

"What is it?" Larina asked.

"When I was in India, the Viceroy, Lord Curzon, asked me to help him in finding and restoring the magnificent Temples and monuments in India which are being destroyed through neglect. They are a heritage to the world, and if someone does not take the trouble to save them and spend money on them, then they will be lost to posterity."

He kissed Larina's forehead again before he said:

"I think that, darling, is something we can both do together, and what is more we will both find it enthralling."

"Do you . . . really . . . want me?" Larina asked in a low voice.

"I want you more than I can possibly explain in words," he answered. "I want you not only because you are so beautiful, but because for me it is also an aching, spiritual need to have you with me for the rest of our lives."

"That is what I want . . . too," Larina murmured.

"We will be married immediately," Wynstan said. "And we will go for our honeymoon to Greece!"

She gave a little cry of sheer delight and he added:

"Would that make you happy?"

"I can imagine . . . nothing more thrilling," Larina answered, "than to see Greece and to be with . . . Apollo!"

# THE INCREDIBLE HONEYMOON

# Author's Note

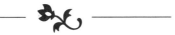

While the main characters in this novel are fictitious, the facts regarding the Siege of Paris are all correct. The British Ambassador and the British Consul did leave on September 19th, an action which provoked considerable anger, both at home and among the British left in Paris.

Balloons carrying dispatches and mail took off at the rate of two or three a week. Sixty-five balloons actually left Paris during the Siege, of which only four fell into enemy hands.

The Siege dragged on. Early in October Parisians began to eat horseflesh; from mid-November the Zoo provided exotic menus. No animal was exempt.

A journalist colleague of Henry Labouchere—the details about him are factual—wrote during the first days of January—"I have now dined off camel, antelope, dog, donkey, mule and elephant."

There was a notable price difference between 'brewery' rats and sewer rats and there were 380 cases of smallpox in January. The final capitulation of Paris to the Prussians took place on January 27th, 1871, but no Prussian troops were to enter Paris for the duration of the armistice which was to last until February 19th.

The terms were harsh; Paris was to pay an indemnity of two hundred million francs, surrender the perimeter forts to the Prussians, and throw the rampart guns into the moats.

Henry Labouchere, having lived through the Siege and the terrible aftermath, returned home to British Political life. It was however observed by his friends that the Siege had markedly aged him.

# CHAPTER ONE

─────── ❧ ───────

# 1870

"**I** have something very important to say to you!"

The Marchioness of Northaw spoke with an intonation in her voice which made the Duke of Doncaster, who was putting the finishing touches to his cravat, pay attention.

He was looking in the mirror and by moving his head slightly to one side he could see the Marchioness lying against the tumbled pillows of the bed, her naked body as beautiful and iridescent as a pearl.

With her fair hair falling over her white shoulders she was in fact the most beautiful woman to whom the Duke had ever made love, and without exception the most passionate.

"What is it?" he asked.

"You will have to be married, Athol!"

The duke was startled into immobility; then he turned round to say with laughter in his voice:

"Surely this is hardly an appropriate moment to speak of the holy bonds?"

"I am serious, Athol, and this is in fact a very appropriate moment."

"Are you suggesting that we should be married?" the Duke enquired incredulously.

"No, of course not!" the Marchioness replied, "although I assure you, Athol, I would like it above all things! But George would never give me a divorce. There has never been a public scandal in the Northaw family."

"Then what is worrying you?" the Duke asked.

There was no doubt she was worried: there was a distinct pucker on the perfection of her oval brow and the blue eyes were clouded with anxiety.

There was a pause, then the Marchioness said:

"The Queen knows about us!"

"That is impossible!"

"Nothing is impossible where the Queen is concerned, as you well know. There is always some spiteful old woman, doubtless one of your relatives or George's, to whisper poison in her ears."

"What makes you think Her Majesty is suspicious?" the Duke asked slowly.

"She more or less told me so," the Marchioness replied.

The Duke sat down on the end of the bed he had so recently vacated.

The Marchioness pushed herself up a little higher against the lace-edged pillows, regardless of the fact that the only covering down to her small waist was her long, silken, golden hair.

She looked, the Duke thought, like the sun rising at dawn, but for the moment her beauty left him cold. He was too concentrated on what she had just told him.

"It was last night at the Ball," the Marchioness explained. "When we had finished dancing and I had returned to the dais, the Queen beckoned me. She was smiling and I sat down beside her, thinking she was in a pleasant mood."

She paused to say viciously:

"I should have remembered that when she smiles she is always at her most dangerous!"

"Go on with what happened," the Duke ordered.

Despite the fact that he had not yet put on his coat, he

looked exceedingly elegant in his fine lawn shirt, embroidered with his monogram surmounted with a coronet, and with his white collar showing against his grey cravat.

He was athletically built with square shoulders and narrow hips. As the Marchioness's eyes rested on him the pucker between her eyes vanished, and as if she could not help herself she put out her hand towards him.

He ignored it.

"Go on," he said, "I want to hear exactly what Her Majesty said."

The Marchioness drew in her breath.

"She said in that ingenuous manner which hides her Machiavellian brain: 'I think, Marchioness, we must find the Duke of Doncaster a wife!'

" 'A wife, Ma'am?' I exclaimed.

" 'It is time he was married,' the Queen said, 'Handsome unattached Dukes are such a disturbing influence'."

The Marchioness made a little gesture.

"You can realise, Athol, I was too astounded for the moment to be able to reply. There was no mistaking the innuendo in the Queen's voice. Then she went on: 'You must use your influence, and of course your tact, Marchioness. They are two qualities I greatly admire and which I always seek in my Ladies of the Bedchamber'."

The Marchioness ceased speaking and the Duke was silent too. Then after a moment she continued:

"You know how much I want to be appointed to the Royal Household! It would be such a snub to all my sour-faced viper-tongued sisters-in-law who have always looked at me down their noses and openly deprecated the fact that George married anyone so young and unimportant."

"You will certainly enliven the gloom at Windsor!" the Duke remarked.

"And Buckingham Palace," the Marchioness said quickly. "You forget the Queen is now coming to London far more than she used to, and naturally I shall try to persuade her to do so as much as possible."

"You really think that in such circumstances we could go on seeing each other?' the Duke asked.

"If you were married—yes!" the Marchioness answered.

"But not otherwise. She would prevent it somehow—you can be certain of that. And I am quite sure she will not appoint me unless you are married or at least engaged."

The Duke rose to his feet to walk to the window and look out at the trees in the square outside.

"So I am to be sacrificed to make a Roman holiday!" he said and there was a sharp note in his voice.

"You have to marry sometime, Athol. You must have an heir."

"I am well aware of that," the Duke replied, "but there is no hurry."

"You are thirty and it is time you settled down," the Marchioness said.

"And do you imagine that is what I would do?" he asked.

Once again there was a note of cynical amusement in his voice.

"I cannot give you up!" the Marchioness cried. "I cannot! I have never loved anyone as I love you, Athol! As you well know, you excite me as no other man has ever been able to do."

"Quite a number have tried!" the Duke remarked.

"That was because I was so unhappy. George is only interested in Greek urns, ancient history and Italian masters."

The Marchioness paused before she said passionately:

"I want to live to-day. I am not interested in the past nor particularly in the future for that matter. I just want you to go on making love to me, for us to be together as we are now."

"I thought we had been so careful," the Duke said beneath his breath, as if he spoke to himself.

"How can anyone be careful in London?" the Marchioness asked. "There are servants who talk; there are people on the other side of the Square who watch the carriages stopping outside my door; and there are all those women who look at you with hungry eyes and who loathe me because you are no longer interested in them!"

The Duke's lips twisted a little at the corners.

"You flatter me, Clarice!"

"It is the truth—you know it is the truth!" the Marchioness retorted. "If I have had a few lovers, it is nothing to the legions of women you have left with broken hearts."

The Duke made an irritated sound and walked back to the mirror to continue adjusting his cravat.

The Marchioness sensed he was annoyed and remembered that he always disliked any reference to his many love-affairs.

But she told herself she was so sure of him that nothing could disrupt the wild ecstasy they found in each other's company.

Never, she told herself, had she known a more passionate or more ardent lover.

Never had she been more determined that, whatever the Queen might say, whatever the difficulties that lay ahead, she would not give him up.

"Listen, Athol," she said now as he stood with his back to her, "I have a solution—the perfect solution to the problem."

"If it involves my giving my name to some nit-witted girl, I am not interested."

"Oh, Athol, do be sensible! You have to marry sooner or later, and I cannot lose the opportunity of becoming a member of the Royal Household. It will give me an aura of respectability I have never had before!"

"I would not be surprised if you found it a mill-stone round your neck!" the Duke remarked.

"It will make everything so easy," the Marchioness said pleadingly. "We shall be able to see each other not only surreptitiously in London but also in the country."

"How do you reason that out?"

"Because where it has been difficult for you to come to the Hall or for me to visit you at Doncaster Park, there will be a thousand excuses if you have a wife and I am friendly with her."

"And you really think my wife would accept you as her friend as well as mine?"

"Of course she will! Especially the girl I have already chosen for you."

The Duke turned round sharply.

"This is too much, Clarice! If you really think I would allow you to choose my wife, you are very much mistaken!"

"Do not be so stupid, Athol!" the Marchioness retorted. "You know as well as I do that you never come into contact with young girls. When are you likely even to meet one moving between White's Club and this house, between Newmarket and Epsom, Ascot or your hunting lodge in Leicestershire?"

"I must admit there are few débutantes to be found in such surroundings," the Duke agreed.

"Then you must leave it to me," the Marchioness said, "and actually, not only can I provide you with a complacent, well-bred, unobtrusive wife, but also with the extra acres of land that you always wanted at the end of 'The Chase' at Doncaster Park."

"You mean Lemsford's land?" the Duke enquired.

"Exactly! When you marry Felicity Wyndham you ask as her dowry the three hundred or so fine acres of her father's estate, that adjoins your own."

"Really, Clarice, you seem to have it all tied up!" the Duke expostulated. "But may I point out that I have never seen this Wyndham girl? In fact I had no idea that she even existed!"

"Why should you?" the Marchioness enquired. "But I am well aware that you have always coveted that particular acreage which would make the ground where you exercise your horses, as you have so often said yourself, into a miniature race-course."

That was true and the Duke could not gainsay it.

It had in the past proved a constant irritant that the Earl of Lemsford, his next-door neighbour in Hertfordshire, should own a piece of land which had once been part of his family estate but had been lost at cards by his great-grandfather.

As if she realised her advantage in the discussion the Marchioness went on:

"The Earl is, I know, extremely hard up and looking for a rich son-in-law. Felicity Wyndham is very pretty, in fact if you do not compare her with me, outstandingly so!"

"I imagine by that remark that she is fair-haired and blue-eyed," the Duke said.

"Exactly!" the Marchioness agreed. "And what could be

more proper for a Duchess? Fair-haired women always show off jewellery so much better than brunettes."

She gave a little sigh.

"Oh, Athol, you must know how much it will hurt me to see another woman at your side and see her glittering with the Doncaster diamonds which are far more magnificent than anything poor George ever possessed!"

Her lips tightened for a moment before she went on:

"But, darling, neither of us can afford a scandal, even if you were prepared to run away with me, which I doubt."

"If I asked you, would you come?" the Duke asked with a cynical twist to his lips.

The Marchioness was still for a moment, then she said:

"I have often asked myself that question and I think, if I am truthful, the answer is no. How could I bear to live abroad, to be ostracised and cut by everyone we know? You would be all right. The man always is. It is the woman who suffers in a *cause célèbre*."

The Duke knew this was the truth.

"Well, Clarice," he said, "you have been very persuasive, but naturally I must have time to think over this extraordinary proposition."

"There is no time to think," the Marchioness said sharply. "You know as well as I do that if there is a vacancy among the Ladies of the Bedchamber, there will be a dozen old harridans manoeuvring for themselves, their daughters, their nieces—or anyone rather than me!"

"Are you really suggesting," the Duke asked, "that I should make up my mind on such an important subject now—at this moment?"

"If you love me you will not hesitate," the Marchioness said. "But you know, Athol, it would be an inexpressible agony if we have to say good-bye to each other. I do not think I could bear it."

There was a break in the soft voice.

"We could go on as we are now," the Duke suggested.

"And do you suppose someone would not tell the Queen?" the Marchioness asked. "How can we meet knowing we are being spied on, that everything we do and perhaps

everything we say is repeated back to that old Spider spinning webs in her Sitting-Room at Windsor?"

"All I will promise you," the Duke said firmly, "is that I
will think seriously about it."

He took his coat from a chair as he spoke, put it on and
pulled it firmly into position over his square shoulders.

He glanced down at the dressing-table to see if there was
anything he had forgotten. Then he walked across the room
to where the Marchioness lay watching him from the bed.

She looked up at him, her eyes very blue against her
white skin.

"I do matter to you?"

"You know you do," the Duke replied. "But love is one
thing, Clarice, marriage is another!"

"It is love which counts," the Marchioness said softly.

The Duke took her hand and raised it to his lips.

"Thank you, Clarice, for making me very happy."

His lips lingered a moment against the softness of her
skin. Then her fingers tightened on his and she drew him
towards her.

"Good-bye, my darling, wonderful, magnificent lover!"
she whispered.

She raised her lips as she spoke towards his.

Just for a moment he hesitated, then as he bent forward
her arms were around his neck pulling him down upon
her . . .

He tried to resist but it was too late.

Her lips, wildly passionate, held him captive, and he felt
the fire that was never far from the surface rising within him
to match the fire which was burning in her.

He had the feeling that he was surrendering himself not
only to her violent exotic desire but also at the same time to
the loss of his freedom.

But for the moment it was not important!

The Earl of Lemsford slit open the letters which lay beside his place at the breakfast table one by one.

The Butler had provided him with a silver letter-opener
engraved with the Lemsford coat of arms.

That it needed cleaning passed unnoticed by the Countess who, seated at the other end of the table, was admonishing her daughter Felicity for having torn her gown the night before.

"I cannot think why you are not more careful, Felicity. If you danced the waltz more sedately these accidents would not happen."

"I could not help the man standing on the train of my gown, Mama. I said when I fitted it that it was too long."

"It looked so elegant when you walked into the room," the Countess said.

Her eyes rested on her elder daughter and the irritation which had expressed itself in lines round her mouth seemed to fade.

Felicity Wyndham was in fact very pretty. She had china-blue eyes, fair hair and a skin which was invariably referred to as 'strawberries and cream'.

She had a beguiling way of looking at her parents that made it hard for them to deny her anything, and the Countess was already calculating how she could persuade her husband to give her enough money to buy Felicity another gown.

On the other side of the table Antonia sat unnoticed.

She had no wish to draw attention to herself; for if she did she was quite certain she would be sent on an errand or made to listen to what was being said while her food grew cold.

Accordingly she applied herself to eating her eggs and bacon without glancing up, until her father gave such a loud exclamation that it seemed to reverberate around the Dining-Room.

"Good God!"

"What is it, Edward?" his wife enquired.

"When did this letter arrive?" the Earl asked.

He picked up the envelope and without waiting for a reply went on:

"It was delivered by hand. It has not been sent by post. Why the devil was it not brought to me at once?"

"Really, Edward, not in front of the girls?" his wife admonished.

"Do you know who this is from?" the Earl enquired.

"No, of course not! How should I?"

"It is from Doncaster!"

The Earl paused, an expectant look on his face as if he were a conjurer about to produce an unexpected rabbit from a hat.

"Doncaster?" the Countess repeated. "Do you mean the Duke of Doncaster?"

"Of course I mean the Duke!" her husband snapped. "There is only one Doncaster as far as I am concerned! Our neighbour in Hertfordshire, Emily, who has never invited me inside his house since he inherited!"

The Earl spoke with a bitterness which showed that this was an old grievance.

"Well, he has written to you now," the Countess said. "What does he want?"

The Earl stared down at the letter as if he could not believe his eyes. Then he said slowly:

"His Grace asks, Emily, if he can call on me at three o'clock to-morrow afternoon. He informs me that he thinks it would be to our mutual advantage to have a closer association between our two families than has hitherto existed and he hopes that he may have the pleasure of making the acquaintance of my daughter!"

The Earl's voice died away and he realised that the three people seated at the table were staring at him with their mouths open, looking not unlike three goldfish in a bowl.

The Countess recovered first.

"I do not believe it!" she said. "Give me the letter, Edward. You must have made a mistake!"

"There is no mistake," the Earl replied, "unless my eyesight is at fault!"

He threw the letter across the table to the Countess. It landed in a dish of marmalade from which it was hastily retrieved.

The Countess held it in her hands, staring at it in the same fascinated manner that her husband had done.

"Why does the Duke say that he wishes to . . . meet me?" Felicity asked in a frightened voice.

The Countess looked at her daughter and there was a sudden light in her eyes that had not been there before.

"You will be a Duchess, Felicity!" she said. "Think of it—the Duchess of Doncaster! I never thought—I never dreamt that we should ever aspire so high!"

"I would have wagered it being 100–1 against Doncaster," the Earl remarked.

"But why? Why me?" Felicity enquired.

"He must have seen you somewhere. He must have fallen in love with you!" the Countess said ecstatically.

"There is nothing like that about it," the Earl remarked sharply. "There is some other reason and I will find out what it is, before I am very much older!"

"Are you inferring, Edward, that the Duke would wish to marry Felicity for any other reason except that he wants her to be his wife?"

"I am not saying, after reading that letter, that he does not wish her to be his wife," Sir Edward replied. "I am merely saying that he has not fallen in love like some beardless boy. Doncaster is a man, Emily, and a man who by all accounts has more women fawning around him than he has horses in his stables. If he wants to marry Felicity—and I find it hard to believe it—then there is something behind it, you can bet your shirt on it!"

"Really, Edward, I do dislike those vulgar racing expressions!" the Countess retorted. "If the Duke does wish to marry Felicity, then we should go down on our knees and thank God for such a miracle without trying to find ulterior motives for his proposal!"

The Earl rose to his feet.

"Where are you going?" the Countess enquired.

"I intend to answer this letter," the Earl replied, "then I am going to White's. If old Beddington is there, which he will be, he will tell me the latest scandal and what Doncaster has been up to lately."

"You will not mention that the Duke is coming here to-morrow?" the Countess said quickly. "We may be mistaken. He may have very different intentions."

"I am not a fool, Emily," the Earl said. "If there is any blabbing to be done, it will not be done by me."

He went from the room, and as the door shut sharply

behind him the three women left at the table looked at each other.

"I can hardly believe it!" the Countess said.

"But I do not want to marry the Duke, Mama!" Felicity said in a small voice.

Her mother did not appear to hear her as she stared down at the Duke's letter as if the words written on the thick vellum paper must be printed indelibly on her mind.

Felicity would have spoken again, when she received a sharp kick on the ankle which made her wince.

She looked across the table and saw her sister frowning at her warningly and the words she was about to say died on her lips.

"We must go upstairs at once and decide what you will wear to-morrow afternoon when the Duke calls," the Countess said after a moment. "I think it will have to be the pale blue: it is so becoming with your eyes. But then, so is the white with the turquoise ribbons threaded through it."

She gave a sound of exasperation.

"There is no time to buy you anything new, so it will have to be one or the other! Oh, dear, I do hope you have not made them dirty!"

Rising from the table the Countess bustled away and her daughters followed her.

Only as they reached the door of Felicity's bed-room did she turn and say sharply:

"There is no reason for you to hang about, Antonia. I am sure you have plenty to do, and if you have not, I will find you something. You know that you have to help tidy the Sitting-Rooms. You cannot expect Janet to do everything!"

"No, of course not, Mama," Antonia replied.

She moved away as she spoke, giving Felicity a warning glance and at the same time a touch on her arm which told her sister she would be back later.

There were always innumerable jobs in the house for Antonia. They were understaffed and she was invariably expected to fill in for deficiencies in housemaids, lady's-maids and even footmen.

It was Antonia who made the Sitting-Rooms presentable, who cut the sandwiches for tea when they entertained, who pressed and mended her mother's and Felicity's gowns, and who was sent on messages from the top of the house to the bottom.

But she was used to it and it did not unduly perturb her.

This morning however she wished that she could be in the bed-room with Felicity while the Countess was choosing her gown for to-morrow, simply because she was afraid that Felicity would betray herself.

To learn that she had not done so was a relief, when finally an hour later Antonia entered Felicity's bed-room to find her alone.

As soon as she saw her sister, Felicity ran across the room to put her arms round Antonia and burst into tears.

"What am I to do? Oh, Antonia, what am I to do? I cannot marry this Duke . . . you know I cannot!"

Antonia held her sister close, then she said:

"Come and sit down, Felicity, and let us talk about it. You can see what it meant to Mama and Papa."

"I know! I know!" Felicity sobbed. "They are not going to listen to me . . . whatever I say . . . but I love Harry. You know . . . I love him, Antonia!"

"Yes, dearest, but Harry is not a Duke."

"He loves me," Felicity said, "and I promised I would marry him as soon as he can approach Papa."

Antonia gave a little sigh as she wondered how she could possibly explain to Felicity that, whatever Harry Stanford might say now, the Earl was not going to listen to him.

The son of the Squire who owned an attractive Manor House on a very small estate, Felicity and Antonia had known Harry ever since they were small children.

They had met him at parties and, as they had grown older, out hunting. It was difficult for Antonia to remember when first she realised he had fallen in love with Felicity and she with him.

They had all known that it was impossible for Harry to approach the Earl when Felicity was only seventeen, and being only three years older himself he had certainly not enough money to keep a wife.

His circumstances were not much better at the moment.

As he was an only child he would inherit on his father's

death, his estate, such as it was, and there was also a bachelor uncle who had always promised to make him his heir.

Harry had wished to ask the Earl's permission to marry Felicity before they came to London for the Season, but Antonia had advised them against it.

"Papa and Mama have been saving up for years so that Felicity can have a proper Season in London and be presented at Court," she said. "As you know, it should have happened last year just before Felicity was eighteen. But when Mama's father died we were all plunged into mourning, and so Felicity's début had to be postponed."

"Supposing she meets someone else?" Harry had asked despondently.

"I think it unlikely," Antonia replied, "that she will ever love anyone but you."

It was strange, seeing that Antonia was a year younger than her sister, that everyone referred their problems and troubles to her, and that was another role she played in the household. Even her mother was more inclined to ask her advice rather than Felicity's.

"What am I to do?" Harry Stanford had enquired helplessly.

"Wait until the Season is over," Antonia advised. "Then when we are back in the country you can approach Papa. I am sure he will be more amenable then."

What Antonia really meant was that there was a chance for him unless Felicity had had a very advantageous offer of marriage.

She privately thought it unlikely.

Although Felicity was extremely pretty and men fluttered around her in the proverbial manner of moths around a flame, they thought twice before proposing marriage to a girl who had no dowry and only the possibility of 500 acres of not particularly productive Hertfordshire land when her father died.

That of course was if the estate was not sold and divided equally between his two daughters, which Antonia always doubted.

But while Felicity had received much flattery and never lacked partners at a Ball, up to date there had been no positive approach to her father and no suggestion of anything more permanent than a flirtation in the garden.

Now out of the blue the Duke of Doncaster had appeared, and Antonia knew that it put to an end any hopes Harry Stanford might have of becoming Felicity's husband.

"I want to marry Harry! I love him! I will never love anyone else!" Felicity was saying.

When she raised her face, looking lovely despite the tears which ran down her cheeks, Antonia felt desperately sorry for her.

"I think you have to face facts, dearest," she said. "Papa would never permit you to marry Harry when you could be a Duchess."

"I have no wish to be a Duchess," Felicity said. "I just wish to live quietly with Harry. I have much enjoyed the Season and the Balls, Antonia, but I kept thinking of him and how much more fun it would all have been at home."

Antonia knew this was the truth, and she thought apprehensively that there was no doubt that Felicity would be unhappy living a life of pomp and circumstance.

She also knew a great deal more about the Duke than anyone else in the family did; she could in fact have answered her father's queries about the Duke's motives for his proposal very nearly as competently as the old crony he was going to consult at the Club.

As their estates marched with each other, the Duke owning some 10,000 acres, Antonia had always been extremely curious, not so much about him as about his horses.

The one love of her life was horse-flesh and while she had ridden since she was a small child she had always been allotted the worst and oldest horses to ride which neither her father nor her sister required.

Nevertheless it was Antonia who managed by some magic of her own to enthuse the laziest and sometimes the most aged beast into action, and who was invariably in front of the field out hunting and in at the kill.

But it was impossible for her not to realise almost since she could walk that just over the boundary hedge were the most magnificent thoroughbreds that any lover of horses could desire.

What was known as The Chase was a long gallop which ended abruptly at the Earl of Lemsford's boundary.

The part of Hertfordshire where Doncaster Park and The Towers, in the Earl's estate, were situated was undulating, wooded and a large part of it was cultivated.

But only a mile from the Duke's mansion The Chase provided a flat, perfect stretch of parkland which had once extended for another quarter of a mile into what was now owned by the Earl of Lemsford.

Ives, the Duke's head groom who had lived in Hertfordshire all his life, soon became aware that there was always a small girl staring wistfully over the fence as he and the stable-lads took the horses for their morning gallop.

As the small girl grew older her friendship with the elderly man meant a great deal to both of them.

He even came to say himself:

"Ye knows as much about horses, M'Lady, as Oi knows meself!"

"I wish that was true," Antonia would answer. "Now tell me about the day the Duke's horse won the Derby."

There is no man who does not enjoy an attractive audience and Ives was no exception.

He had no children of his own and the tales he used to relate to Antonia would hold her spell-bound, her eyes fixed flatteringly upon him until he would describe so vividly the races he had attended that she felt as though she had been there herself.

It was only a question of time before Antonia was introduced to other members of the Duke's household.

Mrs. Mellish, the Housekeeper, who often found that time lay heavy on her hands, was prepared to guide the very appreciative young lady from next door round the great mansion.

But it was the Curator, Mr. Lowry, who taught her the most.

The Earl had no appreciation of the arts and if his ancestors had ever possessed pictures or furniture of any value they had long since been sold.

Only rather badly executed portraits of the Wyndhams

remained, because they were unsaleable rather than because they were appreciated.

But Doncaster Park was filled with pictures, furniture and *objets d'art* and treasures which had been collected over the centuries, each one contributed by a member of the Casterton family and having a history that Antonia found absorbing.

Because Mr. Lowry taught her far more than did the inadequate Governesses provided by the Earl, Antonia, after she was fifteen, spent more time at Doncaster Park than she did in the School-room at The Towers.

The Governesses, realising that she counted the least in the family, were not concerned by her absence and concentrated on trying to instill the very meagre knowledge they themselves possessed into Felicity's mind.

Because she was very pretty they decided, like her parents, that she would not require many talents, and education was therefore not important.

There was only one thing that the Countess did insist upon and that was that both her daughters should speak fluent French.

"All ladies of good breeding can speak French," she said loftily, "and as people are going abroad more and more, just in the same way as foreigners come here, it is essential that you should both speak with a Parisian accent."

The fact that she and her husband were invited to a large party given when Louis Napoleon and the Empress Eugénie came to England in 1857 accentuated her determination that her daughters should not be lacking in this accomplishment even if they possessed few others.

Antonia found French easy and she liked the old retired *Mademoiselle* who came to The Towers from St. Albans twice a week to give her and Felicity lessons.

"I cannot remember all those tiresome verbs," Felicity would cry despairingly.

But Antonia had not only mastered the verbs but was soon chattering away to *Mademoiselle* finding out many things she wanted to know about France and especially Paris.

Unlike the other Governesses who concentrated on Felicity and ignored Antonia, *Mademoiselle* reversed the procedure.

Because Antonia had a natural ear she taught her and let Felicity sit silent, deep in her own thoughts, which certainly did not concern French.

"There are two things anyway I know a lot about," Antonia told herself once. "The first is horses, and that is thanks to Ives, and the second is French, thanks to *Mademoiselle!*"

Mr. Lowry found some books at Doncaster Park which satisfied both interests, and because they seldom conversed with their younger daughter the Earl and Countess would have been surprised if they had known how knowledgeable she was, or how widely and extensively she read.

As soon as the Earl could do so he dispensed with the services of the Governesses, thereby saving their meagre salary and keep. Despite the fact that the family was in mourning Felicity was considered now to be grown up and no longer in need of lessons.

That Antonia was a year younger did not perturb either her father or her mother.

The Countess had already stated categorically that she was not going to have two unmarried daughters 'out' at the same time.

She said it in a way which made Antonia sure that she thought it unlikely that her younger daughter would ever get married, and even if she did it would be to no-one of any importance.

As Antonia regarded herself in the mirror she was not surprised.

Unlike Felicity's her hair was dark, or very nearly so. It was not, unfortunately, the jet black tresses beloved by romantic novelists.

Instead it was an indecisive colour, dark enough to give her dark eye-lashes for her grey-green eyes, but not, she thought, enough to make her skin seem the dazzling white that was so fashionable amongst the young ladies of fashion.

"It is shadowy," Antonia said to herself disparagingly. "I wish it were red and my eyes a vivid green . . . then perhaps someone would notice me!"

It was difficult to look outstanding in the clothes she wore as they were always those which had been discarded by Felicity, and Antonia knew that the colours which suited Felicity's Dresden-china appearance did nothing to flatter her.

But she was too inexperienced and not interested enough to worry about it.

The only thing that did concern her about clothes was her riding habit.

While she was not allowed to be fitted as Felicity was by a London tailor, the local man in St. Albans did his best because he liked Antonia and she was so pleasant to him.

She took him a pot of honey because his wife had a persistent cough during the winter, and she talked to him about his children.

She was also considerate when he told her that he had not finished her habit because a fox-hunting gentleman was wanting a pair of breeches who was a good customer and a better payer than the Earl.

"I understand, Mr. Jenkins," Antonia said. "But do try to make me have a small waist and see that the jacket fits really well over the shoulders. I am not worrying about myself so much, but it does show off to advantage the horse I am riding."

"That's true, M'Lady," Mr. Jenkins replied.

Antonia found later that he had spent far more hours on her habit than the small amount of money he received for it justified.

What she did not tell Mr. Jenkins, and what she certainly would not have told her father, was that Ives occasionally permitted her to ride the Duke's horses.

She exercised them with him and the stable-boys and found it impossible to say how thrilled and delighted she was at the opportunity.

"It's a real pity, M'Lady," Ives remarked, "that ye can't ride one of these horses out hunting. Then ye'd give 'em something to talk about!"

"I would indeed!" Antonia agreed. "And think how jealous everyone would be! But they would be certain to tell His Grace and then I would be back on the other side of the boundary where you first found me."

This was a joke between them and Ives laughed.

"That's true, M'Lady. Oi've never forgotten how ye looked with yer big eyes peeping at me from between the branches. It annoyed me at first to think ye were spying on us, until Oi realised it was a real interest ye were showing and we got to know each other."

"We did indeed, Ives," Antonia replied, "and it was the luckiest day of my life."

She used to think she could put up with any disagreeableness at home so long as she could get away and be with Ives and the horses.

It compensated her for the unhappiness she often felt at being unwanted.

When she had been very young and she had first realised that she was a constant irritation to her father because she was not a boy, she had cried bitterly because she could not please him by changing her sex.

As she had grown older and learnt from the Nurses and other servants that the Countess in bringing her into the world had suffered so badly that the doctors said it was impossible for her to have another child. Antonia began to understand how deeply disappointed her father had been.

"The Earl was convinced he would have a son," the old Nanny told her. "The cot and everything else was decorated with blue ribbons, and he was to be called Anthony, which is a family name as you well know."

"So that is why I was called Antonia!"

"Nobody had thought you would be a girl. Then as they expected both you and your mother to die, you were christened a few hours after you were born.

" 'What name is she to be given?' the doctor asked me.

" 'The baby was to have been called Anthony, Sir,' I replied, seeing that your poor mother was incapable of speech.

" 'Then it had better be Antonia,' he remarked."

Antonia had tried to make up for her unavoidable deficiency by being a son to her father.

She would ask if she could go out shooting with him. She would beg him to take her riding.

But she soon realised that even to look at her annoyed him and reminded him of the son he would never have. So instead she kept out of his way, and soon no-one in the house worried about her unless she was late for meals.

Then she was severely punished.

So she soon learnt to tear herself away from Ives, however absorbed she was in his stories. Or to run into the house after she had been riding, giving herself just time enough to change into a suitable gown and walk breathlessly but demurely into the Dining-Room before the Earl was aware of her absence.

Now, Antonia thought as Felicity sobbed against her shoulder, the attractive and undoubtedly, if she ever met him, irresistible Duke was likely to become her brother-in-law.

It was impossible for her, spending so much time at Doncaster Park, not to hear the servants gossiping, and it was not only the servants who talked of their master but also her mother's friends.

Because the Duke was the most important and certainly the most interesting person in that part of Hertfordshire, he was an endless topic of conversation to everyone in the vicinity of Doncaster Park.

The fact that he never concerned himself with local people when he was in residence did not stop their tongues wagging or their learning in one way or another of his various love-affairs.

Antonia was so insignificant and made herself so quiet and unobtrusive that it was easy for the ladies talking around the tea-table to forget that she was there.

She would hand round the sandwiches and cakes, pass the cups of tea, and then retire into a corner of the Drawing-Room, out of sight, out of mind, but listening with rapt attention to everything that was said when it concerned the Duke.

She knew when one love-affair ended, she knew when the next one began

She heard of jealous husbands who found it difficult to prove what they suspected, she learnt over and over again of women who proclaimed to all and sundry that their hearts were broken and that life would never be the same once the Duke had loved but left them.

It was as fascinating as some of the romantic novels that had been lent to her, not by Mr. Lowry, who would not have allowed anything of that sort in the Library, but by the Governesses who passed the long dreary hours when they were alone in the School-room reading of the love they were never likely to experience in their own lives.

Antonia thought the books a lot of nonsense, until she found that some of the episodes in them were much more true to the Duke's life than ever she had imagined they could be.

"I wonder what it is that makes women go wild where he is concerned?" she asked herself.

She looked at the pictures of him hanging on the walls of Doncaster Park.

Although they showed an exceedingly handsome and fine-looking man she felt there was something missing, something she could not explain to herself but which she was sure was not portrayed by the artists.

She had, it was true, seen the Duke when he was riding on The Chase which he always did when he was staying at Doncaster Park.

But on Ives's instructions she kept well out of sight, merely peering at him over the boundary fence and thinking how magnificently he rode, so that he did in fact seem to be part of his horse.

He was usually at a gallop when he passed her so that it was impossible to see his face closely or the expression in his eyes.

Antonia had always wished to meet him and now it seemed she was likely to do so, not to-morrow, for she was quite certain that her mother and father would not allow her to be present when he called to see Felicity, but later when the engagement was announced.

At the thought of an engagement Antonia's arms tightened around Felicity.

She knew how this was going to hurt her sister and she could not help thinking from what she knew of the Duke that Felicity would be unable to cope with him.

She was a sweet, gentle girl, but as Antonia knew only too

well, extremely stupid in many ways and very vulnerable if she was not cosseted, fussed over and loved.

Would the Duke do that? And was it likely that he would want to?

"What shall I do, Antonia? What shall I do?" Felicity sobbed despairingly.

And Antonia found herself thinking of the Marchioness of Northaw.

# CHAPTER TWO

The Duke was finishing his breakfast, which had been a substantial one, when the Butler came to his side to say respectfully:

"Excuse me, Your Grace, but Lady Antonia Wyndham has called to see you."

The Duke was surprised into thinking that he must have been mistaken.

"Lady Antonia Wyndham?" he repeated.

"Yes, Your Grace."

"At this hour?"

"Yes, Your Grace."

The Duke looked even more astonished.

"Has she come alone?"

"No, Your Grace. She has a maid with her who is waiting in the Hall. I have shown Her Ladyship into the Library."

The Duke put down his knife and fork and lifted a cup of coffee to his lips.

He always ate a large meal at breakfast-time. believing it

to be important to his health. He preferred coffee to any other beverage and was never known to touch alcohol, however much he had indulged the night before.

He had made it a rule, and he organised his life on rules that he made for himself, that he would always rise early.

When he was in London he rode in the Row before it became fashionably crowded with the Ladies of Quality who wished to gossip with their friends and the Pretty Horse Breakers who were intent on showing off their mounts.

To call on him at half past seven in the morning was something which had not yet been attempted by any lady, however persistent she might be in pursuing him.

As he finished his coffee and took a last glance at *The Times* which he had propped up in front of him on a silver stand, the Duke was wondering what this early visit could mean.

How was it possible that the Earl of Lemsford's daughter should not know that it was extremely unconventional, not to say reprehensible, for a lady to call at a bachelor establishment.

He was also irritated to think that she would make him late for his ride.

Already the stallion that he had ordered from the stables would be waiting for him outside the front door, and undoubtedly any delay on the part of his master would make it hard for the stable-boys to hold the animal.

The Duke therefore walked purposefully and without a welcoming expression on his face into the Library.

As he entered the room a small figure turned from the window and at his first glance he realised that the girl who had come to see him was not in the least what he had expected.

He was quite sure that the Marchioness had described her as having fair hair and blue eyes.

Had she not said that was the right colouring for a Duchess and would become the Doncaster diamonds?

Then as he recalled the conversation he remembered that in fact the Marchioness had said that the girl she had chosen for his wife was called Felicity.

The Duke looked at Antonia and was not impressed.

For one thing she was badly dressed in an extremely ill-fitting gown of faded blue gaberdine and her bonnet, which was small and inexpensively trimmed, seemed to obscure most of her hair.

The eyes she raised to him however were very large in her pointed face and he saw that she was nervous.

"I hope Your Grace will . . . pardon me for calling at such an . . . early hour."

"It is certainly an original way of our becoming acquainted," the Duke replied. "Am I correct in thinking it is your sister I am to meet this afternoon?"

"Yes," Antonia replied, "my sister, Felicity."

"I thought I had not been mistaken in the name."

Then with a gesture of his hand the Duke said:

"Will you sit down, Lady Antonia, and tell me to what I owe this unexpected visit?"

Antonia sat down on the edge of a comfortable sofa and regarded her host with wide eyes.

He was far better looking, she thought, than he had appeared when she had seen him riding on The Chase, and now they were at close quarters she realised what it was the artists had not included in their portraits of him.

It was a raffish, perhaps cynical, but certainly mocking look which they had omitted whilst striving to portray his clear-cut features, broad brow and deep-set eyes.

"He is much more attractive than they portrayed him!" Antonia told herself.

The Duke had seated himself opposite her in a wing-back arm-chair.

He crossed his legs and she saw that his riding-boots were exquisitely polished and wondered if it would be impertinent to ask him what was used on them.

Then she remembered that Ives could find this out for her and she determined she would ask him to do so when she next went to Doncaster Park.

"I am waiting, Lady Antonia," the Duke said with just a note of impatience in his voice.

"I . . . I think," Antonia said a little hesitatingly, "and I . . . hope you will not think it an impertinent guess, that when you call on my father this afternoon you will ask for my sister's hand in . . . marriage."

There was a noticeable silence before the Duke replied:
"That was my intention."

"Then would you . . . mind very much asking for . . . me instead?"

The Duke sat bolt upright in surprise. Then as he realised after a perceptible pause that he had not been mistaken in what she had said, he replied:

"I think you should explain yourself a little more clearly. I must admit I am wholly at a loss to understand what is happening or why you have come here with such a suggestion."

"It is quite easy to understand, Your Grace," Antonia replied. "My sister, Felicity, is in love with someone else!"

The Duke was aware of a sensation of relief.

"In which case it is quite obvious that she will refuse my proposal and there is in fact no point in my calling on your father this afternoon."

He thought to himself as he spoke that this set him free from carrying out the Marchioness's plan and she could hardly blame him if the girl she had chosen to be his wife would not accept him.

"Papa is expecting you," Antonia replied, "and is of course extremely excited, and so is Mama, at the thought of having you as a son-in-law."

"I can hardly marry your sister if she does not want me," the Duke said, with a smile on his lips.

"You do not suppose she would be allowed to say so?" Antonia asked scornfully. "As it happens neither Papa nor Mama have the slightest idea that she is in love. Harry, the man in question, has not up to now been able to speak to Papa."

The Duke looked at Antonia, a little uncertainly she went on:

"You cannot be unaware that Felicity would be forced to marry you whatever her feelings are?"

"That is ridiculous!"

Even as the Duke spoke he knew that what this strange girl was saying was undoubtedly the truth.

He was too well versed in the social world not to know that as the most eligible bachelor in the country every match-making Mama would welcome him as a son-in-law.

Any girl he chose as his wife would be compelled to marry him willy-nilly, whatever her secret feelings might be on the matter.

It had however never crossed his mind in this instance that there would be any opposition where Felicity Wyndham was concerned.

He had not really thought of her as a person, but just as a complacent, compliant young woman who would be over-whelmingly grateful that he should condescend to offer for her.

"I am afraid I am not pretty like Felicity," Antonia said, breaking in on his thoughts, "but as it does not really matter to you what your bride looks like so long as she fulfils her duties and produces an heir, I think you will find one Wynd-ham sister is very like another."

The Duke rose to his feet.

"Who told you it did not matter what my wife looked like?" he asked sharply.

Antonia hesitated for a moment and he had the idea that she was choosing her words with care before she replied:

"It is obvious, Your Grace, is it not? You have not seen Felicity and she has never seen you . . . but you are prepared to offer her marriage and everybody has been saying for a . . . long while that you need an . . . heir."

"I cannot help thinking this is the most extraordinary conversation to have with a young girl," the Duke said. "Does your father know you are here?"

"No, of course not!" Antonia replied. "Mama thinks I am attending early Communion with Janet, who is our maid. It was my only possible excuse for escaping from the house when there is so much to do in preparation for your call this afternoon."

"You really wish me to consider your extraordinary pro-posal seriously?"

"Why not?" Antonia enquired. "Felicity has cried all night and is making herself ill at the thought of marrying you. I have to do something to help her, and apart from my looks I would make you a better wife than she would."

There was an irrepressible smile at the corners of the Duke's lips as he asked:

"How can you be certain of that?"

"I would make no demands on you, for one thing," Antonia replied, "and I would be quite happy staying in the country when you were in London. In fact, I would be very content to be at Doncaster Park."

"And you really think you would like to marry me?" the Duke asked.

His question surprised Antonia into telling the truth.

"If I could ride your horses," she answered, "I would marry . . ."

She checked herself quickly.

She had been about to say: 'the devil himself!' but realised it would have sounded extremely rude. So she substituted a little lamely:

". . . the owner of them!"

The Duke had not missed her hesitation before the sentence was finished.

"You sound as if you know my horses," he said. "I suppose, since you live next door, you have seen them?"

"I have watched them on The Chase," Antonia said. "They are magnificent! Especially Red Duster. I think you have a winner there!"

"I think so too," the Duke agreed, "but until a horse has won his first race one can never be sure how he will shape when he is actually on a course."

"Ives is confident that he will prove to be as good as, if not better than his sire," Antonia said.

The Duke looked at her speculatively.

"I have a feeling, Lady Antonia, that you have in fact a more intimate knowledge of my horses than you have gained just by looking over the boundary that separates our lands."

He saw the colour come into her face as Antonia realised she had more or less betrayed herself.

"I am . . . very interested in . . . horses," she said not very convincingly.

"Especially mine!" the Duke said. "So much so that you are prepared to marry me for them!"

"It is not exactly like that," Antonia said a little shyly. "Any girl would be deeply honoured at the idea of being your wife, but Your Grace must admit it is a little difficult to be sure of what a man is like until one has at least met him—or for that matter a horse until one has ridden him!"

She knew the last sentence was impertinent, but she could not help adding it.

"And of course you know my horses better than you know me!" the Duke remarked.

There was a mocking note in his voice which she did not miss.

"I know you must think it very strange for me to come here and make the suggestion that I have. Mama would be absolutely horrified! But there was really nothing else I could do to save Felicity."

Again Antonia realised that her choice of words was not particularly flattering and she added quickly:

"If she were not already in love I feel sure Felicity would have been delighted by your proposal, as any other girl in her position would be."

"And if, as you say, she is in love," the Duke said, "then the only alternative is for me to marry you."

"I really would do my best to make you a good wife," Antonia said gravely. "It is not only that I know a little about your horses, I am also very interested in Doncaster Park and all the treasures it contains. Mr. Lowry has told me about your ancestors and I can understand why you are very proud of them."

The Duke did not speak and after a moment Antonia went on:

"I have not been well educated, except that I have read a lot."

"No doubt the books in my Library?" the Duke remarked.

Antonia realised he was more perceptive than she had imagined he would be.

"Quite a number, Your Grace," she admitted truthfully, then added quickly:

"I hope you will not be angry with Mr. Lowry because he

lent me your books. I have known him for years, ever since I was quite small, and he realised how very inadequate my Governesses were to teach me the things I wanted to know!"

The Duke did not speak and she went on:

"Because I asked so many questions he would often lend me a book on the subject. I was very careful of them!"

Antonia looked at the Duke anxiously.

"I think I must commend Mr. Lowry for adding to your knowledge," he said after a moment, "and I am glad that my books, which I often think are sadly wasted in that large Library, should have been put to some really useful purpose."

Antonia gave a little sigh of relief.

"Thank you, Your Grace. I should be very distressed if Mr. Lowry found himself in trouble on my account."

"You were telling me about your education," the Duke prompted.

Antonia gave him a smile that transformed her pale face.

"I am afraid," she said, "that what I know about horses, the knowledge I have acquired from your books and a capacity for speaking French comprise my entire repertoire."

"You have no other talents?" he enquired.

"None that I know of! I never have time to paint in water colours or embroider cushion-covers."

She gave a little sigh.

"I suppose that shows I am not very feminine, but then I ought to have been a boy!"

The Duke raised his eye-brows and she explained:

"Papa longed for a son and was quite certain that I would be one. I was to have been christened Anthony."

"I see," the Duke said. "So to make up for it you have become what is known as a 'tom-boy'."

He looked as he spoke at the unbecoming bonnet on her hair which he saw was not dressed in a fashionable manner.

He also glanced at her ill-fitting gown which had been made for Felicity and now had been altered, although not at all skilfully.

He had not expected a young girl to have the elegance, the *chic* or the sophistication of women like the Marchioness whom he had found so desirable and indeed so irresistible.

BARBARA CARTLAND

But vaguely at the back of his mind he had thought of a débutante in spotless white with wide innocent blue eyes, golden hair, and looking something like the angels in the picture-books his mother had read to him as a child.

Antonia did not look in the least like an angel and in fact her appearance was not at all what he had envisaged in his wife.

As if she realised what he was thinking Antonia said a little nervously:

"I am sure I could look . . . better than I do now if I could wear a new gown which had been chosen especially for me."

"You mean . . ." the Duke began.

"I am the younger sister, Your Grace!"

Antonia could not help smiling at his perplexity.

What did the Duke know about being poor, she thought, of striving to make ends meet, wondering where the money would come from to pay the bills that poured in day after day?

He had always lived in the lap of luxury. He had always been a rich man with great possessions, the owner of a proud title.

"How can he possibly understand," she asked herself scathingly, "what ordinary people have to put up with in their lives?"

Because she suddenly felt annoyed and at the same time slightly deflated by his scrutiny, Antonia rose to her feet.

"I think, Your Grace, I should go now," she said. "My father will be waiting to greet you at three o'clock this afternoon. If you feel you could not contemplate having me as your wife, I shall quite understand. Felicity is very lovely and perhaps in time she will grow fond of you."

"You appear to have set me a problem, Lady Antonia," the Duke said. "My choice appears to be between a young woman who, if she is truthful, will hate the sight of me, and another who is enamoured of my horses and not in the least of me as a man!"

He spoke sarcastically and Antonia answered him without thinking:

"It might be very inconvenient for Your Grace to have a wife who was much interested in you for yourself."

"What are you suggesting by that?" the Duke enquired and now there was an icy note in his voice that had not been there previously.

"Only that in the sort of marriage you envisage, Your Grace . . . an arranged marriage . . . which is to bring an . . . advantage to both parties, it would be best, if you had . . . other interests, that your wife should have . . . some too!"

There was a pregnant silence. Then the Duke said:

"And where you are concerned it would be my horses?"

"Exactly!" Antonia said.

She had the feeling that he was annoyed, if not positively angry, at what she had suggested and thought despairingly that she had messed up the interview: now there would be no chance of his doing what she wished.

She was certain that when he came to see the Earl in the afternoon he would ask for Felicity's hand and not hers.

"I have tried and failed!" Antonia told herself. "I can do no more."

She curtsied very politely and as she rose said:

"I must thank Your Grace for listening to me, I deeply regret that I have delayed you from going riding."

"I shall think with great care about all you have said to me, Lady Antonia," the Duke said, "and whatever my decision I hope I shall have the pleasure of seeing you this afternoon."

"That, I can assure you, is very unlikely," Antonia replied, "unless of course you ask for me."

She gave him a quick glance and he thought her eyes had a sparkle of defiance in them.

Then before he could reach the door she had opened it herself and was hurrying across the Hall to where her maid was waiting.

The Butler let them out and the Duke stood staring with an expression which was almost one of stupefaction, until the door closed behind them.

"Good God!" he muttered to himself.

He knew that he was more surprised by Antonia's appearance and what she had said to him than by anything that had happened in his life for a very long time.

'The whole situation is absurd—utterly absurd!' he thought as he rode towards the Park.

He avoided the Row where he was certain to meet a number of acquaintances, and galloped in the less fashionable part on the other side of the Serpentine.

Although after an hour's exercise he undoubtedly felt better in himself, he still found it impossible to decide his future.

Everything had seemed comparatively simple when Clarice had persuaded him that Felicity Wyndham was exactly the type of wife he required and beguiled him into writing to the Earl of Lemsford.

It was true, the Duke thought, that at the back of his mind he had assumed that any woman he honoured would be content to live in the country except on special occasions.

Although the Marchioness had said it would be easier for them to see each other when they were both in Hertfordshire he had the uncomfortable feeling that there might be prying eyes and just as many gossiping tongues in the country as there were in London.

Now for the first time the full impact of what he was about to do seemed to strike him like a blow.

Could he really contemplate spending a lifetime with a woman in whom he had no interest and who, even if she did not interfere with his love affairs, might prove an intolerable burden in other ways?

"What would we talk about?" the Duke asked himself as he slowed the stallion, now not so frisky, down to a trot.

If he married Antonia, he told himself, it would undoubtedly be about horses.

He had not missed the light in her eyes when she spoke of them or the excitement in her voice.

The Duke was not used to women showing interest in other subjects when he was present.

If their faces lit up, it was when they looked at *him*! If their voices deepened with excitement, it was because *he* excited them!

Antonia certainly did not look like the type of woman he had envisaged as bearing his name.

Yet there was something about her which made it difficult for him to dismiss her as completely unattractive.

Her clothes were lamentable, but at least she was conscious of their deficiencies and she might, as another woman would put it, 'pay for dressing'.

"The whole thing is ridiculous!" the Duke told himself. "How can I possibly marry a girl who comes to my house early in the morning and offers herself to me in place of her sister?"

Then he thought it was really no more extraordinary than marrying the sister he had never met.

He realised that neither the Marchioness nor himself had for one moment considered the possibility that the girl they had chosen for such an enviable position might positively dislike the idea and in fact be in love with somebody else.

"I will call the whole thing off," the Duke decided. "I will send a note to the Earl—tell him I have made a mistake—that unfortunately circumstances prevent me from calling on him and I have no desire to meet his daughter!"

He knew even as he spoke the words to himself that to do so would be to insult the Earl gratuitously and unforgivably. Moreover it would involve him in explaining to the Marchioness why he could not do what she had asked of him.

She had set her heart on becoming a Lady of the Bedchamber and the Duke knew that the Queen would not have been speaking idly when she had implied it was more or less a condition of the appointment that he should find himself a wife.

"Dammit!" the Duke ejaculated. "Royalty has no right to interfere with one's private life."

But even as he spoke he knew that in the Society in which they moved Royalty was always interfering.

If there were rules and restrictions as regards Buckingham Palace, there were always innumerable difficulties and problems arising for those who were close friends of the Prince of Wales.

The Duke had only to enter Marlborough House and be alone with the Heir to the Throne to find himself involved in situations that required him to strain every intellectual faculty to find a solution.

"You are a good fellow, Athol! I cannot think what I would do without you," the Prince had said not once but a dozen times in the last year.

And the Duke knew that at least he had certainly earned the Prince's gratitude.

In February he had been deeply involved when His Royal Highness had been subpoenaed to appear in the divorce case Sir Charles Mordant brought against his wife.

Twelve letters from the Prince to Lady Mordant, who was by now in a lunatic asylum, were read out in Court.

Although they were innocuous and the Prince was completely exonerated of having any part in the breakup of the marriage, a whirlwind of public condemnation arose.

The Duke, like most of the Prince's friends, had a hard time defending him.

He had vowed then that he would take care never to find himself in a similar position, which the Queen described as being 'painful and lowering'.

But marriage!

He was back with his own problem again.

It had already kept him awake, tossing and turning for two nights before he finally had written to the Earl of Lemsford, and felt that the die was cast.

He realised it was time for him to return home to change after his ride.

He had a meeting to attend in the House of Lords at eleven o'clock and he would be late if he did not hurry.

He felt a sudden reluctance to leave the Park until he had made up his mind one way or the other.

"Shall I marry the girl or shall I somehow get out of the mess in which I find myself?" he asked himself aloud.

His horse pricked his ears at the sound of his voice, and quickened his speed and, as the Duke touched him with his spur, broke into a gallop.

It might not solve anything, but at least he felt better because he was travelling at speed.

"What did he say? What happened?" Felicity asked.

Antonia had only just returned home to be in time for breakfast at half past eight.

When Felicity had looked at her across the table with questioning eyes, she had been unable to give her an encouraging smile for the simple reason she was now sure she had failed in her quest.

The Earl and Countess discussed all through breakfast the Duke's visit in the afternoon, going over and over for the hundredth time what should be said and what the procedure should be.

"You will first see His Grace alone, Edward," the Countess decided. "Then you will send for me, and what we have now to decide is whether I shall bring Felicity in with me or wait until after I have talked with the Duke myself."

Antonia had heard the arguments for and against so many times that she could no longer give it her attention.

Instead she concentrated on deciding exactly what she should say to Felicity.

It would not be fair to raise her hopes. At the same time to tell her categorically she had failed would be to precipitate another flood of tears.

And that, Antonia thought, would solve nothing.

Now walking across Felicity's bed-room, Antonia said slowly:

"The answer is, Felicity, I really do not know!"

"What do you mean, you do not know?" Felicity asked frantically. "Will he marry you instead of me? Surely he must have told you if he would!"

"He said he would think about it."

"How can he want me? How can he?" Felicity asked despairingly. "You told him I was in love with somebody else?"

"I made it quite clear. But after all there is no reason why that should worry him when he is in love with the Marchioness!"

"And if he is, surely it cannot matter to him who he marries, whether it is you or me?"

"I more or less said that," Antonia admitted, "but I am not as pretty as you, Felicity! Duchesses should be outstanding and beautiful, as you well know!"

"You certainly look dreadful in that old gown of mine," Felicity said. "What on earth made you wear it?"

"I have nothing else," Antonia said simply. "Your green one is so tight it is almost indecent! And I have had no time to mend the pink one which had burst its seams through sheer old age! After all, you wore it for years before it was handed down to me."

"If there had been time you could have altered one of my new gowns," Felicity said.

"And what do you suppose Mama would have said to that?" Antonia asked.

She realised how distressed her sister was looking and said soothingly:

"It may be all right, Felicity. We must just pray he will think it better to ask for me, since I am willing to marry him, than for you who cannot bear the idea."

"I will not marry him! I would rather die!" Felicity said dramatically. "I belong to Harry . . . I always have. I could not . . . I could not let another man . . . touch me!"

"I suppose all women feel like that when they are in love," Antonia said as if she was speaking to herself. "But why are men so different? They seem to be able to make love to two or three women at the same time without it perturbing them!"

"That is not love!" Felicity said. "It is something horrid! Harry says that because he loves me he can never even see another woman! They just do not exist where he is concerned!"

Antonia did not answer and Felicity suddenly put her arms around her sister.

"Oh, Antonia, help me, help me!" she cried. "I am so frightened, so terrified that I shall be made to marry this horrible Duke and never see Harry again!"

"I am sure it will be all right," Antonia said soothingly.

At the same time even to herself her voice sounded uncertain.

The Duke arrived at 29 Chesham Street precisely at three o'clock, and as a concession to the importance of the occasion he travelled in a closed carriage.

It was not a great distance from Berkeley Square to Chesham Street in Belgravia where the Earl had a small and comparatively inexpensive residence.

The Duke's London carriage, with his crest on the painted panels and the accoutrements of silver, was extremely impressive. His horses were superlative.

The Duke himself was resplendent in a morning-coat which fitted him like a glove and his striped trousers were in the very latest vogue.

His top-hat which sat on the side of his dark hair had the curled brim which Locke had decreed as the *dernier-cri* and yet everything about him seemed to have that degree of casualness which only a well-bred Englishman could impart to his clothes.

An ancient Butler escorted the Duke up the twisting staircase to the first floor where the Earl was waiting for him in the Drawing-Room.

It had been the subject of another long controversy as to whether it would be more correct for the Earl to be waiting in the small, rather stuffy Study at the back of the house where he habitually sat.

But the Countess had decided it was not impressive enough and the chairs were so shabby that the Duke could not help noticing them.

The Drawing-Room, however, decorated with fresh flowers, was quite a pleasant room, despite the fact that there was a slight stiffness about it as it was usually kept for Receptions or other occasions when the Countess entertained formally.

"Good afternoon, Your Grace," the Earl said with a bluff heartiness. "I am delighted to meet you. I knew your father, but unfortunately I have not had the pleasure of your acquaintance since you were a boy."

Try as he would he could not help a slight resentment creeping into the tone of his voice.

"It has been most remiss of me not to have invited you to Doncaster Park," the Duke replied. "But as you must know, I am seldom in residence, being kept in London by my duties at the House of Lords or finding the Leicestershire packs provide me with better sport than those in Hertfordshire."

"We are not a particularly good hunting county, Your

Grace," the Earl admitted. "Nevertheless we can occasionally get an exceptional day on the southern part of your estate. The coverts at Harmer Green, for instance, gave us the best run of the season last December!"

"I heard about it," the Duke remarked.

"I think everybody who was out enjoyed themselves," the Earl said. "I was unfortunately not in at the kill owing to the fact that I am somewhat of a heavy-weight. I lost my second horse."

"That must have been bad luck," the Duke said lightly, "but I dare say your daughter, Lady Antonia, supplied you with a graphic account of what happened."

"Antonia?" the Earl exclaimed in surprise. "Well, as a matter of fact, she did, Your Grace. She rides well and so of course does my daughter Felicity."

"I am sure both your daughters follow Your Lordship's lead," the Duke said politely.

There was a somewhat uncomfortable silence. Then the Earl ventured:

"You said in your letter, Your Grace, that you had the idea that our families should be more closely associated than they have been in the past. May I ask exactly what you mean by that?"

"I think you must already have a good idea of my intentions," the Duke replied slowly.

"You mean marriage?" the Earl enquired heavily.

"That is what I had in mind," the Duke agreed.

There was no doubt about the look of pleasure in the Earl's face as he said:

"It is of course a suggestion, Your Grace, to which I shall give my whole-hearted consent and support. Although I say it myself, Felicity is a very lovely young woman. I feel sure you would like to meet her. Shall I send for her so that she can join us for a few moments before we go further into this matter?"

Without waiting for the Duke's reply the Earl moved towards the bell-pull hanging at the side of the mantelpiece.

Only as he reached it did the Duke say quietly:

"It was actually, My Lord, your second daughter I had in mind—Lady Antonia!"

The Earl's expression was ludicrous. His hand dropped to his side.

"Antonia!" he ejaculated. "I think Your Grace has made a mistake!"

The Duke's fingers were playing with his gold watch-chain.

"I think not," he said. "Perhaps I was remiss in not stating clearly in my letter to which of your daughters I desired to pay my addresses. It is in fact Lady Antonia!"

"But—I never envisaged such a thing," the Earl gasped, "neither did my wife. Antonia is the younger and . . ."

He paused and the Duke knew he was trying to find words in which to describe his second child.

"I am sorry if I misled you," the Duke said, "But now that it is quite clear may I suggest, My Lord, that you ring the bell, as you intended?"

The Earl seemed too bemused to argue.

He pulled the bell. When the Butler, who had obviously been waiting outside the door, appeared he said sharply:

"Ask Her Ladyship to come here immediately and—alone!"

"Alone, My Lord?"

"That is what I said," the Earl affirmed.

The Butler withdrew and a few moments later the Countess rustling in silk and wearing almost every jewel she possessed, which were not many, came into the Drawing-Room.

Her face was wreathed in smiles and she held out her hand in a welcoming gesture as she said:

"Your Grace! How delightful to see you here! I have always longed to meet our nearest neighbour in Hertfordshire, and it seems unbelievable that the years have passed by without us becoming acquainted!"

"It does indeed!" the Duke answered. "But now, as His Lordship will tell you, the omissions of the past are to be rectified."

"The Duke wishes to marry Antonia!" the Earl said abruptly.

"Antonia?"

The Countess was no less astonished than her husband had been, but quicker than he, she recovered her poise.

"I think you have made a mistake, my dear Duke. You surely mean Felicity, our elder daughter. She is lovely, so very attractive that I have always been certain she will make a brilliant marriage and make some lucky man extremely happy."

"There is no mistake, Emily," the Earl interposed before the Duke could speak. "His Grace means Antonia!"

"I do not believe it!" the Countess exclaimed. "How can you possibly wish to marry Antonia when you can have Felicity?"

The Duke began to grow somewhat bored with the argument.

"Of course," he said addressing the Earl, "if you do not wish to give your consent to such a union I shall quite understand. In which case, My Lord, I can only withdraw and ask your forgiveness for taking up so much of your time."

His words could not have caused more consternation than if he had cracked a whip under the Earl and Countess's noses.

"My dear fellow, I am not saying you cannot marry Antonia if you wish to do so," the Earl said quickly.

"No, indeed!" his wife interrupted. "Of course we should be thrilled and delighted to welcome you as a son-in-law, whichever of our daughters you prefer, but it is just slightly surprising. Antonia is . . ."

The Countess paused for a word.

". . . the younger!" she finished lamely.

"I should like to make Lady Antonia's acquaintance," the Duke said.

"I will fetch her," the Countess answered and casting a despairing glance at her husband went from the room.

"I am afraid I have been remiss in not offering you any refreshment," the Earl said. "I see there is some wine on the table. Would you have a glass of sherry, Your Grace, or would you prefer port?"

"Neither, thank you," the Duke replied. "I make it a rule never to drink in the afternoon. I find at most dinner-parties, especially those at Marlborough House, one has to drink so much that only the most strenuous exercise will shake it off the next day."

"You are right! Of course you are right!" the Earl agreed. "Indeed it is difficult to refuse a drink when one is in convivial company."

The Duke was thinking of a suitable reply to this rather banal chit-chat when the door opened and the Countess returned followed by Antonia.

She was wearing the same gown she had been wearing early in the morning.

But without the ugly bonnet she did in fact look more attractive, and as her eyes met those of the Duke he knew she was trying to tell him without words how grateful she was.

As she curtsied he took her hand and felt her small fingers tighten on his.

"May I introduce my daughter Antonia!" the Earl asked ceremoniously. "Antonia, His Grace the Duke of Doncaster has asked for your hand in marriage! I need not say how fortunate your mother and I consider you to be, and I hope you will be fully appreciative of the honour His Grace has accorded you."

"I am indeed very honoured, Your Grace," Antonia said in a quiet voice.

"I hope I shall make you happy," the Duke said a little stiffly.

"And I hope that I may . . . please you, Your Grace."

"That will be all, Antonia," the Earl said. "His Grace and I have various matters to discuss."

He looked at his wife and added:

"I think, Emily, it would be best if we do so alone."

"Of course, Edward," the Countess agreed meekly. "Good-bye, Your Grace. My husband will, I am sure, invite you to dine with us either this week or next and I feel sure there will be a great many details of the marriage that we must discuss in the near future."

"Of course, Your Ladyship," the Duke replied.

The Countess curtsied and the Duke bowed.

Antonia curtsied.

Only as she turned towards the door and her father could not see her face was the Duke almost certain that she winked at him!

# CHAPTER THREE

"Your health, Athol!"

It was the third or fourth time the gentlemen seated around the Dining-Table had drunk the Duke's health and he fancied that some of them were getting a trifle 'foxed'.

The dinner had been superlative. The Chef had excelled himself in order to impress the Duke's numerous relations who had accepted his invitation to stay at Doncaster Park for his wedding.

The Duke realised that most of them came with not only a sense of relief that he was doing his duty to the family so that he could produce an heir, but also considerable curiosity.

They had none of them met Antonia: their innumerable suggestions that he should take her to Receptions, Dinner-parties or even Balls in London for the purpose of introducing her to the family had met with no response.

'There will be quite enough for them to talk about to-morrow,' he thought.

As if the idea of his wedding weighed heavily upon him, the Duke made an excuse to the cousin sitting next to him and went from the Dining-Room, aware that most of the party had not noticed his departure.

He walked across the huge marble hall which in Adam's inimitable manner was decorated with classical sculpture set in alcoves, and ignoring the row of attentive footmen, walked down the front steps.

Reaching the gravel sweep in front of the house he turned not towards the garden but to the stables.

It was later than he expected it to be. Already the sun had sunk and it was neither light nor dark but twilight which made the great mansion look like the Palace in a fairy tale.

The Duke had meant to arrive at his country home far earlier. He had in fact told Mr. Graham to notify Ives that he would ride over The Chase before dinner.

He had looked forward to doing this, because as the flat-racing season was nearly over he had decided that he would now concentrate on steeple-chasing.

Accordingly he had instructed Ives to have a number of Grand National fences set out on The Chase incorporating some of the new land he had just acquired from the Earl of Lemsford.

It was something he had planned to do for some years, and while he had been phenomenally successful on the flat he felt it was a challenge to see if he could train horses which could prove themselves over steeple-chasing courses.

The Grand National Handicap Steeplechase which had first been run in 1839, took place on the last week in March.

Steeple-chases had meant a good old hell-for-leather match race across any naturally fenced country that was available.

The sudden prominence of the Grand Liverpool Steeple-chase as it was called, was due to the fact that it was the first jumping race for a really desirable prize.

Twelve hundred pounds was the purse in 1839.

It was four miles across country mostly heavily ploughed, with twenty-nine jumps in all, fifteen to be negotiated on the first round, fourteen on the second.

Two years ago in 1868 a horse called The Laird had won

the race although he was only fifteen hands high and he had won it again this year, amid scenes of great enthusiasm.

The Duke was determined that in 1871 his colours would be first past the post!

He had bought a horse called Black Knight which he fancied might be exactly what he required. It was an exceptional animal in appearance, but although he had heard a great deal about its performance he wanted to try Black Knight out himself.

Unfortunately his plan had gone awry because the Marchioness had exerted every wile that she knew to keep him with her.

Like all women, having persuaded him to marry against his better judgment, she was now bitterly regretting that after to-morrow he would no longer be free.

"How can I bear to think of you on your honeymoon, Athol?" she asked. "And how will you bear three weeks, or will it be more, away from England and me?"

"I shall miss you, Clarice, you know that," the Duke said automatically because it was expected of him.

"Promise that when you are in Paris you will think of me every minute, every moment!"

Her arms went round his neck as she said:

"It will not be your wife who perturbs me and makes me so anxious for you, but those exotic, expensive houris with whom you spent so much of your time and money last year.

There was no chance of the Duke refuting this, even if he had wished to do so, because the Marchioness's lips, fiercely, passionately demanding, prevented him from speaking and anyway there was no need for words.

Later the Duke had extracted himself with difficulty but he was so late in reaching Doncaster Park that dinner had to be put back an hour.

There was only time for him to bathe, change and greet his numerous relations before they proceeded into the great Baronial Hall which Adam must have designed with just such an occasion as this in mind.

The Castertons were a good-looking lot, the Duke thought, looking down the table.

His aunts, his cousins and his grandmother all looked, if

not magnificent, certainly aristocratic however old they became.

'Breeding shows itself in bone-structure,' he thought and
was glad that, if he had to marry, his wife should come from
an ancient family with a pedigree that was almost the equal of
his own.

This however was not particularly reassuring when he
thought of Antonia as a person rather than a name on a
genealogical family-tree.

He had in fact seen practically nothing of her since their
engagement had been announced.

Because the Duke felt that the numerous parties that
would be given for them jointly and the endless process of
being looked over by each other's families would prove intolerable, he had insisted on the marriage taking place far
more quickly than his future mother-in-law thought seemly.

There was however the excuse that in July everybody
would be leaving London.

While for economy's sake the Earl had decided that Antonia should be married in the country at their local Church,
the majority of the guests could conveniently come down
from London for the ceremony.

"Indecent haste, I call it!" the Countess remarked tartly.
"At any rate it gives me a good excuse to buy you only a small
trousseau. Your future husband is rich enough to provide
you with anything you need, and what money we have would
better be spent on Felicity."

Her mother was being disagreeable, Antonia knew, simply because she could not adjust herself to accepting the fact
that the Duke had offered for her rather than Felicity.

"I cannot understand it!" the Countess said over and over
again.

Then finally she found an answer to what perplexed her
and the Earl in the fact that Antonia rode so well.

"He has obviously heard what a 'go-er' she is in the
hunting-field," the Earl said.

"Felicity also rides well!" the Countess said, championing
her elder daughter as she always did.

"Not as well as Antonia!" the Earl retorted.

Antonia thought during the weeks that preceded the

wedding that her mother's dislike expressed itself every time she looked at her and every time she spoke.

She had never made any pretence that Felicity was not her favourite child; but now, Antonia thought, what had been mere indifference where she was concerned had changed into something very much stronger and very hurtful.

There was however nothing she could do about it, while Felicity told her over and over again how grateful she was and how both she and Harry would bless her for the rest of their lives.

"As soon as you are married, Harry has decided he will speak to Papa," Felicity said.

"He had better wait until I come back from my honeymoon," Antonia advised. "I will then try to persuade the Duke to say pleasant things about Harry to Papa and Mama and perhaps make them see him in a different light."

"Do you think the Duke would do that?" Felicity asked. "If he would, I am sure Papa would then think Harry was a suitable husband for me."

"I can at least try," Antonia replied.

She wondered as she spoke whether it would be easy to make the Duke do what she wanted and give a helping hand for the second time where Felicity was concerned.

She did not have a chance however of approaching him on any subject and she had the idea that he might be relieved that they saw so little of each other.

The Duke was in fact finding his time fully occupied with the Marchioness.

She had been appointed a Lady of the Bedchamber and she thanked him for making it possible by being even more passionate and voluptuous in their moments of intimacy than she had ever been before.

He wondered sometimes how it was possible for a woman who looked almost angelic to be a ferocious tiger when it came to love-making.

As he walked through the high stone archway which led into the stables the Duke was thinking of the Marchioness.

It was almost as if her arms were still clinging to him

possessively and her lips were still like a consuming fire against his.

Then he realised the stables were very quiet and knew the stable-boys had retired for the night.

He wished now that he had sent for Ives when he first arrived and explained to the old groom why he could not go round the course as he had planned.

Ives he knew would be disappointed.

He had always wanted the Duke to go in for steeple-chasing, and now there would be much they had to discuss and a number more horses to be bought before they could really enter a new field in the racing world.

"I am too late," the Duke told himself. "He will have gone to bed."

The horses were all shut up in their stalls for the night.

He was just wondering if he would have a look at Black Knight when he heard the sound of hoofs at the far end of the buildings.

The stables were so extensive that in the dusk it was hard to see clearly what was happening, so that he heard rather than saw two horses being ridden into the stable-yard to enter the stalls at the far end.

The Duke wondered who was out so late, and told himself that perhaps Ives was having a last look at the jumps and wished that he could have been with him.

He walked on and as he drew nearer heard Ives speak to be answered by a voice he also knew.

"I did it! I did it, Ives! It is the most exciting thing I have ever done in my life!"

"You rode magnificently, M'Lady!" Ives replied. "But you'd no right to take that untried animal over the jumps, as you well know!"

"But he took them like a bird!" Antonia insisted. "He hesitated just for a moment at the Water-Jump, then he stretched himself out and I swear not a drop of water touched his hoofs!"

"Oi be sure of it, M'Lady, but that jump's too big for a woman!"

"Not for me!" Antonia said proudly.

"Oi don't know what His Grace would say, that Oi don't!"

The Duke stood still outside the stable.

He was aware that Ives and Antonia were unsaddling the horses.

There were two stalls side by side in that particular stable, Ives was rubbing down his mount making a whistling sound through his teeth that the Duke could remember hearing ever since he was a boy.

"I am quite certain that Black Knight has a chance of winning the Grand National!" Antonia was saying. "You must tell the Duke so."

"And how am Oi to explain to His Grace what a good jumper the horse is?" Ives enquired.

"He should have been here to see for himself," Antonia answered. "We waited until it was nearly dark."

"That be true, M'Lady."

Antonia gave a little sigh.

"Oh, Ives, I wish I were not going away to-morrow. I want to go round the course again not once, but a dozen times!"

"Ye'll enjoy yourself abroad, M'Lady. Oi hears as ye be going to France. Them Frenchies have some good horses!"

"Do they? Yes, of course they have! I can see them at the races if His Grace will take me there!"

She sighed again.

"But I shall be counting the days until I can be back, to ride Black Knight for the second time."

"Oi'm only hoping, M'Lady that His Grace won't consider the horse too strong for ye."

"You know he is not!" Antonia answered. "I do not think there is a horse I cannot handle!"

"That's true, M'Lady. Ye've a way with animals, as Oi've always told ye. 'Tis something as be born in a person. They either has it, or they hasn't!"

There was a silence during which Ives went on whistling through his teeth and the Duke was aware that Antonia too was rubbing down her horse.

"How does the Marchioness of Northaw ride?" she asked in a low voice.

"A Park-rider, M'Lady!" Ives replied disparagingly. "But she's hard on her horses."

"What do you mean by that?" Antonia enquired.

"A groom from Northaw Place were here t'day asking me what Oi uses as a poultice."

"You mean she has spur-galled her horse?" Antonia asked.

"Oi be afraid so, M'Lady, and pretty bad the groom told Oi it were."

"How can these fashionable women be so cruel . . . so insensitive?" Antonia asked furiously. "Seeing the way they ride, only trit-trotting in the Park, there is no reason for them to use the spur, especially the five-pointed rowel, unless it actually gives them pleasure."

Ives did not answer and after a moment Antonia went on, still with a note of anger in her voice:

"Do you remember what Lady Rosalind Lynke did to the horses when she stayed here two years ago?"

"Oi do indeed, M'Lady. We both worked hard on the horses she damaged."

"I have never forgotten it," Antonia said.

"No more have Oi, M'Lady," Ives agreed. "And very helpful ye were. The horses were that nervous and restless from the harsh treatment they'd received that only ye could calm them while Oi applied the poultices."

"I wondered then, and I wonder now," Antonia said reflectively, "what it is that makes those feminine frilly sort of women so cruel when they are on a horse?"

"Perhaps it be a sense of power, M'Lady. Some women resent a man's superiority, so they takes it out on a dumb beast what can't answer 'em back!"

"I am sure you are right, Ives, and I loathe them for their cruelty! I swear to you I will never wear a spur however fashionable it may be, or whoever tells me it is essential to the training of a horse."

She spoke passionately. The Duke turned and retraced his steps towards the house.

As he went he was thinking not of the Marchioness but of Antonia.

\* \* \*

The carriage decorated behind with two horse-shoes, two old boots, its roof be-speckled with grains of rice, rolled away down the drive.

The Duke sat back against the cushioned seat and thought with a sense of unutterable relief that it was all over!

He had been spared, for which he was extremely relieved, a Wedding-Breakfast which might have lasted interminably, simply because there were too many guests for the Earl to consider entertaining them in such a lavish manner.

Even if they had restricted the Breakfast to relations there would not have been enough accommodation in the Dining-Room at The Towers.

The Church ceremony had therefore been followed by a Reception from which the Duke and his bride could escape in little over an hour.

He had risen in the morning in a depressed mood which he could not shake off, even though he broke his rule of never drinking alcohol at breakfast-time.

The brandy, good though it was, did not seem to alleviate his sense of being pressured into doing something he had no wish to do and also his apprehension about the future.

When he entered the village Church to find it packed to over-flowing and stiflingly hot, he had an almost irresistible impulse to back out of what he told himself was a 'mockery of a marriage'.

It had been Clarice who had instigated the whole thing, and as he came from the vestry accompanied by his Best Man and she smiled at him from the fourth pew, he told himself he would willingly strangle her!

She was looking inexpressibly lovely and he thought that it was most insensitive of her to be present at his wedding.

Since she was a near-neighbour, it might indeed have caused comment if she had refused the Earl's invitation.

At the same time she made him feel uncomfortable and he resented that, just as, he thought savagely, he resented everything else which was happening to him.

There was a stir at the end of the Church and his Best Man whispered:

"The bride has arrived! At least she has not kept you waiting!"

The reason Antonia was on time, the Duke told himself cynically, was not that she was considering his feelings but that she would not wish to keep the horses that were conveying her from her home to the Church waiting in this heat.

Having seen Felicity as she arrived, he could not help asking himself if he would not have been wiser to marry the girl Clarice had originally chosen for him rather than her unimpressive, horsy sister.

Wearing a bridesmaid's gown of pale blue that matched her eyes, and carrying a bouquet of pink roses which echoed the wreath she wore in her fair hair, Felicity looked extremely pretty.

She was in a modest way with her pink and white beauty the counterpart of the Marchioness.

Felicity had curtsied to him, and as she rose she said in a soft voice which only he could hear:

"Thank you! Your Grace must know how very, very grateful I am."

What other man, the Duke asked himself angrily, in his position and with his reputation, would be thanked by a pretty girl because he had *not* asked her to marry him?

He took a quick glance at Antonia as she came up the aisle on her father's arm and told himself again he had made a mistake.

It was very difficult to see what Antonia looked like since she wore a Brussels lace veil over her face.

Her wedding-gown, which had a long train, was carried by two reluctant small children who were being almost forcibly propelled up the aisle by their Nurses.

Behind them, Felicity was the only bridesmaid.

The service was conducted by the Bishop of St. Albans and the local Vicar. The Bishop besides actually joining the couple in matrimony gave them an extremely boring address to which the Duke deliberately closed his ears.

Then there was the drive to The Towers under triumphal arches made in the village with small nosegays of flowers being thrown into the open carriage by the village children.

The Towers, with such a large crowd inside it, seemed even hotter and more oppressive than the Church had been.

By the time Antonia had changed and come downstairs

the Duke was feeling that if he had to wait any longer he would leave alone.

Fortunately—and the Duke had no doubt she was thinking once again of the horses waiting for them—Antonia was a good deal quicker than most women would have been in the circumstances.

But now they had escaped, the Duke thought with satisfaction, as he brushed the rice from his coat and thought that the pelting of the bride and bridegroom with rice as a symbol of fertility was a pagan custom which should have been done away with a long time ago.

"Do you think we ought to stop and tell the coachman to throw away the horse-shoes and the boots which I can hear rattling away behind us?" Antonia asked.

"I have had a better idea than that," the Duke replied. "When we are out of the village, and just before we come to the cross-roads, I have ordered my Phaeton to be waiting for us. It may be unconventional, but I thought it would be a quicker way of reaching London."

"And much more pleasant than being cooped up in here for hours," Antonia exclaimed, "it was clever of you to think of it!"

The admiration in her voice mitigated a little of the Duke's irritation that he had been feeling all the morning.

They drove on in silence, and when the carriage came to a standstill Antonia jumped out eagerly and hurried up the road to where the Phaeton was waiting.

She greeted the grooms in charge, addressing them by name, the Duke noticed, then went to pat the team of four perfectly-matched chestnuts.

She talked to the horses as they tried to nuzzle their noses against her and the Duke was aware of an expression on her face that he had not seen before.

"I am glad Rufus is one of the horses taking us to London," she said to Ives. "He has always been my favourite."

"Yes, M'Lady," Ives replied a little uncertainly.

He was embarrassed that Antonia was talking to him in the Duke's presence and showing a knowledge of the horses that he might find it hard to explain.

"I think we should be on our way!" the Duke said

abruptly. "The guests will soon be leaving your father's house, and it will cause quite a lot of comment if we are seen changing vehicles."

"Yes, of course," Antonia agreed obediently.

The footmen helped her into the Phaeton and a groom sprang up behind them. The Duke set the horses in motion and the four out-riders who were to travel with them to London spread out on either side so as to be clear of the dust.

"This is exciting!" Antonia said. "I was wondering how soon it would be possible for you to drive me in your Phaeton! I was afraid I would have to wait until we came back from our honeymoon."

The Duke glanced down at her and realised that the short satin coat she was wearing over a thin gown was more becoming than anything he had seen her in on previous occasions.

Her bonnet also, trimmed with small ostrich feathers, was fashionable, and he decided that while she did not compare to advantage with her elder sister she had perhaps, although he was yet to find them, attractions of her own.

He was relieved to find that she did not chatter all the time they were travelling.

In fact she appeared to be concentrating on the horses, and as they journeyed on towards London the Duke found that the fresh air and the fact that it was not so hot made him feel less constrained and irritable than he had been before.

After dinner at Doncaster House where they were to stay the first night of the honeymoon, the Duke in fact felt mellow and almost at peace with the world.

He found that he had enjoyed explaining to Antonia during dinner exactly what his plans were as regards Goodwood Races which would take place while they were away.

He was also surprised at her knowledge, not only about his own horses bought in the last five years and improving the stud he had inherited from his father out of all recognition, but also how much she knew about the other stables with which they came into opposition on the race-courses.

"How can you have learnt all this?" he asked at one moment.

She had corrected him over the breeding of one of Lord

Derby's mares and after a short argument he found that she was right.

"I read the racing-papers," Antonia replied with a smile. "Papa would be horrified if he knew that I did so, because in most of them there are also all sorts of scandalous police reports and slanderous innuendos about political and social personalities."

The Duke knew only too well to which papers she referred and he thought they were certainly not the type of reading suitable for a young girl.

He was however too interested in what Antonia had to say to find fault.

They moved from the Dining-Room into the Library although the Duke had suggested they might sit in the Salon upstairs.

"I have learnt that this is your favourite room," Antonia said, "so let us sit here."

"I think the real reason for your choice is that you want to look at my books," the Duke remarked.

"As soon as you have time," Antonia replied, "I want you to show me all the wonderful treasures you have here, which I am told are equally as fine as those at Doncaster Park."

"I have the uncomfortable feeling that you already know more about them than I do," the Duke said.

Antonia did not answer.

He watched her looking round the Library with a faintly amused smile on his lips, being well aware she was far more interested in her surroundings than in him.

As if she realised what he was thinking, she turned her large grey-green eyes towards him and he had an intuition she was going to say something that was of great importance.

"I have . . . something to ask you," she said.

Now her tone was very different and the gay excitement with which she had been talking all the evening seemed to have vanished.

"What is it?" he asked.

He knew she was feeling for words, but at that moment the door opened and the butler announced:

"The Marchioness of Northaw, Your Grace!"

The Duke, after a momentary start, rose slowly to his feet.

Antonia rose too as the Marchioness, radiantly beautiful, glittering with jewels, and looking like a fairy on a Christmas-tree came gliding towards them. The long tulle train of her gown billowed out behind her.

"I am on my way to a Reception at Marlborough House," she said. "But I had to come in for a second just to give you both my good wishes."

Her words included Antonia, but her blue eyes were fixed on the Duke's and they held a message that only he could understand.

She put her ungloved hand in his and he raised it to his lips.

"It is very gracious of you," he said, "and my wife and I appreciate your expression of goodwill, even at such a late hour!"

It was impossible not to hear the rebuke in his voice, but the Marchioness was quite unperturbed.

"Forgive me for troubling you, Antonia," she said, "but I came out without a handkerchief, I wondered if you would kindly lend me one of yours?"

"Yes, or course," Antonia replied.

She crossed the Library but did not go outside into the Hall, being well aware that the Marchioness's request was only so that she could be rid of her.

Instead she went into the room which adjoined the Library, closing the door behind her.

It was an attractive Salon also overlooking the garden and Antonia had the idea that it was a room which might be allotted to her as the Duke used the Library as his special sanctum.

She thought that the Marchioness must be very sure of the Duke's devotion to have forced herself upon them the first night of his marriage.

Although she knew very little about such things, Antonia was sure that in most cases it would be an embarrassment to a man when his first *tête à tête* with his wife was interrupted by a woman who had been his mistress.

Then she asked herself why she was putting the Marchioness into the past tense.

She was making it very obvious that as far as she was concerned the liaison she had with the Duke would continue as soon as they returned from their honeymoon.

Antonia moved round the Salon looking at the gold snuff-boxes which were arranged on one table, at the *Sèvres* china which decorated another.

She thought the blue and white porcelain was like the Marchioness and told herself with a little sigh that there was no china which even remotely resembled herself.

It was a dispiriting thought and with a wistful expression she was contemplating the fine bronzes which ornamented the mantelpiece when the door opened and the Duke came into the room.

"I must apologise, Antonia," he said. "Our uninvited caller had no right to drive you away in that arbitrary manner."

"I realised she wanted to see you . . . alone," Antonia replied and added in a low voice, "She is very . . . beautiful . . . I can . . . understand what you . . . feel for her."

The Duke stiffened.

"Who has been talking to you?"

Antonia looked at him in surprise.

"Did you expect me not to . . . know that you . . . love the Marchioness and she . . . loves you?" she enquired. "Everybody knows . . . that!"

"Everybody?" the Duke asked incredulously.

"But of course!" Antonia replied. "And most people . . . I think . . . know that you . . . married because the Queen had more or less . . . commanded you to do so."

The Duke was absolutely astounded.

"How can such a story have got about?" he enquired. "I cannot credit that anything so intimate and secret could be known except by the people concerned."

"Well, Colonel Beddington told Papa," Antonia answered, "and I . . . I also heard it from another . . . source."

"Who told you?" the Duke asked abruptly.

"I would . . . rather not say," Antonia answered.

"I insist on you telling me," he said. "As you have already said so much, I might as well know the rest. Who told you?"

Antonia hesitated for a moment, then as if the hardness of his voice and the look of his eyes compelled her, she replied hesitatingly:

"The Marchioness's . . . lady's maid is the sister of Mrs. Mellish's daughter-in-law . . . who is . . . married to one of your . . . grooms."

"Good God!"

There was no doubt the Duke was surprised into being almost speechless.

"Are you telling me," he asked after a moment, "that this is known to all the servants at the Park?"

"Not all of them," Antonia answered. "But they always know what you do . . . and they talk . . . just as the ladies talk in Mama's Drawing-Room . . . except that they are not . . . spiteful about it!"

The Duke looked at her enquiringly and she explained:

"The servants you employ are proud of you! They like to think you are a kind of Don Juan, Sir Lancelot and Casanova all . . . rolled into one. They boast about your . . . love-affairs just as they boast about your successes on the race-course. It is a credit to the whole Estate that you should be such a successful . . . lover."

Antonia paused, but as the Duke apparently had nothing to say she went on:

"It is rather different where Mama's . . . friends are concerned. They want to . . . snigger. They do that about everybody . . . but as you are so important and so much more exciting than anyone else . . . naturally everything you do is a special . . . tit-bit with which they regale each other!"

"You absolutely astound me!" the Duke exclaimed.

"I think because you are so . . . attractive and so . . . important," Antonia said after a moment, "you must . . . expect people to be . . . interested in you, and I think too I . . . understand about all the . . . beautiful ladies whom you have loved."

"What do you understand?" the Duke asked.

There was a note in his voice that should have warned

Antonia that he was angry, but she was to intent on following the train of her own thoughts to be aware of it.

"I could not think at . . . first," she replied, "why you had to have so many women in your life. Then I thought perhaps it was rather like having a . . . stable. One would not want only one horse, however good, however . . . outstanding. One would want lots of thoroughbreds! Perhaps it is a sort of race in which they all try to reach the . . . winning-post, the prize being your heart!"

She spoke confidently because it was like a story she had told herself.

"I would have never believed any woman of my acquaintance would say anything so vulgar and ill-bred!" the Duke exclaimed angrily.

He did not raise his voice but his tone was icy and like a whip-lash.

For a moment Antonia was still as he glared at her.

Then he saw the colour flood in a crimson tide up her small face until it burnt itself against her eyes.

He saw her tremble, and she turned away from him to stand at the table which held the snuff-boxes, looking down at them with her head bent.

There was something about her slight figure which made him realise that she was very young and very vulnerable. He felt unaccountably that he had struck a child.

"I am sorry, Antonia, I should not have spoken to you like that," he said after a moment.

She did not reply and he had the feeling that she was fighting to control her tears.

"What you told me was so utterly surprising," the Duke went on, "that I was quite unnecessarily rude. I have asked you, Antonia, to forgive me."

"I . . . I am . . . sorry," Antonia whispered.

"Will you please turn round?" the Duke asked. "I find it difficult to apologise to your back!"

For a moment he thought she would refuse to do as he asked. Then she turned towards him and he saw there was still a stricken look in her eyes which made him feel ashamed.

"Come and sit down, Antonia," he suggested. "I want to talk to you."

She moved across the room and he found himself thinking she was like a young colt, a little unsteady and unsure of herself, yet ready to trust everyone until she learnt the hard way that not everyone was trustworthy.

Antonia sat down on a sofa and the Duke thought her grey-green eyes were more expressive than any woman's he had ever known.

Before the Duke could speak Antonia faltered:

"Because I have . . . never been . . . alone with anyone like . . . you, I said what . . . came into my head without . . . thinking. It was very . . . foolish of me . . . I will try not to do it again."

She seemed so humiliated and spoke so humbly that it made her seem even more vulnerable than she had been before.

"I am the one to do the apologising, Antonia," the Duke insisted. "I want you always to say what comes into your head. I want you to be frank with me. If we are to make our marriage work, I think it is essential there should be no pretence between us. Do you agree?"

Antonia looked down and her lashes were very dark against her cheeks.

"I . . . may say . . . things you do not . . . wish to . . . hear."

"I want to hear about anything and everything that interests you," the Duke said. "I also always want to be told the truth. I made a mistake just now when I snapped at you for telling me just that. My only excuse is that like you I have never been married before!"

He smiled in a manner which much more experienced women than Antonia had found irresistible.

"Is it . . . wrong of me," Antonia asked after a moment, "to speak of the . . . ladies you have . . . loved?"

"It is not wrong," the Duke answered, "but perhaps a little unusual. However I would much rather you talked about them than bottle up inside you what you think."

She looked up at him and once again he was reminded of a colt which having received a blow, was afraid to approach nearer even though it wished to do so.

"Worst of all, I beg you not to take what my Nurse used

to call 'umbridge'," he went on. "It is an emotion to which I have a positive aversion!"

Antonia gave him a wan little smile.

"I will . . . try not to . . . do that."

"I think that, before we were so unnecessarily interrupted a little while ago, you were about to say something to me," the Duke remarked. "Will you tell me what it was?"

As he spoke he saw the colour burn once again in Antonia's cheeks.

"I . . . think . . . perhaps it might make you . . . angry."

"If I promise not be angry but to consider quietly and seriously everything you have to say to me," the Duke asked, "will you tell me what it was you wished to say?"

Antonia turned her head sideways to stare at the empty fireplace.

The Duke noticed for the first time that she had a small straight nose, a firm little chin and delicately curved lips.

It was only a fleeting impression, before Antonia looked back at him.

"I . . . I was going to ask you a . . . favour," she said in a low voice, and the Duke realised she had made up her mind to be frank.

"I realise you will think it very . . . ignorant of me," she went on, "but I do not know, when a man and woman get . . . married, exactly how they have a . . . baby. I think perhaps it is because they . . . sleep together."

She glanced nervously at the Duke, then looked away again.

"I thought," she continued in a very small voice, "that as you are . . . in love with . . . somebody else, and as we do not . . . know each other very well . . . I might ask you just to . . . wait a little before we . . . had a . . . baby."

As she finished speaking and her voice faltered away into silence Antonia gripped her fingers together and held her breath.

The Duke rose to his feet and stood with his back to the mantelpiece.

"I am glad you were brave enough to tell me what you were thinking, Antonia," he said, after a moment.

"You are . . . not . . . angry?"

"No, of course not!" he replied. "I think in the circumstances you have been extremely sensible in sharing with me what was in your mind."

He paused for a moment, then went on slowly.

"You must try to believe me when I tell you I had no idea that my association with the Marchioness was common knowledge in the country or that it would ever reach your ears."

"Perhaps I . . . should not have . . . told you."

"I am very glad you did," the Duke said. "I am glad too, Antonia, that we can start our life together on a solid foundation. Will you promise me something?"

"What is it?" Antonia enquired.

"That you will keep no secrets from me," the Duke replied. "Not at any rate about important things. However difficult they may appear. I feel somehow we can thrash them out together and find a solution even to the most tricky problem."

He smiled at her again and he saw a little of the nervousness go from her eyes as he went on:

"I think what you have suggested is extremely wise, and I agree that we should get to know each other a great deal better before we do anything so fundamentally important as starting a family."

He saw that Antonia was looking puzzled and after a moment he asked:

"What is troubling you?"

He knew that she was looking at him as if she was wondering whether she dare say what she was thinking. Then she said:

"I have told you I am very ignorant . . . but what I cannot . . . understand is why if . . . when you . . . sleep with me we might . . . have a baby . . . while when you sleep with . . . other ladies like . . . the Marchioness, they do not . . . have one?"

The Duke could not help thinking that this was the most extraordinary conversation he had ever had in his whole life. But he replied very carefully:

"That is one of the questions I would like to answer when we know each other better. Please trust me to explain everything in the future which I am a little reluctant to do to-night."

"Yes . . . of course," Antonia said. "Thank you for being so . . . kind and not being . . . angry with me."

"I will try never to be angry with you again," the Duke said. "But like you I am rather inclined to speak without thinking."

"It is so much . . . easier," Antonia said. "And I have a feeling that if everybody thought before they spoke, there would only be many uncomfortable silences."

"That is true," the Duke smiled. "And now, as we are leaving for Paris to-morrow morning, I suggest, Antonia, that you go to bed. You must be tired after all we have been through to-day, and it must also have been rather tiring going over the jumps last night!"

Antonia was very still. Then she said in a frightened voice:

"You . . . knew?"

"Yes, I knew. I heard what you had done," the Duke said, "and I can hardly credit it possible. Those jumps, if Ives carried out his instructions correctly, are the same height as those on the Grand National course!"

"It was your new horse," Antonia said. "It was very . . . presumptuous of me to ride him . . . but we waited until it was nearly dark and you . . . never came."

"It was my loss," the Duke said. "Have you forgotten, Antonia, that my horses are now yours? I distinctly remember saying in the Marriage Service—'With all my worldly goods I thee endow'."

There was an unmistakable light in Antonia's eyes.

"I should be very . . . very grateful and . . . honoured if I might . . . share them with . . . you," she said after a moment.

"Then we will share them," the Duke replied. "Just as we will share our thoughts and perhaps, when we get to know each other better, our feelings!"

# CHAPTER FOUR

The Duke sat in the Café Anglais waiting for Antonia.

He had been surprised, when he had sent his valet to find out what time she would be ready to leave the house with him, to discover she had already left.

He had awakened early, as he always did, and while he ate his breakfast he read the French newspapers. The news had been a shock when he and Antonia had arrived at Calais the day before.

They had travelled in great comfort from London to Dover in reserved carriages on the fastest train of the day.

There they had joined the Duke's yacht which was waiting for them in the harbour and spent a comfortable night on board, the Channel being as flat as the proverbial mill-pond.

On reaching Calais there were again engaged carriages not only for the Duke and Antonia but also for His Grace's valet and their luggage.

A Courier had gone ahead with instructions from Mr.

Graham to have everything booked for the journey and in readiness for when they reached Paris. Owing to his usual genius for organisation there was not a hitch during the whole journey.

When they arrived it was to find that the house which the Duke had been lent by one of his friends was as charming as he had expected it would be.

Situated just off the Champs Élysées, it was decorated in Louis XIV style and, when they arrived, Antonia was entranced by the tapestries, the Boucher and Fragonard pictures and exquisite Aubusson carpets.

Comfortable though it was, it had however been a tiring journey and the Duke had expected Antonia to sleep late.

When he learnt she had left the house by nine o'clock he had thought with a smile that she was not wasting any time.

"Are you very rich?" she had enquired as they were nearing Paris.

It was a question he had been asked before and he replied:

"It depends on what you wish to buy."

"I think you know the answer to that," Antonia said. "Clothes! Even though the few Mama bought for my trousseau are new, I know they are not right for me."

The Duke had looked at what she was wearing and was sure that, while the Countess of Lemsford's taste might be impeccable for her elder daughter, where Antonia was concerned there was, as she put it, something wrong.

It might be the fussiness of the frills and furbelows on the very English-styled gown, it might be the pastel shades she had chosen—he was not sure.

He only knew that Antonia did not give the impression of being anything but a rather 'frumpy' English bride.

He was however too tactful to say so. All he answered, with a smile on his lips, was:

"I am sure you will not bankrupt me! I presume you mean to visit Worth?"

"If you are quite sure you can afford it!"

"I am quite sure," the Duke answered, "and his gowns are superlative. There is no-one, from the Empress down to the least important actress, who does not wish to be dressed by Frederick Worth!"

"Perhaps he will not wish to be bothered by me," Antonia said humbly.

Then she exclaimed:

"But of course, I forgot! I am now a Duchess! That must count for something, even in France!"

The Duke had laughed and he wondered without a great deal of curiosity what the great Worth would make of Antonia.

His thoughts of gowns or even of the amusements of Paris were however overshadowed by the news he had read in the French newspapers.

It appeared, although he could hardly believe it possible, that France was on the brink of war with Prussia.

Everyone in England had been completely sure that although there was always a certain amount of 'sabre-rattling' in Europe it would come to nothing.

In the spring there had been a spirit of content over the whole Continent which had not been seen for many years.

Only two weeks ago the new British Foreign Secretary Lord Granville, had said blithely to the Duke that there was 'not a cloud in the sky'.

Peace was everywhere except, the Duke had learnt, that it was the hottest summer in memory and there were reports of droughts in several parts of France which had the peasants praying for rain.

It was the sort of crisis he was used to in Hertfordshire and to find the French newspapers filled with news of an incipient war had in fact astounded him.

The Duke was quite certain that the Emperor, whom he had known for many years, in fact since he was exiled in England, had no wish for war. But he was to learn that the Emperor was being pushed hard into being aggressive by his heavy-handed Foreign Secretary, the Duc de Graumont.

His hatred of the Prussians was a personal issue because he had never forgotten Bismarck for calling him 'the stupidest man in Europe!"

When the Duke, deprived of Antonia's company, had sought an aperitif in the Palais Royal before luncheon, he

had met several acquaintances who were only too anxious to
discuss the political situation.

"It is the Empress who is determined we shall attack Germany," one of them said. "I have myself heard her declare
dramatically as she pointed to the Prince Imperial" 'This
child will never reign unless we repair the misfortunes of
Sadowa!' "

"I understood the Emperor was not well," the Duke remarked.

"He is not," was the answer. "He has begun to suffer the
tortures of the damned from a stone in the bladder."

"In which case I think it extremely unlikely that you will
go to war," the Duke replied.

He felt however that his friends were not convinced and
as he sat in the Café Anglais reading *Le Figaro* he realised
that the editorial articles and news items were extremely in-
flammatory and obviously intended to whip up the flames of
bellicosity.

"Thank goodness England will not be involved whatever
happens!" the Duke thought to himself.

He was aware that Britain was, if anything pro-German
as was most of Europe.

The Queen with her German relatives was inevitably
more inclined to favour the Prussians than the Emperor
Louis Napoleon, of whose personal behaviour and his irrepressible Capital she had always disapproved.

"I am sure the whole thing will blow over," the Duke told
himself, "and like so many other war-scares will end in nothing but a few diplomatic insults."

He put down the newspaper and looked again at his
watch.

He could not help thinking that if there was a danger of
keeping the horses waiting rather than himself Antonia
would have been here by now.

The Café Anglais, which was the smartest and the most
famous restaurant in Paris, was filling up.

There were a great number of men having luncheon
alone because it was near the Bourse, but there were also
some very attractive women.

They were all wearing the new gowns which had a suggestion of a bustle and were swept back from the front of the body so that the wearer looked like the figure-head on a ship.

Or, as someone put it more poetically, 'like a goddess moving forward against the wind!'

The crinoline had been discarded two years earlier, and although it was still worn in London, in Paris there was not a sign to show it had ever existed.

Instead there was a profusion of beautiful women, so elegant, so *chic* that the Duke wondered why a man would wish to spend his time and amuse himself in any other Capital.

He had found for himself some years ago how alluring Paris could be.

The only demand was for 'pleasure', a criterion set by the Emperor, who never refused the temptation of a new and pretty face.

Louis Napoleon was in fact notorious not only for his love-affairs, but also for his charm and gallantry. Even Queen Victoria had attested to this when she had written:

"With such a man one can never for a
moment feel safe!"

It was, however, not safety which men and women sought in Paris, and the great Courtesans of the period had spent more money and established themselves as having more power and fewer morals than in any other period in history.

Immense fortunes passed through the hands of the *demi-mondaines*. Even Egyptian Beys could be ruined in a matter of two weeks.

The Emperor was said to have given the lovely Comtesse de Castiglione a pearl necklace costing 432,000 francs besides 50,000 a month pin-money, while Lord Hertford, who was reputed to be the meanest man in Paris, had given her a million for the pleasure of one night in which she promised to abandon herself to every known *volupté*.

The Duke had found it all very amusing on his various visits to Paris, and it did not in fact, he remembered, cost him anything like the large sums expended by his fellow-countrymen.

He was not a particularly conceited man, but he did know that the women with whom he had spent his time had welcomed him for himself and were in fact not interested in what he might give them otherwise.

He was just about to draw his watch once again from his waist-coat pocket, when he saw the occupants at other tables near him turn their heads in the direction of the doorway.

The Maître d'Hôtel was speaking to a lady who had just arrived, and although she was some way from the Duke he noticed, as obviously the other gentlemen around him were doing, that she had an exquisite figure.

Dressed in a gown of vivid flamingo pink with touches of white which gave it an indescribable *chic*, it revealed the perfect curves of her breasts and the smallness of her waist before it swept to the ground in a flutter of frills.

As she walked down the restaurant she was the object of every masculine eye, and the Duke could not help ejaculating to himself:

"God! What a figure!"

He was watching the way she moved and it was not until she had almost reached his table that he realised incredulously that the woman he had been admiring was not a stranger and not French—but Antonia!

The Maître d'Hôtel pulled out a chair for her and only then did the Duke rise to his feet, an unconcealed expression of astonishment on his face.

Although he knew that Antonia had large eyes, he had never before realised quite how huge they were or that they filled her small face, which was set on a long, beautifully rounded neck.

Now with her hair swept up in a fashion not yet known in London which gave her a new height, she looked entirely different from the dowdy, insignificant young woman he had brought with him to Paris.

There was something indescribably alluring in the tiny hat perched forward on the very top of her head which consisted of little more than ribbons of the same colour as her gown and a few small white roses.

The angle at which it was set and the shadowy darkness

of her hair gave her a piquancy and fascination, while as to her gown . . .

The Duke glanced again at the perfection of his wife's body, and wondered if he ought to resent the fact that it was obvious to every other man in the room besides himself.

"I did not realise it was you at first," he said.

Antonia's face lit up with a smile.

"That is what I hoped you would say. I do not feel in the least like . . . me!"

"It is a transformation!"

"*Monsieur* Worth has been very kind. He did not wish to see me at first as he is tired and intends leaving the country in a few days."

"How did you persuade him?" the Duke enquired, still so bemused by Antonia's appearance that he found it hard to collect his thoughts.

She laughed.

"I was ready to go down on my knees in front of him, but when he saw me he was so horrified at my appearance that I think he considered it a challenge!"

Antonia sighed contentedly.

"I am so glad you are pleased."

"I suppose I am," the Duke replied. "At the same time I can see that from now on my role of husband is going to be rather different from what I had envisaged!"

He did not have to explain to Antonia what he meant for she exclaimed delightedly:

"That is a compliment and the first you have paid me!"

"Have I really been so remiss?" the Duke enquired.

"You have had nothing to compliment me about," she said, "and do not bother to tell me how terrible I looked! *Monsieur* Worth has said it both in French and in English!"

She gave a little laugh before she went on:

"What is so exciting is that he is coming to England in a month's time and he has already begun to plan a winter trousseau for me. I only hope you are as rich as you are reputed to be!"

"I can see that sooner or later it is going to be a choice between clothes and horses!" the Duke said.

"That is unkind!" Antonia flashed at him. "You know quite well which I should choose!"

It was strange, the Duke thought, as the day progressed, that instead of sitting and talking seriously to Antonia as he had done previously, he now found it quite easy to flirt with his own wife!

It was absurd that clothes should make so much difference, but he knew that instead of being an unfledged country-girl with whom he had nothing in common but horses, she had now in her Worth gown assumed an aura of glamour.

And yet her eyes were still very innocent and he found himself watching them reflecting her reaction to everything that happened and to everything he said to her.

After luncheon they called on some friends the Duke had known on his last visit and inevitably the conversation was of war.

"I do not mind telling you, Duke," one of the guests said pompously, "that I have taken a very large wager that war will be declared, if not to-night, to-morrow!"

"Are you not worried?" Antonia asked.

The Frenchman who had spoken smiled.

"Here in Paris we are as safe as, how do you say, in your country—the Bank of England!" he answered. "And it will only be a few days before our magnificent Army puts those Prussians, once and for all, in their proper place!"

"I have heard that their troops are well trained," the Duke said, "and the railways in Germany in recent years have been planned with a particular eye to Military needs."

"We have something far more important," the Frenchman replied. "We have a destructive device in the cartridge-firing *chassepot* rifle which has nearly twice the range of the Dreyse 'needle-gun'. And we also have a secret weapon called the *mitrailleuse*."

"What is that?" someone asked.

"It is a gun consisting of a bundle of twenty-five barrels which by turning a handle can be fired off in very rapid succession."

The speaker gave a loud laugh.

"The Germans have no answer to that!"

The Duke said nothing, but he was thinking that he had heard of a steel breech-loading cannon which *Herr* Krupp had made for Prussia but which at the time the French military leaders had refused to take seriously.

When they drove back to their house from the Reception Antonia asked:

"You do not think there will be a war?"

"I hope not," the Duke replied. "But if there is it will not be fought here, but in Germany."

"Do you think the French can advance without the Germans stopping them?"

"That is what they believe," the Duke replied.

He had already told Antonia they were dining that night with the Marquise de Barouche before a Ball that she was giving in her magnificent Château near the Bois.

As she changed for dinner Antonia was not only thrilled with the wonderful gown that Worth had delivered for her to wear, but also the fact that she had a French maid.

It was one more arrangement which had been made by the Courier who had gone ahead of them. He had engaged a French woman so that Antonia would be properly looked after when she arrived in Paris.

It was typical, she thought, that everything that concerned the Duke was meticulously planned down to the very smallest detail.

She knew that when she returned to England Mr. Graham would have engaged an English maid to look after her and one who was experienced in attending to riding-habits.

The French maid was vivacious and very efficient.

She chatted away gaily as she arranged Antonia's hair in the manner the *Coiffeur* had done who had come to *Monsieur* Worth's while he was fitting Antonia into the gown in which she had dazzled the Duke at luncheon.

"For no other lady, however important or grand she might be, Your Grace, would I put myself to such trouble," *Monsieur* Worth had said.

"Then why am I so honoured, *Monsieur*?" Antonia had enquired.

"Because, Your Grace, I am English, like yourself, and I am fed up with the French always expecting an Englishwoman to look dowdy, ungainly and to have protruding teeth, as most of them do!"

They had both laughed but Antonia knew it was not only patriotism which made the great man take so much trouble. She also, as she had told the Duke, presented a challenge he could not resist.

"Why did I never realise," she asked herself as she looked in the mirror, "that I had such a good figure?"

She knew the answer was that her mother would have been outraged by the thought of her being conceited about anything so immodest.

Her long neck, her ears which were perfectly shell-shaped, her huge eyes, now they were fully revealed by the up-swept darkness of her hair, were all new and exciting discoveries.

When she went into the Salon where the Duke was waiting to take her out to dinner, wearing a gown of golden orange tulle, glittering with diamanté and ornamented with minosa, she felt for the first time in her life glamorous and romantic.

She saw the glint of admiration in the Duke's eyes as he looked at her, and as she walked towards him she felt she was on a stage waiting for the plaudits of the audience.

"Do you approve?" she asked as he did not speak.

Now there was a touch of anxiety in her eyes.

"I am very proud to be your escort!" he answered and saw the colour come into her cheeks because she was so delighted by his reply.

If she had any doubts left they were soon dispelled by the compliments that were paid to her by the dinner-party guests and the flirtatious attitude of both of her partners at dinner.

"You are enchanting—fascinating!"

"I would never have believed that a star could fall from the sky so early in the evening!"

Antonia told herself that she might have found such exaggeration incredible but despite her inexperience of men she could not help realising that their admiration was sincere.

In fact as soon as the Ball opened she was besieged with partners in a way which made her realise that this was an experience very different from anything that had ever happened to her before.

She returned to the Duke's side after waltzing with a handsome and ardent young Diplomat.

"You are enjoying yourself?" he asked.

"It is wonderful! More wonderful than I could ever have imagined!" Antonia replied. "But I would like . . ."

She was about to say that she would like to dance with him, when their conversation was interrupted by a cry of joy.

"Athol! *Mon Brave!* Why did no-one tell me you were in Paris?"

An entrancingly pretty woman was holding out both hands to the Duke and looking up into his face in a manner which proclaimed all too obviously her interest in him.

"Ludevica!" the Duke exclaimed. "I heard that you had returned to Vienna."

"We went—we came back!" the lady answered. "I missed you—*Hélas!* How I missed you!"

She spoke in a fascinating manner which seemed to make every word have a hidden meaning, both intimate and provocative.

She was holding both the Duke's hands in hers and as if he suddenly remembered Antonia's existence, he said:

"I am here on my honeymoon and we have only just arrived. May I present my wife—Madame La Comtesse de Rezonville."

The nod that Antonia received was so brief as to be almost insulting. Then the Comtesse was holding onto the Duke's arm and looking up into his eyes.

She made it obvious that whatever they had meant to each other in the past, her feelings at any rate were unchanged.

Because she felt embarrassed and at a loss how to behave in such circumstances Antonia glanced round the ballroom and almost immediately her next partner was at her side.

She allowed herself to be escorted onto the dance-floor only to look back and see the Duke with the Comtesse hanging onto his arm disappearing through one of the open windows which led into the garden.

There were Chinese lanterns hanging from the branches of the trees, but otherwise the shadows were dark.

As Antonia had already discovered, there were small arbours discreetly arranged where there were soft cushioned seats and the reassurance that anything that was said could not be overheard.

She could not help feeling that even if the Duke had not asked her to dance he might have taken her into the garden.

If the Marchioness had been present, that was where, she was quite certain, they would have ended up.

She gave a little sigh, then thought to herself that if the Duke had been thinking of the Marchioness while they were on their way to Paris and perhaps earlier to-day, he would certainly not be thinking of her now!

Never had Antonia seen anyone quite so fascinating as the Comtesse de Rezonville.

She gathered from the reference to Vienna that she was in fact Viennese. Her hair was certainly the deep, dark red beloved of the Austrian women who all wished to look like their beautiful Empress.

Yet her eyes were dark, almost purple in their depths, while at the same time they sparkled as everything about her had seemed to glitter and shimmer.

She had made Antonia feel that however elegantly she might be dressed in a Worth creation there was something lacking inside herself which the Comtesse had in superabundance.

"You are very pensive," her partner said, breaking in on her thoughts.

"I was thinking," Antonia replied.

"I wish it could be of me!"

"But I do not know you!"

"That is something that can easily be rectified," he replied. "When may I see you again? Where are you staying in Paris?"

She laughed at him because they were questions that had been asked by all her partners.

The dance came to an end and another Frenchman drew her onto the dance-floor.

Although Antonia glanced frequently towards the windows there was no sign of the Duke returning, nor could she see the fascinating Comtesse.

She lost count of her partners. Then she found herself dancing with a man to whom she did not remember being introduced. She was quite certain he had not written his name on her dance-card.

It did not seem to matter if she exchanged one man for another. They all seemed to say much the same thing, and she was really hoping the Duke would appear so that they could go home.

"You are the Duchess of Doncaster?" her new partner asked as he swung her round to the music of the 'Blue Danube'.

He spoke in a heavy voice almost as if it was an indictment.

"Yes, I am," Antonia replied. "But I have a feeling we have not been introduced."

"Your husband is with you?"

"Yes, of course," Antonia answered. "We are on our honeymoon."

Her partner glanced round the room.

"I do not see him anywhere."

"He is in the garden," Antonia replied, "with a very fascinating and alluring lady whom I suspect of being an old friend and who was certainly very pleased to see him."

"What was her name?"

The question was so sharp, so abrupt that Antonia looked at the man in surprise and almost missed a step.

"The Comtesse de Rezonville."

"So! It is what I suspected!" the Frenchman muttered in a furious tone.

He stopped dancing and taking Antonia by the arm drew her across the room towards the open window.

"We will find them," he said grimly, "doubtless, as you say, in the garden."

There was something so ferocious in the way he spoke that Antonia said quickly:

"I . . . I may have been . . . mistaken. Who . . . who are you? And why are you so interested in my husband?"

"I happen to be married to the fascinating, alluring lady you have just described so vividly!" he replied.

Antonia's heart gave a frightened leap.

She realised by the way he spoke and the manner in which he was pulling her along that the Comte was in a rage and she knew she had precipitated it by what she had told him.

"How could I have known?" she asked herself frantically, "that the man dancing with me was the Comtesse's husband?"

They walked down the steps which led from the terrace into the garden.

The Comte stood looking around as if he was adjusting his eyes from the brilliant lights of the Ball-Room to the darkness which was only relieved by the golden glow of the Chinese lanterns.

"I am sure they are not here," Antonia said hastily. "Let us look in the Supper-Room."

The Comte did not answer her but kept his hand firmly on her arm, pulling her forward and moving her towards the right.

Bordering the lawn there was the first of the arbours screened by ferns or potted-plants where they were not naturally enveloped with climbing roses or flowering creepers.

Still dragging Antonia with him he went up to the first arbour, disturbing a couple who were kissing each other passionately, and looked round with a startled expression on their faces.

"*Pardon, Monsieur, Pardon, Madame,*" the Comte muttered and moved towards the next arbour.

Antonia stood still.

"Stop!" she said. "You cannot do this! I do not know what you suspect but whatever it is, it is quite unfounded. My husband and I are here on our honeymoon. We have only just arrived. I think he will be looking for me in the Ball-Room."

"You will find your husband, Madame, when we find my wife!" the Comte replied.

He drew Antonia on again and she knew that unless she made a scene she could do nothing but go with him.

He was very strong and his fingers seemed to dig into the softness of her arm.

There was a grim determination about him which she found terrifying and which made her feel at the same time weak and helpless.

They visited no less than four arbours and interrupted the couples in them in an embarrassing manner which made Antonia hope that while she could see their faces in the light from the lanterns hanging on the trees, they could not see hers.

Then just as they approached the fifth arbour she heard the Duke's voice.

She could not hear what he said but there was no mistaking his deep resonant tone.

Because she was afraid that he might be embracing the Comtesse or indulging in any of the small intimacies they had seen when interrupting the other couples, she called out:

"Athol! Athol! Where are you?"

She knew her cry annoyed the Comte and he looked at her angrily.

Then he moved her forward quickly, still clasping her arm. In the arbour the Duke and the Comtesse were sitting beside each other on the cushioned seat.

There was nothing to show they had been doing anything intimate but even if they had, Antonia thought with satisfaction, they would have had time to move apart when she had called out to the Duke.

When they saw the Comte it seemed to Antonia as if, for a moment, both the Duke and the Comtesse were carved in stone.

Then the Comtesse gave a little cry.

"Jacques, what an enchanting surprise!" she exclaimed. "I was not expecting you to join me."

"That is obvious!" the Comte replied and his eyes were on the Duke.

"Good evening, Rezonville," the Duke said calmly. "I have only just learnt that you have returned to Paris."

"I warned you when you were here last to keep away from my wife!" the Comte said aggressively.

"My dear fellow," the Duke said, "your wife was just congratulating me, as I hope you will, on my marriage."

"My congratulations are best expressed like this!' the Comte replied.

He was wearing only one glove and he held the other in his right hand.

Now he raised it and slapped the Duke across the face.

The Comtesse gave a shrill cry while Antonia felt as if the breath had been squeezed out of her body.

"I consider that an insult!" the Duke said quietly.

"That is what it is meant to be!" the Comte retorted.

"My seconds will wait on you!"

"I have no intention of waiting," the Comte replied. "We will fight at dawn."

"Certainly!" the Duke replied.

He moved past the Comte and offered his arm to Antonia.

"I think it is time we said farewell to our hostess," he said in a quiet, level voice that was quite expressionless.

Antonia was glad to put her hand on his arm. She had the feeling that otherwise she might have fallen to the ground.

They moved back through the garden towards the house, and as they did so they could hear the Comtesse screaming at her husband, and the anger in his voice as he answered her.

It was impossible to speak—impossible to say anything until the Duke led Antonia into the lighted Ball-Room where the Marquise was standing at the door saying farewell to others of her guests.

"It has been a delightful evening," the Duke said graciously.

"I am so glad you could both come," the Marquise answered. "If you are to be in Paris for some time we must meet again."

"My wife and I will be delighted!" the Duke replied.

He kissed the Marquise's hand, Antonia curtsied gracefully and soon they were driving away towards the Champs Élysées in the carriage that had been waiting for them.

"What does it . . . mean? You cannot . . . fight him!" Antonia said frantically as the Duke did not speak.

"I have no alternative," he replied. "I must apologise,

Antonia, for what must have been a very upsetting experience for you, but the Comte has wanted an excuse to call me out for some time."

Remembering the way the Comtesse had greeted the Duke, Antonia thought that perhaps he had every reason for jealousy, but all she could say in a frightened voice was:

"He may . . . kill you!"

"That is unlikely," the Duke replied. "Most duels are fairly civilised. A small show of blood and honour is satisfied!"

"Can you be . . . sure of that?" Antonia asked.

She was thinking of the Comte's anger and the aggressive manner in which he had deliberately insulted the Duke.

"I assure you, Antonia," the Duke said, "there is nothing to trouble you. By the time you wake to-morrow morning it will all be over!"

"M . . . may I . . . go with you?" Antonia asked.

"No, of course you may not!" the Duke replied. "Spectators are not permitted on such occasions! I assure you the whole thing is just a formality—a salve to the Comte's pride."

"The Comtesse is very attractive," Antonia said.

"Very!" the Duke answered, "and I assure you I am not the first man to have found her so!"

"Then why are you fighting over her?"

"It is a question of honour," the Duke replied. "I am quite prepared to admit, since we are frank with each other, Antonia, that the Comte might have reason to be incensed with me."

"But you . . . cannot fight . . . every man who is . . . jealous of you!" Antonia said hesitatingly.

"I hope not!" the Duke smiled. "But Rezonville has always been a fiery, over-dramatic fellow. At one time he talked of challenging the Emperor to a duel, but fortunately he was persuaded not to make a fool of himself."

"Could not . . . someone persuade him . . . now?" Antonia asked in a very small voice.

"I am not an Emperor!" the Duke answered. "And I assure you I am not afraid of Rezonville or any other man!"

It seemed there was nothing more to be said. When they

reached the house the Duke, having escorted Antonia into the Hall, raised her hand to his lips.

"You will understand that I have arrangements to make," he said. "Sleep well, Antonia, I hope when we have breakfast to-morrow morning all this unpleasantness will be forgotten."

She wanted to hold on to him.

She had a feeling she ought not to let him go, but he turned and went out of the house and she heard the carriage drive away.

She stood indecisively in the Hall and the night-footman who had let them in waited as if he expected her to give him an order.

Antonia made up her mind.

"Fetch Tour to me immediately!" she said.

"*Très bien, Madame.*"

The footman hurried up the stairs to fetch the Duke's valet and Antonia went into the Salon.

It was still very dark under the trees although there was a faint glow in the East while the stars were fading overhead.

Tour led the way through the bushes and shrubs and Antonia followed closely behind him frightened of losing him in the shadows.

After the Duke had left the house, it had taken a great deal of persuasion to make Tour promise he would take her to the Bois. It was only when she threatened to go alone that he finally consented.

"I don't know what His Grace will say to me," he kept murmuring unhappily.

"I will take the blame, Tour. You know as well as I do that you cannot disobey my orders. I command you to take me to the Bois where we can watch the duel just in case His Grace is hurt and needs assistance."

The valet still looked unhappy and Antonia said:

"If His Grace is unharmed, then we will slip away and be back at the house long before he returns."

She had known that it would be difficult to do what she

wished and she had actually heaved a sigh of relief when Tour had finally consented.

He had been with the Duke for years and always travelled with him when he went abroad.

In England the Duke had two younger valets also in attendance, but Tour spoke several foreign languages.

Because she wanted to find out more about the Comte, Antonia insisted on Tour sitting inside the carriage as they drove to the Bois.

She knew he was embarrassed that she should request anything so unusual and he sat opposite her on the small seat, his back straight, his hat held firmly in both his hands.

"Tell me about the Comte de Rezonville," Antonia asked. "Is he a good shot?"

"He has a reputation, Your Grace, for having fought a number of duels."

"All over the Comtesse?" Antonia asked and felt it was a foolish question with only one answer. "Has he ever threatened the Duke before?"

"There was a little trouble two years ago, Your Grace."

"What sort of trouble?"

Tour looked uncomfortable.

"I can guess," Antonia said hastily, "but the Comte did not challenge the Duke on that occasion?"

"He threatened to, but as His Grace was staying in the British Embassy with the Ambassador, I think *Monsieur le Comte* thought it might cause an international incident."

"I see!" Antonia answered.

The Duke now was without the protection of the British Flag and therefore the Comte could take the vengeance which must have been festering in him for two years.

She was suddenly desperately afraid.

As if he knew what she was feeling Tour said:

"Don't you take on, Your Grace. It'll be all right. There's no-one handles a pistol better than His Grace, and he's a sportsman if ever there was one!"

"I am sure he is going to be all right!" Antonia said speaking more to herself than to Tour.

At the same time there was a fear within her which seemed almost like a presentiment of evil.

She could see the clearing in the wood as she peeped through the bushes into which Tour had taken her.

She realised it was the traditional place where the famous Parisian duels were fought and wondered how many men had died in just this spot simply because they had aroused jealousy and anger over some tiresome woman.

There was however little time for introspection.

The duellists were already lined up. She could see the Duke conferring with his seconds and the Comte conferring with his.

There was a man who she imagined was the Referee and another holding a black bag, who she guessed with a sinking of her heart was a doctor.

Dawn had broken and now it was easy to see every detail, the diamond tie-pin glittering in the Comte's cravat, the Duke's signet ring on his little finger.

'I cannot bear it!' Antonia thought.

She wondered if she should run forward and beg them not to fight each other, but she knew she would only embarrass the Duke and that she would be sent away.

If the duel did not take place this morning, it would take place to-morrow.

She fastened her teeth onto her lower lip so that she would not cry out.

Now the Referee was ready and he called the two contestants to him and they stood back to back.

"Ten paces," Antonia heard him say and began to count.

"*Un, deux, trois . . .*"

The Duke was taller than the Comte and he moved slowly and with a dignity which made Antonia feel very proud.

There was something magnificent about him, she thought. Something which seemed to raise him above everything that was squalid and vulgar and made him a man of honour and a sportsman in every fibre of his being.

"*Huit, neuf, dix!*"

Antonia held her breath.

The Duke and the Comte stood sideways to each other and brought their pistols, French fashion, down upon their left arms, which were raised shoulder high, and took aim.

"Fire!"

The Referee gave the word and the Duke with superb marksmanship just grazed the outside of the Comte's arm. A crimson patch appeared on his coat.

The Duke's seconds moved forward.

"Honour is satisfied!" they declared.

The Duke dropped his arms.

"Not as far as I am concerned!" the Comte replied savagely.

Then he fired!

There was the reverberation of his pistol, and Antonia realised that when the Duke had lowered both his arms, he had been off guard and at his ease. He had also turned his body fully towards the Comte.

Just for a moment she thought the bullet had missed, then as the Duke fell she gave a cry that was strangled in her throat and ran towards him.

She was certain as she reached him that he was dead!

# CHAPTER FIVE

Someone . . . a man . . . was screaming . . . crying out . . . making a noise . . .

The Duke wondered how anyone could be so tiresome when he felt so ill. He had heard this man before and resented the commotion which he made.

He could still hear him but he was further away . . . in the distance . . . gradually fading . . . until there was silence . . .

He felt a relief that the noise was no longer there and then a soft voice which he also seemed to have heard many times said:

"Go to sleep. You are safe . . . quite safe. No-one shall hurt you."

He wanted to say that he was not afraid, but it was too much effort to try to speak or to open his eyes.

"Go to sleep, my darling," the voice said tenderly. "But perhaps you are thirsty?"

There was an arm lifting his head very carefully so that

he could drink from a glass which contained something cool and rather sweet.

He was not certain what it was—it was too much of an effort to try and think.

It was strangely comforting to be held closely and his cheek was against something very soft.

There was a sweet fragrance of flowers and now there was a cool hand on his forehead, soothing him, mesmerising him and he knew he was slipping away into oblivion . . .

The Duke came back to consciousness to hear two voices speaking.

"How is he, Tour?"

It was the voice of a woman and vaguely he wondered who she was. Tour he recognised as his valet.

"Much quieter, Your Grace. I have washed His Grace, shaved him and he hardly moved."

"Did the doctor come while I was asleep?"

"He did, Your Grace, and he is very pleased indeed with the wound. He said His Grace must have been in the pink of condition to be healing so quickly."

"You should have awoken me, Tour, I would have liked to talk to the doctor."

"You must sleep sometimes, Your Grace. You cannot be up all night and all day."

"I am all right. There are many more important things to worry about rather than my health."

"You have to think of yourself, Your Grace. Remember I cannot cope without you, especially when His Grace is in one of his restless moods."

"No, that is true. Will you sit with him a little longer, Tour? I am expecting Mr. Labouchere."

"Yes, of course, Your Grace, and afterwards I think you should take a little fresh air."

"I will go into the garden. You will call me if His Grace wakes or is restless?"

"I will do that, Your Grace, I have given my promise and I won't break it."

"Thank you, Tour."

The Duke wondered what it was all about but he was too tired to make the effort of trying to find out. He fell asleep.


Antonia waited in the Salon for Henry Labouchere.

She was sure that when the Duke regained consciousness he would think it strange that the only friend she had in Paris was a journalist.

Henry Labouchere, as it happened, owned a quarter share in the *London Daily News*, and had appointed himself to the Paris office.

An Englishman with Huguenot ancestry, 'Labby' as all his friends called him, was a character. While many people hated him for his sharp and caustic articles, he was many other things as well.

A wit, cynic, stage manager and diplomat, he had filled all these roles and had been elected to Parliament as a Radical and a Republican in 1865.

He had however lost his seat at the same time as he had inherited £250,000 and he now devoted himself to increasing the circulation of the *Daily News*.

Henry Labouchere had come to interview the Duke, having heard rumours of the duel which had taken place in the Bois.

He had found instead a white-faced and very frightened Duchess who told him quite frankly that the Duke's life was in danger and pleaded with him not to write about it in his newspaper.

Henry Labouchere, who had been the lover of a great many attractive women, found Antonia's pleading, worried eyes irresistible.

He not only promised to keep the duel a secret, but as the days passed he became her friend, confidant and adviser when she had no-one else to turn to.

It was Henry Labouchere who kept her up to date with the fantastic events which were happening in Paris.

At first, when everyone expected the war to be over almost immediately, the French went on enjoying themselves without a thought that there might be anything to disturb their pleasure but a celebration of French victories.

On July 28th, the Emperor had taken command of his armies with the Empress's words "Louis, do your duty well," ringing in his ears.

But as he passed through Metz he was in constant pain from the stone in his bladder and to many of his Generals he gave the impression of a man who was utterly worn out.

The Germans had 400,000 men in supreme fighting trim and 1,440 guns concentrated on the far side of the Rhine, while Louis Napoleon had only been able to muster 250,000 soldiers.

His strategic plan was to advance rapidly eastwards into Germany in the hope of swinging the South German States and eventually the reluctant Austrians into war against Prussia.

The gay uniforms of the French army, the joyous fanfares, the confident and dashing officers with their smart 'imperials' worn as a compliment to their Emperor, all made a striking contrast to the Prussian disdain for any kind of ostentation.

On August 2nd, the French captured Saarbrücken from the weak German advance forces and all Paris revelled in the triumph.

A telegram was read out on the Bourse reporting the capture of the Prussian Crown Prince. This caused a famous tenor to sing the Marseillaise from the top of a horse-drawn bus!

Henry Labouchere had related to Antonia the wild scenes that took place in the streets.

She had heard and seen nothing as she nursed a delirious and restless Duke who was running a high fever after the bullet had been extracted from his wound.

At first she was not particularly interested in the news and, although she thanked Mr. Labouchere for coming to see her, she made it obvious that she could only spend a few minutes with him.

All her thoughts were concentrated on the sick-bed.

However, as the week went by and the Duke, though his wound was improving day by day, did not regain consciousness, she found it was impossible to shut her mind to the events occurring outside.

She therefore found herself looking forward to Mr. La-bouchere's visits even though he brought her little but bad news.

Stories of terrible inefficiency drifted back to Paris; of weary troops reaching their destination to find their tents had been mislaid; of gunmen separated from their guns; of magazines discovered to be empty.

After two defeats at Spicheren and Woerth, a long and disheartening retreat began. Orders and counter-orders were issued from a panic-stricken Paris.

A German attack at St. Privat on August 18th inflicted 20,000 casualties on the French and during the night the army fled back in disorder to Metz from where they had started.

The disastrous news had staggered Paris into a state, which was, as Mr. Labouchere put it 'bordering upon mad-ness'.

"I have just seen three or four Germans nearly punched to death," he told Antonia. "Several of the larger cafés have been forced to close! Excited mobs are attacking them be-cause their proprietors are supposed to have German sym-pathies."

What seemed to Antonia to distress him even more was when he told her that the beautiful trees in the Bois were being felled.

"Is everyone leaving Paris?" she asked a few days later.

"On the contrary," he replied. "The French authorities are insisting that it is safer to be in Paris than anywhere else, and people are flooding into the City."

"Then things cannot be too bad," Antonia smiled.

"I do hope you are right," he said. "At the same time I would have liked you and your husband to go home while it is possible."

"It is quite impossible at the moment," Antonia replied, "and surely we are completely safe being British?"

"I expect so," he answered. "But I do advise you against going outside the house except into your own garden. People are arrested on the most trivial suspicions of being a German and there has been a certain amount of dissension on the Boulevards."

"In what way?" Antonia asked.

"When the despatches arrive and they are not favourable, the crowds start shouting: 'Down with the Emperor!' and *'Déchéance!'* "

"Abdication!" Antonia exclaimed. "Can they really be asking that?"

"The French are very intolerant of failure," Henry Labouchere replied.

Because she felt that it might be a long time before they could return to England and therefore they must not be extravagant with what money they had, Antonia, after consultation with Tour, dismissed the majority of the servants in the house.

She kept two who had been there with its owners, a middle-aged couple who were quite content, as there was no entertaining, to do everything that was required.

Antonia found that Tour was a tower of strength. Not only could he speak French fluently, but he knew exactly how to handle the Duke and was, in his own way, she thought, an even better nurse than she was.

It was Tour who told her of the animals massed in the Bois and for the first time Antonia faced the suggestion that the Germans might reach Paris.

"So much food will not be necessary?" she asked Tour in surprise.

"One never knows, Your Grace," he replied in a tone which told her he did not wish to make her nervous. "They say it would be impossible for anyone to take Paris, it is so heavily fortified."

"That is true," Antonia agreed. "I was reading in the Guide Book how the whole City is surrounded by an *enceinte* wall, 30 foot high and divided into 93 bastions. Besides, there is a moat and at varying distances a chain of powerful forts."

She thought of the animals again and said:

"But of course all the trains will be needed to convey food to the troops at the front and I quite understand that in the City we should be self-sufficient."

She asked Henry Labouchere for further news when he next came to see her and in reply he handed her an article he had written for the *Daily News* in England.

She read it, her eyes widening with surprise at the incredible story.

"As far as the eye can reach over every open space, down the long, long Avenue all the way to Longchamps itself, there is nothing but sheep, sheep, sheep! In the Bois alone there must be 25,000 as well as 4,000 oxen."

"Can this really be true?" she enquired.

"We are getting ourselves prepared," Henry Labouchere had laughed, "so you need not be afraid that when the Duke gets better he will not be able to build up his strength with plenty of good meat."

Tour however was not prepared to rely entirely on the Bois. He brought into the house quite a lot of food which would not deteriorate, telling Antonia gloomily that it was getting more expensive every day.

The Duke stirred and instantly Antonia rose from a chair at the open window and came to the side of the bed.

She knelt down beside him and said in the soft voice which he had grown used to hearing these past weeks:

"Are you hot? Would you like a drink, my darling?"

She spoke, he thought, as a woman would speak to a child she loved.

He remembered that when he had been delirious he had thought that his mother had her arms around him and that she was telling him to be good and go to sleep.

He felt very weak and yet for the first time his brain was clear. He knew who he was and remembered that he was in Paris.

Then, as he tried to move he felt a sudden pain in his chest. He recalled the duel and that it would account for what he now knew had been a long illness.

Antonia had lifted him very gently; now she was feeding him with a soup that he thought must be extremely nourishing as it tasted of beef, or was it perhaps venison? He could not be certain.

She placed it against his lips, giving him small spoonfuls, waiting between each one so that he had time to swallow.

There was again the fragrance of flowers coming from her, and when he had taken quite a considerable amount of the soup, she held him close for a moment.

He found that the softness he had felt beneath his cheek so many times before had been the softness of her breast.

"You are better," she said and there was a note of elation in her voice. "The doctor will be very pleased with you to-morrow and now my dearest one, you must go back to sleep again."

He felt her hand cool against his forehead.

"No fever," she said as if she spoke to herself. "How wonderful it will be when it is all gone and you are yourself again."

She laid him down against the pillows, moving them comfortably behind his head. Then she moved away and after a little while he opened his eyes.

He had not realised before that it was night time. There was a candle lit beside his bed, the curtains were drawn back and the windows were open. He thought he could see the sky and the stars.

He lay trying to focus his eyes, and then, as if she knew instinctively that he was awake, Antonia came back to the bed.

She looked down at him and said in a voice that was a little above a whisper:

"Athol, can you hear me?"

He found it impossible to speak but he turned his eyes to look at her.

She made a little sound that was a cry of delight.

"You are awake!" she exclaimed, "and I think you can understand."

She knelt down beside him taking his hand in hers and said softly:

"Everything is all right. You are going to get well and there is nothing to make you afraid."

\* \* \*

Henry Labouchere, looking rather raffish, Antonia thought, came to call at four o'clock in the afternoon.

Tour had let him in and Antonia came into the Salon wearing one of her elegant Worth gowns which revealed her exquisite figure.

"You look happy," he said and raised her hand to his lips.

"I am," she replied. "My invalid has eaten a proper meal today for the first time. He is sitting up in bed and being rather irritable, which Tour tells me is a good sign."

Labby laughed.

"Well, that is a relief at any rate! Perhaps now you will be able to give me more attention."

Antonia looked at him in surprise as he went on:

"I do not think I have ever spent so much time with a woman who would not even know I existed, had the news I brought her not in some way concerned her husband."

Labby spoke resentfully and Antonia laughed. Then she said seriously:

"You know how grateful I am. I should have known nothing of what is happening and been very much more afraid if you had not proved such a very kind friend."

"Friend!" Labby ejaculated. "That is not what I wish to be, as you must be well aware! This friendship, as you call it, will ruin my reputation as a lady-killer!"

"It is a . . . friendship I value very much," Antonia said softly.

She was used by this time to Labby's protestations of love to her, even while he realised better than she did how hopeless it was.

He had never met a woman who concentrated so fiercely on a man who could neither see nor hear her and who from all accounts was not particularly interested anyway.

Labby knew of the Duke's liaison with the Marchioness and his reputation with beautiful women. It did not need Antonia to tell him—which she would not have thought of doing—why the Duke had married.

Labby had at first been touched by Antonia's youth and inexperience.

Then as he saw her day after day, calling at first because

he told himself she was a countrywoman whom he must help and if possible protect, he found himself falling in love.

He could hardly believe it possible that at the age of thirty-nine he should find himself as idealistically enamoured as he had been when in his youth he had once joined a Mexican Circus in pursuit of a lady acrobat.

Yet there was something about Antonia which told him she was different from any of the women he had pursued so ardently in his varied career.

At one time Queen Victoria had referred to him as 'that viper, Labouchere!' She would have been surprised how controlled, gentle and considerate he was to Antonia.

Labby did not only bring Antonia the news, he also made her laugh, something she had almost forgotten to do in her anxiety over the Duke.

Because the eyes of the world were focused on France, inquisitive British and Americans were flooding into the city. Labby had related that enterprising Estate Agents were circulating advertisements which read:

> Notice for the benefit of English gentlemen wishing to attend the Siege of Paris: comfortable apartments, completely shell-proof, rooms in the basement for impressionable personages.

"The Siege of Paris!" Antonia had repeated apprehensively. "Can it possibly come to that?"

"No, of course not," Labby had said confidently. "The Germans will be driven back long before they reach Paris. But there is no doubt that the Army is somewhat disorganised and has retired to the small citadel town of Sedan."

He paused before he added:

"Things cannot be too bad. I hear the French Cavalry blades gave a ball at Douzy last night. It was attended by all the ladies from Sedan who are to watch a triumphant victory tomorrow."

There was no triumph! Two days later Labby had to tell Antonia that the army was trapped, with two powerful Prussian armies moving in.

There was only enough food in Sedan for a few days.

What Labby did not relate to Antonia, even if he was aware of it, was that there was chaos inside Sedan reaching catastrophic proportions. Cannons were jammed wheel to wheel with refugee wagons, while shells from 400 Prussian guns burst in their midst.

Then on September 1st came the bombshell. After Louis Napoleon had ridden amongst his wavering troops outside the walls of Sedan, his face roughed in order to hide how ill he was, he finally had to order a white flag to be hoisted over the citadel.

It was two days later before the contradictory rumours, and there were many of them, reached Paris.

Labby told Antonia that the Empress had flown into a terrible Spanish rage and then retired to her room to weep.

In the streets now there was no doubt of the menacing roar of the crowd or the cry that was heard everywhere:

"*Déchéance! Dé-ché-ance! Dé-ché-ance!*"

"What is the news today?" Antonia asked nervously on September 4th.

It was difficult, because she was so pleased about the improvement in the Duke's health, to force herself to attend to the troubles which were happening outside the house.

She felt sometimes as if they were alone on an island, surrounded by a hostile sea and yet somehow protected from it.

"Paris has learnt that the Emperor has offered up his sword," Labby replied. "And the Empress at last has consented to leave."

Antonia started. She had felt that as long as the Empress stayed in Paris, things could not be too bad.

"Her Majesty has stayed on at the Tuileries until the servants began to desert her, flinging off their livery and pilfering as they went. It was nearly too late," Labby told Antonia. "The mob were accumulating outside and she must have heard the clatter of their muskets in the courtyard and their voices on the main staircase."

"Did she get away?" Antonia asked quickly.

"She left by a side door accompanied by her Lady-in-

Waiting. She was heavily veiled and I have learnt that the two ladies went first to the house of the State Chancellor in the Boulevard Haussmann, but he had already gone. Eventually, after finding the same thing at the house of her Chamberlain, Her Majesty found shelter with her American dentist, a Doctor Evans."

"How extraordinary!" Antonia exclaimed.

"It was sensible, if slightly unconventional," Labby remarked.

The following day Labby was taken by Antonia into the Duke's bed-room. She had already related to him how kind the English journalist had been during the long, frightening weeks of his unconsciousness.

She thought the Duke was slightly sceptical—or was it suspicious—of the warm manner in which she had described Henry Labouchere.

But when she brought him into the bed-room he had held out his hand and said in his most pleasant tone:

"I hear, Labouchere, I have to be very grateful to you."

"There is not reason for you to be grateful, Your Grace," Henry Labouchere replied. "It has been a very great pleasure to be of service to the Duchess."

He smiled at Antonia as he spoke and there was an expression on his raffish face which made the Duke look at him sharply.

What he had suspected was confirmed during the conversation which followed.

Even a less experienced man than the Duke would have noticed the gentleness in Henry Labouchere's voice when he addressed Antonia, and the manner in which he found it hard to take his eyes from her.

"We must leave Paris as soon as I am well enough to travel," the Duke remarked abruptly.

"I am afraid that will not be for some time," Labby replied. "As Your Grace must know by now, you have been very ill indeed."

He smiled at Antonia again as he added:

"I shall be giving away no secrets if I tell you, now the danger is over, that your doctor told me it was a ninety percent certainty that you would die."

Antonia drew in her breath.

"I . . . did . . . not realise it was as bad . . . as that," she faltered.

"You were saved by two things," Labby told the Duke. "The first that the bullet missed your heart and by a miracle did not shatter any bones, and secondly that you were outstandingly fit."

"I am glad you did not tell me until now," Antonia said.

"Do you imagine that I would have distressed you more than you were already?" he asked gently.

The Duke listened to this exchange looking first at Henry Labouchere, then at Antonia.

"I would be grateful, Labouchere," he said after a moment, "if you would tell me exactly what the position is at the moment. As you can imagine, I have a great deal to catch up with and women are never very good at describing the horrors of war."

"Her Grace will have told you that there is a new Government," Henry Labouchere replied. "The Second Empire has ended ignominiously and France has been humiliated. King William has reached Rheims."

"It is hard to believe!" the Duke exclaimed.

"But France still has an army of sorts, all of which General Trochu, our new leader, is concentrating in Paris."

"Is that wise?" the Duke enquired.

"He has little choice," Labby conceded, "and the enrollment of 350,000 able-bodied males in the National Guard is encouraging, while at the same time it reveals the inefficiency of France's war mobilisation."

"I should think that the fortifications will certainly make Paris impregnable," the Duke remarked.

"A visit to the fortifications is rapidly replacing a drive in the Bois as the smart Parisian Sunday afternoon entertainment."

"Good God!" the Duke exclaimed, "do they never take anything seriously?"

"What seems to me extraordinary," Labby went on, "is that no effort is made to get the useless mouths out of the city. The Duchess will have told you of the vast concentration of animals in the Bois. But I should have thought that it would have made more sense to move people out rather than in."

"So should I," the Duke agreed, "but I suppose the last people anyone is likely to listen to are the English."

"That is certainly true," Henry Labouchere agreed, "and it is essential that the Duchess should not attempt to walk in the streets. Spy-mania has led to situations which are far from comic."

"I have warned Tour," Antonia said, "and he assures me that now when he goes out he wears his oldest clothes and looks more French than the French themselves!"

"You need not worry about Tour," the Duke replied, "'but you, Antonia, will stay here with me."

There was an accent on the last word that Antonia did not miss.

After Henry Labouchere had gone she came back into the Duke's bed-room. He looked at her and said:

"I gather you have a new admirer."

"Shall we say my only . . . admirer," Antonia replied.

The Duke's eyes seemed to rest on her speculatively and she flushed a little under his scrutiny.

He realised that she had lost some weight these past weeks when she had been nursing him, but it had not affected the perfection of her figure.

As he looked at the exquisite line of her breasts, and at the smallness of her waist, he wondered what other young woman would have been content to be cooped up indoors, nursing an unconscious and delirious man, without finding herself restricted or apparently bored.

He raised his eyes to her face and realised she was watching him apprehensively.

Her eyes looked very green because the gown she was wearing was the green of the creeper climbing over the balcony of the bed-room.

It had taken Worth, the Duke thought, to realise that only deep vivid or clear colours could make Antonia's skin appear dazzlingly clear and white.

They brought also, both to her eyes and to her hair, strange unpredictable lights that had a fascination all of their own.

He had learnt that Antonia had dismissed her lady's-maid, but he saw that her hair was as elegant and as fashionably arranged as it had been when she had joined him at the Café Anglais and he had not recognised her.

"It is a very dull honeymoon for you, Antonia," he said in his deep voice.

As if she had expected him to say something else the flush which came to her cheeks seemed to bring an expression of happiness to her face.

"It is at least . . . unusual, and if we are . . . besieged in Paris it might last for a . . . very long time!"

"We must prevent that from happening," the Duke said.

"How can we do that?" Antonia asked.

"By getting out of the City as soon as possible and returning to our own country."

Antonia gave a little cry.

"There is no chance of your moving for weeks! You must not think of it! The doctor has been very insistent that you must take things very quietly and build up your strength gradually."

"I will not have you put in any danger," the Duke said obstinately.

"How can there possibly be any danger when we are English?" Antonia asked. "I told you Mr. Labouchere says that English and Americans are pouring into Paris to have a view of the events from the front row of the stalls!"

"He said men were coming," the Duke replied, "not women."

"I shall be safe enough," Antonia insisted, "and have you forgotten that I am not a very feminine woman? In fact you said yourself I am a tomboy."

"That is the last thing you look at the moment."

Antonia glanced down at her exquisitely made gown.

"If we are going to be here a long time I shall regret that I asked *Monsieur* Worth to deliver to me in England nearly all the garments I had ordered."

"I have a feeling that was a very wise instruction," the Duke said. "For the time being neither of us will be attending smart Balls or anything that appertains to victory celebrations."

"At the same time I want to look nice for you."

"For me or your admirer?" the Duke asked, and there was a sharp note in his voice.

There was a little pause and then he saw the colour rise in Antonia's cheeks.

"For . . . you," she said quietly.

She had the feeling in the days that followed that the Duke was watching her.

She could not understand why sometimes, when she thought he was asleep, she would find in fact that he was awake and that his eyes were on her.

She sat in the window of his room or just outside on the balcony in case he should need anything.

There were fortunately some books in the house and Labby brought her more. She became acquainted with the works of Gustave Flaubert, Victor Hugo, George Sand, Dumas and many other romantic authors whom she had never had the chance of reading in England.

Sometimes she found that the excitement the written page held for her was interrupted by the feeling she was being watched, and then she would find the Duke's eyes on her.

She wondered to herself if it was in approval or indifference.

She longed to ask him if he missed the Marchioness; but the frankness with which she had been able to talk to him when they had first been married seemed to have vanished since the duel and his long illness.

She knew the answer to that herself and she only prayed that he would never realise it.

When she had seen him fall to the ground and when she had thought as she reached his side he was dead, she had known that she loved him.

As she and Tour, assisted by the Duke's seconds, had carried him to the carriage and he had been laid on the back seat, his head in her lap, she admitted that she loved him agonisingly.

She had done so, she thought later, from the first moment when she had gone to his house to ask him if he would marry her rather than Felicity.

How, she asked herself, could any woman have resisted that strange, attractive, mocking expression in his eyes and the faintly cynical twist to his lips.

Now she could understand all too vividly what the Marchioness, the Comtesse and what doubtless every woman he had met, felt for him.

No wonder, when a whole world of beautiful women could be his, that he did not wish to tie himself to one dull, unattractive girl with no knowledge of anything except horses.

"I love you! I love you!" she whispered to him in the long nights when she nursed him.

He had cried out deliriously, sometimes talking gibberish she could not understand, but at other times speaking of things that had taken place in his life.

Gradually, after questioning Tour, she could understand what had actually happened.

He had fallen from a tree when he was a small boy and very nearly dislocated his neck.

He had been unconscious for a long time and forced to lie on his back so that the injuries he had done to himself would not become permanent.

He had thought in his delirium it was happening to him again, and as Antonia had held him in her arms, he had cried out for his mother.

When she tried to prevent him from throwing himself about in case he should injure the wound in his chest, Antonia had felt as if she was his mother and he was her child.

"You are all right, darling," she had murmured to him. "You are safe. You will not fall again, see, I am holding you close against me, and you cannot fall."

She felt gradually that her voice got through to him and that he understood.

Then he would turn his head against her breast as if seeking the comfort which only she could give him. She knew, at these times, that she loved him with her whole being as she had never thought she could love anybody.

Another night the Duke had thought he had had a fall hunting. When Antonia questioned Tour, he remembered when he had broken his collarbone and it had been very painful for some time.

He had cried out then for someone, but Antonia suspected that although he mentioned no name, it was not his mother he sought but another woman who he imagined would comfort him.

"It was not possible for me to be in his thoughts," Antonia told herself, "but lucky I am that he should turn to me and need me as I have never been needed before."

Gradually, as her love grew within her day after day, she understood that this was what she had always wanted, someone to love, someone to whom she was important and not just a nuisance and an irritation.

Someone also she could care for not only physically but with her whole heart.

'Even if he does not love me,' Antonia thought, 'I can love him. But he must never know of it!'

Sometimes now when the Duke was asleep she would creep to his bedside to look at him. Then she would feel that her breasts ached because she could not hold him any more in her arms and know that he would turn to her like an unhappy child.

She decided that when the Duke was well enough she would ask him to give her a baby. It would be a part of him which she could love and she was no longer afraid of the idea.

She thought of how foolish she had been not to let him make her his wife the first night they were married.

She wondered now why she had ever thought it important that they should get to know each other first. What really mattered was that she could have given him the heir he wanted and she would have had his child to love.

"When we get back to England," she told herself, "he will go back to the Marchioness, but nothing and nobody can take this time away from me! He is mine . . . mine now and there is no other woman to distract him."

She felt herself quiver with a sudden ecstasy as she whispered:

"I have held him in my arms and . . . kissed his cheek . . . his forehead and his . . . hair."

She schooled herself in the day-time to be very circumspect, so that the Duke would not suspect for one moment how much it had thrilled her when he asked her to lift him up against his pillows, to arrange them behind his head.

She even found herself, as the Duke got better, growing jealous of Tour because he asked so much more from him than he did from her.

She wanted to serve him, she wanted to be useful to him.

But when she had made him well, she remembered he would make love to the Marchioness!

She felt the pain of it strike at her like a dagger in her heart.

# CHAPTER SIX

"How are you feeling?" Antonia asked.

"Well enough to go home," the Duke replied.

He was sitting in an armchair in the window, and Antonia looking at him thought that he did in fact seem much better.

At the same time both she and Tour knew that he was still far from being himself.

Thanks to Labby, who had found a Chinese masseur, the Duke was in fact not as weak in the body as he might have been after such a long time in bed.

At the same time Antonia knew it would be a great mistake, at this stage in his convalescence, to over-tax his strength.

There were however many more difficulties arising from the situation in Paris than they had dared relate to the Duke, because they knew it would worry him.

They had not even told him that the Germans were approaching nearer and nearer day by day.

He had given her an answer and now, when the Duke said much the same thing she had the reply:

"We are British," he said, "so there is no need to think that we cannot leave whenever we might wish to do so."

Antonia hesitated.

"We are, as a Nation, very unpopular."

"Why?" the Duke enquired.

"According to Mr. Labouchere, French opinion has been scandalised by the unfriendly attitude of the British Press."

The Duke made an exasperated sound which she knew meant he thought little of the press one way or another.

"Once Paris was threatened," she went on, "it was widely assumed that Britain would enter the lists to rescue the Fount of Civilisation."

She paused before saying with a nervous note in her voice:

"Now, the feeling against us is so intense that *Les Nouvelles* even proposed that all the British in Paris should be shot at once!"

"Good heavens!" the Duke exclaimed.

"When the street names of Paris were changed after the fall of the Empire," Antonia went on, "the French press demanded that the Rue de Londres should be renamed on the grounds that the name of Londres was detested even more than Berlin."

"I cannot believe this is any more than gutter journalism," the Duke said sharply. "I shall myself call at the British Embassy to-morrow!"

Antonia said nothing for a moment and then changing the subject she asked:

"I can see you have a headache. Will you let me massage your forehead? You know it helps you."

She hoped as she spoke she did not sound too eager. To touch the Duke was such a delight that she found it difficult to hide her feelings in case he should guess how much she loved him.

"Perhaps it will help," he said a little grudgingly.

She rose to stand behind his chair and placed her two hands very gently on his forehead, soothing away the tension in a way he remembered her doing when he had been ill.

"How did you learn to do this?" he asked.

"Ives found that it helped your horses when they had a sprained fetlock," Antonia replied.

The Duke gave a short laugh.

"I might have guessed it was connected with horses!"

"I do not think I should have been allowed to practise on a man," Antonia said with a little smile.

"I am grateful that I can be the first in that field at any rate," the Duke remarked.

There was a slightly cynical and mocking note in his voice, and she wondered why.

Recently he had seemed almost to resent her attentions—or perhaps that was not the right word. It was as if he challenged her in some way which she could not understand.

"We must get away," he said suddenly. 'We must get back to England and a normal life. I am sure that is what you want as much as I do."

With difficulty Antonia prevented herself from crying out that it was the last thing she wanted.

"Or perhaps," the Duke went on, as if he was following the train of his own thoughts, "you would rather be here receiving the attentions of your journalist admirer."

"Mr. Labouchere has been very kind," Antonia said, "and when you are ready to leave I know he will help us."

"I very much doubt if I shall need his help," the Duke said loftily. "As I have already told you, I will go to the British Embassy to-morrow and arrange with Lord Lyon, our Ambassador, our safe conveyance to Le Havre where the yacht will be waiting."

"You must be quite strong enough before we undertake the journey," Antonia insisted.

"I intend to walk in the garden after I have rested this afternoon," the Duke said, "and my masseur assures me that my muscles are in perfect trim. It is just a question of not reopening the wound on my shoulder."

He did not add, Antonia noticed, that each time he got up out of bed he felt rather dizzy.

He resented any form of weakness, fighting against it with a determination which in part was the reason why he had recovered so quickly.

At the same time she knew that once they returned to England she would lose him, and she wished that whatever might happen in Paris they could stay on at least for a little while.

The Duke was resting after luncheon at which he had eaten quite a decent meal, having no idea how difficult it had been to procure, when the manservant announced that *Monsieur* Labouchere was in the Salon.

Antonia went in to him and he lifted her hand to his lips, holding it longer than necessary and looking at her in a manner which made her feel shy.

"You look a little tired," he said in concern. "Are you still nursing your importunate invalid at night?"

"No, of course not," Antonia replied. "I sleep peacefully and my husband has a bell that he rings if he requires anything. He has not woken me for several nights now."

"Yet subconsciously you listen for it," Labby said perceptively.

Antonia smiled.

"You are not to worry about me. My husband wishes to go home."

"He told me so yesterday," Labby replied. "It is not going to be easy."

"He says that he will see the British Ambassador tomorrow."

"That will be impossible," Labby answered. "He left this morning with the last of the British Corps Diplomatique."

"I do not believe it!" Antonia exclaimed.

"I am afraid it is the truth," Labby replied. "I was told that had happened, and because I was thinking about you I called at the Embassy on my way here."

Antonia drew in her breath as he went on:

"There is no official left now in the British Embassy, save a conçierge whose duty, I gather, is to shrug his shoulders to all enquiries and say parrot-wise 'I cannot give you any information'."

"I have never heard of anything so extraordinary!" Antonia exclaimed. "I thought the British Ambassador would stay as long as there were any English in Paris."

"There are some 4,000 still in the City," Labby told her.

"If the Ambassador has gone, then I feel we should go too," Antonia said in a frightened voice. "Are there any trains running?"

"I think it unlikely you will be able to get on one even if there were."

Labby paused and Antonia knew that he was keeping something from her.

"Tell me the truth," she begged.

"I have only just learnt that a train which left the Gare du Nord on September 15th was seized by Prussian outriders at Senlis, which you know is only 27 miles north of Paris."

Antonia gasped but did not speak, and Labby went on:

"I think it was that which must have persuaded Lord Lyon and the British Consul to leave this morning."

"Why did the French Government not insist on all the British leaving earlier?" Antonia asked despairingly.

"The Government and the Council of National Defence has said that large groups of foreigners leaving the City would be . . . demoralising to the Army and the citizens."

"But we are nothing but useless mouths," Antonia persisted.

"That is what a number of British have already said to me," Labby replied, "but I can assure you the French Government will not listen and in my opinion they are making a mess of everything."

He spoke almost savagely and then said:

"I will get you away somehow, I promise you that. At the same time, if I followed my own wishes, I would keep you here."

Antonia glanced at him enquiringly and saw the look in his eyes and quickly looked away.

"I love you, Antonia," he said very quietly. "You know that by this time."

"You must not . . . say such . . . things."

"What harm can it do?" he asked. "I know what your feelings are where I am concerned."

He gave a sigh which seemed to come from the very depths of his being as he said:

"I realise that I am much too old for you. Had I been ten years younger I would have done my damnedest to seduce you. As it is, I will leave you as I found you, perfect and unspoilt—perhaps in a long list of conquests, the only woman I have ever really loved."

There was something in Labby's voice which made Antonia feel curiously near to tears.

There was nothing she could say. She was only perturbed that she should have brought unhappiness to someone who had been so kind.

As if he knew what she was thinking, Labby went on:

"Perhaps one day when you are older you will understand how difficult it has been these past weeks, when we have been so much alone together, for me to behave with an unaccustomed constraint and control."

"It has meant so . . . much to me to have your . . . friendship," Antonia faltered.

"It is not friendship, Antonia," Labby contradicted, "it is love! A love so different from anything I have known or felt in the past that sometimes I think I must be dreaming and you do not really exist, except in my imagination."

"You should not talk to me like . . . this, as you . . . well know," Antonia said.

But she wondered even as she spoke why she should prevent him from doing so.

The Duke would not care if another man made love to her. After all he was in love with the Marchioness. When they returned to England she would have nobody in her life, neither the man she loved, nor the man who loved her.

She had half turned away and Labby, as he was speaking, put his hands on her shoulders to turn her round to face him.

"What is it about you that is so different to other women?" he asked. "You are not outstandingly beautiful, and yet I cannot be free of the fascination of your face."

She saw the pain in his eyes as he went on:

"I hear your voice in my ears, your figure makes any other woman look coarse and ungainly, and I find it almost impossible to think of anyone else but you."

There was a depth of passion in his tone which made Antonia feel shy and a little afraid.

Then he released her and walked across the Salon to stand at the window looking into the garden.

"When you leave," he said, "all I shall have are my dreams. I have the uncomfortable feeling that they will haunt me for the rest of my life."

Antonia made a little helpless gesture.

"What can I . . . say?" she asked. "You know I do not wish to . . . hurt you."

"It is banal to say 'it is better to have loved and lost than never to have loved at all'," Labby replied in the tone of a man mocking at himself. "In my case it happens to be true. You have done a wonderful thing for me, my sweet Duchess."

"What is that?" Antonia asked.

"You have restored my faith in women. I have watched the manner in which they defamed and prostituted in every possible way the Second Empire. I saw their greed, their hypocrisy, their perfidy! You have shown me that women can be pure and faithful, true and uncorrupted."

He gave her one of his cynical smiles as he said:

"I have always thought that each woman a man loves, leaves a tombstone in his life. On yours will be written—'She gave me faith'."

"Thank you, Labby," Antonia said very softly.

Then without waiting for him to say good-bye she went from the Salon and left him alone

"I do not believe you!" the Duke ejaculated angrily.

"It is true," Henry Labouchere replied. "The Uhlans from two Prussian armies joined hands yesterday, September 20th, near Versailles which surrendered without a shot."

There was silence for a moment. Then the Duke said:

"That means that Paris is now severed from the rest of France. I can hardly believe it!"

"What do the people feel?" Antonia asked.

"At the moment the mood is 'Let them come, Let the cannon thunder! It has been too long!' " Labby replied, "but retribution has been enacted violently upon the wretched deserters."

"If they desert, they deserve all they get!" the Duke said in a hard voice.

"I cannot help being sorry for them," Labby answered. "According to reports they were not only badly led, but many of them were without arms. The young Zouaves panicked the first time they were shelled by a well-trained Prussian field-gun battery."

"What is happening to them now?" Antonia enquired.

"Montmartre is full of them and an angry mob was spitting in their faces and threatening to lynch them until the *Garde Nationale* escorted them with many prods of their rifle butts into the centre of the City."

"And what else is taking place?" the Duke enquired.

"The great difficulty is going to be to get news out of the City," Labby replied. "A possible solution may be balloons."

"Balloons!" the Duke exclaimed in surprise.

"A number have been located," Labby replied, "unfortunately most of them in various states of disrepair. It is however an idea, though not where passengers are concerned."

"I was not thinking we should fly from Paris!" the Duke said sharply. "What I am considering is whether it could be any use appealing to the French to negotiate with the Germans for a special pass."

"I thought of that," Labby answered. "The Duchess has already requested me to find some way in which you could leave."

"Is it possible?" the Duke enquired.

"This morning I watched four Britons who I happened to know, climbing gaily into a carriage loaded with hampers of provisions, luggage and with an English flag flying."

"What happened?" the Duke asked.

"They got as far as Pont de Neuilly where they were seized and taken before General Ducrot. He said to them, 'I cannot understand you English: if you want to get shot, we will shoot you ourselves to save you trouble'."

Labby paused for a moment and then went on:

"My friends swear they will try again to-morrow, but I should think it unlikely they will get through."

"Then what can we do?" the Duke asked.

"Give me a little time," Labby begged. "The Prussians are

bringing up their big guns. The bombardment will not start yet."

Antonia looked frightened.

"You think they will bombard us?"

"Naturally," Labby replied. "It is the obvious thing to do if they want a quick surrender."

That night, Antonia lay awake wondering if she would hear the shells thudding and exploding in the centre of the City, but everything was quiet and she thought that perhaps Labby had exaggerated the danger.

There was however no doubt that the Duke took him seriously and in the next few days he became more and more restless.

He was only prevented with difficulty from going out of the house to see for himself what was occurring.

It was Antonia who finally managed to dissuade him by saying she would be frightened if she were left alone.

"I cannot stay here like a caged animal," the Duke said irritably.

"S . . . suppose you were . . . killed, or . . . arrested," Antonia said. "What would happen to . . . me?"

It was an unanswerable argument, and the Duke had listened to Labouchere when he said that if he went to the French Authorities and declared who he was, they could take two courses of action.

They might consider an English Duke so important that they would give him no chance of ever leaving Paris in case he fell into the hands of the Prussians.

"Or else," Labby went on, "they will arrest you on some trumped up charge merely to force the British Government to pay more attention to the siege of Paris!"

Both, the Duke realised, were quite viable arguments, but he was now more determined than ever that they must leave Paris somehow without anybody realising who they were.

However, when he had suffered nearly a week's inactivity, while getting stronger day by day, he said to Antonia:

"You know I would not wish deliberately to take you into danger, but I am quite convinced that the siege is going to get very much worse before the French surrender."

"You think they really will surrender?" Antonia asked in surprise. "Surely someone will come to their rescue."

"Who is likely to do so?" the Duke asked, and she knew there was no answer.

"But if Paris holds out without relief from outside, the siege might last indefinitely."

"It can only last as long as there is enough food to eat," the Duke replied.

"But surely there will be enough for a very long time?"

Antonia thought as she spoke of all the animals in the Bois.

"Tour has told me," the Duke replied, "that people are talking, if things get really bad, of slaughtering the animals in the Zoo. And there is no doubt that cats and dogs will be in danger of their lives as soon as what meat is obtainable in the Butchers' shops is priced beyond the purse of the very poor!"

Antonia gave a little cry.

"I cannot bear to think of it."

"Nor can I where you are concerned," the Duke said. "And that is why I have to decide whether it would be best to risk our being caught or shot by the Prussians outside Paris, or to stop here and starve, as undoubtedly the Parisians will do eventually."

Antonia did not hesitate.

"I know what you would prefer," she said, "and I am prepared to take any risk that you wish."

"Thank you, Antonia," the Duke said. "I knew I could rely on you to show courage."

He smiled at her in a way she found irresistible as he added:

"Perhaps it will be no more frightening and no more dangerous than leaping over the high hedges and the water-jump on The Chase!"


The soldiers guarding the Port de St. Cloud watched a wooden cart trundling towards them drawn by a frisky young mule.

It was driven by a woman muffled in shawls despite the

heat and with a dirty cotton handkerchief tied under her chin.

As the cart drew near to the gate she began to cry out loudly and defiantly:

"*La Vérole!*"

"*Danger!*"

"*Contagieuse!*"

The Corporal in front of the gate held up his hand and with a little difficulty she drew the mule to a stand-still.

"What is all this?" he asked.

"*La Vérole*," she replied, jerking her thumb backwards to where he could now see a man lying on the straw of the wooden cart.

"Smallpox!"

The Corporal took a step backwards.

"I have my papers if you want to see them," the woman said speaking in argot, "but I should be careful how you touch them."

She held them out to the soldier who made no effort to take them.

"Where do you think you are going, *Madame*?"

"We've been turned out," she answered. "There's not a man amongst the sniffling cowards in this City who'll touch a smallpox case as bad as his!"

Without moving his feet the Corporal peered over the edge of the cart. He could see the face of the man lying on the straw was covered with flaming red pox-marks and shuddered.

"Go on, get out of here!" he said harshly, "and the quicker the better!"

The woman whipped the mule, the gate was opened and they proceeded until they came to the Prussian out-post just outside the town of St. Cloud.

Here the same explanation was given, but the papers signed by the doctor were inspected and there was some delay while a junior Officer was produced.

"The man you are conveying, *Madame*," he said in guttural but just intelligible French, "may have smallpox, but that is no reason why you should leave the City with him."

She did not answer, but pulled back a ragged cuff that

covered her wrist. On her skin he could see two flaming red pox-marks! Hastily he handed her back the papers.

"Go away as far as you can from Paris," he ordered.

"We're going to Nantes, *Mein Herr*," the woman said. "That's if we reach it before we die!"

The German officer was however not listening, as he hurried away to wash his hands after touching her papers. The soldiers watched them go with a look of relief on their smileless faces, and one of them said:

"I would rather die from a bullet than that disease."

"For such filth it would be a waste of ammunition," the other answered.

Antonia's back was very straight as she drove away, and it was an effort not to look behind her.

She touched the mule with her whip and made him go faster. Only when the Prussian out-post was out of sight did the Duke sit up from the floor of the wooden cart and say:

"I am being rattled to bits!"

"You can come up here and drive," Antonia replied over her shoulder.

"It is certainly what I would prefer," he answered.

Antonia slackened the speed of the mule a little, but she did not pull up to a stand-still.

The Duke climbed into the front of the cart and took the reins from her.

"Is it safe to wipe this blasted paint off my face?" he asked.

"I should leave it for the moment," she replied. "There will be, as Labby warned us, Germans all over the place and whatever happens we must not get captured."

"I am aware of that," he said, "but according to reports they have not yet reached Amiens."

"Can we trust the reports?"

"Tour will get to Le Havre all right," the Duke said.

The valet had left two days earlier in the company of some Americans who had managed by some extraordinary good luck to obtain permits both from the French and Germans.

There had been no chance however, even if they had

wished to do so, of taking anyone extra with them. The pass was merely for themselves and their servants.

Only by bribing the American's French servant with what seemed to Antonia an almost astronomical amount of francs had Tour persuaded the man to stay in Paris while he took his place.

Once Henry Labouchere and the Duke had worked out a plan of campaign, they had instructed Tour down to the minutest detail as to what he should do.

Horses were to be left for Antonia and the Duke at a village which Labby was certain was not at the moment under Prussian occupation.

"Buy the best you can," the Duke said, "and then hire the fastest conveyance that is obtainable and get to Le Havre where the yacht will be waiting."

"The Prussians will not touch a British ship," Labby had said firmly.

"No, but they might prevent us boarding her," the Duke replied, "and that is why if Le Havre is under Prussian occupation, Tour must somehow get in touch with my Captain and tell him to take the yacht to Cherbourg."

"It is much, much further," Antonia said nervously.

"I know that," the Duke said, "but I intend to take no risks where you are concerned. Somehow, if it is necessary, we will make our way across country, and we may be lucky."

"The reports at the moment," Labby told them, "but of course they are not completely reliable, are that the Prussians have not advanced, at least in any strength, further than St. Quentin."

"In which case Versailles and Evreux will be all right," the Duke said, "but I do not intend to visit any towns. We will keep to the fields and we may find something to eat in the small villages."

"Having seen the way the people were behaving in Paris, Your Grace," Tour said, "I should not rely on it, if they have any food, I am quite certain that the French, when they fear that they themselves might go hungry, will not give away or even sell anything that is edible to passing travellers."

"I am afraid that may be true," Labby agreed. "Hundreds of stragglers have brought the Army into disrepute with the locals. I am told French farmers have barred their doors and threatened to fire on the starving troops begging for food."

"We will take what we can with us," Antonia said quietly. "Otherwise we shall just have to be hungry for a day or two until we reach the yacht."

As she spoke she felt worried not for herself, but for the Duke.

He was much better, but she knew this journey would be a tremendous strain and she wondered what she would do if he collapsed, perhaps in some hostile French village where there would be no doctor.

But when they set off the Duke was in good spirits simply because he was at last being active.

He had laughed at the clothes that Labby had bought for them as a disguise, and when he saw the wooden cart and the mule that was to carry them from Paris he had said to Antonia:

"I am sure, Your Grace, you will find this as impressive, though perhaps not so fast, as the Phaeton in which we set out on our honeymoon."

"I only wish Rufus was drawing it!' Antonia replied.

"So do I," he said quietly.

She had felt a sudden warmth within her because they were sharing their love of horses and a secret which was their own.

But when they had driven away from the house leaving Labby staring after them with an expression of despair in his eyes, Antonia felt frightened.

It would be bad enough if the French penetrated their disguise, but what if the Prussians did!

She felt herself tremble at what might happen, knowing that it would be hard to explain who they were or to get anyone to believe them.

Then she told herself that whatever happened she was with the Duke.

The secret island on which they existed in a strange unreal world had now been left behind. They were crossing the hostile sea which she had sensed was always waiting for them outside.

But she told herself almost despairingly that, while the

Duke would be travelling to safety and to England, she was returning to loneliness, to being unwanted as she had been all her life.

Once he was back with the Marchioness there would be no-one for her to look after, to comfort, to sustain.

Perhaps sometimes, she told herself, he would want her to massage his forehead.

Perhaps because they had been through so much together there would be things to talk about which other women could not share.

But when she thought of the Marchioness's beauty, she knew that even a Worth gown could not make her look like a fairy on a Christmas tree, or have the unbelievable loveliness of the woman who called in uninvited to see them the first night they were married.

"It is hopeless!" Antonia told herself.

At the same time there were two, perhaps three days left when she would be alone with the Duke!

Even to sit beside him in the front of the cart, realising how grotesque they both looked in their ragged clothes, the Duke's face painted with small-pox eruptions, was still an indescribable thrill.

The village where Tour was to leave the horses for them was 10 miles out of Paris and off the beaten track.

They left the main road for a dusty and twisting lane.

Antonia realised with relief that they were getting into an uninhabited part of the country where there were thick forests and only occasional small and unimportant hamlets.

Labby had suggested they should leave by Port de St. Cloud because the Prussian lines of investment were nearer to Paris there than at any other place.

"The sooner you are away from the City and its environment, the better. There is always the chance that you might encounter some officious French Official who would turn you back. And whatever you do, keep north when you are through the German lines otherwise you will find yourself in Versailles which is full of Uhlans."

"Do you think we are going in the right direction," Antonia asked the Duke tentatively.

"I have a good bump of location," he answered, "and I

have studied the map very carefully. Once we have found the horses we should have an uninterrupted ride across country."

He spoke in a calm, matter of fact manner. Then he said:

"You are not frightened, Antonia?"

"No . . . no," she answered, "not . . . when I am with . . . you."

He looked down at her, muffled in her ragged shawls and said with a hint of laughter in his voice:

"I have said it before: this is an incredible honeymoon."

"It will be something to tell our grandchildren," Antonia replied.

Even as she spoke she realised she had assumed that they would have grandchildren and that entailed first having children.

The Duke did not say anything and merely drove on, keeping the mule at a steady pace and handling the reins with an expertise that he would have shown towards his own superb horses.

They came upon the village unexpectedly at a turn of the road and the Duke drew to a stand-still.

"Is it . . . safe?" Antonia asked.

"I am just making certain that everything is quiet and there is no sign of any Prussians. If there is anything suspicious I will lie down in the back of the cart. It is always best to be prepared, Antonia, and not to take risks."

"Yes, of course," she said, "you think of everything."

"I am thinking of you," he said sharply.

But she wondered if in fact he was resenting that he must look after a woman instead of being able to forge ahead and hurry back to England.

She was well aware that if she had not been with him he would have left several days earlier.

It was not only because he doubted his own strength that he had listened to her pleadings and to Labby's good common sense, but also because he realised that having Antonia with him was an added responsibility.

The village appeared quiet and safe in the morning sunshine.

The Duke approached a small Inn, called Le Coq d'Or.

He drove the mule into the yard and handed Antonia the reins.

Then jumping down from the cart he went to the pump in the centre of the yard and washed his face.

'It may be taking a risk,' Antonia thought, 'but it would certainly be unwise to frighten the French who are holding the horses for us.'

She slipped the papers they had used to escape through the barriers, down the front of her dress.

Then as the Duke disappeared into the Inn she climbed down from the cart and went to the mule, patting his neck and talking to him in a voice which all horses seem to understand whatever their nationality.

The Duke came back with a thick-set elderly man, who Antonia guessed was the proprietor of the Inn.

She noticed that the Duke had removed the ragged garments which he had been wearing over his riding-clothes, except that he still had on his feet a pair of disreputable toe-less shoes.

Antonia burrowed in the straw and produced his riding-boots.

Then as she heard the two men talking inside the stable she took off the shawls and the full, ragged skirt which covered her own riding-habit.

It was very elegant because she had not thought to bring with her the one she had bought in London, knowing it would be far too severe to be worn riding in the Bois.

Instead she had on a habit of thin piqué which the Empress had made all the vogue and in which Worth had dressed all the fashionable Courtesans as well as the Ladies of Quality.

The only thing Antonia had not dared to bring with her was her riding-hat, but she had a scarf of the same colour as her riding-habit with which she could cover her hair.

She was however aware that her hair must look lamentable without the fashionable coiffure which had done so much to change her appearance from a dowdy English bride to the *chic* woman with whom Labby had fallen in love.

Realising the mule had found some grass to eat amongst

the weeds growing in the courtyard she left him and went
into the Inn.

A woman, whom she guessed to be the wife of the proprietor, was very willing to show her upstairs to a poorly
furnished bed-room, where however she could wash and
there was a mirror in which she could arrange her hair.

She was as quick as she could be because she was quite
certain the Duke would wish to get away. In a few minutes
she was at least more presentable and had arranged the gauze
scarf over her up-swept hair before she hurried downstairs.

As she had expected, she found the Duke waiting for her
impatiently. The horses were saddled and Antonia saw that
Tour had managed to procure a side-saddle for her.

They were rough-looking, not particularly prepossessing
beasts, but she realised they were sturdy and would undoubtedly endure the long journey better than well-bred and faster
animals.

The Duke had a glass of wine in his hand and the proprietor handed one to Antonia.

She was just about to protest that she did not need anything alcoholic to drink, when she thought that the Duke had
ordered it for her, and it might be a long time before they
would get anything else to drink.

This idea however was dispelled when the proprietor
said:

"I put the food the gentleman ordered for you, *Monsieur*,
in the saddle-bag, and there are two bottles of wine in *Madame*'s."

"Thank you again," the Duke said. "I am extremely grateful."

He tipped the man and helped Antonia onto her saddle.

For a moment she was close to him, his hands were touching her, and she felt a thrill like quicksilver run through her.

Then the Duke had mounted his own horse, and without
speaking they rode from the Inn, through the small village
and out into the open country.

"So far so good, Antonia," the Duke said with a note of
satisfaction in his voice, after they had travelled some way.

"Tour has obviously got through."

"And so have we," the Duke smiled. "As you said just

now, Antonia, this is a story that will undoubtedly enthrall our children."

He did not look at her as he spoke but Antonia felt the colour rise in her cheeks.

"Please God, let him give me . . . a child," she prayed in her heart. "I love him . . . I love him so desperately."

# CHAPTER SEVEN

Antonia thought she was lying on a soft cloud. She felt as if she was sinking into it deeper and deeper until it enveloped her whole body.

Then gradually she became aware that everything was very quiet and there was in fact a pillow under her head.

Slowly her mind began to work and she realised she had been asleep for a very long time. She opened her eyes slowly as if she were afraid, until as she saw the outline of the cabin she knew where she was.

She was on the yacht, they had reached safety, they had won!

Antonia turned over onto her side and could not remember coming aboard. She could recall the moment when they had arrived at the Quay at Le Havre and seen the Duke's yacht at anchor, gleaming white against the blue of the waves.

She had stood staring at it, feeling now she no longer had the support of her horse that if she moved she would fall down from sheer exhaustion.

Vaguely she had recalled someone helping her into a boat, then she must have fallen asleep.

"How is it I can remember nothing of what happened next?" she asked herself, and saw her arm was naked.

She moved the blanket which covered her and realised someone had removed her riding-habit.

She was wearing only her full petticoats and a silk chemise. Even the waist of the petticoat had been undone so that she would not be restricted.

She knew who must have undressed her and felt herself blush at the thought.

How could she not have known that he was touching her?

Perhaps he had carried her to her cabin; but she had been so tired, so utterly and completely exhausted that everything had been swept away in her need for sleep.

Even the first day had been tiring because she had not been riding for nearly two months. But she had been too preoccupied in worrying about the Duke to think of herself.

They had ridden hard and said very little. Watching him however Antonia knew that he was tense every time they saw people in the distance, or were in sight of a main road.

The highways seemed unaccountably crowded although whether it was with Germans, stragglers from the French Army or refugees, Antonia had no idea.

She guessed that the Duke was as apprehensive of meeting French deserters who were living off the land, as he was of encountering the invaders.

'They would rob us,' Antonia thought, 'and would undoubtedly take our horses.'

She understood why the Duke skirted even the smallest hamlets and kept to the open fields.

They stopped for a very short while to eat some of the food which Tour had ordered for them. There was crisp French bread, a rough local pâté, cheese and fruit, which they finished the first day.

It seemed delicious, but by dinner time they were both too tired to feel hungry and were only grateful for being able to drink a little wine from the bottles in Antonia's saddle-bag.

It was nearly dusk when the Duke reined in his horse

which was now moving much more slowly than it had done before and said:

"We must find somewhere to sleep, Antonia, but I am afraid your accommodation for to-night must be in a wood."

"I think I would sleep on top of a mountain and on bare rocks at this moment," Antonia smiled.

"You are tired?" he asked sharply.

"Very,' she replied truthfully, "and so are you."

She had in fact been worrying about him for several hours, aware that he was over-taxing his strength.

But knowing too that as he concentrated on getting them away, he would not acknowledge his own weakness or the fact that his wound was doubtlessly hurting him.

They stopped in a small wood surrounded by open fields which would make it, if they were watching out, impossible for anyone to approach them unawares.

Having unsaddled the horses and made quite certain they could not wander away, the Duke flung himself down on the moss-covered ground beside Antonia and she saw the lines of fatigue on his face.

"If you will put your head in my lap," she suggested tentatively after they had finished eating, "I will massage your forehead."

"You will do nothing of the sort, Antonia!" the Duke replied. "You will lie close to me and go to sleep. I want to leave here at dawn."

Thinking there was no point in arguing, Antonia did as she was told.

After he had moved restlessly for several minutes as if he were in pain, she knew by his even breathing that he was fast asleep.

Very, very carefully she moved herself a little higher up the soft ground so that she could put her arm beneath his head and hold him close against her breast.

'This may be for the last time,' she thought, 'I may never be able to do this again.'

Very gently she massaged his forehead with the soothing strokes she had used when he was delirious.

As she did so she felt him relax, and knew that he was

sleeping deeply, too deeply for her to waken him inadvertently.

It was then she kissed his hair, telling him wordlessly how much she loved him.

"I love you! Oh, my darling . . . I love you!"

She held him closer still, his head heavy against her, and she thought that for the moment she had never been so happy.

"I must move away," she told herself, "before I fall asleep . . ."


The next thing Antonia knew was that the Duke was calling her. He was already up and had saddled both the horses.

Hurriedly she got the food and wine ready for them to have a scanty breakfast before they set out again.

The bread was stale by now and not very appetising, but it was not a moment to be fastidious.

The next day was very much like the first and Antonia knew that Tour's choice of their horses had been a wise one.

Like their riders they might be tired, but they kept going at a fair pace and Antonia knew that the miles between them and Le Havre were lessening every hour.

"Do you know where we are?" she asked the Duke once.

"I have a good idea," he replied briefly.

He obviously did not want to talk and Antonia was silent, knowing that as they rode the Duke was always on the alert for any unexpected danger.

They stopped a little earlier than they had the night before, simply because both they and the horses found it difficult to go any further.

The heat of the day had changed when the sky became overcast and a chill wind began to blow across the open countryside.

For the first time Antonia wished that her smart piqué habit was more substantial, and that she had not thrown away all the shawls in which she had disguised herself for leaving Paris.

She did not complain, but the Duke must have known what she was feeling because a mile later he said:

"I see a barn ahead. If, as it appears, it is not connected to a farm-house, I think that is where we will stay the night."

The barn was in fact some distance from the farmhouse which lay about a quarter of a mile away.

What was more, it was half full with hay, which provided not only fodder for the horses but a comfortable resting-place for two very tired people.

They ate a little of the dry bread and the pâté which still tasted quite pleasant, although rather monotonous. Then Antonia sank down into the hay.

"I would not change this," she said, "at the moment for the most comfortable mattress in Doncaster Park!"

The Duke picked up some handfuls of hay and covered her with it.

"This will keep you warm just as effectively as a woollen blanket," he said. "I should have thought to suggest that you brought a riding-cloak with you."

"I should have thought of it myself," Antonia replied, "but it was so hot in Paris."

"I think it is going to rain."

The Duke lay down on the hay and they neither of them heard the rain pouring down in the night.

But when they left the barn in the morning the earth felt fresh and the horses seemed to respond to the coolness in the air.

They stopped to water the animals at the first stream and then they were off again.

Antonia hoped and prayed that they would reach the end of their journey before nightfall. She would not have admitted it to the Duke but her body was feeling very stiff and the saddle was not a comfortable one.

The day seemed unaccountably long, but she knew hopefully that the end was near when the Duke insisted on her drinking quite a lot of the last bottle of wine and then threw it away.

"Only a few more hours," he said encouragingly.

"You can manage?" Antonia asked anxiously.

"I am worrying about you and not myself!" the Duke answered.

"That is ridiculous!" she protested. "You are the invalid."

She knew as she spoke she had said the wrong thing.

"I am nothing of the sort, Antonia," he said almost sharply, "and this would be a taxing journey for any woman, even an Amazon like yourself."

He was teasing her and she felt happy because he was well enough to do so.

As the hours dragged by she grew tireder and tireder.

Fortunately the horses kept together and when she thought the Duke was not watching her she was able to hold on to the pommel of her saddle.

"I must not fail him now," she kept telling herself. "We have got so far. I cannot let him down at the very last moment."

But the very last moment seemed far away and when finally they clattered over the cobbled streets of Le Havre she thought that if a whole battalion of Prussian soldiers was waiting for them she would be unable to make any effort to escape.

Now she made no pretence of not holding on to the pommel with both hands, and the Duke reached out to take the bridle of her horse as they rode down to the Quay.

She had heard him giving orders; she felt him lift her down from the saddle and help her into a boat. Then there was a blank.

"He should have been the one to collapse, not me," Antonia told herself and was ashamed that she had so little fortitude.

She wondered what time it was and even as she thought about it, the door of the cabin opened very softly and she knew someone was peeping inside.

"I am . . . awake!" she said and her voice sounded hoarse and strange.

"I thought you might be, Your Grace."

Tour came into the cabin and pulled back the curtains over the portholes.

"We are safe!" Antonia exclaimed.

"You are indeed, Your Grace. There are no dangers in Southampton Harbour."

"Southampton!" Antonia queried. 'But how can we have got here so quickly?"

Tour smiled.

"You slept all of yesterday, Your Grace, in fact you have been asleep for two nights, a whole day and it is now nearly noon!"

"I cannot believe it!' Antonia exclaimed. "And His Grace?"

She waited apprehensively in case Tour should tell her the Duke was ill.

"His Grace also slept the whole way over. He had a little dinner last night and went straight back to sleep."

"He is all right?" Antonia enquired.

"Fit as a fiddle, Your Grace. There is no need to worry about him."

"And the journey did not hurt his wound?"

"It appears to me not to have changed in any way since I last saw it in Paris."

"Thank God for that!" Antonia exclaimed.

"And thank God you and His Grace arrived safely," Tour said solemnly.

"And you," Antonia added. "Was it a difficult journey?"

"It had its unpleasant moments, but I will tell Your Grace about them another time."

He bent down as he spoke and Antonia saw him pick up her dusty travel-stained riding-habit which was lying on the floor.

"I expect Your Grace would like a bath," he said, "and I have some good news for you."

"What is it?" Antonia asked.

"When I came aboard I found that when six weeks ago, *Monsieur* Worth passed through Le Havre on his way to England, he saw the yacht in the harbour and asked to whom it belonged."

Tour paused to make what he had to say even more dramatic.

"When he learnt it belonged to His Grace, he sent aboard

the trunks in which he was conveying Your Grace's purchases to England."

"Oh, Tour, I cannot believe it!" Antonia cried. "How wonderful! Bring me my bath, and then I will make myself look respectable for His Grace."

"His Grace has gone ashore, so there is no hurry," Tour replied. "First I must get Your Grace something to eat."

Antonia smiled.

"As you mention it," she said, "I do feel ravenously hungry."

She ate what seemed to her an enormous amount of eggs and bacon, while Tour filled her bath with hot water and brought one of the trunks that *Monsieur* Worth had left for her into the cabin.

There was a fascinating choice of garments, but knowing it was likely to be colder in England than it had been in Paris, especially late in September, Antonia chose a gown of heavy satin.

It had a short jacket fastening into the waist and was trimmed with a collar of ermine, with the same fur on the cuffs.

She washed her hair and was appalled at the amount of dust it had accumulated on the ride and from sleeping in the hay in the barn.

While she had a little difficulty in arranging it, when it was surmounted by one of Worth's *chic* little hats she looked very fashionable and very un-English.

She knew when she went on deck that the Captain and the crew looked at her in undisguised admiration, and she only hoped the same expression would be echoed in the Duke's eyes.

He was standing near the gangway, exceedingly smart and looking as if he had undertaken nothing more strenuous than a ride in the Park.

Antonia found it hard to look at him.

Now they were back to normal life and there was no danger, no urgency, she felt as if they were drifting apart.

She wanted to cling onto him and to beg him not to leave her.

"I love you, I love you," she wanted to cry, but instead with a commendable control, she said:

"Good morning, Your Grace. It is delightful to be home."

"Are you ready to go for a drive?" he asked.

"A drive?" she questioned. "I thought we should be taking the train to London."

"We are not going to London," he replied. "Not unless you particularly wish to do so."

She waited for him to explain and he went on:

"I have a cousin, the Earl of Manford, who lives near Southampton. I have already called at his house to find that he and his wife are in Scotland. I have therefore arranged with his Secretary who is in charge, that we shall stay there for a few days. I think we have both done enough travelling for the moment."

He smiled at Antonia as he spoke and she felt her heart turn over in her breast with excitement.

She was not to lose him immediately! He was not in such a hurry as she had feared to see the Marchioness again.

They would be together and she could not imagine anything that would be more wonderful.

The Earl's house was only a few miles outside Southampton and the Duke drove her there in the smart Phaeton which he explained also belonged to his cousin and which was drawn by two horses.

Antonia had to exclaim in delight at the sight of them. Then she said:

"Perhaps they only appear so superbly well-bred after the two which carried us from Paris."

Then she added quickly:

"Do not think I am disparaging their splendid performance in bringing us to safety. I only wish we could have explained to them how grateful we were."

"I gave them to the man who owns the local Livery Stables," the Duke said. "I also gave him quite a considerable sum for their keep on condition he rested them for at least a week. I think he will appreciate their worth."

"That was generous of you," Antonia said gratefully.

"I do not think either of us will forget that ride or the horses that carried us," he said quietly.

"I could never forget it," Antonia said in her heart. "We were alone . . . he was with me both by day and by night . . . for perhaps the last time!"

The house belonging to the Earl of Manfred was impressively Georgian with a delightful garden.

There was a staff of well-trained servants and Antonia was shown into a large, elegantly furnished bed-room which compared favourably with the State rooms at Doncaster Park.

There was a canopied and curtained bed in a rose pink that she thought was particularly becoming to herself. Only she remembered that the colour was of no importance as she would be sleeping alone!

The last two nights she had slept beside the Duke her body had been touching his and the first night she had held him in her arms.

"That will never happen again," she told herself miserably.

Suddenly the fact that they were back in civilisation swept over her with a feeling of despair! Now she would lose him!

She had had him to herself for so long that she could hardly remember what it was like before he had been there. To the exclusion of all else, she had concentrated all her thoughts, her feelings and love on him.

Yet she had promised him when he had asked her to marry him that she would be unobtrusive and would make no demands upon him. Now she must keep her promise.

'I cannot imagine anything more humiliating,' she thought, 'if he realises that I love him and he had to make it clear to me that he is not interested.'

What was more, she thought, such knowledge might make him feel uncomfortable, perhaps embarrassed, in which case she might see even less of him than she would do otherwise.

"I have to be very sensible, and very brave about this," she told herself, but was near to tears.

She forced herself to take an interest in her trunks which had been brought to the house by Tour and had followed them from Southampton in a travelling carriage also provided by the Earl's staff.

Before she had left the yacht, Antonia had remembered to ask about the Duke's clothes.

She learnt that he always had an extra wardrobe kept aboard the yacht in case he wished to embark at a moment's notice without the necessity of waiting for a valet to pack for him.

He was therefore looking resplendent and just as elegant as on their wedding night, when Antonia entered the Salon before dinner.

The sun was sinking and the crimson and gold sky cast a warm glow into the long room with its French-windows opening out onto a balustraded terrace.

Antonia stood just inside the door, her eyes seeking the Duke's and for a moment it was hard to move forward.

She had spent a long time choosing what she would wear, changing her mind a dozen times.

Finally she had let the maids dress her in a gown of cardinal red which made her skin seem almost translucent.

It was however not a heavy gown despite the depth of colour.

It was ornamented with the soft tulle, expensive satin ribbons, frills and fringes which Worth had made fashionable. They accentuated the perfect curves of Antonia's figure and gave her an alluring femininity that was unmistakable.

Slowly she walked towards the Duke.

"These surroundings are somewhat different from our lodgings last night," he said with a smile, "and although I had a good luncheon I am still hungry."

His eyes were on her face as he spoke, and she had the feeling that he was talking as if he had to bridge a certain awkwardness which lay between them. But what it was she did not know.

Then as he raised her hand to his lips, she wanted desperately to hold on to him because she was afraid he would vanish.

'He will leave me now we are home,' she thought despairingly, but aloud she said:

"Tour tells me your shoulder has withstood the journey well."

"I am well," the Duke said firmly. "It is what I have waited for, for a long time, Antonia."

She looked at him enquiringly, but at that moment dinner was announced and she put her hand shyly on his arm as he led her towards the Dining-Room.

The Earl's chef was not as skilled as the one employed by the Duke in London, but Antonia thought that never had a meal tasted more delicious.

She kept remembering how dry and hard the bread had been the last day of their journey, and how tired she had been of the pâté which seemed less appetising every time they sampled it. The cheese too had been over ripe from being carried in the saddle-bag.

She thought now that the fish, fresh from the sea; the beef, from the Earl's own herd; the pigeons, roasted until they were exactly the right tenderness, were an epicurean feast.

The Duke insisted that she should drink a little champagne.

"It will take away the last vestige of tiredness," he said.

The Duke had found out the latest news from France and he told her that Strasbourg had surrendered after a gallant defence, following the bombardment which had destroyed the magnificent old library and killed many civilians.

"War is such a waste!" Antonia exclaimed. "It destroys not only people but also history."

"That is true," the Duke agreed, "and it seems incredible that the French should have gone to war without finding out more accurately the strength of the German armies."

"I suppose the Prussians are very pleased at the way things are going," Antonia said in a low voice.

"Cock-a-hoop!" the Duke replied, "and I am quite certain they will extract every ounce of humiliation possible from the French."

"We can only pray that Paris will be spared," Antonia said quietly and hoped that Labby would be safe.

When dinner was over she and the Duke moved into the Salon. The sun had now sunk and it was twilight outside, with a few stars in the sky.

The candles had been lit in the Salon and the curtains

were drawn in all the windows except one. Antonia stood
looking out, and then drawing a deep breath she said in a
very small voice:

"I have . . . something to . . . tell you."

She turned round as she spoke to walk back towards the
Duke who was standing in front of the fire-place.

A fire was lit in the grate in case, as the Butler had explained, they should feel cold, but Antonia at the moment
was cold, not from the temperature, but because she was
extremely nervous.

The Duke set down on the mantelpiece the glass of
brandy he held in his hand.

"What is it?" he asked.

"It is . . . something which may make you very . . . angry,"
she answered, "but I . . . have to tell . . . you."

"I promised you the night we married that I would try
never to be angry with you, so I cannot imagine what it can
be."

"It is . . . something of which I am very . . . ashamed."

She twisted her fingers together as she trembled, and he
said quietly:

"It is not like you to be afraid, Antonia."

"I am . . . afraid of making you . . . angry."

"Then I will not be."

"You have every . . . right to be," she said miserably.

There was silence and after a moment the Duke
prompted:

"I am waiting to receive the momentous confession."

His voice sounded almost apprehensive but for a moment Antonia thought she was struck dumb and would never
be able to speak again.

"It is my . . . fault that you ever had to . . . fight the . . .
duel."

The words came out with a rush and as she looked up at
him for a fleeting second he saw the stricken consternation in
her eyes.

"I spoke without . . . thinking," she went on. "I did not
know the Count was the husband of the lady you were . . .
with."

And there was a little sob in her voice as she continued:

"When he asked me where you were I replied you were in the garden with a very fascinating and alluring lady . . . whom I . . . suspected of being an old . . . friend."

Antonia's voice faded away and then she added:

"How could I have been so foolish . . . so idiotic to say such a thing without . . . knowing to whom I was . . . speaking?"

There was so much self-accusation in her voice that it seemed to vibrate in the air.

The Duke gave a sigh, almost as if it was one of relief, Antonia had no idea what he might have been afraid of hearing.

"You must not blame yourself," he said quietly. "The Count would have found an excuse sooner or later to fight me as he had always wished to do."

"You will . . . forgive . . . me?" Antonia pleaded.

"I think you have made it impossible for me not to do so, seeing how well you nursed me," the Duke replied.

"But you might have . . . died," Antonia said. "And it would have been my . . . fault. How could I have gone on . . . living knowing that I had . . . caused your death?"

She thought she was going to burst into tears, and having no wish to lose her self-control, she turned away to walk back to the window.

She stood there looking out into the darkness, tipping back her head a little so that the tears would not brim over and run down her cheeks.

"As we are being frank with each other," she heard the Duke saying behind her, "and because once we agreed that there could be no pretence between us, I also have something to tell you, Antonia."

There was something especially solemn in the way he spoke and she waited, digging her nails into the palms of her hands. She could guess what he was going to say to her now they were back in England.

"What I have to tell you," the Duke said, "is that I am in love."

It was what she had expected to hear him say, but it was like a mortal blow which struck at her very heart.

Just for a moment she felt numb, and then it was an agony so intense, so violent that it tore her apart. It was only with the greatest difficulty she did not scream and cry out.

In a voice which did not seem to be her own, she said:

"I . . . understand and I will . . . go to Doncaster Park as we . . . arranged."

"Do you think you will be happy there?" the Duke asked.

It was hard to fight back tears, but a pride she did not know she possessed made Antonia reply:

"I will be . . . all right."

"Alone?"

"I shall . . . have the . . . horses."

"I thought we agreed to share them."

She did not understand and after a moment she said hesitatingly:

"You . . . mean you will want . . . some of them for the . . . Marchioness?"

"Turn round, Antonia!"

She wanted to obey him but she was afraid he would read in her face what she was feeling.

She did not move and she heard him come nearer.

"You are under some misapprehension," he said quietly. "It is not the Marchioness with whom I am in love."

"Not the Marchioness?"

Now Antonia was surprised into turning round and she found he was nearer than she had thought. After one quick glance at him she looked away.

"But I . . . thought . . ." she said hesitatingly.

"So did I for a short time," the Duke said, "but I was mistaken.'

'Then there is someone else?' Antonia thought and wondered desperately who it could be.

She could not believe it was the Comtesse after the way her husband had behaved during the duel.

"The person I am in love with," the Duke said very quietly and slowly as if he was choosing his words, "is someone who I think loves me as she might love a child. What I wish to find out, Antonia, is whether she loves me as a man."

It was difficult for Antonia to breathe!

Something strange had happened to her throat, and something wild and wonderful that she dare not acknowledge was rising in her breast.

"Do . . . you . . . mean . . . ?" she tried to say.

"I love someone," the Duke said very softly, "who held me in her arms and talked to me in the voice of love and who kissed my cheek and my forehead."

Antonia made a little inarticulate murmur, and then instinctively she moved towards him and hid her face against his shoulder.

His arms went round her, holding her very close.

"Can you love me as a man, my precious one?" he asked. "I am so afraid that I might lose you now I am well again."

He felt her quiver against him and then very gently he put his fingers under her chin and turned her face up to his.

"You kissed me, my darling," he said. "It is only fair that I should now be allowed to kiss you."

His lips were on hers and she felt a strange and wonderful thrill streak through her whole body. It was like no feeling she had ever known before, and yet it was a part of the love that she had already given him.

It was so perfect, so rapturous, so overwhelming, that she thought no-one could feel such an emotion and not die of sheer happiness.

He kissed her until the room disappeared and they were alone, as she had thought they had been in Paris, on a secret island where there was no-one except themselves.

Only now it was so marvellous, so divine, that she felt she must be dreaming and this could have no substance or reality.

It was only when he raised his head to look down into her eyes and saw the wonder in them did he say tenderly:

"Now tell me how you love me."

"I . . . love you. Oh, Athol, I love . . . you with all of . . . me . . . as I have loved you I know now . . . from the very first."

"My brave, wonderful, uncomplaining little wife," he said. "How could I know that there was any woman who could be so perfect and at the same time so courageous."

"I was never . . . afraid because I was with . . . you," Antonia murmured.

"As you always will be," he answered.

His arms tightened round her as he said:

"There are so many things for us to do together, and I think for the moment we neither of us have any wish to be in

London, to be fashionable, or to clutter our house with friends."

Antonia felt that he was thinking of the Marchioness and she whispered:

"You will not be . . . bored in the country?"

"I should never be bored anywhere with you," he answered. "But we must not forget our horses! We will school them for the steeple-chasing and win the prizes together. I think that will keep us fully occupied for the moment."

His lips sought hers before she could reply and now his kisses were demanding, insistent and very passionate.

They made her feel as if her whole being dissolved into his and yet there was a fire beneath the warm wonder of them, and she surrendered herself to him feeling that they were one and completely indivisible.

"I love you," he said later, a little unsteadily. "I love everything about you, not only your exquisite body, and your eyes which are as fascinating as looking into a crystal ball."

He kissed them before he continued:

"But I love the music of your voice, the softness of your hands, your sweetness, gentleness and compassion."

His voice deepened as he went on:

"I never realised before that those were the things I wanted from a woman but which I knew were always missing."

"I have been so . . . jealous of the . . . Marchioness," Antonia whispered.

"Not half as jealous as I have been of that damned journalist who was making love to you when I was too ill to do so myself!"

Antonia looked at him in surprise.

"You were . . . jealous?"

"Crazily so!" the Duke replied harshly. "And I promise you, my darling, if I find other men looking at you as he did I shall be fighting not one duel, but hundreds!"

"Oh, no! That I could never allow," Antonia exclaimed. "I could never go through that anxiety and misery again, thinking that it was I who had nearly killed you and that if you knew the truth you would never . . . forgive me."

"I have to forgive you."

"Why?"

"Because I realise now I cannot live without you," the Duke answered. "I want you, Antonia, because you are mine, because we belong to each other."

The fierce passion in his voice made her hide her head against his shoulder.

"I thought," she said after a moment, "that when . . . we came back to . . . England you would leave . . . me to go to the . . . Marchioness, and then . . . I was . . . going to ask . . . you . . ."

She paused and the Duke said tenderly:

"What were you going to ask me?"

"If you . . . would give me . . . a baby . . . because he would be . . . part of . . . you and I would . . . have something to . . . love," she whispered.

The Duke held her so tightly she could hardly breathe.

"I will give you a baby, Antonia, but only if you promise me one thing."

"What is . . . that?" she asked a little apprehensively.

"That you will not love it more than you love me," he answered. "I am prepared to share a small part of you with our children, but only so long as you love me best. That you hold me in your arms as you held me when I was ill, and make me sure that I never need be afraid of losing you or of being hurt."

Antonia's eyes seemed to hold all the stars in the sky as she looked up at him.

He knew that while she had never been really beautiful before, love had made her lovelier than any woman he had ever known.

"Do you promise?" he asked, his lips very close to hers.

"I promise to . . . love you always and for . . . ever," she answered, "more than . . . anything else in the world or . . . in Heaven. I am yours . . . completely and . . . absolutely yours, my darling, and I love you."

The last words were lost against the Duke's lips as he carried her once again away to their secret island where there were only themselves and no-one else could ever encroach.

# KISS THE MOONLIGHT

Dedicated to the ex-Ambassador to the Court of St. James, His Excellency General Nicholas Broumas and his lovely wife, Clary, whose warmth, generosity and affection to my son and me was everything that we had hoped to find in Greece.

# Author's Note

In 1899 the French archaeologists moved the village of Delphi and discovered underneath it the wonders of the bronze Charioteer, the altar of Athena and many statues and friezes of great beauty.

I visited Delphi in 1976 and found that the Shrine to Apollo had a strange, ecstatic serenity which is indescribable. The Shining Cliffs, rising protectively behind the broken columns, look over the loveliest view in Greece.

The Temple of Athena, surrounded by olive trees, has a mystic charm which is different from any other Temple I have visited.

In 1837 an historian wrote that the whole of Greece was infested with brigands whom the Bavarian Government were unable to hold in check. This was one of the causes of the revolution of 1862 which drove King Otho from his throne.

# CHAPTER ONE

———— ❧ ————

# 1852

Athena came out of her bed-room window onto the balcony to stand looking at the vista in front of her.

Every time she saw a view in Greece she thought it more beautiful than it had been a moment before, and yet it seemed impossible that anything could be lovelier than the blue sea of the Gulf of Corinth.

The setting sun turned the coast-line to gold until in the distance it became purple merging to misty grey where it met the sky.

Athena knew that behind the Palace the sun would be throwing fantastic shadows on the mountains against which the Summer Palace of the Princes of Parnassus gleamed like a pearl.

Everything, she felt, had a mystery and a wonder about it that she had never envisaged, even though she had been sure that Greece would in fact be even more breathtaking than her wildest dreams.

All her life she had longed to come to Greece.

Ever since she had been a small child her grandmother, the Dowager Marchioness, had regaled her with stories of the Greek gods and goddesses; of Pan who blew his pipes under the olive trees, and of Zeus who sat in all his majesty on the summit of Mount Olympus.

While other children had read the story of Cinderella, of Hansel and Gretel, Athena had read of the adoration in which her namesake was held.

Not that in England anyone thought of her as Athena.

To her family she was Mary Emmeline, and to the outside world she was Lady Mary Emmeline Athena Wade, daughter of the 4th Marquess of Wadebridge, and as such an important social figure.

The sun sank a little lower and now the whole sea was suddenly shimmering with glittering gold and the light from it combined with the translucence of the sky seemed almost blinding.

She could remember her grandmother saying: "The Greeks were never tired of describing the appearance of light. They loved the glitter of moist things, of stones and sand washed by the sea, of fish churning in the nets, and their Temples glowed like pillars of light."

"It is what I feel," Athena thought.

She compared the sunset with this morning when she had risen very early to see "the rosy fingered dawn" and imagined that the whole body of Apollo was pouring across the sky, flashing with a million points of light, healing everything he touched and defying the powers of darkness.

Apollo was very real to her for, as her grandmother had explained, he was not only the sun but the moon, the planets, the Milky Way, and the faintest stars.

"He is the sparkle on the waves," the Dowager Marchioness had said, "the gleam in one's eyes, the strange glimmer of fields on darkest nights."

Athena had remembered the lines from Homer, "Make the sky clear and grant us to see with our eyes."

She had read all she could find of the Greek poets who wrote of the light. She found herself often murmuring the lines from Pindar's ode—

*"We are all shadows, but when the shining comes
from the hands of the gods,
Then the heavenly light falls on men."*

Would the heavenly light ever fall on her, she wondered; and if it did, what would she feel?

The setting sun carried a prayer from her heart, but Athena was aware that time was passing and she would be expected downstairs for dinner.

She turned from the balcony, crossed her bed-room floor and stepped onto the landing at the top of the stairs.

Again there was beauty to make her draw in her breath —the curve of the stone staircase, the mosaics against the white walls, the golden light coming through the long windows through which she could see the brilliant flowers which filled the green garden.

She paused instinctively because it was so beautiful, and as she did so she heard a man's voice below say in Greek:

"Do you mean to tell me that you have brought me no news of His Highness?"

Athena knew who was speaking. It was the deep, rather hoarse voice of the Prince's Comptroller, Colonel Stefanatis.

"No, Sir," a younger voice replied. "I have been to all the places you instructed me, but there was no sign of His Highness."

There was a pause before the Colonel said:

"You called at Madame Helena's Villa?"

"Yes, Sir. She left a week ago and the servants have no idea where she has gone."

There was another pause which Athena felt was somehow pregnant with meaning. Then the Colonel said as if he spoke to himself.

"It is an impossible situation—impossible!"

Suddenly he said sharply:

"You had better rest, Captain. I shall require you to start out again to-morrow morning."

"Very good, Sir."

Athena heard the young officer's heels click as he drew himself to attention and he walked away, his spurs jingling as he moved across the marble floor.

With difficulty she forced herself to descend the stairs slowly and in an unconcerned manner, as if she had not overheard what had been said.

But if the Colonel thought the situation was impossible, to her it was incredible.

She had come to Greece from England because it had been arranged by her grandmother that she should marry Prince Yiorgos of Parnassus.

It was the result of negotiations with which the Dowager Marchioness had been concerned for nearly two years.

Although Xenia Parnassus was only a distant relative of the Prince, the ties of family and the blood of her ancestors pulsated in her veins and never let her rest.

Extremely beautiful she had taken English Society by storm from the moment the 3rd Marquess of Wadebridge searching for Grecian antiquities had brought back with him not only a collection of vases, statues and urns, but also a wife.

The Greeks were extremely profligate with their treasures and, as Athena had learnt in Athens, not particularly interested in what they called "Ruins".

From the time that Lord Elgin had committed what Lord Byron had raged over as "vandalism" in shipping the Acropolis Marbles to England, dozens of aristocrats with a yearning for culture had journeyed to Greece to see what they too could pillage from the past.

> *"Dull is the eye that will not weep to see*
> *Thy walls defaced, thy mouldering shrines removed."*

Lord Byron had thundered, but no-one listened.

Country houses in England and museums all over Europe were packed with the spoils from Greece.

Xenia Parnassus, once she had become the Marchioness of Wadebridge, had never returned to her own country.

She had however presented her adoring husband with six extremely good-looking children, although none of them had measured up to her idealised standard of beauty until her grandchild, Athena, had arrived.

The Marchioness had known when she first saw the baby that it was what she had always wanted; a child who resembled the goddess who meant more to her than all the saints in the Church calendar.

"I insist that she is given the name of Athena," she said firmly.

The family protested: the Wades had never gone in for fancy names and the Marquess's first daughter must be christened Mary, as was traditional, then Emmeline after a famous ancestor whose portraits hung on the walls at Wadebridge Castle.

It had taken a great deal of persistence for the Marchioness to get her way but finally her granddaughter had been christened Mary Emmeline Athena. The third name however was never used except by the Dowager Marchioness and her granddaughter herself.

"Of course I want to be called Athena, Grandmama," she had said when she was nine years old. "It is a pretty name, and I think the name Mary is dull and Emmeline is ugly."

She wrinkled her small nose, which even when she was a baby had the straightness of the statues which the Dowager Marchioness took her to see in the British Museum.

From then on the goddess Athena was as real to her as a member of her own family.

The Dowager Marchioness told her of Athena the Warrior shaking her spear; of Athena the companion, almost the lover; of Athena of the household presiding over the young weavers—the goddess of all things fair who gazed down on her charges with maternal solicitude.

Most important of all there was Athena, the Virgin, immaculate and all powerful, resolved to protect the chastity of her city, who was also Athena, goddess of love.

"It was she to whom the women prayed when they wished for children," the Dowager Marchioness explained.

"And she brought them love?" Athena asked.

"Because they loved and were loved they had beautiful children—beautiful, both in body and soul," the Dowager Marchioness replied.

The rest of the family found the Dowager Marchioness as she grew older somewhat of a bore with her predilection for Greece and her endless stories of the ancient gods.

But to Athena they were always absorbing, always exciting.

It therefore seemed quite natural when as she reached eighteen her grandmother told her that her marriage had been arranged with the Prince of Parnassus and she would journey to Greece to meet him.

Vaguely she had thought from the various things her grandmother had said that this had been intended for some time and was why the Dowager Marchioness continually extolled the virtues and the charms of a young man she had never seen.

"He is strong and handsome; a good Ruler and a man whom his people trust," the Dowager Marchioness said positively.

Because he was Greek, Athena was perfectly prepared to believe that he was all these things.

But here she was in the Prince's Palace having been sent out to meet him and knowing that inevitably the story would end with wedding-bells—but there was no Prince.

It was perhaps, Athena thought, her Aunt's fault that he had not been waiting as they had expected on the Quay when the ship which had carried them from the Port of Germeno had docked in the small harbour of Mikis.

He had written a charming letter to her Aunt, Lady Beatrice Wade, saying he was unfortunately unable to meet them in Athens but would be waiting to greet them at his Summer Palace as soon as they wished to join him.

It had been at first planned that they should stay in Athens after their arrival from England for at least three weeks.

There were many members of the family for them to meet and King Otho asked that the future bride of the Ruler of one of the States should be presented to the Court.

Greece after winning her independence had later become a Kingdom in 1844 and King Otho, although he was a Bavarian, had shown himself a little more interested in the people over whom he ruled but he was extremely unpopular.

But even King Otho, Athena thought, could not at this moment conjure up a Prince who had mysteriously disappeared at the moment he should be meeting his future bride.

Lady Beatrice had quite a lot to say on the subject when they were alone.

"I cannot understand it, Mary," she said sharply. "And I cannot believe that your father would consider it anything less than an insult that the Prince should not be there to greet you."

"He obviously expected us to stay longer in Athens," Athena answered.

"I sent a messenger ahead of us," Lady Beatrice replied, "and quite frankly I do not believe a word of the story that he is visiting some obscure part of his territory where they cannot get into communication with him."

"Then where else can he be?" Athena asked a little helplessly.

If it was not an insult, it was hardly an encouraging welcome for a bride who had come all the way from England to meet her bridegroom.

As she spoke, however, she looked out to sea.

She had learnt on arrival in Athens that the Prince wore a beard, and when she seemed surprised she had been told it was because he had served in the Greek Navy and like most Greeks was more at home on the sea than he was on the land.

Perhaps he had sailed to the opposite shores, Athena told herself, or even through the narrow Straits forming the western exit of the Gulf into the Ionian Sea.

There he could have visited some of the many islands and perhaps forgotten who would be waiting for him on his return to the Palace.

Yet however much one explained it away it was still a depressing thought, and now three days had passed since she and her Aunt had arrived and there was still no sign of the Prince.

The conversation she had heard from the landing offered an explanation she had not suspected previously.

Who was Madame Helena?

Athena had been brought up in the country and was very ignorant of the intrigues and loose behaviour of the social world; but she could not have read Greek mythology without realising that love had pre-occupied the gods and they had been continually enraptured by beautiful women.

For the first time since Athena had set our from England she questioned whether her marriage was likely to be a happy one.

She had been so swept away by all her grandmother had told her, by the stories which had coloured her youth and by her own instinctive yearnings for romance, that until now she had not really considered the Prince as a man.

He had been a mythical figure as attractive, and in a way as awe-inspiring, as one of the gods themselves.

But she had not envisaged him as a human being, a man to whom she would belong, a man with the desires and emotion of other men.

Now suddenly, as if she awoke from a dream, Athena realised that the Prince was flesh and blood, and never having seen her how could he be interested in her as she had been interested in him primarily because he was Greek?

To him there was nothing particularly romantic and certainly nothing mysterious or ethereal about her being English.

He would not have invested her with the mystery which to her surrounded the gods, and indeed he might dislike the very thought of her as his wife.

It was almost as if Athena had been drenched with cold water when she least expected it.

There had been a dream-like quality about the whole arrangement, the voyage from England, her arrival in Athens and most of all her first sight of the Palace.

Never had she believed anything could look so exquisite or that the mountains behind it could be so impressive.

She knew they were part of the Parnassus Range which extended north-west from the borders of Attica rising between the Boeotian plain and the sparsely inhabited northern shores of the Gulf of Corinth, the whole region rich in mythology and history.

Further to the east lay the rugged slopes of Mount Kitheron which was associated with the haunts of Pan and his goat-like satyrs and the sacred Mount Helicon where the nine Muses dwelt.

Far to the north in the centre of Greece stretched the mountain range which held as its highest peak the sacred

Mount Olympus from where the gods themselves had once ruled.

Lady Beatrice was not concerned with mountains.

"As I have already told you, Mary," she said insistently, "this is the Summer Palace of the Princes of Parnassus. I believe their main Palace which is near Lividia is far more impressive, although sadly in need of repair."

There was a note in her Aunt's voice which told Athena all too clearly why she was accentuating the fact at this particular moment.

The whole reason that the marriage had been arranged, and her grandmother had not deceived her on this score, was that the Prince of Parnassus was in need of money.

The centuries of oppression under Turkish rule and the protracted struggle for freedom had left the country poverty-stricken and had taken its toll of what had once been a rich and proud family.

The obvious course for the Prince was to marry a rich wife, and that was where the Dowager Marchioness had played her trump card in the shape of Athena.

"When I was young," she said to her granddaughter, "it would have been deemed impossible for the head of our family to marry anyone who was not a Royal; but times have changed and the Wadebridges are one of the oldest and most important families in England."

"Yes, Grandmama," Athena had agreed dutifully.

"What is more," the Dowager Marchioness continued, "you are singularly fortunate in that you were left so much money by your godmother."

She had smiled in a way which was almost mischievous.

"I must take the credit for that, Athena, because your father and mother were very much against giving you an American godmother!"

Athena had laughed.

"So it was you who chose such a good fairy for me?"

"She indeed proved to be that," the Dowager Marchioness replied, "but who would have imagined that even though she had no children she would have made you her sole heiress?"

"Who indeed!"

"Money carries with it a great deal of responsibility, as I have always told you," the Dowager Marchioness went on, "and that is why, Athena, I can imagine nowhere where your fortune could be better spent than in Greece."

Athena had agreed with her, and it had seemed, until this moment, almost as if she was marrying a country rather than a man.

When she reached the hall the Colonel had moved into the Salon.

Before she joined him Athena tried to compose herself, knowing she must not let him realise she had overheard and understood his conversation with the young Captain.

She had not let the Prince's Comptroller know she could speak Greek. Her grandmother had been most insistent that she should speak the language ever since she was a child and she had hoped it might prove a delightful surprise to the Prince.

The members of the Prince's household automatically spoke in English to answer their Master's questions and Lady Beatrice had no knowledge of any language other than her own and French.

"Perhaps it is a good thing they do not realise I understand everything that is said," Athena told herself.

Then she was afraid of what else she might discover.

She found it difficult at dinner to listen to the conversation between her Aunt and the Colonel or to answer the conventional, stiffly polite comments of the other officers who were present.

The Prince's mother was staying in the Palace, but she was in ill-health and invariably, Athena found, retired to bed before dinner.

She was a shy person which made her appear somewhat stiff in her manner to strangers, and Athena had felt ever since she arrived somewhat uncomfortable in her presence.

But now she wondered if it was because the Princess was not in fact pleased to accept her as a daughter-in-law.

"I am sure she would have wanted her son to marry a Greek," Athena told herself and wondered if the rest of the Parnassus family were prepared to swallow her like a nasty medicine only because she was rich.

It was a discouraging thought and remembering the people she had met in Athens and her reception at Court she recalled the somewhat searching looks they had given her.

Had this been because they were wondering why as she was so rich she should wish to marry a Greek Prince, unless it was for his title?

This idea was almost as much of a shock as the thought that the Prince might not be interested in her as a woman.

"How could they think such a thing?" Athena asked herself indignantly.

Yet it was, she admitted, the obvious explanation they would put upon her acceptance of a man she had never seen.

The whole marriage which up to now had been invested with a strange unearthly magic became something quite different.

Quite suddenly she felt horrified at everything that was happening.

How, she wondered wildly, had she ever been persuaded into setting out on a voyage to meet a man to whom she could mean nothing and who in fact could mean nothing to her.

Yet, because her grandmother had invested Greece with a splendour and a glory that was sacred she had accepted the suggestion of marriage almost as if it had been a gift from the gods.

"I must have been mad!" Athena thought.

Then she realised that while she had been thinking dinner had come to an end and she had not in fact heard one word of what had been said to her since about half-way through the meal.

Her Aunt led the way into the Salon.

"You seem a little distant this evening, Mary," she said. "The Colonel asked you the same question three times before you answered him."

"I am sorry, Aunt Beatrice, I think perhaps I am a little tired."

"It is the hot sun. You are not used to it," Lady Beatrice said. "As the Prince will doubtless be arriving shortly and I want you to look your best, it would be wise to go to bed and have a good night's rest."

"Yes, of course, Aunt Beatrice, I will do that."

Lady Beatrice glanced towards the door before she said in a low voice:

"The Colonel tells me they are still having difficulty in getting in touch with the Prince, but he is certain that His Highness will be here to-morrow. Nevertheless I am considering whether we should return to Athens. This waiting is extremely embarrassing."

"Perhaps we should have remained in the City the three weeks they expected us to stay." Athena suggested.

"That is what we should have done," Lady Beatrice agreed, "but it is too late to think of it now. Everything has been planned by Mama and I am afraid I accepted her arrangements without questioning them. It was stupid of me."

For her Aunt to admit that she was at fault meant, Athena knew quite well, that she was extremely perturbed.

Because she herself felt so worried at the Prince's non-appearance, she felt it would not make the situation any better to discuss it.

"Do not worry, Aunt Beatrice," she said, "I am sure it will be all right. And it is so lovely here."

"It is quite an intolerable situation!" Lady Beatrice replied. "I must say I have always believed that the Greeks had good manners—until now!"

"The people we met in Athens were certainly very polite," Athena remarked.

"They all spoke most warmly of His Highness," Lady Beatrice said.

"Yes, indeed," Athena agreed.

But to herself she was wondering exactly what thoughts and intentions had lain beneath the complimentary manner in which they had talked about the Prince.

Had they been glad that he should have the money he urgently needed for his people?

The Parnassus country was, Athena knew, quite a large territory, stretching east of the mountains and being only partly productively fertile.

Travelling to Greece in one of its country's steam-ships, Athena had imagined herself riding over the land beside the Prince, deciding how they would improve the lot of the poorest, perhaps building better ports for the fishermen and raising the standard of education.

Now she suddenly felt uncertain and afraid.

Supposing he wished to do none of those things with her? Suppose Madame Helena, whoever she might be, should have his complete confidence and companionship?

She said good-night to her Aunt and retired to her own room before the Colonel and the other gentlemen came from the Dining-Room into the Salon.

When she was undressed she dismissed the maid who had waited on her and walked out onto the balcony to gaze once again on the sea.

Dusk was falling and there was the last glimmer of gold and crimson on the horizon. The stars were coming out in the velvet darkness over-head.

There was no wind, and although the great heat of the day had gone it was still warm.

She leaned over the balcony, her arms on the cool stone, and stared into the darkness.

"Why am I here?" she asked herself. "Why have I allowed myself to come to a place where I am not wanted as a person, but only as the purveyor of wealth?"

The idea horrified her.

Always she had been very conscious of herself as a person.

"Know thyself," one of the Seven Sages had said, and she tried to follow it because she knew it was the foundation of Greek thought to be honest and to understand her own feelings.

Looking back she knew she had been bemused as a child would be with fairy-stories. She had not faced reality. She had just let herself drift into a day-dream that had seemed real simply because she had wanted it to be.

Now she had woken up.

"What can I do?"

The question was insistent, almost as if someone had asked it aloud, and Athena shivered.

She saw how easily she had been manipulated by her grandmother into accepting the idea of marriage and she saw only too clearly that she was now involved almost to the point of no return.

"Supposing I hate the Prince and he hates me?" she asked herself. "What can I do about it?"

She remembered the effusive manner in which the Courtiers at the Palace and the King himself had spoken of the Prince.

Now she suspected that their praise of him had not come from their hearts but it was merely because they wished to assure her that she was doing the right thing in bringing her money into their country.

For the first time since she had realised she was a great heiress Athena was afraid.

Her future had not actually meant anything to her in the past. She had been told the money had been left to her and she was very rich, but her father was a wealthy man and she had never wanted for anything since she had been a child.

She had accepted her wealth as she might have accepted the gift of a necklace or a new horse.

She was pleased, but she had not thought about it continually and it did not seem of any particular consequence.

Now she realised how important it was—a passport to marriage. A marriage in which she had no choice and which, even more frightening, the bridegroom had no choice either.

It was an arrangement—a *mariage de convenance* the French called it—and every instinct in Athena fought against the idea.

Now the Prince suddenly assumed frightening proportions.

A man—a man who could make demands upon her because she bore his name, a man who would use her fortune, which would become his on marriage, a man who had no other interest in her as a person.

"I have been . . . crazy!" Athena said into the darkness. "How could I have accepted anything so horrible without considering it?"

She put her head back and looked up at the stars. They seemed immeasurably far away and she felt very small and insignificant.

"What does it matter what happens to you?" she felt as if someone asked mockingly.

Then she replied fiercely:

"It *does* matter! I am I. I will not be over-ruled and humiliated in this fashion. I must escape."

The words seemed to come to her almost as if it was a light in the darkness.

Escape! But how? Where could she go? What could she do?

She stared out at the sea, feeling that there must be an answer in the gentle movement of the waves.

Almost-mockingly the idea came to her that if she had been a Greek in the old days she would have consulted the Oracle.

The Oracle of Delphi, as her grandmother had always explained to her, had guided and inspired those who consulted it for nine hundred years.

The Greeks had believed that Apollo spoke through the lips of the Pythia. She sat in a cave near the great Temple of Apollo and was a pure young girl trained in priesthood and in the worship of the god.

The Dowager Marchioness had explained to Athena so often what occurred.

"On the day of the Oracle the Pythia bathed in the waters of Castalia and drank from the holy spring. She put on the special robes of prophecy and was led to the Temple of Apollo."

"What happened then, Grandmama?"

"She passed through the main halls of worship until she reached the adyton, the most sacred part of all, the living place of the god where only the priests were allowed to enter."

"Was she afraid?"

"No, dearest, she was dedicated to her work. She took her place on Apollo's throne and she may have taken a branch of the holy laurel in her hand or perhaps she fumigated herself with burnt laurel leaves."

"I knew the laurel was sacred to Apollo," Athena remarked, "but I do not think the leaves could have smelt very nice."

The Dowager Marchioness ignored her.

"Music was played," she went on, her eyes half-closed as if she herself remembered it happening, "and incense was burned."

"And then . . . ?" Athena prompted.

"Then the Pythia fell into a trance and when she was possessed by the god she uttered strange and often wild words that were carefully taken down and later a priest put them into verse."

The Dowager Marchioness went on to tell many stories of what the Pythia had said and how her prophecies had come true.

Athena had sat wide-eyed, listening, believing and almost seeing the pictures her grandmother conjured up.

"If the Oracle was there to-day," she said to herself, "I could go to Delphi and ask Apollo to help and guide me."

Suddenly she was very still.

She knew how near Delphi was to the Summer Palace.

Just around the corner, so to speak, of the promontory projecting into the Gulf of Cornith there was the Krisaean Gulf at the head of which lay the Port of Itea.

This Athena knew, was where the pilgrims, who nearly all went by sea, used to disembark when visiting Delphi. It was in fact at Itea that Lord Byron had landed when he had visited Delphi over thirty years ago.

Athena remembered reading how he and his friend John Hobhouse had been rowed in a strong Cephaloniot ten-oared boat.

Winding in and out of the rocky bays that lined the Gulf they saw a mass of anchored merchant vessels swaying in the moonlight and finally at midnight reached the Port of Itea.

"It is not far away," Athena whispered to herself. "I could go there."

She moved from the balcony into her bed-room and sat down on the bed.

Now a plan was beginning to fall into place almost as if it was a puzzle which she was solving piece by piece.

She had mentioned Delphi to Colonel Stefanatis, but he had not seemed interested.

She had imagined before she left England that all the

Greeks, like her grandmother, would be obsessed by their glorious past and by the wonders which still lay only half discovered in their country.

But she learnt from the Greek passengers on board the steamer that they were far too concerned with modern politics to worry much about the past, or else, Athena thought humbly, they had not been interested in talking about their national heritage to her.

But Delphi had shone in her heart like a lighted candle, and she knew that one of the first things she planned to do in Greece was to follow the Sacred Way to the Shrine of Apollo.

Now she knew it would be far easier not to take the long laborious road across the arid foot hills of Parnassus which thousands of pilgrims had trod wearily in the past. Instead she could do what Lord Byron had done and approach Delphi from the sea.

For the first time in her life Athena felt a desire to be independent, to do what she wished without asking approval, without everything being planned for her.

It was almost as if the spirit of Greece that she had felt so strongly like a shining light had entered into her and awoken her to new possibilities within herself.

She felt a wild springing within her mind which had never been there before, a desire to enquire, to find, to know on her own—without being dictated to, without being told what to do.

She was certain as if the Oracle had already spoken, that she must first find her way to Delphi.

She had a guide-book which she had bought in Athens and it had a rough map of Greece in the front of it.

It was badly printed and badly written, and yet it showed her clearly what a little way she had to travel from where she was now to Port Itea.

That was all that concerned her at the moment, and she knew that once Itea was reached, Lord Byron had climbed towards Delphi which stood above it, built on the cliffs of the mountains where they overlooked the valley of the River Pleistos.

"I will go there, and nothing will stop me," Athena told herself.

As if she could not keep still she walked about her bed-room, thinking out ways and means.

Of one thing she was quite certain—if she asked in the Palace for any help, they would try to stop her.

She would be put off with the usual excuses: nothing could be arranged until the Prince returned—doubtless His Highness had his own plans for taking her to Delphi, just as he would wish to show her other parts of the country!

But how could anyone know that was what he intended?

Doubtless he was as uninterested in the "Ruins" as every-body else appeared to be.

She had been so sure when she left England that, if nothing else, they would have one taste in common which was all-important, the love of Ancient Greece.

A reverence for its teaching, the belief that the whole world owed to the Greeks the beginning of Science and the beginning of philosophical thought.

This was what her grandmother had taught Athena and she had been convinced that the Prince would be still fighting to restore to the world the splendour of the miraculous fifty years when Athens became the centre of civilisation and Apollo and Athena became the gods of Greece.

Now everything she had anticipated was lying in ruins at her feet.

Of course the Prince would not think like that! Why should he? He would be like the other men at the Court of King Otho who laughed and gossiped and argued about politics.

No-one had offered to take Athena to see the Acropolis, and when she suggested it they had pushed the idea aside as if it was too commonplace and uninteresting to be given a second thought.

She had been too shy to insist, and she had told herself that perhaps the Prince would want to take her there himself.

Then they could dream amongst the marble pillars of the glory of the years when the Acropolis in all its brilliance glowed with light and it served both as a fortress and the sacred sanctuary of Athena.

Athena had imagined that the Prince would explain to her how the Parthenon had looked drenched with colour, blue, scarlet and gold, and containing treasures from all over the Greek world.

They would have walked together, she had thought, to the Erechtheion—the most mysterious and sacred place on the whole Acropolis. Here was the golden lamp that was never allowed to go out, the olive tree Athena had called forth from the ground and the fountain which had sprung up when Poseidon had struck the earth with his trident.

She had imagined herself listening to the stories he would tell her in a deep voice unlike her grandmother's and she had felt herself thrill because she would not be only reliving the story of Greece but would also be with a Greek who loved it as she did.

"Those were just childish dreams," she told herself bitterly. "How could I have been so naïve—so utterly absurd to imagine he would wish to do anything of the sort?"

"I will go home," she decided. "When I meet the Prince I will be strong enough to tell him that I have made a mistake. We have both made one. Perhaps I can give him some of my money in compensation—but I cannot marry him!"

She paused to add:

"I *will* not marry him!"

Then she felt herself tremble because she knew how difficult it would be to make not only the Prince but also her Aunt realise she was serious.

It would seem inconceivable to both of them that at the last moment after coming all this way she should decide not to be a sacrifice to the Prince's need for money.

"Even if he is pleasant and nice to me at the beginning," she told herself, "he will soon want to return to Madame Helena."

The whole impact of what she was thinking and saying to herself swept over her almost like a tidal wave in which she must drown because she had not the strength to swim against it.

Then she told herself that she would survive; but first she must have the strength to refuse to do what everyone wanted, however hard they might try to over-rule her.

It was not going to be easy, Athena was well aware of that.

Her father was a very domineering man and she had always done as he wished ever since her childhood.

Her mother had died when she was ten, and although she remembered her tenderly she had never been an important influence in her life.

It was her grandmother to whom she had turned for affection, for understanding and for guidance.

And now she saw that her grandmother had been concerned less with her than with the Parnassus family.

In arranging this marriage Athena knew she had not thought of her granddaughter's feelings, but of the benefit her money would bring to the reigning Prince of the House of Parnassus.

"How could I have been so stupid, so foolish as not to understand what was happening before I left England?"

Athena knew that if she had been firm and had appealed to her father, who had never been particularly interested in her grandmother's enthusiasm for her native land, she could have prevailed upon him not to agree to her leaving home.

But it was too late to think of that now.

What she had to do now was to extract herself one way or another from the trap into which she had fallen all too willingly, and too easily.

It was a trap—there was no other word for it—and her grandmother had baited it with the glory that had once been Greece, but was certainly not to be found in the Court of their Bavarian King, King Otho.

"I hate them all! I hate them!" Athena cried.

She felt as if they were all intriguing against her, encompassing her about with ropes of silk, which would incarcerate her in Greece with a man who was interested in another woman.

"And why not?" Athena enquired.

She did not blame the Prince.

Of course there were other women in his life. Doubtless there were women he wished to marry but could not afford to do so.

But being married to a rich Englishwoman would not prevent him from loving where he wished and doing what he wanted.

There would be nothing left for her but a cage of pomp and circumstance and a title in which she was not in the least interested.

"What shall I do?"

The question came again and she knew the answer.

She would go to Delphi and if she could not consult the Oracle at least she felt that somehow she would be near the gods who had once reigned in Greece—the gods whose Empire had not been over great tracts of land or a subject people.

In the person of Apollo the Greeks had conquered the world by the power of beauty.

He had no earthly resources, no Army, no Navy, no powerful Government, but he had captured men's minds, and in the silence Athena was still certain she would hear the voice of the god calling to her own heart to seek the light.

"I will go to Delphi."

Nothing, she told herself, was impossible!

At Delphi she would know what to do and she would no longer be afraid.

She caught a glimpse of herself in the mirror as she moved across the bed-room and it seemed to her that in the past hour she had grown from a very young English girl into a woman.

She did not know how it had happened—she only knew that, as she had always known they would, the gods had helped her and were showing her the way.

# CHAPTER TWO

The caique with the wind in its sails rounded the tip of the promontory and Athena gave a sigh that was one both of relief and joy.

She had done it! She had escaped!

Even now she could hardly believe she was free of the Palace and the ship now out of sight of anyone who might be looking out at such an early hour.

She had made her plans very carefully and it had given her an excitement she had never known to arrange matters for herself. She had tried to think of every detail, not only of her requirements, but also of eventualities that might betray her at the last moment.

She had of course been unable to sleep, but she had lain on her bed after packing in the Greek bag which had been woven by native craftsmen the few necessities she thought she might need.

She had written a letter to her Aunt in which she had said that as she was tired of waiting for the Prince she had decided to stay for a night or perhaps two with friends who lived nearby.

She begged her Aunt not to worry and said that she would be perfectly safe and they would look after her.

She smiled as she wrote the pronoun, thinking her Aunt would not appreciate the fact that "*they*" as far as she was concerned were the gods who dwelt at Delphi.

She had drawn back the curtains from her window and from her bed she could watch the sky. Long before dawn, when she saw the stars beginning to fade, she had risen to dress herself.

This was quite a feat as she was used to having a maid or even two in attendance.

She had chosen her gown very carefully the night before.

All those in her trousseau were elaborate, their full skirts decorated with lace and frills.

But one was comparatively simple with a plain skirt and for the tiny waist a blue sash which a child might have worn.

Athena chose her plainest bonnet to go with it, and thinking it might be cool in the ship she carried over her arm a warm shawl.

When she was dressed she knew the most difficult part of the whole adventure was to get out of the Palace without being seen.

But she had listened during the night to the movements of the night-watchmen walking around inside and the footsteps of the sentries pacing outside.

Methodically she had calculated the exact time when she could get down the stairs without being noticed and when she could cross the garden to reach the sanctuary of the bushes before the sentry turned and marched back in the direction from which he had come.

The actual exit from the Palace was easy, because she had found a door into the garden the previous day which she noted without realising it at the time was easy to open from the inside.

The top half of the door was of glass and she had thought that it seemed a vulnerable place to leave unguarded when the great door of the Palace itself had sentries on either side of it.

As she sped across the garden into the shade of the hibiscus bushes she thought that if a sentry saw her in her white gown he would think she was a ghost or some sprite from the underworld bemusing his senses and would not challenge her.

But actually the sentry was looking in the opposite direction and Athena climbed over the low wall which separated the Palace from the road which ran along the cliffs, and stood looking down at the sea beneath her.

The Palace had been built high up on the mountainside and the Harbour of Mikis at which she had arrived was on the west coast of the Gulf while beyond it was a small town of the same name.

She had realised when she arrived that from the harbour to the Palace on the twisting, turning road which made the climb easy for the horses was at least two miles.

But by going straight downhill Athena reckoned that the harbour in actual fact was not more than a quarter of that distance away.

It proved to be a little further than she had anticipated, but Athena was a country girl and used to walking and riding long distances. She reached the Harbour of Mikis without being unduly fatigued and in surprisingly quick time.

Now the sky had lightened perceptibly and all around was the translucent grey of the prelude to the rising of the sun.

It would have been impossible, Athena thought, to imagine there could be so many shades of that mysterious, elusive colour, ranging from the silver grey of the sea and the pigeon-feathered grey of the cliffs on the other side of the water, to the deep almost purple-grey of the mountains.

There was however, no time for day-dreaming or even for admiring the view.

She found as she had expected that the fishermen were already astir, carrying their yellow nets aboard their caiques, shouting cheerily to each other or singing a song as they got their boats ready for the sea.

She found an elderly man who seemed less busy than the others and told him what she required.

She spoke slowly in her perfect Greek and he understood her without any difficulty.

"A ship to take you to Itea, lady?" he asked scratching his head. "They'll be going fishing."

"I will make it worth their while," Athena promised. "I will pay for the journey there and for the return. It will doubtless come to more than they would earn by a day's fishing."

It took a little time and quite an amount of argument before the elderly man persuaded the crew of one of the caiques to accept the large sum of money which Athena offered in return for their services.

Finally with a great many smiles and good-humoured chaffing they agreed to abandon their nets and the caique set off.

The dawn wind billowed out its sails, and when the twelve men dipped their oars into the waves the water fell from them like glittering diamonds.

As they moved Athena kept looking apprehensively over her shoulder at the Palace high above them.

She was quite certain that no-one would be watching the Harbour at this hour of the morning, and yet at the same time she was thankful now finally they were out of sight and round into the Gulf of Krisa.

Now the mountains rose high on each side of the gulf and as the first rays of the sun came up over the horizon their tops were turned to gold and every other colour of the rainbow filtered across them.

It was so lovely that Athena felt as if the time she was at sea sped past and she could hardly believe they had been travelling for some hours when at last they reached the Port of Itea.

There were several anchored merchant vessels with their three high sail-less masts swaying on the waves, but there was not the galaxy of them that Lord Byron had seen.

She found on arrival as she stepped out of the boat that there were a few gaily decorated houses and donkeys waiting to carry anyone who engaged them up the long steep climb to Delphi.

Athena, who had a good knowledge of horse-flesh, re-

fused the donkeys which were pressed on her by their owners, and chose instead a young horse which she felt would
carry her more swiftly.

She also liked the honest, good-humoured face of its
owner.

All the animals soliciting the tourists had thick saddles
made of sacking covered with a woolen rug on which the
rider could sit sideways in comparative comfort.

It meant that no horsemanship was required because the
owner of the animal led it up the hill, and Athena had a
sudden longing to ride on her own without restrictions as she
had once imagined she might ride with the Prince over his
land.

But she was aware that the owner of the young horse was
obviously both fond and proud of his possession and would
not let the bridle out of his hands.

She was therefore prepared to be carried without any
effort up the winding stony path which was so steep that she
felt at times it was almost cruel to make her horse carry any
weight on its back even someone as light as herself.

The countryside was extraordinarily beautiful and Athena kept turning her head from side to side, afraid she might
miss some exquisite piece of scenery simply because she was
looking the other way.

At the bottom of the valley there was the River Pleistos
and on either side of it rolled grove upon grove of silvery
olive trees, their ancient trunks and twisting branches seeming to Athena to be redolent with history.

They passed caves which she longed to explore and she
remembered that Lord Byron had almost been lost in one.

But her goal was Delphi and she did not dare to linger on
the way.

High above her she was vividly conscious of her great
Shining Cliffs, the Phaedriades, which scintillated in the sunlight with a myriad points of multi-coloured reflected light.

She remembered how her grandmother had told her that
when Apollo left the holy island of Delos to conquer Greece
a dolphin had guided his ship through the Krisaean Gulf
which lay beneath the Shining Cliffs.

"The young god," the Dowager Marchioness had said,

"leapt from the sea disguised as a star at high noon. Flames soared from him and the flash of splendour lit the sky."

She paused dramatically, then she said softly:

"Then the star vanished and there was only a handsome young man armed with a bow and arrows."

Athena had listened breathlessly.

"He marched up the steep road to the lair of the dragon," the Dowager Marchioness went on, "and when it was slain he announced in a clear rising voice to the gods that he claimed possession of all the territory he could see from where he was standing."

"It was a lovely place," Athena had murmured.

"Apollo was amongst other things the god of good taste and he had chosen the most haunting and satisfying view in Greece," the Dowager Marchioness replied.

Half way up the steep ascent Athena looked back and knew that her grandmother had not exaggerated.

There was the blue sea in the distance, the valley of silver-grey olive trees below, the blue mountains curving away to the left and the right and the River Pleistos like a silver ribbon running through the centre of the valley.

She turned her head to look up. The Shining Cliffs rose ahead, grey and silver, they seemed to glitter in the sunshine and she had the feeling that the valley, the mountains and the sea were slowly revolving in front of them.

The man leading her horse brought her back to reality by telling her that there used to be wolves in the caves they had just passed but they had not been seen for some years.

Athena was not afraid of the wolves; what excited her far more than wild animals were the flowers.

Never had she imagined the grassland up which they were climbing could be so vivid with colour.

She recognised grape hyacinths, the star of Bethlehem, narcissus, anemones, poppies, and of course the redolent thyme. There were also wild orchids and vividly blue blossoms to which she could not put a name besides the wild iris, the flower of the gods.

Higher and higher they climbed, even the young horse finding it hard going, until finally they had reached the narrow dusty road which had been the Sacred Way and stood below the Shining Cliffs themselves.

Above her through the blossoming fruit trees Athena could see several broken pillars and the outline of what appeared to be a Temple and she knew that she had reached her goal.

It all lay to the right of a small, untidy village, many of the houses built precariously on the very edge of the cliff, the others lying haphazard amongst the ruins, children were sitting astride a great marble block and making mud-pies on the flat surface of another.

Athena dismounted, paid the man so generously that he was almost over-profuse in his thanks, then stood staring up at the cliffs above her.

She saw wheeling high against the sky a bird that she was sure was an eagle and remembered that Lord Byron had seen a flight of twelve which he had taken as a sign that Apollo and the Muses had accepted his offering of "Childe Harold."

Athena was certain that the eagle was a good omen for her too, and now because she was impatient to see what had brought her here she started to climb up the hillside.

She found steps amongst the grasses and occasionally exquisite pieces of carving that she felt should be taken away to safety rather than left uncared for and unattended.

She had known that little was left of the great Temple of Apollo except a few broken columns. But she was not primarily looking for remnants of the antiquities: she was really seeking to feel and understand what this sacred place had meant to the Ancient Greeks.

When she was a little higher up the mountainside the white stone gleamed like fire and she had a feeling of quietness and serenity and that the Shining Cliffs protected something very precious and sacred.

Avoiding the village she climbed higher and higher still, finding the walking hard until finally she found what she knew must be the Stadium.

There were only what must have been the upper row of seats above the ground and the rest was overgrown with grasses and moss.

Athena tried to imagine the competitors with their perfect, athletic bodies competing amongst themselves.

She sat down to get her breath and recited the ode written by Pindar in praise of the Aeginetan Aristomenes, who had won a wrestling match here at Delphi in 446 B.C.

> *"He who has won some new splendour*
> *Rides on the air*
> *Borne upwards on the wings of his human vigour*
> *In the fierce pride of hope, rejoicing*
> *In no desire for wealth, enjoying*
> *For a brief space the exaltation of glory."*

All the Athletes competed naked, their slim, muscular bodies as perfect as those of the gods they worshipped.

Athena sat for a long time in the Stadium. Then slowly she began the descent back to the Temple of Apollo, then lower still, seeking to the left of it the ravine where the Oracle had been.

It was, however, difficult for her to know the exact spot where the prophecies had taken place.

Then because she remembered that her grandmother had spoken of the Temple of Athena below the Sacred Way, she crossed the road and found hidden among the olive trees three perfect columns on a circular foundation which she knew had been dedicated to Athena.

They seemed to have a special light about them and the grasses which grew round the stones which had fallen from the Temple seemed to contain brighter and more brilliant flowers then any she had seen before.

Athena stared at them for a long time, and then because she was conscious that her legs were aching from the stiff climb up to the Stadium she sat down amongst the grasses and rested her back against a block of white marble.

She felt as if the faith of all those who had worshipped here so many centuries ago was still vibrant and alive, and she felt the prayers of those who had brought the Goddess Athena their petitions still lingered on the warm air.

A movement in the sky attracted her attention. Athena lifted her head and looked up.

There were eagles just as she imagined they would be hovering over the Shrine. There were six of them and the great span of their wings made them seem omnipotent— King of Birds—surveying in awful majesty the weakness of the mortals beneath them.

Silhouetted against the sun they seemed to shine with a light of their own and she watched them fascinated, until it seemed to her as if she herself was amongst them soaring in the sky, moving always higher and higher towards the sun . . .

How long she slept Athena had no idea but she came slowly back to mortal consciousness to realise that she was not alone. Someone was with her.

For a moment it was only a shadowy thought and she was still with the eagles.

Half-asleep, hardly conscious of what she was doing or saying Athena murmured:

"I was . . . flying into the . . . sun."

The sound of her own voice made her open her eyes.

Sitting looking at her as she lay amongst the flowers was a man. For a moment she looked at him hazily, finding it hard to focus her sight.

"I was certain you were a goddess," he said in an amused voice, "but I am not sure if you are Aphrodite or Athena herself."

Without thinking, without considering what she was saying, Athena answered him.

"My name is Athena," she said, and woke up completely.

"Then I offer you my most respectful homage," he said a little mockingly.

Athena sat up and put her hands to her hair. She had taken off her bonnet as she had climbed down the twisting path from the Stadium because it had been so hot.

Now she realised that she must look very strange lying bareheaded amongst the flowers and what was more, talking to a strange man to whom she had not been introduced.

He was certainly very unlike the men she had met at home, and yet despite his appearance she was sure he was well-bred.

He was wearing a white shirt without a tie and with the

sleeves rolled up above the elbows of his sun-burnt arms. But when she looked at his face Athena forgot everything else.

He had in fact the perfect classical features she had expected to find on every Greek, only at the Court of King Otho, at any rate, to be disappointed.

As she stared at him he smiled at her and the smile took away the almost severe perfection of his face and made him very human.

His deep set eyes were twinkling and she thought to herself that they had the light of Apollo in them.

"We have now established that you are the goddess Athena," the strange man said, still speaking in English. "Perhaps I should introduce myself or would you prefer to guess my identity?"

His tone made Athena feel self-conscious and the colour rose in her cheeks as she said a little uncomfortably:

"I . . . I am sorry . . . I was asleep when you spoke to me . . . and I did not know what I was . . . saying."

"You told me you were flying into the sun," the man said, "and surely no human being—if you are human—could ask for more."

Athena made a movement as if she would rise.

"I think . . . I should be . . . going."

"Going where?" the man asked. "Unless you are returning to Olympus from whence you must have come."

She smiled at him because she could not help it.

"You are very . . . flattering," she said. "But I feel this is a very strange conversation to have with . . . someone I have never met . . . before."

"We have met now," he said firmly, "and you have not answered my question."

As if it was a game in which she must take part, Athena said:

"You are not Apollo—you are too dark."

"I assure you I would not presume to such an exalted position as that of the god of light," her companion said, "even though I am a pale reflection of him. Try again."

Athena thought for a moment, then she said:

"Then you are not Hermes. I was thinking of him as I came up the hill from the Port, feeling he would protect me because after all he is the god of travellers as well as the messenger of the gods."

"If that is who you wish me to be, then I am quite content to become Hermes," the man answered, "but actually my name is Orion."

"The most famous and the most beautiful of all the constellations of stars!" Athena exclaimed.

"Now I am indeed flattered. Is your name really Athena?"

She nodded her head.

"Yes, really."

"And yet you are English?"

"Is it so obvious?"

"Only because you speak English. Otherwise you might be pure Greek, Athena when very young—not yet old enough to be the goddess of wisdom, but old enough to be the goddess of love."

Again Athena blushed, and now she picked her bonnet up from where she had laid it beside her.

"Do not put it on," Orion said quickly. "Your hair is perfect. Just the right colour against the marble and your eyes are the grey of the sea in the early morning."

Instinctively Athena's face turned towards the Gulf of Krisa as it could be glimpsed through the rocks beyond the carpet of olive trees.

"Also your nose is pure Greek," Orion finished.

"That is what I have been told before," Athena replied, "and it makes me very . . . proud."

"You would like to be Greek?"

"I have a little Greek blood in my veins and perhaps that has made me want all my life to be here, as I am now."

There was a little throb in her voice which told the man listening how much it moved her.

"And you came here alone?" he asked in surprise.

He looked beyond her through the trees as if he thought somebody else might be slumbering there whom he had not yet perceived.

"Quite alone," Athena answered.

Then she wondered if she had been indiscreet in telling him so much about herself.

"That was brave of you," he said. "English ladies are seldom so adventurous. They come here in a party, and if the majesty of Apollo makes them feel awe-inspired they giggle with each other because they are embarrassed to admit the emotions he arouses in them."

"You are speaking very scathingly," Athena said. "Do you not like the English?"

"Not very much," he admitted. "Not the ones I have met so far."

"Then it is certainly time for me to leave."

"You know I did not mean that," he said in his deep voice.

Now he looked into her eyes.

"You are different—different from the average English-woman. But everyone who comes to Delphi is a pilgrim and as such acceptable to the gods, wherever they may have been born."

"How I wish I could have seen this place in all its glory," Athena sighed.

"There have been many Temples in this particular place," Orion said quietly. "The first was a very small shrine made of bees-wax and feathers. The second was of ferns twisted together."

He paused.

"The third of laurel-boughs; the fourth of bronze with golden song-birds perched on the roof."

"I would like to have seen that one," Athena interposed softly.

"The fifth was of stone," he went on, "which was burnt down in 489 B.C., the sixth was destroyed by an earthquake, finally about 400 A.D., the seventh was plundered and torn down by the Christian Emperor Arcadius."

He hesitated for a moment before he continued:

"But long before that the Emperor Nero had robbed the Sacred Shrine of seven hundred bronze statues and removed them to Rome."

There was a note in his voice which told Athena how he resented the manner in which the Romans had appropriated treasures that were Greek. Then thinking of the Elgin Marbles she was silent.

"So much has been taken from us," Orion went on, "but they cannot take away the feeling that Apollo is still here."

*"No shelter has Apollo, nor sacred laurel leaves;*
*The fountains now are silent; the voice is stilled."*

Athena spoke in a low voice and he turned to look at her in surprise.

"Is that what you feel?"

"No," she answered, "that is what the Oracle said to the Emperor Julian the Apostate when he came here in A.D. 362 and asked what he could do to preserve the glory of the god."

"How do you know all these things?" Orion enquired. "Who has taught you?"

"I have heard the stories of Greek mythology ever since I was a child," Athena answered. "That is why I have always longed to come here and why, even though I see how little there is left to see, I am not disappointed."

She felt that his eyes lit up at her words.

"You belong here," he said quietly, and she knew that he could not have paid her a greater compliment.

They sat talking for a long time.

Orion who obviously knew everything that was known about Delphi, told to her more details of the Oracle than her grandmother had told her and described many of the ceremonies which had taken place when the pilgrims landed in the Port below and flooded along the Sacred Way.

Apollo had ordered them to come in high summer and the scorching sunlight flashed off the rocks and the white and gold glory of his Temple must have shimmered almost blindingly.

"They came very slowly," Orion said, "and yet there were always those who wished to lay their heart and their soul at the feet of Apollo. On one single day 50,000 pilgrims crowded through the Port of Itea."

He paused, then he said:

"To-day there is hardly a visitor and after all what is there for them to see?"

"Perhaps like us," Athena said, "they come to feel the presence of Apollo, and perhaps to hear within themselves the voice of the Oracle."

Orion looked at her in surprise.

"Is that why you are here?"

She did not wish to tell him the truth, but she felt as if he forced it from between her lips.

"Yes."

"The Oracle has gone," he said, "but I think that not the Pythia but Athena will speak to you. How could she fail to listen to her namesake?"

"Perhaps no-one can solve our problems except ourselves," Athena said.

She wondered as she spoke how she could be talking to a man she had never met before in this intimate manner.

Yet because he was a stranger, because he had appeared from nowhere while she was asleep, and because he could be of no importance in her life, it seemed easy and natural.

With anyone from her own world she would have felt constrained. Besides never had she been able to talk to any man of her thoughts and feelings or of the gods and goddesses that to her were so real.

Always the conversation must be of sport or of general affairs; but this man, whoever he might be, was different.

It was obvious that to him Apollo and Athena were as real as they were to her, and so she was able to say what came into her mind and after the first few moments of waking not to feel embarrassed.

The olive trees sheltered them from a sun that was scorchingly hot in the first part of the afternoon, then gradually the air grew a little cooler and finally almost regretfully, because she could not bear the thought that their conversation must come to an end Athena said tentatively:

"Perhaps you could tell me of a place where I could find something to eat and stay the night?"

"You intend to stay here?" Orion asked.

Athena looked down into the valley.

It would take her at least two hours, she thought, to reach the Port of Itea.

It would be getting late when she arrived there and she was certain that it would be difficult to persuade the fishermen to venture out into the dark on the voyage round to Mikis.

It would be better to leave early in the morning. She would be back at noon and perhaps, she thought, then she would feel stronger to face her Aunt's anger at the manner in which she had disappeared.

Somehow she could not bear this perfect day to be disrupted by disagreeableness as must inevitably occur if she arrived back at the Palace very late to-night.

Orion appeared to be waiting for her answer and after a moment she said:

"I would like to stay here if it is possible. I feel too tired to go all the way back to Itea, even if the horse on which I came here has waited to convey me down again."

"It has doubtless waited," Orion said with a smile, "as his owner knows that you will require his services. At the same time I think you are wise to stay the night. There is only one Taverna I can recommend. It is on the other side of the village and it is primitive. But it is clean and you will be welcome."

"Would you be so kind as to show me the way there?" Athena asked.

There did not seem to her to be anything reprehensible in asking this stranger for guidance. Somehow she had the feeling that he would protect her.

Perhaps because she had been so cosseted and looked after all her life it had made her more trusting than another woman might have been.

At the same time because of what they had said to each other and the manner in which they had talked together she felt a confidence in him that she had never felt for any other man.

"If you have had nothing to eat all day you must be very hungry," he said. "I should have thought of it before, but we were feeding our minds rather than our bodies."

That was what Athena thought and she flashed him a smile as she rose to her feet.

He picked up the bag in which she had put her few requirements and she remembered how heavy it had seemed when she had to carry it all the way up to the Stadium.

She did not attempt to put on her bonnet, not only because Orion had asked her not to but also because it gave her a feeling of freedom and lightness to be without it.

She was well aware that her Aunt and all her other relations would think it very reprehensible for a lady to be walking about without a covering on her head and especially to be accompanied by a man in his shirt sleeves with his collar open.

Then Athena told herself they would never understand why she was here or what it had meant to her to come to Delphi.

She admitted that her delight had been not only in the Sacred Shrine but also in having someone who understood, to talk to about it. Someone who she felt now was in fact protecting her and looking after her as the god Hermes might have done.

They moved through the olive trees, then climbed some rough steps onto the road above.

For a moment they both stood looking up at the Shining Cliffs and at the great ravine on one side of it from which a cascade of water fell silver and shimmering onto the rocks below.

"Is that the water of Castalia which Byron found to have a 'villainous tang'?" Athena asked.

"It may have been," Orion replied, "but I think you need something more sustaining than water, however blessed. So I suggest we seek the Taverna where they have quite a passable local wine and delicious coffee."

"You are making me feel thirsty, and I admit to feeling very hungry," Athena said. "It is rather lowering to realise that while our minds and hearts are in the heights our bodies are still mundane enough to remain very material."

"I shall never believe that of your body," Orion replied. "As I suspected when I saw you this afternoon, you move like a goddess with a grace that only the nymphs that sprang from the spray of the waves could emulate."

Athena gave a little laugh.

"I like your compliments," she said. "They are so different from any I have ever received before."

"And you have obviously received very many," he said mockingly.

"Not really," she answered.

Now there was a wistful note in her voice as she remembered that the compliments she had received in Athens and which at first had seemed so delightful had doubtless been lip-service to her fortune rather than to herself.

It struck her as they moved along through the village that was built above and below the Sacred Way that this was the first time in her life that anyone was talking to her without being aware of her background or her rank as her father's daughter.

To this strange man, Orion, she was just Athena. He accepted that as her name and asked no further questions.

Yet they had conversed as equals in the manner of two scholars who had met each other across the centuries of time and to whom there was nothing of importance except the searchings of each other's minds.

"While I commend your courage," Orion was saying as they walked along, "at the same time I do not advise you to make many such expeditions in Greece without being accompanied either by someone older than yourself or at least a courier."

"Why not?" Athena enquired.

"The first reason is obvious," he replied. "You are young and you are very beautiful."

"And another?"

"There are always bandits in this part of the world."

"Bandits?" Athena exclaimed.

"Bandits—brigands—whatever you like to call them," he replied. "They have no respect for property nor in some cases for the female sex."

Athena remembered that when she was in Athens she had soon found that the most talked about person at Court was an Albanian General.

She had been told with bated breath that he was a Pallikare who was certainly amongst the most striking of the many races who were crowded into the city.

"They are a legendary lot," someone had said in her presence, "mercenaries and cut-throats, and originally bandits from the Albanian mountains."

"It is all very well to disparage them," another man answered, "but they fought magnificently in the War of Independence and it is to keep them amiably disposed that the King has named their Chief, General Xristodolous Hadji-Petros as one of his *aides-de-camp*."

The General was certainly a splendid figure, Athena thought.

Ferocious-looking, he wore an Albanian costume with crimson and gold embroideries and he bristled with pistols and *yetaghans*.

His horses' bridles and saddles were decorated with gold and silver and his men, with long moustachios, swaggered about in great shaggy cloaks and looked like bears.

It was during the week that Athena had spent in Athens that a sensational scandal had broken.

A famous English beauty, Lady Ellenborough, who after a very chequered career in which, it was whispered, she had been not only King Otho's mistress but also previously that of his father, King Ludwig of Bavaria, had run away with the General into the mountains.

Despite his magnificent appearance he was over sixty, a widower with children.

But among those who had been very conscious of his attractions was Queen Amelia, and apparently she, as Athena heard, was furious and jealous that the General should have eloped with someone who moved in Court circles.

No-one, Athena remembered, had talked of anything else and she suspected that one of the reasons that her Aunt had been so insistent on leaving Athens for the Prince's Palace at Mikis was to prevent her hearing more about the scandal that had left everyone gasping at its audacious impropriety.

But at Delphi, amongst the untidy houses which were little more than huts or hovels, she could not imagine she would find a brigand looking like the Albanian General.

As if he read her thoughts Orion said:

"There are brigands and brigands, some are extremely picturesque, but others can be dangerous and that is why I am warning you against them, Athena."

"I am not inviting their company," Athena laughed.

He stopped still and looked at her and because he had ceased walking she was forced to do the same.

"Look at me," he said.

Wondering she turned her eyes up to his.

He was so much taller than her that his head seemed to be silhouetted against the sky.

"You must take care of yourself," he said very quietly but insistently. "You are so beautiful—so unbelievably beautiful—and I realise so innocent, that you have no idea of the dangers that might be waiting for you. Promise me, promise me by everything you hold sacred that you will be careful."

The solemnity in his voice gave her a very strange feeling.

No-one had ever spoken to her like that before, no-one's voice had ever suggested so much concern—and another emotion to which she could not put a name.

"I will . . . be careful."

"You promise?"

"I promise!"

It was an easy promise to make, she thought, for after to-morrow she was quite certain there would never be another chance to escape.

They would be watching for her, and if she was brave enough, as she intended, to tell the Prince she could not marry him, she would go back to the safety of England where there were no brigands, but also no gods or sacred shrines.

They walked on and now as if Orion was thinking deeply he did not speak.

When they left a larger part of the village behind, the narrow road began to slope upwards.

Finally they climbed steeply to where on the outskirts of the other houses there stood what was obviously a Taverna with a breath-taking view over the valley beneath them.

It was a very simple building of two storeys and like all the houses in the village had a flat roof. It had a front porch made simply of dried branches of trees supported by wooden struts.

Beneath it were a number of deal tables at which were sitting several elderly men looking, Athena thought, as if they were customers of long standing.

They said good-evening in a friendly manner to Orion

when they both appeared, and he answered them, calling them by their names as if they were his close friends.

Carrying Athena's bag and putting a hand under her elbow as if to support her he drew her through the doorway and into the house itself.

There was a large kitchen, a table in the centre of it and a stove at one side.

A middle-aged woman and a young girl dressed in peasant costume were preparing a meal while a thickset man whose hair was turning grey was sitting in an arm-chair, smoking a pipe.

They looked up as Orion and Athena entered and there was no doubt of the curiosity in their expressions.

"Madame Argeros, I have brought you a lady who requires a bed for the night," Orion said. "I told her that you will welcome her and she will be safe in your comfortable house, safe from the brigands and the 'sharks' in the village who batten upon tourists."

Madame Argeros laughed.

"Any friends of yours, Orion, is welcome," she said. "The lady can have Nonika's room. She can move in with us."

They spoke in Greek but Athena understood.

"I would not wish to be any trouble," she said in their language.

Orion stared at her in astonishment.

"You speak Greek!" he exclaimed. "We have been together all the afternoon and you did not tell me."

"You did not ask me, and you spoke English so well that I might have been put to shame."

"But you speak with perfection!" he said. "Like everything else about you."

The last words were spoken in English so that only she could understand them. Athena felt shy and did not look at him.

"Let me introduce you," Orion said. "Madame Argeros, the best cook in the whole province, Dimitrios Argeros, her husband, the owner of this comfortable Taverna and Nonika, the prettiest girl for miles around."

Nonika blushed and dropped her eyes, Dimitrios Argeros gave Athena a respectful nod, but he did not rise from the chair on which he was sitting.

"Come and sit down," Madame Argeros suggested. "Nonika will get your room ready."

"We are both thirsty and hungry, Madame," Orion said. "I have not eaten since breakfast and I have not asked my friend when she last enjoyed a meal."

"As it happens it was last night," Athena replied, "with the exception of an orange which one of the boatmen gave me on my way here."

She spoke in Greek and Madame Argeros gave a little cry of horror.

"You must be starving!" she said. "Sit down, child, and I will find you something to eat, but dinner is not yet ready."

Obediently Athena sat down at the large deal table and Madame put down in front of her a loaf of bread and a cheese made from sheep's milk which Athena had tasted before and found delicious.

There were black olives ripe from the sun and red tomatoes sliced into their own juice, besides a cucumber hastily cut and added to the plate of tomatoes.

The bread was crisp and delicious and without waiting Athena cut herself a slice and spread on it the white sheep's-milk cheese.

As she did so Orion brought a bottle of wine to the table, opened it and poured her out a glass.

She sipped it.

"A feast for the gods," she smiled. "I do not believe that even ambrosia and nectar could taste better when I am so hungry."

He laughed, helped himself to the olives and also cut a large piece of the bread.

"You are not to spoil your appetite, Orion," Madame admonished from the stove. "I have cooked all your favourite dishes as you are leaving us to-morrow."

"Shall I guess?" he asked. "Or shall I tell you I can already smell the fragrance of baby lamb?"

"It is to be a surprise," Madame said severely. "There is *Moussaka* to start and I only hope your friend enjoys it as much as you do."

"She will," Orion answered.

He smiled at Athena as he spoke and as he did so it suddenly struck her that she had never been so happy in the whole of her life.

She was with people who welcomed her because she was herself.

She was with a man who was speaking to her as an intellectual equal.

This was what she had always wanted, what she had always missed. It could be summed up in one word—happiness.

# CHAPTER THREE

Nonika came shyly into the kitchen to tell Athena her room was ready.

"I expect you would like Nonika to show you the way upstairs," Orion suggested.

"Thank you, I would," Athena replied.

She picked up the hand-woven bag and her bonnet from where they were laid on a chair and followed Nonika.

They climbed a narrow, rather rickety staircase, and on the low-ceilinged small landing at the top Athena saw there were two doors, one on the right the other on the left.

Nonika opened the one on the left and Athena followed her into a room which contained a bed, a wool rug on the wooden floor and a chest-of-drawers on which there was a small mirror.

Another table contained a washing basin and there was one chair, but nothing else against the white-washed walls. But it was spotlessly clean, and smelt of bees-wax and wild thyme.

"It is very kind of you to give me your room," Athena said.

"I only sleep here when there are no guests," Nonika replied. "Orion has the other room."

"You know him well and he stays here often?" Athena enquired.

She felt perhaps she had no right to ask the question. At the same time she could not help feeling curious about Orion's position in the household.

He was so obviously a different class from the Argeros family, but they appeared to treat him as if he was a favoured son rather than a client of their Taverna.

While they were eating Madame had admonished him for having missed the midday meal, and her husband had cracked jokes and repeated some incident that had happened in the village to people who were apparently known to them both.

In answer to Athena's question Nonika gave a little shrug of her shoulders.

"He comes—he goes," she said enigmatically. "Sometimes we do not see him for a long time, but always he returns and is welcome."

She gave Athena a smile as she added:

"As you are welcome as his friend."

She shut the door as she spoke and Athena felt herself warm at the sincerity of her words.

How charming and simple these people were, she thought, so different from the sharp-eyed, wise-cracking society notabilities whom she had met in Athens.

Even the Parnassus relations who had come to call on her had seemed very social-minded in their outlook and the women were extremely fashionable in their appearance.

She realised that the whole of Athenian society centred around the Court and the gossip that enthralled them left little room for any other interest or amusement.

It was not extraordinary that the Courtiers and notabilities who circled around King Otho and Queen Amelia should have a passion for scandal.

It ran through the Salons and cafés of the whole city and was in keeping with its many other Oriental traits.

Athens had surprised Athena in that it was not in the least what she had expected from the Greek capital.

"It is part Turkish, part Slav and part Levantine," one of the King's *aides-de-camp* had explained to her, and she realised when she drove through the busy city that he was right.

There were the seething Turkish Bazaars, the cafés where at least half the population spent most of their time smoking their *nargailyes* and drinking innumerable cups of coffee.

But what had delighted Athena was the noisy crowded streets where she could see the exotic costumes which were characteristic of the islands and the provinces.

This was where she longed to wander by herself if she had been allowed, to watch the people and have the opportunity of entering the dark churches, decorated with Icons, from where, as she passed, she could hear the chanting of the monks.

The King's Palace, plain, square and uncompromisingly Bavarian, had set the standard for the taste of Greek Society, who were determined to be as European as possible.

But however conventional they might wish to be, Athens remained a conglomeration of booths and Palaces, noisy *gargottes* and Byzantine churches.

"You would hardly believe it," someone said to Athena: "the city has over twenty thousand inhabitants but only two thousand houses."

"Then where do they all sleep?" Athena asked.

"Many of them in the streets," was the answer.

In the short time she was there Athena realised that the tiny capital attracted like a magnet pleasure seekers from all over the Balkans.

Rich Moldavian nobles travelled for weeks over immense distances to indulge in riotous living; fezes, turbans, and the lambskin hats of the Caucasians intermingled with tasselled caps.

A mixture of yashmaked kohl-eyed women wrapped anonymously in black rubbed shoulders with colourful peasants, and ladies wearing silks and satins direct from Paris.

It was only in the Palace and in its splendid gardens that Athena had felt lonely among the chattering groups of nobles and her eyes went continually toward the Parthenon standing sentinel over the city as it had done for more than two thousand years.

She wanted to say with Byron:

*"Ah! Greece! They love thee least who owe thee most;*
*Their birth, their blood and that sublime record*
*Of hero sires, who shame thy now degenerate horde!"*

But because she was so anxious to love everything in the land in which she was to live and because she wanted to immerse herself in everything that was Greek, she would not admit that Athens had disappointed her or that the Greek people whom she met had not in any way measured up to her expectations.

But to-day she had found in Orion the type of man she had hoped to meet.

This was how she had imagined all Greek men would look and that they would be proud of their past, trying within themselves to revive the spirit which had made Greece the foundation on which European civilization was built.

As she washed, then tidied her hair, Athena could not help wishing that she could change her dress and put on one of the exquisite gowns she had brought with her from London in her trousseau.

But she laughed at the idea of going downstairs to the kitchen bedecked in silk and tulle or wearing one of the off-the-shoulder gowns edged with a lace bertha which was the fashion.

At the same time something very feminine within her wanted Orion to see her at her best.

How could he judge what she was like in the very plain dress she had chosen in which to travel to Delphi?

Then she told herself she was being ridiculous.

"To-morrow he is leaving and I shall never see him again," she told her reflection and wondered why the thought gave her a pain that was almost physical within her breast.

Laughing at her vanity, and yet at the same time driven by it, she arranged her hair more fashionably.

She brushed the ringlets on either side of her face until they shone as if they had caught the sunlight, and made certain that the parting down the centre of her small head was absolutely straight.

The face she saw in the mirror had changed, she felt, in some way from its look before she had come to Delphi.

Her large grey eyes which dominated the oval of her face had a light in them that had not been there before, there was a touch of colour in her cheeks and her lips were soft and parted with excitement.

Only her small straight nose which her grandmother had always said was exactly like that of the goddess after whom she was named, remained the same.

Yet the whole effect was different, though Athena could not explain exactly how.

She remembered when Homer wished to describe the goddess Athena he called her "the bright-eyed one," and that he had spoken of Helen of Troy as "wearing a shining veil."

"That is what is happening to me now," Athena said to herself. "I am shining with a reflection from the Shining Cliffs and from the light that I felt in the Temple."

Because she was in a hurry to go downstairs to see Orion again and talk to him, she did not linger long in her bedroom.

Just for a moment she glanced out through the window at the stupendous view that lay beneath.

Now as the sun was sinking the valley was in deep shadow, the olive trees no longer silver-grey but like a dark carpet of purple.

But the little Port of Itea still glowed in the setting sun and the tops of the mountains were burnished with gold.

Athena drew in her breath. Then spurred by an urgency that she was afraid to explain to herself she hurried below.

There was a cloth on the table in the kitchen and when Orion rose at her entrance she saw that he had put on a black velvet coat over his shirt.

He wore nothing so formal as a tie, but a silk scarf inside the collar of his shirt which made him not only appear tidier, but also in some way gave him a new dignity.

It made Athena find it hard to look at him as she approached the table, but his eyes were on her face and it would have been impossible for her to go anywhere except to his side.

"Dinner is ready," he said speaking in Greek and she answered him in the same language.

"I am very hungry, I hope Madame Argeros will not think I am greedy."

"There is plenty for everyone," Madame said.

She set a dish down on the table and Athena saw that it was the famous *Moussaka* which she had eaten before and which she had learnt varied from place to place and from kitchen to kitchen.

It might be a Greek speciality, but she thought it resembled very closely the Shepherd's Pie that she had eaten so often at home and which in the School-Room always appeared on Monday made from the left-overs of the Sunday joint.

However with Greek olives, herbs, aubergines and various other vegetables added she found Moussaka very delectable and because she was hungry ate without speaking.

Orion filled her glass with the golden wine and by the time they had consumed large portions of baby lamb roasted on the spit the edge of Athena's hunger and, she thought, Orion's too had gone.

They started to talk to the Argeros family who had joined them at the table, but either Nonika or her father kept rising to attend the customers sitting outside the Taverna.

They continually and loudly demanded bottles of wine or cups of coffee, but with the exception of olives and an occasional plate of cheese, they did not ask for food.

Athena commented on this.

"The Greeks eat very late," Orion explained. "Madame Argeros panders to my preference for an early dinner, but if I was not here I doubt if she would begin cooking until it was nearly ten o'clock."

"But they get up very early," Athena answered, remembering that the streets of Greece had been crowded when she had looked out at six or even five o'clock in the morning.

"Every Greek enjoys a long siesta during the hottest time of the day," Orion said, "just as you took yours this afternoon."

"But I did it inadvertently," Athena replied almost defensively.

"Consciously or unconsciously you conformed with the customs of my country," he smiled.

His eyes were on hers as he spoke and she remembered how she had awoken to find him sitting beside her when she had been dreaming that she was flying with the eagles.

She felt herself blush at what she thought he must be thinking and was glad when Madame Argeros broke the tension by saying:

"We have bad news to-day."

"Bad news?" Orion questioned.

"There was trouble at Arachova last night."

Athena knew that Arachova was a small town about four hours from Delphi on the road over the mountains leading to Athens.

It was where the wine came from and the inhabitants wove tufted rugs which were famous all over Greece.

She had been shown several of them when she was in Athens and had made up her mind to buy one because they were so attractive.

"What happened in Arachova?" Orion asked.

"Kazandis was there!"

Orion seemed to stiffen in his seat.

"I thought he was in prison."

"Apparently he escaped," Madame replied. "He swept down on the town last night and although they tried to drive him away he stole a considerable number of things before he left."

"That is serious," Orion remarked.

"Who is Kazandis?" Athena enquired.

"A bandit," Orion answered, "of the type that I was warning you about. He is a dangerous man who is thought to have murdered a number of people in the valleys."

"They should have hanged him when they had the chance," Madame Argeros said shrilly. "No-one can feel safe in their houses when Kazandis is at large."

"The trouble was that no-one would bear witness against him," Orion said. "They were too frightened of the vengeance he would wreak upon them."

He brought his fist down hard on the table making the glasses rattle.

"How could the Military be so stupid as to allow him to escape? He was committed to prison for a long sentence."

"From all I hear there is a great deal of corruption in the State Prisons," Argeros said from the head of the table.

"I have heard that too, but it is difficult to prove," Orion replied.

"There must be something wrong when a man like Kazandis can escape," Madame Argeros said sharply. "He is a menace, and if he has managed to free himself from gaol I am quite certain he will have left a number of dead bodies behind him."

Orion turned towards Athena.

"Now you understand why you should not be travelling alone, especially in this part of the world."

"There are always dragons wherever one may travel," she answered, "but perhaps too there is an Apollo, or maybe a Hermes, to save me from them."

She spoke lightly but Orion's expression was serious.

"I am worried about you," he said in English.

"I shall be all . . . right," she answered.

At the same time, because he was so concerned she felt a little flicker of fear within herself.

Up to now she had not thought there might be any dangers other than being prevented from coming to Delphi.

Now it seemed there were indeed dragons that she had not anticipated, but she thought it very unlikely that she would encounter one.

"The whole trouble with the country is that too much attention is paid to what happens in the city and not enough in the Provinces," Dimitrios Argeros said provocatively.

"That was inevitable while we were a divided nation," Orion replied. "But now we are a Kingdom things should improve, and I understand that representations on that very subject had been made to the King."

"The King!" There was a world of meaning in the way Argeros said it. "He is a good man, but he is not a Greek."

"That is true," Orion agreed.

"Only a Greek can understand Greece," Argeros went

on. "Only a Greek can sympathise with us when our crops fail, when the sea does not yield its fish, when the gods withhold the rain, or drown the soil."

Then the arguments started, arguments which Athena thought she had listened to in England, the countryman against the town-dweller, the farmer against the artisan, and all against the Government.

She liked the way each man put his point, concisely and eloquently, and the manner in which as if they fought a duel they tried to make their point and defeat the other with the flash and sparkle of words.

Sometimes Madame Argeros joined in but Nonika listened, wide-eyed, only having to rise to attend to the noisy orders of those outside on the porch.

Finally when the wine and the coffee were finished Orion rose to his feet.

"We agree in principle," he said to his host.

"Which is more than the Government does," Argeros grumbled and Orion laughed.

"Come along, Athena," he said. "You could stay here listening all night to Greek politics, but I doubt if you would be any the wiser at the end of it. The whole trouble with this country is that there is too much talk and not enough 'do'."

He said this as a parting shot at Argeros who laughed and made a remark that Athena did not understand but which made Orion laugh too.

Then they had left the Taverna behind and were descending the road up which they had climbed earlier in the day.

While they had been eating and talking the sun had sunk and the stars had come out in the sky and with them the moon.

· It was not yet full, but there was light enough to see the way.

As they passed the houses of the village and came near to the Sacred Shrine Athena could see that a mist hung over the valley so that the Shining Cliffs seemed to be floating over a vast and mysterious chasm.

Now the broken marble columns and the strange shapes

lying among the grasses were haloed with silver and acquired a new form and grace that they had not had before.

It was very silent save for a dog barking far away in the village; Athena could hear the water flowing from the chasm and the air was filled with the fragrance of wild thyme.

In silence she and Orion climbed the broken steps and moved through the long flower-filled grasses towards the Temple of Apollo.

He put his hand under her elbow to help her and with the feeling of his fingers on her bare skin she felt a strange little tremor go through her and she thought perhaps it was because the mystery and darkness of the night was so awe-inspiring.

They climbed until they had passed the columns of Apollo and had reached the theatre above it.

Below them it was possible to make out the complete shape of the Temple and the white stones and columns seemed to make a pattern that Athena had not been able to perceive in the daytime.

Now they shone like crystals and there were strange shadows in the sanctuary which made her feel it was peopled with the priests and pilgrims of the past, and with the presence of the god himself.

Far below she could just make out the sea glimmering through the gap in the great dark mountain rocks.

As she looked the moon came out fuller throwing a shimmering icy lightness over the whole valley, and now it seemed to her that the very air was filled with a mysterious quivering and the beating of silver wings.

A light blinded her eyes so that she felt as if Apollo himself materialised before her and she could see him in all his glory surrounded by stars.

She almost felt as if she could take wing and fly towards him. Then she heard Orion's deep voice speaking for the first time since they had left the Taverna.

"Tell me what you feel."

"It is wonderful! Lovely! So beautiful," Athena murmured almost beneath her breath, "that I want to . . . hold the moonlight in my arms. I want to . . . kiss it and make it . . . mine."

"That is what I want."

Then he turned her round and his lips were on hers.

For a moment Athena was so bemused by her feelings that she could hardly believe that it was Orion kissing her rather than Apollo.

She felt his lips hard and possessive against the softness of her own.

Then as if it was part of the whole magic of the night, the moonlight and the Shining Cliffs, she found herself without conscious volition melt closely against him.

She surrendered her mouth to his, feeling as if everything that was happening was inevitable—pre-ordained and what in the depths of her heart, she had expected.

His arms tightened and now his lips seemed to draw not only her soul from her but also her life itself.

She became one with the moon, the stars and of course Orion.

It was so wonderful that Athena felt as though she was disembodied, and at the same time the moonlight was not only all around but within her.

It was hers and she held it in her arms and in the innermost sanctuary of her soul.

Time stood still.

She was aware of a rapture and an ecstasy that was not of the world but belonged to Olympus. Orion was not a man but a god, and she was Athena, goddess of love.

How long they stood there it was impossible to know, a century might have passed or more.

Slowly Orion raised his head and looked down at Athena with her eyes shining as they stared up at him, her lips soft and warm from his kisses, and a radiance in her face that gave her a spiritual beauty that was indescribable.

For a moment they looked at each other, then with an inarticulate sound that seemed to come from the very depths of his being he was kissing her again.

Kissing her now demandingly, possessively, until she clung to him even closer, aware of strange sensations within herself which she had not known existed.

Finally when she felt as if he carried her as the eagles had up into the sky so that she no longer had her feet on the ground, he released her so suddenly that she staggered and almost fell.

As he put out his hand to steady her, she sat down on one of the stone seats of the Theatre.

She stared up at him, her fingers entwining themselves as if only by touch could she believe that she was still human, still flesh and blood.

He stood looking at her for a long moment, then sat down beside her.

"You have never been kissed before."

His voice was very deep and moved.

She shook her head. Her voice had died in her throat from the sheer wonder of what she had just experienced.

"Then you know now that this is how a kiss should be, pure and sacred as only the gods understand purity."

Athena did not reply and after a moment he said in what she knew was a different tone:

"This has been a dream, Athena. We both have to go back to reality, but I think neither of us will ever forget."

Athena drew in her breath.

Somehow it seemed to her as if he was speaking to her from very far away and was difficult to understand.

"Y . . . you are . . . going away," she managed to say at length and her voice sounded very unlike her own.

"I am leaving early to-morrow morning," he replied, "before you are awake. But I wanted to say good-bye to you here, for nowhere else would have seemed so right."

There was a silence in which the moonlight shining on the pillars beneath them seemed to look almost like tears. Then Athena said hesitatingly:

"Must . . . it be . . . good-bye?"

She did not know what she really meant or what alternative she could offer, she only knew that every instinct in her body cried out against losing him, against being separated from the wonder and magic of his lips.

There was a pause. He was looking down into the valley and his clear-cut profile was silhouetted against the broken and moss covered tiers of the theatre, which had once held an enraptured audience.

"This has been a dream, Athena," he said slowly. "A

dream sent to us by the gods and I think neither of us could bear to spoil it."

He drew in his breath as he went on:

"It has been a moment of utter perfection; a moment which is engraved on my heart for all time."

"And on . . . mine," Athena whispered.

"That is why there is nothing we can say to each other. There is no need for explanations. I could not bear to ask for them—or make them."

She knew what he was trying to say and she accepted that it was inevitable.

They were strangers, and because they had met in the abode of gods they had for a moment assumed a god-like isolation from the rest of their lives.

They had been swept away from the normal into a spiritual existence which nether of them had ever known before. They had been disembodied, touched with the divinity of the gods themselves and for one ecstatic moment had become divine.

Now they must face reality and Athena wished that she could have died while his lips were on hers.

Then she would have achieved immortality: there would have been no problems, no difficulties, no human needs to which she must return.

She wanted to cry out at the pain of relinquishing the wonder she had known in Orion's arms, then to weep perhaps with despair. But because she knew that nothing she could say could alter their destiny she kept silent.

"There is no need for me to tell you that this is something which has never happened to me before in my life," Orion was saying, "and which I am certain will never happen again. You were rightly named, Athena, you are the goddess of love and you have brought me love which I believed existed but had never found."

"That is how . . . love should . . . be," Athena murmured.

"That is why the pilgrims came here," he said. "That is why there are pilgrims all over the world seeking love, the love which has led, guided and inspired man since the beginning of time."

"It was the . . . love they gave . . . Apollo," Athena said softly.

"And the love Athena gave to them."

They sat looking down at the ruined Temple and the valley beyond it and although he was not touching her Athena felt as if she was still in his arms.

Finally with a sigh he rose to his feet.

"I must take you back."

She rose too to stand looking at him, her face raised to his, the moonlight shining in her eyes.

He knew without words what she asked and what she wanted of him and he said quietly:

"I will not kiss you again because after to-night our paths will never cross each other's and I dare not repeat that moment when we both reached the heights of bliss and were one with the gods."

Athena's eyes were on his and he looked at her as if he was spellbound and he could not look away.

"I am after all only a man," he said, "and if as a man I kissed you again I might try to change the pattern of our lives, and that would be a mistake."

Athena wanted to protest, wanted to tell him that she wanted above all things, the pattern of her life to be changed, to be with him, to have him kiss her and that nothing else was of any consequence in the whole world.

"You are lovely!" he said hoarsely, "more lovely than I believed any woman could be. That is why, having known you, I am convinced that no other woman will ever matter to me again."

Athena felt her heart leap.

It was like a streak of joy running through her and he must have seen it in her eyes, for almost as if she had spoken he said firmly:

"No! No, Athena!"

Then he turned and walked back down the twisting stone path that led to the road.

After a moment she followed him because there was nothing else she could do.

As she went, finding it difficult at times to keep her balance without his supporting hand, she felt that he would disappear away from her into the shadows so that she would never find him.

"Perhaps," she thought wildly, "he never existed. Perhaps he is part of my dreams or perhaps he is in fact not human, but has come from the constellation of stars whose name he bears."

But he was waiting for her when she reached the road.

She thought his expression was stern and that his jaw was set so that it seemed as if he had already left her and she was alone as she had been alone before they met.

They walked up the road without speaking, past the shuttered village, and although light gleamed in many of the windows there was a silence that seemed now to Athena not magical, but oppressive.

Several dogs barked as they passed and Athena felt that they were hostile because she was an intruder and did not belong.

After the steep climb to the Taverna, they could see the lights glowing golden from its windows. But the porch was empty and the old men had gone home.

The chairs were stacked tidily on the tables as Orion opened the door into the house. The warmth of the kitchen after the cold of the moonlight was almost like a shock.

Madame Argeros and her husband were sitting at the table. He was smoking and they each had a cup of coffee in front of them, but there was no sign of Nonika.

Madame smiled as they entered.

"You are back!" she exclaimed. "That is good. I have kept some coffee warm for you."

"How kind of you, Madame," Orion said conventionally.

Athena moved towards the other door which led to the stairs.

"I think I will go to bed," she said in a voice which sounded strangled in her throat.

"You will not have some coffee?" Madame Argeros asked.

"No . . . thank you . . . I am tired . . . it has been a . . . long day."

She did not look at Orion although she was vividly conscious that he had walked to the table. He pulled out a chair and sat down opposite Dimitrios Argeros.

She wanted to stay beside him. She wanted to eke out the last minutes that she could be with him, but she felt it might somehow spoil the wonder of all they had experienced.

The glory of his kiss still pulsated within her, even while she knew inevitably the rapture of it was fading.

Soon it would be gone and she felt despairingly that there would be nothing but an aching void that would be with her all the rest of her life.

"We wish you good-night," Madame said. "May you sleep well."

"Thank you," Athena answered.

Then as she would have turned away the door of the Taverna was flung violently open.

The noise of it made them all turn instinctively to see entering the kitchen a huge man.

He was wearing a short sheep-skin coat with a fur hat set jauntily on the side of his head.

He was very dark with bushy eye-brows, a long curling moustache, the ends of it reaching almost to his chin where they had been curled fastidiously.

There was a pistol stuck in his belt, besides a long knife, and as his black eyes looked around the kitchen searchingly and somehow insolently Madame Argeros gave a scream.

"Kazandis!"

"Yes, Kazandis," the Bandit answered. "Are you surprised to see me? You should have expected me, for where else in these regions can I get better food?"

He walked forward as he spoke and pulling out a chair from the table sat down at the end of it.

"I want food," he said, "money and . . ."

He paused for a moment and he stared towards Athena.

Mesmerized she stood in the open doorway, her hair golden in the light from the lamp, her skin very white against the dark walls of the kitchen.

She felt as Kazandis looked at her that somehow he stripped her naked and her heart gave a frightened leap as he finished his sentence.

". . . and a woman!"

There was silence in the kitchen, then Orion rose to his feet.

Swiftly as he moved the Bandit was swifter.

He drew the pistol from his belt and pointed it at him.

"Any position from you," he said, "and not only you will die but also the Argeros' and anyone else who interferes with me!"

"You shall have your food," Madame interrupted. "You are fortunate there is some left. Here is wine."

She set a bottle down on the table with a bang as she spoke and walked towards the stove. No-one else moved. Then slowly, without the impetuosity he had shown the first time, Orion rose.

"Madame will provide you with your needs," he said, "and I shall make no effort to interfere. But this woman is my wife. We have not been married long, but she is with child."

The Bandit looked across the room at Athena and at the slimness of her figure.

"That is why she is retiring to bed," Orion said firmly. "Do you understand?"

The Bandit looked at him as if to make certain he was telling the truth. Orion's eyes met his fairly and squarely.

After a moment he grunted, poured out a glass of wine and swilled it down without speaking.

Orion crossed the room, put his arm around Athena and took her through the door which led to the stairs. He deliberately left it open as if to let the Bandit see that they were not escaping.

"Go up to bed and lock your door. You will be quite safe," he said in English.

"You are . . . sure?"

Athena was trembling.

"Quite sure," he answered.

He did not touch her, but he watched her as she climbed the stairs, and heard her go into the room overhead.

There was no lock on the door, but there was a bolt made of wood and Athena pushed it into place.

The shutters over the window were closed and she made no effort to open them, she could not bear to look at the moonlight. Nonika had left a rush candle burning and by the light of it Athena undressed and got into bed.

She thought it would be impossible to think of anything

but the Bandit sitting downstairs, but although she could hear the murmur of their voices she began to relive the moment when Orion had kissed her in the Sacred Shrine.

With her eyes closed she could still see the outline of the Temple, the silver mist in the valley and the glimmer of the sea.

It all seemed to glow within her with the shining light which she knew came from Apollo himself.

It was perfect, it was wonderful, and even now she could hardly believe that her spirit, having soared to the Heavens in Orion's arms, was back within the confines of her body.

She would never see him again. He was leaving her, as strangely and mysteriously as he had come. Orion—the stranger who was no longer a stranger but a part of herself.

She felt cold with the pain and misery of it. She wanted him, wanted him with an intensity that was violent.

How could she lose him? How could she forget the moment when she gave herself to him completely and absolutely, keeping back nothing, merging her whole being into his until they were one person?

She wanted to cry out in despair, and yet her eyes were dry and she knew there were no words by which she could express her feelings, not even to him.

For one moment of her life she had been transformed from a conventional English girl into, as he had said, the goddess of love.

Now when he left her, she would return to what she had been before except that nothing could ever be the same again.

Having once touched the very fount of happiness and of ecstasy, having once known the rapture of the initiated into the mysteries of the gods, how could she return to ordinary life?

How could she face commonplace people and the thought of living perhaps three-score-years-and-ten without the man she loved?

Put into words it seemed incredible.

How could she love a man she had never met until this afternoon? Yet she knew inexorably and irrefutably that this, as Orion had said, was the love that all men sought.

Journeying as pilgrims, following twisting philosophies and innumerable religions they sought in their souls what she and Orion had captured in one immortal moment on the broken steps of the theatre.

"I love him!"

She said the words to herself, and they seemed to be emblazoned across the darkness in letters of fire.

"I love him! I love him! He is the only person who understands."

To anyone else the story would sound ridiculous: they would laugh and tell her she was just an imaginative, romantic girl, carried away by the moonlight.

But Athena knew it was something fundamental and eternal.

It was soul reaching out to soul, spirit reaching out to spirit, a woman finding the man who was hers and to whom she had belonged from the beginning of creation.

This was love, this was fate which drew two people to each other, so that whatever the appearances against it they became one in the real and spiritual sense of the word.

"When Orion leaves to-morrow he takes my heart with him," Athena whispered to the darkness.

A long time later she heard him coming up the stairs.

There was silence below and she guessed that the Bandit must have gone, doubtless taking with him all the money the Argeros' had in the house and anything else of value he fancied.

As Orion reached the landing and opened the door of his room she fancied that he stood for a moment listening as if to ascertain that she was all right.

She wanted to cry out to him, but she knew that that was something he did not want—and anyway modesty kept her silent.

Orion went into the other room and shut the door.

She heard him walking about on the uncarpeted floor then she heard the bed move beneath him.

She wondered what he looked like asleep, perhaps younger and gentler, and not so overwhelmingly masculine as he had looked when his deep-set eyes sought hers and she felt shy yet excited by the expression in them.

"I love him! I love him!" Athena whispered to herself.

She knew that he intended to rise early in the morning before she was awake, but she was sure that after all that had happened she would be unable to sleep, and if he made the slightest sound she would hear it.

It would be a worse agony than anything she could imagine to hear him going downstairs and leaving the house without saying good-bye.

And yet what could they say to each other that had not already been said?

It would be a bathos that was unthinkable to shake hands or even to kiss each other perfunctorily after what had happened at the shrine.

No—there would be nothing she could do but listen to him leaving, and know that after he had gone she must return to the world from which she had escaped for one brief ecstatic day.

"However long I live I shall never be able to love anyone else," Athena thought.

Deep in her thoughts she was vaguely aware of a scrabbling sound against the wall of the house.

She had not really noticed it, but now she distinctly heard a footstep overhead.

It was not loud, and yet it was followed by another one, and she looked up apprehensively in the darkness at the ceiling.

Again she heard a noise and now with a sudden shock of terror she knew what it was.

Someone was on the roof over her head and it was not difficult to guess the intruder's identity. He was obviously trying to open the trap-door which was built in most flat-roofed houses to let in the cool night air when the weather was hot.

Athena sat up in bed.

It was Kazandis who was overhead—and she knew that he intended to enter her room from the roof above.

He would know where she was sleeping because he would have heard her moving about when she went to bed, and although he had pretended to accept Orion's story that she was his wife and with child it was doubtful if he had been deceived.

Terror-stricken, she realised that the trap-door in the roof was opening.

It was obviously stiff through not having been used since last year, but although she could not see in the darkness she felt that strong fingers were already raising it.

There was a creaking noise, then a faint light above her!

With a cry like a frightened animal Athena jumped out of bed.

She ran across the room and groped with frantic, trembling fingers for the bolt on the door.

Then she pulled the door open, ran across the landing and grasped the handle of Orion's door.

It turned, and unable to breathe from sheer terror Athena let herself in.

# CHAPTER FOUR

Orion had opened his shutters when he went to bed, and in the moonlight flooding into the room he could see, as he sat up, Athena at the door.

She turned to push in the bolt which was similar to the one on the door of her bed-room, then frantically she ran across the room to him.

"What is the matter? What has happened?" he asked.

Without thinking she threw herself against him and his arms went around her.

"Th . . . that man," she managed to gasp, "he is . . . getting into my bed-room f . . . from the . . . roof."

Orion's arms tightened for a moment. Then he said quietly:

"Shut your eyes. I am going to get out of bed."

He moved as he spoke, and hardly understanding what was happening Athena had a glimpse of his body, slim, athletically muscled, silver in the moonlight, and realised he was naked.

Hastily she covered her face with her hands.

She sat trembling on the bed, her back towards him until, as he moved about, he said:

"Get into the bed. I will not let him touch you."

Fearfully she turned her head to see that Orion dressed in his trousers and shirt was pulling the furniture in front of the door.

Automatically, still too bemused really to know what she was doing, she got into the bed as he had ordered and pulled the sheet over her.

It was a large bed, larger than the one in her room, but she sat upright watching Orion dragging first the chest-of-drawers, then a table and various other pieces of furniture in front of the door, piling them up one upon the other.

He made a considerable noise while he was doing it, and she thought that if Kazandis was by this time in her bed-room he must realise what was happening.

She knew now that Orion had gambled on the Bandit respecting her because he had said she was not only a married woman but also carrying a child.

Perhaps he had believed, as she did, the age-old saying of the Ancient Greeks that the three most beautiful things in the world were a ship in full sail, a cornfield blowing in the wind, and woman with child.

He had been mistaken.

Kazandis respected nothing and nobody, and Athena trembled as she thought that if she had been asleep he would have entered her bed-room and been beside her before she was aware of his presence.

Then there would have been no escape.

Even now when she thought of the huge man with his pistol and his knife and the lustful expression in his eyes she could not be sure she was free of him.

She looked up at the ceiling trying to see if there was a trap-door to the roof in Orion's room as there had been in hers.

Then she realised that even if there were Kazandis would not have risked entering the room by such a method when there was a man in it.

He would be too vulnerable to assault as he descended,

for there would be no other way of coming down except feet first.

Then even as she thought about it she heard a heavy footstep on the landing outside.

Kazandis must have got into her bed-room as he intended only to find that his prey had flown.

He would have guessed where she had gone and he would know now that he had been right in assuming that Orion had lied to him when he said they were man and wife.

Athena held her breath, and fancied that Orion standing back a little way from the door and listening was also holding his.

She noticed that while he had pulled most of the furniture against the door there was a strongly made wooden chair beside him.

She guessed he intended if necessary to use this as a weapon and thought despairingly that although it might prove effective against an un-armed man, it would be useless against a bullet from a pistol with which Kazandis was doubtless an expert.

There was no sound of movement outside on the landing, and yet he was certainly there.

It was almost as if they could hear him breathing, almost as if they could see, mentally, his brain working, wondering if he should force his way into the room and overpower Orion, which he could be quite capable of doing, and then take Athena as he wished to do.

It must have been only a few seconds, but it seemed to Athena as if hours ticked by.

She was conscious only of the frenzied beating of her heart and the straining of her ears.

Then abruptly, unexpectedly, they heard Kazandis stump noisily down the stairs.

It was as if by the very noise he made he defied them and refused to acknowledge defeat.

They heard him fling open the door leading into the kitchen, cross the room beneath and let himself out of the Taverna, slamming the door behind him.

Athena felt her whole body relax and it was almost painful because the tension had been so strained.

Now Orion turned to face her and she saw in the moonlight that he was smiling.

"He has gone."

He came across the room towards her and sat down on the bed facing her, his eyes taking in the thin white muslin nightgown she was wearing, trimmed with lace, her fair hair falling over her shoulders and her eyes wide and frightened, looking into his.

"You are safe, Athena," he said again as if she had not understood. "He has gone."

"Suppose he . . . comes back?" she whispered.

"He will not. I should have anticipated that something like this would happen and I apologise for not taking better care of you."

"It was not your . . . fault," Athena said. "I thought he . . . believed you."

"I hoped he did, but marriage vows mean nothing to Kazandis and he has a reputation with women as with everything else."

"Can there be . . . women who like a man . . . like that?" Athena asked. Then she added wonderingly, "I did not . . . understand that men could . . . feel that way."

"About what?" Orion asked.

She was silent for a moment, then said in a voice he could hardly hear:

"He . . . asked for food and a . . . woman as if they were the . . . same kind of thing."

There was something so shocked in the tone of her voice that Orion reached out and put his hand over hers.

"Forget it," he said. "In the sheltered life I imagine you have led and will continue to lead when you go home you are never likely to meet another man like Kazandis. But you see, I was right in warning you that you must take care of yourself."

Athena drew in her breath.

"If . . . you had . . . not been . . . there . . ." she whispered.

"But I was here," Orion said firmly. "Forget it, Athena, it is something that might happen once in a million times, and then only to someone like yourself who has run away from those who are looking after her."

He paused before he asked:

"You have run away, have you not?"

Athena's eyes flickered and she looked down.

"Yes," she admitted after a moment.

"I can understand your wanting to go to Delphi alone," he said. "The presence of other people can spoil such an unforgettable experience as a first visit to the Shrine. At the same time you are too beautiful, Athena, to take chances with yourself."

There was a note in his voice which made her glance up at him quickly, and then it was impossible to look away.

For a moment they both stared at each other and Athena knew that something magnetic passed between them and she felt as if once again she was in his arms and his lips were on hers.

Abruptly Orion rose to his feet.

"I know you will not wish to go back to your own room," he said, "so we will change places."

Without thinking Athena put out her hands towards him.

"No . . . do not . . . leave me," she begged. "Please . . . do not . . . leave me."

She did not realise what she was asking, she only knew the fear of what had happened swept over her, and her whole body shrank from being alone and from the fear that however securely Orion might fasten the door Kazandis would somehow reach her.

There were two windows in this room and she was sure there was also a trap-door in the ceiling.

In her imagination she could almost see Kazandis killing Orion while he slept. Then there would be no-one to protect her or to prevent him from battering down the door and coming to her if he wished to do so.

It was the cry of a frightened child as she repeated:

"I . . . cannot be alone . . . I could not . . . bear it."

Orion walked to the window to stand in the moonlight.

She could see his profile with its perfect Greek features etched against the lintel and she thought, as she had thought before, that no man could be so handsome or indeed so irresistible.

"I understand what you are feeling, Athena," he said

after a moment, and she thought that his voice was deliberately controlled. "So you will stay here and I will stay with you, but you must understand that it will be difficult for me and I dare not touch you."

"Why?" Athena whispered.

She felt as if his words conjured up an enchantment that crept over her insidiously like a warm wave.

Now she was trembling, but not with fear.

She felt the same excitement she had felt when he kissed her and carried her up into the sky, where they had ceased to be human beings and had become gods.

"You know the answer to that," Orion answered harshly. "We said good-bye to each other, Athena. It is something we had to do because you have your life to live and I have mine. I had steeled myself not to see you again."

He sounded reproachful and Athena replied:

"I am . . . sorry."

She knew as she spoke that she was nothing of the sort, since now that the horror that had driven her to him was over, he was there.

She could look at him, she could listen to his voice even if it were only for a short time until once again they must leave each other.

"We can mean—nothing to each other in the future," Orion went on almost as if he spoke to himself, "and this is only prolonging the agony for me, if not for you."

It was a worse agony for her than he imagined, she thought.

Whatever the responsibilities to which he had to return, he did not understand that she had to go back to Mikis to tell the Prince that she would not marry him, to face her Aunt's anger and undoubtedly his.

She had thought before she came to Delphi that it would be very difficult, creating arguments and a situation with which she felt very inadequate to cope.

But now, having met Orion, she knew that not only to marry a man she did not love was impossible but whatever happened she would never now consent to marry the Prince.

Perhaps, she thought to herself, her bravery when she left the Palace had been superficial, and if the Prince had proved as pleasant and as charming as everybody averred she might have allowed herself to give in to the pressure that would undoubtedly have been put on her.

It would be, Athena was well aware, ignominious and humiliating to return to England unmarried.

She would have to make explanations not only to her family but also to those relatives and friends who had been let in on the secret of what her journey to Athens actually entailed.

There was also the Greek Ambassador and members of his staff who had come to Wadebridge Castle to discuss the proposals with her father and grandmother.

At the thought of the Dowager Marchioness Athena felt much more apprehensive than she did in regard to the rest of her family.

Her grandmother had always meant so much to her. She had taken her mother's place after she had died, and she had adored her from the moment she was old enough to recognise anyone.

The Dowager Marchioness was now old and in ill health, and Athena feared that after setting her heart on arranging this marriage between the Prince of her House and her favourite grandchild, to learn that her arrangements had failed would be almost like a death-blow.

"I cannot help it," Athena thought. "Much as I love Grandmama I cannot do as she wishes, not after having met Orion and learning what love between two people really means."

This was not the bloodless comradeship between a man and a woman who had common interests or who were prepared, because they met more or less on equal terms, to find friendship and perhaps even a sexual satisfaction in each other.

What she felt for Orion was love.

She looked at him across the room and she thought that his face shone with a light that was echoed in her own.

Together they had found perfect love, together they had penetrated the mystic innermost shrine of life itself.

How could either of them afterwards ever be satisfied with second best?

"I shall never marry," Athena thought wildly, and re-membered how often she had been told that marriage meant more to a woman than to a man.

Orion would find himself a wife—for all she knew he might have one already and she would merely remain in his mind as a moment of enchantment.

Perhaps he would remember her when the moon was full or when he came to Delphi again.

She felt as if her whole body cried out in protest, and yet what could she do?

As if with an effort Orion turned from the window.

"You must rest," he said. "Lie down, Athena, and try to go to sleep. You are quite safe while I am here and I am almost certain that we shall hear no more of Kazandis."

He paused to add:

"He has taken a large sum of money from Argeros, and as his action will doubtless be reported to the Military as will his robbery of last night at Arachova he will know that the soldiers are looking for him and will keep away from this region for some time."

Athena knew that he was talking to reassure her.

Looking round the bare room she said:

"What will . . . you do?"

"I am going to take one of the pillows from the bed," Orion said, "and there is a blanket in the cupboard. I prom-ise you I shall be quite comfortable on the floor. I have slept in worse places and everything in the Taverna is very clean."

"I . . . I would not wish you to be . . . uncomfortable. If you want to go to my room I will try to be . . . brave and you could leave the doors open so that you will hear if I . . . called out to you."

"Did you call or scream when you knew Kazandis was breaking into your room from the roof?" Orion enquired.

She did not answer and he smiled.

"I know exactly what happened. Your voice died in your throat. It is what happens to most people when they are really afraid."

He moved around to the other side of the bed and picked up a pillow.

"So we will do things my way, Athena. Lie down and try

to relax. You have had a long day and I feel quite certain you will sleep."

"And . . . you?"

"I am used to going without sleep," he answered, "and if I do doze off, it will be with one eye open, like wild animals who are seldom taken by surprise."

He walked across the room with the pillow in his hand and she had the feeling that he deliberately did not look at her when he came to the bed.

There was a cupboard on the opposite wall and on a shelf at the top of it was a folded blanket.

Orion drew it out and put it down on the floor in a patch of silvery light made by the moon-beams.

"Now you can see me," he said, "and you will not feel afraid. Good-night, Athena. Try to sleep."

"You will not . . . go in the . . . morning without . . . telling me?" she pleaded.

"I suspect that however carefully I move you will hear me," he answered, "but I shall be leaving very early. My horse has been ordered and to-night I told the man who brought you from Itea that you would be leaving at about seven o'clock. Madame Argeros will give you breakfast before you go."

He had arranged everything, Athena thought despairingly, and felt as if he almost told her what she must do for the rest of her life.

She wondered what he would say if she confided in him.

Would he, because he was Greek, tell her that her duty lay in marrying the Prince? Would his patriotism mean more to him than his feelings for her?

She could not believe that any man feeling as he must have felt when he swept her up to the stars would wish to hand her over tamely to another man who might teach her to love him.

And yet after all what did she know about Orion? They had talked together for a few brief hours.

Yet they had found the secret of eternity together and that meant more than a lifetime of knowledge.

"Shall I tell him?" Athena asked herself.

Then she thought there was really no point. He had already given her the answer to her problem and as far as she was concerned it was "no".

It was not only that she knew she could not bear another man to touch her; it would also be intolerable to live in Greece with the knowledge that once she was married somehow, by some chance, she might encounter Orion again.

She knew it would be impossible not to look for him in every crowd, at every party, in every street.

She would be searching the faces of every man she saw for those perfect features, for that slim, athletic body, for the curve of his dark head.

And if they did meet—what then?

She had no idea what he did. All she knew with certainty was that he was the most cultured and civilised man she had ever met.

That was not to say that he might not live in very humble circumstances while she . . . she would be a Princess!

"I must go away," Athena thought. "I must return to England and forget there was ever such a country as Greece and one man who means to me everything that was the splendour, the beauty and the inspiration of the past."

Orion had arranged his hard bed to his satisfaction and now he said:

"You are not lying down, Athena, as I told you to do. Shut your eyes and think of all the happiness we have known to-day. Forget everything else."

He was still thinking that she was afraid, Athena knew. But her thoughts were far away from Kazandis, and instead she was thinking only of Orion and what it would mean to lose him.

But because of the note of authority in his voice she did as he told her. She lay down, pulling the sheet over her shoulders and turning her cheek against the soft pillow.

"Good-night, Athena," Orion said as he lay down on the floor.

"Will you . . . always remember to-day?" she asked softly.

"You know the answer to that question," he replied. "It would be impossible for me ever to forget."

His words were somehow comforting but she wanted to

ask him so much more. Yet instinctively she knew that if she did he would not give her the right answers.

All the time they had been together she had known without being told in words that there was a deep reserve about him and it was that reserve which she knew now was like an impregnable wall between them.

And after all, what could she suggest?

That they should meet after she returned to the Palace? That was impossible!

That she should not return to the Palace?

Athena knew in her heart that was what she wanted!

She wanted Orion to ask her to stay with him, and unbelievable though it seemed, she knew what her answer would be.

Whatever the hardships she might encounter, whatever the heart-breaks, if they came, it would be worth everything to be with him if only for a year, a month, a week, any time however short, so that their love would be complete.

How strange it was, Athena thought, that while most people looked forward to living perhaps seventy years, all she wanted to live was just one moment of time however brief in the arms of one man.

It was difficult to express even to herself, but she knew that the life that had been hers for eighteen years had not been the fulfillment of everything of which she was capable.

There was no reason to think, however many years she lived in the future, that they would be any different.

In those minutes, when Orion kissed her and she had experienced a wonder and glory that was not of this world, she had lived—perhaps a whole lifetime—to the fullest of what any man or woman was capable and still remain human.

"How can I lose it? How can I let it go?" she asked herself and knew there was no answer.

Athena was very innocent, but she could not help feeling that any other man in the world in the situation in which she was now would not be lying on the floor on the other side of the room but beside her.

She attracted Orion, he felt about her as she felt about him, and yet deliberately he would not accept the fact that she was all too willing to surrender herself. He would not allow his desires to overthrow the conviction of his mind.

She respected him for it as she knew he would respect her, and yet her whole being wanted him so insistently, so violently, that only a lifetime of self-control prevented Athena from running to lie down beside him.

She wanted to feel herself close against him, she wanted to find in his arms not only the wonder and the glory of love but the protection and the sense of safety which she knew only he could give her.

She felt as if her whole heart cried out to him to understand.

She dared not put what she was feeling into words, and although she knew he was not asleep he did not speak to her again.

Slowly the hours of the night passed, the moonlight gradually began to fade and the silver light was no longer so intense in the little room.

It was then, just before dawn came, that Athena knew Orion was asleep.

For the first time she heard his even breathing and she wondered if any two people had ever spent a stranger night, both needing each other, both awake and both respecting a silent separation that was self-imposed.

"I love him!" Athena thought to herself. "I love him so completely and intensely that even if he wishes to crucify me, as indeed he is doing, I will obey him and do what he wants."

"I will go back," she told herself.

Because she had known Orion, she would face all the difficulties and all the unpleasantness that awaited her with a courage and a self-control which he himself would show in such circumstances.

She would be quite firm—she would promise the Prince large sums of money for the poor of Parnassus.

She had learnt that the whole country was in desperate need of money, suffering from centuries of crippling taxes levied by the Turks and now by the King.

It would not be like accepting the money for himself, and she was certain she could give it to him in such a way that he would not feel humiliated by her generosity.

Then she would go home.

She had no wish to see Athens again; she had no wish to see any other part of Greece.

She just wanted to return in an English ship to the quiet life of Wadebridge Castle.

She knew her father liked having her there with him and she would devote herself to him for the rest of his life.

They would ride together, hunt in the winter, and now that she was old enough she would play hostess instead of her grandmother.

Although she supposed there would be men who would want to make love to her and to marry her, she knew it would be impossible to accept them.

"I shall be dedicated to an ideal," she told herself a little bitterly, "and ideals can be very . . . cold and . . . lonely . . . especially when one grows . . . old."

She would fill her days, she would make certain of that. Only as far as her heart was concerned it had been given to one man and it would be impossible for her to give it to any other.

She thought of the many orphanages that her father had on his enormous Estate.

Perhaps when he died, Athena thought, there would be a child to whom she would take a fancy and whom she could adopt.

Anyway there would be plenty of children for her to spend her huge fortune on and England would benefit instead of Greece.

It was easy to plan, but as she sat up very, very carefully so as not by a sudden movement to awaken Orion, she could see him in the gradually lightening sky, lying fast asleep.

Lying on his back with his shirt open nearly to the waist he looked, Athena thought, like a fallen god, perhaps like one of the statues that had once stood in Delphi and which Nero had carried away to Rome.

She had also meant to go to Rome, but now she knew that was another place that was barred to her.

How could she bear to find carved in marble or cast in bronze the man she had known as a living, pulsating being who had sent her blood racing through her veins?

"If I were an artist," Athena thought, "I would try to draw him as he is now. Then when I felt unhappy and miserable I could look at the sketch and remember what he meant to me."

But she knew there was no need for a drawing, a painting or even a sculpture.

Each line of Orion's face was indelibly etched in her mind and she knew that every time she shut her eyes and thought of him he would be there in her consciousness.

"I love you! I love you!" Athena thought looking at him. "Wherever you go, wherever you may be, my love will be with you, protecting you, keeping you, perhaps inspiring you, even if you are unaware of it."

If one believed in prayer, she thought, one must also believe in thought-transference: her prayers and thoughts and living sparks from within herself would wing out across the sea towards Orion and find him.

They would form an aura of protection around him, and perhaps because of it the light that she sensed came from him would bring inspiration and help to all those with whom he came into contact.

"If that is all I can do for you, my beloved," Athena told him silently, "then at least it will be some small way by which I can express my love."

She sat looking at him as the room grew lighter and lighter.

When the first rays of the sun appeared over the horizon suddenly there was a golden glow and the whole room was transformed.

It was then that Orion awoke.

He opened his eyes and sat up abruptly and saw that Athena was looking at him.

"I have been asleep."

"You did not sleep for a very long time," she answered.

"It must be late!" he exclaimed, "and I meant to leave early."

"Does it matter so . . . tremendously?"

"I did not mean to see you again."

"But that was . . . impossible: you could not have . . . left without . . . waking me."

"Then as I am so late," Orion said, "I will see you off first. I want to make sure that you are safe, and perhaps that is what I should have arranged in the first place."

He was trying to speak in an ordinary, matter-of-fact manner, and she knew that having looked at her once he deliberately looked away and did not glance again in her direction.

Now he started to move the furniture from the door, putting it back in the places where it stood normally.

After he had finished he walked onto the landing and crossed into her room; she knew that he was satisfying himself that it was safe for her to go there.

He came back into the bed-room.

"I am going downstairs to wash and shave," he said, "and as I am sure Madame Argeros will be awake by now I will order breakfast for both of us. I will also see that your horse is ready for you when you have eaten."

"Thank you," Athena said.

She knew he had taken charge and there was nothing for her to do except to obey his orders.

Orion turned towards the door, then as he reached it he looked back at Athena as he had not done since the first moment of waking.

"You are very beautiful in the morning," he said in a deep voice. "You look like Persephone must have done when she came back from the darkest bowels of the earth to bring spring and hope to mankind."

His eyes seemed to take in everything about her, the soft outline of her breasts beneath the thin nightgown, the gold of her hair falling over her shoulders, the light in her grey eyes which seemed to hold the reflection of the sunlight.

Then he was gone and she heard him clattering down the stairs and a moment later his voice talking to Madame Argeros.

She got out of bed and went to her own room.

She washed in cold water which was no hardship as she realised that soon the sun would be very hot.

She dressed herself and because she knew Orion liked her without a bonnet she decided to carry hers as she had done the day before.

Then she packed her nightgown and all the small things she had brought with her in her Greek bag, stuffing her shawl on the top of them.

She glanced round the room to see that she had forgotten nothing, then for the first time glanced up apprehensively at the trap-door in the ceiling.

It was open and she could see the sky through it.

It was a large aperture and now she saw as she had not noticed before that in one corner of the room there was a ladder which was obviously used in the great heat of the summer by those who wished to sleep on the roof as many Greeks did.

She felt herself shiver as she thought of Kazandis letting himself down into her room.

They had been lucky that he had not forced the issue once he knew where she had gone and sought her across the landing.

She could not have borne, she thought, to watch a fight between Orion and that great hulking Bandit with his huge body and evil eyes.

Of one thing she was quite certain, that he would not have fought fairly and he would undoubtedly have been prepared to fire his pistol and murder Orion if it suited him.

Because the mere thought of what might have happened made her shiver and because above all things she wanted to be with Orion again Athena ran down the stairs.

He was sitting at the table in the kitchen and Madame Argeros was cooking at the stove.

"Good-morning," Madame said as Athena appeared. "Because you are here Orion has asked for an English breakfast and the eggs are ready."

"I am hungry enough to eat a dozen," Orion smiled.

He had risen as he spoke and pulled out a chair so that Athena could sit next to him.

"There's not a dozen," Madame replied, "so you'll have to make do with bacon from the pig we killed only a few weeks ago—and very good it has proved."

"Even Kazandis admitted you had the best food in the whole region," Orion said.

"Kazandis! Don't speak of the man," Madame said bitterly. "He has taken all our money. I warned Dimitrios openly yesterday that we had too much in the house, but what man ever listens until it's too late?"

"I am sorry for you, Madame," Athena said. "You must tell me what I owe you for staying here last night."

"You owe me nothing," Madame said almost sharply. "You are a friend of Orion's, and that is enough. We are not so poverty-stricken—Kazandis or not—that we have to take from our friends."

"But . . . I cannot let you . . ." Athena began only to feel Orion's hand on her arm.

She looked at him in perplexity; but he shook his head and she understood that she must accept Madame's gesture of generosity and not argue about it.

"It is kind of you," Athena said, "and thank you very much."

But she felt as if she must do something for them and so she said:

"As it is going to be very hot to-day I shall not need my shawl and I wonder if I might leave it for Nonika as she was kind enough to give up her room, and I am sure she will find it useful."

She drew the shawl as she spoke from her bag and remembered that it had in fact been an expensive purchase and had come from Bond Street.

Madame's face softened.

"That would be very kind," she said. "Nonika is collecting things for her trousseau, but for all Greek girls, as things are expensive, it takes a long time and the shawl will therefore be most acceptable."

"Then I am very glad for her to have it," Athena said.

She glanced at Orion as she spoke, hoping that he approved, and knew by his smile and the expression in his eyes that he did.

She felt a warm feeling within her because he was pleased with her, but when she looked at him he looked away and she knew that their parting was near and he was as conscious of it as she was.

Their eggs and bacon were set down in front of them. There was hot coffee, crisp bread and honey which Orion explained came from the bees around Delphi.

"Perhaps they are specially sanctified," he said, "for I

always think that the honey here is the most delicious in Greece, although quite a number of my countrymen will tell me I am mistaken."

"Does honey differ in flavour from province to province?" Athena asked.

"Yes, it does," Madame exclaimed before he could speak, "and perhaps the honey from Mount Olympus is the best of all."

"I still continue to disagree with you, Madame," Orion said helping himself to another spoonful.

"You are prejudiced!" Madame Argeros laughed, "but as long as you go on thinking that we have the best, I for one am satisfied."

"Could you ever question it?" he asked.

They finished their breakfast and now Dimitrios Argeros appeared in the doorway to say that their horses were waiting outside.

Athena rose to her feet.

"You are not going in the same direction as I am?" she asked.

He shook his head.

"No. I am riding home over the mountains," he replied, "but I have already spoken to Spiros which, by the way, is the name of the man who brought you here, and he will take very good care of you—as you must take care of yourself."

He spoke the last words in English in a low voice, and Athena looked up at him and for a moment they were both very still.

He walked towards the door.

Athena thanked Madame Argeros for her kindness, then followed him.

Outside their two horses were waiting and she saw that Orion's was very different from the animal that had brought her up from Itea.

His was a black stallion, extremely high-spirited, and the man who was holding it was having some difficulty in keeping it under control.

It was plunging and bucking and it seemed doubtful that his hold on the bridle would be effective.

"Better not waste much time in mounting that animal,"

Dimitrios Argeros said. "I hear it nearly kicked a stable down during the night."

"He needs exercise and it is his way of telling me that I have stayed here for too long."

"It has been our gain," Dimitrios Argeros said with surprising eloquence for him. "Come again soon, Orion. You are always welcome—you know that."

"Thank you," Orion replied.

Then as he held out his hand his horse gave another terrific plunge and nearly swept the man holding the bridle off his feet.

"You had best go," Athena said hastily. "There is no hurry for me."

"Perhaps you are right."

He looked at her for a moment, but did not attempt to take her hand. Then as if he had no words in which to express himself he moved away and with surprising ease swung himself into the saddle of the plunging and bucking stallion.

Almost immediately it seemed the animal knew that his master had taken control, and although he fidgeted he no longer proved to be so obstreperous.

Then, as if he was as eager as the horse he was riding to be gone, Orion turned and started to descend the steep road towards the village.

Athena felt as if she could not bear to watch him go and went towards her own horse.

A line written by Lord Byron was ringing in her ears.

*"Gone shimmering through the dream of things that were."*

"How can I bear it, how can I live without him?" she asked despairingly.

Spiros was greeting her delightedly.

"Good-morning, Lady—very nice day for ride to Itea."

She forced a smile to her lips.

"I have not yet said good-bye to Nonika," she said to Dimitrios Argeros.

"I'll call her," he said and he turned and went into the Taverna.

As he went Athena heard a footstep behind her.

She turned thinking that Nonika must have approached from another direction, but coming round the side of the Taverna through some bushes where he must have been hiding was Kazandis!

For a moment she could not credit that it was really the Bandit and that he was actually walking towards her.

She felt her heart give a terrified jerk within her breast.

Without speaking, without saying anything, he came nearer still and before she had tine to move away or obey her impulse to run he picked her up in his arms and flung her over his shoulder.

The shock of the impact on the hardness of his body took her breath away. Then as she heard Spiros shout she managed to scream.

She screamed and screamed again and it was to Orion she called, her screams gradually giving way to his name which seemed stifled and ineffectual as she lay head downwards over Kazandis's shoulder.

He turned back through the bushes the way he had come, and moving at what seemed to Athena to be a tremendous speed, he started to climb the mountain behind the Taverna.

She tried to strike at him with her arms, but hanging down his back she was quite ineffectual and he held her tightly below the knees so that it was very difficult to struggle in any way at all.

He was climbing, climbing, and she tried to see if anyone was following them. But it was impossible for her to raise her head with the blood flowing into it.

Stones fell, dislodged by his feet, bouncing and rumbling their way down the steep mountainside, and as he zig-zagged she knew that he was keeping to the goat-paths and also that he knew the way without faltering.

By now she was breathless and unable to scream any more or cry out for Orion. She could only fear that in fact he had gone too far and not heard Spiros call or her own screams.

If he had not heard, she wondered if Spiros would ride after him and tell him what had occurred.

There was so much discomfort in hanging head downwards over Kazandis's back with the fur of his sheepskin coat tickling her face and smelling most unpleasant, that it was difficult to think clearly.

As they went higher there seemed to be a strange and uncanny silence around them. Athena wished to struggle again but she was too afraid.

She could see even with limited vision that the mountainside was very steep. There were patches of moss and occasionally twisting tree-trunks and small trees, their green leaves a strange contrast to the bare rocks.

She was well aware that where they were going was almost as steep and perilous as the Shining Cliffs, and should she fall she would roll down the mountainside in a manner which if it did not kill her would certainly bruise and maim her whole body.

'What can I do . . . what can I do?' Athena thought frantically.

She knew that she was in Kazandis's power and supposed it would be impossible now for Orion to save her.

She thought that she must die before he touched her and wondered if it would be possible for her to shoot herself with his pistol or stab herself with his knife.

What was happening was so terrifying that her brain seemed to be paralysed by the horror of it.

The position in which he carried her made her feel almost apoplectic, and yet she knew that her only salvation lay in Orion.

She felt her whole being calling to him as she had managed to cry out at first, if only briefly.

Surely he would understand? Perhaps he would get a gun from somewhere in the village. Perhaps he would bring soldiers to her assistance.

But then she knew that even if he did so it would be too late.

What Kazandis intended to do to her would be done long before the Military could climb the cliff or Orion come to her assistance.

"I must . . . die. God . . . help me. I have to . . . die!"

She felt that the God to whom she had prayed in the quietness and security of England was very far away, and she thought that now only Apollo or perhaps Hermes, the god of Travellers, could help her.

Higher and higher Kazandis climbed and now the stones beneath each foot-fall had become a kind of shower, and yet still he twisted and turned, obviously sure of his way between the craggy rocks.

Vaguely Athena realised that he was moving all the time to the left but there was a whole range of the Parnassus mountains to choose from and it was impossible to speculate which way he was likely to go or where he was taking her.

Now it seemed to her that she had sudden glimpses of what seemed to be a sheer precipice beneath them, and because beside the horror of what was happening, it was terrifying to think of rolling down it, she shut her eyes.

Kazandis must have been carrying her for nearly half an hour, and Athena with the blood in her head found it impossible to think any longer, but only to feel choked and dizzy.

Suddenly he took a step upwards, bent his head then set her down roughly on the ground.

For a moment everything seemed to go black and she thought she was dying.

Then as Athena opened her eyes she realised she was in a cave.

It was not a large cave and the roof under which she was lying only just enabled Kazandis to stand upright.

He was looking down at her and, dazed and bewildered though she was, the look in his eyes instinctively made her try to shrink away from him while her hands went to her breasts.

"Kazandis does not give up easily," he said in the boastful tones he had used in the Taverna the night before. "I want you and now you're mine!"

Athena could not speak, she could only stare up at him in terror.

"Yes, mine!" he repeated with satisfaction. "Get your breath. No-one will find you here."

It was not so much a question of her getting her breath, but of him getting his.

Perhaps because he had been in prison for so long, the

burden of carrying her up the mountain had taken its toll even on such a strong man.

There were beads of sweat running down his forehead and over his cheeks.

He pulled off his sheepskin coat and flung it down on the ground and she saw that his shirt was stained and his hairy arms were wet.

He walked further into the cave and as her eyes followed him apprehensively she saw that the cave opened out and was far larger than it had first appeared from where she was lying.

From the darkness of the shadows Kazandis produced a bottle and pulling out the cork he lifted it to his lips and drank noisily.

"Have some?"

He held the bottle out to her and when she shook her head he said:

"Please yourself! There's plenty if you change your mind."

Now taking a dirty rag from his pocket, which he doubtless thought of as a handkerchief, he wiped his forehead and his cheeks and rubbed his hands on it before he flung it to the floor of the cave.

"You're a pretty piece," he said, "although you've not much to say for yourself."

"Let . . . me . . . go," Athena managed to articulate. "If you . . . want money . . . I can . . . give it to you . . . I am . . . rich."

"Rich—when you are staying in a Taverna?" he laughed.

"It may seem . . . strange," Athena answered, "but I am in fact . . . very rich . . . if you will let me . . . go to . . . safety . . . I will pay you . . . well."

"And how shall I collect it?" Kazandis asked jeeringly, "or will you ask the Military to hand it to me?"

"I will see you have it . . . and that no-one will . . . molest you," Athena said earnestly. "That I . . . promise."

He laughed and the noise of it seemed to echo and re-echo round the cave.

"I've got all the money I want for the moment," he said, "and when I want more—I shall take it! But now I want you!"

He wiped his lips as he spoke with the back of his hand, and Athena thinking it was preliminary to kissing her gave a little cry of terror.

The mere fact that she was frightened seemed to please Kazandis and he smiled.

Then as he stepped towards her and she thought despairingly she must somehow try to snatch his knife and kill herself, he glanced towards the opening of the cave.

As if a thought had suddenly struck him, he went to it and looked out.

As Athena watched him it seemed to her that something seemed to hold his attention and he did not move but remained looking down below them.

A faint hope stirred within her, and moving for the first time since he had thrust her down onto the sandy floor, she got to her knees and edged forward so that she too could look out through the opening.

She saw what had attracted Kazandis's attention.

They were high up over what appeared to be almost an impassable precipice of steep rock.

Far beneath, almost directly below them, a man was climbing, not zig-zagging as they had done, but climbing directly upwards.

With an indescribable feeling of relief and gratitude Athena knew it was Orion.

# CHAPTER FIVE

Kazandis stood staring down for some moments, then gave a grunt like an animal.

"You had better let me go," Athena said. "If people are coming to rescue me, you will not get the money I have offered you."

She thought for a moment that the Bandit was considering what she said. Then he laughed the same loud, jeering laugh which once again echoed round the cave.

"You think they'll find me?" he asked. "They'll never find me here, and I've caves, many caves which only the wolves know."

He came back into the cave and because she felt giddy looking down from such a great height, Athena also moved backwards.

He looked at her and his eyes narrowed unpleasantly and he moved as if he would touch her.

She gave a scream and before he could stop her she

moved back again to the entrance of the cave and leaned out of it shouting:

"Orion! Orion! I am here! Save me!"

Her voice seemed to be swept away from her by the height and she felt it was shrill and ineffective; but it obviously disturbed Kazandis, for he seized her roughly and pulling her back into the cave threw her down on the floor.

"You be quiet!" he commanded.

There was something ferocious in the way he spoke, and although Athena tried to be brave she winced away from him in a manner which told him all too clearly how fearful she was.

"If you betray me you suffer for it!"

He raised his arm menacingly and for a second she thought he was going to strike her. Then as if another idea came to him he grunted again and moved further into the cave, disappearing into the shadows.

She wondered where he had gone.

Then because she could not believe that he was speaking the truth when he said it would be impossible for Orion to find her, she went once again to the opening and looked down.

For a moment she could not see him and she felt an icy hand clutching at her heart in case he had fallen or given up the climb as impossible.

Then she saw he was rounding a rock and perhaps following the track that Kazandis had taken.

She was staring down at him wondering whether she should scream to him again and risk Kazandis's anger, when she heard the Bandit coming back from the darkness.

She moved away, ashamed that she should be so afraid, unable to prevent an instinctive sense of self-protection.

Then she saw he was not looking at her, but instead was carrying in his hand a long-barrelled gun.

She looked at it with horror, until as he started to load it she asked in a quivering voice:

"Wh . . what are you . . . going to . . . do?"

"Kill the dog that's following me!" he answered.

She gave a cry.

"B . . but you . . . cannot do that!"

"Who'll stop me?"

He tipped the powder into the breech and said as if he spoke to himself:

"Still dry after all this time. There's no better gun in the whole of Parnassus!"

With an effort Athena forced herself to speak quietly.

"I have told you that I am rich," she said. "Very rich. I will give you a thousand pounds . . . five thousand pounds . . . ten thousand pounds, if you do not fire at that man who is following us."

Kazandis did not answer and after a moment Athena said:

"Perhaps you do not understand pounds. I will give you drachmas, a million if you like. You will be a rich man . . . a very rich man. You can buy anything you like . . . go anywhere you want."

She thought for a moment that he might be tempted by her offer. But then he looked up at her and she saw the sneer on his face as he said:

"Give it to me now and you can go!"

"Of course I cannot give it to you now," Athena replied. "I have not so much money here with me. But as I have told you I am rich, a very rich Englishwoman."

"I'm no fool," Kazandis said slowly. "Rich English tourists don't travel alone. They have friends with them, Guides, Couriers. They hire many donkeys and horses and have much luggage."

"All the things I own are in Mikis," Athena said, "and I have money there, a lot of money."

"With many people to guard it?"

There was no doubt that he did not believe her and thought she was lying.

Athena watched him white-faced as he finished loading the gun, then went to the mouth of the cave.

He crouched on the edge of it looking down and she knew that he was waiting until Orion presented him with a good target.

"You cannot do this . . . you cannot!" she said frantically. "Listen to me . . . please listen! I will give you all the money I promised you and I will be to you anything you want if you will spare the man down there. I will be your woman . . . your wife . . . whatever you require . . . but please do not kill him!"

"I have you here with me," Kazandis answered. "I've all the money I need. Why should I bargain?"

"Because I can give you so much more," Athena said frantically. "You must believe me. You must listen to what I tell you. A million drachmas shall be yours and I will stay with you and not go away, so long as you will spare the life of that man who you say will not be able to find us and is therefore doing you no harm."

Kazandis laughed. It was not a pleasant sound.

"I kill many men. Why should I spare this one?"

He put his gun to his shoulder as he spoke and looked down the barrel.

"Spare him! . . . please spare him!" Athena pleaded. "What can I say . . . what can I offer you to make you understand that you must . . . not do this . . . terrible thing?"

She drew in her breath before she went on, her voice low and intense:

"It will be murder . . . sheer murder and all the soldiers will be determined that you shall be found. They will find you wherever you may hide, and this time they will hang you . . . there will be no escape."

"They'll not find me," Kazandis said confidently.

"They will! They will!" Athena cried.

Once again he was looking down the barrel, and now, although Athena could not see Orion, she realised that he must be below them but a little to the left.

Kazandis shifted his position so that the gun was pointing almost directly downwards.

He was taking aim, his finger was on the trigger.

"No! No!" Athena cried desperately.

Then as she thought he must fire and Orion would die she flung herself against him in an effort to snatch the gun from his hands.

She took him by surprise and although she was not strong the fact that she snatched at the gun made him lose his hold on it and it slipped from his hands.

He reached out towards it, grasping in the air to catch it before it slipped from his reach. As he did so, hardly realising what she was doing, Athena pushed his shoulder with all her strength.

For a moment it seemed as if she made no impact upon him, then Kazandis strove to keep his balance and fell.

He gave one last grunt and with a cry which was like that of an animal in agony he disappeared from sight.

One moment he was there, a monstrous figure in the opening of the cave, and the next minute he was gone and all she could see was the sky and the sun was blinding her eyes.

Athena had also lost her balance in her effort against Kazandis, and she lay sprawled on the sandy floor, too bemused, too shocked by what had happened to move.

Then suddenly the horror of it swept over her.

She had killed a man!

Killed him intentionally and deliberately . . . although it had all happened so quickly that it was hard to know the exact moment when she had meant it to happen.

She lay panting. Then because she could not bear to look below and see the broken remains of the man she had killed, she moved back into the cave and sat with her back against the wall and covered her face with her hands.

It seemed as if she had passed through a nightmare from which now she could not awake.

It seemed altogether unreal: her discomfort and fear while being carried up the mountain; the terror she felt at Kazandis's presence; the agony she had suffered knowing he intended to kill Orion!

Now he was dead—and she was responsible.

She sat trembling, trying to think clearly, but all she was conscious of was the violent beating of her heart and a kind of indescribable horror that prevented her thinking of anything but Kazandis's scream as he fell.

Then suddenly there was a sound and without taking her hands from her face she knew that someone had entered the cave.

For a moment it was impossible to move or to breathe; then Orion's arms were around her and he was holding her close to him.

"It is all right, my darling," he said. "It is over. You are safe."

"I . . . killed him! Oh, Orion . . . I killed . . . him!"

He held her a little closer and after a moment she said:

"He meant . . . to shoot you . . . and nothing I could . . . say . . . nothing I could . . . offer him would . . . stop him."

"He is dead," Orion said quietly. "That is all that matters. He did not hurt you, my precious little goddess?"

"N . . no," Athena whispered.

"Put your hands down and listen to me."

Athena felt so weak that she was prepared to do anything she was told.

She lowered her hands and raised her eyes.

He was very near her and now that she could look at him the feeling of horror began to recede.

"I know what you have been through," Orion said in a low voice, "but darling, you are to forget it ever happened, and you are to tell no-one—no-one, do you understand?—that it was due to you that Kazandis died."

"B . . but I k . . killed him."

"To save me," he said, "and it was very brave and very wonderful of you. But I would not wish you to be interrogated, because that is what it would mean, by the Military. And I do not want you in the future to be pointed out as the woman who killed Kazandis."

"Was it very . . . wrong and very . . . wicked of me?" Athena asked.

He smiled and it seemed to illuminate his face.

"My darling, it is what hundreds of people have been trying to do for a very long time. He was an animal, a reptile, an enemy of the people, a man without morals, without principles and without mercy. The world is well rid of him."

Athena gave a little sigh and laid her head against Orion's shoulder.

"Remember, my sweet, that he over-balanced and fell— that is what happened."

He drew her close, as he went on:

"How could I imagine that such a terrible thing would happen to you the moment I left your side?"

"He was . . . hiding in the bushes by the Taverna," Athena said. "When he carried me . . . away I was only afraid you would not . . . hear me calling for . . . you."

"I heard Spiros and I heard you scream," Orion replied. "I could not imagine what had occurred."

"But you . . . came back."

"Of course I came back," he answered. "I knew that you of all people would not scream unless something very terrible had occurred."

Athena gave a little sigh.

"What did you . . . feel when you . . . knew what had . . . happened?"

For a moment Orion did not reply, and because she was surprised she looked up at him.

His eyes on hers and after a moment he said:

"I knew that not only must I rescue you, but also that I must never lose you again."

Athena looked at him wide-eyed, then he said:

"You belong to me, my darling. I knew it when we first met, and when we kissed in the moonlight and together touched the summit of bliss."

Athena made a little movement as if she would draw nearer to him, but she did not speak and after a moment he went on:

"I thought I was doing the right thing for both of us when I decided that we must go our separate ways, and we would remember as if it were a dream what we had meant to each other."

"And now . . . ?"

"Now I know that I cannot live without you. You are mine, Athena, and nothing and nobody shall ever keep us apart."

Athena felt as though the whole cave was illuminated with a brilliant light.

There was a tremor in her voice as she asked:

"Do you . . . mean that? Are you . . . sure of what you are . . . saying?"

"Quite, quite sure," he answered. "I love you, my darling and I know that you love me."

His voice seemed to ring out as he went on:

"It is not just a question of love, it is because your spirit is my spirit, as my soul is your soul. We belong to one another.

We are one and I will spend the whole of my life protecting you and taking care of you."

"That is all I . . . want," Athena whispered. "I love . . . you! I have loved you from the very first moment I met you and although it has been . . . wonderful it has also been . . . agonising."

Her voice broke on the words.

"My precious, my poor little love. You shall not suffer any more," he said with a deep tenderness in his voice.

Then his lips found hers and she knew she surrendered her whole self, body and soul, to his kiss.

Later when they had told each other of their love, and kissed again and again, Orion smoothed back Athena's hair from her flushed cheeks and said:

"Now, my darling, I think we should make plans to return to civilisation. It is still quite early in the day, but there is a lot to do if we are to be married this evening."

"M . . married?"

Athena gazed at him wide-eyed.

"I thought that was what we were talking about," he said with a smile, "but of course I have not really asked you. Will you marry me, my lovely one?"

He saw the expression in her eyes, then he put his hand under her chin and tipped her face up to his.

"I know," he said. "I know all the things we ought to say—'we do not know each other very well'—but we do! 'We have only just met'—but that is not true! We have known each other since the beginning of time! 'We ought to have a conventional ceremony with all our relatives present'—but do either of us want that?"

"No . . . no," Athena said instinctively.

"That is exactly what I feel," he said, "and because I dare not let you out of my sight—because I have no intention of losing you—I intend to marry you this evening. Nothing else is of any consequence."

"Oh, Orion . . . do you really . . . mean it?" Athena asked.

"You have not answered my question," he said with a smile. "Will you marry me?"

Just for a moment Athena thought of her family, of her Aunt waiting for her in the Palace, of her grandmother, of the King in Athens. Then she knew that Orion was right, and that none of them mattered.

"I want to marry you," she said, "more than I have ever wanted anything in my whole life."

"Then let us get married," Orion smiled.

"I wondered when you were . . . leaving me whether in fact you had a . . . wife already."

He laughed.

"You need have no fears on that score, and I am not going to ask if you have a husband. No-one could be so soft and sweet, so innocent, and not be as pure as Athena herself."

Because there was a note in his voice that made her feel shy, Athena hid her face against his neck.

He kissed her hair, then said:

"There are a thousand things we have to tell each other which will give us something to talk about on our honeymoon! But all that concerns me at this moment is that you should be my wife and that no-one—and I mean no-one—shall take you from me."

She supposed he was thinking of Kazandis, but her thoughts went to the Prince.

Supposing by marrying her Orion should incur the hostility of the Prince he had supplanted?

Then she remembered how rich she was and knew that if the Prince resented their marriage and made trouble for them in Greece they could go elsewhere.

The whole world was theirs, and she need not be afraid.

"But in order to get married," Orion was saying, "we have to get away from this eagle's nest."

He went to the mouth of the cave as he spoke and stood looking down.

After a moment Athena followed him.

She took one glance at the precipice beneath them; then afraid that she might see Kazandis's body lying somewhere at the foot of it she looked away and said:

"I am . . . afraid of . . . heights."

"I thought perhaps you might be," he answered, "and

this is no ordinary height. Kazandis hid himself very cleverly, but fortunately I guessed where he had gone."

"How could you have guessed?" Athena asked.

"After he was captured two years ago, a survey of the mountains showed the most likely spots in which he had his hiding-places. There are a large number of caves of all sorts in this part of the world, and when I saw him carrying you up the mountain I knew the whereabouts of this particular cave and was sure that was where he was taking you."

"It was lucky ... very lucky that you should have ... known that," Athena exclaimed.

She could not help remembering the expression on Kazandis's face as he looked at her and the lust she had seen in his eyes.

As if he knew what she was thinking, Orion put his arms around her and kissed first her eyes, then her cheeks, and lastly her mouth.

"You are to think of no-one but me," he said masterfully. "I am jealous even of Kazandis if he occupies your thoughts."

"I want ... only to ... think of ... you," Athena murmured.

He kissed her again, then he went to the entrance of the cave and gave a shout of joy.

"Here they come!" he said. "I thought Dimitrios Argeros would not fail me."

"What is it? Who is there?" Athena asked.

"I shouted to him as I started to climb after you for some of the men from the village to bring ropes with them," Orion answered. "I was sure there must be an easier way than climbing directly up the mountainside, but I could not wait to take it myself."

Athena knew with a little throb of her heart why he had realised only too well that there was every reason for haste.

He was aware why Kazandis had carried her away, and if he had not arrived until now it would have been too late.

"Could any man be more wonderful?" she asked herself.

Athena thought only of Orion all the time he and the men from the village were helping her down the mountainside.

It was not easy although she was roped to Orion and he to several others.

There were moments when the world below seemed to swim before her eyes, and she thought that however tightly they held her she must fall as Kazandis had fallen to die on the rocks below.

Somehow, although they took a long time, they managed it and when finally they came down into the village Madame Argeros was waiting to fold Athena in her arms and kiss her as if she was her own long-lost child.

It was difficult to say anything amid the babble of noise, the congratulations that were showered upon Orion, and the excited comments of everyone, including the children.

Madame Argeros took Athena into the Taverna and made her sit down on a chair.

"You must be exhausted," she said. "There's some coffee waiting for you and that will do you more good than the wine which Orion will be opening as soon as he can get here."

"I would . . . rather have coffee," Athena managed to say.

"Drink it up," Madame admonished, "then you are going straight upstairs to lie down on the bed. I will bring you up something to eat."

Because Athena really did feel exhausted she drank her coffee as Madame had ordered, and went upstairs.

"You will be more comfortable in the big bed," Madame Argeros said. "Nonika has put fresh sheets on it."

Athena was only too glad to agree.

She knew it was stupid of her but she felt an aversion to the other room where she had been so frightened when Kazandis let himself down from the roof in search of her.

Madame Argeros helped her out of her gown. Then, slipping on her night-dress which had been left behind in her bag on the horse, Athena lay back against the pillows with a little sigh.

"I'll cook something light and appetising," Madame Argeros said, "and Nonika shall bring it up."

"Thank you, Madame. You are very kind."

"We are ashamed and humiliated that such things should happen to a lady like you when you have been our guest,"

Madame Argeros said, "but now that evil man is dead there will be no more troubles."

"Are there no more bandits?" Athena asked.

"Plenty of them," Madame replied, "but they are not like him. Most bandits are only beggars, who are hungry and want to eat. They're poor and they ask for a little money! But Kazandis was different, he was a murderer!"

She went from the room as she spoke and Athena shivered.

Kazandis might be a murderer, but she had murdered him! Then she told herself she must not think about it, but only of Orion, as he had told her to do.

She was to be married to Orion!

Somehow she could hardly believe it was true that she was to be his wife as she longed to be; there would be no problems about the Prince to be solved, no question of whether she should return to England or not.

The astonishment and inevitable reproaches of her relatives did not concern her.

For the moment she would only have to cope with Aunt Beatrice, but later she would have to tell her father what had happened and of course her grandmother.

It was the Dowager Marchioness who would mind most and feel that Athena had betrayed her trust.

"They will love Orion when they meet him," Athena told herself confidently.

But any such meeting was a long way off and for the moment there was only one thing to worry about, and that was the attitude the Prince might take.

Athena did not know anything about Greek law, but she expected that the Nobility and certainly minor Royalties in every country were important and powerful and to offend one of them could result in penalties which were not only social ones.

Then she told herself again that if things became difficult she and Orion would leave Greece.

In which case, she thought uneasily, they would have to live on her money.

Here was another difficulty she had not faced before.

She knew nothing about Orion, and yet instinctively she was aware that he was proud.

She was sure he was a man who would think it beneath him to accept money from a woman: a man must always be the master in his own house and that included his wife.

"I shall have to tell him who I am," Athena thought, but she felt afraid.

He loved her enough to marry her whoever she might be, but she supposed that he thought of her as a quite ordinary Englishwoman from an ordinary family, with perhaps a little money of her own, enough at any rate to travel round the world.

But that was very different from marrying a great heiress and a woman who had come to Greece to marry one of the reigning Princes.

"If I tell him he might not . . . marry me," Athena thought.

She felt herself trembling and knew here was something she must avoid at all costs.

He had told her nothing about himself, he had asked no questions where she was concerned; but the moment would come eventually when they must be frank with each other.

Then if she was not already his wife Orion might refuse to go through with the marriage which he himself had suggested.

She knew as she thought of it that she could not—she dare not—lose him for the second time.

It had been a pain and an agony unlike anything she had ever known in the whole of her quiet life when she had watched him ride away from her on the black stallion and knew that he was riding out of her life forever.

And because her suffering had been so intense she had hardly had time to realise that it was tearing her into pieces when Kazandis appeared and carried her away.

Now she knew that what she had suffered was like dying a thousand deaths and she could not go through that again.

"I will not . . . tell him," she decided. "I will tell him . . . nothing until we are married. Nothing . . . nothing!"

In her mind she said the words defiantly as if she chal-

lenged the fates themselves to wrench her happiness from
her at the eleventh hour.

As if in answer she heard at that moment Orion's feet
coming up the stairs.

He knocked at the door of her room but it was open and
even as he knocked he could see her lying in what had been
his bed.

He came towards her and she thought she had never
seen a man look so happy.

"Madame Argeros told me you were resting, my darling,"
he said, "but I had to see you."

Athena stretched out her hands towards him.

"I wanted to see you."

"You are all right? You do not feel ill?"

She shook her head.

"Only a little tired."

"That is not surprising," he said, "and I want you to rest.
I will arrange for our wedding to take place in the cool of the
evening, but I am afraid that the whole village will wish to
celebrate afterwards—do you mind?"

"I mind nothing as long as I can be your wife."

He took her hand in his and kissed her fingers one after
another, then pressed his lips into the softness of her palm.

"I can hardly believe that everything that happened this
morning really took place," he said. "But now you are safe—
and you belong to me!"

She felt herself thrill at his tone of voice.

But when instinctively she lifted her face towards his, her
lips ready for his kiss, he looked down at her and said:

"You are not to tempt me, Athena. I want you to rest, but
if I start kissing you now it will be very difficult for me to stop
or to leave you alone as I intend to do."

"You will not go . . . far?"

There was a touch of fear in her voice.

"Only to the Church, because I have to speak with the
Priest," he said. "Do you mind, my darling, being married in
the Greek Orthodox religion to which I belong?"

"I do not mind how we are married . . . as long as we . . .
are," Athena answered.

"I really feel we should be married in the Temple of

Apollo," Orion smiled, "but the Priests are long dead, and I am determined to tie you to me by every vow and nuptial bond that exists so that you can never escape."

"I would never want to," Athena murmured.

They looked into each other's eyes and she knew that Orion drew in his breath.

It was almost impossible, Athena thought, to be closer to one another than they were at this moment in their love for each other.

Then with an effort Orion kissed her hand again.

"I am going now, my darling. There was really only one thing I came to ask you and it seems extraordinary after all that has happened that I do not know your name."

Athena had anticipated this question. A lot had been written about her in the newspapers in Athens when she arrived with her Aunt and she was afraid that if she told him her real name Orion might connect it with the English heiress who was visiting Greece and had been received by the King.

Yet when she first thought of it she asked herself whether if she was married by any other name it would be legal.

Then she remembered, almost as if fate had provided for such an emergency, what she had been told had happened at her christening.

Her American Godmother, Mrs. Mayville, who had later left her the huge fortune, had been asked to hold the baby in her arms. She had been instructed that when the Parson said: "Name this child," she would reply: "Mary Emmeline Athena."

But Athena's Godmother was not only delighted with her Godchild, but also wished to give her something of herself.

She must have thought over what she intended to do while the Service began and the baby lay sleeping peacefully in her arms wrapped in the long lace-edged robe in which every member of the Wade family had been christened for centuries.

Finally when the Godparents had promised to "renounce the devil and all his works" and sanctified the water in the font the Parson turned to Mrs. Mayville. She handed him the baby, and he said:

"Name this child."

"Mary Emmeline Athena Mayville," she answered.

There was a little gasp from the Marquess and the other relatives, but before they could think what to do the Parson had intoned solemnly:

"Mary Emmeline Athena Mayville I baptise thee In the Name of the Father, of the Son and of the Holy Ghost. Amen."

Athena's head had received the Holy Water and for the first time she cried, "Letting the devil out of her!" as her Nanny said later with satisfaction.

Afterwards the Marquess had stormed in a fury about it.

"I told you the Wades have never been given fancy names! Athena Mayville! Have you ever heard of such a combination?"

"I am sorry, dearest," Athena's mother replied. "I had no idea that my friend intended anything quite so unexpected. But there was nothing we could do."

"I should have stopped the ceremony," the Marquess said. "It is outrageous that my daughter should be saddled for life with such names!"

"Perhaps we could just forget them," the Marchioness said soothingly. "After all, we shall always call her Mary and there is no reason for her ever to use any other name."

The Marquess was gradually reassured, but Athena learnt as she grew older that her Godmother was in disgrace and was seldom invited back to Wadebridge Castle.

However, when she died and left all her money to Athena, the Marquess's antagonism was noticeably modified and he no longer flew into a rage if she was mentioned in his presence.

Now Athena thought her Godmother had done her a good turn.

Her name indeed was Athena Mayville legally, and she was quite certain that once married it would be impossible for the ceremony to be annulled because she had not used all her other names.

Orion was waiting for her answer and she smiled up at him.

"Athena Mayville," she said. "And now it is only fair that you should tell me yours."

"It is very Greek," he answered. "Theodoros."

"I like it," she said. "I shall be very proud to be Athena Theodoros."

She spoke with such sincerity in her voice that Orion could not prevent himself from kissing her.

It was a hard, quick kiss but, as if he no longer trusted himself, he rose to his feet and walked towards the door.

"Sleep now, my darling," he said. "There is nothing to make you afraid. I shall rest later in the next room, and if you want me you have only to call."

"I shall remember . . . that," Athena answered.

As it happened she fell asleep almost as soon as he had left her and she did not hear Nonika bring her food or take it away again.

She slept and slept, dreaming happily of Orion and not even in her dreams did the shadow of Kazandis disturb her.

She awoke drowsily to find Nonika was coming into her room carrying a can of hot water.

"I thought you would want to wash," she said in her shy manner as Athena opened her eyes, "and I've brought you some coffee. Mama is cooking you an omelette."

"Thank you."

"And I have sponged your gown and pressed it," Nonika went on, "but I am afraid it does not look very nice."

Athena sat up in bed.

She was to be married and for the first time she realised that she had nothing to wear.

She could hardly bear to think that on what was the most important day in her life she had only the gown that she had worn yesterday, and which she knew had been in a terrible state by the time they had brought her down the mountain-side.

The ropes had marked the waist, and the bushes, some of them with thorny claws, had clutched at her skirts as she passed them.

The dust and dirt from the bare rocks had done the rest.

Nonika laid it over a chair, but even though the full skirt was uncreased it was still badly marked.

"Oh, Nonika!" Athena exclaimed. "How can I be married in that?"

It was woman calling to woman, a cry for help that was very feminine.

Nonika was silent for a moment, then she said:

"I have a suggestion, but I would not like you to think it impertinent."

"I would not think anything you suggested impertinent," Athena said, "especially if it was helpful."

She rose from the bed as she spoke and walked across the room in her bare feet to look at the gown.

"I do want to look beautiful for Orion," she said almost beneath her breath.

"I understand," Nonika said, "I would feel the same. I have a gown that I could lend you, but you might not like it."

"Could I see it?" Athena asked.

She saw the smile in Nonika's eyes before she ran from the room, then Athena wondered what she could possibly provide that would not make her look even more shabby than she would appear in her own soiled gown.

She thought of all the beautiful dresses she had brought to Greece in her trousseau and longed for Orion to see her in them.

It was easy, Athena thought, to say that clothes did not matter beside one's feelings, but there was no woman in the whole world who did not wish to look beautiful and at her best on her wedding-day.

She almost felt as if she would rather postpone the wedding than be married looking drab and bedraggled, as was inevitable unless Nonika could provide her with something different.

But what could the daughter of a Taverna-keeper have to offer?

Athena did not ask the question disparagingly but practically.

All the gowns she had brought with her to Greece had been from the most expensive dressmakers in London.

If she had not been conscious that she must be extremely smart and impressive when married to the Prince of Parnassus, her grandmother had certainly been determined that she should outshine every member of the fashionable Athenian Society.

"The Queen is noted for her elegance," the Dowager Marchioness had said, "and when there are women in Athens like Lady Ellenborough you cannot afford to be anything but very smart."

It was the first time that Athena had heard of Lady Ellenborough, but there were plenty of people to tell her of the English Beauty's adventures and her flamboyant behaviour with one lover after another.

The stories of Lady Ellenborough, or the Countess Theotoky as she was now, lost nothing in the telling. She was called "The Queen of Love and Beauty", and her loveliness was framed by exquisite clothes.

"Perhaps Orion knows women like that," Athena thought now. "How can I marry him looking little better than a beggar-maid?"

It did not help to recall that she was very much the opposite, which was something she was still afraid to tell her future husband.

It only made her feel sadly that some of the happiness and glamour of her wedding was being taken from her simply because she did not look as a bride should.

She walked to the small mirror which stood on the chest-of-drawers and stared at her reflection.

Orion thought her beautiful—she knew that—but because she wanted him to go on thinking so for the rest of his life she could imagine nothing more depressing than for him to start off their wedded life together by feeling sorry for her.

And that undoubtedly was how he would feel when he saw her in her old gown.

Almost despairingly Athena waited as she heard Nonika coming back up the stairs.

Had she a solution? Was there anything she could offer as an alternative to her own clothes?

Nonika entered the room, and Athena drew in her breath.

In her arms she carried almost reverently a gown which Athena knew instinctively was to be Nonika's own wedding-dress and she recognised it as a native costume of Parnassus.

It was very elaborate and beautiful.

The gown was white, made simply with open sleeves, the soft material edged both at the hem and on the sleeves with the most intricate and exquisite coral and gold embroidery.

The same colours richly embroidered with gold formed an apron and the front of the bodice was embellished in the same way.

To be worn round the neck was a huge necklace of wrought gold fringed with coins, set with five rows of turquoises and corals of varying sizes encircled with what appeared to be small diamonds.

Athena gasped and Nonika explained:

"The necklace has been in our family for many, many years, all Greek families have them."

She paused to add sadly:

"Or they did have them, many have had to be sold for food or to pay the terrible taxes."

"It is perfectly lovely," Athena exclaimed.

"The dress was made by me and my mother," Nonika continued. "We embroidered all through the winter, and now at last it is finished!"

"But you cannot wish anyone else to wear it!" Athena protested.

"You will look very beautiful in it," Nonika replied. "A Greek bride for Orion."

"Will you really lend it to me?"

"I should be honoured."

"It is kind ... so very kind of you," Athena answered, "but you must show me how to wear it, how to put it on."

"I will show you," Nonika agreed. "It is not difficult."

When she had been staying in Athens Athena had seen many Greek girls wearing their native costume and thought how attractive they looked.

But Nonika's gown was not only lovelier than those she had seen, it was also particularly becoming to her.

There was a white veil with which she covered her hair and perched on the top of it was a little gold cap, also embellished with turquoises and coral and with a row of gold coins which outlined her forehead.

When she looked at herself in the mirror she thought she looked quite different from the way she had looked before and yet it seemed a more fitting frame for her oval face and huge grey eyes than anything else she had ever worn.

"You look lovely! Lovely!" Nonika exclaimed. "And now we will show you to Orion."

Athena took a last look at herself in the mirror.

Would he think her beautiful, she wondered, or would he perhaps think what she wore was too like fancy-dress?

Then she told herself that this was after all, the type of costume which all Greek girls wore and as Nonika had said she was to be a Greek bride.

Nonika ran ahead of her down the stairs to say she was coming and as Athena moved a little shyly into the kitchen Orion rose from the table at which he had been sitting.

She only needed one glance at his eyes, one look at his face to know exactly what he thought.

There was no need for words.

To him she was as beautiful as he had expected her to be.

# CHAPTER SIX

The men were dancing the *zeimbekiko* with a verve and a vigour that was exciting for those who watched them.

Athena thought it would be impossible for a single other guest, however thin, to squeeze into the kitchen of the Taverna.

They were certainly a colourful throng to look at, all wearing what she realised were their best and most treasured costumes, the women brilliant in red and blue, yellow and magenta.

Those who could not get inside the Taverna were sitting outside on the verandah or leaning through the open windows into the room.

It was hot, it was noisy, and yet at the same time it had a spontaneous gaiety that she had never encountered before.

The whole village had turned out for their wedding.

When she had come out from the Taverna with Orion she found that they had already congregated outside around the ancient, open carriage that was to carry them to the Church.

The horse which drew it was decorated with flowers, even the hubs of the wheels had bows of ribbon on them, and the closed hood was piled with hibiscus, bougainvillaea and blossoms from other shrubs.

A cheer went up as Athena and Orion appeared, and as he helped her into the carriage she realised that if she had borrowed her wedding-gown he also must have borrowed the clothes he wore.

He was wearing the full-sleeved traditional white shirt and over it a gold edged bolero which was exquisitely embroidered with flowers in all colours of the rainbow.

There was a red silk handkerchief around his neck and a red cummerbund around his waist, but instead of the stiff-pleated, white-skirted *fustanella* that many of the other men wore he had on tight-fitting black trousers which were extremely becoming.

He did in fact look so handsome and attractive that Athena felt her heart turn over with happiness.

As the horse started off he took her hand in his.

"All these people love you," she said as the crowd cheered and followed the carriage, the children running beside it excitedly down the narrow road towards the village.

"As everyone you meet in my country will love you, my darling," he answered.

She looked into his eyes and found it hard to remember anything except that she was to be his wife and that already she belonged to him in everything but name.

It was only a short distance to the Church which was small and built Byzantine fashion in the shape of a cross.

As Athena walked into it on Orion's arm and found the Priest waiting for them, she realised it would have been quite impossible for even a tenth of the people following them to get inside the small building.

But she soon realised that Orion had thought of this and everything was arranged.

Only the Argeros family followed them into the Church, while the rest stood outside the open door in respectful silence.

Although Athena had seen the Priests of the Greek Orthodox religion walking about the streets with their black beards and flowing black robes, she had not before seen one of the brilliantly coloured vestments such as was worn by the Priest who was waiting to marry them.

Of shimmering silver and gold the embroidery seemed to be part of the flowers outside, and the fragrance in the building itself reminded her of the grasses around the shrine of Apollo.

Innumerable candles and the seven silver sanctuary lamps glittered on the mosaics and gold carvings with which the Church was decorated, and they also illuminated the dozens of sacred Icons which hung on every available wall.

Athena had been afraid that she would not understand the ceremony, but as soon as it started she realised that the Priest was conducting the Service in Katharevousa, which was the Greek she knew.

She and Orion made their vows and when they knelt in front of the Priest, Dimitrios Argeros held over both their heads the linked wreaths which symbolised their union as man and wife.

Nonika, wearing a pretty gown, but very simple compared to the one she had lent to Athena, had held the bride's bouquet during the Service.

Orion had placed it in the carriage and it was a small posy fashioned of white irises. Athena knew that as they were the flowers of the gods it was for both of them a symbolic gift.

The service in the small Church was very beautiful, and as the fragrance of the flowers and the incense mingled together Athena felt that nothing could be more inspiring or more holy.

She dedicated herself for all time to Orion and felt that he did the same to her.

When he placed the ring on her finger she saw the expression on his face and knew that he was deeply moved. She thought that in marrying the man she loved and who loved her she was the most fortunate woman in the whole world.

Whatever difficulties lay ahead, whatever obstacles they might encounter, however many recriminations awaited them because of their action in getting married so quietly and secretly, it would always be the supreme moment in their lives.

Athena knew that nothing could be more fitting or indeed more wonderful than that she should marry Orion without a fashionable congregation, surrounded only by those who loved him for himself and had nothing to give or take except true friendship.

The Priest blessed them, then as they rose to their feet Orion put his arms around her and kissed her.

It was a kiss which was sacred and holy and she knew she would ask nothing more of God than that she should be his wife.

"My heart, my mind and my soul," he said very softly in English so that only she could hear.

As they turned to go out into the sunshine where their friends were waiting both of them radiated a happiness that was not of this world.

But the villagers of Delphi were not to be deprived of their fun.

Athena and Orion were driven back up the hill, but now the carriage was invaded and there were men and children hanging on to the sides and the back and flowers were thrown at them by the women until they sat knee-deep in blossom.

At the Taverna Madame Argeros had laid out a spread of food which made Athena gasp.

She could only guess that all the women of the village must have contributed, for it would have been impossible for any one person to cook so much in so short a time.

There were tables groaning under plentiful but not expensive food—for the villagers were poor—but the best each could contribute.

Bottles were opened, and Athena and Orion were toasted a hundred times as they sat together at the top of the table.

Athena was too excited to want to eat but Madame Argeros pressed the delicacies upon her and she did not wish to be disappointing.

When the food was finished and the tables taken away the dancing began and now Athena could see as she had wanted to ever since she came to Greece the folk dances.

These had evolved through the centuries containing in

each one of them the taste of the different nationalities, creeds and cultures which had been part of Greece at one time or another.

And Athena heard for the first time the real Greek music which was something she had not been able to listen to at the Court in Athens.

Now she saw the *aulos,* or reed pipe, which she knew was associated with the wine-god Dionysus. Beside the pipes, there was the flute and the lyre, and the *tympanon* which was a hand beaten frame drum and the *crotala,* hand-clappers, and the *cymbala,* which were cymbals.

As if as a concession to modernity there was also an accordion played by a young man wearing a *fustanella* and the Greek cap with the long black tassel that reached to his waist.

Those who were musical seemed to Athena to be more vividly and exotically dressed than the others.

The entertainment which had been put on for the bride and bridegroom started with the *chassapiko* which Orion told her was "the butchers' dance" originating from Constantinople and was danced by four men who hissed and snapped their fingers to a rhythm clearly marked by their foot-beats.

It was gay and amusing and was followed by the arrival of the *bouzoukia* which was a large awkward-looking mandolin which added to the other music nostalgic notes which sometimes seemed weighted with sorrow.

Each performance was greeted with cheers and prolonged applause and shouts of "Bravo!"

A quick and lively *serviko* which Athena thought was probably of Slav origin had everybody stamping their feet and swaying their shoulders.

She was certain that if there had been room everybody would have joined in.

Now, as the men performed the *zeimbekiko,* their arms reaching across each other's shoulders and having strangely enough a grace which she had not expected, she found herself wondering why in England dancing was considered to be only a feminine accomplishment.

There was no doubt that the Greek men enjoyed every moment of their rhythmic movements and they danced because they loved dancing.

It gave them a feeling of warmth and camaraderie towards those with whom they shared this pleasure.

The *zeimbekiko* evoked frenzied applause. Then with the soft throbbing of the *bouzoukia* a man began to sing the timeless strain of a lover's serenade.

It was a flowing melodic Ionian *cantade* which Athena knew had the power to ravish the ear and melt the heart of all those who listened to it.

Now everyone was silent, their dark eyes filled with emotion.

Because she too was moved by the singer's deep voice which had an unmistakable throb in it, Athena sought Orion's hand.

She felt his spontaneous reaction almost crush her fingers bloodless. Then as the singer finished and after a moment's pause of appreciation more congratulatory than any other expression, the noise broke out.

It was then that Orion pulled Athena to her feet and they slipped away into the back of the kitchen almost before anybody realised they had moved.

She thought he intended to take her upstairs, but instead he opened a door at the side of the building which she did not know existed and they stepped out into the star-strewn night.

There was a path leading through the bushes which led them to the road without having to pass through the crowds outside the Taverna.

Athena did not speak, she only let Orion lead her where he would and felt a rising excitement because at last they were alone together.

The road through the village now seemed empty and deserted. They walked along it and gradually the music from the Taverna grew fainter and fainter.

It was almost like stepping into another world and Athena was aware of the quietness and the inexpressible serenity which was part of the Sanctuary.

The stars were vivid in the sky and the moon was rising.

She felt her pulses quicken at the thought that Orion was taking her to where they had known the wonder of their first kiss and she had given him her heart for all time.

But when they reached the narrow path that led up to the Temple of Apollo and beyond again to the Theatre, Orion kept on down the road.

Athena glanced at him enquiringly, but he did not speak and because there was no need for words between them she did not ask where they were going.

She knew instinctively that he was taking her to where he had found her, to the shrine of her namesake—the Temple of Athena.

Their footsteps made no sound on the dry, sandy road and Athena felt almost as if they floated past the ravine through which gushed the Castalian Cascade, until they came to the steps which led down to the shrine.

Now they had to pass through the closely growing olive trees until in the clearing they saw the three lovely Doric columns of the Tholos.

The moonlight was shining on their fluted marble so that they seemed to sparkle with almost a crystalline beauty.

Then as she looked at them wonderingly Orion's arms went round her and her thoughts were only of him.

"My wife!" he said softly as if he wished to convince himself that the words were true.

It was the first time he had spoken since they left the Taverna.

Holding her close he looked down at her face and the moonlight revealed to each of them the expressions in their eyes.

"You are more beautiful, my darling, than I believed it possible for any woman to be!" he said. "And now you are mine—mine for eternity—because if we have been separated before, we cannot be separated again."

"I love . . . you! Oh, Orion . . . I love . . . you!" Athena whispered.

"Love is such an inadequate word for what I feel for you," he answered. "Everything about you is perfect, not only your beauty, my precious one, but your sweetness, your kindness, and most of all your courage."

"I am not really . . . brave," Athena replied. "Only when I think of . . . you."

She raised her lips to his as she spoke, his mouth came

down on hers and she felt as if a streak of fire ran through her, magical, ecstatic and with a radiance that was desire.

Orion held her close and still closer. Then with his lips still keeping her captive his hands removed the little gold embroidered cap on her head and the veil which covered her hair.

He drew out the pins which held it in place so that it fell over her shoulders as it had done when she had been lying in his bed.

Gently he unfastened the huge gold necklace and then she felt his fingers unbuttoning her wedding-gown.

It was difficult to think of anything but the wonder of his lips and the fact that the fire he had evoked in her seemed to run over her whole body, burning its way from the top of her head to the very point of her toes.

Athena felt her dress fall to the ground followed by the garments she wore beneath it.

She was not shy. She felt as if she was lifted by Orion's lips into a mystic rapture which swept away all human emotions and she was ethereal and spiritually one with the night.

Orion raised his head and looked at her.

"You are divine!" he said hoarsely. "The goddess at whose feet I worship!"

Just for a moment he stood not touching her, then he pulled her into his arms and carried her beneath an ancient olive tree.

Athena felt the grass and flowers bending beneath her body and there was the fragrance of wild lilies and the scent of thyme.

She looked up and her eyes were dazzled by the brilliance of the moon-shafts shining through the branches. And she was conscious of a strange glitter in the air.

For a second she thought she had lost Orion, only to find him standing above her and she looked as she had seen him once before, his slim, athletic body silver in the moonlight.

She felt that he was haloed by the stars after which he was named and that he shimmered with them until she was looking at a constellation.

Then he was beside her, touching her so that she quivered and trembled because of the sensations he awakened and the fire in her breasts seemed to burst into a flame.

He moved and his heart beat against her heart and she could no longer think.

She only knew that he carried her up into the sky. She was conscious of a strange glitter in the air and there was the beat of silver wings as, glorious and omnipotent, they were gods.


Riding down the incline which led them South from the Sanctuary, Athena turned to smile at Orion who was still having a little difficulty in keeping his stallion under control.

It would be hard to explain to him, she thought, how during her journey up from Itea to Delphi she had longed to ride as she was riding now, free and untrammeled in the early morning sunshine.

But as if he understood without words what she was thinking he drew his horse alongside hers and said:

"Are you happy, my precious one?"

There was no need for Athena to answer him in words, her eyes met his and he thought he had never known a woman could look so radiant, so lovely.

They had left the Taverna very early, in fact Athena felt that she had hardly closed her eyes before Orion awakened her.

"We have a long ride ahead of us, my darling love," he said. "As I do not wish you to be exhausted by the heat I would like to start as soon as you are ready."

"Is . . . it morning?" Athena asked drowsily.

"Yes, darling, it is morning," he answered, "and the first day of our marriage."

She opened her eyes at that and lifted her arms towards him, but he took her hands and kissed them one after another before he said:

"If I kiss your lips my beautiful, adorable wife, I shall come back to bed and stay with you there for the rest of the day!"

Athena blushed and he said:

"You look more lovely than I have time to tell you, but remind me not to forget to do so to-morrow morning."

His words awakened Athena very effectively; for she could not help wondering where they would be to-morrow and what would happen between now and then.

When they arrived back at the Taverna all the guests had gone and everything was quiet.

She knew then that Orion had made plans and that she must come back from the heights of ecstasy to face reality.

"I shall have to tell him the truth sooner or later," she told herself.

Then because she knew she was afraid that it might in some way spoil their happiness she shied away from that moment like a horse frightened by a shadow on the road.

But Orion was already dressed in the clothes in which she had first seen him, and when he left the room Athena rose.

She realised with a sudden depression that she would have to put on the gown of which she had been so ashamed and which Nonika had saved her from having to wear as her wedding gown.

However there was no time to worry about such details. Orion was waiting downstairs and she knew how it infuriated her father if he was ever kept waiting by his womenfolk.

She washed and tried not to think of how unbelievably wonderful and perfect everything had been the night before.

There would be time later to remember, to recall the ecstasy she found with her husband, and he with her.

Now she must try to be practical.

Nonika's beautiful wedding-gown was lying on a chair and Athena turned to the cupboard, expecting to find her own gown hanging there, but the cupboard was empty.

Even as she thought she must call down stairs and ask for it, there was a knock on the door and Madame Argeros came in carrying her gown followed by Nonika.

"Good-morning," Madame Argeros said. "You must hurry, for your husband has already started his breakfast and he tells me you have a long way to go."

"I am nearly . . ." Athena began, then broke off.

She looked at her gown which Madame Argeros was carrying, and realised that it had been washed and pressed and

looked almost as fresh as it had been when she had first put
it on, what now seemed a century ago, in the Palace.

"You have washed my gown!" she exclaimed. "Oh, Madame Argeros, it must have taken you half the night! How
can I ever thank you?"

"I could not have you leaving us in such a state," Madame
Argeros said, "especially as it was through no fault of your
own that your dress was dirtied."

"But you have done it so beautifully," Athena cried.

The gown had in fact been exquisitely laundered as the
Greek woman wash their own blouses and their men's shirts.

It glowed with a whiteness that seemed to reflect the sunshine.

As Athena slipped it on she thought with delight that
now she would not be ashamed for Orion to see her.

"You have been so kind—so very kind," she said to Nonika, because Madame had already hurried down the stairs.

"We are glad we could be of help to Orion's wife," Nonika
replied.

"You have been more than that," Athena said. "I felt like
a real bride in your beautiful gown, and it has brought me so
much happiness that I know it will do the same for you."

"I hope so," Nonika smiled.

"And as a wedding present," Athena went on, choosing
her words with care, "I hope you will allow me to send you a
part of your trousseau. I thought perhaps you would like
some nightgowns like mine, and perhaps some petticoats and
other garments made of the same material."

She saw Nonika's eyes widen in sheer astonishment. Then
the Greek girl said stammeringly:

"D . . do you really . . . mean that? I thought your nightgown so . . . pretty that I might try to . . . copy it."

"I will send you a dozen," Athena said. "In the meantime
keep this one if it is any use to you as a pattern."

Nonika drew in her breath, then she said:

"It is too kind . . . too generous. Perhaps I should not . . .
take such a gift."

"I should be very hurt and disappointed if you refused,"
Athena replied. "After all, you lent me something of such

inestimable value, which could never be calculated in any currency except that of friendship."

She smiled as she went on:

"We are friends, Nonika, and that is what I hope we shall be all our lives. Nothing is too good or too precious to give in return for friendship."

"You are right," Nonika said, "and I can only say thank you."

She paused, then she said as if it was impossible to suppress the words:

"You will not . . . forget?"

"No, I promise, I shall not forget," Athena laughed.

She put her arms round Nonika's shoulders and kissed her; then picking up her bonnet she ran down the stairs, eager to be with Orion again.

There were so many good-byes to say when they had hastily eaten their breakfast that it was only when they were outside that Athena looked at the horse she was to ride, expecting it to be the one belonging to Spiros.

But she found it was in fact a very different animal which awaited her.

Although it did not equal the well-bred qualities of Orion's stallion, it was obviously a horse capable both of endurance and of speed.

Athena looked questioningly at Orion and he explained with a smile:

"Your first wedding-present, my darling. I bought it for you this morning. It is the best the village can provide."

"I am delighted with it," Athena answered.

"At least it will carry you where we have to go," he said, "and you have not yet told me where that is."

Her eyes widened and she laughed.

"I know it cannot be far," he went on, "because you came to the Port of Itea."

"It is ridiculous how little we know about each other," she said.

"On the contrary," he replied. "I know everything about you, everything that is important, and to me our love is a miracle!"

She blushed at the passion in his voice and her eyes fell before his.

They were talking in English so that no-one else could understand. Then she said, having already decided what to say:

"I am staying at Mikis."

"At the Hotel Poseidon, I suppose?" he said. "It is a favourite spot for tourists, but I thought you were more likely to be at Ossios."

"Mikis is nearer," Athena replied, realising that Ossios was on the opposite shore to the promontory on which the Palace was built.

Orion helped her onto the horse, arranged her full skirts over the pommel and said a little anxiously:

"Do you think you will be comfortable? We have a long way to go."

"I am used to riding," she answered, "and I seldom find it tiring."

"That is what I thought you would say."

"How did you know I could ride?"

"I knew you would ride superbly well, like everything else you do," he answered, and she smiled from sheer happiness.

He swung himself onto the stallion's back who was behaving in his usual obstreperous manner. Then amid the cheers of the crowds who had come to see them off they rode down and along the first part of the thirty mile road which led eventually to Thebes.

After they had left Delphi behind there was a long and lonely descent from the mountainside.

Athena stopped and drew her horse to a standstill as Orion suggested she should look back.

Now she could see almost the whole range of the Parnassus mountains and there was snow on the tops of some of them, gleaming dazzlingly in the sunlight, and there was also a superb view over Delphi itself.

"I hate to say good-bye," Athena said in a low voice.

"It is only *au revoir*," Orion replied. "We will come back perhaps every year to celebrate, and in the years to come we will bring our children, and I shall show them where I found a goddess asleep amongst the ruins of her own Temple."

Athena's eyes met his and he said hoarsely:

"If you look at me like that I shall have to kiss you and that means we shall never reach our destination."

"Do we . . . have to go . . . back?" Athena asked.

There was a little pause before he replied:

"I cannot help feeling that your relatives must be getting worried by now, unless you gave them a very good explanation for your disappearance. We would not wish them to send out a search-party looking for you."

"No, of course not!" Athena exclaimed.

"Leave everything to me, my darling," Orion said. "I promise you I will sort it out with the minimum of difficulty and trouble. Do you trust me?"

"You know I do."

"Then let us go on," he said. "The sooner we are free of all such tiresome obligations, the sooner we can think of ourselves, which means that I can think of you."

As if his words spurred them on they set off at a sharp pace and after proceeding for some miles they left the main road to begin what Athena knew was the descent which would lead them eventually to the sea and Mikis.

The land was very undulating and it was impossible to ride direct since they had to take various detours to avoid the hill-tops.

But away from the heights of Delphi the flowers intensified in beauty and the blossom was richer on the trees, and it also grew a great deal hotter.

Athena was glad after all that she had worn her bonnet for the journey, because the sun would have been too hot on her head. She hoped that her white skin would not be sunburnt, even though she thought that the brown of Orion's bare neck and arms was exceedingly becoming to him.

About eleven o'clock they stopped in the shade of some trees to eat the luncheon with which Madame Argeros had provided them.

"I thought it would be more fun for us to be alone," Orion said, "than to eat in some small Taverna where doubtless the food would be indifferent and the wine flavoured with resin, which you would not like."

"I am feeling hungry even though it may be unromantic," Athena smiled.

"Then suppose you unpack what there is to eat, while I cool the wine in that small cascade," he suggested.

Athena followed the direction of his eyes and saw a waterfall in a ravine near where they had stopped.

He walked away towards it, having given her some packages from his saddle-bag.

Athena opened them to find as she expected that Madame Argeros, despite the earliness of their departure, had cooked them a whole lot of delicious Greek specialties that would have tempted the appetite of anyone far less hungry than they were.

She was not certain what all the things were although she recognised *dolmades* which were vine-leaves folded over mince-meat and rice.

But whatever was provided Orion was prepared to eat it, and he lay on the ground beside her and somehow there was no need to talk because they were so happy.

Only when they had finished nearly everything that Madame Argeros provided for them and Orion was drinking the last of the wine, did Athena realise that now was the moment when she should tell him about herself.

"What are you thinking about?" he asked unexpectedly.

"You," she replied.

"That is the right answer, my darling, you should always be thinking of me, as I am thinking about you."

"What were you thinking about me?" Athena asked.

"I was thinking how much I love you," he answered, "and how fortunate I am—the luckiest man in the world—to have found you."

"That is what I feel about you."

"We think the same, we feel the same, we are the same," he said softly.

He stretched out his arms.

"Come here!"

It was a command and for one moment Athena hesitated. Then she knew that she wanted the touch of his lips so urgently, so insistently, that she could not wait.

What was the point of talking when they could be kissing?

Why should she spoil this moment with what might prove to be unpleasant information?

She moved swiftly towards him, and close in his arms it was impossible to think of anything else but him.

When they rode on there was a flush on Athena's cheeks and she felt warm and weak with sheer happiness.

She did not wish to make decisions, she did not wish to force herself to choose the right moment in which to make revelations about herself to Orion.

She only wanted to know that she was loved.

She loved him so overwhelmingly that she was afraid, as she had never been afraid in her whole life, that her happiness was only a glorious iridescent bubble and it might burst if it was roughly handled.

"I adore you!" Orion said as he lifted her into the saddle and that was all she wanted to think about as she rode along beside him.

They had come a long way since the morning, and two hours later, in the distance Athena had her first glimpse of the blue of the Gulf of Corinth.

It was still a long way ahead but growing nearer all the time, and when suddenly they dropped down to sea level she realised with a frightened leap of her heart that she had still not said what must be said.

"Are we far from Mikis now?" she asked in a small voice.

"Only about a mile or so," Orion replied. "You are not too tired, my darling? It has been a long way, but you have ridden magnificently and it was really much easier than if we had come by sea. If we had done that I would not have known what to do with my horse."

"We could hardly put him in the boat," Athena smiled, "or make him swim behind us."

Orion laughed.

"That is what I thought."

"Orion . . ." she began in a tremulous little tone, but he did not seem to hear her because he said:

"I have decided what we will do. I will leave you at the

Hotel and as now it is getting on for two o'clock I suggest you follow everyone else's example and have a siesta.

"When the whole world stirs again at about four you can tell your relations that you are married and that I shall be arriving at six. You can then introduce me and explanations can be made on either side."

He smiled as he added:

"I do not think they will be too angry with you, my precious. I promise that I will give a good account of myself."

"I am . . . sure you . . . will . . . but . . ." Athena began.

Again what she was about to say was lost because Orion had spurred his horse and they were moving more quickly than they had moved before over a piece of flat grassland to where in the distance there were the roofs and the dome of the Church in the small Harbour of Mikis.

"I will have to tell him later," she thought and hurried her own horse forward to catch up with him.

Orion drew his stallion to a standstill when they were within a hundred yards of the Hotel Poseidon which stood above the town looking down on the harbour.

It was quite an impressive looking building and had, Athena thought, only recently been built.

One of the results of a united Constitution and peace within the country was that visitors were now flocking back to Greece and there was every likelihood that the tourist trade would bring the Government the foreign currency they needed so badly to balance their economy.

"I am going to leave you now, my precious," Orion said. "Go straight to the Hotel and, if you can have a rest before you become involved in explanations for your absence, so much the better."

He paused then added:

"I will come to you at six o'clock. Do not be worried or upset in the meantime. There is no need for it—that I promise you!"

"You will not . . . forget?" she asked, as Nonika had done.

"That would be impossible, Heart of my Heart!"

He put out his hand and she laid her fingers in it.

"I love you, my darling," he said. "I love you, completely and overwhelmingly, and I swear to you that never again will we be parted for a single moment. We will be together and nothing and nobody shall come between us."

"You are . . . sure of . . . that?" Athena asked in sudden fear.

"Trust me."

"I do trust you."

He raised her fingers to his lips. Then as if he had no wish to say more he moved his horse.

"Go straight to the Hotel, my precious," he said. "I shall watch until you are safely there so that nothing can happen to you when my back is turned."

"I will be . . . all right."

Athena smiled at him and rode off conscious that he was watching her.

As she went she decided she would have to go to the Hotel to make certain he did not see her ride up the twisting road towards the Palace.

When she reached the Hotel entrance she looked back. Although there was no sign of Orion she could not be certain that he was not watching her from the hillside, so she dismounted and went inside.

Having told a groom to hold her horse for a few minutes she ordered herself a glass of lemonade.

When she had drunk a little of it she paid the waiter who seemed to be half asleep and resentful at having to attend to her when he might be dozing, and went outside.

The groom helped her back into the saddle.

She was certain that by now Orion would no longer be watching for her but had gone to his own home, wherever it was in the vicinity.

Although it was only two o'clock, she felt there was a lot to do before she must be back in the Hotel to meet Orion at six. So she forced her horse as fast as possible up the road to the Palace.

It did not take long and as she rode in past the sentries she thought how lovely the building looked, gleaming white against the mountainside, its garden a riot of colour with two fountains playing on the green lawns.

But she was no longer interested in the Palace and intent

only on planning exactly how she should behave once she was inside it.

As she had expected, everything was very quiet and there were only a few junior servants on duty who did not seem in the least surprised at her appearance.

Without making any explanations as to why she had returned she merely told the senior amongst them to inform Lady Beatrice Wade when the siesta was over that Lady Mary was in her bed-room.

The servant bowed and Athena knew that he would obey her orders and would not think of disturbing her Aunt for at least two and a half hours.

Then she went upstairs and once inside her own room rang for her maid.

Because she wished to obey Orion she undressed and got into bed.

"Call me at four o'clock," she told the maid, "when I would like a bath."

Athena realised as she spoke that she was almost too tired to say the words and literally as her head touched the pillow she fell asleep.

She awoke to realise that she had been dreaming of the sound of rushing water that came from the Castalian spring, but it was in fact her bath being prepared next door.

The bathrooms in the Palace had been designed in the Roman manner, sunk deep into the floor and Athena thought there was something very attractive in stepping down into her bath and sitting with the cool water reflecting the tiles which had been copied from some of the ancient Roman Villas.

The thought of bathing got her out of bed, and only when she had washed and was drying herself with the big white Turkish towel did she begin to think apprehensively of what she must say to her Aunt and even more important the explanation she must make to the Prince.

It was not going to be easy—she was aware of that—and what frightened her more than anything else was that the Prince might try to denounce Orion as a "fortune-hunter."

It was a thought that had lain at the back of her mind and now the idea forced itself upon her.

"It is so obvious that to discredit him they will say that he must have known all along who I am and married me so hastily to make quite certain that my money became his.

"How could anyone think such things of Orion?" Athena asked indignantly.

But she knew it was because she had come back from the sacred peace and serenity of Delphi to the world where people's minds were suspicious and bad motives were easier to believe than good.

"Orion will answer for himself," she thought proudly.

At the same time she knew that she was a coward because she was afraid.

Her maid was waiting for her in the bed-room and as she put on the beautiful lace-trimmed underclothes like those she had promised Nonika for her trousseau Athena was thinking deeply.

She was dressed as far as her petticoats and was arranging her hair in the mirror when the door was flung open and Lady Beatrice came into the room.

"Mary!" she exclaimed. "I have just learned that you have returned! How could you go away in such an irresponsible manner without even leaving an address?"

"I am sorry, Aunt Beatrice," Athena said rising, "but . . ."

"I dare say you have a good explanation," Lady Beatrice interrupted, "but I have no time to hear it now. All I can say is that I consider it extremely thoughtless of you."

"I am sorry," Athena began again.

"You will have to tell me all about it later," Lady Beatrice added. "But hurry now and put on your best gown and make yourself look presentable."

"Why?" Athena asked in surprise.

"Why?" Lady Beatrice echoed. "Because the Prince is here! Luckily I shall not have to make any explanation for your absence. That would have been embarrassing, to say the least of it."

"The . . . Prince is . . . here?" Athena repeated almost stupidly.

"Yes, at last!" Lady Beatrice said. "Goodness knows, we

have been waiting for him long enough! Now come along, Mary. There is no point in keeping him waiting, despite the manner in which he has behaved to us."

She hurried across the room as she spoke to pull open the wardrobe doors.

"You had better put on your blue grenadine," she said. "That is the gown your grandmother thought you should wear when you first met him. It is certainly one of the most becoming creations we have brought with us."

"Y . . yes . . . I will wear the blue," Athena said.

She was thinking as she spoke that it did not matter what the Prince thought, but she would like Orion to see her in the blue grenadine.

It was a very elaborate gown with a huge skirt of wide frills each one trimmed at the edge with real lace. It had the very becoming off-the-shoulder, boat-shaped neckline which had been made so fashionable by Queen Victoria.

"No jewellery, I think—no—perhaps your pearls," Lady Beatrice was saying. "You do not want to look ostentatious. At the same time it is important that he should admire you."

"Aunt Beatrice . . . I have something to tell you . . ." Athena began hesitatingly.

She knew the maid who was doing up her gown could not understand English, and she felt she must tell her Aunt now what she was going to say when she met the Prince.

"You can tell me later, Mary," Lady Beatrice said quickly. "There is really no time now. Just hurry! I know Colonel Stefanatis is waiting for us in the hall."

There was nothing Athena could do but clasp the pearls round her neck, slip her lace mittens over her hands and pick up a handkerchief.

"Come along! Come along!" Lady Beatrice was saying impatiently. "First impressions are very important, as I have told you often enough, and to be late is always inexcusable."

She went ahead of Athena down the stairs at such a pace that her niece almost had to run to keep up with her.

When they reached the hall Colonel Stefanatis bowed to Lady Beatrice, then to Athena, giving her at the same time a look that she thought was both curious and reproachful.

She was quite sure that he had worried over her disappearance perhaps more than her Aunt had done.

"This way, ladies, please," he said in his most pompous manner.

He led the way down a broad corridor towards a room which Athena knew she had hitherto not seen.

'How shall I . . . begin?' she thought frantically. 'What shall I . . . say?"

She wondered if it would be easier to speak to the Prince in English or Greek, and she decided that having greeted him she would ask if she could speak to him alone.

Everybody would think it very forward and unconventional but after all what did it matter?

They were moving through a part of the Palace which she thought must be exclusively the Prince's because now there were sporting pictures on the walls, ancient guns and several portraits.

There was one which she felt sure must be the Prince himself as it was of a young man with a short dark beard.

She would have liked to stop to look at it and prepare herself for the man she was to meet. But her Aunt and the Colonel were walking so quickly that she could only give the picture a cursory glance as she was forced to keep up with them.

Ahead she saw two liveried servants, one on either side of a pair of mahogany doors and the Colonel looked back to make sure that she was still there.

Then the doors opened and he stepped through them.

Athena drew a deep breath.

"Lady Beatrice Wade, Your Highness," she heard Colonel Stefanitis announce, "and Lady Mary Wade!"

Athena realised that her heart was beating violently in her breast.

'There is no need to be frightened,' she thought, 'Orion will look after me! Help me, oh my darling, help me to be brave!'

She said his name over and over to herself as if it was a talisman.

She realised that her Aunt was curtsying in front of her and heard a man's voice say:

"You must forgive me, Lady Beatrice. I am more apologetic than I can possibly convey that I have been delayed and that you should have arrived here sooner than I expected."

Athena raised her eyes.

Somehow the voice seemed curiously familiar.

Then she saw standing at her Aunt's side raising her gloved hand perfunctorily to his lips a man wearing a white uniform coat with gold epaulettes.

For a moment it was difficult to focus her eyes, until as he straightened himself after bowing over her Aunt's hand he turned to face her and the whole world seemed to stand still.

It was impossible to think—impossible to breathe and it seemed as if he too had been turned to stone.

Then as their eyes met it was as if they reached out and touched each other and everybody and everything else vanished.

"Athena my precious!" Orion exclaimed. "What are you doing here?"

# CHAPTER SEVEN

Athena walked out onto the balcony and stood looking at the last glimmer of the sun as it sank into the blue of the sea.

It turned the hills and the coastline to every kind of gold; gold facing to russet brown, gold shot through with black, green and purple in the fading light.

And the gold patterns on the sea shimmered against the golden outline of the shore.

She leant over the balustrade thinking she had not seen this view of the sea from the room she had previously occupied in the Palace.

Now she was in the Prince's Suite and the room behind her was so magnificent and at the same time so artistically beautiful that she felt as if it belonged to a fairy-tale.

But then nothing had seemed real, nothing since that moment when she discovered that Orion was the Prince, and regardless of everybody else in the room he had held her close in his arms and she had known that she need no longer be afraid.

They had dined very early because he had thought she must be tired, and now her maids had arrayed her in one of the lovely gauze negligées which she had brought from London in her trousseau.

It barely concealed the curves of her figure as she stood staring at the last glimpse of Apollo before he vanished into the sable of the night.

She heard a footstep behind her but she did not turn her head, and after a moment's pause Orion came and stood beside her.

It was the first time they had been alone since he had left her early in the afternoon to go to the Hotel Poseidon.

He did not speak, but she knew his eyes were on her face and after a moment she said:

"How . . . could I have known . . . how could I have even suspected for . . . one moment that you might be the . . . Prince? I was told he had a beard."

"A beard can prove to be a very effective disguise," he said with laughter in his voice, "but to remove it can be equally effective."

"You have done that before?"

"Several times when I wanted to go to Delphi," he admitted. "It was fascinating the way I could walk out of the Palace and nobody gave me a second glance."

There was a moment's silence, before she said:

"Colonel Stefanatis . . . looked for . . . you at the . . . Villa of . . . Madame Helena."

She thought Orion might stiffen at the name, but instead he leant over the balustrade beside her and said:

"How do you know that?"

"The Colonel did not realise that I could speak Greek," Athena answered, "and I . . . overhead what he was saying to the officer who had been looking for you."

"Do you want me to explain?"

"No."

It was the truth, Athena thought. There were really no explanations needed between them.

Of course there had been women in his life before they

met, but she knew now without his telling her that if they had mattered to him once they were pale shadows beside what he felt for her.

"Then I will tell you," he said with a faint smile. "The affection I had for Helena, who is an extremely intelligent and cultured woman, was over before I reluctantly accepted the suggestion that for the sake of my people I should marry an English heiress."

He paused, then added:

"I was not hiding in her Villa for the simple reason that she is leaving Greece and building a house for herself in the South of France."

Athena did not speak and after a moment he said:

"If you were surprised at learning my identity, how do you think I could have imagined that the cold-blooded, stiff, awe-inspiring heiress from England should prove to be my own little goddess, warm, loving and with a fire within her which echoes the fire in me?"

Athena felt herself tremble at the passion in his words. Then he asked:

"Why did you not tell me?"

"I . . . meant to," Athena said, "I tried to when we were having luncheon together . . . but then you . . . kissed me and nothing else . . . seemed to matter."

"Nothing else ever will matter."

He did not touch her but moved a little nearer to her before he said:

"I went to Delphi because at the last moment I panicked into thinking that even to help my poor people—and they are very poor—I could not saddle myself with a woman I did not love."

Athena turned to look at him.

"I went there for the same . . . reason. When I came to Greece I expected the Prince would be a man like you but I was terrified when I met the gossiping, pleasure-seeking Courtiers at the Palace in Athens."

"I loathe the place—that is why I never go there."

"You are not . . . angry with me for having . . . kept my secret? I was preparing to tell the Prince I could not marry

him . . . and the thought that . . . Orion was waiting for me
. . . gave me the courage to do so."

"I am still waiting, my darling."

She looked in his eyes and made a little movement as if
she would go closer to him. But then she said:

"Our marriage is . . . legal? We will not have to be married again?"

"It is completely legal," he replied, "and I know that like
me you could not bear to repeat what to both of us was an
unforgettable experience."

"I loved becoming your . . . wife in that dear little Church
with only the . . . people who . . . love you present," Athena
said in a low voice.

"I have learnt from your Aunt that you were christened
'Athena Mayville'," Orion said, "and Count Theodoros is actually one of my titles."

"Then I am really your wife!"

"Do you want me to prove it?"

He would have taken her in his arms but with a faint
gesture Athena stopped him.

"I want you to know one thing," she said. "Even if you
had been quite poor and of no social consequence, I would
still have been happy . . . wildly, crazily happy with you . . .
even if you refused to touch my money."

"You anticipated that I might do that?"

Athena looked away from him a little shyly.

"I was sure you were very proud," she said, "and I was
afraid that the Prince might . . . revenge himself on you in
. . . some manner, in which case we should have been obliged
to use my fortune to leave Greece! Otherwise I anticipated
that you might feel it a . . . humiliation to live on your wife's
. . . wealth."

"You would have cooked for me and looked after me?"
Orion asked.

"I would have tried to be as good a cook as Madame
Argeros," Athena answered.

Orion gave a laugh of sheer happiness.

"My darling! Was there ever anyone like you?" he asked.
"I said you were perfect, but there are degrees of perfection

of which even I was not aware. You are everything Athena should be."

He touched her cheek with his hand as he went on:

"You have her beauty, her clear-sighted intelligence and, having put her armour away, like her you cultivate the feminine graces and of course the olive groves."

He was half-serious, half-teasing, and now Athena moved close against him.

"Shall we cultivate the . . . olive-groves together?" she whispered.

His arms went round her and his lips were on her hair as he said:

"There are so many things I want to do with you and as the goddess of wisdom I know that you will guide, inspire and help my people—they need you desperately!"

"And . . . you?" Athena enquired.

He looked down at her, his eyes searching her face as he said:

"I cannot live without you—does that answer your question?"

"I love you, Orion! I love you and I am afraid that . . . this is a . . . dream from which we might both . . . awaken."

"It is a dream that will stay with us all the days of our lives," he answered, "and every moment, every second that I am with you, my darling little goddess, I fall more deeply, more overwhelmingly in love."

He felt a quiver run through her at his words and his arms tightened around the softness of her body which seemed to melt into his.

The last golden finger of the sun touched them both and illuminated them with a golden aura.

Orion looked down into Athena's eyes shining in the light that came not only from the sun but also from the glory within herself.

"You are tired, my precious," he said, "but if you look at me like that it will be hard for me to let you rest and not make love to you as I want to do."

"I . . . want your love," Athena said. "I want to make sure that I am really your . . . wife and that I need no longer be afraid of . . . losing you."

"You will never do that," he answered, "and I think you realise as I do, my dearest love, that we have been joined together not only by the Church but also by the power of Apollo and Athena goddess of love."

He paused and his voice deepened as he said:

"I believe with all my heart that they brought us together. We were meant for each other since the beginning of time, and an instinct which was part of the divine took us both to Delphi."

"I think that too," Athena said. "In fact I am sure of it."

"Fate moved in strange ways, and there is always a pattern behind everything," Orion went on. "There is a reason for us meeting and loving each other, which will affect the lives and the future of all those with whom we come in contact."

"You mean that . . . together we can do something for . . . Greece?" Athena asked.

"Nothing ever really happens by chance, and nothing is ever wasted," Orion replied. "That is why, my darling, there are gods who plan our destiny."

"As long as I am with you," Athena whispered, "and as long as we can do what is right and good . . . that is all I ask of the future."

She had been moved by the solemnity of his tone, and now he turned towards the sea and the mountains in the distance, which were bathed in the pale transparent limpid grey of the dusk.

"Once this country gave to the world the power to think," he said quietly. "Men's minds moved quicker here and their hearts were lifted in a manner which has never been forgotten."

He paused before he continued:

"That should be the goal of all Greeks to-day, to find again the vision of perfect beauty and of clear thinking which was our contribution to the world."

There was a radiance in Orion's expression and his voice seemed to have a special vibrance as he said:

"Once the Greeks saw holiness wherever they walked and they translated it into beauty."

Athena thought of Delphi and of the Parthenon, and understood what he was trying to say, as he went on:

"That holiness and beauty must come again for it has been too long from the earth. That is the ideal, my darling, to which we in our way must dedicate ourselves."

"I will do that . . . if you will . . . help me," Athena said.

"We will do it together," he answered. "You and I will try to find the light of the gods and bring it to those who need it desperately."

As he spoke the grey of the sky deepened to sable and the mystery of the darkening night enfolded them.

And yet it seemed to Athena that some light within themselves remained. It came from their hearts and was in fact some of the splendour that had once belonged to Greece.

Because she was a little over-awed and at the same time deeply moved by the way Orion had spoken, she moved closer to him as if for protection, half afraid of the greatness of his vision and all he asked of her.

Because he understood he held her very close and his lips were against the softness of her cheek.

"Such ideals lie in our souls and cannot be shown to ordinary people because they would not understand," he said quietly, "but our love and happiness in each other is different."

His mouth moved over her skin before he went on:

"I believe that, in itself, will bring happiness to others, as you, my beautiful one, gave happiness yesterday to the simple friends I have in Delphi."

"They have no idea who you are?" Athena asked.

"To them I am Orion, someone they love because I love them. I like to keep it that way so that there is always somewhere I can go and just be myself, and there are no demands made on me except as a man."

"I love you as a . . . man," Athena said, her voice deepening on the word, "but I also love you as Orion and last night when you . . . made me your . . . wife I thought that the . . . constellation of stars shone . . . around you."

"We were enchanted," he said, "and I think that the light of Apollo brought us both an ecstasy that is only given to those favoured by the gods."

His lips found her mouth.

At first it was a kiss without passion, but something more perfect, more sacred, like the moonlight on the Sanctuary at Delphi.

Then the closeness of him and his lips awakened the fire that had burnt within Athena the night before and she felt it rise in him.

They clung together feeling the flames of love uniting their bodies and exciting their minds.

"I love you! I love you, Orion," Athena whispered.

Now his kiss became more demanding, fiercely, insistently passionate and with it an exaltation and a rapture which made her feel that once gain he would carry her up into the sky until they reached the stars that were just appearing in the velvet darkness above them.

Then with his lips on hers, and holding her close against his throbbing heart, both of them aware of the urgency of their need for each other, Orion drew Athena from the balcony and into the room behind them.

On the sea the reflection of light from the rising moon touched the softly moving waves with silver as if they caressed the body of the goddess of love.

# A KISS IN ROME

# *Author's Note*

The first time I visited Rome I was entranced by the beauty of its treasures and the history which one finds at every turn.

It is undoubtedly one of the most beautiful Cities in the world and every stone appears to have a story attached to it.

The Villa Borghese, which I have described in this novel and which in the past was called a Palace, is one of the jewels of Europe.

It is breath-taking in the beauty of its rooms and their contents.

It was built originally by Cardinal Camillo Borghese in 1605 when he came to the Papal throne, taking the name Paul V.

The treasures were added to year by year with each generation.

But it makes one's heart sink to learn that the famous collection of antique sculpture to which had been added the Masterpieces of Bernini, making in all 523 pieces, was given by Camillo Borghese, the husband of the beautiful Pauline Bonaparte, to his brother-in-law Napoleon in 1807 and was carried off bodily to Paris.

This is typical of conquerors all down the ages.

Fortunately, however, most of these were returned eventually to Rome, where we may still see them.

The exquisite statue of Pauline Borghese, who was the

second wife of Prince Camillo Borghese, is the masterpiece of Antonio Canova (1757–1822).

It is now on show in one of the rooms and was sculpted in 1805.

It shows Pauline semi-nude, reclining on a divan, half raised up and holding in her left hand the apple of victory won—as Venus—for her beauty.

I have written another novel which includes the Borghese Palace, called *The Coin of Love*.

In this novel, which I wrote after my visit in 1988, I have described the magic of the Trevi Fountain and the glory of the Colosseum.

But one has only to arrive in Rome and visit a list of the places that move one and excite the imagination to find there are hundreds more waiting for one's appreciation.

Rome is known as the "Eternal City" and as long as its treasures remain it will always have a place in the hearts of those who love beauty.

# CHAPTER ONE

Alina Langley looked around the room and wondered miserably if there was anything left to sell.

Everything that was of any real value had already gone.

The patches on the wall where the mirrors had hung and the gap where the pretty inlaid *secrétaire* had stood made her want to cry.

"What can I do?" she asked. "What can I do?"

It seemed incredible that everything had happened so quickly.

From feeling safe and happy in the world around her, she now felt as if the ceiling had crashed down on her head.

When her Father a year ago had had a fall out hunting and broken his spine, it was for her Mother as if the world had come to an end.

They had been extremely happy together.

They were not rich, but had enough money to enjoy their horses and the few acres of land by which they were surrounded.

Then, when Sir Oswald died, it was found that he had run up a mountain of debts.

They were certainly not due to riotous living.

He had not paid his taxes and he owed a great deal to his Coach-Builder and to the builders for repairs to the house.

What was worse, shares in Companies in which he had invested both his wife's and his own money had proved worthless.

Lady Langley, however, was not the slightest perturbed by this.

She only knew that without her husband she had no wish to go on living.

To Alina it was horrifying to see her Mother fading away.

She was still so young and beautiful and had always seemed like a girl.

As she had no wish to live, Lady Langley simply died so that she could be with her husband again.

It was then that Alina knew she was alone in the world and, what was even more frightening, that she had no money.

The house was hers because she was an only child, but how could she keep it up?

Anything that was valuable had been sold off to pay her Father's debts.

A few other things which she cherished she had had to sell to pay for special food and medicines for her Mother.

It was just a waste of money, for Lady Langley never got better, and had never intended to do so.

Alina walked to the window to look out at the garden.

The daffodils made a golden patch of colour beneath the trees.

The almond trees were just coming into bloom, and the grass was growing on the lawns.

The sun was shining and she opened the window.

She could hear the song of the birds and the buzz of the bees hovering over the blossom.

It was so familiar.

She felt as if they were telling her that they sympathised with her in her predicament and how they wished they could help.

"What can I do?" she asked the wrens who were watching

her from a bush that was just beginning to show the green leaves of Spring.

It was then, to her surprise, that she heard in the distance wheels approaching the front-door.

She wondered who it could be.

The only people who had called on her after her Mother's Funeral had been from the village, and they had walked.

She thought it might be the Doctor, who had always been a friend.

Then she remembered that he had gone away, on a short holiday.

Slowly, because she almost resented being disturbed in her loneliness, she walked from the Drawing-room out into the Hall.

The woman who came to clean in the morning had already left and she opened the door herself.

A very smart carriage was standing outside.

There was a face at its window that made her cry out in astonishment.

"Denise! Is it really you?"

She ran down the steps, and as the elegantly dressed figure got out of the carriage, she flung her arms around her.

"Denise, how wonderful to see you!" she exclaimed. "I thought you had forgotten all about me."

"No, of course not," Denise Sedgwick replied, "but I have come to ask for your help."

"My help?" Alina repeated in surprise.

She could not imagine how Denise Sedgwick could possibly want her help.

Her Mother had been a distant Cousin of the Sedgwicks and had been devoted to Denise's Mother before she had died in childbirth.

Because Alina and Denise were almost the same age, with Denise just a few months older, it was arranged that they should take lessons together.

Every Monday Alina would ride over to the large house, which was only three miles away across the fields, and stay there until Friday.

On Friday she returned home to be with her Father and Mother.

It had been a very satisfactory arrangement from Lady Langley's point of view.

Because Denise's Father was wealthy, he could afford the best-educated Governesses.

They also had a number of Tutors for various additional subjects in which he wanted his daughter to be educated.

Alina enjoyed her lessons and loved being with Denise.

She was very lovely; in fact, both girls were outstandingly beautiful.

Perhaps Denise was the more sensational of the two, having perfect features and chestnut hair that was tipped with little flames of red.

Her eyes were the green of a forest stream.

It was no surprise when, just before her eighteenth birthday, Denise went to London to be presented at Court by her Grandmother.

She had been an outstanding success.

In fact, she was such a sensation that Alina lost touch with her.

At first the two girls had corresponded frequently.

But soon Alina found that she was writing three letters to one hurried note from Denise.

She therefore thought that perhaps she was imposing on their friendship and wrote only occasionally.

Lately she had not written at all.

Now Denise was saying:

"Dearest, you must forgive me for not having come to see you sooner. I have not been at home or with my Grandmother, but staying in all sorts of exciting houses, for house-parties which I am longing to tell you about."

"You look lovely!" Alina exclaimed.

She was looking, as she spoke, at the very elegant travelling-coat which Denise was wearing, and at her hat trimmed with feathers.

She noted too the elegance of her gloves, her shoes, and her hand-bag—in fact, everything about her.

They went into the Drawing-Room and Denise gave a cry of surprise.

"What has happened?" she exclaimed. "What have you done? Where are all the mirrors and the pictures?"

"I have a lot to tell you," Alina said quietly.

Denise waited and Alina went on:

"After Papa died we found we were very poor."

"I was so upset to hear about his accident," Denise murmured sympathetically. "But I had always imagined you were very comfortably off."

"We thought we were," Alina replied, "but there were a great many debts, and Papa's investments did not pay any dividends."

Denise clasped her hands together.

"Oh, dearest, how terrible! I wish I had known. Of course I would have wanted to help you."

Alina drew in her breath.

"I do not think you know," she said, "that Mama . . . died three weeks ago."

Denise gave a little cry of horror and flung her arms round Alina.

"I had no idea—oh, Alina, I am so sorry! I know how much you loved her, and I loved her too."

"Everybody loved Mama," Alina said, "but she could not go on living without Papa."

Denise sat down on a sofa that needed repairing.

"You must tell me all about it," she said. "I had no idea that anything like this had happened. When I decided to come to you for help, I expected, of course, to find your Mother here with everything as beautiful as I remembered it to be."

"We had to sell everything that was saleable," Alina said in a low voice.

There was a little pause before she added:

"We will talk about that later. I want to hear about you and the success you have been, and, of course, why you have come to me for help."

She saw by the expression in her friend's eyes that something was really wrong.

After a moment Denise said:

"Oh, Alina, I have been such a fool! You will not believe how stupid I have been."

Alina sat down beside her.

"Tell me about it."

"That is what I decided to do and why I came," Denise replied, "and I was sure you would help me."

Alina reached out and took Denise's hand in hers.

"Start at the beginning," she said.

"Well, as you heard, I was a success in London. I really was a great success, Alina, and it would be stupid to deny it."

"How could you be anything else?" Alina asked fondly. "You are so lovely and you have all those beautiful clothes that you wrote and told me about."

"My Grandmother was very generous," Denise said, "and, of course, Papa was prepared to pay for anything I wanted."

There was a smile on her lips as she added:

"I really was the Belle of every Ball I went to!"

"Of course you were!" Alina said loyally.

"It is not only looks that count in London," Denise said. "There are plenty of sophisticated Beauties who fascinate the Prince of Wales and all the smart gentlemen who frequent Marlborough House."

"I am sure none of them could be as beautiful as you!" Alina said.

"They think they are far more beautiful, and the men who go after them are not interested in *débutantes*."

Alina waited, wondering what was wrong.

"However, I have had dozens of proposals," Denise said, "and finally, Alina, I lost my heart!"

"How exciting!" Alina exclaimed. "Who is he? And are you very happy?"

Denise gave a deep sigh.

"He is very handsome and he is the Earl of Wescott, so Papa was only too delighted at the idea of my marrying him."

"You are going to be married?" Alina exclaimed.

"That is what has gone wrong," Denise answered.

"But what has happened?"

"I cannot understand how I can have been such a fool!" Denise said. "Henry was in love with me, very much in love with me, and asked me to marry him."

Alina was listening wide-eyed.

She could not understand what she was hearing.

"I do not know what came over me," Denise continued, "but I think it was because Henry rather took it for granted that I would accept him. Although there could be no question of my doing anything else, I prevaricated."

"You mean," Alina said, "that you did not accept him."

"I did—in a way—but told him he would have to wait a little for us to be quite certain that we really loved each other."

"And he disagreed?"

"No. But, Alina, I was so stupid! Just to make him more in love with me and a little jealous, I flirted with a lot of other men, until finally I went too far."

"What happened then?" Alina asked.

"Henry wrote me a letter saying it was quite obvious that I did not really care for him, and he left England!"

There was a note of despair in Denise's voice which Alina did not miss.

"He left England?" she questioned. "But where has he gone?"

"He has gone to Rome to stay with his Grandmother," Denise replied, "and I am terrified—yes, terrified—that I shall never see him again."

"But, surely, if you write to him . . ." Alina began.

"I am not going to do that," Denise said. "I have decided to go to Rome and see him. I know when he sees me again, everything will be all right. I can tell him that I love him more than anything on earth, and we will be married."

Alina thought for a moment before she said:

"I am sure that is a sensible solution."

"But it will be difficult," Denise said, "and that is why I have come to see you."

"What can I do?" Alina asked.

"Well, Papa has agreed that I can go to Rome, and, as it happens, my Cousin, Lord Teverton, whom you have never met, is going there on a special mission on behalf of the Prime Minister. I can travel with him, but, of course, I have to have a chaperon."

Alina nodded.

She could understand that it would be impossible for a young girl to go abroad without one.

"That is why I came to see you," Denise said, "because I have been trying to remember the name of that Governess we had for a short while when Miss Smithson was ill. She was a married woman, and a very pleasant lady."

"A Governess?" Alina repeated. "But, surely . . . ?"

"I know what you are thinking," Denise said, "exactly the same as Papa did, that I should take one of my relatives with me. An Aunt, or an elder Cousin."

She threw out her hands in a very expressive gesture.

"Can you imagine what they would be like? They would be coy and say 'Now, you young people want to be alone together,' which would make me feel hot with embarrassment. Or else they will play the strict chaperon and never allow me to be alone with Henry for an instant."

Alina laughed.

She had met some of Denise's relatives and knew that was exactly the way they would behave.

"I went over a whole list of them," Denise was saying, "and each one seemed worse than the last. I have to be very clever with Henry, as I have really upset him."

She made a sound that was almost a sob as she said:

"His letter was such a shock to me. I know he has taken umbrage at the way I behaved, and I have somehow to make him forgive me."

She sighed again, then with a little flash in her eyes she added:

"But I am not going to crawl at his feet, which would be very bad for his ego. He is quite authoritative enough as it is!"

Alina laughed again.

"I can see your problem, but Mrs. Wilson, which is the name of the lady about whom you were asking, is working for the French Ambassador, teaching his children to speak English. At the moment she is with them in France."

"Oh, bother!" Denise said. "She was the only person I could think of who could be tactful and at the same time satisfy Papa that she was the right sort of chaperon for me."

"I am sure you can think of somebody else," Alina said hopefully.

"I simply cannot think who—" Denise began.

Then she gave a sudden scream.

It was so loud that it made Alina start, and she looked at her friend in surprise.

"But of course—I have solved the problem!" Denise said. "It is quite easy. You will come with me!"

"Me?" Alina asked. "But, dearest, I am not a married woman, and two girls together could not chaperon each other."

"Of course I understand that," Denise said sharply. "What I am thinking of, and it is really clever of me, is that you should come as your Mother."

"M-my . . . Mother?"

"You know how lovely your Mother was and how young she looked," Denise said, thinking it out in her mind. "After all, we all know the story of how she married when she was seventeen, so she cannot have been quite thirty-seven when she died."

"That's true," Alina said, "but—"

"There are no 'buts,'" Denise interrupted. "I shall tell Papa, who is leaving this afternoon for a week's racing at Doncaster, that Lady Langley is chaperoning me to Rome. In fact, when I left the house he said:

"'Remember me to Lady Langley. She was always a very charming woman and I am sorry we have not seen more of her.' He has obviously not heard of her death."

Alina was staring at her friend as if she could not believe what she was hearing.

Then, as Denise stopped speaking, she said:

"It is a wonderful idea, darling, and you know I would adore to come with you to Rome, but no-one in their senses would believe I was Mama . . . even if I dressed up in her clothes."

"Why not?" Denise argued obstinately. "People used to say that you and your Mother looked more like sisters. If you did your hair in a more sophisticated style and wore a little powder and rouge as the Beauties do in London, I am sure you would look a lot older."

Alina did not speak, and after a moment Denise continued:

"I remember all the flattering praise you used to get at the Christmas parties when we put on those Charades and

Plays for Papa's guests. I used to be jealous because they always said you were a much better actress than I was."

She put her fingers up to her forehead in thought.

Then she added:

"You remember the Restoration Play we put on the Christmas before I went to London? You played two parts in it: one was a very sophisticated and witty woman who was supposed to be at least forty."

"Acting on a stage is one thing," Alina said, "but if I was doing it at close quarters, I am quite certain no-one would be deceived."

Denise threw out her hands.

"Who is there to be deceived?" she asked. "Papa will have left for the Races. My Cousin, Lord Teverton, has never met you, nor has my lady's-maid and the Courier who will be escorting us."

Alina did not speak, and she went on:

"When we get to Rome, all I want you to do is to let me see Henry alone, and I am sure you can amuse yourself by looking at the Colosseum and all those other places about which we used to read with Miss Smithson."

There was a sudden light in Alina's eyes.

She was thinking of how much she had longed to see all the places they had read about.

She often thought about them when she was alone at night.

She pretended she was actually seeing them with her eyes instead of just remembering what she had read.

Then she told herself she had to be firm about this.

"Dearest Denise," she said at length. "You know I would do anything to help you—anything in the world—except something which is wrong and might cause trouble for you, one way or another."

"What you can do for me is quite simple," Denise answered. "You will come with me to Rome as my chaperon, and you will make quite certain that Henry Wescott forgives me and we become officially engaged."

Alina thought it all sounded too easy to be true.

Then she said in a frightened voice:

"Y-you are quite certain I would not . . . make a mess of it?"

"Why should you?" Denise enquired. "We will not see anyone who has ever seen your Mother, and you have to admit that she did look very young."

"Yes . . . everyone said so," Alina agreed.

"Then all you have to do is to make yourself look a little older than you are now. Good gracious! If you cannot act the part of a Lady who is a suitable chaperon for me, what can you do?"

Alina laughed.

"You are being ridiculous! At the same time, you know, dearest, because I do want to help you and also because, if I am honest, I would love to go to Rome, I am longing to say 'Yes.' "

"That is wonderful!" Denise cried. "We leave in three days' time."

"Three . . . days?" Alina repeated.

"That will be plenty of time for you to decide which of your Mother's clothes you are going to wear, and I will provide you with everything else."

She put her hand over Alina's as she said:

"I am so ashamed of myself for not realising before now how poor you are. I have mountains of clothes, really mountains of them, which I could have sent you, but I was so selfish I did not think of it."

"You are not to blame yourself," Alina said, "and what would I do with mountains of clothes in Little Benbury?"

"You can wear them," Denise answered, "but the gown you have on now is a disaster!"

"I have had it for years," Alina admitted, "and it is rather threadbare."

"Throw it away—throw everything you have away, and I am sure there are furs and jewels that belonged to my Mother of the kind you would be expected to wear."

Alina looked at her questioningly, and Denise said:

"Now, let us work this out carefully. You are not coming as the country-bred and impoverished Lady Langley who is chaperoning me because Papa is paying her to do so."

Alina made a little sound and she went on:

"I will of course pay you myself. I have an absolute mint of money! But you will have to look rich and a Lady of Fashion, or people will not be impressed by you."

"Why do you want them to be impressed?" Alina asked.

"I want Henry to be impressed, for one," Alina said. "I have no wish for him to think I am just running after him. I have got to arrive in Rome with a different reason for going there, and that could be that I am accompanying Lady Langley, who is a friend of my family, because she has recently been widowed and is feeling lonely."

"You are making a whole drama out of it," Alina protested.

"That is what I intend to do," Denise said. "And I will write your part just as you used to write one for me in the past. Now I will do it for you."

Alina laughed.

"Oh, Denise, you are incorrigible!" she said. "But I am sure you are making a terrible mistake. There must be plenty of people more suitable than I am to go with you to Rome. Suppose I make mistakes and give the show away?"

"I have never known you to fail at anything," Denise said. "You are much cleverer than I am. Every one of my Governesses, Tutors, or anyone else who taught us always used to say:

" 'Now, come along, Miss Denise, try and be as clever as your Cousin who, after all, is younger than you!' "

Denise was mimicking a Tutor's voice, and Alina threw her arms round her neck and kissed her.

"Oh, Denise, it is such Heaven being with you again," she said. "I have missed you so much and all the things we used to laugh about together."

"That is what we are going to do all the way to Rome. Otherwise I shall just sit here and mope," Denise answered. "You have to keep me laughing and sparkling so that when Henry sees me he realises what a mistake he made in leaving me."

"I cannot think why he should have done so, seeing how beautiful you are," Alina said.

"It was my own fault," Denise said in a low voice, "and if

I lose him, Alina, it would break my heart. I could never love anyone else in the same way."

She was speaking in a very different tone of voice. Then she reached out and took her Cousin's hand.

"Help me . . . please . . . help me!" she begged. "I know my whole happiness is at stake. If I lose Henry, nothing else will ever be the same again."

There was a cry in her voice that tore at Alina's heart.

She knew she would do anything, however difficult, if it would help Denise.

"I will come," she said, "but you will have to tell me exactly how I should behave. Remember, I have never been to London or seen any of the smart, sophisticated women I am to impersonate."

"They are all very much alike," Denise answered. "They behave as if the world were made for them to walk on and believe that every man at whom they smile is very lucky and should feel as if he has just won a million pounds on the Race-Course."

Alina giggled.

"Can you see me behaving like that?"

"Of course I can," Denise said, "and that is exactly what you have to do. You are very grand, very self-important, and very rich!"

"I would certainly need to be a good actress to make them believe that!" Alina remarked.

"Why did you not tell me?" Denise asked. "I cannot bear to think of your selling all the lovely things in this room."

"I was just wondering before you arrived what else I could possibly sell, or how I could work to earn some money."

"You have got it," Denise replied. "You are going to work for me and I am prepared to pay you anything you ask."

She put her arms around Alina as she spoke and kissed her.

"I love you, Alina," she said, "and we shall have a marvellous time together. When I am married to Henry, I will find you a husband who is just as rich as he is!"

"I shall be quite content for the moment just to see the Colosseum and St. Peter's," Alina said.

"From what I have been told," Denise answered, "Rome

is packed with marvellous treasures of every sort. So if you are prepared to go sightseeing, you will be able to do so from morning to night."

"That is all I want," Alina said, "and I shall certainly not interfere with you and the Earl."

There was a pause before Denise said with almost a sob:

"Oh, Alina . . . do you think he has . . . forgotten me already? Supposing he has found an . . . Italian girl who is more . . . beautiful than I am?"

"I do not believe it possible," Alina answered, "and if he has, it means that he is not really in love with you. You know we always used to say when we were younger that what we wanted to find was real love, which means we have found the other half of ourselves."

"That is true," Denise said. "Do you remember Miss Smithson saying the Ancient Greeks believed that after God had made man and thought he wanted a companion, He cut him in half and called the soft, gentle, sweet part of him woman?"

"I remember her saying that," Alina said, "and what we are searching for is the other half of ourselves."

"Of course," Denise agreed, "and that is what Henry is to me—I know he is!"

"How could you have been unkind to him?" Alina asked. "He must have been very unhappy to have rushed away from you in that abrupt manner."

"Do not talk about it," Denise begged. "I was a fool—I know I was a fool! I just wanted to make him a little jealous so that he would be more in love with me than he was already. But I . . . went too . . . far!"

Alina put her arm around her friend's shoulders.

"Do not worry, dearest," she said. "I am sure you will be able to get him back, and I will pray very hard that he is as miserable without you as you are without him."

"I remember your prayers," Denise said. "You always said they were answered."

"That is what I am thinking of it at this moment. When I pray for a solution to my own problems, I even ask the birds outside for help!"

"And here I am, ready to help you," Denise replied. "Now, let us make plans."

Because she was so determined to take Alina with her to Rome, Denise worked it out very intelligently.

First of all, as her Father was going away immediately, she thought it would be possible for Alina to come to Sedgwick House, her own home.

Then they thought that the servants would know her and that could be dangerous.

"I will pick you up here on Wednesday morning," Denise decided, "and we will drive to the train together. When we reach London, Lord Teverton will be waiting for us at his house in Belgrave Square."

"I have no idea what he is like," Alina said. "Supposing he is suspicious?"

"You need not worry about him," Denise said. "He is extremely angry that I am to travel with him to Rome, so I doubt if he will so much as speak to us."

Alina looked surprised.

"Why not?" she asked.

"Because he is stuck up and interested only in himself!" Denise said. "He is a huge success in London and a close friend of the Prince of Wales."

She lowered her voice, almost as if she were afraid she would be overheard.

"He also has affairs with the great Beauties, and I am told that when he leaves them, they cry their eyes out!"

Alina did not understand.

"Leaves them?"

"You know what I mean," Denise said.

She saw that her Cousin was looking perplexed and explained:

"He has what are called *affaires de coeur,* and because he is so smart and also so rich, the women run after him as if he were a golden apple at the top of a pear tree!"

Alina laughed.

"I do not believe it!"

"It is true!" Denise said. "He gives himself frightful airs and behaves as if everybody is beneath his condescension."

"He sounds horrible!" Alina said.

"I have disliked him for years," Denise replied. "He always speaks to me as if I were a mentally deficient child!"

"I cannot believe this!"

"It is true, and it is only because he enjoys riding my Father's horses that he comes to stay with us at all. And, of course, they meet on the Race-Course."

She gave a little laugh before she said:

"I saw his face when Papa asked him to take me with him to Rome."

"He was not pleased at the idea?" Alina said.

"He was horrified!" Denise answered. "I could see him thinking up a dozen different excuses for refusing. Then finally, very grudgingly, he accepted the responsibility of having me with him, providing I had a chaperon."

Alina thought indignantly that it was incredible that anyone could be unkind to someone as pretty and sweet as Denise.

She remembered her Father once saying that the young men in London thought *débutantes* were a bore.

Therefore, the sooner they were married off to a suitable husband, the better.

"Why has your Cousin never married!" she asked now. "How old is he?"

"All of thirty," Denise replied, "and he can hardly marry any of the women to whom he makes love because they are always already married."

Alina's eyes widened.

"Surely their husbands object?"

"They do not know about it. You would be amazed at how extraordinarily women behave in London. The Prince of Wales always associates with married women who are beautiful, witty, and very sophisticated. My Cousin, Marcus Teverton, behaves in the same way."

"Well, I think it is horrid!" Alina said firmly. "I cannot imagine Papa would have behaved like that, and, if he had, it would have broken Mama's heart."

"Your Father and Mother were so different from anybody else," Denise said. "I never thought of her dying. She always seemed so young and happy."

"She was until she lost Papa," Alina said softly, "but then

the light went out, and she could not bear to be in the darkness alone."

There was a break in her voice as she spoke.

It was still hard to speak of her Mother without the tears coming into her eyes.

"Poor Alina!" Denise said. "I know how much you must miss her. It would be the best thing in the world for you to come to Rome, and I am sure it is what she would want you to do."

Alina hesitated.

"Perhaps Mama would be shocked at the idea of my telling lies and playing a part that is deceitful."

"If you ask me," Denise said, "I think she would consider it a great joke. You know how she used to laugh at the 'fuddy-duddy' people in the County who disapproved of everything we did."

She saw Alina was looking a little happier and went on:

"Do you remember when they said the hedges we jumped were too high for us, and we acted like young hooligans? It was your Mother who said she thought it was a very good thing for women to be able to ride well and not be afraid of a high jump."

Alina nodded.

"That is what we are going to do now," Denise continued. "We are going to take a high jump and you will forget all your problems. You will see Rome and all the beautiful things it contains."

Alina gave a little cry.

"Do you really think, Denise, that I can do it? I want to, and it will be a great adventure!"

"Of course it will," Denise agreed, "and I will supply the happy ending when I marry Henry and make sure he never leaves me again."

"Oh, dearest," Alina said, "I do want you to be happy."

# CHAPTER TWO

Denise arrived the next afternoon.

Alina watched in astonishment as the coachman and footman carried in a number of trunks.

They put them in Alina's bed-room and as soon as they had done so Denise started to open them.

"I have brought you Mama's luggage," she said. "It has her initials on it and looks, I am sure, much more luxurious than anything you have."

Alina was aware of that and she also saw the initials "A.L." on the trunks.

Before she could ask the question, Denise said:

"You must remember that Mama's name was Alice."

"Of course it was!" Alina exclaimed. "I had forgotten."

"I suddenly thought of the luggage when I was driving home," Denise said with glee. "As soon as I told Papa that Lady Langley was chaperoning me—and he was delighted about it—I went upstairs to the attics. All Mama's things were there—and look what I found!"

She opened the trunks one by one.

First she lifted out an evening-cloak of black velvet trimmed with ermine.

Alina made a little murmur of delight.

Denise then produced another cloak which was of blue velvet trimmed with Russian sables.

"They are lovely!" Alina exclaimed.

"Wait!" Denise said.

She then produced a sable stole with lots of tails.

Alina knew most Ladies of Fashion wore this type of fur if they could afford it.

There was also a number of sunshades which were very elegant.

Then Denise opened a large hat-box.

"I thought Mama's other clothes were far too out of date for you to wear them," she said, "except for a few evening-gowns. But hats have altered very little since she died; in fact, they are now only more elaborate."

She removed a number of hats trimmed with feathers and bows of ribbon.

Alina realised they would make her look older.

She could also take the decoration from one hat to make another look more spectacular.

"You know how elaborate everything is to-day," Denise was saying, "and that is why I am sure we can add lace and frills to the evening-gowns so that they look up-to-date."

The bustle, which had been very prominent when Denise's Mother was alive, had gradually become more a part of the skirt.

But for older women the evening-gowns with their trains were still very much the same as they had been.

"I am sure we can find a Dressmaker in Rome who can smarten up some of these gowns," Denise said. "In the meantime, I have brought you every gown of mine that does not look obviously as if it belonged to a *débutante*."

There were a great number of them, and Denise unpacked them quickly, saying:

"I always thought that one unbecoming because it was too dark, and this one I bought in a bad light. I really think it would become you, while on me it is a disaster."

Certainly the darker dresses with their rich colours threw into prominence Alina's very fair hair and the whiteness of her skin.

Finally Denise brought a small box from the last trunk with an air of triumph.

"Look what I found also in the attic!" she said.

She opened the box and Alina saw that inside there was face-powder, mascara, and a tiny pot of rouge.

"How could your Mother have had that?" she asked.

"That is a question that worried me," Denise replied, "until I remembered one of our Cousins who was very smart and very sophisticated coming to stay. I could not have been very old at the time, but I can remember her laughing at Mama and saying she was 'old-fashioned.' After she left, a small parcel arrived which was a present from her."

" 'What do you think Gwen has sent me?' I heard my Mother ask Papa.

" 'I have no idea,' he replied.

"She opened the box and showed him what was inside," Denise went on.

"And what did your Father say?" Alina enquired.

"I remember him roaring in fury:

" 'I am not having my wife looking like an actress!'

"My Mother laughed at him.

" 'If we go to London,' she said, 'you will be ashamed of me for looking so countrified.'

" 'That is how I like you,' Papa replied, and put his arms around her.

"So she never used it," Denise finished, "but now you will find it very useful."

"But ... I have no wish to look like an actress!" Alina protested.

"Gwen sent Mama the present ten years ago," Denise said. "Since then things have changed. All the smart women in London use a little powder, a touch of rouge, and their lips are always invitingly pink."

Alina laughed.

"Well, I shall be inviting nobody, but if you want me to look the part, I suppose I shall have to accept the 'stage props.' "

"Of course you must," Denise insisted.

She did not stay long but hurried away, leaving Alina to put all the clothes she had brought back into the trunks.

She added some clothes that had belonged to her Mother.

Lady Langley had always been elegantly dressed, even though she could not spend a lot of money on her clothes.

But they were certainly very much smarter than anything Alina now owned.

She therefore left her own dress hanging in the wardrobe.

She found, which had belonged to her Mother, a very pretty travelling-gown in a deep blue satin.

It was fortunate that it could go under a cloak which Denise had brought her of almost the same shade of blue.

It was trimmed with just a little fur, which made it not look too smart for a journey.

There was a hat which Alina thought was really very becoming.

She added a few small feathers and a velvet bow to the crown.

Among the sunshades there was a hand-bag.

"I am afraid there is only one of those," Denise had said as she took it out of the box. "But Papa gave a lot of Mama's belongings away to her relations after she died. They all asked for hand-bags because they knew the ones Mama possessed all came from a very expensive shop in Bond Street."

"I am delighted to have that one," Alina said. "I am afraid that if anyone saw the bag I have been using, they would not for a moment believe I was rich enough to have any money inside it."

"Then throw it away," Denise said, "because that is the sort of thing that might make people suspect you are not what you are pretending to be."

There were plenty of pairs of suede and kid gloves and silk stockings which Alina had never expected to own.

There were also nightgowns and *negligées* as well as petticoats trimmed with real lace.

When she looked at them, Alina sent up a little prayer of thankfulness to God.

She at last owned the lovely things she had always longed to have.

By the time she had finished packing it was quite late. She went to bed and slept peacefully.

Mrs. Banks from the village came in early in the morning to prepare her breakfast.

She looked in surprise at the pile of luggage.

"You goin' away, Miss?" she enquired.

"I am going to stay with some friends," Alina said, "but I hope, Mrs. Banks, you will come in and look after the house, and I will arrange for the Vicar to pay you your money every week."

Yesterday Denise had actually been on her way downstairs when Alina had said to her in a rather embarrassed manner:

"I hate to ask you, Denise, but could you possibly let me have just a few pounds so that the woman who looks after the house can be paid? Otherwise, it will get in a dreadful state."

Denise stopped on the bottom step and gave a cry of horror.

"How stupid of me to forget to give it to you!" she apologised. "Of course I have brought you some money, and remember there is plenty more whenever you need it."

"I am ashamed to ask you, when you have given me so much," Alina murmured.

"I have given you nothing that has cost me anything!" Denise said honestly. "Here is the envelope I brought ready for you."

She pulled an envelope out of her hand-bag and put it into Alina's hand.

Then she hurried to where the carriage was waiting outside and drove off.

When she opened the envelope Alina saw there were twenty-five pounds in it.

For a moment she thought it impossible to accept so much money from her Cousin.

When she saw her the next day she would give some of it back.

Then she remembered how much she owed in the village.

As soon as she was dressed she went first to the Vicarage and handed the Vicar ten pounds.

"I do not know how long I will be away," she said, "but will you please pay Mrs. Banks every week, and if there is any dilapidation to the roof, which keeps happening, will you ask Barker to come and repair it?"

"Of course I will," the Vicar said. "I am so delighted that you are having a holiday. I have been very worried about you."

"I will be with my Cousin Denise Sedgwick, with whom, you may remember, I did lessons for so many years."

"It is the best thing that could happen," the Vicar said, "and do not worry about your house or anything here. I will see to it."

He hesitated before he added:

"You have been very brave and I know things have been difficult for you. But I prayed that God would help you, and I think He has answered my prayers."

"I know He has," Alina replied. "But please, go on praying for me."

"Of course I will," the Vicar said as he smiled.

Alina then paid the Grocer, the Banker, and the Butcher.

She had, in fact, forgotten how much she owed.

There was also a bill owing to the man who had replaced some broken panes of glass in the windows.

When she went back to the house she found she had only three pounds left.

"I must try and make it last," she told herself. "I cannot keep bothering Denise for money when she has already been so kind and generous."

The carriage arrived the following morning soon after eight o'clock.

When she finally put the newly-decorated hat on top of her head she looked at herself in surprise.

It was certainly very becoming.

She had done her hair in a fashionable manner that she had seen illustrated in the *Ladies' Journal*.

The Vicar's wife often lent it to her.

Now she thought that she looked exactly as Denise would expect her to.

There was no doubt that anyone seeing her for the first time would assume that she was very much older than she was.

As Denise jumped out of the carriage and came into the house, Alina waited for the verdict.

Denise took one look at her Cousin and gave a shout of delight.

"That is marvellous!" she said. "You look absolutely stunning and exactly how a chaperon should look!"

Alina had not used the cosmetics because she was afraid of over-doing them.

But as soon as they were on the road which led to the Station, Denise insisted on her powdering her nose.

She also made her add a little rouge to her lips.

"Now, that is how I want you to look from this moment onwards," she said.

Alina stared at herself in the small mirror which fitted into her hand-bag and asked nervously:

"You . . . you do not think you have used . . . too much lip-salve?"

"Too little!" Denise said firmly. "And before we get to London I will add a touch of rouge to your cheeks."

She did this as soon as they were alone in their reserved carriage.

When Denise had finished adding the rouge to her cheeks, she said:

"What about Mama's jewellery?"

"I have on the ear-rings," Alina said quickly, "but I thought that would be enough."

"Not nearly enough," Denise said scornfully.

She had brought the jewellery in a special crocodile case which she had told Alina to carry as well as her hand-bag.

Now she looked for the case and took out two rows of pearls which she put round Alina's neck.

There was a diamond ring for her third finger and a wedding ring.

As if this was not enough, Denise added an emerald and pearl bracelet and a brooch in the shape of a butterfly.

"Will it be safe to wear them when we are travelling?" Alina asked.

"We have plenty of people looking after us," Denise replied, "including, of course, the intimidating Marquis of Teverton!"

In the excitement of preparing for the journey, Alina had forgotten about him.

Now she asked:

"Will he be with us?"

"I am afraid so," Denise answered, "but he will make quite certain he travels in another carriage on the train to Dover, and keeps his own cabin on the ship."

Alina looked surprised.

"Do not forget," Denise explained, "he does not want us, and although we have to stay in the house where he is staying, I am quite sure we will see him only passing us on the stairs."

Alina looked at her Cousin questioningly, and she said:

"I told you that Papa tricked him into taking me to Rome, and he fell without realising it into the trap Papa set for him."

"What trap?" Alina asked.

"Papa said quite casually:

" 'I suppose you are staying at the British Embassy?'

" 'Oh, no,' Cousin Marcus replied. 'I have been lent a considerable house by one of my friends. If there is one thing that bores me, it is Diplomatic Dinners!'

" 'A house?' Papa exclaimed. 'How very fortunate! As I have a great dislike of my daughter staying in Hotels, I know you will be kind enough to have Denise and her chaperon with you.' "

Denise laughed.

"You should have seen the expression on Cousin Marcus's face, but there was nothing he could say except to agree we could stay in his house."

Alina longed to say that she was going to feel very uncomfortable staying in a house where they were not welcome.

Then she knew that Denise would not listen to her.

She hoped, therefore, that the Marquis would not be as fierce as his Cousin made out.

The rest of the way to London Denise talked only of Henry Wescott.

There was a Courier waiting for them at the London terminus to see to their luggage.

He was to travel with Denise's lady's-maid in another reserved carriage.

Alina thought they were certainly doing things in style.

They did not mention Lord Teverton again until they were driving from the station to Belgrave Square in a smart carriage.

The Courier, Denise's lady's-maid, and the luggage followed in another.

"Now, do not forget," Denise said, "when you meet Cousin Marcus, be very cool, and do not let him think you are the slightest bit impressed by him. You are an important person yourself, and are not prepared to think that anyone— whoever he may be—is superior to you!"

Alina laughed.

"Oh, Denise, you do make things difficult! Can you really imagine me feeling grander than Lord Teverton, or any of the smart Society people in London?"

"You are better than he is because you are much nicer!" Denise said firmly. "But if he tries to ignore you and me, just make him aware that you in turn intend to ignore him!"

Alina thought this was quite impossible, but there was no point in saying so.

They arrived at the impressive house in Belgrave Square.

Alina noticed as she entered it that there was a Butler with four footmen in attendance in the Hall.

The Butler bowed to them and led them across the Hall into what was obviously a Study.

It was a very elegant room, the walls lined with books.

Sitting at a flat-topped Regency desk by the window was the intimidating Lord Teverton.

At first glance Alina thought he was far better-looking than she had expected.

When he rose, and it seemed almost reluctantly, she could understand what Denise felt about him.

"Here we are, Cousin Marcus!" Denise said brightly, as if there were no awkwardness in the situation. "And let me introduce you to Lady Langley, who is being kind enough to take me with her to Rome."

Lord Teverton held out his hand to Denise, then turned towards Alina.

She thought she saw a faint flicker of surprise in his eyes before he said:

"How d'you do, Lady Langley! I do not think we have met before."

"It is unlikely," Alina said in what she hoped was a somewhat crushing tone, "as I live in the Country."

They shook hands and Lord Teverton said, drawling the words:

"I think we should leave at once for the station, and I have arranged that we will eat luncheon in the train. My Chef has prepared it for us."

"That is good news!" Denise remarked. "Papa has always said you have the best Chef in London."

"I make certain that is true," Lord Teverton said in the same lofty manner. "Now, let us be on our way."

He opened the door for them to leave the Study first.

Alina saw with amusement that one footman was holding his hat, another his travelling-cloak, a third his gloves, and a fourth his stick.

The Butler ushered them down the steps and into the carriage.

It was then Alina realised that Lord Teverton was not driving with them, but was alone in a carriage behind theirs.

Another vehicle containing his luggage and Valet was drawn up beside the one that contained Denise's lady's-maid.

Because she could not imagine anyone traveling in such state, she wanted to laugh.

She managed, however, to suppress her feelings until the carriage doors were closed and the horses moved off.

Then she said to Denise:

"This is just like a Funeral procession!"

They both laughed until the tears came into their eyes.

"I knew you would think it funny," Denise said. "You can see how furious Cousin Marcus is at having to escort us to Rome."

"I think the whole thing is ridiculous!" Alina giggled. "Can you imagine the necessity for four carriages for only six people?"

They laughed again until Denise said:

"We must be serious! I am sure Cousin Marcus will assume it is the way we behave when we are at home."

"I only hope he never sees me there," Alina said.

"I am quite certain he would not be interested enough to do that," Denise remarked. "I have learned that he is having a tremendous affair with the lovely Countess Gray, who is definitely one of the most famous Beauties in London."

"I think I have seen a picture of her in the *Ladies' Journal*," Alina said.

"I expect you have," Denise agreed. "She is dark and very exotic-looking and has dozens of men in love with her!"

"If Lord Teverton is one of them," Alina said, "why is he leaving her to go to Rome?"

"Oh, Papa can tell you the answer to that. He often goes on special missions for Earl Granville, who is the Secretary of State for Foreign Affairs."

Alina looked surprised.

"That sounds adventurous and exciting!"

"I doubt it," Denise said. "I expect he only has to talk privately to a King, or the Pope, or somebody like that. Then, when he brings back a favourable answer, he will get another decoration on his evening-coat. It is almost covered with them already!"

Because it sounded so funny, they both started laughing again.

They arrived at the station.

As His Lordship had driven there alone, Alina was not surprised to find they had separate carriages on the train to Dover.

They were escorted by the Station-Master, resplendent in his uniform with a cap ornamented with gold braid.

They were bowed into their reserved carriage.

The door of Alina and Denise's carriage was locked so that it was impossible for anyone to intrude on them.

The Courier saw that a large hamper was placed on one of the empty seats before he withdrew to his carriage.

Lord Teverton did not come to enquire if they were comfortable, or to ask if there was anything he could do for them.

He entered the carriage which had been reserved solely for him.

Alina thought it was really rather rude of him.

She could see that her Cousin was right in saying that His Lordship resented being accompanied by two women he did not want.

"Now we can enjoy ourselves," Denise said, "and you can take off your hat. This is an Express train, so no-one will see you until we reach Dover."

Alina did as she suggested.

Then, as Denise opened the hamper, she realised they were really living in luxury.

Alina was very hungry.

She had eaten a very small breakfast and had had only an egg which she had cooked for herself for supper.

The hamper contained everything a *gourmet* could enjoy.

There was a delicious *pâte*, lobster claws, cold chicken, and salad with a Hollandaise sauce. This was followed by a pudding of chocolate and cream that was so rich it would be impossible to manage a second helping, however one felt.

There was champagne to drink and coffee in a hay-box which kept it warm.

"If we are to eat like this every day," Alina said as they finished, "I shall never be able to get into any of my clothes because, as you know, Mama was very slim."

"And you are too thin," Denise answered. "I am sure you have been economising on food."

"Not economising," Alina replied, "just unable to afford anything that was expensive."

Denise put her hand on Alina's.

"That is all over now, dearest," she said. "I am going to look after you in the future, and you will never be hungry—or lonely—again."


In the next carriage Lord Teverton ate very little luncheon but drank several glasses of champagne.

He had been with the Countess Gray until it was nearly dawn.

He had, therefore, when he was called, awoken in a bad temper.

To begin with, he had no wish to go to Rome.

He had, however, been unable to refuse the Secretary of State for Foreign Affairs when he had begged him to do so.

"You know, Teverton, you have been so much more successful with the King and his Advisers than any of our Diplomats."

"What about the Ambassador?" Lord Teverton asked.

"You know without my saying so what I think about him," Lord Granville said. "So for goodness sake stop prevaricating and assist me. I would not have asked you if it was not urgent."

Lord Teverton sighed.

"Very well," he said. "But this is the last time you ask me to leave London just when I am enjoying myself."

"She is very attractive," Lord Granville said, "and you will not be away long."

"I will take good care of that!" Lord Teverton remarked.

He had therefore been all the more furious when he had been obliged out of sheer politeness to accept the request of Denise's father, not only to escort her to Rome, but also to have her to stay in his house there.

"What does she want to go to Rome for?" he had asked. "After all, from what I hear, your daughter has been a great success in London."

"An enormous success!" the Honourable Rupert Sedgwick replied. "But she has set her heart on going to Rome, and I find it difficult to refuse."

To refuse was what Lord Teverton also wanted to do, but he had the same difficulty.

'Here I am,' he thought, 'saddled with a boring *débutante* who will chatter away without having a sensible idea in her head, and a chaperon, who will doubtless be a middle-aged old body who will make every possible excuse to gush over me.'

That happened far too often with women who toadied to him because he was so good-looking, and because he was so rich.

He enjoyed his importance.

He was well aware that Earl Granville was not the only Minister who sought his advice and his help when the occasion arose.

He often thought that if he had been a poor man, he would have gone into the Secret Service because that work intrigued and amused him.

As it was, he found himself more and more in demand by Ministers.

They realised that he knew how to manage foreigners far better than most of those in the Foreign Office, who were paid to do so.

As the train gathered speed and Lord Teverton sipped his third glass of champagne, he thought Lady Langley was something of a surprise.

He had certainly not expected anyone so unusually lovely.

In fact, she was beautiful in a different way from any woman he had met previously.

He could not quite explain to himself the difference, but knew it was there.

Then he told himself that in some extraordinary way she looked something more than human.

He was used to women with flashing eyes, pouting lips, and an inviting expression which told him without words what they wanted.

He had the strange feeling that Lady Langley would never look like that.

Then he told himself he was not in the least interested in his unwelcome guests, and the less he saw of them, the better.

In fact, now that he thought about it, there was no reason why he should see them at all.

He had things to do in Rome which certainly did not concern them.

He was quite certain that their friends in Rome would have no points of contact with his.

Because he was going to Rome, he was reminded of the beauty of the Princess Cecilia Borghese.

When he had last seen her he had been well aware that she found him attractive, just as he found her very beautiful.

She was the wife of the reigning Prince Borghese.

Unless his memory was at fault, the Prince was constantly called away from Rome with interests which did not at all concern his wife.

There was a faint smile on Lord Teverton's hard lips.

He thought that as a relief from the task set for him by the Earl Granville he would call at the Borghese Palace.

He was quite certain he would be welcome.

The train steamed on and Lord Teverton found his head nodding.

He had not had more than three hours sleep last night.

As often happened when he left a warm bed for the cold dawn, he wondered if the pleasures he had enjoyed with the lovely Lady Gray had been worthwhile.

It was this question of his impulses and desires which invariably brought his *affaires de coeur* to an end far sooner than expected.

If he was honest, he found that however lovely were the women he pursued and who pursued him, they were all exactly alike.

"What do I want?" Lord Teverton asked himself. "What am I looking for?"

It was a question which far too often came at dawn.

When day broke he would feel, although it was ridiculous, that he was disillusioned and somewhat cynical.

Because he was intelligent, he tried to laugh at himself.

'A cynic at thirty!' he thought. 'In which case, what shall I be like at forty?'

He did not want to know the answer.

All he wanted was to feel that his life was full, complete, and there was nothing wanting, nothing he could not attain.

Inevitably he found his brain, as always disastrously critical, would ask the same questions, especially after a night of passion.

"What am I looking for? Where am I going? What is my ultimate goal?"

It was a case of having had too much too soon, his mind told him.

He wished that he could turn off the self-examination as another man might turn off a tap.

But it continued.

Then he knew as the train seemed to go even faster that although it seemed extraordinary even to him, he would not be seeking out Lady Gray when he returned.

# CHAPTER THREE

When they reached Calais, Lord Teverton was annoyed.

He realised he would have to share his special Drawing-Room carriage, which was attached to the Rome train, with his Cousin and her chaperon.

He had crossed the Channel in peace and quiet, sitting in his own cabin reading *The Times* and *The Morning Post*.

He had not really thought about the journey to Rome until they disembarked.

He carried out many diplomatic missions and he was also a very rich man.

He therefore always travelled in the same style and comfort as Queen Victoria.

He had a Drawing-Room carriage specially attached to the train.

It consisted of a comfortable Sitting-Room with a sofa and arm-chairs, and two bed-rooms.

If he was travelling alone with his Valet, his Valet had a

bed put up in the space provided to accommodate the luggage.

On this journey his valet and Denise's lady's-maid would have an ordinary carriage reserved for themselves.

What annoyed him when he boarded the train was to remember that of the two bed-rooms, one was larger than the other.

The former, of course, was the one he always occupied.

Now a second bed had been installed in it so that it could be shared by his Cousin and her chaperon.

He went into the smaller sleeping-compartment and thought that women were a nuisance, especially when they were connected with him only by birth.

There was, however, nothing he could do about it.

He changed from his travelling-clothes into something more comfortable.


Alina, like Denise, was delighted with the Drawing-Room carriage.

"I have never been in one before," Denise said, "but Papa has told me how the Queen travels, and he himself had a carriage like this when he went to Vienna with Mama."

"It is delightful!" Alina exclaimed. "I love the comfortable chairs and the sofa. And although we are going to be rather cramped in the sleeping-compartment, it will be fun to be with you."

"Of course it will," Denise agreed, "but we must be careful what we say in front of Cousin Marcus."

They took off their hats and cloaks and Alina said:

"Let us change. We have been in the same clothes all day, and this gown is rather tight."

"You look very pretty in it," Denise answered, "but let us change. Can you remember in which trunk the gown you want is packed?"

It was a difficult question.

It took Alina some time to find a simple, thin afternoon-gown which she thought suitable for dinner on a train.

Denise put on one of the white gowns she had bought in London.

When they had arranged their hair they went into the Drawing-Room.

Lord Teverton was seated in an arm-chair, reading some papers.

He looked up as they appeared and made a perfunctory gesture to rise.

"We do not wish to disturb you, Cousin Marcus," Denise said quickly. "If you are busy working, we can wait in our sleeping-compartment until dinner is ready."

"It is being prepared now," Lord Teverton replied, "so sit down, as the train will soon be increasing speed."

He spoke with his usual drawl, as if it were an effort to talk to Denise.

When he was not looking, she made a grimace at Alina.

They had hardly seated themselves before Stevens, Lord Teverton's Valet, and a steward brought in dinner.

They would move into their own compartment when the train stopped at a station.

As Alina had expected, Lord Teverton had brought the dinner with him from London.

It was just as delicious as the luncheon they had on the way to Dover.

Lord Teverton also had a small glass of brandy when the meal was finished.

They talked very little at first. Then Alina said to Denise:

"I am looking forward to seeing Rome. I have read about its history, but I never thought I would see the treasures about which I have read with my own eyes!"

"You have read about Rome?" Lord Teverton asked before Denise could speak.

"Many, many books about it," Alina replied.

She was thinking that it had been one of her Father's favourite places.

He had talked to her about the Forum and all the buildings which had been the background to the formation of the great Roman Empire.

"I am surprised," Lord Teverton replied.

Alina looked at him.

"That I should be interested particularly in Rome, or that I should read any serious books?" she enquired defensively.

There was a faintly mocking smile on his lips as he replied:

"Both."

"That is so unfair!" Alina objected. "If I were a man, you would have expected me to be interested in Roman History and the astonishing way in which their Empire expanded, to include even England."

She made a gesture with her hand before she went on:

"But because I am a woman you assume immediately that I read only the *Ladies' Journal* and occasionally a novel."

Lord Teverton laughed, and it was a genuine sound of humour.

"I apologise! Of course I apologise," he said. "But most of the women I have known do, as you say, read magazines from cover to cover and find little time to read anything else."

"Then I hope you will be more generous to my sex in the future," Alina said, "for I assure you I am not the only woman who is interested in History. But perhaps they do not move in the social circles you patronise."

"*Touché!*" Lord Teverton remarked, and his eyes were twinkling.

Denise was listening, entranced.

Alina was behaving just as she wanted her to do.

She thought it was very good for her stuck-up Cousin to be challenged by a woman instead of their fawning all over him as they usually did.

Lord Teverton demanded to test Alina to see if she really had read the History of Rome.

He spoke first of St. Peter's Basilica of which, as it happened, she knew a great deal.

"I always think," she said, "'it is a wonderful story how Constantine the Great, the first Christian Emperor, built the first Basilica of St. Peter over the actual spot where St. Peter was buried after he had been martyred in the reign of Nero."

Denise, watching, realised that her Cousin Marcus raised his eye-brows as if he were surprised, and was temporarily silenced.

Alina went on, following her own thoughts:

"Now you are being more feminine," Lord Teverton remarked. "I have never met a woman yet who did not want to make a wish in the fountain."

"How do you have to wish in it?" Denise asked.

"It was built by Nicolò Salvi in 1762," Lord Teverton replied. "It is very beautiful and reputed to be extremely lucky. Anyone who throws two coins into the fountain standing with their back to it has two wishes."

"How exciting!" Denise exclaimed.

"One is that you will return to Rome," Alina took up the story, "the second is your personal wish which, unless the Story-Tellers lie, is always fulfilled."

Denise clasped her hands together.

"Then that is the first place we will go!"

"Of course," Alina answered.

She knew exactly what her Cousin would wish for.

As she looked at Denise, she guessed she was thinking rapturously of Henry Wescott.

"I think perhaps you are raising Denise's hopes unduly," Lord Teverton drawled. "After all, I cannot believe that everybody who wishes at the Trevi Fountain is so fortunate."

Alina threw up her hands.

"You are not to spoil our illusions," she said. "You have been to Rome before, but for Denise and myself it is an adventure, and we want to believe in everything, enjoy everything, and be very, very grateful for having the opportunity to be there."

She spoke so sincerely that Lord Teverton was again silent.

He could not help thinking that Lady Langley was very different from what he had expected.

She was totally different from the many women he had known in London.

He thought the enthusiasm in her voice was touching.

He was sure that because she had lived in the Country she was unspoilt.

Everything she saw would be exciting for her.

At the same time, he was genuinely overwhelmed by her beauty.

He had thought her lovely the first time he had seen her.

Now, without a hat, she looked younger and even more beautiful.

He wondered how old she was, but knew it was a question he could not ask.

She had certainly, he thought, had a very generous husband.

Denise saw his eyes on the necklace she had put round Alina's long neck after she had changed her gown.

It was a small one, otherwise it would have been out of place on a train-journey.

But the diamonds were a blue-white and matched earrings and the brooch Alina wore on her breast.

Denise smiled to herself, thinking her Cousin Marcus was being completely deceived, exactly as she wanted him to be.

She told herself she had been very clever.

Once launched on an historical discussion, Alina found it difficult not to continue.

She had missed her Father so desperately after he was killed because he had always talked to her as if she were his contemporary.

They had entered into intellectual discussions on many different subjects.

History had been their favourite, but her Mother had taken no part in the cut and thrust of their debates.

Lady Langley had been quite content to listen to the two people she loved.

She would tell them when it was all over how clever they both were.

"We shall have to be careful, darling," she had said once to her husband, "Otherwise Alina will become a 'blue-stocking,' and you know how frightened men are of a woman who is too clever."

"If a woman is that clever," her husband replied, "she will not let a man feel inferior to her, however stupid he may be!"

Alina and her Mother had laughed at this.

But after her Father's death Alina had thought desparingly that never again would she enjoy similar intellecutal discussions.

Now she found herself enjoying an argument with Lord Teverton.

It was not only that she was obeying Denise's instructions to stand up to him and make him be impressed with her.

However, it had been a very long day, and when Denise yawned, Alina knew it was time they went to bed.

"What time do we arrive in Rome?" she asked Lord Teverton.

"Late in the afternoon," he replied, "so there will be no need for you to hurry up for breakfast, although Stevens will have it ready at about nine o'clock."

"Anyhow, do not wait for us," Denise said.

"I have no intention of doing so," Lord Teverton replied.

Now he was drawling again in the way she most disliked.

When they went into their sleeping-compartment, Denise said in a whisper:

"You were splendid! But you do see how he treats me? As if I were still in the cradle!"

"I agree with you, he is rather frightening," Alina said.

"But you stood up to him," Denise said as she smiled, "and he was obviously surprised that you were so intelligent."

They undressed and got into bed.

When Lord Teverton went to his own compartment he could hear his two companions laughing together.

He thought it was a very young sound.

He was used to women who had been told their laughter was like the tinkling of bells, though it was in fact always contrived.

The two women in the adjoining sleeping-compartment sounded like School-girls.

"It is obvious in some ways that Lady Langley comes from the Country," he said. "At the same time, although she is not aware of it, she would be a sensation in London!"

He had noticed the graceful way she walked.

He knew that with her strange beauty, the Prince of Wales would find her entrancing.

Then he thought it would be a shame for her to be spoilt.

She was like a Lily-of-the-Valley.

It would be a mistake to change her into an orchid, which was exotic in its own way but had no fragrance.

'Dammit all, I am becoming poetical!' he thought. 'The sooner I get to Rome and contact the Princess, the better!'

When he was in bed he found himself lying awake.

He was listening to the voices he could still hear even above the rattle of the train.

He did not know what they were saying.

Yet the lilt and youth of their voices was recognisable.

It was a long time before he fell asleep.

The next day Alina was thrilled by what she could see from the window.

She made no effort to talk to Lord Teverton after they had breakfast, which surprised him.

He was used to women, even before he showed any interest in them, looking at him expectantly.

They then did everything in their power to attract his attention.

Alina, on the contrary, had just gone to a comfortable chair by the window..

She was absorbed in looking out at the countryside through which they were passing.

She occasionally exclaimed to Denise:

"Oh, look at those peasants working in the fields!" or "Do look at that exquisite Villa! I am sure it is still occupied by a Nobleman whose family have inherited it for centuries."

Lord Teverton, reading the papers which required his attention before he reached Rome, could not help listening.

They had already crossed the border into Italy and the countryside was quite different.

Alina was thrilled by the tall spires of the Churches, the structure of the houses, and the picturesque villages.

"I can see," Lord Teverton remarked somewhat mockingly as they sat down to luncheon, "that you intend to be an ardent sight-seer when we reach Rome."

"But of course!" Alina replied. "It would be very foolish if I did not visit everything I can and store it in my memory in case I never have the chance to return."

"So your Trevi wish may not come true!" Lord Teverton said as if he had scored a point.

"Then I shall return in another life," Alina said, "and doubtless I was a Roman in a life before this one."

Lord Teverton found it impossible not to challenge her belief in reincarnation.

They were arguing fiercely.

Unexpectedly, like everything else she did, Alina insisted on sitting by the window.

"In case," she explained, "I miss anything important in the scenery."

Lord Teverton picked up his papers again.

As he did so, he told himself he could never remember an occasion when a woman to whom he was giving his full attention found the scenery, or anything else, more interesting than him.

'Lady Langley is certainly unusual,' he thought cynically.

By the time they arrived in Rome they were tired.

As the train was late, it was dark before they reached the house which Lord Teverton had been lent.

It was larger than Alina had expected and situated near the top of the Spanish Steps.

She learnt soon after she arrived that the magnificent Park on one side of it was known also as Villa Borghese.

She had read about the beautiful Princess Pauline Borghese, who had been Napoleon Bonaparte's sister.

The memory of what she had read about her came back.

Now she found herself excited by the idea that they were not very far from the Palazzo Borghese, which lay below them near the River Tiber.

Then she sighed as she thought:

'I am not likely to enter it, although perhaps I shall see it as we pass.'

Denise was thinking only of Henry Wescott and asking Alina a thousand times how she should get in touch with him.

"Whatever happens," she kept saying, "he must not think I have come here especially to see him."

"You know where he is staying?" Alina asked.

"'Yes, of course. He is with his Grandmother, the Dowager Countess, who lives in Rome because the climate suits her so much better than that of England."

She smiled before she added:

"I also think she dislikes the idea of seeing her grandson in her husband's place, although she keeps telling Henry he should marry and have a family."

"And that is, of course, exactly what he should do!" Alina agreed.

Finally they decided that Denise should send the Earl a short note.

She could tell him she had arrived in Rome to keep her friend Lady Langley company, and it would be fun to see him again.

It took some time to compose the note.

Before they went to bed they handed it to a servant and asked him to take it to the Dowager Countess's villa first thing in the morning.

When Denise kissed Alina good-night she said:

"You are praying? Tell me you are praying, Alina, that everything will be all right."

"Of course I am, dearest," Alina replied, "and you are not to worry. We will go to the Trevi Fountain first thing in the morning, throw our coins in the water, and wish that you and Henry will live happily ever after."

"I do believe that whatever you wish at the Fountain will come true—despite what Cousin Marcus said!" Denise declared.

"He is just being cynical and deliberately argumentative," Alina replied.

"I told you he was awful," Denise reminded her.

"Not awful," Alina corrected her Cousin. "I can see he is clever, but for some reason that I cannot understand I think he despises women."

"Despises them?" Denise queried. "Good Heavens! He is always making love to some woman or other! I have listened to the Mothers of the other girls talking about him, and my Grandmother, who presented me, warned me that he was the 'Casanova of London,' and she hoped I never married a man like that."

"I can understand it would be misery," Alina agreed, "but I did rather enjoy arguing with him."

"It is an enjoyment you will not experience again," Denise said. "He made it clear, when Papa arranged for us to stay in his house, that he would not be able to give us a minute of his time."

Alina laughed.

"I am sure we will manage quite well in Rome without him. So go to sleep and believe, even before we start wishing, that everything will come true."


It might have been a prophecy!

Next morning, just after they had finished breakfast, the Earl arrived.

He was, Alina thought with relief when he entered the room, extremely prepossessing.

Very English-looking, he had a frank, open face that she liked.

He was announced after they had left the Dining-Room and had moved into the Sitting-Room.

They were deciding what they should do during the day.

Lord Teverton, needless to say, had breakfast alone, and they had not seen him when they came downstairs.

Now, as the Earl walked across the room, Alina was sure the expression in his eyes was one of love.

"How is it possible that you are here?" he asked Denise. "I never imagined you would come to Rome."

With difficulty Denise had suppressed a cry of delight when he was announced.

Now she managed to say in quite a casual manner:

"Oh, Lady Langley asked me to come with her, and it seemed too good an opportunity to miss."

She turned to Alina, saying:

"I do not think you have met the Earl of Wescott."

"How do you do?" the Earl said politely. "May I welcome you to Rome—and it is delightful to have Denise here."

"Thank you," Alina said, "and we are just planning all the things we want to see."

As she spoke, she turned towards Denise and said:

"Forgive me, dearest, if I just go upstairs and fetch that book I was telling you about. It has very good descriptions of the places we want to visit, and it will help us to decide our programme."

"Shall I fetch it for you?" Denise asked.

"I think I had better go myself," Alina replied. "I am not quite certain in which trunk I put it, and I shall have to instruct the maid."

She went from the room as she spoke, feeling she had been very tactful.

As soon as Henry Wescott closed the door behind her he walked back toward Denise.

She was standing beside the fireplace.

She did not speak, but waited until he was standing beside her.

"Have you come here to torture me?" he asked.

"I . . . I do not know . . . what do you mean?," Denise replied.

"You drove me mad!" he declared. "I came away because I intended never to see you again."

"How could . . . you be so . . . unkind?"

"Did it seem unkind to you—or were you glad I had gone?"

"Of course I was not . . . glad! I could not . . . believe you would do anything so . . . cruel as to just . . . leave me for no reason . . . whatsoever."

"There was reason enough as far as I was concerned," Henry said. "You were behaving abominably with Charles Patterson, and, short of killing him in a duel, there was nothing I could do about it."

He spoke aggressively.

Then suddenly Denise could no longer keep up the pretence.

"Can we . . . forget about . . . Charles?" she asked in a low voice. "I was so . . . happy before . . . you became so . . . angry."

"Is that true?" Henry asked.

"I swear to you it is."

Their eyes met and they were both very still.

"I love you!" Henry said. "You know that. But I want you to love me too."

Denise wanted to answer, but somehow the words would not come to her lips.

It was then, as if he had to know the truth, Henry put his arms round her.

He drew her close to him.

Her lips were waiting for his, and as he kissed her he knew there was no need for words, no need for explanations.

He kissed her until the world seemed to spin dizzily round them.

When he raised his head, Denise put her face against his neck.

"Oh . . . Henry!" she said in a broken little voice.

"You love me!" he said triumphantly. "'You love me! Now tell me you will marry me."

Because she had wanted him so desperately and been terribly afraid it would not happen, Denise felt the tears come into her eyes.

Very gently Henry put his fingers under her chin and turned her face up to his.

When he saw her tears and that her lips were trembling, he looked at her for a long moment.

Then he pulled her a little closer.

"We will be very happy," he said.

Then his lips were on hers.


Upstairs Alina finished unpacking her trunks.

She arranged her new clothes so that she would be able to know herself exactly where they were.

Then she looked out the window.

She wondered how long Denise would be downstairs.

She was longing to go out and discover Rome.

There was so much to see, so much to do, and she thought she could not bear to miss a minute of it.

Time seemed to pass very slowly.

She was beginning to wonder if she would have to stay the rest of the morning in her bed-room.

Then the door burst open and Denise rushed in.

She flung her arms around Alina, saying:

"It is all right! Everything is all right! He loves me . . . he loves me and we are to be married! Oh, Alina . . . I am so happy."

Alina kissed her.

"And I am so happy for you."

"We are going now to visit Henry's Grandmother, and he wants you to come too," Denise said.

"I am sure you do not want me," Alina replied.

"Henry says his Grandmother is a stickler for convention, and would think it scandalous if he and I should arrive in a carriage together without a chaperon!"

"Then of course I will come with you," Alina said. "I hope I look respectable enough for the Dowager Countess."

"Put on your most impressive hat," Denise said, "while I go and dress."

She ran to her own bed-room.

Alina did as she was told and took the most elaborate of the hats she had re-trimmed out of the wardrobe.

Picking up her hand-bag and gloves, she hoped that the Dowager Countess would be impressed.

Denise was in a hurry to be with Henry, so she managed to change into one of her best gowns in only a few minutes.

When they went downstairs together, Henry was waiting for them in the Hall.

Alina held out her hand.

"I must congratulate you, My Lord," she said, "and I know that you and Denise will be very happy."

"Thank you," the Earl said, smiling, "we shall, I promise you, be blissfully happy once we are married. But my Grandmother will want to give a party for us, or perhaps several, before we leave Rome."

Alina felt her heart leap.

She had been desperately afraid while she was waiting for Denise.

She was thinking that if she and Henry were engaged, they would have to return immediately to England.

Now she hoped there would be at least a few days in which to see everything she wanted to see.

The Earl had arrived in an open carriage drawn by two horses which was waiting for them.

The coachman and the footman were on the box.

They set off, but Henry and Denise could only sit looking at each other.

Alina thought it would be difficult to find two people who were more in love.

She was so glad that her prayers had been answered.

At the same time, she knew that every second that was passing was precious because she was in Rome.

However many wishes she might make at the Trevi Fountain, she was certain that it would never be possible for her to come here again.

"This is the Park known as the Villa Borghese," the Earl was saying as they drove along the road, "and actually we are dining at the Palace to-night."

"Dining there?" Denise asked.

"The Prince and Princess invited my Grandmother some time ago, and she was delighted by the idea, especially as I am staying with her. Now, of course, she will ask if we may bring you and Lady Langley to the party as well as Lord Teverton."

Alina felt excited.

She had read about the Borghese Palace, how it contained the most marvellous collection of treasures in the whole of Rome.

It had been started in 1605 by Cardinal Camillo Borghese before he became Pope.

She had never thought she would have the chance of seeing inside the Palace.

Now she knew it was the most exciting thing that had ever happened to her.

She wanted to tell the Earl so.

Then, when she turned her face towards him, she saw that he was looking at Denise.

They were in an enchanted world of their own.

# CHAPTER FOUR

The Dowager Countess lived in a very luxurious Villa surrounded by a large garden.

She was nearly eighty, but still had remains of the beauty which had made her famous.

She obviously adored her grandson.

After they had had luncheon, waited on by efficient if ancient servants, the Earl took Denise into the garden.

When they were alone, the Dowager Countess said to Alina:

"I am delighted that Henry is marrying such a charming young girl. I have been eager for him to settle down and get married."

"He could not have chosen a lovelier bride," Alina said, "and Denise is truly in love with him."

The Dowager Countess clasped her hands together.

"That is what I wanted to hear. I have always been so afraid that he would be married for his title and his money."

"I know they are ecstatically in love with each other," Alina said, "and that is all that matters."

"Of course," the Dowager Countess agreed.

She then looked at Alina and said:

"I do not remember meeting you, or any of your family, when I lived in England."

"We have always lived very quietly in the Country," Alina said quickly.

"That would account for it," the Dowager Countess said, "and that is what I hope Henry and Denise will do."

She was obviously interested in nothing but her grand-son.

Alina gave a little sigh of relief.

She had been afraid that she might be cross-questioned by English people.

They could easily think she looked too young for the part she was playing.

They stayed with the Dowager Countess until she was beginning to look tired.

Alina was certain that, living in Italy, she had adopted the custom of the Country of taking a short *siesta* after luncheon.

She therefore signalled to Denise that they should leave.

The Dowager Countess did not press them to stay.

When they were outside the door Denise asked:

"Would you mind if Henry and I go to St. Peter's? We want to pray that our marriage will be a happy one."

"That is exactly what you should do," Alina agreed, "and of course I do not mind. I will walk back to the house."

"You will do nothing of the sort," Henry said firmly.

He hailed a Hackney carriage that was standing in the Square a little way from the Villa.

As he did so, Denise said to Alina in a low voice.

"I do not think you have any Italian money."

"I had forgotten that," Alina replied.

She had only what she had brought with her from England.

When Henry was not looking, Denise slipped several Italian notes into her hand.

Then she jumped into Henry's carriage and they drove off.

Alina got into the Hackney carriage.

When the driver asked her where she wanted to go, she answered in Italian.

She told him the address of the house where they were staying.

Then she had a sudden idea.

"I have changed my mind," she said. "I want to go to the Trevi Fountain."

There was no need to give the address.

The Italian grinned and whipped up his horse.

The carriage was open.

Alina enjoyed the sunshine, the crowded streets, and the trees coming into bloom.

Everything about Rome was so lovely.

She only hoped she would have a chance to see everything before Denise and Henry were ready to return to England.

It took a little time, because the narrow streets were crowded, to reach the Trevi Fountain.

Alina realised it was impossible to drive right up to it.

The carriage stopped in a road from which there was a pavement leading to the Fountain.

Alina thought she could find her way back to the house at the top of the Spanish Steps.

She therefore paid the coachman what he asked and put the change into her hand-bag.

Feeling excited, she walked through the passage which took her to the front of the Fountain.

There were only a few people on the two rows of stone steps.

They were sitting looking at the water pouring out from beneath a huge statue of Neptune.

He was in a wheeled chariot drawn by two horses.

For a moment Alina could only stand staring at the beautiful sculpture.

The water caught the sunlight which also glittered on the coins lying in the stone basin.

She remembered that she must wish, and looked in her hand-bag.

Apart from some small Italian notes, she had three

pounds of English money—two sovereigns and two half-sovereigns.

It seemed very extravagant!

Then she asked herself what could be more important than making a wish.

She remembered it was customary that the first wish should be that one would return to Rome.

However, for her, that was so unlikely it seemed a waste.

"What I shall wish for first," she decided, "is that Denise will be happy for ever with her Earl, and the other wish will be for myself."

She took out the two half-sovereigns and closed her bag.

After looking entranced at the Fountain, she turned round and closed her eyes.

Holding one half-sovereign in her right hand, she wished with all her heart, and it was a prayer that Denise would be happy.

Then she threw the coin over her shoulder.

She held the second half-sovereign in the same way.

As she shut her eyes again she knew that what she wanted was to find for herself the love that Denise and Henry had for each other, the happiness she had seen in their faces when their eyes met.

"Give me love," she wished, "real love, because I am so alone, and that is what I want to find."

She threw the coin.

As she did so, she felt her hand-bag tugged from her left hand.

For a moment she could not think what was happening.

Then as she opened her eyes she saw a small boy.

Bare-footed and wearing ragged clothes, he was leaping like a fawn over the stone steps.

Then he ran through the passage by which she had approached the Fountain.

"Stop!" she cried out in English, then again: "*Alt! Alt! Alt!*"

She ran as quickly as she could after the small boy, but he had vanished into the street outside.

She knew she could not catch him.

She stood still, feeling a sense of shock at what had occurred.

She wondered what she should do.

Suddenly a voice beside her asked in the drawl she knew so well:

"Now, what can have happened to make you look so concerned?"

It was Lord Teverton. Without even turning her head, Alina replied:

"My hand-bag has been . . . stolen with . . . all my money . . . in it!"

"That certainly is a disaster," Lord Teverton said slowly, "but I imagine you mean all the money you had brought out with you this morning."

For a moment, because she was so concerned about her loss, Alina hardly realised what he was saying.

Then after a short pause she said:

"Y-yes . . . yes of course . . . that is what I mean. How could I have been so . . . foolish as to . . . close my . . . eyes?"

"You were wishing at the Fountain?" Lord Teverton asked. "But as that is the correct ritual, you can hardly blame yourself if one of those pestilential little Gypsy boys stole your hand-bag."

"It is the . . . only one . . . I have," Alina murmured to herself.

"Then suppose we remedy the loss of something so necessary," Lord Teverton said. "I will drive you to a shop not far from here, where I believe they have the best selection of bags in the whole of Rome."

Quite suddenly Alina realised what he was saying.

She could not afford to buy a hand-bag, nor had she now any money to put in it.

"No . . . no . . . of course . . . not," she said. "I am sure Denise will . . . lend me . . . one."

"My Chaise is very close," Lord Teverton persisted. "It would be no trouble to take you to the shop, and it is in fact on our way home."

"I would much rather . . . return to the house," Alina said.

She was thinking frantically what excuse she could give for not going shopping.

Then the words came to her lips.

"I think Denise will be back by now, and I came to the . . . Fountain only on an . . . impulse."

"I learnt at the house you had gone out to luncheon with Wescott," Lord Teverton said, "so I suppose Denise is still with him. I feel sure they can manage quite well without you. Incidentally, why are you alone?"

"Denise and the Earl have gone to St. Peter's."

"St. Peter's?" Lord Teverton exclaimed in astonishment. "Why should they do that?"

"Oh, I forgot—you do not know," Alina said. "It all happened so suddenly, but this morning soon after breakfast the Earl called on Denise, and they have now become engaged to be married."

"That is a surprise!" Lord Teverton said.

He thought for a moment, then added:

"I presume that is the reason why she was so eager to come to Rome."

Alina thought this was uncomfortably perceptive of him, and she said:

"They are very happy, and I came to the Fountain to make a wish that their happiness would last for ever."

"Very commendable and unselfish of you," Lord Teverton said mockingly. "But surely you also wished for yourself?"

He was much too perceptive, Alina thought.

He was looking at her in a penetrating way, and she knew with annoyance that she was blushing.

She could see a little way ahead of them the Chaise in which he must have arrived.

"It would be very kind if you would drive me back," she said quickly, "just in case I am wanted."

"Of course!"

He helped her into the Chaise, then got into the driver's seat.

The groom who had been holding the two horses sprang up into the small seat behind.

Lord Teverton drove the Chaise skillfully but carefully

through the throng of vehicles, all of which seemed to be converging on the entrance to the Fountain.

As they moved into a wider street, he said:

"So you had luncheon with Wescott—where?"

"With his Grandmother, the Dowager Countess," Alina replied.

"I remember her," Lord Teverton remarked, "a charming woman who must have been very beautiful in her day."

"That is what I thought," Alina said.

"Shall I prophesy," he went on, "that you will be very beautiful for many years? It will be a very long time before old age withers you, as it must do eventually."

Alina glanced at him in surprise, and he said:

"You must be aware that you look very young. I suppose you would not care to tell me your age?"

"Of course not!" Alina replied quickly. "I have always been told that it is very rude to speculate about a lady's age!"

"Not when she looks as young as you, Lady Langley," Lord Teverton said. "At the same time, Denise tells me you had been happily married for many years."

Alina thought this was becoming a more and more uncomfortable conversation, and after a moment she said:

"How lovely Rome is! Every house in the street is a picture in itself! And the Fountain was far more beautiful than I expected."

"You are changing the subject," Lord Teverton said accusingly. "I thought every woman liked to talk about herself."

"Then I must be the exception," Alina said. "I have no wish to talk about myself, but about Rome."

There was a twinkle in Lord Teverton's eyes as he drove on.

He was thinking that any other woman with whom he was alone would have said they wished to talk about him.

They were once again driving through very narrow streets.

As he had to negotiate his horses carefully, both he and Alina were silent.

Only as they climbed up the hill towards the house in which they were staying did she say:

"I expect Denise will tell you that we are all dining to-night at the Borghese Palace."

Lord Teverton raised his eye-brows.

He had, in fact, been on his way to call at the Borghese Palace himself.

But he had seen Lady Langley driving in a Hackney carriage towards the Fountain and had decided, out of curiosity, to follow her.

He had had luncheon with the British Ambassador, which he had found very boring.

He had then intended to go to the Borghese Palace.

He was actually waiting until it was the correct time to call on the Princess.

Alina was explaining to him that a special party had been arranged for the Dowager Countess.

"While we were having luncheon with her," she went on, "she sent a message to the Princess to say that her grandson was engaged to Denise, although it was a secret that would not be announced until they were back in England. However, she was sure the Princess would not mind if she brought Denise, you, and myself to the party to-night."

"I am sure Her Highness will be delighted," Lord Teverton said. "She is known to be a very generous hostess."

"I am so excited at the thought of seeing the Borghese Palace," Alina said. "I thought I should never have the opportunity."

"Well, now you will see it in style," Lord Teverton answered, "and let me warn you that Italian women are very smart, or, as the French say, *chic*. So put on your best gown and all the dazzling frills and furbelows you possess."

He was mocking her, Alina knew, but she merely laughed and said:

"I will do my best to do credit to the Union Jack, but you must not blame me if I fail."

Lord Teverton brought his horses to a standstill outside the house.

"Thank you for bringing me home," Alina said.

He helped her out of the Chaise and she walked into the Hall.

She asked the man-servant at the door if Miss Sedgwick had returned, but he shook his head.

She then went upstairs to the bed-room.

She thought it would be a mistake to be alone with Lord Teverton in case he questioned her further about her bag.

"How could I have been so foolish?" she asked herself.

It would be embarrassing to have to borrow one of Denise's.

It was even worse to have to admit that all she had left of the money Denise had given her in England was two pounds.

Now that had been stolen.

She had not been in her room very long and had only taken off her hat when Denise appeared.

"I heard you were back," she said, "and oh, Alina, it is so beautiful in St. Peter's! I am sure that Henry and I had a very special blessing, and we will never lose each other again."

"I am sure you will not do that," Alina said as she smiled.

"Henry is downstairs talking to Cousin Marcus," Denise said. "He told us that you had your hand-bag stolen."

"Oh, dearest, I am so sorry," Alina said, "but I had wished that you and Henry would be happy together. I shut my eyes, and just as I was making my second wish a small boy snatched my bag and ran off with it."

"Well, I can easily lend you another one," Denise said. "Was there much money in it?"

There was a little pause before Alina said apologetically:

"All the money I . . . had left of what you had so kindly given me in England. Fortunately, however, I had paid all the bills at home that were owing before I came away."

"Well, that was sensible, so I suppose that horrid boy did not get very much."

"Two sovereigns . . . and one or two of the Italian notes you gave me," Alina admitted.

Denise laughed.

"Is that all there was? There is no need to cry over so little."

"I feel ashamed to keep taking money from you," Alina said, "when you have done so much for me already."

"Do not be so ridiculous," Denise replied. "Look what you have done for me. Without you I could not have come to

Rome and found Henry! And you were very, very tactful in leaving us alone together, just as I wanted you to do."

She kissed Alina and said:

"Stop worrying. I am going downstairs to say good-bye to Henry. Then we have to plan what we are going to wear to-night. I can tell you it will be a very, very smart occasion."

"That is what Lord Teverton told me it would be," Alina replied.

"He is right," Denise said. "And it will be very exciting to see the Palace. But for Henry's sake we must not look like 'Country Bumpkins.'"

She paused for a moment before she went on.

"Oh, Alina, I am so happy! He is so sweet, and I want him to think me the prettiest person at the party."

"Which you will be!" Alina replied.

"I will go down and say good-bye to him, then we must have a conference about what you shall wear."

She ran from the room.

Alina thought she had never seen her look happier or more beautiful.

Because she wanted to look her best to-night, she went to the wardrobe and looked at the gowns hanging there.

Those given to her by Denise were very attractive.

But she had not yet had time to make them as elaborate as the gowns that would be worn by the older women present.

Finally Alina decided on a gown of her Mother's which had been her best.

She had worn it to a Ball given by the Lord Lieutenant and everybody had admired her.

When Denise returned, she agreed that that would be the most suitable gown for Alina to wear.

She herself intended to wear the gown in which she had been presented at Court.

It had been extremely expensive.

"I have ordered a hairdresser to come to do our hair," Denise said, "and we had better not be late or I am sure Cousin Marcus will be very disagreeable."

Alina thought he had in fact been very kind to her when she had lost her hand-bag.

Later, just as she was ready to have her bath, a parcel was brought to her room.

She thought at first the servant had made a mistake and it was intended for Denise.

But he insisted it was for her.

When she opened it she found it contained an extremely expensive hand-bag, even smarter than the one that had been stolen.

She stared at it in surprise until she saw there was a card inside.

It bore Lord Teverton's name and written on the back was:

*"A present from Rome"*

Now she stared at the bag in sheer astonishment.

How could Lord Teverton, of all people, give her anything so expensive and, of course, exactly what she needed?

Because she was so surprised, she ran from her room into Denise's.

"Look, Denise!" she cried. "Just look what your Cousin has given me! I can hardly believe it!"

Denise admired the hand-bag and said:

"His stuck-up Lordship has certainly 'come up trumps' for once!"

"I feel embarrassed," Alina said, "because when he suggested taking me to a shop to buy another bag, I refused. It was, of course, because I could not afford it, but perhaps he thought I was really asking for a present."

"I should not worry about that," Denise said. "Cousin Marcus can afford a million hand-bags if he wants to buy them. It is a blessing, as far as I am concerned, that he has not taken a dislike to you and made things difficult."

She laughed before Alina could reply and said:

"You know as well as I do he was furious at having us with him. If you think about it, he could hardly have been ruder on the journey, short of shutting us up in the Guard's Van!"

"He has certainly made amends for it now," Alina answered, "but perhaps I ought to refuse to accept such an expensive present."

"Oh, for goodness' sake, Alina, do not make difficulties!

You never know how Cousin Marcus will react. Now that he is being pleasant, as he is to you, make the most of it!"

"But . . . I do feel embarrassed and . . . rather shy," Alina confessed.

Denise gave a cry of horror.

"That is the last thing you must feel! Do you not realise that the sort of lady with whom my Cousin spends his time would not think a hand-bag nearly good enough unless it bore her initials in diamonds and its fittings were made of pure gold!"

"I do not believe it!" Alina exclaimed.

"It is true," Denise replied. "He is expected by the Society Beauties to give them the most expensive gifts because he is so rich. I was told he gave the Countess Gray a necklace of rubies that is worth a King's ransom!"

Listening, Alina realised that in that case it would be ridiculous to make a fuss about a hand-bag.

"Take everything you can get," Denise was saying, "and do not be over-grateful or he will think you are toadying to him."

This was all good advice.

Yet, when Alina went downstairs before they left for the Borghese Palace, she felt nervous.

Although she knew that Denise would laugh at her, she nevertheless felt shy.

When she went into the Study where they were all to meet, Lord Teverton was alone.

He was looking particularly impressive, she thought, in his evening-clothes.

There were several decorations on his coat and one round his neck.

As she walked toward him she felt that he was appraising her.

She saw him look at the tiara she wore on her head, and the necklace of diamonds which matched her ear-rings and her bracelets.

He did not move, and by the time she reached him she felt breathless.

"I want to . . . thank you so . . . very much. It was very . . .

kind of you to . . . give me that . . . beautiful hand-bag, and I will be very . . . careful not to . . . lose it."

She had no idea that her cheeks were flushed as she spoke, and her eye-lashes flickered.

"No more wishes!" Lord Teverton admonished. "And if you must shut your eyes, beware of small boys!"

"I shall be very . . . very . . . careful in the . . . future," Alina promised.

"May I tell you," he said, "that you are looking very beautiful? I will be extremely proud of the two ladies I am escorting to the Borghese Palace."

"You have said exactly the right thing," Alina replied, "because Denise wants to shine so as to impress the Earl."

Lord Teverton smiled.

"I think Henry Wescott is quite impressed enough already. He is obviously very much in love!"

"That is exactly what he should be," Alina said.

"It is what would be expected in Rome," Lord Teverton went on.

Alina did not answer, and he said:

"And what about you, Lady Langley? Are you feeling the Romance of Rome beginning to make your heart beat faster?"

"Perhaps that is . . . something that will . . . happen before I leave," Alina managed to say, "but for the moment I have . . . seen only a . . . small part of Rome, and there is so much . . . more I want to . . . discover."

"Of course," Lord Teverton agreed, "so I will keep that question for a later date."

As he spoke, Denise joined them.

She was looking so lovely that Alina felt it would be impossible for anyone not to be overwhelmed by her.

Lord Teverton, however, hurried them into the carriage.

They set off for the Borghese Palace.

The horses carried them along the streets which were just beginning to be lit up for the evening.

Alina thought this was a greater adventure than anything she had experienced so far.

She would see the most famous Palace in Rome with its

fabulous collection of treasures about which her Father had often spoken.

She would meet some of the most important Italians.

It would be something she would remember when she went back to England.

Just for a moment she saw in her imagination her Drawing-Room at home with the marks on the walls from which the mirrors and pictures had been removed to be sold.

She could see the faded sofas and chairs and the mantel-piece from which all the pretty ornaments had disappeared.

Then she forced the picture away from her mind.

To-night Cinderella was going to the Ball.

She was not a penniless young woman who would have to earn her own living somehow, who had no assets apart from a house she could not afford to keep up.

To play her part she must believe she really was the rich Lady Langley, owning diamonds and elegant gowns.

Even as she thought of it, she saw Lord Teverton's eyes looking at her piercingly, and she was afraid.

The horses pulled up outside the Borghese Palace.

They had to wait while several other guests ahead of them stepped out of their carriages.

There were flares so that they could see their way up a flight of steps covered with a red carpet.

As they moved into the vast Hall in which they were to be received, Alina felt as if her breath were taken away from her.

Never had she seen anything so beautiful as the ceiling rioting with angels and cupids and the walls decorated with a brilliance beyond what she had ever seen or imagined.

Then they were being greeted by the Prince and Princess Borghese.

The glorious background, the glittering jewels, the splendidly-liveried servants, were everything that a Fairy-Tale Princess could desire.

More guests were announced as they moved on, and a handsome dark-eyed young Italian held out his hand to Lord Teverton.

"How are you, My Lord?" he said. "It is good that you are in Rome again."

"I am delighted to be here, Your Highness," Lord Teverton replied.

The Italian then glanced towards Alina, and Lord Teverton said:

"Lady Langley, may I present His Highness Prince Alberto Borghese!"

Alina held out her hand.

To her surprise, the Italian Prince took it in both of his.

"I know now," he said, "that this evening is going to be a very important one, because I have met you!"

# CHAPTER FIVE

The Dining-Room was beautiful.

Alina looked around the huge table which seated forty people.

She realised that the seating had been altered because she and Denise had joined the party.

As would be expected, the Dowager Countess was sitting on the right of their host.

Alina herself had been placed on his left.

At the other end of the table Lord Teverton was seated next to the Princess and the Earl was on her right.

Denise, of course, was seated next to him.

The party consisted of a number of what Alina thought must be the Dowager Countess's special friends, because they were mostly much older.

Prince Alberto, who was on her left, informed her that a number of people were coming in later.

"We had thought," he said, "as the party was for the Countess of Wescott, that we would have singers from the

Opera. However, as my sister is young, she wanted to dance, and I thought the Earl, despite his impressive title, was young enough to want to do the same."

Alina laughed.

"I am sure either entertainment would be delightful," she said. "And your Palace is so beautiful that what one feels about it could be expressed only in music."

"I wish I were musician enough to express in that way what I feel about you," the Prince said.

For a moment she looked at him in surprise.

Then she realised that he was flirting with her.

He continued to do so all through dinner.

It was for her a new experience, but one she might have expected because she was pretending to be an older and sophisticated woman.

She could see that the Princess at the end of the table was behaving very intimately with Lord Teverton.

She was not certain, however, whether he was flirting with her, or she with him.

Denise and Henry had eyes only for each other, and were not interested in the rest of the party.

When Alina looked down the table, she saw, as Lord Teverton had warned her, that the Italian Ladies were very smart indeed.

They all seemed also to be pouting their lips and flashing their eyes at the men next to them.

"I suppose I should try to flirt," Alina said to herself, "but I have no idea how to start."

Instead, she found herself blushing and feeling shy at the compliments Prince Alberto showered upon her.

"You are lovely, exquisitely lovely!" he said. "Just like an English rose!"

"That is a symbol which everybody uses," Alina managed to say. "As an Italian, you should think of something more original."

She tried to sound crushing, as she thought a famous London Beauty would be.

But the Prince merely said:

"I have a number of very original things to say to you, but not here at this table."

However, as dinner progressed, he became even more daring.

Alina was eager to change the subject from herself.

She asked if the famous statue of Princess Pauline Borghese, which had been sculpted by Antonio Canova, was in the Palace.

"I will show it to you after dinner," the Prince replied.

"I have always heard it is one of the most alluring as well as one of the most famous statues in the world," Alina said.

"Her skin was like yours," the Prince commented, "and when she bathed in her house in Paris, a Negro servant carried her naked from her bath to her bed-room so that she could see the contrast between his skin and hers."

This was something Alina had not heard before.

But before she could say anything, the Prince said in a lower voice:

"I will carry you myself. I am sure the closeness if not the contrast between our skins will be very exciting!"

Because she could not meet the expression in his eyes, Alina blushed and looked away.

Then she realised that from the other end of the table Lord Teverton was watching her.

She thought—although of course she could not be certain—that he was looking contemptuous.

When the elaborate and delicious meal was finished, the ladies and gentlemen all left the Dining-Room together.

They went into a very large and beautifully decorated room with exquisite pictures.

An Orchestra was already playing.

The Prince did not ask her to dance; he merely put his arms round her waist.

When she and Denise were doing lessons together, among their instructors they had an excellent dancing-teacher.

Alina had always longed to dance at a Ball.

However, by the time she was old enough to go to one, her Father had died and she was in mourning.

Now, she thought, it was thrilling to be dancing in such a marvellous Palace.

She was aware, too, that it was an exceptionally good

orchestra, while to complete the story she was dancing with a handsome Prince.

The Prince was holding her a little too close.

Because she was engrossed in trying to make him keep his distance, she found it hard to listen to what he was saying.

"You are beautiful! Gorgeously beautiful!" he said as they moved round the room. "Even the pictures pale before your loveliness!"

Alina told herself he doubtless said this sort of thing to every woman with whom he danced.

She therefore did not reply, but looked round the room at the other guests.

She saw Lord Teverton was dancing with the Princess Borghese.

The Princess was looking up at him in what Alina thought was a very intimate manner.

She wondered if they were old friends and if he had ever made love to the Princess.

Then she was shocked at her own thoughts.

How could she think of such things?

Such thoughts had never occurred to her when she was living quietly at home in the Country.

"I must behave as Mama would expect me to behave," she told herself.

It was rather difficult with the Prince saying such intimate things in her ear.

She was relieved when the dance came to an end.

"Now I want to look at the pictures," she said firmly.

She moved across the room to where there was a very lovely picture of the Madonna and Child with St. John.

It was by Credi and she wanted to discuss it with Prince Alberto.

Instead, he said:

"That is one of my favourite pictures, and I know now why it has always attracted me."

"Why?" Alina asked unwarily.

"Because the Madonna has a slight resemblance to you," he said. "Only you in fact are more lovely than when Credi created her. Now I will always be dissatisfied with the picture because, although it reminds me of you, it is not you."

Alina could not think what to reply.

It was a relief when the Earl asked her for the next dance, and she accepted his invitation eagerly.

She thought he was being polite.

Then she realised that Denise was dancing with their host, Prince Borghese.

When they were moving round the floor he said:

"Denise has been telling me how kind you have been to her, and I am very grateful."

"It is delightful to have her with me," Alina said, remembering just in time that she was supposed to be not herself, but her Mother.

"Denise has also told me that Lord Teverton did not pay you much attention on the journey. In fact, that he travelled in his own compartment on the train to Dover, and in his own cabin crossing the Channel."

"I can understand it was tiresome to have two women thrust upon him," Alina said.

She felt she must somehow make excuses for Lord Teverton, as he had been kind enough to give her a hand-bag.

"According to Denise, he has a strangely cynical attitude towards women," the Earl went on. "But my Grandmother informed me after you had been to luncheon at the Villa that he was crossed in love when he was very young. This perhaps may explain it."

Alina was interested.

"Crossed in love?" she asked. "What happened?"

"According to my grandmother, there was a very beautiful girl whom Lord Teverton's Father and Mother were eager for him to marry. He genuinely fell in love with her despite the fact that he was being pressured in asking her to be his wife. But in proposing he made a terrible mistake."

"What do you mean by that?" Alina asked.

"She accepted him, but fortunately, just before the engagement was announced, he discovered the truth."

"And what was the truth?"

"She was marrying him entirely because he was rich, and her Father, who was a Nobleman, was heavily in debt."

The Earl paused.

Then as he swung her round to the music he added:

"As a matter of fact, the girl was already in love with somebody else."

Alina did not say anything.

She thought that now she could understand.

Lord Teverton's cynical and supercilious air where women were concerned was due to a woman having hurt him.

She was sure that because he was so good-looking, this had been a blow to his pride.

That would be another reason why he was autocratic, also why he was apparently unfeeling when he left a woman weeping.

However, she did not say anything of this to the Earl.

It was inevitable that a few seconds later he was talking about Denise.

She then danced with her host.

She thought he looked much older than his wife and was somewhat boring.

He danced badly, almost shuffling round the room.

He was obviously not enjoying the evening in the same way as everybody else.

She tried to talk to him about the pictures, but got little response, as when she spoke of the magnificent statues in the room.

She would have loved to know much more about them. Then she mentioned the garden.

Now there was a spark more interest in her partner's eyes than there had been previously.

Finally when she spoke of the Park, she learnt that he had recently installed deer and gazelles.

He was now considering having a private Zoo and importing wild animals like tigers and lions from overseas.

This was something Alina had not expected to find in Rome.

She thought it was another detail that she would remember with interest.

The dance ended and Prince Alberto was once more at her side.

"I have done my 'duty dances,' " he said, "and now I can enjoy myself with you."

Alina could hardly say that she had any "duty dances" to do.

She therefore danced again with Prince Alberto.

Then he said:

"I want to show you the garden."

"I have just been talking about it," Alina answered, "and I think it is a fascinating idea that he should import wild animals for the Park."

"I think it is quite unnecessary," Prince Alberto replied. "However, the garden is very beautiful, and I know you will enjoy it."

He led Alina out through one of the long windows.

She saw that quite a lot of the garden had been illuminated.

There were lights under the firs and cypress trees, and others lit up the statues.

The fountains were throwing their water iridescently into the air because there were lights hidden in the basins beneath them.

"How lovely!" Alina exclaimed, clasping her hands together.

"Very lovely!" the Prince echoed in a deep voice, but he was looking at her.

She went down some steps to look at one fountain more closely and found it was exquisitely sculptured.

The water was pouring out of a cornucopia held in the arms of a cupid.

"There is another one which is even more attractive farther on," Prince Alberto said.

They moved farther away from the house.

Alina was standing looking up at a very elaborate statue.

Suddenly she realised that the Prince was putting his arms around her.

"No . . . no . . . please!" she said quickly, trying to move away from him.

But he merely tightened his arm and asked:

"How can I stop myself when I find you irresistible!"

"I . . . I ought to . . . go back," Alina said in a frightened voice.

She was aware that they were much farther from the Palace than she had realised.

The boughs of the trees almost encompassed them.

"You excite me," the Prince said, "and I want to excite you. Are you really an icicle like so many other English-women, or could I create a fire in your heart?"

"I . . . am an . . . icicle!" Alina answered quickly.

She was trying to escape from his arms.

But he was much taller than she was and, as she realised, very strong.

"I want you, Alina," he said in a deep voice, "and I will teach you about love—the love which is fiery, passionate, and Italian. It has nothing in common with the dull, milk-like emotion that an Englishman calls love."

His face was very near to hers, and she knew he intended to kiss her.

With a little cry she tried to thrust him away.

"No . . . no!" she exclaimed. "How can . . . you behave . . . like this when . . . we have . . . only just met?"

"I have known you for a million years," the Prince answered, "and I have searched for you ever since I have been a man. Now I have found you!"

His lips were against the softness of her cheek.

Alina gave a little scream.

He pulled her closer still.

She knew she was helpless and imprisoned by him, when a drawling voice said:

"I think, Lady Langley, that this is our dance!"

For a moment both Alina and the Prince were startled into immobility.

Then, as his arms slackened, Alina pulled herself free.

She ran toward Lord Teverton, who was standing just beside the cypress trees.

"I . . . I am . . . afraid I had . . . forgotten," she stammered.

"Then shall we go back to the Ball-Room?" Lord Teverton suggested.

"Y-yes—of . . . course."

She did not look at the Prince, who she knew was standing beside the statue.

She just walked ahead of Lord Teverton until they were clear of the trees.

Only when she thought they were out of earshot did she say in a small, hesitating voice:

"Thank you . . . thank . . . you! I was . . . frightened and did not know . . . what to . . . do."

"Surely you know that it is a mistake ever to go into a garden alone with a man?" Lord Teverton asked scathingly.

"I . . . I never . . . thought about it. I . . . I was . . . looking at the . . . fountains and . . . then—"

She paused.

It suddenly struck her that there was no reason for her to make excuses to Lord Teverton.

He did not speak.

They walked on until they came back to the Palace.

Instead of taking her in through the window by which she had left with the Prince, he took her to a side-door.

It had a portico.

As they stepped into it, they were in shadow.

Feeling nervous and upset, Alina waited for Lord Teverton to open the door.

Then unexpectedly he said:

"Try to behave with a little more propriety before we leave!"

He spoke scathingly.

Alina looked up at him, wondering what she should say.

He put his hand under her chin.

"If you are so hungry for kisses," he said, "why not seek them from someone of your own nationality?"

Before she could understand what he was saying, she felt his lips on hers.

She could not believe it was happening.

Then, while she was still bewildered, he opened the door.

He walked inside, leaving her standing in the portico.

It was a relief when half-an-hour later the Dowager Countess declared it was time she had to leave.

Denise and the Earl said they were ready to leave too.

Alina realised that they wanted the chance to be alone.

She drove back with them and the Dowager Countess.

But as soon as they reached the house, she went upstairs, leaving them in the Study together.

There had been no sign of Lord Teverton.

The Earl suggested it was quite unnecessary for them to wait for him.

"I will take you home, Grandmother," he had said to the Dowager Countess, "and then escort Denise and Lady Langley to where they are staying."

"Thank you, dear boy," the Dowager Countess answered.

When Alina reached her own room she stared at her reflection in the mirror.

It was as if she were seeing herself for the first time.

How was it possible that Lord Teverton, of all people, should have kissed her?

Then she knew that he was showing her in his own subtle manner how cheap she had made herself.

His kiss was really a punishment for bad behaviour.

It was not because she attracted him in any way.

It was the first time she had been kissed.

It was not the least what she had expected a kiss would be like.

His lips had been hard, and she knew it was because he was angry.

But why should he be angry with her?

She was no concern of his in any possible regard except, of course, as a chaperon for his Cousin in whom he was clearly not at all interested.

It was like a conundrum that kept whirling round in her head.

It always came back to the same point.

Lord Teverton had kissed her.

Although he had been angry, it was an experience which she felt she would not forget.

Now, as she thought about it, she realised she had at first been stunned into surprise.

Then, before he had taken his lips from hers, she had felt a little flicker within her breast.

It was like the water rioting from the fountain, a sensation she had never known before.

It was strange yet exciting, but she had felt it for only the passing of a second.

Then he had released her and walked into the Palace, leaving her alone outside.

"I think perhaps I have shocked him," she told herself.

She had no wish for him to despise her for the way she had behaved.

"Why does he not understand that I did not deliberately do it?" she asked her reflection.

Then she knew the answer.

Like the Prince, Lord Teverton assumed her to be a sophisticated woman of a sensible age, a woman who accepted the men who pursued her as her right.

"How can he be expected to know," she asked herself pathetically, "that I am only a stupid girl from the Country who has never been kissed before?"

Now she had been kissed.

Not by a man who was excited and attracted by her—but by Lord Teverton, who despised her!

Alina went to bed in tears.

It seemed foolish, and she was annoyed with herself for weeping.

But somehow the evening, which had started so gloriously, had ended in disaster.

She kept telling herself that there was nothing to be upset about.

It really did not matter one way or the other what Lord Teverton thought or did not think.

Yet all her thoughts came back to the same point: he had left her on the doorstep.

It was as if she were something to be discarded.

When she reached the Ball-Room there had been no sign of him.

Then when with the Dowager Countess they had said good-night, the Princess was not there.

It might just be coincidence.

Yet, remembering how the Princess had looked at Lord

Teverton during dinner, Alina could not help thinking they were together.

They were somewhere in her beautiful Palace.

The statues, the pictures, and the vast collection of treasures were, she thought, a perfect background for love.

She had not understood all the compliments Prince Alberto had paid her.

He must have been surprised, she thought, at the way she had behaved, like a School-girl rather than a woman, and certainly out of keeping with her appearance.

She was vividly conscious of the powder and rouge on her cheeks, and the colour of her lips.

She knew Denise was right.

It made her look not only older, but also like every other woman who was a social success.

In Lord Teverton's eyes she was simply one of the sophisticated Beauties who frequented Marlborough House in London.

'Underneath I am just a gauche *débutante* who does not know how to behave!" Alina thought bitterly.

Denise did not come in to say good-night to her.

Alina cried herself to sleep although she was not certain why she was doing so.


When morning came, Alina chided herself for being so absurd.

"You are in Rome. You have a chance of seeing everything that is beautiful, and yet you are making a fool of yourself!"

She also remembered that she had no reason to be concerned with Lord Teverton.

It was no business of his what she did or did not do.

"I am not a *débutante*, I am a widow, and I must not behave like a frightened, half-witted girl!"

When very late she went downstairs to breakfast, it was a relief to find there was nobody in the Breakfast-Room.

She was just finishing her coffee when Denise came in.

"What a wonderful, wonderful evening!" she cried.

"Thank you, dearest Alina, for letting me be alone with Henry. He did not leave until two o'clock."

"Two o'clock?" Alina exclaimed. "What about Lord Teverton?"

"There was no sign of Cousin Marcus—thank goodness!" Denise replied. "I expect he was enjoying himself elsewhere, otherwise he would have been home earlier."

"Yes . . . I expect . . . he was," Alina said in a dull voice.

"Henry is calling for me at eleven o'clock," Denise said. "You will not mind, dearest, if we go alone, will you?"

"No, of course not," Alina answered, "but I hope nobody will be shocked."

"They will not see us," Denise said eagerly. "We are going to drive out of Rome to a place in the Country which Henry has discovered and where he says the food is delicious!"

She gave a little laugh.

"I only hope I can taste it, for actually I can think of nothing but him!"

"You do not . . . think," Alina asked a little nervously, "that your Cousin Marcus will consider it . . . wrong of . . . me to let . . . you go off . . . alone?"

"Henry thought of that, and when he comes he is going to say that he is taking me to see his Grandmother—that is, if Cousin Marcus is interested enough to ask the question."

Denise pushed her plate away before she went on:

"The best thing we can do is to avoid seeing him. I am going upstairs now to get ready. As soon as Henry arrives, I shall run down and jump into whatever vehicle he is driving, and we will be gone!"

Denise seemed to have everything organised.

Alina thought it would be a mistake for her to argue about it.

She merely hoped, because she disliked lying, that Lord Teverton would not ask her any questions.

Finally when she had finished her breakfast she went upstairs.

Denise, with her hat on, was ready and waiting for the Earl.

"Do not forget," she said, "there are a lot of things for you to see in Rome which you have not yet seen. And I have here, dearest Alina, some money, which I am sure you will need."

Reluctantly, but thinking it foolish to make a fuss, Alina accepted it from her.

"You are . . . so kind and . . . generous," she murmured.

"The kindness you have done me cannot be expressed in money, not if it were a million pounds," Denise answered, "and Henry is very grateful to you too."

She gave a little laugh before she added:

"Can you imagine what it would be like if I had one of my pompous, ultra-respectable relatives with me? She would be determined that we should speak to each other only when she was present!"

Alina laughed too.

"I am sure you are exaggerating."

"You do not know how stuffy they are," Denise said, "and Henry's Grandmother is very much the same. Whatever you do, do not go near her to-day, or she may ask you why you are not with me."

"I will keep out of sight," Alina promised

A servant came up to announce that the Earl was downstairs.

Denise gave a cry of delight.

Picking up her hand-bag, she ran down to him without even saying good-bye.

They drove away immediately.

Alina followed Denise down the stairs, and now she wondered what she could do.

There was so much in Rome that she wanted to see, but she had no idea where to begin.

There was a Guide-Book, she knew, in the Study which Denise had left there.

She went to the Study and found the book.

She was just going back upstairs, when Lord Teverton walked in.

If he had gone to bed late last night, he certainly did not show any sign of it this morning.

He was looking, she thought, very smart and extremely English.

"Good-morning, Lady Langley!" he said. "Where is my Cousin?"

There was a little pause before Alina forced herself to say:

"She has gone with the Earl to see the Dowager Countess."

"I saw them driving away," Lord Teverton remarked. "It was in the opposite direction—but no matter!"

'He would catch me out again!' Alina thought to herself.

Feeling it best to say nothing, she moved towards the door.

"What are you going to do with yourself today?" Lord Teverton enquired.

"I came here to fetch the Guide-Book," Alina answered.

"I had an idea," Lord Teverton said, "that one of the things you would want to see before leave would be the Colosseum."

"Yes, of course."

"Well, as I have finished my business for the morning," Lord Teverton said, "let me take you there."

Alina looked at him in surprise.

"Do you . . . mean that?" she asked. "It would be an awful . . . nuisance for . . . you, and I am sure you have . . . been there a . . . thousand times!"

"Then this will be the thousandth-and-first!" Lord Teverton said. "Put on your hat and we will leave as soon as you are ready."

"I will be only a few minutes," Alina promised.

She went from the room.

The depression she had felt since getting up had vanished.

She suddenly felt Lord Teverton was not still angry with her.

He had actually offered to take her to see the Colosseum.

She had had no wish to go there alone.

It was wonderful that she could go with him.

Suddenly it struck her that perhaps he was apologising for the way he had behaved last night.

For a moment she was still.

Then she told herself that what was past was past.

What was the point of worrying about it?

"He is going to accompany me to the Colosseum!" she told her reflection in the mirror.

Then she was smiling.

And the sun was shining more brightly than she had ever known it to do.

# CHAPTER SIX

They walked into the Colosseum and stood in one of the Galleries.

Quietly Lord Teverton began to explain what it had been like when it was first built.

He described the scene very vividly with its huge crowd of more than fifty thousand spectators.

They were seated according to rank in the Galleries, with women allowed in the top Gallery only.

In the arena Gladiators fought one another to the death.

Men were pitted against wild beasts, beasts against other beasts.

It could even be flooded for mimic sea-battles.

All were spectacles to delight the blood-thirsty mob.

He described how the animals were hoisted up in cages from the dens below the arena.

He told her that whips had been found which had been used on them.

He made Alina shiver to think of the crowd becoming wildly excited by watching the cruelty and blood.

The smell of it intoxicated them as if it were wine.

The shrieks and cries from the Galleries were even louder than those of the victims and the roar of the enraged animals.

She could not only see it all happening, but feel it.

Suddenly she felt overcome, as if the spectacle were actually taking place below her.

She must have looked very pale, because at once Lord Teverton stopped speaking.

Slipping her hand through his arm, he helped her down the steps to the exit.

His Chaise was waiting just outside.

He lifted her onto the seat, then sat beside her and picked up the reins.

They drove for a little way in silence.

Then Alina said in a low voice:

"I . . . I am . . . sorry."

"There is nothing to be sorry for," Lord Teverton replied. "It is what I felt myself the first time I visited the Colosseum."

She looked at him in surprise.

She had never imagined that he would feel as she had, that he would be upset by the thought of what both humans and animals had suffered there.

She wanted to ask him to tell her more, but for the moment she felt too weak.

She therefore said nothing.

They drove on until they came to a Restaurant.

"I thought we would have luncheon here," Lord Teverton said. "I found when I was here before it served the best fish in the whole of Rome."

Alina felt her weakness pass.

It was wonderful to think she would have luncheon with Lord Teverton.

Perhaps he would talk to her as interestingly as he had talked to her in the Colosseum.

The Restaurant was small.

The fish were displayed attractively so that a customer could choose what he wished to be cooked.

Lord Teverton did not ask Alina what was her preference.

He chose what he thought was the best.

Then they sat down in a comfortable corner seat with a window looking out onto a court-yard at the back.

In it were flowers and shrubs, and the sun was shining.

Alina found she had recovered completely from her weakness.

Lord Teverton, however, insisted that she drink a glass of golden wine.

When she obeyed him she said:

"It was . . . silly of . . . me to be upset . . . I hope you . . . you . . . will . . . forgive me."

"I am interested, perhaps the right word is 'curious,' to know why you felt just as I did," he replied. "I have taken quite a number of people, at one time or another, to see the Colosseum, but their reaction has been very different."

He then began to speak of other things, and he did not refer to the Colosseum again.

When they finished luncheon he drew his gold watch from his waist-coat pocket.

"I must take you back," he said a little ruefully. "I have an appointment with the King for which I must not be late."

"No . . . of course not."

Alina picked up the hand-bag he had given her and walked from the Restaurant.

She thanked the Proprietor for a delicious meal as he bowed them out into the street.

Lord Teverton drove the horses rather quicker than he had done during the morning.

When they arrived at the house, Alina said:

"Thank . . . you. Thank you . . . very much for being . . . so kind. I enjoyed . . . my luncheon . . . enormously."

Lord Teverton did not reply.

He merely smiled at her, lifted his hat, and drove on as if he were afraid of being late.

Alina went into the house, thinking it unlikely that Denise would be back.

There was no sign of her until five o'clock.

Then she rushed in excitedly to say that she had a fascinating time with Henry.

He wanted to take her out to dinner.

"There is a place he knows where no-one will see us, and we can be together and talk," Denise said. "You do not mind, dearest?"

"No, of course not," Alina replied.

"I feel mean leaving you alone, but perhaps Cousin Marcus will be dining in."

"Do not worry about me," Alina said. "I have a number of books I want to read, and it would be a mistake to let your Cousin know that I am not with you."

"Yes, of course," Denise agreed. "I am sure he would think it reprehensible that Henry and I want to be alone."

Alina therefore went to her bed-room.

Settling herself on the sofa, she opened one of the books she had brought upstairs from the study.

She thought when Lord Teverton did return he would let her know if he was dining in.

Then she would have to pretend that Denise and Henry were dining with his Grandmother.

No-one came near her until, when it was nearly eight o'clock, there was a knock on her door.

"Come in," she said, and a footman appeared.

Speaking in Italian, he said:

"Milord is sending a carriage for Your Ladyship at nine o'clock."

Alina's eyes widened with delight, and she jumped up from the sofa.

Lord Teverton was taking her out to dinner.

She supposed if he was sending a carriage for her, it meant he could not get away until the last minute.

Hastily she rang for the maid.

Instead of the Italian woman who had been looking after her, Denise's English lady's-maid answered the bell.

"I am going out to dinner with His Lordship," Alina said. "Please be very kind and help me with my hair and to choose a gown which I have not yet worn."

Jones, the maid, smiled.

"I'm glad Your Ladyship's going out," she said. "It's a waste being in Rome for you to sit here alone."

"That is what I thought," Alina agreed.

Jones ordered her bath to be brought in immediately.

While it was being prepared, they went to the wardrobe to decide which gown Alina should wear.

There was a very pretty one with lace draped over a full skirt of sky-blue satin.

It was not really elaborate enough for an older woman.

Alina thought, however, if she wore plenty of the jewellery that Denise had lent her, it would make her look older.

Jones dressed her hair in a particularly becoming manner.

Then she put on a necklace of turquoise and diamonds with large ear-rings to match.

Alina thought she would be very foolish if she did not know that she looked her best.

"Thank you so much!" she said to Jones.

"The gown's a little loose at the back," Jones said. "I'll just give it a stitch now, and if Your Ladyship'll ring for me when you get back, I'll undo it. To-morrow I'll sew on a hook and eye."

Alina thanked her again.

She picked up the wrap which went with the gown.

It was too hot to wear any of the capes that Denise had brought her.

Instead, she just had a scarf of the same material as the gown itself, but edged with lace.

"You looks beautiful, M'Lady!" Jones said with satisfaction.

A few minutes later a footman announced that the carriage was at the door.

Alina ran down the stairs excitedly.

She stepped into the closed carriage.

She thought as she did so that Lord Teverton was very lucky to be allowed to use his friend's stables as well as staying in his house.

The two horses drove off.

She wondered as they did so where Lord Teverton was taking her.

Would it be an even more delightful Restaurant than the one in which they had luncheon?

It was growing dark outside.

It was difficult to see much of the street through which they were passing.

Unexpectedly, they were no longer in a street.

Instead, they were moving between some trees.

Alina thought she must be in a Park.

Then the horses came to a standstill and there were lights.

She could not, however, see any large building, but there was a door ahead which was invitingly open.

She got out of the carriage.

Lord Teverton had certainly thought of somewhere original for them to have dinner.

As she walked in she could see ahead of her not a large room, as she had expected, but a terrace and beyond it the shimmering water of a lake.

A question came to her mind.

Even as it did so, a man stepped forward from between two pillars.

It was Prince Alberto.

Alina stared at him in sheer astonishment until he said:

"Welcome, my beautiful one! I cannot tell you how thrilled I am that you are here."

"Wh-where am I?" Alina asked. "I was asked out to dinner by Lord Teverton.

The Prince laughed.

"As I knew that His Lordship would be dining with His Majesty, I thought it would save a great deal of argument if I invited you to dine with me in his name."

Alina gasped.

"How could you do such a thing?" she demanded. "I think it very deceitful of you!"

"I adore you when you are angry!" he replied. "In fact, I adore you in whatever mood you are in."

He put out his hand.

"Come—our dinner is waiting, and we are both hungry."

Alina felt it was difficult to protest.

She knew now where she was.

She was in the little Temple of Aesculapius in the Borghese Park.

She had read about it and seen it from a distance.

She thought it was exquisite, but she had never imagined she would ever be actually inside it.

Now she was aware that a dinner-table had been laid for two on the terrace.

On a side-table there were a number of dishes set out attractively.

There was no sign of any servants.

Alina realised she was alone with the Prince.

She felt very nervous.

At the same time, she was sensible enough to know that if she tried to run away from him, he could easily prevent her from doing so.

Moreover, it would be impossible for her to find her way home through the Park.

"I must behave as the sophisticated lady I am pretending to be," she told herself.

She took off her gloves and sat down at the table.

It was decorated with several exquisite pieces of gold craftsmanship.

There was also a profusion of white orchids.

The Prince placed a dish of *pâte* in front of her before he sat on the opposite side of the table.

"I want to look at you," he said. "I have dreamt of how we could be together like this and I could tell you how beautiful you are!"

"I would much rather you told me about the Temple," Alina said. "It is very fine and I am wondering when it was built."

"In 1787," the Prince replied. "Now tell me when you were born."

Alina found it difficult to keep the conversation from herself.

The Prince asked her questions and paid her compliments.

As he did so, he looked at her with burning dark eyes which made her feel embarrassed.

She found it difficult to know what she was eating.

She was careful to drink very little.

She was aware that whenever she took a sip from her glass he filled it up again.

As they ate, the stars came out overhead.

A full moon shone over the lake, turning the water to silver.

It was very romantic.

But Alina kept wishing she was not with the Prince and that he would not be so effusive.

He was certainly very good-looking.

Yet for some reason she could not explain, he did not attract her in any way.

His exaggerated compliments made her feel uncomfortable.

She was afraid to meet his eyes because of the expression in them.

When they had finished what she thought must be the last course, she said:

"I must not be late in going back. Denise is dining with the Dowager Countess, and she will expect me to be waiting for her when she returns."

The Prince laughed.

"They may deceive you," he said, "but I am quite certain that Henry and your little *protégée* are dining somewhere secretly together and are as happy to be alone as we are."

"I am not at all happy to be alone with Your Highness," Alina retorted. "You brought me here by a trick, and I must insist that you send me back very shortly."

"How can you tell me to do anything so ridiculous?" the Prince asked.

He rose from the table and held out his hand.

"I want to show you what else the Temple contains."

Slowly, because she did not want to touch his hand, Alina rose.

She tried to avoid him.

However, the Prince took hold of her hand and drew her into the Temple.

There was a thin passage through which she had entered.

Then she was aware there were rooms on either side of it.

"This is what I want to show you," the Prince said.

He opened a door and she saw a small but beautifully decorated room.

There was a large divan at one end of it which was as big as a double-bed.

There was a window looking onto the Park at the other end.

The room was lit with candelabra in the shape of cupids, each holding three candles.

The air was fragrant with the scent of roses.

As Alina looked around her, she was aware that the Prince was taking off his evening-coat.

He flung it down on a chair as she said hastily:

"Thank you for showing me this pretty room, and now I must go!"

He walked towards her in his shirt-sleeves.

"Do you really think I will let you leave?" he asked. "My precious, my beautiful little Madonna, I have brought you here to teach you about love, of which, like all English-women, you know very little. But after tonight it will be different."

Alina gave a little cry of horror.

He reached out his arms.

She ran away from him through the door he had left open back onto the terrace.

She looked first to one side, then to the other.

She realised in horror that the Temple was built out onto the lake.

There was no way on either side of the terrace by which she could reach the Park.

Because the Prince was aware of her predicament, he did not run after her.

He merely walked slowly until he was standing beside her.

"You are shy and elusive," he said, "and that, my sweet, excites me all the more! I want you—God knows I want you—and I intend to have you!"

He put out his arm, and Alina knew despairingly there was no way of escape.

He would carry her back to the room they had just left.

However much she might protest, he would make her his.

"Oh . . . God . . . save me," she prayed.

In that instant she knew the answer.

Taking the Prince by surprise, she moved away from him, not as he might have expected, either to one side or the other, but straight ahead into the lake.

The water rose first up to her knees, then nearly to her waist.


Lord Teverton, who had dined with the King and Queen, left the Palace as early as he could.

It was a privilege to be invited to what was an informal dinner.

At the same time, he found it somewhat heavy-going and had no wish to linger when the meal was finished.

He thanked Their Majesties profusely for their hospitality.

He accepted an invitation from the King to discuss further proposals put by the Prime Minister.

To present them had been the reason for his coming to Rome.

Then with a sigh of relief he stepped into his carriage.

It was still comparatively early and he wondered if Alina had gone to bed.

He was still thinking that the way the Colosseum had upset her this morning was rather intriguing.

As he had said to her quite truthfully, it was how he had felt himself on his first visit.

He had been only twenty and a student at Oxford.

He had never known anybody else who had felt the same.

He thought there must be some rapport between himself and Lady Langley which he had not expected.

She was beautiful—that he recognised.

But there was something different about her beauty which he could not quite explain.

The carriage drew up outside the house and he walked into the Hall.

He waited for a footman to remove the evening-cloak from his shoulders.

Before he could do so, Jones, the lady's-maid who had accompanied his Cousin from London, appeared.

"But where's Her Ladyship, M'Lord?" she asked. "She hasn't come back with you?"

Lord Teverton stared at her.

"Come back with me?" he asked. "What are you talking about?"

"Her Ladyship said she was going to dinner with Your Lordship," Jones explained. "I'm waiting up so that I can help her undress."

"I am afraid you are mistaken," Lord Teverton replied. "I have been dining at the Palace with Their Majesties."

Jones stared at him.

"That's very strange, M'Lord! A message came for Her Ladyship to say you'd be sending a carriage for her at nine o'clock."

For a moment Lord Teverton was still.

Then he reacted quickly.

"Stop the carriage!" he said sharply to the footman who was standing nearest to the door.

The horses were just being driven away.

The footman quickly ran out, shouting to the coachman, who heard him and pulled them to a standstill.

Lord Teverton looked at the other footmen.

"Who took the message to Her Ladyship?" he asked.

Lord Teverton spoke extremely fluent Italian.

One of the footmen who spoke no English replied:

"I did, Milord."

"And who brought it?" Lord Teverton asked.

"A man. He were wearing livery, Milord."

"Did you recognise whose livery it was?"

The man thought for a moment.

"I think, now Your Lordship mentions it, 'twas the livery of the Prince Borghese."

Lord Teverton did not wait to hear any more.

He ran down the steps and climbed into the carriage.

As he did so he gave the coachman instructions as to where he wanted to go.

At dinner he had listened to an attractive woman who was seated on his left.

She told him scandalous tales of what was going on in Rome.

"It is Prince Alberto," she had said, "who keeps us all on tenter-hooks as to what he will do next. He is a very naughty boy, but, of course, we enjoy his endless *affaires de coeur*. He keeps us all guessing as to who is to share with him his next *amore*."

Lord Teverton had not been particularly interested.

He thought the Prince a somewhat tiresome young man, but his dinner-partner continued:

"His Highness takes whoever he fancies to the small Greek Temple in the Borghese Park. He has made an alluring bed-room at the back of the Temple and keeps the whole of Rome guessing as to who will be its next occupant!"

She had laughed.

The gentleman on her other side had confirmed what she said, adding a few anecdotes of his own to which Lord Teverton had listened.

He knew now who had spirited Alina away in his absence and where she would be.

He was angry, extremely angry, at the impertinence of it.

At the same time, his cool, calculating mind was thinking shrewdly.

It would be a mistake to let this become a Diplomatic incident.

There was always the possibility that it could disrupt the mission he was carrying out on behalf of the Prime Minister.


Standing up to her waist in water, Alina was afraid to go any farther.

If the bottom of the lake sloped down any lower, she would be out of her depth.

She could swim, but not very well.

She thought that nothing could be more humiliating than to have the Prince rescue her from drowning.

Astonished by what she had done, he was standing on the edge of the terrace.

She knew he was wondering what he should do.

"Come back, Alina!" he said finally. "You have made yourself wet for no reason whatsoever, and I will dry you to prevent you from catching cold."

Alina did not answer.

She was trying to think of some way by which she could avoid retracing her steps.

But she felt despairingly that sooner or later that was what she would have to do.

Then, as she felt her body sinking a little lower into the water, she moved nervously.

At that moment she heard a drawling voice say:

"Good-evening Your Highness. As I was passing, I thought I would give Lady Langley a lift home."

The Prince, utterly astonished, turned.

Lord Teverton was standing just behind him.

For the moment he was so taken aback at his unexpected appearance that he could think of nothing to say.

Lord Teverton walked forward to the edge of the terrace.

Then he looked with an expression of surprise at Alina, standing in the lake.

"It is a warm night, Lady Langley," he drawled, "but I think it would be a mistake for you to linger in your present position for too long."

With a feeling of irrepressible relief Alina began to move back slowly.

Her skirt, clinging to her legs in the water, was impeding her embarrassingly.

The Prince swore a lewd oath beneath his breath and walked away.

When Alina reached the place where Lord Teverton was standing, he put out both his hands.

He had to pull her up beside him.

The water was pouring off her satin and lace skirt.

She bent down to try to squeeze some of it from the folds.

Without saying anything, Lord Teverton removed his evening-cape and put it over her shoulders.

Having done so, he drew her from the front of the Temple and down the passage.

The door was open and his carriage was outside.

"I will make the carriage very wet," Alina said in a whisper.

"It is of no importance," Lord Teverton answered.

He helped her onto the back seat.

Then he went round to the other side of the carriage and got in beside her.

Her hands were clasped together, her wet skirt making a pool of water on the floor.

As they drove off, Alina whispered:

"I . . . I thought I was being taken to dine with y-you."

"I learned that when I returned to the house," Lord Teverton replied.

"Thank . . . God you . . . c-came . . . I was so . . . frightened . . . very . . . frightened. There was . . . no other way I could . . . escape . . . from h-him."

The words tumbled out of her mouth almost incoherently.

"Forget him!" Lord Teverton said. "And it would be a great mistake for you to talk about what occurred to-night."

"O-of course . . . I would not . . . talk about it! How . . . can you . . . think I . . . would?"

She tried to speak defensively.

At the same time, she was very near to tears.

Lord Teverton did not reply, and they drove on in silence.

It was only a short distance to the house, and when they arrived Lord Teverton said:

"Go straight upstairs, and if your maid asks questions, simply say it was an accident."

He was speaking sharply, as if he were addressing a naughty School-boy.

As Alina went up the stairs to her room, she thought miserably that he must despise her.

And he must be ashamed of her too for being so foolish.

Jones was horrified by the state of her gown as she helped her out of it.

"Never mind, M'Lady," she said, "I'll hang it somewhere to dry, and when I press it, I'm sure it'll look as good as new."

Alina thanked her and got into bed.

In the darkness she thought how lucky she was that Lord Teverton had come at exactly the right moment.

She was sure that otherwise she would have been unable to escape from the Prince.

He would have done what he intended, no matter how much she pleaded or protested.

"Lord Teverton saved me!" she whispered.

She knew that only he could have been clever enough to find her.

Only he could have carried off the whole incident so diplomatically.

The Prince had not raged at him or, worse still, challenged him to a duel.

Duels were still fought in Italy, as they were occasionally, if secretly, in London.

'I am sure to-morrow His Lordship will be very angry with me,' she thought.

Then she knew she could not bear it if he were.

She did not want him to despise her for her stupidity, but to admire her.

She was suddenly very still.

Incredible though it seemed, she was in love!

In love with Lord Teverton, who was finding her nothing but a nuisance!

"I love . . . him! I love . . . him!" she said in the darkness.

She felt a little quiver in her breast. Then she realised the same thing happened when his lips had touched hers.

# CHAPTER SEVEN

Alina awoke with a start.

Somebody was shaking her shoulder.

She opened her eyes and saw that it was Denise.

"What is it?" she asked.

She felt as if she had been asleep for only a few minutes, although actually it had been several hours.

"I am sorry to wake you, dearest," Denise said, "but we have to leave for England almost immediately."

Alina gave a little gasp and sat up in bed.

"Wh-what has . . . happened?" she asked.

"When Henry got back last night to his Grandmother's," Denise exclaimed, "he found a cable from England to say that his sister, who is older than he is and a widow, is desperately ill."

"I am . . . sorry," Alina said.

"He came here at eight o'clock to tell me," Denise went on, "and I went downstairs to talk to him. He is now arranging with Cousin Marcus for us to travel back in his private railway carriage."

"And we . . . are going . . . at once?" Alina asked in a small voice.

"You have a little over an hour before we leave the house," Denise said. "As soon as Jones has finished my packing, she will attend to yours, but I think you should start on it at once."

"Yes . . . of course," Alina agreed.

Denise went from the room, and Alina got out of bed.

She walked to the window, looking out over the roofs of Rome.

So this was the end.

She had been in this enchanting City for such a very short while.

Now the fairy-story was finished and she would go back to England to be herself again.

She felt as if there were a hard stone in her breast.

She knew that the real reason for her unhappiness was not that she was leaving Rome, but, rather, Lord Teverton.

She was aware that he would not come home with them.

He had not finished the work he had come here to do.

That meant that she would never see him again.

While she was thinking what this would mean, two Italian maids came hurrying into the room.

They brought with them one of her trunks.

Alina quickly dressed herself.

By the time she went downstairs for breakfast, the maids had practically emptied the wardrobe and the drawers.

There were only a few more things left to pack in the last trunk.

There was nobody in the Breakfast-Room.

When a servant brought in a fresh pot of coffee, Alina could not help asking:

"Has His Lordship had breakfast?"

"His Lordship has gone out, Milady."

Alina knew her last hope had vanished.

When the Earl arrived, he confirmed it.

"I am very sorry, Lady Langley, that we have had to do

everything in such a hurry, but I am sure you will understand that I must go home immediately, as my sister is so ill."

"Of course you must," Alina agreed.

"She has been under the care of the doctor for some time," the Earl went on, "but they do not seem to know what is wrong with her. I only hope it is nothing really serious."

Alina gave a little murmur of sympathy.

Before she could say anything, he went on:

"I know you will understand that I will be able to cope with everything once I am back in England, even if it means an operation."

He paused for a moment, then added:

"Oh, and by the way, Lord Teverton asked me to say how sorry he is that he could not say good-bye to you. He had a very important meeting with His Majesty, which, of course, he could not ask to be postponed."

"I understand," Alina said.

She went upstairs and tipped the maids who had done her packing.

Then she collected the warm cloak she had worn on the outward journey.

When she came down again, the carriage was outside.

The Courier who had escorted them to Italy was attending to the luggage.

They drove off, all three of them sitting on the back-seat of the carriage.

Denise was holding the Earl's hands to comfort him.

It was a great achievement that at such short notice Lord Teverton's Drawing-Room carriage had been attached to the Express.

It was because, Denise explained, her Cousin ranked as an Ambassador for England.

He could therefore get things done quickly.

They boarded the train.

Alina remembered how Lord Teverton had travelled with them so reluctantly on the journey out.

He had made it quite clear from the very beginning that he had no wish for their company.

Yet he had been so kind to her once they were in Rome.

She would never forget how yesterday he had taken her

to the Colosseum and afterwards they had luncheon together.

Then in the evening he had taken the trouble to save her from Prince Alberto.

Perhaps, therefore, if nothing else, he felt friendly towards her.

Then, like a blow from a dagger piercing her heart, she understood.

He still thought of her as an older woman, not as the unfledged girl she really was.

If he ever guessed at the truth, he would never want to see her again.

It was most unlikely anyway that he would take the trouble to do so.

One thing was absolutely certain.

She had seen how he behaved towards Denise and knew he had no time for girls.

The wheels of the train as they rumbled under her were saying over and over again:

"It is finished . . . finished . . . finished . . . finished . . ."

Lord Teverton had arranged that they should have hampers of food as they had on the journey from England.

But the Chef in Rome had very little time to prepare them.

The food was therefore not as inviting as it had been before.

The Earl's Valet waited on them and was very attentive.

Somehow, however, everything to Alina seemed different and flat.

She was glad she was tired and had an excuse for going to bed early.

She left Denise talking to the Earl in the Drawing-Room.

She was, however, still awake when Denise came to bed.

Denise undressed, then said to Alina in a low voice:

"There is something I have to say to you, dearest."

"What is it?" Alina asked, also speaking very softly.

She guessed that Denise did not want the Earl to hear what they were saying from his sleeping-compartment.

"You do understand," Denise whispered, "that when we reach London you must go home immediately?"

"Yes, of course . . . I know that," Alina agreed.

"I have no wish for Henry to learn or to guess I have lied to him about you," Denise said. "Although he has forgiven me for the way I behaved with Charles, he has not forgotten it. I must not do anything which seems to him underhanded or unconventional."

"I understand that," Alina agreed, "and as soon as we reach London, I will go straight home."

"What we have been deciding," Denise went on, "is that if Henry's sister is dangerously ill, we will be married quickly, before she dies."

She paused before she added:

"You will understand better than anyone that I could not bear to have to wait until the six-month period of mourning is over before I could marry Henry."

"I think it is wise of you to marry him at once," Alina replied, "even if it will have to be a very quiet wedding."

"That is what we have decided," Denise said. "But what I mind more than anything else is that you cannot be present at the wedding."

"I will . . . pray for your happiness . . . wherever I am," Alina promised.

"I am hoping that later, perhaps in a year or so," Denise went on, "I can tell Henry that your Mother is dead, and how much you mean to me, having shared our lessons together. Then, of course, we can see each other again and he will not be suspicious of you, even if you resemble your Mother so closely."

"I think you have thought it all out very sensibly," Alina said.

"I know I seem to be behaving very selfishly," Denise went on, "but I suspect, although I am so happy with Henry, that he is still a little doubtful of my love. So I must be very careful."

"Do not worry," Alina replied. "I will disappear, and when we do meet again he will not have the slightest idea that I am anything but a young girl . . . a year younger . . . than you."

Denise gave a little laugh.

"It was clever of me to think of having you with me," she said. "You have been perfectly wonderful! I know that if it had been anybody else who chaperoned me, they would not have allowed me to be alone with Henry as I had to be in order to convince him that I really do love him."

"And now you will live happily ever after!" Alina said. "I do think you would be wise to marry as quickly as possible."

"I shall see to that," Denise said, "and, dearest Alina, I can never thank you enough."

She put out her hand towards the other bed and laid it on Alina's.

"What I am going to do," she said, "is to send you all the clothes I have now when I buy my trousseau. I have also written you a cheque for two-hundred pounds, which I slipped into your hand-bag when I was undressing."

"It is . . . too much!" Alina protested. "I cannot . . . take it!"

"Do not be silly," Denise replied. "You have to live, and I cannot bear to think of you trying to earn money in some servile or mean occupation. The two-hundred will keep you comfortable until we can be together in the future."

"But, I . . ." Alina began.

"Do not argue!" Denise interrupted. "It will only upset me and make me worried about you even on my honeymoon. You could not be so unkind as to make me do that!"

"Thank you, darling, thank you!" Alina said.

Denise had been so kind to her that she felt she wanted to cry.

She knew this was not her only reason for tears.


They were fortunate in that they did not have to change trains at Paris.

After a long stop they set off again for Calais.

By the time they reached London they were all very tired.

The Earl was on edge because he was worried about his sister.

He was also afraid, Alina suspected, that she might already have died, in which case it would be impossible for him to marry Denise for some months.

He had telegraphed ahead and carriages were waiting for them.

The coachman was able to tell him that his sister was alive.

The carriage for Alina took her directly to Paddington Station.

The Courier had ascertained that there was a train to the station nearest to her village.

She could catch it with only a three-quarters-of-an-hour's wait.

On the Earl's instructions the Courier went with her.

She sat in the Waiting-Room until he escorted her to the platform where the train was waiting for a Reserved Carriage for her.

She thought it was an extravagance she could not really afford.

But she learnt that either the Earl or Denise had paid for everything.

All she had to do was to thank the Courier, which she did most profusely.

He said good-bye and walked away, having also tipped the Porter.

'Denise has been so kind, so very kind!' Alina thought as the train left the Station.

Then once again she felt she was being carried farther and farther away from Lord Teverton.

She suspected that by now he was enjoying having the house in Rome to himself.

He could spend his time with the beautiful Princess Borghese or somebody like her.

Alina had not forgotten he had told her how *chic* Italian women were.

If he admired them, there was no doubt that they would admire him.

"I must be sensible," she told herself. "It was an adventure which I shall always remember, but it is no longer part of my life and I have to live without it from now on."

What she was really thinking was that she would have to live without Marcus Teverton.

However sensible she tried to be about it, the agony was there in her heart.

Her love seemed to grow as swiftly as the train carried her out of his life and back into her own.


It was the fifth day since she had come home.

Alina came in from the garden carrying a bunch of roses.

She had already filled several vases in the Drawing-Room, and there were red roses in a large bowl in the Hall.

There had been a great deal to do when she had first returned home.

First she had unpacked her trunks.

Then she called on the Vicar to thank him for looking after the house.

She had gone round inspecting everything.

Staying in the beautiful mansion at the top of the Spanish Steps had made her aware of how shabby her own home had become.

She was therefore determined, without being extravagant, to make it as beautiful as she could, even without the many things she had sold.

She cleaned the walls until the marks where the mirrors and pictures had been were no longer visible.

She washed the covers of the chairs and sofas.

They certainly looked brighter and more attractive.

She was now determined to darn the patches where they were threadbare.

Mrs. Baker had helped her to clean the carpets so that she felt they looked almost like new.

This was an exaggeration.

The whole room, however, did look very much better, and the flowers made up for the absence of the china ornaments.

She put the roses down on the table by the window.

As she arranged them in the bowl she had left there, she was wondering why she was taking so much trouble.

Who was to see the improvements she had made except herself?

Then she knew that in some strange way it was her love for a man she would never see again which was making her fastidious, not only about her home, but about herself.

She and Lord Teverton had shared an identical experience in the Colosseum.

If he did think of her sometimes, she wanted him to admire her.

She did not want him to think of her as the rather untidy, gauche girl which she actually was.

She wanted him to remember her as the elegant, exquisitely dressed woman whom he had said was beautiful.

There had been a genuine admiration in his eyes before he had taken her to dine at the Borghese Palace.

That was how she wanted him to think of her for ever.

It might be childish!

It might be just creating dreams that could never come true!

She vowed she would never again allow herself to become dowdy and despondent.

This morning she had put on one of the pretty gowns which Denise had given to her.

She felt it made her look very young.

It was of white muslin with little touches of blue ribbon threaded through the *broderie anglaise* with which it was trimmed.

There was a blue sash round her small waist.

It had a bow at the back which was like a bustle.

She had arranged her hair in the same attractive manner as Jones had done for Denise.

When she looked at herself in the mirror, she had thought it was becoming.

She finished the arrangement of the roses in the bowl.

In her mind they were a symbol of the beauty she found in Rome.

She wished she could offer them as a gift to the man she loved.

Her task finished, she went to the window. Should she go out again into the garden, or stay in the house?

Suddenly, as if she were dreaming, she heard a voice behind her drawl:

"The door was open, and as no-one answered the bell, I came in!"

For a split second she thought that what she was hearing was only in her mind.

It was one of the stories she told herself.

Then she turned her head.

Although it seemed incredible, he was there—standing just inside the Drawing-Room door and looking at her.

It was impossible to move, impossible to breathe.

He walked forward, and she knew that he was real.

She was not just seeing him in her dreams.

At last, as he reached her, Alina found her voice.

"W-what . . . has happened?" she asked. "W-why . . . are you . . . h-here?"

She thought there was a faint smile on Lord Teverton's lips as he replied:

"I wished to apologise for having been unable to say good-bye to Lady Langley before she left Rome, but I had some difficulty in finding her."

Alina's eyes seemed to fill her whole face as she murmured:

"Y-you . . . wanted to find . . . her?"

"Naturally I wanted to find her!" Lord Teverton replied. "But when I asked my Cousin Denise where she was, she was very evasive in her replies."

He paused.

Because Alina felt his eyes were looking at her in a penetrating manner, she looked away from him.

There was a short silence before Lord Teverton said:

"Wescott was equally uninformative. Then I thought of asking Denise's father, who proved far more helpful."

Alina felt as if she were still holding her breath.

It was impossible to think coherently.

It flashed through her mind that Lord Teverton did not think she was her Mother.

He believed her to be who she was in actual fact—her Mother's daughter.

"Rupert Sedgwick," Lord Teverton continued, "was kind

enough to tell me where Lady Langley lived, and I therefore made the journey to Little Benbury."

There was another silence before he added:

"What I learnt when I entered the village was that Lady Langley was dead."

Alina clasped her fingers together.

He was obviously waiting for an answer, and after a moment she said:

"Y-yes . . . Mama is . . . dead."

"I also learnt," he went on, "that the Funeral took place a month ago."

So he knew the truth.

Alina looked up at him pleadingly.

"Forgive me," she said, "please . . . forgive me . . . but Denise desperately wanted to go to . . . Rome with a chaperon who would not prevent her from . . . being alone with the Earl and especially . . . she did not . . . wish him to think . . . that she was . . . following . . . him."

"So you pretended to be your Mother in order to act as her chaperon!" Lord Teverton exclaimed.

"It may have been very . . . wrong of me," Alina said unhappily, "but . . . Denise is very happy now . . . and there was no reason why anyone . . . especially you . . . should guess that I was . . . not who I . . . pretended . . . to be."

"Why—especially me?" Lord Teverton enquired.

"Because . . . you would have been . . . shocked and might have . . . told the family," Alina answered.

She gave a little cry and begged:

"Oh, please . . . you will not speak of what has . . . happened to . . . anyone? Denise does not . . . want the Earl or her Father or any of her . . . relatives to know. They . . . would be . . . very angry."

"And quite rightly," Lord Teverton said. "How could you have thought that someone as young as you would be a sufficient chaperon?"

"I am sorry . . . I have said I am sorry," Alina said. "Unless, however, you talk . . . nobody will . . . ever know."

"But *I* know!"

"You have found out," Alina said, "but, please . . . I beg you . . . keep the . . . secret!"

He did not answer, and after a moment she said:

"Oh, why did you have to come here and . . . discover the truth? I cannot . . . believe it was . . . just because you . . . had not said . . . good-bye to me . . . in Rome!"

"No," he agreed. "There was another reason."

She looked at him enquiringly.

She was thinking as she did so how handsome he was and how smart.

Because he was standing so near to her, her heart was beating tumultuously.

She was afraid he must hear it.

'I love him! I love him!' she thought. "But he must . . . never have the . . . slightest suspicion that . . . that is how I feel!"

She was waiting for the answer to her question.

When he did not speak, she asked again:

"W-what . . . was the . . . reason?"

She thought somehow it was important.

To her surprise, Lord Teverton moved a step closer to her.

"I had to know," he said very quietly, "whether your lips were really as soft and pure and innocent as they seemed when I kissed you."

Alina stared at him in astonishment.

Before she could move, his arms went round her.

"I have come a long way to learn the truth," he said.

Then his lips were on hers, and she felt as though the whole world had come to an end.

He kissed her and now his lips were not hard, but gentle.

As her body seemed to melt into his, his kiss became more demanding, more possessive.

Alina felt that he drew her heart from between her lips and made it his.

The love they felt for each other seemed to envelop them.

It was as if the sun had come into the room and surrounded them with its dazzling light.

Lord Teverton raised his head.

"Now, tell me," he said, "what you feel about me."

"I . . . I love you," Alina whispered. "I . . . cannot help it

. . . but I love you . . . and I thought I would . . . never see you again."

As she spoke, her eyes filled with tears.

"And I love you!" he said, and his voice was very deep. "But how could you have done anything so outrageous as to pretend you were a sophisticated woman rather than a girl who had never been kissed?"

"Did I seem . . . so very . . . inexperienced?" Alina whispered.

"I kissed you because you were so beautiful," Lord Teverton said. "But I thought that like all other women, you were flirting outrageously with every man you met, and were perhaps just pretending to be afraid of the advances that Prince Alberto was making to you."

"How could . . . you think . . . such things about . . . me!" Alina asked.

She knew the answer without his having to say it.

She was painted and rouged.

She looked like the sophisticated Beauties with whom he spent his time in London.

There was a little pause.

"Yes, that is the answer—until I kissed you! Is it true that you had never been kissed before?"

"Nobody has . . . ever kissed me . . . except . . . you," Alina said.

There was a little catch in her breath.

Now several tears had run from her eyes onto her cheeks.

He pulled her close to him and kissed them away.

Then his lips were again on hers.

He held her captive and made her feel as if she were flying in the sky and her feet were no longer on the ground.

She was breathless as he asked in an unsteady, deep voice:

"How can you do this to me?"

"Do . . . what?" she whispered.

"Make me feel as I believed I would never feel about any woman. It means, my darling, that I am very much in love!"

"Is . . . that true?" Alina asked. "Can it be . . . true? How can . . . you love . . . me?"

Lord Teverton smiled.

"Very easily, and I promise you, my precious, that if we feel as we do now, this is only the beginning."

He saw the question in her eyes, and said:

"I am asking you, my darling, how soon you will marry me?"

Alina felt her heart turn a dozen somersaults before she managed to say:

"Are you . . . are you really . . . asking me to . . . be your wife?"

"As quickly as possible," Lord Teverton replied.

He thought as he spoke that he had never seen a woman look more radiant, so exquisitely happy, or so beautiful.

Then Alina gave a little gasp.

"But . . . how can we be married?" she asked. "If I . . . marry you, it will be the most . . . wonderful . . . miraculous thing that has ever happened to me. But the Earl will then guess . . . the truth . . . and I could not . . . spoil Denise's happiness!"

"Denise or no Denise," Lord Teverton replied firmly, "I am going to marry you. We must just be as clever as you were, my lovely one, and think out an explanation of which nobody will be suspicious."

"But . . . you were . . . suspicious!" Alina pointed out.

"I was suspicious only after I kissed you," Lord Teverton replied, "and I assure you, nobody is ever going to kiss you in the future except me. Prince Alberto was very lucky that I did not kill him the other night—or at least throw him into the lake!"

Unexpectedly Lord Teverton laughed.

"Only you, my darling, could think of anything so surprising as to walk into the lake to save yourself from the amorous advances of the Prince!"

"I . . . I was frightened . . . and I could . . . find no . . . other way of . . . escape."

"I realised that," Lord Teverton said, "and it was very clever of you. But it is something which will not happen again because I will never let you out of my sight. You are far too beautiful—far too alluring—not to be *properly* chaperoned, and that is the right word."

Alina moved a little closer to him.

"Do you . . . really think . . . that I would . . . want any-body to kiss me . . . except you?" she asked. "I thought the Prince was . . . repulsive! Of course I . . . realise now that . . . I thought of him . . . like that because . . . I was already . . . in love."

"Not half as much as I intend you to be in the future," Lord Teverton replied.

Alina rested her cheek against his shoulder.

"Is it true . . . really true . . . that you . . . love me? I felt as I came . . . away from Rome that . . . every minute was . . . taking me farther and farther . . . away from you . . . until you were . . . completely out of . . . reach."

"I came to England determined to see you the moment I arrived," Lord Teverton said. "When Denise was so vague about your whereabouts, I began to be terrified in case I could never find you again."

"But . . . suppose . . . when we are . . . married you are . . . disappointed in me?" Alina asked. "After all, I am . . . only a g-girl . . . and you . . . you hate . . . girls!"

Lord Teverton moved his lips over the softness of her skin.

"That is something you will not be for very much longer!"

"But . . . how can we be . . . married without . . . hurting Denise?"

"I have been thinking about that, and it is really quite easy," Lord Teverton replied. "You are resident in this Parish and your Vicar will marry us secretly to-morrow morning."

Alina gave a little start, but she did not speak and he went on:

"We will then leave immediately for my yacht which is at Folkestone Harbour."

His lips moved nearer to hers as he went on:

"We are going to have a very long honeymoon, my darling. I will teach you about love and it will be the most exciting thing I have ever done in my life!"

Alina waited for his kiss, but he continued:

"As soon as we have left England, your Mother's death will be announced. Then three or four months from now, or whenever we are ready to come home, we will announce our marriage."

He smiled reassuringly before he went on:

"There is no reason why anybody, not even Wescott, should suspect that my Cousin Denise's friend with whom she had lessons and who is now my wife, has pretended to be anything but herself."

"You are so clever," Alina said, "and it will be like . . . Heaven to be with you . . . wherever . . . we go."

"That is exactly what I was thinking," Lord Teverton said. "We think alike, we feel alike, and, my darling, I know now you will be mine for eternity."

"That . . . is what I want you to say . . . and to think. Because I love you . . . I love you and there are . . . no other words in which I can tell you what I feel."

She saw the happiness in his eyes.

Then he was kissing her wildly, possessively, and now very passionately.

She felt that every nerve in her body responded to him.

He created a fire within her that was part of the fire she could feel on his lips.

It was so exciting, so rapturous, that she knew they had both found real love.

It was the love that she and Denise had talked about when they were young.

It was the love that is part of the Divine, the love that she had wished for at the Trevi Fountain.

The Fountain had granted her wish, and God had answered her prayers.

"Thank You, thank You!" she said in her heart.

Then, as Lord Teverton's kisses carried her high into the sky, she knew they were reaching out towards the Gates of Heaven.

# About the Author

BARBARA CARTLAND, the world's best known and best-selling author of romantic fiction, is also an historian, playwright, lecturer, political speaker and television personality. She has now written over five hundred and sixty-one books and has the distinction of holding *The Guinness Book of Records* title of the world's bestselling author, having sold over six hundred and twenty million copies all over the world.

Miss Cartland is a Dame of Grace of St. John of Jerusalem; Chairman of the St. John Council in Hertfordshire; one of the first women in one thousand years ever to be admitted to the Chapter General; President of the Hertfordshire Branch of the Royal College of Midwives, President and Founder in 1964 of the National Association for Health, and invested by her Majesty the Queen as a Dame of the Order of the British Empire in 1991.

Miss Cartland lives in England at Camfield Place, Hatfield, Hertfordshire.

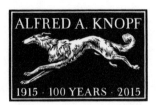

ALFRED A. KNOPF

1915 · 100 YEARS · 2015

# THE GIRL IN THE
# SPIDER'S WEB

# THE GIRL IN THE SPIDER'S WEB

# David Lagercrantz

*Translated from the Swedish by George Goulding*

ALFRED A. KNOPF   NEW YORK   2015

THIS IS A BORZOI BOOK
PUBLISHED BY ALFRED A. KNOPF

Translation copyright © 2015 by George Goulding

All rights reserved. Published in the United States by Alfred A. Knopf,
a division of Penguin Random House LLC, New York. Originally published
in Sweden as *Det som inte dödar oss* by Norstedts, Stockholm, in 2015.
Copyright © 2015 by Norstedts Agency. This translation simultaneously
published in Great Britain by MacLehose Press, an imprint of Quercus, London,
by agreement with Norstedts Agency. Published by arrangement with
Quercus Publishing PLC (U.K.).

www.aaknopf.com

Knopf, Borzoi Books, and the colophon are registered trademarks
of Penguin Random House LLC.

Cataloging-in-Publication Data is available at the Library of Congress.

ISBN 978-0-385-35428-8 (hardcover); ISBN 978-0-385-35429-5 (eBook)

Jacket photograph courtesy of Paul De Koninck, Laval University,
Quebec City, Canada
Jacket design by Peter Mendelsund

Manufactured in the United States of America
First United States Edition

# Continuing Characters from the Millennium Series

LISBETH SALANDER, an exceptionally talented hacker with tattoos, piercings, and a troubled past.

MIKAEL BLOMKVIST, an investigative journalist at *Millennium* magazine. Salander assisted him with one of the biggest stories of his career, about the disappearance of Harriet Vanger. He later helped to vindicate Salander when she was on trial for murder.

ALEXANDER ZALACHENKO, also known as Zala, or by the alias Karl Axel Bodin. A Soviet spy who defected to Sweden and was protected for years by a special group within the Swedish Security Police who later murdered him. He is Lisbeth Salander's father, and used to violently abuse her mother, Agneta. He was also the head of a criminal empire.

RONALD NIEDERMANN, Salander's half-brother, a blond giant impervious to pain. Salander arranged for his murder.

CAMILLA SALANDER, Lisbeth Salander's twin sister, from whom she is estranged.

HOLGER PALMGREN, Salander's former guardian, a lawyer. One of the few people who know Salander well and whom she trusts.

DRAGAN ARMANSKY, Salander's former employer, the head of Milton Security. Another of the few she trusts.

PETER TELEBORIAN, a sadistic psychiatrist at the clinic where Salander was institutionalized as a child. The chief prosecution witness in her murder trial.

. . .

ERIKA BERGER, editor-in-chief of *Millennium* magazine, occasional lover of Blomkvist.

GREGER BECKMAN, Erika Berger's husband.

MALIN ERIKSSON, managing editor of *Millennium.*

CHRISTER MALM, art director and part owner of *Millennium.*

ANNIKA GIANNINI, Blomkvist's sister, a lawyer who represented Salander in her trial.

HARRIET VANGER, scion of a wealthy industrial family, who disappeared as a girl and was found by Blomkvist and Salander at the behest of her great-uncle, Henrik Vanger. She became a shareholder in *Millennium.*

HANS-ERIK WENNERSTRÖM, a corrupt financier who tricked Blomkvist into publishing a defamatory article in *Millennium* about his business, landing Blomkvist in prison for libel. Salander emptied Wennerström's bank accounts in retribution.

SVAVELSJÖ MC, a motorcycle gang closely associated with Zalachenko. Members of the gang were critically injured by Salander.

HACKER REPUBLIC, a coalition of hackers, among whom Salander, who goes by the handle "Wasp," is the star. Includes the hackers Plague, Trinity, and Bob the Dog.

SÄPO, the Swedish Security Police, which harbored a secret faction known as "the Section," dedicated to protecting Zalachenko.

JAN BUBLANSKI, a detective inspector with the Stockholm police, who headed the team investigating the Salander case. Now promoted to chief inspector. Known as "Officer Bubble."

SONJA MODIG, a police officer who works closely with Bublanski.

JERKER HOLMBERG, a crime scene investigator on Bublanski's team.

HANS FASTE, a police officer who clashed with Bublanski and leaked information to Ekström during the Salander investigation.

RICHARD EKSTRÖM, the prosecutor who brought the case against Salander. Now chief prosecutor. A manipulative and venal man, believed within the police to be interested only in self-advancement.

# THE GIRL IN THE SPIDER'S WEB

# PROLOGUE

# ONE YEAR EARLIER

This story begins with a dream, and not a particularly spectacular one at that. Just a hand beating rhythmically and relentlessly on a mattress in a room on Lundagatan.

Yet it still gets Lisbeth Salander out of her bed in the early light of dawn. Then she sits at her computer and starts the hunt.

# PART 1

# THE WATCHFUL EYE

NOVEMBER 1–21

The NSA, or National Security Agency, is a U.S. federal authority that reports to the Department of Defense. The head office is in Fort Meade, Maryland, by the Patuxent Freeway.

Since its founding in 1952, the NSA has been engaged in signals surveillance—these days mostly in connection with Internet and telephone traffic. Time after time its powers have been increased, and now it monitors more than twenty billion conversations and messages every twenty-four hours.

# CHAPTER 1

# EARLY NOVEMBER

Frans Balder had always thought of himself as a lousy father.

He had hardly attempted to shoulder the role of father before and he did not feel comfortable with the task now that his son was eight. But it was his duty, that is how he saw it. The boy was having a rough time living with Balder's ex-wife and her obnoxious partner, Lasse Westman.

So Balder had given up his job in Silicon Valley, gotten on a plane home to Sweden, and was now standing at Arlanda airport, almost in shock, waiting for a taxi. The weather was hellish. Rain whipped onto his face and for the hundredth time he wondered if he was doing the right thing.

That he of all self-centred idiots should become a full-time father, how crazy an idea was that? He might as well have gotten a job at the zoo. He knew nothing about children and not much about life in general. The strangest thing of all was nobody had asked him to do it. No mother or grandmother had called him, pleading and telling him to face up to his responsibilities.

It was his own decision. He was proposing to defy a long-standing custody ruling and, without warning, walk into his ex-wife's place and bring home his boy, August. No doubt all hell would break loose. That damn Lasse Westman would probably give him a real beating. But he put that out of his mind and got into a taxi with a woman driver who was dementedly chewing gum and at the same time trying to strike up a conversation with him. She would not have succeeded even on one of his better days. Balder was not one for small talk.

He sat there in the backseat, thinking about his son and everything that had happened recently. August was not the only—or even the main—

reason why he had stopped working at Solifon. His life was in turmoil and for a moment he wondered if he really knew what he was getting himself into. As the taxi came into the Vasastan neighbourhood Balder felt as if all the blood was draining from his body. But there was no turning back now.

He paid the taxi on Torsgatan and took out his luggage, leaving it just inside the building's front entrance. The only thing he took with him up the stairs was an empty suitcase covered with a brightly coloured map of the world, which he had bought at San Francisco International. He stood outside the apartment door, panting. With his eyes closed he imagined all the possible scenarios of fighting and screaming, and actually, he thought, you could hardly blame them. Nobody just turns up and snatches a child from his home, least of all a father whose only previous involvement had consisted of depositing money into a bank account. But this was an emergency, so he steeled himself and rang the doorbell, resisting the urge to run away.

At first there was no answer. Then the door flew open and there was Westman with his piercing blue eyes and massive chest and enormous fists. He seemed built to hurt people, which was why he so often got to play the bad guy on screen, even if none of the roles he played—Balder was convinced of this—were as evil as the person he was in real life.

"Christ," Westman said. "Look what we have here. The genius himself has come to visit."

"I'm here to fetch August," Balder said.

"You what?"

"I'm taking him away with me, Lasse."

"You must be joking."

"I've never been more serious," he tried, and then Hanna appeared from a room across to the left. True, she was not as beautiful as she had once been. There had been too much unhappiness for that and probably too many cigarettes and too much drink as well. But still he felt an unexpected wave of affection, especially when he noticed a bruise on her throat. She seemed to want to say something welcoming, even under the circumstances, but she never had time to open her mouth.

"Why should you care all of a sudden?" Westman said.

"Because August has been through enough. He needs a stable home."

"And you think you can provide that, you freak? Since when have you done anything except stare at a computer screen?"

"I've changed," he said, feeling pathetic, in part because he doubted that he had changed one little bit.

A shiver ran through Balder as Westman came towards him with his mighty bulk and his pent-up rage. It became crushingly clear that he would have no means of resistance if that madman let fly. The whole idea had been insane from the start. But surprisingly there was no outburst, no scene, just a grim smile and then the words:

"Well, isn't that just great!"

"What do you mean?" Hanna asked.

"That it's about time, isn't it, Hanna? Finally some sense of responsibility from Mr. High and Mighty. Bravo, bravo!" Westman clapped his hands theatrically. Afterwards that was what Balder found the most frightening— how easily they let the boy go.

Perhaps they saw August only as a burden. It was hard to tell. Hanna shot Balder some glances which were difficult to read and her hands shook and her jaw was clenched. But she asked too few questions. She should really have been cross-examining him, making thousands of demands, warning him and worrying that the boy's routine would be upset. But all she said was:

"Are you sure about this? Will you manage?"

"I'm sure," he said. Then they went to August's room. Balder had not seen him for more than a year and he felt ashamed. How could he have abandoned such a boy? He was so beautiful and strangely wonderful with his curly, bushy hair and slender body and serious blue eyes, engrossed in a gigantic jigsaw puzzle of a sailboat. His body seemed to cry out, "Don't disturb me," and Balder walked up to him slowly, as if approaching an exotic creature.

He nonetheless managed to get the boy to take hold of his hand and follow him out into the corridor. He would never forget it. What was August thinking? What did he imagine was happening? He neither looked up at him nor at his mother and of course he ignored all the waving and the words of farewell. He just vanished into the lift with Balder. It was as simple as that.

August was autistic. He was most likely also mentally disabled, even though they had not received unequivocal advice on that point and anyone who saw him from afar might suspect the opposite. His exquisite face radiated an air of majestic detachment, or at least suggested that he did not think it worth bothering with his surroundings. But when you looked at him closely there was something impenetrable in his gaze. He had yet to say his first word.

In this he had failed to live up to all the prognoses made when he was two years old. At the time, the doctors had said that August probably belonged to that minority of autistic children who had no learning impairment, and that provided he was given intensive behavioural therapy his prospects were quite good. But nothing had turned out as they had hoped and Balder had no idea what had become of all that remedial care and assistance or even the boy's schooling. Balder had run away to the United States and lived in his own world. He had been a fool. But now he was going to repay his debt and take care of his son.

Right away he ordered casebooks and called specialists and educational experts and it became immediately apparent that none of the money he had been sending had gone towards August's care, but instead had trickled out to pay for other things, probably Westman's extravagances and gambling debts. The boy seemed to have been left pretty much to his own devices, allowed to become set in his compulsive ways, and probably worse—this was also the reason why Frans had come home.

A psychologist had called to express concern about unexplained bruises covering August's arms and legs, chest and shoulders. According to Hanna they were because the boy had fits and hurt himself thrashing back and forth. Balder had witnessed one already on the second day, and it scared him out of his wits. But that could not account for the sheer number and type of bruises, he thought. He suspected violence and turned for help to a GP and a former policeman whom he knew privately. Even if they were not able to confirm his fears with any degree of certainty he grew more and more angry about it and set about submitting a series of formal letters and reports.

He almost forgot all about the boy. It was easy to forget him. August spent most of his time sitting on the floor in the room Balder had prepared for him in the house in Saltsjöbaden, doing his exceedingly difficult jigsaws, assembling hundreds of pieces only to break them up and start afresh.

At first, Balder had observed him in fascination. It was like watching a great artist at work, and sometimes he was taken by the fantasy that the boy would glance up at any moment and say something grown-up. But August never uttered a word. If he raised his head from the puzzle it was to look straight past him towards the window overlooking the sea and the sunshine reflected on the water, and eventually Balder just left him alone. Balder seldom even took him outside into the garden.

From a legal point of view he did not have custody of the boy and he did not want to take any chances until he had sorted this out. So he let the housekeeper, Lottie Rask, do all the shopping—and all the cooking and cleaning. Balder was no good at that side of things. He understood computers and algorithms but not much else, and he immersed himself in them even more. At night he slept as badly as he had in California.

Lawsuits and storms loomed on the horizon and every evening he drank a bottle of red wine, usually Amarone, and that probably did little good either, except in the short term. He began to feel worse and worse and fantasized about vanishing in a puff of smoke or taking himself off to some inhospitable place, somewhere remote. But then, one Saturday in November, something happened.

It was a cold, windy evening and he and August were walking along Ringvägen in the Södermalm district, feeling frozen. They had been having dinner at Farah Sharif's on Zinkens väg. August should have long since been asleep, but dinner had gone on late and Balder had revealed far too much. Farah Sharif tended to have that effect on people. She and Balder had known each other since they had read computer sciences at Imperial College in London and now Sharif was one of the few people at his level in Sweden, or at least one of the few who was by and large able to follow his thinking. It was an incredible relief for him to meet someone who could understand.

He also found her attractive, but despite numerous attempts he had never managed to seduce her. Balder was not much good at seducing women. But this time he had received a farewell hug that almost turned into a kiss, which was a big step forward. He was still thinking about it as he and August passed Zinkensdamm sports centre. Maybe next time he should get a babysitter and then perhaps . . . Who knows? A dog was barking some ways off and there was a woman's voice shouting behind him, but it was hard to tell if she was upset or happy. He looked over towards Hornsgatan and the intersection where he could pick up a taxi or take the tunnelbana down to Slussen. It felt like it might rain. Once they got to the crossing, the light turned to red and on the other side of the street stood a worn-looking man in his forties who seemed vaguely familiar. At precisely that moment Balder took hold of August's hand.

He only wanted to make sure his son stayed on the sidewalk, but then he felt it: August's hand tensed as if the boy were reacting strongly to something. His look was intense and clear, as though the veil which always seemed to cover his eyes had been magically drawn aside, and instead of staring inwards at his own complexities, August had apparently understood something uniquely deep and great about that intersection. So Balder ignored the fact that the light had turned green. He just let his son stand there and observe the scene, and without knowing why, he was overcome by a strong emotion, which he found strange. It was only a look, after all, and not even an especially bright or joyful one at that. Yet it rang a distant bell, stirred something long dormant in his memory. For the first time in an age he felt hopeful.

## CHAPTER 2

# NOVEMBER 20

Mikael Blomkvist had slept for only a few hours because he had stayed up reading a detective novel by Elizabeth George. Not a particularly sensible thing to do. Ove Levin, the newspaper guru from Serner Media, was due to present a strategy session for *Millennium* magazine later that morning and Blomkvist ought to be rested and ready for combat.

But he had no desire to be sensible. Only reluctantly did he get up and make himself an unusually strong cappuccino with his Jura Impressa X7, a machine which had been delivered to his home a while ago with a note saying, "According to you, I don't know how to use it anyway." It now stood there in the kitchen like a memorial to a better time. He no longer had any contact with the person who had sent it. Nor did he feel that his work was particularly stimulating these days. Over the weekend he had even considered looking around for something new, and that was a pretty drastic idea for a man like Mikael Blomkvist. *Millennium* had been his passion and his life, and many of his life's best, most dramatic events had occurred in connection with the magazine. But nothing lasts forever, perhaps not even a love for *Millennium*. Besides, this was not a good time to own a magazine dedicated to investigative journalism. All publications with ambitions for greatness were bleeding to death and he could not help but reflect that while his own vision for *Millennium* may have been beautiful and true on some higher plane, it would not necessarily help the magazine survive.

He went into the living room sipping his coffee and looked out at the waters of Riddarfjärden. There was quite a storm blowing out there. From an Indian summer, which had kept the city's outdoor restaurants and cafés open well into October, the weather had turned nightmarish with gusts of wind and cloudbursts, and people hurried bent double through the streets. Blomkvist had stayed in all weekend, not only because of the weather. He had been planning revenge on an ambitious scale, but the scheme had come to nothing, and that was not like him, neither the former nor the latter.

He was not an underdog, and unlike so many other big media figures in Sweden he did not suffer from an inflated ego which needed constant boosting and soothing. On the other hand, he had been through a few tough years. Barely a month ago the financial journalist William Borg had written a piece in Serner's *Business Life* magazine under the heading: MIKAEL BLOMKVIST'S DAYS ARE OVER.

The fact that the article had been written in the first place and been given such prominence was of course a sign that Blomkvist's position was still strong. No-one would say that the column was well written or original, and it should have been easy to dismiss as yet another attack from a jealous colleague. But for some reason, incomprehensible in retrospect, the whole thing blew up. At first it might have been interpreted as a spirited discussion about journalism, but gradually the debate began to go off the rails. Although the serious press stayed out of it, all kinds of invective were being spewed out in social media. The offense came not only from financial journalists and industry types, who had reason to set upon their enemy now that he was temporarily weakened, but also from a number of younger writers who took the opportunity to make a name for themselves. They pointed out that Blomkvist was not on Twitter or Facebook and should rather be seen as a relic of a bygone age in which people could afford to work their way through whichever strange old volumes happened to take their fancy. And there were those who took the opportunity to join in the fun and create amusing hashtags like #inblomkvistsday. It was all a lot of nonsense and nobody could have cared less than Blomkvist—or so he persuaded himself.

It certainly did not help his cause that he had not had a major story since the Zalachenko affair and that *Millennium* really was in a crisis. The circulation was still OK, with 21,000 subscribers. But since advertising revenue was falling dramatically and there was no longer additional income from their successful books, and since one of the shareholders, Harriet Vanger, was not willing to put up any more capital, the board of directors had, against Blomkvist's wishes, allowed the Norwegian Serner newspaper empire to buy 30 percent of the shares. That was not as odd as it seemed, or not at first sight. Serner published weekly magazines and evening papers and owned a large online dating site and two premium TV channels as well as a football team in Norway's top division and ought not to have anything to do with a publication like *Millennium*.

But Serner's representatives—especially the head of publications, Ove Levin—had assured them that the Group needed a prestige product and that "everybody" in the management team admired *Millennium* and wanted only for the magazine to go on exactly as before. "We're not here to make money!" Levin said. "We want to do something significant." He immediately arranged for the magazine to receive a sizeable injection of funds.

At first Serner did not interfere in the editorial work. It was business as usual, but with a slightly better budget. A new feeling of hope spread among the editorial team, sometimes even to Blomkvist, who felt that for once he would have time to devote himself to journalism instead of worrying about finances. But then, around the time the campaign against him got under way—he would never lose the suspicion that the Serner Group had taken advantage of the situation—the tone changed and they started to apply pressure.

Levin maintained that of course the magazine should continue with its in-depth investigations, its literary reporting, its social fervour. But surely it was not necessary for all the articles to be about financial irregularities, injustices, and political scandals. Writing about high society—about celebrities and premieres—could also produce brilliant journalism, so he said, and he spoke with passion about *Vanity Fair* and *Esquire* in America, about Gay Talese and his classic piece, "Frank Sinatra Has a Cold," and about Norman Mailer and Truman Capote and Tom Wolfe and heaven knows who else.

Blomkvist did not actually have any objections to that, not at the time. Six months earlier he had himself written a long piece about the paparazzi industry, and as long as he could find a serious angle then he was content to profile just about any lightweight. In fact he always said it isn't the subject that determines good journalism, it's the reporter's attitude. No, what he objected to was what he sensed was there between the lines: that this was the beginning of a longer-term assault and that, to the Group, *Millennium* was just like any other magazine, a publication you can damn well shift around any which way you want until it becomes profitable—and colourless.

So on Friday afternoon, when he heard that Levin had hired a consultant and commissioned several consumer surveys to present on Monday, Blomkvist had simply gone home. For a long time he had sat at his desk or lain in bed composing various impassioned speeches about why *Millennium* had to remain true to its vision: There is rioting in the suburbs; an openly racist party sits in Riksdagen, the parliament; intolerance is growing; fascism is on the rise and there are homeless people and beggars everywhere. In many ways Sweden has become a shameful nation. He came up with lots of fine and lofty words and in his daydreams he enjoyed a series of fantastic triumphs in which what he said was so relevant and compelling that the whole editorial team and even the entire Serner Group were roused from their delusions and decided to follow him as one.

But when sobriety set in, he realized how little weight such words carry if nobody believes in them from a financial point of view. Money talks, bullshit walks. First and foremost the magazine had to pay its way. Then they could go about changing the world. He began to wonder whether he could rustle up a good story. The prospect of a major revelation might boost the confidence of the editorial team and get them all to forget about Levin's surveys and forecasts.

Blomkvist's big scoop about the Swedish government conspiracy that had protected Zalachenko turned him into a news magnet. Every day he received tips about irregularities and shady dealings. Most of it, to tell the truth, was rubbish. But just occasionally the most amazing story would emerge. A run-of-the-mill insurance matter or a trivial report of a missing person could be concealing something crucial. You never knew for sure. You had to be methodical and look through it all with an open mind, and so on Saturday morning he sat down with his laptop and his notebooks and picked his way through what he had.

He kept going until 5:00 in the afternoon. He did come across the odd item which would probably have gotten him going ten years ago, but which did not now stir any enthusiasm. It was a classic problem, he of all people knew that. After a few decades in the profession most things feel pretty familiar and even if something looks like a good story in intellectual terms it still might not turn you on. So when yet another squall of freezing rain whipped across the rooftops he stopped working and turned to Elizabeth George.

It wasn't just escapism, he persuaded himself. Sometimes the best ideas occur to you while your mind is occupied with something completely different. Pieces of the puzzle can suddenly fall into place. But he failed to come up with anything more constructive than the thought that he ought to spend more time lying around like this, reading good books. When Monday morning came and with it yet more foul weather he had ploughed through one and a half George novels plus three old copies of the *New Yorker* which had been cluttering up his bedside table.

So there he was, sitting on the living-room sofa with his cappuccino, looking out at the storm. He had been feeling tired and listless until he got to his feet with an abrupt start—as if he had suddenly decided to pull himself together and do something—and put on his boots and his winter coat and went out.

It was a parody of hell out there. Icy, heavy, wet squalls bit into his bones as he hurried down towards Hornsgatan, which lay before him looking unusually grey. The whole of Södermalm district seemed to have been drained of all colour. Not even one tiny bright autumn leaf flew through the air. With his head bent forward and his arms crossed over his chest he continued past Maria Magdalena kyrka to Slussen, all the way until he turned right onto Götgatsbacken and as usual he slipped in between the Monki boutique and the Indigo pub, then went up to the magazine on the fourth floor, just above the offices of Greenpeace. He could already hear the buzz when he was in the stairwell.

An unusual number of people were up there. Apart from the editorial team and the key freelancers, there were three people from Serner, two consultants and Levin, who had dressed down for the occasion. He no longer looked like an executive and had picked up some new expressions, among others a cheery "Hi."

"Hi, Micke, how's things?"

"That depends on you," Blomkvist said, not actually meaning to sound unfriendly.

But he could tell that it was taken as a declaration of war and he nodded stiffly, walked in and sat down on one of the chairs which had been set out to make a small auditorium in the office.

Levin cleared his throat and looked nervously in Blomkvist's direction. The star reporter, who had seemed so combative in the doorway, now looked politely interested and showed no sign of wanting to have a row. But this did nothing to set Levin's mind at ease. Once upon a time he and Blomkvist had both temped for *Expressen*. They mostly wrote quick news stories and a whole lot of rubbish. But afterwards in the pub, they had dreamed about the big stories and talked for hours of how they would never be satisfied with the conventional or the shallow but instead would always dig deep. They were young and ambitious and wanted it all, all at once. There were times when Levin missed that, not the salary, or the working hours, or even the easy life in the bars and the women, but the dreams—he missed the power in them. He sometimes longed for that throbbing urge to change society and journalism and to write so that the world would come to a standstill and the mighty powers bow down. Even a hotshot like himself wondered: Where did the dreams go?

Micke Blomkvist had made every single one of them come true, not just because he had been responsible for some of the big exposés of modern times, but also because he really wrote with that passion and power that they had fantasized about. Never once had he bowed to pressure from the establishment or compromised his ideals, whereas Levin himself . . . Well, really *he* was the one with the big career, wasn't he? He was probably making ten times as much as Blomkvist these days and that gave him an enormous amount of pleasure. What use were Blomkvist's scoops when he couldn't even buy himself a country place nicer than that little shack on the island of Sandhamn? My God, what was that hut compared to a new house in Cannes? Nothing!

No, it was Levin who had chosen the right path. Instead of slogging it out in the daily press, he had taken a job as media analyst at Serner and developed a personal relationship with Haakon Serner himself, and that had changed his life and made him rich. Today he was the most senior journalist responsible for a whole series of newspaper houses and channels and he loved it. He loved the power, the money, and all that went with it, yet he was not above admitting that even he sometimes dreamed about that other stuff, in small doses, of course, but still. He wanted to be regarded as a fine writer, just like Blomkvist, and that was probably why he had pushed so hard for the Group to buy a stake in *Millennium.* A little bird had told him that the magazine was up against it and that the editor-in-chief, Erika Berger, whom he had always secretly fancied, wanted to keep on her two latest recruits, Sofie Melker and Emil Grandén, and she would not be able to do so unless they got some fresh capital.

In short, Levin had seen an unexpected opportunity to buy into one of the most prestigious brands in Swedish media. But Serner's management was not enthusiastic, to put it mildly. On the contrary, people were heard to mutter that *Millennium* was old-fashioned and had a left-wing bias and a tendency to end up in fights with important advertisers and business partners, and if Levin had not argued his case so passionately, the plan would have come to nothing. But he had insisted. In a broader context, he argued, investing in *Millennium* represented a negligible amount, which might not yield vast profits but could give them something much greater, namely credibility. Right now, after the cutbacks and blood-letting, Serner's reputation wasn't exactly their prime asset. Taking a stake in *Millennium* would be a sign that the Group did after all care about journalism and freedom of expression, even if Serner's board was not conspicuously keen on either. This much they were able to understand, and Levin got his acquisition through, and for a long time it looked like a winning outcome for all parties.

Serner got good publicity and *Millennium* kept its staff and was able to concentrate on what it did best: carefully researched, well-written reportage, with Levin himself beaming like the sun and even taking part in a debate at the Writers' Club, where he said in his usual modest way, "I believe in virtuous enterprise. I have always fought for investigative journalism."

But then . . . he did not want to think about it. At first he was not bothered by the campaign against Blomkvist. Ever since his former colleague's meteoric rise in the reporting firmament, Levin had rejoiced secretly whenever Blomkvist was sneered at in the media. This time, though, his joy did not last. Serner's young son Thorvald spotted the commotion—social media made a big thing of it. Even though he was not a man who took any interest in what journalists had to say, he did like power and intrigue, and here he saw a chance to score some points or simply to give the older generation on the board a good drubbing. Before long Thorvald had encouraged the CEO—who until quite recently had not concerned himself with such trivial matters—to declare that *Millennium* could not be given any special treatment, but would have to adapt to the new times like all of the other products in the Group.

Levin, who had just given Berger a solemn promise that he would not interfere in the editorial line, save perhaps as a "friend and adviser," all of a sudden felt that his hands were tied. He was forced to play some intricate games behind the scenes. He did everything he could to get Berger, Malin Eriksson, and Christer Malm at the magazine to buy into the new policy, which was never in fact clearly expressed—something that flares up in a panic rarely is—but which somehow entailed making *Millennium* younger and more commercial.

Naturally Levin kept repeating that there could be no question of compromising the magazine's soul and provocative attitude, even if he was not sure what he meant by that. He only knew that to keep the directors happy he needed to get more glamour into the magazine and reduce the number of lengthy investigations into industry, since they were liable to irritate advertisers and make enemies for the board. But of course he did not tell Berger this.

He wanted to avoid unnecessary conflict and, standing there in front of the editorial team, he had taken the trouble to dress more casually than usual. He did not want to provoke anyone by wearing the shiny suits and ties which had become all the rage at the head office. Instead he had opted for jeans and a white shirt and a dark-blue V-necked pullover which was not even cashmere. His long curly hair—which had always been his rebellious little gimmick—was tied in a ponytail, just like the edgiest journalists on TV. But most important of all, he kicked off in the humble tone he had been taught in his management courses:

"Hello, everybody," he said. "What foul weather! I've said it many times before, but I'm happy to repeat it: We at Serner are incredibly proud to be accompanying you on this journey, and for me personally it amounts to even more than that. It's the commitment to magazines like *Millennium* which makes my job meaningful; it reminds me why I went into this profession in the first place. Micke, do you remember how we used to sit in the Opera Bar and dream about everything we were going to achieve together? And we weren't exactly holding back on the booze, ha ha!"

Blomkvist did not look as if he remembered. But Levin was not put off.

"Don't worry, I'm not going to get all nostalgic," he said, "and there's no reason to do so. In those days there was much more money in our industry. Just to cover some piddling little murder in the middle of nowhere we would hire a helicopter and book an entire floor at the poshest hotel, and order champagne for the after party. You know, when I was about to go off on my first overseas trip I asked Ulf Nilson, foreign correspondent at the time, what the Deutschmark exchange rate was. 'I have no idea,' he said, 'I set my own exchange rate.' Ha! We used to pad our expenses, do you remember, Micke? Maybe we were at our most creative back then. In any case, all we had to do was knock out some quick copy and we still managed to sell any number of issues. But a lot has changed since then—we all know that. We now face cut-throat competition and it's not easy these days to make a profit in journalism, not even if you have Sweden's best editorial team, as you do. So I thought we should talk a little bit today about the challenges of the future. Not that I imagine for one moment that I can teach you anything. I'm just going to provide you with some context for discussion. We at Serner have commissioned some surveys about your readership and the public perception of *Millennium*. Some of it may give you a bit of a fright. But instead of letting it get you down you should see it as a challenge, and remember, there are some totally crazy changes happening out there."

Levin paused for a moment and wondered if the term "totally crazy" had been a mistake, if he had tried too hard to appear relaxed and youthful and whether he had started off in too chatty and jocular a vein. As Haakon Serner would say, "It is impossible to overestimate how humourless underpaid journalists can be." But no, he decided, I'll fix this. I'll get them on my side.

Blomkvist had stopped listening more or less at the point when Levin explained that they all needed to reflect on their "digital maturity," so he did not hear them being told that the younger generation were not aware of *Millennium* or Mikael Blomkvist. Unfortunately that was precisely the moment at which he decided he had had enough and went out to the coffee room. So he had no idea either that Aron Ullman, the Norwegian consultant, quite openly said, "Pathetic. Is he so scared that he's going to be forgotten?"

In fact nothing could have worried Blomkvist less at that moment. He was angry that Levin seemed to think consumer surveys might be their salvation. It was no bloody market analysis that had created the magazine. It was passion and fire. *Millennium* had gotten to where it was because they had all put their faith in it, and in what felt right and important, without trying to guess which way the wind was blowing. For a time he just stood there in the pantry, wondering how long it would take before Berger came to join him.

The answer was about two minutes. He tried to calculate how angry she was by the sound of her heels. But when she was standing next to him she only gave him a dejected smile.

"What's going on?" she said.

"I just couldn't bear to listen."

"You do realize that people feel incredibly uncomfortable when you behave like that?"

"I do."

"And I assume you also understand that Serner can do nothing without our agreement. We still have control."

"Like hell we do. We're their hostages, Ricky! Don't you get it? If we don't do as they say they'll withdraw their support and then we'll be sitting there with our arses hanging out," he said, loudly and angrily. When Berger hushed him and shook her head he added sotto voce:

"I'm sorry. I'm being a brat. But I'm going home now. I need to think."

"You've started to work extremely short hours."

"Well, I reckon I'm owed a fair bit of overtime."

"I suppose you are. Would you like company this evening?"

"I don't know. I honestly don't know, Erika," he said, and then he left the magazine offices and went out onto Götgatsbacken.


The storm and the freezing rain lashed against him and he swore, and for a moment considered dashing into Pocketshop to buy yet another English detective novel to escape into. Instead he turned onto Sankt Paulsgatan and as he was passing the sushi restaurant on the right-hand side his mobile rang. He was sure that it would be Berger. But it was Pernilla, his daughter, who had chosen the worst possible time to get in touch with a father who already felt bad about how little he did for her.

"Hello, my darling," he said.

"What's that noise?"

"It's the storm, I expect."

"OK, OK, I'll be quick. I've been accepted into the writing course at Biskops Arnö school."

"So, now you want to be a writer," he said, in a tone which was too harsh and almost sarcastic, and that was unfair in every way.

He should have simply congratulated her and wished her luck, but Pernilla had had so many difficult years hopping between one Christian sect and another, and from one course to another without finishing anything, that he felt exhausted by yet another change of direction.

"I don't think I detected a whoop of joy there."

"Sorry, Pernilla. I'm not myself today."

"When are you ever?"

"I'm just not sure writing is such a good idea, given how the profession is looking right now. I only want you to find something that will really work for you."

"I'm not going to write boring journalism, like you."

"Well, what are you going to write, then?"

"I'm going to write for real."

"OK," he said, without asking what she meant by that. "Do you have enough money?"

"I'm working part-time at Wayne's Coffee."

"Would you like to come to dinner tonight, so we can talk about it?"

"Don't have time, Pappa. It was just to let you know," she said, and hung up. Even if he tried to see the positive side in her enthusiasm it just made his mood worse.

He took a shortcut across Mariatorget and Hornsgatan to reach his apartment on Bellmansgatan. It felt as if he had only just left. He got a strange sense that he no longer had a job and that he was on the verge of entering a new existence where he had oceans of time instead of working his fingers to the bone. For a brief moment he considered tidying the place up. There were magazines and books and clothes everywhere. But instead he fetched two Pilsner Urquell from the fridge and sat down on the sofa in the living room to think everything through more soberly, as soberly as one can with a bit of beer in one's body.

What was he to do?

He had no idea, and most worrying of all was that he was in no mood for a fight. On the contrary, he was strangely resigned, as if *Millennium* were slipping out of his sphere of interest. Isn't it time to do something new? he asked himself, and he thought of Kajsa Åkerstam, a quite charming person whom he would occasionally meet for a few drinks. Åkerstam was head of Swedish Television's Investigative Taskforce programme and she had for years been trying to recruit him. It had never mattered what she had offered or how solemnly she had guaranteed backing and total integrity. *Millennium* had been his home and his soul. But now . . . maybe he should take the chance. Perhaps a job on the "Investigative Taskforce" programme would fire him up again.

His mobile rang and for a moment he was happy. Whether it was Berger or Pernilla, he promised himself he would be friendly and really listen. But no, it was a withheld number and he answered guardedly.

"Is that Mikael Blomkvist?" said a young-sounding voice.

"Yes," he said.

"Do you have time to talk?"

"I might if you introduced yourself."

"My name is Linus Brandell."

"OK, Linus, how can I help?"

"I have a story for you."

"Tell me."

"I will if you can drag yourself down to the Bishops Arms across the street and meet me there."

Blomkvist was irritated. It wasn't just the bossy tone. It was the intrusion on his home turf.

"The phone will do just fine."

"It's not something which should be discussed on an open line."

"Why do I feel so tired talking to you, Linus?"

"Maybe you've had a bad day."

"I *have* had a bad day. You're right about that."

"There you go. Come down to the Bishop and I'll buy you a beer and tell you something amazing."

Blomkvist wanted only to snap: Stop telling me what to do! Yet without knowing why, or perhaps because he didn't have anything better to do than sit in his attic apartment and brood over his future, he said, "I pay for my own beers. But OK, I'm coming."

"A wise decision."

"But Linus . . ."

"Yes?"

"If you get long-winded and give me a load of wild conspiracy theories to the effect that Elvis is alive and you know who shot Olof Palme, then I'm going straight home."

"Fair enough," Brandell said.

# CHAPTER 3

# NOVEMBER 20

Edwin Needham—Ed the Ned, as he was sometimes called—was not the most highly paid security technician in the United States. But he may have been the best.

He grew up in South Boston, Dorchester, and his father had been a monumental good-for-nothing, a drunk who took on casual work in the harbour but often disappeared on binges which not infrequently landed him in jail or in hospital. These benders were the family's best time, a sort of breathing space. When Ed's father could be bothered to be around, he would beat his mother black-and-blue. Sometimes she would spend hours or even whole days locked inside the toilet, crying and shaking. Nobody was very surprised when she died from internal bleeding at only forty-six, or when Ed's older sister became a crack addict, still less when the remains of the family soon afterwards stood teetering on the brink of homelessness.

Ed's childhood paved the way for a life of trouble and during his teenage years he belonged to a gang that called themselves "The Fuckers." They were the terror of Dorchester and got mixed up in everything from muggings to robbing grocery stores. There was something brutal about Ed's appearance from an early age and this was not improved by the fact that he never smiled and was missing two upper teeth. He was sturdy, tall, and fearless, and his face usually bore the traces of brawls with his father or gang fights. Most of the teachers at his school were scared to death of him. All were convinced that he would end up in jail or with a bullet in his head. But there were some adults who began to take an interest in him—no doubt because they discovered that there was more than aggression and violence in his intense blue eyes.

Ed had an irrepressible thirst for knowledge, an energy which meant that he could devour a book with the same vigour with which he could trash the inside of a public bus. Often he was reluctant to go home at the end of the school day. He liked to stay on in what was known as the technology room, where there were a couple of computers. He would sit there for hours. A physics teacher with the Swedish-sounding name of Larson noticed how good he was with machines, and after social services got involved he was awarded a scholarship and transferred to a school with more motivated students.

He began to excel at his studies and was given more scholarships and distinctions and eventually—something of a miracle in view of the odds against him—he went on to study Electrical Engineering and Computer Science at MIT. In his doctoral thesis he explored some specific fears around new asymmetric cryptosystems like RSA, and then went on to senior positions at Microsoft and Cisco before being recruited by the National Security Agency in Fort Meade, Maryland.

He did not have the ideal CV for the job, even leaving aside his criminal behaviour as a teenager. He had smoked a lot of grass at college and flirted with socialist or even anarchist ideals. He had also been arrested twice for assault: bar fights. He still had a volcanic temper and everyone who knew him thought better of crossing him.

But at the NSA they recognized his other qualities. Besides which it was the autumn of 2001, and the American security services were so desperate for computer technicians that they hired pretty much anybody. During the ensuing years, nobody questioned Needham's loyalty—or patriotism, for that matter—and if anyone thought to do so, his advantages always outweighed his shortcomings.

Needham was not just amazingly gifted. There was an obsessive streak to his character, a manic precision and a furious efficiency which boded well for a man in charge of building IT security at America's most highly classified agency. Nobody was damn well going to crack his system. It was a matter of personal pride for him. At Fort Meade he quickly made himself indispensable to the point where people were constantly lining up to consult him. Not a few were terrified of him. He was often verbally abusive and had even told the head of the NSA himself, the legendary Admiral Charles O'Connor, to go to hell.

"Use your own busy fucking head for things you might just be able to understand," Needham had roared when the admiral had attempted to comment on his work.

But O'Connor and everyone else let it happen. They knew that Needham screamed and yelled for the right reasons—because colleagues had been careless about security regulations, or because they were talking about things beyond their understanding. Not once did he interfere in the rest of the agency's work, even though his level of clearance gave him access to pretty much everything, and even though in recent years the agency had found itself at the centre of a heated storm of opinion, advocates of both the right and the left seeing the NSA as the devil incarnate, Orwell's Big Brother. As far as Needham was concerned, the organization could do whatever the hell it wanted, so long as his security systems remained rigorous and intact.

And since he did not yet have a family he more or less lived at the office. Apart from the occasional drinking session, during which he sometimes turned alarmingly sentimental about his past, there was no suggestion that he had ever told outsiders what he was working on. In that other world he remained as silent as the grave, and if ever questioned about his profession, he stuck to a well-rehearsed cover story.

It was not by chance, nor was it the result of intrigue or manipulation, that he had risen through the ranks and become the NSA's most senior security chief. Needham and his team had tightened internal surveillance "so that no new whistle-blowers can pop up and punch us in the nose" and during countless sleepless nights created something which he alternately called "an unbreakable wall" or "a ferocious little bloodhound."

"No fucker can get in, and no fucker can dig around without permission," he said. And he was enormously proud of that.

He had been proud, that is, until that disastrous morning in November. The day had begun beautiful and clear. Needham, who had put on a belly over the years, came waddling over from the coffee machine in his characteristic way. Because of his seniority he completely ignored dress codes. He was wearing jeans and a red-checked lumberjack shirt, not quite buttoned at the waist, and he sighed as he settled down at his computer. He was not feeling great. His back and right knee hurt and he cursed the fact that his long-time colleague Alona Casales had managed to persuade him to come out for a run the night before. Sheer sadism on her part.

Luckily there was nothing super-urgent to deal with. He only had to send an internal memo with some new procedures for those in charge of COST, a programme for cooperation with the large IT companies—he had even changed the codenames. But he did not get far. He was just beginning to write, in his usual turgid prose:

```
<To keep you all on your toes as good paranoid cyber
agents, so that no-one will be tempted to fall back
into idiotic habits, I would just like to point out>
```

when he was interrupted by one of his alerts.

He was not particularly worried. His warning systems were so sensitive that they reacted to the slightest divergence in the information flow. It was going to be an anomaly, a notification perhaps that someone was trying to exceed the limits of their authorization, or some minor interference.

As it turned out, he never had time to investigate. In the next moment something so uncanny happened that for several seconds he refused to believe it. He just sat there, staring at the screen. Yet he knew exactly what was going on. A RAT had been put on the intranet, NSANet. Anywhere else he would have thought, *Those fuckers, I'll crush them.* But in here, the most tightly closed and controlled place of all, which he and his team had gone over with a fine-toothed comb a million times just this last year to detect every minuscule little vulnerability, here, no, no, it was impossible, it could not be happening.

Without realizing it he had closed his eyes, as if hoping that it would all vanish so long as he wasn't watching. But when he looked at the screen again, the sentence he had begun was being completed. His `<I would just like to point out>` was continuing on its own with the words: `<that you should stop with all the illegal activity. Actually it's pretty straightforward. Those who spy on the people end up themselves being spied on by the people. There's a fundamental democratic logic to it.>`

"Jesus, Jesus," he muttered—which was at least a sign that he was beginning to recover some of his composure.

But then the text went on: `<Chill out, Ed. Why don't you`

`stick around for a ride? I've got Root>` at which point he gave a loud cry. The word "Root" brought down his whole world. For about a minute, as the computer raced through the most confidential parts of the system at lightning speed, he genuinely believed that he was going to have a heart attack. He was only vaguely aware that people were beginning to gather around his desk.

There was not much of a crowd down at the Bishops Arms. It was only early in the afternoon, and the weather was not encouraging people to venture out, not even to the local pub. Blomkvist was nevertheless met by shouts and laughter, and by a hoarse voice bawling:

"Kalle Blomkvist!"

It came from a man with a puffy red face, a halo of frizzy hair, and a fussy moustache whom Blomkvist had seen many times in the area. He thought his name was Arne. Arne would turn up at the pub as regularly as clockwork at 2:00 every afternoon, but today he had clearly come earlier than that and settled down at a table to the left of the bar with three drinking companions.

"Mikael Blomkvist," Blomkvist corrected him, with a smile.

Arne and his friends laughed as if Blomkvist's actual name was the greatest joke ever.

"Got any good scoops?" Arne said.

"I'm thinking about blowing wide open the whole murky scene at the Bishops Arms."

"You reckon Sweden's ready for a story like that?"

"No, probably not."

In truth Blomkvist quite liked this crowd, not that he ever talked to them more than in throwaway lines and banter. But these men were a part of the local scene which made him feel at home in the area, and he was not in the least bit offended when one of them shot out, "I've heard that you're washed up."

Far from upsetting him, it brought the whole campaign against him down to the low, almost farcical level where it belonged.

"I've been washed up for the last fifteen years, hello to you brother bottle, all good things must pass," he said, quoting the poet Fröding and looking around for someone who might have had the gall to order a tired journalist down to the pub. Since he saw no-one apart from Arne and his gang, he went up to Amir at the bar.

Amir was big and fat and jolly, a hardworking father of four who had been running the pub for some years. He and Blomkvist had become good friends. Not because Blomkvist was an especially regular customer, but because they had helped each other out in completely different ways; once or twice when Blomkvist had not had the time to get to the state liquor store and was expecting female company, Amir had supplied him with a couple of bottles of red wine, and Blomkvist in turn had helped a friend of Amir's, who had no papers, to write letters to the authorities.

"To what do we owe this honour?" Amir said.

"I'm meeting someone."

"Anyone exciting?"

"I don't think so. How's Sara?"

Sara was Amir's wife and had just had a hip operation.

"Complaining and taking painkillers."

"Sounds like hard work. Give her my best."

"Will do," Amir said, and they chatted about this and that.

But Linus Brandell did not show up and Blomkvist thought it was probably a practical joke. On the other hand there were worse tricks to fall victim to than to be lured down to your local pub, so he stayed for fifteen minutes discussing a number of financial and health-related concerns before he turned and walked towards the door, and that is when Brandell appeared.


Nobody understood how Gabriella Grane had ended up at Säpo, Swedish Security Police, least of all she herself. She had been the sort of girl for whom everybody had predicted a glittering future. Her old girlfriends from the classy suburb of Djursholm worried that she was thirty-three and neither famous nor wealthy nor married, either to a rich man or to any man at all for that matter.

"What's happened to you, Gabriella? Are you going to be a policeman all your life?"

Most of the time she could not be bothered to argue, or point out that she was not a police officer but had been head-hunted for the position of analyst, and that these days she was writing far more challenging texts than she ever had at the Foreign Ministry or during her summers as a leader writer for *Svenska Dagbladet*. Apart from which, she was not allowed to talk about most of it in any case. So she might as well keep quiet and simply come to terms with the fact that working for the Swedish Security Police was considered to be about as low as you can go—both by her status-obsessed friends and even more so by her intellectual pals.

In their eyes, Säpo was a bunch of clumsy right-leaning idiots who went after Kurds and Arabs for what were fundamentally racist reasons and who had no qualms about committing serious crimes or infringements of civil rights in order to protect former senior Soviet spies. And indeed, sometimes she was on their side. There was incompetence in the organization, values that were unsound, and the Zalachenko affair remained a major blot. But that was not the whole truth. Stimulating and important work was being done as well, especially now after the shakeout, and sometimes she had the impression that it was at Säpo, not in any editorial or lecture hall, that people best understood the upheavals that were taking place across the world. But she still often asked herself: How did I end up here, and why have I stayed?

Presumably some of it came down to flattery. No less a person than Helena Kraft, the newly appointed chief of Säpo at the time, had contacted her and said that after all the disasters and bad press they had to rethink their approach to recruitment. We need to "bring on board the real talents from the universities and, quite honestly, Gabriella, there's no better person than you." That was all it had taken.

Grane was hired as an analyst in counter-espionage and later in the Industry Protection Group. Even though as a young woman, attractive in a slightly proper sort of way, she got called a "daddy's girl" and "snotty upper-class bitch," she was a star recruit, quick and receptive and able to think outside the box. And she could speak Russian. She had learned it alongside her studies at the Stockholm School of Economics, where needless to say she had been a model student but never that keen. She dreamed of something bigger than a life in business, so after her graduation she applied for a job at the Foreign Ministry and was accepted. But she did not find that especially stimulating either—the diplomats were too stiff and neatly combed. It was then that Helena Kraft had gotten in touch. Grane had been at Säpo for five years now and had gradually been accepted for the talent that she was, even if it was not always easy.

It had been a trying day, and not just because of the ghastly weather. The head of the division, Ragnar Olofsson, had appeared in her office looking surly and humourless and told her that she should damn well not be flirting when she was out on an assignment.

"Flirting?"

"Flowers have been delivered."

"And that's my fault?"

"Yes, I do think you have a responsibility there. When we're out in the field we have to show discipline and reserve at all times. We represent an absolutely key public agency."

"Well, that's great, Ragnar dear. One always learns something from you. Now I finally understand that I'm responsible for the fact that the head of research at Ericsson can't tell the difference between normal polite behaviour and flirting. Now I realize that I should blame myself when men indulge in such wildly wishful thinking that they see a sexual invitation in a simple smile."

"Don't be stupid," Olofsson said, and he disappeared.

Later she regretted having answered back. That kind of outburst rarely does any good. On the other hand, she had been taking shit for far too long. It was time to stand up for herself. She quickly tidied her desk and got out a report from GCHQ in Britain about Russian industrial espionage against European software companies, which she had not yet had time to read. Then the telephone rang. It was Kraft, and that made Grane happy. She had never yet called to complain or moan. On the contrary.

"I'll get straight to the point," Kraft said. "I've had a call from the United States, it may be a bit of an emergency. Can you take it on your Cisco? We've arranged a secure line."

"Of course."

"Good, I'd like you to interpret the information for me, see if there's anything in it. It sounds serious, but I can't get a handle on the person who's passing it on—who, by the way, says that she knows you."

"Put me through."

It was Alona Casales at the NSA—although for a moment Grane wondered if it really *was* her. When they had last met, at a conference in Washington, D.C., Casales had been a self-assured and charismatic lecturer in what she somewhat euphemistically described as active signals surveillance: hacking, in other words. Afterwards she and Grane had gone out for drinks, and almost against her will, Grane had been enchanted. Casales smoked cigarillos and had a dark, sensuous voice well suited to her punchy one-liners and frequent sexual allusions. But now on the telephone she sounded confused and sometimes unaccountably lost the thread of what she was saying.


Blomkvist did not really know what to expect, a fashionable young man, presumably, some cool dude. But the fellow who had arrived looked like a tramp, short and with torn jeans and long, dark, unwashed hair, something slightly sleepy and shifty in his eyes. He was maybe twenty-five, perhaps younger, had bad skin, and a rather ugly mouth sore. Linus Brandell did not look like someone who was sitting on a major scoop.

"Linus Brandell, I presume."

"That's right. Sorry I'm late. Happened to bump into a girl I knew. We were in the same class in ninth grade, and she—"

"Let's get this over with," Blomkvist interrupted him, and led the way to a table towards the back of the pub.

When Amir appeared, smiling discreetly, they ordered two pints of Guinness and then sat quietly for a few seconds. Blomkvist could not understand why he felt so irritated. It was not like him; perhaps the whole drama with Serner was getting to him after all. He smiled at Arne and his gang, all of whom were studying them keenly.

"I'll come straight to the point," Brandell said.

"That sounds good."

"Do you know Supercraft?"

Blomkvist did not know much about computer games, but even he had heard of Supercraft.

"By name, yes."

"No more than that?"

"No."

"In that case you won't know that what makes this game different, or at least so special, is that it has a particular AI function: it allows you to communicate with a player about war strategy without being really sure, at least to begin with, whether you're talking to a real person or a digital creation."

"You don't say," Blomkvist said. Nothing interested him less than the finer points of a damn game.

"It's a minor revolution in the industry and I was actually involved in developing it," Brandell said.

"Congratulations. In that case you must have made a killing."

"That's just it."

"Meaning what?"

"The technology was stolen from us and now Truegames is making billions while we don't get a single öre."

Blomkvist had heard this line before. He had even spoken to an old lady who claimed that it was actually she who had written the Harry Potter books and that J. K. Rowling had stolen everything by telepathy.

"So how did it happen?" he said.

"We were hacked."

"How do you know that?"

"It's been established by experts at the National Defence Radio Establishment. I can give you a name there if you want, and also by a . . ."

Brandell hesitated.

"Yes?"

"Nothing. But even the Security Police were involved, you can talk to Gabriella Grane there. She's an analyst and I think she'll back me up. She mentioned the incident in a report which she published last year. I have the reference number here . . ."

"In other words, this isn't news," Blomkvist interrupted.

"No, not in that sense. *New Technology* and *Computer Sweden* wrote about it. But since Frans didn't want to talk and on a couple of occasions even denied that there had been any breach at all, the story never went very far."

"But it's still old news."

"I suppose so."

"So why should I be listening to you, Linus?"

"Because now Frans seems to have understood what happened. I think he's sitting on pure dynamite. He's become completely manic about security. Only uses hyper-encryption for his phones and e-mail and he's just got a new burglar alarm with cameras and sensors and all that crap. I think you should talk to him. That's why I got in touch with you. A guy like you could get him to open up. He doesn't listen to me."

"So you order me down here because it seems as if someone called Frans may be sitting on some dynamite."

"Not someone called Frans, Blomkvist, it's none other than Frans Balder, didn't I say that? I was one of his assistants."

Blomkvist searched his memory: the only Balder he could think of was Hanna Balder, the actress, whatever might have become of her.

"Who's he?" he said.

The look he got was so full of contempt that he was taken aback.

"Where've you been living, Mars? Frans Balder is a legend. A household name."

"Really?"

"Christ, yes!" Brandell said. "Google him and you'll see. He became a professor of computer sciences at just twenty-seven and for two decades he's been a leading authority on research in artificial intelligence. There's hardly anyone who's as far advanced in the development of quantum computing and neural networks. He has an amazingly cool, back-to-front brain. Thinks along completely unorthodox, groundbreaking lines and as you can probably imagine the computer industry's been chasing him for years. But for a long time Balder refused to let himself be recruited. He wanted to work alone. Well, not altogether alone, he's always had assistants he's driven into the ground. He wants results, and he's always saying: 'Nothing is impossible. Our job is to push back the frontiers, blah blah blah.' But people listen to him. They'll do anything for him. They'll just about die for him. To us nerds he is God Almighty."

"I can hear that."

"But don't think that I'm some starstruck admirer, not at all. There's a price to be paid, I know that better than anyone. You can do great things with him, but you can also go to pieces. Balder isn't even allowed to look after his own son. He messed up in some unforgivable way. There are a lot of different stories, assistants who've hit the wall and wrecked their lives and God knows what. But although he's always been obsessive he's never behaved like this before. I just know he's onto something big."

"You just know that."

"You've got to understand, he's not normally a paranoid person. Quite the opposite. He's never been anywhere near paranoid enough, given the level of the things he's been dealing with. But now he's locked himself into his house and hardly goes out. He seems afraid and he really doesn't do scared."

"And he was working on computer games?" Blomkvist said, without hiding his scepticism.

"Well . . . since he knew we were all gaming freaks he probably thought we should get to work on something that we liked. But his AI programme was also right for that business. It was a perfect testing environment and we got fantastic results. We broke new ground. It was just . . ."

"Get to the point, Linus."

"Frans and his lawyers wrote a patent application for the most innovative parts of the technology, and that's when the first shock came. A Russian engineer at Truegames had thrown together an application just before, which blocked our patent. It can hardly have been a coincidence. But that didn't really matter. The patent was only a paper tiger. The interesting thing was how the hell they had managed to find out about what we'd been doing. Since we were all devoted to Frans even to the point of death, there was only one possibility: we must have been hacked, in spite of all our security measures."

"Is that when you got in touch with Säpo and the National Defence Radio Establishment?"

"Not at first. Balder is not too keen on people who wear ties and work from nine to five. He prefers obsessive idiots who are glued to their computers all night long, so instead he got in touch with some weirdo hacker he had met somewhere and she said straightaway that we'd had a breach. Not that she seemed particularly credible. I wouldn't have hired her, if you see what I mean, and perhaps she was just talking drivel. But her main conclusions were nevertheless subsequently borne out by people at the NDRE."

"But no-one knew who had hacked you?"

"No, no, trying to trace hacker breaches is often a complete waste of time. But they must have been professionals. We had done a lot of work on our IT security."

"And now you suspect that Balder may have found out something more about it?"

"Definitely. Otherwise he wouldn't be behaving so strangely. I'm convinced he got wind of something at Solifon."

"Is that where he worked?"

"Yes, oddly enough. As I told you before, Balder had previously refused to let himself be tied up by the big computer giants. No-one has ever banged on as much as he did about being an outsider, about the importance of being independent and not being a slave to commercial forces. But out of the blue, as we stood there with our trousers down and our technology stolen, he suddenly accepted an offer from Solifon, of all companies. Nobody could understand it. OK, they were offering a megasalary, free rein, and all of that crap, like: Do whatever the hell you want, just work for us, and that probably sounded cool. It would definitely have been cool for anyone who wasn't Frans Balder. But he'd had any number of offers like that from Google, Apple, and all the others. Why was this suddenly so interesting? He never explained. He just packed his stuff and disappeared and from what I've heard it went swimmingly at first. Balder continued to develop our technology and I think Solifon's owner, Nicolas Grant, was beginning to fantasize about revenues in the billions. There was great excitement. But then something happened."

"Something that you don't actually know so much about."

"No, we lost contact. Balder lost contact with pretty much everyone. But I understand enough to know that it must have been something serious. He had always preached openness and enthused about the Wisdom of Crowds, all that stuff; the importance of using the knowledge of many, the whole Linux way of thinking. But at Solifon he apparently kept every comma secret, even from those who were closest to him, and then—wham bam—he gave notice and went home, and now he's sitting there in his house in Saltsjöbaden and doesn't even go out into the garden or give a damn how he looks."

"So what you've got, Linus, is a story about a professor who seems to be under pressure and who doesn't care what he looks like—though it's not clear how the neighbours can see that, if he never goes outside?"

"Yes, but I think . . ."

"Listen, this could be an interesting story. But unfortunately it isn't for me. I'm no IT reporter—as someone so wisely wrote the other day, I'm a caveman. I'd recommend you contact Raoul Sigvardsson at the *Swedish Morning Post*. He knows everything about that world."

"No, no, Sigvardsson is a lightweight. This is way above his head."

"I think you underestimate him."

"Come on, now, don't chicken out. This could be your comeback, Blomkvist."

Blomkvist made a tired gesture towards Amir, who was wiping a table not far from them.

"Can I give you some advice?" Blomkvist said.

"What? Yes . . . sure."

"Next time you have a story to sell, don't try to explain to the reporter what's in it for him. Do you know how many times people have played me that tune? 'This is going to be the biggest thing in your career. Bigger than Watergate!' You'd do better with just some basic matter-of-fact information, Linus."

"I just meant . . ."

"Yes, what actually *did* you mean?"

"That you should talk to Frans. I think he would like you. You're the same uncompromising kind of guy."

It was as if Brandell had suddenly lost his self-confidence and Blomkvist wondered if he had not been unnecessarily tough. As a general principle, he tended to be friendly and encouraging towards people who gave him tip-offs, however weird they sounded. Not just because there might be a good story even in something that sounded crazy, but also because he recognized that often he was their last straw. There were many who turned to him when everyone else had stopped listening. He was the last hope, and there was never any excuse to be scornful.

"Listen," he said. "I've had a really bad day and I didn't mean to sound sarcastic."

"That's OK."

"And you know," Blomkvist said. "There's one thing which interests me about this story. You said you had a visit from a female hacker."

Alona Casales was not one to become nervous easily and she rarely had trouble staying on topic. She was forty-eight, tall, and outspoken, with a voluptuous figure and small intelligent eyes which could make anybody feel insecure. She often seemed to see straight through people and did not suffer from a surfeit of deference to superiors. She would give anyone a dressing down, even the Attorney General if he came calling. That was one of the reasons why Ed the Ned got on so well with her. Neither of them attached much importance to status; all they cared about was ability.

Nevertheless, she had completely lost it with the head of Sweden's Security Police. This had nothing to do with Helena Kraft. It was because of the drama unfolding in the open-plan office behind her. Admittedly they were all used to Needham's explosions of rage. But something told her right away that what was going on now was on an altogether different scale.

The man seemed paralyzed. While Casales sat there blurting some confused words down the line, people gathered around him and all of them, without exception, looked scared. But perhaps because she was in a state of shock, Casales did not hang up or say that she would call back later. She let herself be put through to Gabriella Grane, that charming young analyst whom she had met and tried to seduce in Washington. Even though Alona had not succeeded in taking her to bed, she had been left with a deep feeling of pleasure.

"Hello, my dear," she said. "How are you?"

"Not so bad," Grane answered. "We're having some terrible storms, but otherwise everything's fine."

"I really enjoyed that last time we saw each other."

"Absolutely, it was nice. I was hungover the whole of the next day. But I don't suppose you're calling to ask me out."

"Unfortunately not. I'm calling because we've picked up signs of a serious threat to a Swedish scientist."

"Who?"

"For a long time we had trouble understanding the information, or even working out which country it concerned. The communication was encrypted and used only vague codenames, but still, once we got a few small pieces of the puzzle we managed . . . what the *hell* . . ."

"What?"

"One second . . ."

Casales's computer screen blinked, then went blank, and as far as she could see the same thing was happening all over the office floor. For a moment she wondered what to do, but carried on the conversation; it might just be a power outage, after all, although the overhead lights seemed to be working.

"I'm still here," said Grane.

"Thanks, I appreciate it. Sorry about this. It's complete chaos here. Where was I?"

"You were talking about pieces of the puzzle."

"Right, yes, we put two and two together, because there's always one person who's careless, however professional they try to be, or who . . ."

"Yes?"

"Um . . . talks, gives an address or something, in this case it was more like . . ."

Casales fell silent again. None other than Commander Jonny Ingram, one of the most senior people in the NSA with contacts high up in the White House, had come onto the office floor. Ingram was trying to appear as composed as usual. He even cracked some joke to a group sitting further away. But he was not fooling anyone. Beneath his polished and tanned exterior—ever since his time as head of the cryptological centre in Oahu he was suntanned all year round—you could sense something nervous in his expression. Now he seemed to want everybody's attention.

"Hello, are you still there?" Grane said on the other end of the line.

"I'm going to have to leave you, unfortunately. I'll call you back," Casales said, and hung up.

At that moment she became very worried indeed. There was a feeling in the air that something terrible had happened, maybe another major terrorist attack. But Ingram carried on with his soothing act and, even though there was sweat on his upper lip and forehead, he kept repeating that it was nothing serious. Most likely a virus, he said, which had found its way into the intranet, despite all the security precautions.

"To be on the safe side, we've shut down our servers," he said, and for a moment he really did manage to calm things down. "What the hell," people seemed to be saying, "a virus isn't such a big deal."

But then Ingram started spouting such vague statements that Casales could not stop herself from shouting:

"Tell us what's actually happening!"

"We don't know that much yet. But it's possible that our systems have been hacked. We'll get back to you as soon as we know more," Ingram said, looking concerned, and a murmur ran through the room.

"Is it the Iranians again?" somebody wondered.

"We think . . ." Ingram said.

He got no further. Ed Needham, the person who should have been standing there in the first place, explaining what was happening, interrupted him brusquely and got to his feet, a bear of a man. At that moment there was no denying that he was an imposing sight. Gone was the deflated Needham from a minute before; he now exuded a tremendous sense of determination.

"No," he hissed. "It's a hacker, a fucking superhacker, and I'm going to cut his balls off."

"The female hacker doesn't really have anything to do with this story," said Brandell, nursing his beer. "She was more like Balder's social project."

"But she seemed to know her stuff."

"Or she was just lucky. She talked a lot of rubbish."

"So you met her?"

"Yes, just after Balder took off for Silicon Valley."

"How long ago was that?"

"Almost a year. I'd moved our computers into my apartment on Brantingsgatan. My life was not great, to put it mildly. I was single and broke and hung over, my place looked like hell. I had just spoken to Frans on the telephone, and he'd been going on like some boring old dad. There was a lot of: Don't judge her by how she looks, appearances can be deceptive blah blah, and hey, he said that to *me*! I'm not exactly the ideal son-in-law myself. I've never worn a jacket and tie in my entire life, and if anyone knows what people look like in the hacker community, then I do. Whatever, so I was sitting there waiting for this girl. Thought that she would at least knock. But she just opened the door and walked in."

"What did she look like?"

"Bloody awful . . . but then, she was also sexy in a weird way. But dreadful!"

"Linus, I'm not asking you to rate her looks. I just want to know what she was wearing and if she maybe mentioned what her name was."

"I have no idea who she was," Brandell said, "although I did recognize her from somewhere—I had the feeling that it was something bad. She was tattooed and pierced and all that crap and looked like a heavy rocker or goth or punk, plus she was as thin as hell."

Hardly aware that he was doing it, Blomkvist gestured to Amir to pull him another Guinness.

"What happened?" Blomkvist said.

"Well, what can I say? I guess I thought that we didn't have to get going right away, so I sat down on my bed—there wasn't much else to sit on—and suggested that we might have a drink or something first. But do you know what she did then? She asked me to leave. She ordered me out of my own home, as if that was the most natural thing in the world. Obviously I refused. I was like: 'I do actually live here.' But she said: 'Piss off, get lost,' and I didn't see what choice I had so I was out for a while. When I got back she was lying there on my bed, smoking—how sick is that? And reading a book about string theory or something. Maybe I gave her some sort of dodgy look, what do I know, and she said that she wasn't planning on having sex with me, not even a little. 'Not even a little,' she said, and I don't think she looked me in the eye even once. She just announced that we'd had a Trojan, a RAT, and that she recognized the pattern in the breach, the level of originality in the programming. 'You've been blown,' she said. And then she walked out."

"Without saying goodbye?"

"Without a single damn word."

"Christ."

"But to be honest I think she was bullshitting. The guy at the NDRE, who did the same investigation a little while later, and who probably knew much more about these kinds of attacks, was very clear that you couldn't draw any conclusions like that, and that however much he searched through our computer he couldn't find any spyware. But still his guess was—Molde was his name, by the way, Stefan Molde—that we'd been hacked."

"This woman, did she ever introduce herself in any way?"

"I did actually press her, but all she would say was that I could call her Pippi. Pretty surly she was too. It was obvious that that wasn't her real name, but still . . ."

"What?"

"I thought it suited her somehow."

"You know," Blomkvist said, "I was just about to head home again."

"Yes, I noticed that."

"But now everything's changed in a pretty major way. Did you say that your professor Balder knew this woman?"

"Well, yes."

"In that case I want to talk to him as soon as possible."

"Because of the woman?"

"Something like that."

"OK, fine," Brandell said thoughtfully. "But you won't find any contact details for him. He's become so bloody secretive, like I said. Do you have an iPhone?"

"I do."

"In that case you can forget it. Frans sees Apple as more or less in the pocket of the NSA. To talk to him you'll have to buy a Blackphone or at least borrow an Android and download a special encryption programme. But I'll see to it that he gets in touch with you, so you can arrange to meet in some secure place."

"Great, Linus, thanks."

# CHAPTER 4

# NOVEMBER 20

Grane had just put on her coat to go home when Casales called again, and at first she was irritated, not only because of the confusion last time. She wanted to get going before the storm got out of hand. The news on the radio had forecast winds of up to sixty-seven miles per hour and the temperature falling to −10°C, and she was not dressed for it.

"I'm sorry it took a while," Casales said. "We've had an insane morning. Total chaos."

"Here too," Grane said politely, looking at her watch.

"But I do have something important to tell you, as I said, at least I think I do. It isn't that easy to analyze. I just started checking out a group of Russians, did I mention that?" Casales said.

"No."

"Well, there are probably Germans and Americans involved and possibly one or more Swedes."

"What sort of group are we talking about?"

"Criminals, sophisticated criminals who don't rob banks or sell drugs. Instead they steal corporate secrets and confidential business information."

"Black hats."

"They're not just hackers. They also blackmail and bribe people. Possibly they even commit old-fashioned crimes, like murder. I don't have much on them yet, to be honest, mostly codenames and unconfirmed links, and then a couple of real names, some young computer engineers in junior positions. The group is active in suspected industrial espionage and that's why the case has ended up on my desk. We're afraid that cutting-edge American technology has fallen into Russian hands."

"I understand."

"But it isn't easy to get at them. They're good at encryption and, no matter how hard I try, I haven't been able to get any closer to their leadership than to catch that their boss goes by the name of Thanos."

"Thanos?"

"Yes, derived from Thanatos, the god of death in Greek mythology, the one who's the son of Nyx—night—and twin brother to Hypnos—sleep."

"Real cloak-and-dagger stuff."

"Actually, it's pretty childish. Thanos is a supervillain in Marvel Comics, you know that comic book series with heroes like the Hulk, Iron Man and Captain America. First of all it's not particularly Russian, but more than that it's . . . how do I put this . . . ?"

"Both playful and arrogant?"

"Yes, like a bunch of cocky college kids messing around, and that really annoys me. In fact there's a whole lot that worries me about this story, and that's why I got so worked up when we learned through our signals surveillance that someone in the network may have defected, somebody who could maybe give us some insight—if only we could get our hands on this guy before they do. But now that we've looked more carefully, we realize it wasn't at all what we thought."

"Meaning what?"

"The guy who quit wasn't some criminal, but the opposite, an honest person who resigned from a company where this organization has moles, someone who presumably stumbled on some key information . . ."

"Keep going."

"In our view this person is now seriously under threat. He needs protection. But until recently we had no idea where to look for him, we didn't even know which company he'd worked at. But now we think we've zeroed in," Casales said. "You see, in the last few days one of these characters mentioned something about this guy, said that 'with him all the bloody Ts went up in smoke.'"

"The bloody Ts?"

"Yes, cryptic and strange, but it had the advantage of being specific and highly searchable. While 'bloody Ts' didn't give us anything, Ts generally, words beginning with T in conjunction with companies, high-tech firms of course, kept leading us to the same place—to Nicolas Grant and his maxim: Tolerance, Talent, and Teamwork."

"We're talking Solifon here, right?" Grane said.

"We think so. At least it felt like everything had fallen into place, so we began to investigate who had left Solifon recently. The company always has such high staff turnover, it's part of their philosophy—that talent should flow in and out. But then we started to think specifically about those Ts. Are you familiar with them?"

"Not really."

"They're Grant's recipe for creativity. By tolerance he means that you need to be open to unconventional ideas and unconventional people. Talent—it doesn't just achieve results, it attracts other gifted people and helps create an environment that people want to be in. And all these talents have to form a team. As I'm sure you know, Solifon was a remarkable success story, producing pioneering technology in a whole series of fields. But then this new genius popped up, a Swede, and with him . . ."

". . . all the bloody Ts went up in smoke."

"Exactly."

"And it was Frans Balder."

"I don't think he normally has any problem with tolerance, or with teamwork for that matter. But from the beginning there was apparently something toxic about him. He refused to share anything and in no time at all he managed to destroy the rapport among the elite researchers at the company, especially when he started accusing people of being thieves and copycats. There was a scene with the owner, too. But Grant has refused to tell us what it was about—just that it was something private. Soon after, Balder gave notice."

"I know."

"Most people were probably relieved when he took off. The air at work became easier to breathe, and people began to trust each other again, at least up to a point. But Grant wasn't happy, and more importantly his lawyers weren't happy either. Balder had taken with him whatever he had been developing at Solifon, and there was a rumour—maybe because no-one really knew what it was—that he was onto something sensational that could revolutionize the quantum computer, which Solifon was working on."

"And from a purely legal point of view whatever he'd produced belonged to the company and not to him personally."

"Correct. So even though Balder had been going on about theft, when all was said and done he himself was the thief. Any day now things are likely to blow up in court, as you know, unless Balder manages to use whatever he has to frighten the lawyers. That information is his life insurance, so he says, and it may well be true. But in the worst-case scenario it could also be . . ."

". . . the death of him."

"That's what I'm afraid of," Casales said. "We're picking up stronger indications that something serious is getting under way, and your boss tells me that you might be able to help us."

Grane looked at the storm that was now raging outside, and longed desperately to go home and get away from it all. Yet she took off her coat and sat down again, feeling uneasy.

"How can I help?"

"What do you think he found out?"

"Do I take that to mean that you haven't managed either to bug him or hack him?"

"I'm not going to answer that one, sweetheart. But what do you think?"

Grane remembered how Frans Balder had stood in the doorway of her office not so long ago and muttered about dreaming of "a new kind of life"—whatever he may have meant by that.

"I assume you know," she said, "I met him before he joined Solifon, because he claimed that his research had been stolen. I didn't warm to him much, at first. Then there was talk in-house of getting him some form of protection, so I met him again. His transformation over the last few weeks was incredible. Not only because he had shaved off his beard, tidied up his hair and lost some weight. He was also mellower, even a little bit unsure of himself. I could tell he was rattled and at one point he did say that he thought there were people who wanted to harm him."

"In what way?"

"Not physically, he said. It was more his research and his reputation they were after. But I'm not so sure, deep down, he believed it would stop there, so I suggested he get a guard dog. I thought a dog would be excellent company for a man who lived out in the suburbs in far too big a house. But he wouldn't hear of it. 'I can't have a dog now,' he said rather sharply."

"Why's that, do you think?"

"I really don't know. But I got the feeling there was something weighing on him: he didn't protest too much when I arranged for a sophisticated alarm system in his house. It has just been installed."

"By whom?"

"A company we often use, Milton Security."

"Good. But my recommendation is to move him to a safe house."

"Is it that bad?"

"We think the risk is real."

"OK," Grane said. "If you send over some documentation I'll have a word with my superior right away."

"I'll see what I can do, but I'm not sure what I can get my hands on. We've been having . . . some computer issues."

"Can an agency like yours really afford that sort of thing?"

"No, you're right. Let me get back to you, sweetheart," she said, and hung up.

Grane remained quite still and looked out at the storm lashing against the window with increasing fury. Then she picked up her Blackphone and rang Balder. She let it ring and ring. Not just to warn him and see to it that he move to a safe place at once, but also because she suddenly wanted to know what he had meant when he said: "These last few days I've been dreaming about a new kind of life."

No-one would have believed that at that moment Balder was fully occupied with his son.

Blomkvist remained sitting for a while after Brandell had left, drinking his Guinness and staring into the distance. Behind him, Arne and his gang were laughing at something. But Blomkvist was so engrossed in his thoughts that he heard nothing, and hardly even noticed that Amir had sat down next to him and was giving him the latest weather forecast.

The temperature was dropping. The first snow of the year was expected to fall, and not in any pleasant or picturesque way. The misery was going to come blasting in sideways in the worst storm the country had seen for a long time.

"Could get hurricane-force winds," Amir said, and Blomkvist, who still was not listening, just said, "That's good."

"Good?"

"Yes . . . well . . . better than no weather at all."

"I suppose. But are you all right? You look shaken up. Was it a useful meeting?"

"Sure, it was fine."

"But what you got to hear rattled you, didn't it?"

"I'm not certain. Things are just a mess right now. I'm thinking of quitting *Millennium*."

"I thought you basically *were* that magazine."

"I thought so, too. But I guess there's an end to everything."

"That's probably true," Amir said. "My old man used to say that there's even an end to eternity."

"What did he mean by that?"

"I think he was talking about love everlasting. It was shortly before he left my mother."

Blomkvist snorted. "I haven't been so good at everlasting love myself. On the other hand . . ."

"Yes, Mikael?"

"There's a woman I used to know, she's been out of my life for some time now."

"Tricky."

"Well, yes it is. But now I've suddenly had a sign of life from her, or at least I think I did, and perhaps that's what's got me looking a bit funny."

"Right."

"I'd better get myself home. What do I owe you?"

"We can settle up another time."

"Great, take care, Amir," he said. He walked past the regulars, who threw a few random comments at him, and stepped into the storm.

It was a near-death experience. Gusts of wind blew straight through his body, but in spite of them he stood still for a while, lost in old memories. He thought about a dragon tattoo on a skinny, pale back, a cold snap on

Hedeby Island in the midst of a decades-old missing person case, and a dug-up grave in Gosseberga that was nearly the resting place of a woman who refused to give up. Then he walked home slowly. For some reason he had trouble getting the door open, had to jiggle the key around. He kicked off his shoes and sat at his computer and searched for information on Frans Balder, Professor.

But he was alarmingly unfocused and instead found himself wondering, as he had so many times before: Where had she disappeared to? Apart from some news from her one-time employer, Dragan Armansky, he had not heard a word about her. It was as if she had vanished off the face of the earth and, although they lived in more or less the same part of town, he had never caught a glimpse.

Of course, the person who had turned up at Brandell's apartment that day could have been someone else. It was possible, but not likely. Who else would come stomping in like that? It must have been Salander, and Pippi . . . that was typical.

The nameplate on her apartment door on Fiskargatan was V. Kulla and he could well see why she did not use her real name. It was all too searchable and associated with one of the most high-profile trials the country had ever seen. Admittedly, it was not the first time that the woman had vanished in a puff of smoke. But ever since that day when he had knocked on her door on Lundagatan and given her hell for having written a personal investigation report about him which was rather too thorough, they had never been apart for so long. It felt a little strange, didn't it? After all, Salander was his . . . well, what the hell was she in point of fact?

Hardly his friend. One sees one's friends. Friends don't only get in touch by hacking into your computer. Yet he still felt this bond with Salander and, above all, he worried about her. Her old guardian Holger Palmgren used to say that Lisbeth Salander would always manage. Despite her appalling childhood, or maybe because of it, she was one hell of a survivor, and there was probably a lot of truth in that. But one could never be sure, not with a woman of such a background, and with that knack for making enemies.

Perhaps she really had gone off the rails, as Armansky had hinted when he and Blomkvist met over lunch at Gondolen about six months ago. It was a spring day, a Saturday, and Armansky had offered to buy beer and snaps and all the rest of it. Even though they were ostensibly meeting as two old friends, there was no doubt that Armansky only wanted to talk about Salander and, with the help of a few drinks, indulge in a spot of sentimentality.

Among other things, Armansky told Blomkvist that his company, Milton Security, had supplied a number of personal alarms to a nursing home in Högdalen, good equipment, he said.

But not even the best equipment in the world will help you if the electricity goes off and nobody can be bothered to fix it, and that is precisely what happened. There was a power outage at the home late one evening, and in the course of that night one of the residents, a lady called Rut Åkerman, fell and broke her femur, and she lay there for hour after hour pressing the button on her alarm to no avail. By the morning she was in critical condition and, since the papers were just then focusing heavily on negligence in care for the elderly, the whole thing became a big deal.

Happily, the old lady pulled through. But she also happened to be the mother of a senior figure in the Swedish Democrats party. When it emerged on the party's website, Unpixelated, that Armansky was an Arab—which incidentally he was not at all, although it was true that he was occasionally called "the Arab" in jest—there was an explosion in the posted comments. Hundreds of anonymous writers said that's what happens "when you let coons supply your technology." Armansky took it very badly, especially when the trolling affected his family.

But then suddenly, as if by magic, all those posts were no longer anonymous. You could see the names and addresses of those responsible, their job titles and how old they were. It was beautifully neat, as if they had all filled in a form. You could say that the entire site had been unpixelated, and of course it became clear that the posts did not just come from crackpots, but also from many established citizens, even some of Armansky's competitors in the security business. For a long time the hitherto-anonymous perpetrators were completely powerless. They could not understand what had happened. Eventually someone managed to close the site down, but nobody had any idea who lay behind the attack—except for Dragan Armansky himself.

"It was classic Salander," he said. "You know, I hadn't heard from her for ages and was convinced that she couldn't give a damn about me, or anybody else for that matter. But then this happened, and it was fantastic. She had stood up for me. I sent an effusive thanks by e-mail, and to my surprise an answer came back. Do you know what she wrote?"

"No."

"Just one single sentence: 'How the hell can you protect that creep Sandvall at the Östermalm clinic?'"

"And who's Sandvall?"

"A plastic surgeon to whom we gave personal protection because he'd been threatened. He'd pawed a young Estonian woman on whom he had performed breast surgery and she happened to be the girlfriend of a known criminal."

"Oops."

"Precisely, not such a clever thing to do. I answered Salander to say that I didn't think Sandvall was one of God's little angels any more than she did. But I pointed out that we don't have the right to make that kind of judgment. Even male chauvinist pigs are entitled to some degree of security. Since Sandvall was under serious threat and asked for our help we gave it to him—at double the usual rate."

"But Salander didn't buy your argument?"

"Well, she didn't reply, at least not by e-mail. But I suppose you could say she gave a different sort of answer."

"What do you mean?"

"She marched up to our guards at the clinic and ordered them to keep calm. I even think she gave them my regards. Then she walked straight past all the patients and nurses and doctors, went into Sandvall's office and broke three of his fingers and made the most terrifying threats against him."

"Jesus!"

"That's putting it mildly. Stark staring mad. I mean, to do something like that in front of so many witnesses and in a doctor's office on top of it all. And of course there was a huge fuss afterwards, a lot of brouhaha about lawsuits and prosecutions and the whole damn thing. You can just imagine: breaking the fingers of a surgeon who's lined up to perform a string of lucrative nips and tucks . . . It's the kind of thing that gets top lawyers seeing dollar signs everywhere."

"What happened?"

"Nothing. It all came to nothing, apparently because the surgeon himself didn't want to take things any further. But still, Mikael, it was insane. No person in their right mind steams into a top surgeon's office in broad daylight and breaks his fingers. Not even Salander."

Blomkvist actually thought that it sounded pretty logical, according to Salander logic, that is, a subject in which he was more or less expert. He did not doubt for one second that that doctor had done far worse than grope the wrong girlfriend. But even so, he could not help wondering if Salander hadn't screwed up in this case, if only on the score of risk analysis.

It occurred to him that she might have *wanted* to get into trouble again, maybe to put some spice back into her life. But that was probably unfair. He knew nothing of her motives or her current circumstances. As the storm rattled the windowpanes and he sat there in front of his computer Googling Frans Balder, he tried to see beauty in the fact that they had now bumped into each other in this indirect way. It would seem that Salander was the same as ever and perhaps, who knows, she had given him a lead. Linus Brandell had irritated him from the word "go," but when Salander dropped into the story, he saw it all with new eyes. If she had taken the time to help Frans Balder then he could at least take a closer look at it, and with some luck find out a bit more about Salander at the same time.

Why had she gotten herself involved in the first place?

She was not just some itinerant IT consultant, after all. Yes, she could fly into a rage over life's injustices, but for a woman who had no qualms about hacking to get indignant about a computer breach, that was a little bit surprising. Breaking the fingers of a plastic surgeon, fine. But hackers? That was very much like throwing stones at glass houses.

There must be some backstory. Maybe she and Balder knew each other. It was not inconceivable and so he tried Googling their names together, but without getting any hits, at least not any that had relevance.

He focused on Frans Balder. The professor's name generated two million hits but most of them were scientific articles and commentaries. It did not seem as if Balder gave interviews, and because of that, there was a sort of mythological gloss over the details of his life, as if they had been romanticized by admiring students.

Apparently it had been assumed that Balder was more or less mentally disabled as a child until one day he walked into the headmaster's office at his school on Ekerö island and pointed out a mistake in the ninth grade maths books to do with so-called imaginary numbers. The mistake was corrected in subsequent editions and the following spring Balder won a national mathematics competition. He was reported as being able to speak backwards and create his own long palindromes. In an early school essay later published online he took a critical view of H. G. Wells's novel *The War of the Worlds* on the grounds that he could not understand how beings superior to us in every way could fail to grasp something so basic as the differences between bacterial flora on Mars and on Earth.

After graduating from secondary school he studied computer sciences at Imperial College in London and defended his thesis on algorithms in neural networks, which was considered revolutionary. He became the youngest ever professor at the Royal Institute of Technology in Stockholm and was elected to the Royal Swedish Academy of Engineering Sciences. These days he was regarded as a world authority on the hypothetical concept of "technological singularity," the state at which computer intelligence will have overtaken our own.

In most photographs he looked like a dishevelled troll with small eyes, his hair standing on end. Yet he married the glamorous actress Hanna Lind. The couple had a son who, according to evening newspaper coverage, under the headline HANNA'S GREAT SORROW, was mentally disabled, even though the boy did not—at least not in the picture accompanying the article—look in the least bit impaired. The marriage fell apart and, amidst a heated custody battle in Nacka district court, the *enfant terrible* of the theatre, Lasse Westman, stepped into the fray to declare aggressively that Balder should not be allowed to look after his son because he cared more about "the intelligence of computers than that of children." Blomkvist concentrated his efforts on trying to understand Balder's research, and for a long time he sat engrossed in a complicated text about quantum processors in computers.

Afterwards he went into Documents and opened a file he had created a year or so earlier. It was called [*Lisbeth stuff*]. He had no idea whether she was still hacking into his computer, but he could not help hoping that she did and wondered if he should not after all type out a little greeting. Long, personal letters were not her thing. He would do better to go for something brisk and a bit cryptic. He wrote:

```
<What should we make of Frans Balder's artificial
intelligence?>
```

# CHAPTER 5

# NOVEMBER 20

The words blinked onto the computer screen:

```
<Mission accomplished!>
```

Plague gave a hoarse, almost deranged, yell, and that may have been unwise. But even if the neighbours had happened to hear, they could not have dreamed what it was about. Plague's home was not an obvious setting for high-level international security coups.

It felt more like a place where a social welfare case might hang out. Plague lived on Högklintavägen in Sundbyberg, a markedly unglamorous area with dull, four-storey, faded brick houses, and the apartment itself had nothing much going for it. It had a sour, stale smell, and his desk was covered in all sorts of rubbish: McDonald's containers and Coca-Cola cans, crumpled-up pages from notebooks, unwashed coffee cups, and empty candy wrappers. Even though some had actually made it into the waste-paper basket—which had not been emptied for weeks—you could hardly take a step in the room without getting crumbs or grit under your feet. But none of this would have surprised anyone who knew him.

Plague was not a man who normally showered or changed his clothes much. He spent his whole life in front of the computer even when he was not working: a giant of a man, overweight, bloated, and unkempt, with an attempt at an imperial beard that had long since turned into a shapeless thicket. His posture was dreadful and he had a habit of groaning when he moved.

But the man had other talents. He was a wizard on the computer, a hacker who flew unconstrained through cyberspace and was probably second only to one person in the field, a woman in this particular case. The mere sight of his fingers dancing across the keyboard was a joy to behold. He was as light and nimble online as he was heavy and clumsy in the other, more material world, and as a neighbour somewhere upstairs, presumably Herr Jansson, now banged on the floor, he answered the message he had received:

> <Wasp, you bloody genius. They ought to put up a statue to you!>

Then he leaned back with a delighted smile and tried to run through in his mind the sequence of events, savouring the triumph for a little while longer before going on to pump Wasp for every detail, and to ensure that she had covered her tracks. No-one must be able to trace them, no-one!

This was not the first time they had messed with a powerful organization. But this was on a new level, and many in Hacker Republic had actually been against the idea, Wasp herself most of all.

Wasp could take on just about any authority or person you would care to name, if it were necessary. But she did not like picking a fight for its own sake. She disliked that sort of childish hacker nonsense. She was not someone who hacked into supercomputers merely to show off. Wasp wanted to have a clear objective, and she always damn well analyzed the potential consequences. She weighed long-term risks against whatever need was being satisfied in the short term, and from that point of view it could not be said it made sense to hack into the NSA. Still, she let herself be talked into it. Nobody could quite understand why.

Maybe she was bored and wanted to stir up a bit of chaos so as not to die of tedium. Or else, as some in the group claimed, she was already in conflict with the NSA and therefore the breach amounted to little more than her personal revenge. But others in the group questioned even that and maintained she was looking for information, that she had been on the hunt for something ever since her father, Alexander Zalachenko, had been murdered at Sahlgrenska hospital in Göteborg.

Nobody knew for sure. Wasp had always had her secrets and actually her motives were unimportant, or so they tried to persuade themselves. If she was prepared to help, then they should just accept gratefully and not worry about the fact that, to begin with, she had not shown much enthusiasm, or hardly any feelings at all for that matter. At least she was no longer being awkward about it, and that seemed as much as anyone could expect.

Hacker Republic knew better than most that the NSA had outrageously overstepped its boundaries in recent years. These days the organization did not confine itself to eavesdropping on terrorists and potential security risks, or even just foreign heads of state and other powerful figures, but listened in on everything, or nearly everything. Millions, billions, trillions of communications and activities online were spied on and archived, and with each passing day the NSA went further and further and pried deeper and deeper into every private life. The agency had become one immeasurable, watchful, evil eye.

It was true that nobody in Hacker Republic could claim the moral high ground here. Every single one of them had made their way into parts of the digital landscape where they had no business being. Those were the rules of the game, so to speak. A hacker was someone who crossed the line, for better or for worse, someone who by virtue of his occupation broke rules and broadened the frontiers of his knowledge, without always being concerned about the distinction between private and public.

But they were not without ethics and above all they knew, also from their own experience, how power corrupts, especially power without control. None of them liked the thought that the worst, most unscrupulous hacking was no longer carried out by solitary rebels or outlaws, but by state behemoths who wanted to control their populations. Plague and Trinity and Bob the Dog and Flipper and Zod and Cat and the whole Hacker Republic gang had therefore decided to strike back by hacking the NSA and messing with them in one way or another.

That was no simple task. It was a little bit like stealing the gold from Fort Knox, and like the arrogant idiots they were they did not content themselves with breaking into the system. They also wanted superuser status, or "Root," in Linux language, and for that they needed to find unknown vulnerabilities in the system, for what was called a Zero-day Exploit—first on the NSA's server platform and then further into the organization's intranet,

NSANet, from which the authority's signals surveillance went out across the world.

They began as usual with a little social engineering. They had to get hold of the names of systems administrators and infrastructure analysts who held the complex passwords for the intranet. It would not do any harm either if there was a chance that some careless oaf was being negligent about security routines. Through their own contacts they came up with four or five names, among them one Richard Fuller.

Fuller worked in the NISIRT, the NSA Information Systems Incident Response Team, which supervised the intranet, and he was constantly on the lookout for leaks and infiltrators. Fuller was a decent sort of fellow: a Harvard law graduate, Republican, former quarterback, a dream patriot if one were to believe his CV. But through a former lover, Bob the Dog managed to discover that he was also bipolar, and possibly a cocaine addict.

When Fuller got excited he would do all sorts of stupid things, such as opening files and documents without first putting them in a so-called sandbox, a required security protocol. Furthermore he was very handsome and a little smarmy. Someone, probably Bob the Dog himself, came up with the idea that Wasp should travel to his home in Baltimore, go to bed with him, and catch him in a honey trap.

Wasp told them all to go to hell.

She also rejected their next idea, that they would compile a document containing information which looked like dynamite, specifically about infiltrators and leaks at the head office in Fort Meade. This would then be infected with malware containing an advanced Trojan with a high level of originality, which Plague and Wasp were to develop. The plan was to put out leads online which would lure Fuller to the file, and with a bit of luck get him so worked up that he would be careless with security. Not a bad plan at all—it could take them into the NSA's computer system without an active breach that might be traceable.

But Wasp said that she was not going to sit around waiting for that block-head Fuller to put his foot in it. She did not want to have to rely on other people making mistakes. She was being generally contrary and bloody-minded, so no-one was surprised when she suddenly wanted to take over the whole operation herself. Even though there was a certain amount of protest, in the end they all gave in, but not without issuing a series of instructions. Wasp did carefully write down the names and details of the systems administrators which they had managed to obtain, and she did ask for help with the so-called fingerprinting: the mapping of the server platform and operating system. But after that she closed the door on Hacker Republic and the world, and Plague had no reason to think that she paid any attention to his advice, for example that she should not use her handle, her alias, and that she should not work from home but rather from some remote hotel under a false identity, in case the NSA's bloodhounds managed to track her down. Needless to say, she did everything her own way and all Plague could do was sit at his desk in Sundbyberg and wait, his nerves in tatters. Which is why he still had no idea how she had gone about it.

He knew one thing for certain: what she had achieved was legendary, and while the storm howled outside he pushed aside some of the rubbish on his desk, leaned forward, and typed on his computer:

```
<Tell me! How does it feel?>
```

`<Empty>`, came the answer.


Empty.

That was how it felt. Salander had hardly slept for a week and she had probably also had too little to drink and eat, and now her head ached and her eyes were bloodshot and her hands shook and what she wanted above all was to sweep all of her equipment to the floor. In one sense she was content, though hardly for the reason Plague or anyone else in Hacker Republic would have guessed. She was content because she had been able to get some new information on the criminal group she was mapping out; she had found evidence of a connection which she had previously only suspected. But she kept that to herself, and she was surprised that the others could have imagined that she would have hacked the system for the hell of it.

She was no hormone-fuelled teenager, no idiot show-off looking for a kick. She would only embark on such a bold venture because she was after something very specific, although it was true that once upon a time hacking had been more than just a tool for her. During the worst moments of her childhood it had been her way of escaping, a way to make life feel a little less boxed in. With the help of computers she could break through barriers which had been put in her way and experience periods of freedom. There was probably an element of that in the current situation too.

First and foremost she was on the hunt and had been ever since she woke up in the early light of dawn with her dream of that fist beating rhythmically, relentlessly on a mattress on Lundagatan. Her enemies were hiding behind smoke screens and this could be the reason why Salander had been unusually difficult and awkward of late. It was as if a new darkness emanated from her. Apart from a large, loudmouthed boxing coach called Obinze and two or three lovers of both sexes, she saw hardly anyone. More than ever she looked like trouble; her hair was straggly, her eyes threatening, and even though she sometimes made an effort she had not become more fluent at small talk. She spoke the truth or said nothing at all. As for her apartment here on Fiskargatan . . . that was a story in itself. It was big enough for a family with seven children, although in the years since she had acquired the place nothing had been done to decorate it or make it homey. There were only a few pieces of Ikea furniture, placed seemingly at random, and she did not even have a stereo system, perhaps because she did not understand music. She saw more melody in a differential equation than in a piece by Beethoven. Yet she was as rich as Croesus. The money she had stolen from that crook Hans-Erik Wennerström had grown to a little more than five billion kronor, so she could afford whatever she wanted. But in some way—which was typical of her—her fortune had not made any mark on her personality, unless perhaps it had made her yet more fearless. She had certainly done some increasingly drastic things of late.

She may have crossed a line by wandering into the NSA's intranet. But she had judged it necessary, and for several days and nights she had been totally absorbed. Now that it was over she peered out of tired, squinting eyes at her two work desks, set at a right angle. Her equipment consisted of the regular computer and the test machine she had bought, on which she had installed a copy of the NSA's server and operating system.

She had run her own fuzzing programme, which searched for errors and tiny vulnerabilities in the platform against the test computer. She then followed that up with debugging and black box penetration testing and various beta test attacks. The outcome of all that formed the basis of her root kit, including her RAT, so she could not afford to neglect a single point. She was scrutinizing the system from top to bottom and that was why she had installed a copy of the server here at home. If she had set to work on the real platform, the NSA technicians would have noticed it immediately.

This way she was able to work without distraction, day after day, and if she did happen to leave the computer, then it was only to doze off for a while on the sofa or to put a pizza in the microwave. Apart from that, she kept at it until her eyes hurt, especially with her Zero-day Exploit, the software which exploited the unknown security vulnerabilities and which would update her status once she had actually gotten in. It was completely mind-boggling. Salander had written a programme which not only gave her ownership over the system, but also the power to control remotely pretty much anything on an intranet of which she had only patchy knowledge.

That was the most extraordinary part. She was not just going to break in. She was going further, into NSANet, which was a self-contained universe barely connected to the ordinary net. She might look like a teenager who had failed all of her subjects at school, but give her source codes in computer programmes and a logical context and her brain just went click, click. What she had created was nothing less than wholly new and improved malware, an advanced Trojan with a life of its own.

She found the pay-as-you-go card she had bought from T-Mobile in Berlin and put it into her telephone. Then she used it to go online. Maybe she should have been far away in another part of the world, dressed up as her alter ego, Irene Nesser. If the security people at the NSA were diligent and on top of things, they just might be able to trace her to Telenor's base station here on the block. They would not get all the way through, at least not with the technology now available, but it would still be close enough and that would be very bad news. Yet she reckoned the advantages of sitting here at home outweighed the risk, and she did take all the security precautions she could. Like so many other hackers, she used Tor, a network by which her traffic bounced about among thousands and thousands of users. But she also knew that not even Tor was watertight—the NSA used a programme called EgotisticalGiraffe to crack the system—so she spent a long time further improving her own personal security. Only then did she go on the attack.

She sliced into the platform like a blade through paper, but she could not afford to become over-confident as a result. Now, quickly, she had to locate the systems administrators whose names she had been given and inject her Trojan into one of their files, thereby creating a bridge between the server network and the intranet, none of which was simple, not by any means. No warning bells or antivirus programmes must be allowed to start ringing. In the end she used the identity of a man called Tom Breckinridge to penetrate NSANet and then . . . every muscle in her body tensed. Before her eyes, her over-worked, sleepless eyes, the magic unfolded.

Her Trojan took her further and further in, into this, the most secret of the secret, and she knew exactly where she was going. She was on her way to Active Directory—or its equivalent—to upgrade her status. She would go from unwelcome little visitor to superuser in this teeming universe, and only once that was done would she try to get some sort of overview of the system. It wasn't easy. It was more or less impossible, in fact, and she did not have much time either.

She worked fast to get a grip on the search system and to pick up all the passwords and expressions and references, all the internal gibberish. She was at the point of giving up when she finally found a document marked TOP SECRET, NOFORN—no foreign distribution—not particularly remarkable in itself. But together with a couple of communications links between Zigmund Eckerwald at Solifon and cyber agents at the Department for the Protection of Strategic Technologies at the NSA, it turned into dynamite. She smiled and memorized every little detail. Then she caught sight of yet another document that seemed relevant. It was encrypted and she saw no alternative but to copy it, even if that would set alarm bells ringing at Fort Meade. She swore ferociously.

The situation was becoming critical. Besides, she had to get on with her official assignment, if "official" was the right word. She had solemnly promised Plague and the others at Hacker Republic to pull down the NSA's trousers, so she tried to work out whom she should be communicating with. Who was to get her message?

She settled for Edwin Needham, Ed the Ned. His name invariably came up in connection with IT security and as she quickly picked up some information about him on the intranet, she felt a grudging respect. Needham was a star. But she had outwitted him.

For a moment she thought twice about giving the game away. Her attack would create an uproar. But an uproar was exactly what she was looking for, so she went ahead. She had no idea what time it was. It could have been night or day, autumn or spring, and only vaguely, deep in her consciousness, was she aware that the storm over the city was building up, as if the weather was synchronized with her coup. In distant Maryland, Needham began to write his e-mail.

He didn't get far, because in the next second she took over his sentence and then continued: <Those who spy on the people end up themselves being spied on by the people. There's a fundamental democratic logic to it>, and for a moment it felt as if those sentences hit the mark. She savoured the hot, sweet taste of revenge and afterwards she dragged Ed the Ned along on a journey through the system. The two of them danced and tore past a whole flickering world of things that were supposed to remain hidden at all costs.

It was a thrilling experience, no question, and yet ... when she disconnected and all her log files were automatically deleted, then came the hangover. It was like the aftermath of an orgasm with the wrong partner. Those sentences that had seemed so absolutely right a few seconds ago began to sound increasingly childish and more and more like the usual hacker nonsense. Suddenly she longed to drink herself into oblivion. With tired, shuffling steps she went into the kitchen and fetched a bottle of Tullamore D.E.W. and two or three beers to rinse her mouth with, and sat down at her computers and drank. Not in celebration. There was no sense of victory left in her body. Instead there was ... well, what? Defiance perhaps.

She drank and drank while the storm roared and congratulatory whoops came streaming in from Hacker Republic. But none of it touched her now. She hardly had the strength to stay upright and with a wide, hasty movement she swept her hand across the desktops and watched with indifference as bottles and ashtrays crashed to the floor. Then she thought about Mikael Blomkvist.

It must have been the alcohol. Blomkvist had a way of popping up in her thoughts when she was drunk, as old flames do, and without quite realizing what she was doing she hacked into his computer. She still had a shortcut into his system—it was not exactly the NSA—and at first she wondered what she was doing there.

Could she care less about him? He was history, just an attractive idiot she had once happened to fall in love with, and she was not going to make that mistake again. She'd much rather get out of there and not look at another computer for weeks. Yet she stayed on his server and in the next moment her face lit up. Kalle Fucking Blomkvist had created a file called [*Lisbeth stuff*] and in that document there was a question for her:

```
<What should we make of Frans Balder's artificial
intelligence?>
```

She gave a slight smile, in spite of it all, and that was partly because of Frans Balder. He was her kind of computer nerd, passionate about source codes and quantum processors and the potential of logic. But mostly she was smiling at the fact that Blomkvist had stumbled into the very same situation she was in. Even though she debated for some time whether just to shut down and go to bed, she wrote back:

```
<Balder's intelligence isn't in the least bit
artificial. How's your own these days?>
<And what happens, Blomkvist, if we create a
machine which is a little bit cleverer than we
are?>
```

Then she went into one of her bedrooms and collapsed with her clothes on.

# CHAPTER 6

# NOVEMBER 20

Despite his best intentions to be a full-time father, and in spite of the intense moment of hope and emotion on Hornsgatan, Frans Balder had sunk back into that deep concentration which could be mistaken for anger. Now his hair was standing on end and his upper lip was shiny with sweat. It was at least three days since he had shaved or taken a shower. He was even grinding his teeth. For hours the world and the storm outside had ceased to exist for him, and he even failed to notice what was going on at his feet. They were small, awkward movements, as if a cat or an animal had crept in under his legs; it was a while before he realized that August was crawling around under his desk. Balder gave him a dazed look, as if the stream of programming codes still lay like a film over his eyes.

"What are you after?"

August looked up at him with a pleading, clear look in his eyes.

"What?" Balder said. "What?" And then something happened.

The boy picked up a piece of paper covered in quantum algorithms which was lying on the floor and feverishly moved his hand back and forth over it. For a moment Balder thought the boy was about to have another attack. But no, it was rather as if August were pretending to write. Balder felt his body go tense and again he was reminded of something important and remote, the same feeling as at the crossing on Hornsgatan. But this time he understood what it was.

He thought back to his own childhood, when numbers and equations had been more important than life itself. His spirits rose and he burst out, "You want to do sums, don't you? Of course, you want to do sums!," and the next moment he hurried off to fetch some pencils and ruled A4 paper which he put on the floor in front of August.

Then he wrote down the simplest series of numbers he could think of, Fibonacci's sequence, in which every number is the sum of the preceding two, 1, 1, 2, 3, 5, 8, 13, 21, and left a space for the next number: 34. Then it occurred to him that this was likely too simple, so he also wrote down a geometric sequence: 2, 6, 18, 54 . . . in which every number is multiplied by three and the next number should therefore be 162. To solve a problem like that, he thought, a gifted child would not need a great deal of prior knowledge. Balder slipped into a daydream that the boy was not disabled at all, rather an enhanced copy of himself; he, too, had been slow to speak and interact socially, but he had understood mathematical relationships long before he uttered his first word.

He sat beside the boy for a long time and waited. But nothing happened. August just stared at the numbers with his glassy look. In the end Balder left him alone, went upstairs and drank some fizzy water, and then settled down at the kitchen table to continue to work. But now his concentration had vanished and he started absentmindedly flicking through the latest issue of *New Scientist*. After half an hour or so he went back downstairs to August, who was still sitting on his heels in the same immobile posture in which he had left him. Then Balder noticed something intriguing.

A second later he had the sense of being confronted by something totally inexplicable.


Hanna Balder was standing in the kitchen on Torsgatan smoking a filterless Prince. She had on a blue dressing gown and worn grey slippers and although her hair was thick and beautiful and she was still attractive, she looked haggard. Her lip was swollen and the heavy make-up around her eyes was not there purely for aesthetic reasons. Hanna Balder had taken another beating.

It would be wrong to say that she was used to it. No-one gets used to that sort of abuse. But it was part of her everyday existence and she could scarcely remember the happy person she had once been. Fear had become a natural element of her personality and for some time now she had been smoking sixty cigarettes a day and taking tranquilizers.

She had known for a while that Lasse regretted having been so generous to Frans. In fact it had been a mystery from the start. Westman had been relying on the money Balder sent them for August. For long periods they had been living off it and often he would make Hanna write an e-mail full of lies about unforeseen expenses for some educational expert or remedial therapy, which obviously the funds had never gone anywhere near. That's what made it so odd. Why had he given up all of that and let Balder take the boy away?

Deep down Hanna knew the answer. It was hubris brought on by alcohol. It was the promise of a part in a new detective series on TV4 which had boosted his confidence still further. But most of all it was August. Westman found the boy creepy and weird even though to her that was incomprehensible. How could anyone detest August?

He sat on the floor with his puzzles and did not bother anyone. Yet he had that strange look which was turned inwards rather than outwards, which usually made people smile and say that the boy must have a rich inner life, but which got under Westman's skin.

"Jesus, Hanna! He's looking straight through me," he would burst out.

"But you say that he's just an idiot."

"He is an idiot, but there's something funny about him all the same. I think he hates me."

That was nonsense, nothing more. August did not even look at Westman or at anyone else for that matter, and he did not have it in him to wish anybody ill. The world out there disturbed him and he was happiest inside his own bubble. But Westman in his drunken ravings believed that the boy was plotting some form of revenge, and that must have been the reason he let August and the money slip out of their lives. Pathetic. That at least is how Hanna had interpreted it. But now as she stood there by the sink smoking her cigarette so furiously and nervously that she got tobacco on her tongue, she wondered if there had not been something in it after all. Maybe August *did* hate Westman. Maybe he *did* want to punish him for all the punches he had taken, and maybe—Hanna closed her eyes and bit her lip—the boy hated her too.

She had started having these feelings of self-loathing and wondered whether she and Westman might not actually have damaged August.

.  .  .

It was not the fact that August had filled in the right answers to the numeri-cal sequences. That sort of thing did not particularly impress a man like Balder. No, it was something he saw lying next to the numbers. At first sight it looked like a photograph or a painting but it was in fact a drawing, an exact representation of the traffic light on Hornsgatan which they had passed the other evening. It was beautifully captured, in the minutest detail, with a sort of mathematical precision.

There was a glow to it. No-one had taught August anything at all about three-dimensional drawing or how an artist works with shadow and light, yet he seemed to have a perfect mastery of the techniques. The red eye of the traffic light flashed towards them and Hornsgatan's autumn darkness closed around it, and in the middle of the street you could see the man whom Balder had noticed and vaguely recognized. The man's head was cut off above the eyebrows. He looked frightened or at least uncomfortable and troubled, as if August had disconcerted him, and he was walking unsteadily, though goodness knows how the boy had managed to capture that.

"My God," said Balder. "Did you do this?"

August neither nodded nor shook his head but looked over towards the window, and Balder had the strangest feeling that his life would never be the same again.


Hanna Balder needed to do some shopping. The refrigerator was empty. Lasse could come home at any moment and he would not be happy if there was not even a beer for him. But the weather outside looked ghastly so she put it off, and instead she sat in the kitchen smoking, even though it was bad for her skin and bad in general.

She scrolled through her contacts two or three times, in the hope that a new name would come up. But of course there were just the same old people, and they were all tired of her. Against her better judgment she called Mia. Mia was her agent and once upon a time they had been best friends and dreamed of conquering the world together. These days Hanna was Mia's guilty conscience and she had lost count of all her agent's excuses: "It's not easy for an actress to grow older, blah blah." Why not just say it straight out: "You look worn out, Hanna. The public doesn't love you any-more."

But Mia did not answer and that was probably just as well. The conversation would not have done either of them any good. Hanna could not help looking into August's room just to feel that stinging sense of loss which made her realize that she had failed her life's most important mission, motherhood. In some perverse way she took comfort in her self-pity, and she was standing there wondering whether she shouldn't go out and get some beer after all, when the telephone rang.

It was Frans. She made a face. All day she had been tempted—but did not dare—to call him to say that she wanted August back, not just because she missed the boy, still less because she thought her son would be better off with her. It was simply in order to avoid a disaster.

Lasse wanted to get the child support again. God knows what would happen, she thought, if he were to turn up in Saltsjöbaden to claim his rights. He might even drag August out of the house, scare him out of his wits, and beat Frans to a pulp. She would have to warn him. But when she picked up and tried to say that to Frans, it was impossible to get a word in edgewise. He just went on and on about some strange story which was apparently "totally fantastic and completely amazing" and all that sort of thing.

"I'm sorry, Frans, I don't understand. What are you talking about?" she said.

"August is a savant. He's a genius."

"Have you gone mad?"

"Quite the opposite, my love. I've come to my senses at last. You have to get over here, yes, really, right now! I think it's the only way. You won't be able to understand otherwise. I'll pay for the taxi. I promise, you'll flip out. He must have a photographic memory, you see? And in some incomprehensible way he must have picked up the secrets of perspective drawing all by himself. It's so beautiful, Hanna, so precise. It shines with a light from another world."

"What shines?"

"His traffic light. Weren't you listening? The one we passed the other evening—he's been drawing a whole series of perfect pictures of it, actually more than perfect . . ."

"More than . . ."

"Well, how can I put it? He hasn't just copied it, Hanna, not just captured it exactly. He's also added something, an artistic dimension. There's such a strange fervour in what he's done, and paradoxically enough also something mathematical, as if he even has some understanding of axonometry."

"Axo . . . ?"

"Never mind! You have to come here and see," he said, and gradually she began to understand.

Out of the blue August had started to draw like a virtuoso, or so Frans claimed, and that would of course be fantastic if it were true. But the sad thing was that Hanna was still not happy, and at first she could not understand why. Then it dawned on her. It was because it had happened at Frans's house. The fact was, the boy had been living with her and Lasse for years and absolutely nothing like this had happened. He had sat there with his puzzles and building blocks and not uttered a word, just having those unpleasant fits when he screamed with that piercing voice and thrashed backwards and forwards. Now, hey presto, a few weeks with pappa and he was a genius.

It was too much. Not that she was not happy for August. But still, it hurt, and the worst thing was: she was not as surprised as she should have been. On the contrary, it felt as if she had almost seen it coming, not that the boy would draw accurate reproductions of traffic lights, but that there was something more beneath the surface.

She had sensed it in his eyes, in that look which, when he was excited, seemed to register every little detail of his surroundings. She had sensed it in the way the boy listened to his teachers, and the nervous way he leafed through the maths books she had bought for him, and most of all she had sensed it in his numbers. There was nothing so strange as those numbers. Hour after hour he would write down series of incomprehensibly large sums, and Hanna really did try to understand them, or at least to grasp the point of it all. But however hard she tried she had not been able to work it out, and now she supposed that she had missed something important. She had been too unhappy and wrapped up in herself to fathom what was going on in her son's mind, wasn't that it?

"I don't know," she said.

"Don't know what," Frans said in irritation.

"I don't know if I can come," she said, and at the same time she heard a racket at the front door.

Lasse was coming in with his old drinking buddy Roger Winter, and that made her flinch in fear, mutter an apology to Frans, and for the thousandth time dwell on the fact that she was a bad mother.


Balder stood on the chequered floor in the bedroom, the telephone in his hand, and swore. He had had the floor laid because it appealed to his sense of mathematical order, with the squares repeating themselves endlessly in the wardrobe mirrors on either side of the bed. There were days when he saw the multiplication of the squares reflected there as a teeming riddle, something with a life of its own rising up out of the schematic in the same way that thoughts and dreams arise from neurons or computer programmes emerge from binary codes. But just then he was lost in quite different thoughts.

"Dear boy. What has become of your mother?" he said.

August, who was sitting on the floor beside him eating a cheese-and-gherkin sandwich, looked up with a concentrated expression, and Balder was seized by a strange premonition that he was about to say something grown-up and wise. But that was obviously idiotic. August remained as silent as ever and knew nothing about women who were neglected and had faded away. The fact that the idea had even occurred to Balder was due to the drawings.

The drawings—by now there had been three—seemed to him to be proof not only of artistic and mathematical gifts, but also of some sort of wisdom. The works seemed so mature and complex in their geometric precision that Balder could not reconcile them with August's mental limitations. Or rather, he did not want to reconcile them, because he had long ago worked out what this was about.

As the father of an autistic son, Balder had suspected that many parents hoped the notion of a savant would be the consolation prize to make up for a diagnosis of cognitive deficiencies. But the odds were against them.

According to a common estimate, only one in ten children with autism have some kind of savant gift, and for the most part these talents, though they often entail a fantastic memory and observation of detail, are not as startling as those depicted in films. There are, for example, autistic people who can say on which day of the week a certain date falls, within a range of several hundred years—in extreme cases within a range of forty thousand years.

Others possess encyclopaedic knowledge within a narrow field, such as bus timetables or telephone numbers. Some can calculate large sums in their heads, or remember what the weather had been like every day of their lives, or are able to tell time to the second without looking at a watch. There are all kinds of more or less remarkable talents and, from what Balder gathered, people with these skills are called talented savants and capable of quite outstanding accomplishments given the fact that they are otherwise handicapped.

Another far less common group is where Balder hoped that August belonged: the so-called prodigious savants, individuals whose talents are sensational whichever way one looks at them. Kim Peek, for example, who was the basis for Rain Man, was severely mentally handicapped and could not get dressed by himself. Yet he had memorized twelve thousand books and could give a lightning-quick answer to almost any factual question. He was known as Kimputer.

Or Stephen Wiltshire, an autistic English boy who was extremely withdrawn as a child and uttered his first word when he was six—it happened to be "paper." By the age of seven Stephen was able to draw groups of buildings perfectly and in the minutest detail, having seen them for just one brief moment. He was flown above London in a helicopter and when he landed he drew the entire city in a fantastic, dizzying panorama, and with a wonderfully individual touch.

If Balder understood it all correctly, he and August must have looked at that traffic light in very different ways. Not only because the boy was plainly so much more focused, but also because Balder's brain had with lightning speed eliminated all nonessential elements in order to concentrate on the traffic light's key message: go or stop. In all probability his perception was also clouded by his thinking about Farah Sharif, while for August the crossing must have appeared exactly as it was, in precise detail.

Afterwards he had taken the image away with him like a fine etching, and it was not until a few weeks later that he had felt the need to express it. The strangest thing of all was, he had done more than simply reproduce the traffic light and the man. He had charged them with a disquieting light, and Balder could not rid himself of the thought that August had wanted to say something more to him than: Look what I can do! For the hundredth time he stared at the drawings and it was as if a needle had gone into his heart.

It frightened him. He did not entirely understand it. But there was something about that man. His eyes were bright and hard. His jaw was tense and his lips strangely thin, almost nonexistent, although that could hardly be held against him. Still, the longer he stared at him, the more frightening he looked, and all of a sudden Balder was gripped by an icy fear.

"I love you, my boy," he murmured, hardly aware of what he was saying, and possibly he repeated the sentence once or twice because the words began to sound increasingly unfamiliar to his ears.

He realized with a new sort of pain that he had never uttered them before and once he had recovered from the first shock it occurred to him that there was something contemptible in that. Did it take an exceptional talent to make him love his own child? It would be only too typical, if so. All his life he had had an absolute obsession with achievement.

He had never bothered with anything which was not innovative or highly skilled, and when he left Sweden for Silicon Valley he had hardly given a thought to August. Basically his son was no more than an irritant in the scheme of brilliant discoveries which Balder himself was busy making.

But now, he promised himself, things would be different. He would set aside his research and everything that had tormented him these last few months, and devote his full attention to the boy.

He would become a new person.

# CHAPTER 7

# NOVEMBER 20

Something else had happened at the magazine, something bad. But Berger did not want to give any details over the telephone. She suggested coming round to his place. Blomkvist had tried to put her off.

"You're going to freeze off that beautiful bum of yours!"

Berger had paid no attention and, but for the tone in her voice, he would have been happy that she was so stubborn. Ever since he left the office he had been longing to speak to her, and maybe also pull her into the bedroom and tear all her clothes off. But something told him this was not going to happen now. She had sounded upset and mumbled "I'm sorry," and this only made him more worried.

"I'll get a taxi right away," she said.

It was a while before she appeared, and out of boredom he went into the bathroom and looked in the mirror. He had certainly seen better days. His hair was dishevelled and needed a cut and he had bags under his eyes. That was basically Elizabeth George's fault. He swore and left the bathroom to set about cleaning up.

That was one thing at least that Berger would not be able to complain about. However long they had known each other, and however interwoven their lives were, he still suffered a complex when it came to tidiness. He was a labourer's son and a bachelor, she the upper-class married woman with the perfect home in Saltsjöbaden. In any case it could do no harm for his place to look a little respectable. He filled the dishwasher and wiped the sink and put out the rubbish.

He even had time to vacuum the living room, water the flowers on the windowsill, and tidy up the bookshelf and magazine rack before the doorbell rang. There was both a ring and an impatient knock. When he opened the door he was horrified. Berger was frozen stiff.

"Ricky!" he said. "Are you all right?"

She shook like a leaf, and not just because of the weather. She was not even wearing a hat. The wind had ruined her neat hairstyle and there was something that looked like a graze on her right cheek, which had not been there that morning.

"I've frozen off that beautiful bum of mine. Couldn't get a taxi."

"What happened to your face?"

"I slipped and fell. Three times, I think."

He looked down at her dark-red high-heeled Italian boots.

"You've got perfect snow boots on, too."

"Yes. Ideal. Not to mention my decision to go without thermals this morning. Brilliant!"

"Come on in and I'll warm you up."

She fell into his arms and shook even more as he hugged her tightly.

"I'm sorry," she said again.

"What for?"

"For everything. For Serner. I've been a fool."

"Don't exaggerate now, Ricky."

He brushed the snowflakes from her hair and forehead and took a careful look at her cheek.

"No, no, I'll tell you everything," she said.

"But first get your clothes off and climb into a hot bath. Would you like a glass of red?"

She would, and she stayed in the bath for a long while with her glass, which he refilled two or three times. He sat on the lid of the toilet listening to her story, and despite all the ominous news there was something of a reconciliation about their conversation, as if they were breaking through a wall they had lately been building up between themselves.

"I know you thought I was being a fool right from the start," she said. "No, don't argue, I know you too well. But you have to understand that Christer and Malin and I could see no other solution. We had recruited Emil and Sofie, and we were so proud of that. They were just about the hottest reporters around, weren't they? It was incredibly prestigious for us.

It showed that *Millennium* was on the move and there was a great buzz, with really positive coverage in *Resumé* and *Dagens Media*. It was like the good old days, and personally I felt strongly about the fact that I had promised both Sofie and Emil a secure future at the magazine. Our finances are stable, I said. We have Harriet Vanger behind us. We're going to have the money for fantastic, in-depth reporting. You know I really believed it, too. But then . . ."

"Then the sky fell in."

"Exactly, and it wasn't just the newspaper crisis, or the collapse of the advertising market. There was also that whole situation at the Vanger Corporation. I'm not sure you realize what a mess it was. Sometimes I see it almost as a political coup. All those reactionary old men in the family, and women too for that matter—well, you know them better than anyone. The old racists and regressives got together and stabbed Harriet in the back. I'll never forget that call from her. I've been steamrolled, she said. Crushed. Of course it was her efforts to revive and modernize the corporation which had annoyed them, and then her decision to appoint David Goldman to the board, the son of Rabbi Viktor Goldman. But we were also part of the picture, as you know: Andrei had just written his report on beggars in Stockholm, which we all thought was the best thing he'd ever done, and which was quoted everywhere, even abroad. But which the Vanger people—"

"Thought was lefty rubbish."

"Worse than that, Mikael, they called it propaganda for 'lazy buggers who can't even be bothered to get themselves a job.'"

"Is that what they said?"

"Something along those lines. My guess is that the story itself was irrelevant, it was just their excuse, a pretext for further undermining Harriet's role within the corporation. They wanted to put a stop to everything that Henrik and Harriet had stood for."

"Idiots."

"My God, yes, but that didn't exactly help us. I remember those days. It was as if the rug had been pulled from under our feet, and I know, I know—I should have involved you more. But I thought we'd all benefit if we left you to concentrate on your stories."

"And still I didn't deliver anything decent."

"You tried, Mikael, you really tried. But what I'm coming to is that it was then, when it seemed as if we'd hit rock bottom, that Levin rang."

"Someone had presumably tipped him off about what had happened."

"Without a doubt, and I don't even need to tell you that I was sceptical at first. Serner felt like the trashiest sort of tabloid. But Levin gave it the works, with his usual torrent of words, and invited me down to his big new villa in Cannes."

"What?"

"Yes, I'm sorry, I didn't tell you that either. I suppose I felt ashamed. But I was going down to the film festival in any case, to do a profile on the Iranian film director. You know, the one being persecuted because she made the documentary about nineteen-year-old Sara, who had been stoned, and I didn't think it would do any harm if Serner helped us with the travel costs. In any event, Levin and I sat up all night and talked and I remained sceptical. He was absurdly boastful and came on with all this sales talk. But eventually I began to listen to him, and do you know why?"

"He was a fantastic lay?"

"Very funny, no, it was his relationship to you."

"Did he want to sleep with me, then?"

"He has boundless admiration for you."

"Bullshit."

"No, Mikael, that's where you're wrong. He loves his power and his money and his villa in Cannes. But more than that, it bugs him that he's not as cool as you. If we're talking cred, he's poor and you're stinking rich. Deep down he wants to be like you, I felt that right away, and yes, I should have realized that that sort of envy can become dangerous. You do know what the campaign against you is all about, don't you? Your uncompromising attitude makes people feel pathetic. Your very existence reminds them just how much they've sold out, and the more you're acclaimed, the punier they themselves appear. When it's like that the only way they can fight back is by dragging you down. The bullshit gives them back a little bit of dignity—at least that's what they imagine."

"Thanks, Erika, but I really couldn't care less about that campaign."

"I know, at least I hope I do. But what I realized was that Levin really wanted to be in with us, and feel like one of us. He wanted some of our reputation to rub off on him and I thought that was a good incentive. If his ambition was to be cool like you then it would be devastating for him to turn *Millennium* into a run-of-the-mill commercial Serner product. If he became known as the man who destroyed one of the most fabled magazines in Sweden, any cred he might still have would be scuttled for good. That's why I really believed him when he said that both he and the Group needed a prestigious magazine, and that he only wanted to help us produce the kind of journalism we believed in. Admittedly he did want to be involved in the magazine, but I put that down to vanity, that he wanted to be able to show off and say to his yuppie friends that he was our spin doctor or something. I never thought he would dare to have a go at the magazine's soul."

"And yet that's precisely what he's doing now."

"Unfortunately, yes."

"And where does that leave your fancy psychological theory?"

"I underestimated the power of opportunism. As you saw, Levin and Serner's behaviour were exemplary before this campaign against you got going, but since then . . ."

"He's been taking advantage of it."

"No, no, somebody else has. Somebody who wanted to get at him. I only realized later that Levin didn't have an easy time persuading the others to support him in buying a stake in the magazine. As you might imagine, not everybody at Serner suffers from a journalistic inferiority complex. Most of them are just ordinary businessmen. They despise all talk of standing up for things that matter. They were irritated by what they described as Levin's 'fake idealism,' and in the campaign against you they saw an opportunity to put the squeeze on him."

"Dear, oh dear."

"You have no idea. At first it looked OK. We were to adapt somewhat to the market, and, as you know, I thought some of that sounded pretty good. I have, after all, spent a fair amount of time wondering how we could reach a younger readership. I really thought that Levin and I were having a productive dialogue so I didn't worry too much about his presentation today."

"I noticed that."

"But that was before all hell broke loose."

"What are you talking about?"

"The uproar when you sabotaged his presentation."

"I didn't sabotage anything, Erika. I just left."

Berger lay in the bath, took a sip of her wine, and then she smiled a wistful smile.

"When will you learn that you're Mikael Blomkvist?" she said.

"I thought I was beginning to get the hang of that."

"Apparently not, because otherwise you'd have realized that when Mikael Blomkvist walks out in the middle of a presentation about his own magazine it's a big deal, whether Mikael Blomkvist intends it to be or not."

"In that case I apologize for my sabotage."

"I'm not blaming you, not anymore. Now I'm the one saying 'sorry,' as you can see. I'm the one who's put us in this position. It probably would have gone pear-shaped anyway, whether you'd walked out or not. They were just waiting for an excuse to take a swing at us."

"What actually happened?"

"After you disappeared we all felt deflated, and Levin, whose self-esteem had taken yet another knock, no longer gave a damn about his presentation. 'There's no point,' he said. He rang his boss to report back, and he probably laid it on a bit thick. I suspect that the envy on which I had been pinning my hopes had changed into something petty and spiteful. He was back again after an hour or so and said that the Group was prepared to give *Millennium* its full backing and use all its channels to market the magazine."

"You didn't like the sound of that."

"No, and I knew before he'd even said one word about it. You could tell by the look on his face. It radiated a mixture of fear and triumph and at first he couldn't find the right words. He was mostly waffling and said that the Group wanted to have more insight into the business, plus content aimed at a younger readership, plus more celebrity news. But then . . ."

Berger shut her eyes, drew her hand through her wet hair, then knocked back the last of her wine.

"Yes?"

"He said that he wanted you off the editorial team."

"He *what*?"

"Of course neither he nor the Group could say it straight out, still less could they afford to get headlines like 'Serner sacks Blomkvist,' so Ove put it neatly by saying that he wanted you to have a freer rein and be allowed to concentrate on what you're best at: writing reportage. He suggested a strategic relocation to London and a generous stringer arrangement."

"London?"

"He said that Sweden's too small for a guy of your calibre, but you get what this is about."

"They think they can't push through their changes if I stay on the editorial team?"

"Something like that. Still, I don't think any of them was surprised when Christer, Malin, and I just said no, that it wasn't even negotiable. Not to mention Andrei's reaction."

"What did he do?"

"I'm almost embarrassed to tell you. Andrei stood up and said that it was the most shameful thing he'd heard in his whole life. That you were one of the best things we had in this country, a source of pride for democracy and journalism, and that the whole Serner Group should hang their heads in shame. He said that you were a great man."

"He does tend to exaggerate."

"But he's a good kid."

"He really is. What did the Serner people do then?"

"Levin was prepared for it, of course. 'You're always welcome to buy us out,' he said. 'It's just—'"

"That the price has gone up," Blomkvist completed the sentence.

"Exactly. He claimed that whichever basis you use for valuing the business would show that any price for Serner's interest should be at least double what it was when the Group went in, given the additional value and goodwill they've created."

"Goodwill! Have they gone mad?"

"Not at all, apparently, but they're bright, and they want to mess us about. And I wonder if they don't want to kill two birds with one stone: pull off a good deal and get rid of a competitor by breaking us financially, all in one go."

"What the hell should we do?"

"What we're best at, Mikael: slug it out. I'll take some of my own money and we'll buy them out and fight to make this northern Europe's best magazine."

"Sure, Erika, but then what? We'll end up with a lousy financial situation which even you won't be able to do anything about."

"I know, but it'll be OK. We've come through more difficult situations than this. You and I can waive our salaries for a while. We can manage, can't we?"

"Everything has to end some time, Erika."

"Don't say that. Ever."

"Not even if it's true?"

"Especially not then."

"Right."

"Don't you have anything in the pipeline?" she said. "Something, anything that will stun Sweden's media?"

Blomkvist hid his face in his hands and for some reason he thought of Pernilla, his daughter. She had said that unlike him she was going to write "for real," whatever it was that was not "real" about his writing.

"I don't think so," he said.

Berger smacked her hand hard on the bath water so that it splashed out onto his socks.

"Jesus, you must have something. There's no-one in this country who gets as many tip-offs as you do."

"Most of it's junk," he said. "But maybe . . . I was just in the process of checking something."

Berger sat up in the tub.

"What?"

"No, it's nothing," he backtracked. "Only wishful thinking."

"In a situation like this we have to think wishfully."

"Yes, but it's a load of smoke and nothing you can prove."

"Yet there's something inside you that believes in it, isn't there?"

"Maybe, but that's because of one little detail which doesn't have anything to do with the story itself."

"What?"

"That my old comrade-in-arms has also been at the story."

"The one with a capital S?"

"The very one."

"Well, that does sound promising," Berger said, and stepped out of the bath, naked and beautiful.

# CHAPTER 8

# NOVEMBER 20—EVENING

August was kneeling on the chequered floor in the bedroom, looking at a still-life arrangement with a lit candle on a blue plate, two green apples, and an orange which his father had set out for him. But nothing was happening. August stared emptily out at the storm and Balder wondered: Does it make sense to present the boy with a subject?

His son only had to glance at something for it to be embedded in his mind, so why should his father of all people choose what he was supposed to draw? August must have thousands of images of his own in his head. Maybe a plate and some pieces of fruit were as wrong as could be. Once again Balder asked himself: Was the boy trying to convey something in particular with his traffic light? The drawing was no casual little observation. On the contrary, the stop light shone like a baleful glowering eye and maybe—what did Balder know?—August had felt threatened by the man on that pedestrian crossing.

Balder looked at his son for the umpteenth time that day. It was shameful, wasn't it? He used to think that August was simply weird and unfathomable. Now he wondered if he and his son were not in actual fact alike. When Balder was young, the doctors did not go in so much for diagnoses. In those days, there was a far greater tendency to dismiss people as being odd. He himself had definitely been different from other children, much too serious—his facial expression never changed—and no-one on the school playground thought he was much fun. Nor did he find the other children particularly entertaining either—he sought refuge in numbers and equations and avoided talking more than he was required to.

He would probably not have been considered autistic in the same sense as August. But nowadays they probably would have stuck an Asperger's label on him. He and Hanna had believed that the early diagnosis of August would help them, yet so little had been done, and it was only now, now that his son was eight, that Balder discovered the boy had a special mathematical and spatial talent. How come Hanna and Westman had not noticed?

Even if Westman was a bastard, Hanna was fundamentally a sensitive and good person. Balder would never forget their first meeting. It was an evening function of the IVA, the Royal Swedish Academy of Engineering Sciences, at Stockholm's Rådhuset, where he was being given some prize that he cared nothing about. He had spent a boring evening longing to get home to his computer when a beautiful woman whom he vaguely recognized—Balder's knowledge of the world of celebrity was limited—came up to him and started to talk. Balder still thought of himself as the nerd from Tappström school who got nothing but contemptuous looks from the girls. He could not understand what a woman like Hanna saw in him. At the time—as he was soon to find out—she was at the height of her career. But she seduced him and made love to him that night like no woman had done before. Then followed maybe the happiest time in his life and yet . . . the binary codes won out over love.

He worked until the marriage fell apart. Lasse Westman arrived on the scene and Hanna went downhill and probably August did as well, which should of course have made Balder wild with fury. But he knew that he too was to blame. He had bought his freedom and not bothered about his son and perhaps what was said during the custody hearing was true, that he had chosen the dream of artificial life over that of his own child. What a monumental idiot he had been.

He got out his laptop and went on Google to learn more about savant skills. He had already ordered a number of books, and in his usual way meant to teach himself everything there was to know. No damn psychologist or educationalist would be able to catch him out and tell him what August needed at this point. He would know that better than any of them and so he continued searching until his attention was caught by the story of an autistic girl called Nadia.

What happened to her was described in Lorna Selfe's book *Nadia: A Case of Extraordinary Drawing Ability in an Autistic Child* and in Oliver

Sacks's *The Man Who Mistook His Wife for a Hat.* Balder read in fascination. It was a gripping story and in many ways there were parallels. Like August, Nadia had seemed perfectly healthy when she was born, and only gradually did her parents realize that something was amiss.

The girl did not start speaking. She did not look people in the eye. She disliked physical contact and did not respond to her mother's smiles or attempts at communication. She was for the most part quiet and withdrawn and compulsively tore paper into narrow strips. By the time she was six she had still not spoken a word.

Yet she could draw like Leonardo da Vinci. Already at the age of three, and out of the blue, she had begun to draw horses. Unlike other children she did not begin with the entire animal, but instead with some little detail, a hoof, a rider's boot, a tail, and the strangest thing of all was that she drew fast. In a tearing hurry she put together the parts, one here, one there, until she had a perfect whole, a horse which galloped or walked. From his own efforts when he was a teenager, Balder knew how exceptionally difficult it is to draw an animal in motion. However hard you try, the result is unnatural or stiff. It takes a master to tease out the lightness in the movements. Nadia was a master already at the age of three.

Her horses were like perfect stills, drawn with a light touch, and obviously not the result of any long training. Her virtuosity burst out like a breaking dam, and that fascinated her contemporaries. How was it possible for her to leapfrog centuries of development in the history of art with just a few quick hand movements? The Australian specialists Allan Snyder and John Mitchell studied the drawings and in 1999 presented a theory, which has gradually won general acceptance, to the effect that we all have an inherited capacity to reach that level of virtuosity, but that in most of us it is blocked.

If we see a football, for example, we do not immediately understand that it is a three-dimensional object. Instead, the brain processes a series of details at lightning speed: the way in which shadows fall and the differences in depth and nuance, from which it then draws certain conclusions about shape. We are not conscious of this. But it requires an examination of the separate parts before we can register something as simple as the fact that what we see is a ball and not a circle.

It is the brain which then produces the final form and, when it does, we no longer see all the detail we first registered. We cannot see the trees for the forest, so to speak. But what struck Mitchell and Snyder was that if only we could reproduce the original image in our minds, we would be able to see the world in an entirely new way, and perhaps even re-create it, as Nadia had done without any training whatsoever.

Nadia saw the myriad details before they had been processed, which is why she began each time with an individual part, such as a hoof or a nose, because the totality as we perceive it did not yet exist in her mind. Balder found the idea appealing, even if he saw a number of problems with the theory, or at least had a number of questions.

In many ways this was the sort of original thinking he always looked for in his research; an approach which took nothing for granted but looked beyond the obvious, down to the small details. He grew more obsessed with the subject and read on with increasing fascination until, quite suddenly, he shuddered and even swore out loud, staring at his son with a stab of anxiety. It had nothing to do with the research findings, rather with the description of Nadia's first year at school.

Nadia had been put in a school for autistic children, where the teaching was focused on getting her to talk for the first time. The girl made some progress—the words came, one by one. But there was a high price to pay. As she started to talk, her brilliance with crayons disappeared and, according to the author Lorna Selfe, it was likely that one language was being replaced by another. From having been an artistic genius, Nadia became a severely handicapped autistic girl who was able to speak a little but who had entirely lost the gift that had astounded the world. Was it worth it, just to be able to say a few words?

No, Balder wanted to shout out, possibly because he had always been prepared to do whatever it took to become a genius in his field. Anything but the ordinary! That had been his guiding principle all his life, and yet . . . he was clever enough to understand that his own elitist principles were not necessarily a good pointer to the right way forward now. Maybe a few fabulous drawings were nothing as compared to being able to ask for a glass of milk, or exchange a few words with a friend, or a father. What did he know?

Yet he refused to be faced with such a choice. He could not bear to give up the most wonderful thing that had happened in August's life. No . . . that was simply not an option. No parent should have to decide. After all, no-one could anticipate what was best for the child.

The more he thought about it, the more unreasonable it seemed, and it occurred to him that he did not believe it, or perhaps that he simply did not *want* to believe it. Nadia's was after all only one case.

He had to find out more. But just then his mobile rang. It had been ringing a lot over the last few hours. One call had been from a withheld number and another from Linus, his former assistant. He had less and less time for Linus; he was not even sure he trusted him—certainly he did not feel like talking to him now.

Yet he answered, maybe out of sheer nervousness. It was Gabriella Grane, the lovely analyst at the Security Police, and that put a little smile on his face. After Farah Sharif, Gabriella came a close second. She had sparklingly beautiful eyes and she was sharp-witted. He had a weakness for smart women.

"Gabriella," he said. "I'd love to talk, but I don't have the time. I'm right in the middle of something."

"You've definitely got time for what I have to tell you," she said with uncharacteristic severity. "You're in danger."

"Oh, nonsense, Gabriella! I told you, they may try to sue the shirt off my back—but that's all."

"Frans, I'm sorry, but some new information has come through, and from an extremely well-informed source at that. There does appear to be a genuine risk."

"What do you mean?" he said, distracted. With the telephone clamped between his shoulder and ear, he was skimming another article on Nadia's lost gift.

"I'm finding it hard to assess the information, I admit, but it's worrying me, Frans. It does have to be taken seriously."

"In that case, I promise I'll be extra-careful. I'll stay indoors as usual. But I'm a bit busy just now, as I was saying. Besides, I'm all but convinced that you're wrong. At Solifon—"

"Sure, sure, I could be wrong," she cut in. "That's possible. But what if I'm right, what if there's even a tiny risk that I am?"

"Well—"

"Frans, listen to me. I think you're right. Nobody at Solifon wants to do you physical harm. It's a civilized company, after all. But it seems as if someone or even more than one person in the company is in touch with a criminal organization operating out of Russia and Sweden. That's where the threat is coming from."

Balder took his eyes off the computer screen for the first time. He knew that Zigmund Eckerwald, head of a special division of Solifon, was cooperating with a group of criminals. He had even picked up some codenames for the leader of that group, but could not understand why they would go after him. Or could he?

"A criminal organization?" he muttered.

"Yes," Grane said. "And isn't it logical, in a way? That's more or less what you've been saying, isn't it? That once you've started stealing someone else's ideas, and made money from them, then you've already crossed the line. It's downhill from there on."

"I think what I actually said was that all you needed was a gang of lawyers and you could safely steal whatever you like. Lawyers are the hit men of our times."

"OK, maybe so. But listen to me: I haven't yet got approval for your personal protection, so I want to move you to a secret location. I'm coming to collect you."

"What are you saying?"

"I think we have to act immediately."

"Not a chance. Me and . . ."

He hesitated.

"Do you have someone else there?"

"No, no, but I can't go anywhere right now."

"Aren't you listening to what I'm saying?"

"I hear you loud and clear. But with all due respect it sounds to me as if it's mostly speculation."

"Speculation is an essential tool in assessing risk, Frans. And the person who got in touch with me . . . I suppose I shouldn't really be saying this . . . is an agent from the NSA who has this particular organization under surveillance."

"The NSA!" He snorted.

"I know you're sceptical of them."

"Sceptical doesn't even begin to describe it."

"OK. But this time they're on your side, at least this agent is. She's a good person. By eavesdropping she's picked up something which could very well be a plan to eliminate you."

"Me?"

"There's a lot to suggest that."

"'Could very well' and 'suggest' . . . it all sounds vague."

August reached for his pencils, and Balder concentrated on that for a moment.

"I'm staying where I am," he said.

"You've got to be joking."

"No, I'm not. I'd be happy to move if you get more information, but not right now. Besides, the alarm Milton installed is excellent. I've got cameras and sensors everywhere. And you know I'm a stubborn bastard."

"Do you have a weapon of any kind?"

"What's got into you, Gabriella? A weapon! The most dangerous thing I own is my new cheese slicer."

"You know . . ." she said, letting the words hang.

"Yes?"

"I'm going to arrange protection for you, whether you want it or not. I doubt you'll even notice it. But since you're going to be so damn obstinate, I have another piece of advice for you."

"Tell me."

"Go public. Tell the media what you know—then if you're lucky there'll be no point in someone getting rid of you."

"I'll think about it." Balder had detected a note of distraction in Grane's voice. "Yes?" he said.

"Wait a moment," she said. "I've got someone else on the line. I have to . . ."

She was gone, and Balder, who should have had much else to mull over, found himself thinking of only one thing: Will August lose his ability to draw if I teach him to talk?

"Are you still there?" Grane asked after a short while.

"Of course."

"I'm afraid I have to go. But I promise to see to it that you get some sort of protection as rapidly as possible. I'll be in touch. Take care!"

He hung up with a sigh and thought again of Hanna, and of August and the chequered floor reflected in the wardrobe doors, and of all kinds of things which seemed irrelevant just then. Almost absentmindedly he said to himself, "They're after me."

He could see that it was not unreasonable, even though he had always refused to believe that it would actually come to violence. But what, in fact, did he know? Nothing. Besides, he could not be bothered to address it now. He continued his search for information on Nadia, and what implications this might have for his son, but that was insane. He was burying his head in the sand. Despite Grane's warning he kept surfing and soon came upon the name of a professor of neurology, an expert on savant syndrome named Charles Edelman. Instead of reading on as he normally would—Balder always preferred the written to the spoken word—he called the switchboard at the Karolinska Institute.

He soon realized how late it was. Edelman was unlikely to be at work still, and his home number was not on the website. But wait a moment . . . he was also the head of Ekliden, an institution for autistic children with special abilities. Balder tried calling there. The telephone rang a number of times before a woman answered and introduced herself as Nurse Lindros.

"I'm sorry to disturb you so late in the evening," Balder said. "I'm looking for Professor Edelman. Might he possibly still be there?"

"Yes, in fact he is. No-one is setting off for home in this dreadful weather. Who may I say is calling?"

"Frans Balder," he said, and in case it might help he added: "Professor Frans Balder."

"Just a moment," Nurse Lindros said, "I'll see if he's available."

Balder stared down at August, who was once again gripping his pencil hesitantly, and that worried him somehow, as if it were an ominous sign. "A criminal organization," he muttered again.

"Charles Edelman," a voice said. "Am I really talking to Professor Balder?"

"The very same. I have a little—"

"You can't know what an honour this is," Edelman said. "I'm just back from a conference at Stanford where we discussed your work on neural networks; in fact we were even asking ourselves if we neurologists don't have a great deal to learn about the brain through the back door, as it were, through AI research. We were wondering—"

"I'm flattered," Balder interrupted. "But right now I have a quick question for you."

"Oh, really? Is it something to do with your research?"

"Not at all. I have an autistic son. He's eight years old and hasn't yet said a single word, but the other day we passed a traffic light on Hornsgatan and afterwards . . ."

"Yes?"

"He just sat down and drew it at lightning speed, completely perfectly. It was astonishing!"

"And you want me to come and take a look at what he's done?"

"I'd like that. But that's not why I called. The fact is that I'm worried. I've read that perhaps drawing is the way in which he interacts with the world around him, and that he might lose this ability if he learns to talk."

"I can tell you've been reading about Nadia."

"How do you know that?"

"Because she's always mentioned in this context. But . . . may I call you Frans?"

"Of course."

"Excellent, Frans, and I'm so glad you called. I can tell you straightaway that you have nothing to worry about, on the contrary. Nadia is the exception that proves the rule, no more than that. All research shows that speech development actually enhances savant abilities. It can happen, of course, that children lose those skills, but that is mostly due to other factors. They get bored, or there's a significant event in their lives. You probably read that Nadia lost her mother."

"I did."

"Maybe that was the reason, even though neither I nor anyone else can know for sure. But there's virtually no other documented case of a similar evolution, and I'm not just saying this off the top of my head, or because it happens to be my own hypothesis. There is broad consensus today to the effect that savants have everything to gain from developing their intellectual skills on all levels."

"Do you mean that?"

"Yes, definitely."

"He's also good at numbers."

"Really?" Edelman said thoughtfully.

"Why do you say that?"

"Because it is extremely rare for artistic ability to be combined with mathematical talent in a savant. These two different skills have nothing in common, and sometimes they seem even to block each other."

"But that's how it is with my son. There's a kind of geometric precision about his drawings, as if he had worked out the exact proportions."

"How fascinating. When can I see him?"

"I don't know. For the time being I only wanted some advice."

"In that case my advice is clear: Make an effort with the boy. Stimulate him. Let him develop his skills in every way."

"I . . ." Balder felt a strange pressure in his chest and found it hard to get the words out. "I want to thank you," he said. "Really thank you. Now I have to . . ."

"It's been such an honour to talk to you, it would be wonderful to be able to meet you and your son. I've developed quite a sophisticated test for savants, if I may boast a little. I could help you get to know the boy better."

"Yes, of course, that would be terrific. But now I must . . ." Balder mumbled, without knowing what he wanted to say. "Goodbye, and thank you."

"Oh, my pleasure. I hope to hear from you again soon."

Balder hung up and sat still for a moment, his hands crossed over his chest, and looked at his son. August was still looking at the burning candle, the yellow pencil in his hand. A shudder went across Balder's shoulders, and the tears came. Whatever else you might say about Professor Balder, he was not one to cry easily.

In fact he could not remember when it had last happened. Not when his mother died, and definitely not when watching or reading anything. He thought of himself as a block of stone. But now, in front of his son with his rows of pencils and crayons, the professor cried like a child and he just let it happen.

It had been Charles Edelman's words. August would be able to learn to speak and could keep drawing, and that was overwhelming news. But Balder was not crying just because of that. There was also the drama at

Solifon. The death threat. The secrets he was privy to and the longing for Hanna or Farah or anyone who could fill the gap in his heart.

"My little boy!" he said, so emotional he failed to notice his laptop switch itself on and show pictures from one of the surveillance cameras outside the house.

Out in the garden, in the blustering storm, there was a tall, thin man in a padded leather jacket, with a grey cap pulled down to conceal his face. Whoever it was knew that he was being filmed, and even if he seemed lean and agile there was something in his swaying walk which was reminiscent of a heavyweight boxer on his way into the ring.

Grane was sitting in her office at Säpo searching the Web and the agency's records. She did not really know what she was looking for. But something worrying was gnawing away at her.

Her conversation with Balder had been interrupted by Helena Kraft, chief of Säpo, who was looking for her again to discuss the same matter as before. Then Alona Casales at the NSA had called to continue their conversation; this time she sounded calmer, and again a little flirtatious.

"Have you managed to sort out your computers?" Grane said.

"Yes, that was a circus, but I don't think it's anything serious. I'm sorry if I was a little cryptic last time. I don't have much of a choice. I just want to stress again that the level of threat against Professor Balder is both real and serious, even though we know nothing for certain. Did you have time to deal with it?"

"I've spoken to him. He refuses to leave his house, told me he was in the middle of something. I'm going to arrange protection."

"Fine. As you might have guessed I've done more than quickly check you out. I'm very impressed, Miss Grane. Shouldn't someone like you be working for Goldman Sachs and earning millions?"

"Not my style."

"Not mine either. I wouldn't say no to the money, but this underpaid snooping is more my thing. Now, honey, here's the situation. As far as my colleagues are concerned this isn't a big deal—which I happen to disagree with. And not just because I'm convinced that this group represents a threat to our national economic interests. I also think there are political implications. One of those Russian computer engineers I mentioned, a guy called Anatoli Chabarov, is also linked to Ivan Gribanov, a member of the Russian Duma. He's notorious, and a major shareholder in Gazprom."

"I understand."

"But most of it so far is just dead ends. I've spent a lot of time trying to crack the identity of the person at the top."

"The man they call Thanos."

"Or woman."

"Woman?"

"I could be wrong. This type of group tends to *exploit* women, not promote them to leadership positions, and this figure has mostly been referred to as a he."

"Then what makes you think it might be a woman?"

"A sort of reverence, you could say. They talk about 'Thanos' in the same way men through the ages have spoken about women they desire."

"A beauty, in other words."

"Right. But maybe I'm just picking up some homoeroticism. Nothing would make me happier than if Russian gangsters and bigwigs were to indulge more in that department."

"Ha, true!"

"In fact I mention it only so that you'll keep an open mind if this mess ends up on your desk. You understand, there are also quite a few lawyers mixed up in it. What else is new, right? Hackers steal and lawyers legitimize the theft."

"True. Balder's said to me that we're equal before the law—if we pay the same amount."

"If you can afford a strong defence you can get away with whatever you want these days. You do know who Balder's legal opponents are, don't you? The Washington firm, Dackstone & Partner."

"Sure."

"In that case you know that the firm is also used by large tech companies to sue the shit out of inventors and innovators hoping to get some modest reward for their creations."

"I discovered that when we were dealing with the lawsuits of that inventor Håkan Lans."

"Grim, wasn't it? But the interesting thing is that Dackstone crops up in one of the few conversations we've managed to track down and decrypt from this criminal network, although there the firm is simply referred to as DP, or even D."

"So Solifon and these crooks have the same lawyers?"

"It looks like it, and that's not all. Dackstone is about to open an office in Stockholm—do you know how we found that out?"

"No," said Grane, who was beginning to feel stressed. She wanted to finish the conversation and ensure that Balder got police protection.

"Through our surveillance of this group," Casales went on. "Anatoli Chabarov mentions it in passing, which suggests that there are ties to the firm. They knew about the office opening even before it became public. Also Dackstone & Partner is setting up in Stockholm together with a Swedish lawyer named Brodin. He used to be a criminal lawyer, and if you remember he was known for getting a little too cozy with his clients."

"I do remember that classic picture in the evening papers—Kenny Brodin out on the town with some gangsters, his hands all over some call girl," Grane said.

"I saw that. I'd bet Mr. Brodin is a good place to start if you want to check out this story. Who knows, maybe he's the link between big business and this group."

"I'll take a look at it," Grane said. "But right now I've got a number of other things to deal with. I'm sure we'll be in touch again soon."

She called the duty officer for Säpo's Personal Protection Unit, who that evening was none other than Stig Yttergren. Her heart sank. Yttergren was sixty, overweight, known to be a heavy drinker, and most of all he liked to play cards online. He was sometimes called "Officer No-Can-Do." She proceeded to explain the situation in her most authoritative tone and demanded that Professor Frans Balder in Saltsjöbaden be given a bodyguard as quickly as possible. As usual Yttergren responded by saying that it would be extremely difficult, perhaps not possible at all. When she countered by saying that this was an order from the chief of Säpo herself, he muttered something which might even have been "that stroppy cunt."

"I didn't hear that," Grane said. "Just make sure this is put in place immediately." Which of course it was not. While she was waiting and drumming her fingers on her desk, she searched for information on Dackstone & Partner and anything else she could find linked to what Casales had been telling her—and that is when she was overcome by a sense of something horribly familiar.

She could not put her finger on it. Before she could find what she was looking for, Yttergren called back to say that no-one from Personal Protection was available. There was an unusual amount of activity for the royal family that evening, he said, some sort of public engagement with the Norwegian crown prince and princess, and the leader of the Swedish Democrats had had an ice cream thrown at his head before his guards could intervene, which meant that they had to provide reinforcements for his late speech in Södertälje.

So Yttergren had sent out "two great guys from the regular police," Peter Blom and Dan Flinck, and Grane had to make do with that, even if their names reminded her of Kling and Klang in *Pippi Longstocking.* For a moment she had serious misgivings. Then she got angry with herself.

It was so typical of her snobbish background to judge people by their names. She might have had more cause for concern if they had a posh name like Gyllentofs or something and been irresponsible layabouts. *I'm sure this'll be fine,* she thought.

She got back to work. It was going to be a long night.

# CHAPTER 9

# NOVEMBER 20–21—NIGHT

Salander woke up lying straight across the king-size bed and realized that she had been dreaming about her father. A feeling of menace swept over her like a cloak. But then she remembered the start of the evening and concluded that it could as easily be a chemical reaction in her body. She had a terrible hangover. She got up on wobbly legs and went into the large bathroom—with the jacuzzi and the marble and all the idiotic luxuries—to be sick. But nothing happened, she just sank to the floor, breathing heavily.

Then she stood up and looked at herself in the mirror, which was not particularly encouraging either. Her eyes were red. On the other hand it was not long after midnight. She must have slept for only a few hours. She took a glass from the bathroom cupboard and filled it with water. But at the same moment the details of her dream came flooding back and she crushed the glass in her hand. Blood dripped to the floor, and she swore and realized that she was unlikely to be going back to sleep.

Should she try to crack the encrypted NSA file she had downloaded? No, that would be pointless, at least for now. Instead she wound a towel around her hand and took from her bookshelves a new study by Princeton physicist Julie Tammet, which described how a big star collapses into a black hole. She lay down on the sofa by the windows overlooking Slussen and Riddarfjärden.

As she began to read she felt a little better. Blood from the towel did seep onto the pages and her head would not stop hurting, but she became more and more engrossed in the book, every now and then making a note in the margin. None of it was new to her. She knew better than most that a star stays alive as a result of two opposing actions, the fusion at its core forcing it outwards and the gravitational pull keeping it together. She saw it as a balancing act, a tug of war from which a victor eventually emerges, once the fuel for the reactions runs out and the explosions weaken.

When gravity gains the upper hand, the celestial body shrinks like a punctured balloon and becomes smaller and smaller. In this way, a star can vanish into nothing. Salander liked black holes. She felt an affinity to them.

Yet, like Julie Tammet, she was not interested in black holes per se, but rather in the process which creates them. Salander was convinced that if only she could describe that process, she would be able to draw together the two irreconcilable languages of the universe, quantum physics and the theory of relativity. But it was no doubt beyond her capabilities, just like the bloody encryption, and inevitably she began again to think about her father.

When she was a child, that revolting specimen had raped her mother over and over again, right up until the time her mother received injuries from which she would never recover. Salander herself, then twelve, hit back with a horrific force. At the time she could have no idea that her father was an important spy who had defected from the GRU, the Soviet military intelligence service, nor could she know that a special department within the Swedish Security Police, referred to as the Section, was protecting him at any cost. Yet even then she understood that there was some mystery surrounding the man, a darkness no-one was allowed to approach in any way. That even applied to so simple a thing as his name: Zala, or Alexander Zalachenko, to be more precise.

Other fathers could be reported to the social services and the police. But Zala had forces behind him which were above all that.

It was this and one other thing which for her were true black holes.


The alarm went off at 1:18 a.m. and Balder woke with a start. Was there someone in the house? He felt an inexplicable fear and reached across the bed. August was lying beside him. The boy must have crept in as usual, and now he whimpered with worry, as if the wailing of the siren had made its way into his dreams. My little boy, Balder thought. Then he stiffened. Were those footsteps?

No, he must be imagining things. All you could hear was the alarm. He cast a worried look towards the storm beyond the windows. It seemed to have grown worse. The sea was beating against the jetty and the shore. The windowpanes shook and arched. Could the alarm have been set off by a gust of wind? Perhaps it was as simple as that.

He still had to check to see if that protection Gabriella Grane was organizing had arrived at last. Two men from the regular police were supposed to have been there hours ago. It was a farce. They had been delayed by the storm and by a series of conflicting orders. It was either one thing or another and he agreed with Grane, it seemed hopelessly incompetent.

He would have to deal with that in due course. Now he had to make a call. But August was beginning to wake up and a hysterical child banging his body against the headboard was the last thing Balder needed right now. The earplugs, it occurred to him, those old green earplugs he had bought at Frankfurt airport.

He took them from the bedside table and gently pushed them into his son's ears. Then he tucked him in and kissed him on the cheek and stroked his curly, tousled hair, straightened the collar on the boy's pyjamas, and made sure that his head was resting comfortably on the pillow. Balder was frightened and should have been in a hurry, or had every reason to be. Yet he took his time and fussed over his son. Perhaps it was a sentimental moment in the midst of a crisis. Or he wanted to put off confronting whatever awaited him out there. For a moment he wished he did have a weapon. Not that he would have known how to use it.

He was a programmer, for heaven's sake, who had developed some paternal instinct in his old age, that was all. He should never have gotten into this mess. To hell with Solifon and the NSA and all criminal gangs! But now he had to get a grip. With stealthy, uncertain steps he went into the hallway, and before doing anything else, before even looking out at the road, he turned off the alarm. The racket had set his nerves on edge and in the sudden silence which followed he stood stock-still. Then his mobile rang and even though it startled him he was grateful for the distraction.

"Yes," he said.

"Hello, this is Jonas Anderberg, I'm on duty tonight at Milton Security. Is everything all right?"

"What, well . . . I think so. My alarm went off."

"I know that and, according to our instructions, when this happens you're supposed to go down to a special room in the cellar and lock the door. Are you down there?"

"Yes," he lied.

"Good, very good. Do you know what's happened?"

"No idea. The alarm woke me up. I have no clue what set it off. Could it have been the storm?"

"Unlikely . . . One moment please."

Anderberg's voice sounded a bit unfocused.

"What is it?" Balder said nervously.

"It seems . . ."

"For God's sake, tell me what's going on."

"Sorry, just take it easy, take it easy . . . I'm going through the picture sequence from your cameras, and it does look as if . . ."

"As if what?"

"As if you've got a visitor. A man, well, you can see for yourself later, a lanky man with dark glasses and a cap has been prowling around your property. He's been there twice, as far as I can see, but as I said . . . I've only just noticed it now. I'd have to look at it more closely to be able to say more."

"What sort of person is it?"

"Well, it's hard to say."

Anderberg seemed to be studying the picture sequences again.

"But maybe . . . I don't know . . . no, it's too soon to be speculating," he said.

"Go on, please go on. I need something specific. It would make me feel better."

"OK, in that case there's at least one reassuring thing I can tell you."

"And what's that?"

"His walk. The man walks like a junkie—like a guy who's just taken a load of speed. There's something cocky and stilted about the way he moves, and that could be a sign that he's just an ordinary druggie and petty thief. On the other hand . . ."

"Yes?"

"He's done a very good job of hiding his face and then . . ."

Anderberg fell silent again.

"Keep going!"

"One moment."

"You're making me nervous, you know that?"

"Don't mean to. But you know . . ."

Balder froze. The sound of a car engine could be heard from his garage drive.

". . . you're getting a visitor."

"What should I do?"

"Stay where you are."

"OK," said Balder, more or less paralyzed. But he was not where Anderberg thought he was.

When the telephone rang at 1:58, Blomkvist was still awake. But his mobile was in the pocket of his jeans on the floor and he did not manage to answer it in time. In any case the call was from a withheld number, so he swore and crawled back into bed and closed his eyes.

He could really do without another sleepless night. Ever since Berger had fallen asleep a little before midnight, he had been tossing and turning and thinking about his life. Not much of it felt right, not even his relationship with Berger. He had loved her for many years, and there was every reason to think that she felt the same way about him. But it was no longer as simple as it had once been. Perhaps Blomkvist had started to feel some sympathy for Greger. Greger Beckman was Erika's husband, an artist, and he could not be accused of being grudging or small-minded. On the contrary, when Greger had realized that Erika would never get over Blomkvist or even be able to stop herself from tearing his clothes off, he had not lost his temper. He had made a deal:

"You can be with him—just so long as you always come back to me." And that's how it became.

They set up an unconventional arrangement with Berger mostly sleeping at home with her husband in Saltsjöbaden, but sometimes here with Blomkvist on Bellmansgatan. Over the years Blomkvist had thought that it really was an ideal solution, one which many couples who lived under the dictatorship of monogamy ought to have adopted. Every time Berger said

"I love my husband more when I can also be with you," or when at some cocktail party Beckman put his arm around him in a brotherly embrace, Blomkvist had thanked his lucky stars for the arrangement.

Yet he had lately begun to have doubts, perhaps because he had had more time to think and it had occurred to him that an agreement is not necessarily always agreeable to all.

On the contrary, one party might advance their self-interest under the guise of a common decision, and in the long run it often becomes clear that someone is suffering, despite assurances to the contrary. Berger's call to her husband that evening evidently had not been well received. Who knows, maybe Beckman was also lying awake right now.

Blomkvist tried to put it out of his mind. For a little while he even tried daydreaming. But that did not help much, and in the end he got up, determined to do something more useful. Why not do some reading on industrial espionage or, better still, sketch out an alternative funding plan for *Millennium*? He got dressed, sat down at his computer, and checked his in-box.

Most of it was rubbish as usual, even if some of the e-mails did give him a bit of a boost. There were shouts of encouragement from Malm and Eriksson, also from Andrei Zander and Harriet Vanger in the light of the coming battle with Serner, and he answered them with more of a fighting spirit than he actually felt. After that he checked Salander's document, without expecting to find anything there. But then he lit up. She had answered. For the first time in ages she had given a sign of life:

```
<Balder's intelligence isn't in the least bit
artificial. How's your own these days?>
<And what happens, Blomkvist, if we create a
machine which is a little bit cleverer than we
are?>
```

Blomkvist smiled and thought of the last time they had met at Kaffebar on St. Paulsgatan. It took a while before he noticed that her message contained two questions, the first one a friendly little jibe which perhaps regrettably contained a grain of truth. What he had written in the magazine lately had lacked intelligence and genuine newsworthiness. Like so many journalists, he had just been plugging away, occasionally trotting out clichés. But that's how it was for the moment and he was much keener to ponder Salander's second question, her riddle, not so much because in itself it interested him especially, but because he wanted to think of some clever response.

If we create a machine that is cleverer than we ourselves are, he thought, what happens then? He went to the kitchen, opened a bottle of Ramlösa mineral water, and sat at the kitchen table. Downstairs Fru Gerner was coughing rather painfully, and in the distance amid the hubbub of the city an ambulance wailed away in the storm. Well, he mused, then we get a machine that can do all the clever things which we ourselves can do, plus a little bit more, for example . . . He laughed out loud and understood the point of the question. A machine like that could go on to produce something more intelligent than itself in turn, and then what happens?

The same would be true of the next machine and the next one and the next one, and soon the very source of it all, man himself, would be no more interesting to the latest computer than a lab rat. An explosion of intelligence beyond all control, as in the *Matrix* films. Blomkvist smiled and went back to his computer and wrote:

```
<If we create such a machine then we'll get a
world where not even Lisbeth is so cocksure.>
```

After that he sat looking out through the window, insofar as one could see anything beyond the swirling snow. Every now and then he looked through the open door at Berger, who was sleeping soundly and who knew nothing about machines more intelligent than human beings, or at least was not concerned about that right now.

He thought he heard his mobile give a ping, and sure enough: he had a new voicemail. That worried him, he was not sure why. Apart from ex-girlfriends who call when they're drunk and want to have sex, you usually only get bad news at night. The voice in the message sounded harried:

*My name is Frans Balder. I know it's rude to call this late. I apologize for that. But my situation has become somewhat critical, at least that's how I see it. I've just discovered that you were looking for me, which is really a strange coincidence. There are a few things I've been wanting to tell you about for some time now, I think they might interest you. I'd be grateful if you could get in touch as soon as possible. I have a feeling that this might be a bit urgent.*

Balder left a telephone number and an e-mail address and Blomkvist jotted them down and sat still for a while, drumming his fingers on the kitchen table. Then he dialled the number.

Balder was lying in bed, agitated and scared. Yet he was feeling a little calmer now. The car coming up his drive had been the police guard arriving at long last. Two men in their forties, one tall and one quite short, both looking cocky and with the same short, trendy haircut. But they were perfectly polite and apologized for the delay in taking up their post.

"Milton Security and Gabriella Grane at the Security Police briefed us on the situation," one said.

They were aware that a man wearing a cap and dark glasses had been snooping around the property and that they had to be on their guard. Therefore they turned down the offer of a cup of hot tea in the kitchen. They wanted to check out the house and Balder thought that sounded sensible. Otherwise they did not make a hugely positive impression, but then he did not get an overwhelmingly negative impression either. He had taken their telephone numbers and gone back to bed to join August, who was still sleeping, curled up with his green earplugs.

But Balder had not been able to fall asleep again. He was listening for noises out there in the storm and eventually he sat up in bed. He had to do something, or he would go mad. He checked his mobile. He had two messages from Linus Brandell, who sounded bad-tempered and defensive all at the same time. At first Balder felt like hanging up. But then he caught a couple of things which were interesting after all. Linus had spoken to Mikael Blomkvist at *Millennium* magazine and now Blomkvist wanted to get in touch and Balder began to think. "Mikael Blomkvist," he muttered.

Is he to be my link with the outside world?

Balder knew very little about Swedish journalists. But he did know who

Blomkvist was, and was aware of his reputation as someone who always went right to the heart of his stories, never yielding to pressure. That in itself did not necessarily make him the right man for the job—plus, somehow Balder seemed to recall hearing other, less flattering things—so he called Gabriella Grane again. She knew just about everything there was to know about the media scene and had said that she would be staying up late.

"Hello," she answered right away. "I was about to get in touch. I'm looking at that man on the CCTV. We really ought to move you now, you know."

"But, my God, Gabriella, the police are here—finally. They're sitting right outside the front door."

"There's nothing to suggest that the man will come through the front door."

"Why would he come back at all? The man from Milton said he looked like an old junkie."

"I'm not so sure about that. He was carrying some sort of box, something technical. We should play this safe."

Balder glanced at August lying next to him.

"I'm quite happy to move tomorrow. That might help my nerves. But I'm not going anywhere tonight—your policemen seem professional, professional enough at any rate."

"If you're going to be stubborn I'll see to it that Flinck and Blom make themselves conspicuous and cover the entire property."

"Fine, but that's not why I'm calling. You said I ought to go public, remember?"

"Well . . . yes . . . That's not the kind of advice you would expect from the Security Police, is it? I still think it would be a good idea, but first I'd like you to tell *us* what you know. I'm feeling a little apprehensive about this story."

"In that case let's talk tomorrow morning, when we've had a good sleep. But one thing, what do you think of Mikael Blomkvist at *Millennium*? Could he be the right sort of person to talk to?"

Grane gave a laugh.

"If you want my colleagues to have an apoplectic fit, then definitely talk to him."

"Is it as bad as that?"

"At Säpo people avoid him like the plague. If you find Blomkvist on your doorstep, then you know your whole year is shot, they say. Everybody here, including Helena Kraft, would advise against it in the strongest terms."

"But it's you I'm asking."

"Well, my answer is that your reasoning is sound. He's a damn fine journalist."

"Hasn't he also come in for some criticism?"

"For sure, people have been saying that he's past his prime and that his writing isn't positive or upbeat enough, or whatever. But he's an old-fashioned investigative reporter of the highest calibre. Do you have his contact details?"

"My ex-assistant gave them to me."

"Good, great. But before you get in touch with him, you must first tell us what you have. Do you promise?"

"I promise, Gabriella. Now I'm going to sleep for a few hours."

"Do that, and I'll keep in touch with Flinck and Blom and arrange a safe house for you first thing in the morning."

After he had hung up he tried again to get some sleep. But it proved as impossible this time as before. The storm made him increasingly restless and worried. It felt as if something evil was travelling across the sea towards him, and he could not help listening anxiously for any unusual sounds.

It was true that he had promised Grane he would talk to her first. But he could not wait—everything he had kept bottled up for so long was throbbing to get out. He knew it was irrational, nothing could be that urgent. It was the middle of the night and, regardless of what Grane had said, he was by any reckoning safer than he had been for a long time. He had police protection and a first-rate security system. But that did not help. He was agitated and so he got out the number Linus had given him and dialled it, but of course Blomkvist did not answer.

Why would he? It was far too late. Balder left a voice message instead in a slightly forced, whispered voice so as not to wake August. Then he got up and put on his bedside light. On the bookshelf by the bed there was some literature which had nothing to do with his work, and both absent-minded and worried, he flicked through an old novel by Stephen King, *Pet Sematary*. But that made him think even more about evil figures travelling through the night. For a long time he just stood there with the book in his hand—then he felt a stab of apprehension, which he might have dismissed as nonsense in broad daylight but which now seemed totally plausible. He had a sudden urge to speak to Farah or better still Steven Warburton at the Machine Intelligence Research Institute in Los Angeles, who would be certain to be awake, and while imagining all sorts of unpleasant scenarios, he looked out to sea and the night and the clouds scudding across the sky. At that moment his mobile rang, as if it had heard his prayer. But it was neither Farah nor Warburton.

"My name is Mikael Blomkvist," the voice said. "You've been looking for me."

"Correct. I'm sorry to have called so late."

"No problem. I was awake anyway."

"Can you talk now?"

"Absolutely, I was actually just answering a message from a person whom I think we both know. Lisbeth Salander."

"Who?"

"Sorry, maybe I've gotten hold of the wrong end of the stick. I thought you had hired her to go through your computers and trace a suspected data breach."

Balder laughed.

"Yes, my God, she's a strange girl, that one," he said. "She never revealed her surname, even though we had a lot of contact for a while. I assumed she had her reasons, and I never pushed her. I met her at one of my lectures at the Royal Institute of Technology. I'd be happy to tell you about it; it was pretty astonishing. But what I meant to ask was . . . well, you'll probably think it's a crazy idea."

"Sometimes I like crazy ideas."

"You wouldn't feel like coming over right now? It would mean a lot to me. I'm sitting on a story which I think could be explosive. I'll pay for your taxi here and back."

"Thanks, but I always pick up my own tab. Tell me, why do we have to talk now, in the middle of the night?"

"Because . . ." Balder hesitated. "Because I have a feeling this is urgent, or actually it's more than a feeling. I've just been told that I'm under threat, and an hour or so ago someone was snooping around my property. I'm frightened, to be honest, and I want to get this information off my chest. I no longer want to be the only one in the know."

"OK."

"OK what?"

"I'll come—if I can manage to get hold of a taxi."

Balder gave him the address and hung up, then called Professor Warburton in Los Angeles, and had an intense conversation with him on an encrypted line for about thirty minutes. Then he put on a pair of jeans and a black cashmere polo and went in search of a bottle of Amarone, in case that was the kind of thing Blomkvist might enjoy. But he got no further than the doorway before he started in fright.

He thought he had seen a movement, something flashing past, and looked anxiously towards the jetty and the sea. But it was the same desolate, storm-lashed scene as before, and he dismissed whatever it was as a figment of his imagination, a product of his nervous frame of mind, or at least he tried to. He left the bedroom and walked along the large window on his way towards the upper floor. Suddenly gripped by a new fear, he spun around again and this time he really did glimpse something over by the house next door.

A figure was racing along in the shelter of the trees, and even if Balder did not see the person for more than a matter of seconds, he could make out that it was a powerfully built man with a backpack and dark clothes. The man ran in a crouch and something about the way he moved had a trained look to it, as if he had run like that many times before, perhaps in a distant war.

It took a few moments for Balder to fumble for his mobile, and he tried to work out which of the numbers on his call list belonged to the policemen out there. He had not put their names into his contacts, and now was uncertain. With a shaking hand he tried one which he thought was right. No-one answered, not at first. The ring tone sounded three, four, five times before a voice panted out, "Blom here, what's up?"

"I saw a man running along the line of trees by my neighbour's house. I don't know where he is now. But he could very well be up by the road near you."

"OK, we'll check it out."

"He seemed . . ." Balder said.

"What?"

"I don't know, quick."

Dan Flinck and Peter Blom were sitting in the police car chatting about their young colleague, Anna Berzelius, and the size of her bum.

Both had recently gotten divorced. Their divorces had been painful at first. They both had young children, wives who felt let down, and parents-in-law who to varying degrees called them irresponsible shits. But once the dust had settled and they had gotten shared custody of the children and new, if modest, homes, they had both been struck by the same realization: that they missed their bachelor days. Lately, during the weeks when they were not looking after the kids, they had lived it up as never before. Afterwards, just like when they were in their teens, they had discussed all the parties in detail, especially the women they had met, reviewing their physiques from top to bottom, and their prowess in bed. But on this occasion they had not had time to discuss Anna Berzelius in as much depth as they would have liked.

Blom's mobile rang and they both jumped, partly because he had changed his ringtone to an extreme version of "Satisfaction," but mainly because the night and the storm and the emptiness out here had made them edgy. Besides, Blom had his telephone in his pocket, and since his trousers were tight—his waistline had expanded as a result of all the partying—it took a while before he could get it out. When he hung up he looked worried.

"What's that about?" Flinck said.

"Balder saw a man, a quick bastard apparently."

"Where?"

"Down by the trees next to the neighbour's house. The guy's probably on his way up towards us."

Blom and Flinck stepped out of the car. They had been outside many times over the course of this long night, but this was the first time they shivered right down to the bone. For an instant they just stood looking awkwardly to the right and the left, shocked by the cold. Then Blom—the taller of the two—took command and told Flinck to stay up by the road while he himself went down towards the water.

It was a short slope which extended along a wooden fence and a small avenue of newly planted trees. A lot of snow had fallen, it was slippery and at the bottom lay the sea. Baggensfjärden, Blom thought, and in fact he was surprised that the water had not frozen over, but that may have been because of the waves. Blom cursed at the storm and at this night duty which wore him out and ruined his beauty sleep. He tried to do his job all the same, not with his whole heart perhaps, but still.

He listened and looked around, and at first he could not pick out anything. It was dark. Only the light from a single lamppost shone into the property, immediately in front of the jetty, so he went down toward it, past a garden chair which had been flung about in the storm.

In the next moment he could see Balder through the large windowpane. Balder was standing some way inside the house, bent over a large bed, his body in a tensed position. Perhaps he was straightening the covers, it was hard to tell. He seemed busy with some small detail in the bed. Blom should not be bothering about it—he was meant to be keeping watch over the property—yet there was something in Balder's body language which fascinated him and for a second or two he lost his concentration before he was brought back to reality again.

He had a chilling feeling that someone was watching him, and he spun around, his eyes searching wildly. He saw nothing, not at first, and had just begun to calm down when he became aware of two things—a sudden movement by the shiny steel bins next to the fence, and the sound of a car up by the road. The engine stopped and a car door was opened.

Neither occurrence was noteworthy in itself. There could easily be an animal by the trash bins and cars could come or go here even late at night. Yet Blom's body stiffened and for a moment he just stood there, not knowing how to react. Then Flinck's voice could be heard.

"Someone's coming!"

Blom did not move. He felt that he was being observed and almost unconsciously he fingered the service weapon at his hip and thought of his mother and his ex-wife and his children, as if something serious really was about to happen. Flinck shouted again, now with a desperate tone in his voice, "Police! Stop right there!" and Blom ran up towards the road, although it did not seem the obvious option even then. He could not rid himself of the apprehension that he was leaving something threatening and unpleasant down by the steel bins. But if his partner shouted like that, he did not have a choice, did he? and he felt secretly relieved. He had been more frightened than he cared to admit and so he hurried off and came stumbling onto the road.

Up ahead, Flinck was chasing after an unsteady man with a broad back and clothes that were far too thin. Even though he hardly fit the description of a "quick bastard," Blom ran after him. Soon afterwards they brought him down by the side of the ditch, right next to a couple of mailboxes and a small lantern which cast a pale light over the whole scene.

"Who the hell are you?" Flinck bellowed with surprising aggression— he had also been scared—and the man looked at them in confusion and terror.

He was not wearing a hat, he had hoarfrost in his hair and in the stubble on his chin, and you could tell that he was cold and in pretty bad shape. But above all there was something extraordinarily familiar about his face.

For a few seconds Blom thought that they had arrested a known and wanted criminal and he swelled with pride.

Balder had gone back to the bedroom and tucked August in again, perhaps to hide him under the blanket if anything should happen. Then he had a crazy thought, prompted by the sense of foreboding he felt, accentuated by his conversation with Warburton. Probably his mind was just clouded by panic and fear.

He realized it was not a new idea but something which had been developing in his subconscious during many sleepless nights in California. So he got out his laptop, his own little supercomputer connected to a series of other machines for sufficient capacity, opened the AI programme to which he had dedicated his life, and then . . .

He deleted the file and all of the backup. He barely thought it through. He was like an evil God snuffing out a life, and perhaps that was exactly what he *was* doing. Nobody knew, not even he himself, and he sat there for a little while, wondering if he would be floored by remorse and regret. It was incomprehensible, wasn't it? His life's work was gone, with just a few taps of a key.

But oddly enough it made him calmer, as if at least one aspect of his life was protected. He got to his feet and once more looked out into the night and the storm. Then the telephone rang. It was Flinck, the second policeman.

"I just wanted to say that we apprehended the man you saw," the policeman said. "In other words, you can relax. We have the situation under control."

"Who is it?" Balder said.

"I couldn't say. He's very drunk and we have to get him to quiet down. I just wanted to let you know. We'll get back to you."

Balder put the mobile down on the bedside table, next to his laptop, and tried to congratulate himself. Now the man was under arrest, and his research would not fall into the wrong hands. Yet he was not reassured. At first he did not understand why. Then it hit him: the man who had run along the trees had been anything but drunk.

It took a full minute or more before Blom realized that they had not in fact arrested a notorious criminal but rather the actor Lasse Westman, who did often enough play bandits and hit men on screen, but who was not actually wanted for any crime. The realization did not make Blom feel any calmer. Not just because he again suspected it had been a mistake to leave the area by the trees and the bins, but because this whole episode could lead to scandal and headlines in the press.

He knew enough about Westman to be aware that whatever that man did all too often ended up in the evening papers, and you could not say that the actor was looking particularly happy. He puffed and swore as he scrambled to get to his feet and Blom tried to work out what on earth the man was doing out here in the middle of the night.

"Do you live in the area?" he said.

"I don't have to tell you a fucking thing," Westman hissed, and Blom turned to Flinck in an attempt to understand how the whole drama had begun.

But Flinck was already standing a little way off talking into his telephone, apparently with Balder. He probably wanted to show how efficient he was by passing on the news that they had seized the suspect, if indeed he was the suspect.

"Have you been snooping around Professor Balder's property?" Blom said.

"Didn't you hear what I said? I'm not telling you a fucking thing. What the hell, here I am strolling around perfectly peacefully and along comes that maniac waving his pistol. It's outrageous. Don't you know who I am?"

"I know who you are, and if we have over-reacted then I apologize. I'm sure we'll have a chance to talk about it again. But right now we're in the middle of a tense situation and I demand that you tell me at once what brought you here to Professor Balder. Oh, no, don't you try to run away now!"

Westman was probably not trying to escape at all. He was just having trouble keeping his balance. Then he cleared his throat rather dramatically and spat right out into the air. The phlegm did not get far but flew back like a projectile and froze to ice on his cheek.

"Do you know something?" he said, wiping his face.

"No?"

"I'm not the bad guy in this story."

Blom looked nervously down towards the water and the avenue of trees and wondered yet again what he had seen there. Still he remained standing where he was, paralyzed by the absurdity of the situation.

"Well then, who is?"

"Balder."

"How so?"

"He's taken my girlfriend's son."

"Why would he have done that?"

"You shouldn't bloody well be asking me! Ask the computer genius in there! That bastard has absolutely no right to him," Westman said, and fumbled in the inside pocket of his coat.

"He doesn't have a child in the house, if that's what you think," Blom said.

"He sure as hell does."

"Really?"

"Really!"

"So you thought you'd come along here in the middle of the night, pissed as a newt, and fetch the child," Blom said, and he was about to make another crushing comment when he was interrupted by a sound, a soft clinking sound coming up from the water's edge.

"What was that?" he said.

"What was what?" answered Flinck, who was standing next to him and did not seem to have heard anything at all. It was true that the sound had not been all that loud, at least not up here.

Yet it still made Blom shudder. He was just about to go down to investigate when he hesitated again. As he looked around anxiously he could hear another car approaching.

It was a taxi which drove past and stopped at Balder's front door, and that gave Blom an excuse to stay up on the road. While the driver and the passenger settled up he cast yet another worried look down to the water. He thought he heard another sound—that didn't reassure him.

He did not know for sure, and now the car door opened and a man climbed out whom Blom, after a moment's confusion, identified as the journalist Mikael Blomkvist, though God only knew why the hell all these celebrities had to congregate right here in the middle of the night.

# CHAPTER 10

# NOVEMBER 21—EARLY MORNING

Balder was standing in the bedroom next to his computer and his mobile, looking at August, who was whimpering restlessly in the bed. He wondered what the boy was dreaming. Was it about a world which he could even understand? Balder wanted to know. He wanted to start living, to no longer bury himself in quantum algorithms and source codes and paranoia. He wanted to be happy, not tormented by that constant weight in his body; he wanted instead to launch himself into something wild and magnificent, a romance even. For a few intense seconds he thought about the women who had fascinated him: Gabriella, Farah, and others too.

He also thought about the woman who it turned out was called Salander. He had been spellbound by her, and as he now remembered her he saw something new in her, something both familiar and strange: she reminded him of August. That was absurd of course. August was a small autistic boy. Salander was not that old either, and there may have been something boyish about her, but otherwise she was his polar opposite. Dressed in black, a bit of a punk, totally uncompromising. Still it occurred to him now that her eyes had that same strange shine as August's, when he had been staring at the traffic light on Hornsgatan.

Balder had encountered Salander at the Royal Institute of Technology in Stockholm, while he was giving a lecture on technical singularity, the hypothetical state when computers become more intelligent than the human being. He had just begun by explaining the concept of singularity in terms of mathematics and physics when the door opened and a skinny girl in black strode into the lecture hall. His first thought was that it was a shame there was no other place for junkies to go. Then he wondered if the girl really was an addict. She did not seem strung out, but on the other hand she did look tired and surly, and did not appear to be paying any attention to his lecture. She just sat there slouched over a desk. Eventually, in the middle of a discussion of the moment of singularity in complex mathematical calculation, the point where the solution hits infinity, he asked her straight out what she thought of it all. It was mean of him to pick on her. But what had happened?

The girl looked up and said that, instead of bandying fuzzy concepts about, he should become sceptical when the basis for his calculations fell apart. It was not some sort of real world physical collapse, more a sign that his own mathematics were not up to scratch, and therefore it was sheer populism on his part to mystify singularities in black holes when it was so obvious that the main problem was the absence of a quantum mechanical method for calculating gravity.

With icy clarity—which set off a buzz in the hall—she then presented a sweeping critique of the singularity theorists he had quoted, and he was incapable of coming up with any answer other than a dismayed: "Who the hell are you?"

That was their first contact. The girl was to surprise him a few times more after that. With lightning speed or just one bright glance she immediately grasped what he was working on. When he realized that his technology had been stolen, he had asked for her help, and that had created a bond between them—they shared a secret.

Now he was standing there in the bedroom thinking of her. But his thoughts were interrupted. He was overcome by a new chilling sense of unease and he looked through the doorway towards the large window overlooking the water.

In front of it stood a tall figure in dark clothes and a tight black cap with a small lamp on his forehead. He was doing something to the window. He pulled across it with a swift and powerful movement, like an artist starting work on a fresh canvas, and before Balder even had time to cry out, the whole window fell in and the figure moved towards him.


Jan Holtser usually told people that he worked on industrial security issues. In actual fact he was a former Soviet special forces soldier who spent his time breaking into security systems. He had a small skilled staff and for operations like this one, as a rule the preparations were so painstaking that the risks were not as great as one might imagine.

It's true that he was no longer a young man, but for fifty-one he kept himself in good shape with hard training and was known for his efficiency and ability to improvise. If fresh circumstances cropped up, he thought about them and took them into consideration in his planning.

His experience tended to make up for his lack of youthful vigour, and occasionally, in the limited circle within which he could talk openly, he would speak of a sort of sixth sense, an acquired instinct. He had learned over the years when to wait and when to strike and although he had been through a bad patch a couple of years earlier and betrayed signs of weakness—humanity, his daughter would say—he now felt more accomplished than ever before.

He was once more able to take pleasure in his work, that old sense of excitement. Yes, he did still dose himself with ten milligrammes of Stesolid before a mission, but that was only because it enhanced his accuracy with weapons. He remained crystal clear and alert at critical moments, and most important: he always carried out the tasks he was assigned. Holtser was not someone who let people down or bailed out. That was how he thought of himself.

And yet tonight, even though his client had stressed that the job was urgent he had considered calling it off. The bad weather was a factor. But the storm in itself would never have been enough to get him to consider cancelling. He was Russian and a soldier who had fought in far worse conditions than these—he hated people who moaned about trivial things.

What bothered him was the police guard, which had appeared out of nowhere. He did not think much of the policemen on the property. From his hiding place he had seen them snooping around with the vague reluctance of small boys told to go outside in bad weather. They would rather have stayed sitting in their car talking rubbish, and they were easily frightened, especially the taller of the two who seemed to dislike the dark and the storm and the black water. As he stood there staring from among the trees a little while ago, he had appeared terrified, presumably because he had sensed Holtser's presence, but that was not something that worried Holtser. He could have slit the man's throat swiftly and soundlessly.

Still, the policemen were not good news.

Their presence considerably raised the level of risk; above all it was an indication that some part of the plan had leaked out, there was a heightened readiness. Maybe the professor had started to talk, in which case the operation would be meaningless, it might even make their situation worse. Holtser was determined not to expose his client to any unnecessary risks. He regarded that as one of his strengths. He always saw the bigger picture and, despite his profession, he was often the one who counselled caution.

He had lost count of the number of criminal gangs in his home country that had gone under because they had resorted too often to violence. Violence can command respect. Violence can silence and intimidate, and ward off risks and threats. But violence can also cause chaos and a whole chain of unwanted consequences.

All those thoughts had gone through his mind as he sat hidden behind the trees and the line of bins. For a few seconds he was resolved to abort the operation and go back to his hotel room. Yet that did not happen.

A car arrived, occupying the policemen's attention, and he spotted an opportunity. Without stopping to evaluate his motivations he fitted the elastic of the lamp over his head. He got out the diamond saw from his left-hand jacket pocket and drew his weapon, a 1911 R1 Carry with a custom-made silencer, and weighed them, one in each hand. Then, as ever, he said:

"Thy will be done, amen."

Yet he could not shake off the uncertainty. Was this right? He would have to act with lightning speed. True, he knew the house inside out and Jurij had been here twice and hacked the alarm system. Plus the policemen were hopeless amateurs. Even if he were delayed in there—say the professor did not have his computer next to his bed, as everyone had said, and they had time to come to his aid—Holtser would be able to dispose of them too without any problem. He looked forward to it. He therefore muttered a second time:

"Thy will be done, amen."

Then he disengaged the safety on his weapon and moved rapidly to the large window overlooking the water. It may have been due to the uncertainty of the situation, but he felt an unusually strong reaction when he saw Balder standing there in the bedroom, engrossed in something. He tried to persuade himself that everything was fine. The target was clearly visible. Yet he still felt apprehensive: Should he call the job off?

He did not. Instead he tensed the muscles in his right arm and with all his strength drew the diamond saw across the window and pushed. The window collapsed with a disturbing crash and he rushed in and raised his weapon at Balder, who was staring hard at him, waving his hand as though in a desperate greeting. The professor began to say something confused and ceremonious which sounded like a prayer, a litany. But instead of "God" or "Jesus," Holtser heard the word "disabled." That was all he managed to catch, and in any case it did not matter. People had said all sorts of things to him.

He showed no mercy.

Quickly and almost soundlessly the figure moved through the hallway into the bedroom. In that time Balder registered with surprise that the alarm had not gone off and noticed a motif of a grey spider on the man's sweater, also a narrow, oblong scar on his pale forehead beneath the cap and the lamp.

Then he saw the weapon. The man was pointing a pistol at him. Balder raised his hand in a vain attempt to protect himself. But even though his life was on the line and fear had set its claws into him he thought only of August. Whatever else happens, even if he himself has to die, let his son be spared. He burst out:

"Don't kill my child! He's disabled, he doesn't understand anything."

Balder did not know how far he got. The whole world froze and the night and the storm seemed to bear down on him and then everything went black.

Holtser fired and as he had expected there was nothing wrong with his aim. He hit Balder twice in the head and the professor collapsed to the floor like a flapping scarecrow. There was no doubt that he was dead. Yet something did not feel right. A blustery wind swept in off the sea and brushed across Holtser's neck as if it were a cold, living being, and for a second or two he had no idea what was happening.

Everything had gone according to plan and over there was Balder's computer, just as he had been told. He should take it and go. He needed to be efficient. Yet he stood as if frozen to the spot and it was only after a strangely long delay that he realized why.

In the large double bed, almost completely hidden by a duvet, lay a small boy with unruly, tousled hair watching him with a glassy look. Those eyes made him uncomfortable, and that was not just because they seemed to be looking straight through him. There was more to it than that.

Then again it made no difference. He had to carry out his assignment. Nothing must be allowed to jeopardize the operation. Here was someone who was clearly a witness, especially now that he had exposed his face, and there must be no witnesses, so he pointed his weapon at the boy and looked into his glowing eyes and for the third time muttered:

"Thy will be done, amen."


Blomkvist climbed out of the taxi in a pair of black boots and a white fur coat with a broad sheepskin collar, which he had dug out of the cupboard, as well as an old fur hat that had belonged to his father.

It was then 2:40 in the morning. The Ekot news bulletin had reported a serious accident involving an articulated truck which was now blocking the main Värmdö road. But Blomkvist and the taxi driver had seen nothing of that and had travelled together through the dark, storm-battered suburbs. Blomkvist was sick with exhaustion. All he had wanted was to stay at home, creep into bed with Erika again, and go back to sleep.

But he had not felt able to say no to Balder. He could not understand why. It might have been out of some sense of duty, a feeling that he could not allow himself any easy options now that the magazine was facing a crisis, or it might have been that Balder had sounded lonely and frightened, and Blomkvist was both sympathetic and curious. Not that he thought he was going to hear anything sensational. He was cynically expecting to be disappointed. Maybe he would find himself acting as a therapist, a night watchman in the storm. On the other hand, one never knew, and once again he thought of Salander. Salander rarely did anything without good reason. Besides, Balder was a fascinating figure, and he had never before given an interview. It could well turn out to be interesting, Blomkvist thought, as he looked about him in the darkness.

A lamppost cast a blueish light over the house, and a nice house it was too, architect-designed with large glass windows, and built to look a little like a train. Standing by the mailbox was a tall policeman in his forties, with a fading tan and somewhat strained, nervous features. Further down the road was a shorter colleague of his, arguing with a drunk who was waving his arms about. More was happening out here than Blomkvist had expected.

"What's going on?" he said to the taller policeman.

He never got an answer. The policeman's mobile rang and Blomkvist overheard that the alarm system did not seem to be working properly. There was a noise coming from the lower part of the property, a crackling, unnerving sound, which instinctively he associated with the telephone call. He took a couple of steps to the right and looked down a hill which stretched all the way to a jetty and the sea and another lamppost which shone with the same blueish light. Just then a figure came charging out of nowhere and Blomkvist realized that something was badly wrong.


Holtser squeezed the first pressure on the trigger and was just about to shoot the boy when the sound of a car could be heard up by the road, and he checked himself. But it was not really the car. It was because of the word "disabled" which cropped up again in his thoughts. He realized that the professor would have had every reason to lie in that last moment of his life, but as Holtser now stared at the child he wondered if it might not in fact be true.

The boy's body was immobile, and his face radiated wonder rather than fear, as if he had no understanding of what was happening. His look was too blank and glassy to register anything properly.

Holtser recalled something he had read during his research. Balder did have a severely retarded son. Both the press and the court papers had said that the professor did not have custody. But this must surely be the boy and Holtser neither could nor needed to shoot him. It would be pointless and a breach of his own professional ethics. This recognition came to him as a huge relief, which should have made him suspicious had he been more aware of himself at that moment.

Now he just lowered the pistol, picked up the computer and the mobile from the bedside table and stuffed them into his backpack. Then he ran into the night along the escape route he had staked out for himself. But he did not get far. He heard a voice behind him and turned around. Up by the road stood a man who was neither of the policemen but a new figure in a fur coat and fur hat and with quite a different aura of authority. Perhaps this was why Holtser raised his pistol again. He sensed danger.

The man who charged past was athletic and dressed in black, with a head-lamp on his cap, and in some way Blomkvist could not quite explain why he had the feeling that the figure was part of a coordinated operation. He half expected more figures to appear out of the darkness, and that made him very uncomfortable. He called out, "Hey you, stop!"

That was a mistake. Blomkvist understood it the instant the man's body stiffened, like a soldier in combat, and that was doubtless why he reacted so quickly. By the time the man drew a weapon and fired a shot as if it were the most natural thing in the world, Blomkvist had already ducked down by the corner of the house. The shot could hardly be heard, but when something smacked into Balder's mailbox there was no doubt what had happened. The taller of the policemen abruptly ended his call, but did not move a muscle. The only person who said anything was the drunk.

"What the fuck's going on here? What's happening?" he roared in a voice which sounded oddly familiar, and only then did the policemen start talking to each other in nervous, low tones:

"Is someone shooting?"

"I think so."

"What should we do?"

"Call for reinforcements."

"But he's getting away."

"Then we'd better take a look," the taller one said, and with slow, hesitant movements, as if they wanted the assailant to escape, they drew their weapons and went down to the water.

A dog could be heard barking in the winter darkness, a small, bad-tempered dog, and the wind was blowing hard from the sea. The snow was whirling about and the ground was slippery. The shorter of the two policemen nearly fell over and started flailing his arms like a clown. With a bit of luck they might avoid running into the man with the weapon. Blomkvist sensed that the figure would have no trouble at all in getting rid of those two. The quick and efficient way in which he had turned and raised his weapon suggested that he was trained for situations like these.

Blomkvist wondered if he should do something. He had nothing with which to defend himself. Yet he got to his feet, brushed the snow from his coat, and looked down the slope again. The policemen were working their way along the water's edge towards the neighbour's house. There was no sign of the black-clad man with the gun. Blomkvist made his way down too, and it was at once clear that a window had been smashed in. There was a large gaping hole in the house. But before he could summon the police-men, he heard something, a strange, low whimpering sound, so he stepped through the shattered window into a corridor with a fine oak floor whose pale glow could be seen in the darkness. He walked slowly towards a door-way where the sound was coming from.

"Balder," he called out. "It's me, Mikael Blomkvist. Is everything all right?"

There was no answer. But the whimpering grew louder. He took a deep breath, walked into the room—and froze, paralyzed with shock. Afterwards he could not say what he had noticed first, or even what had frightened him most. It was not necessarily the body on the floor, despite the blood and the empty, rigid expression on its face.

It could have been the scene on the large double bed next to Balder, though it was difficult to make sense of it. There was a small child, perhaps seven, eight years old, a boy with fine features and dishevelled, dark-blond hair, wearing blue checked pyjamas, who was banging his body against the headboard and the wall, methodically and with force. The boy's wailing did not sound like that of a crying child, more like someone trying to hurt himself as much as he could. Before Blomkvist had time to think straight he hurried over to him. The boy was kicking wildly.

"There," Blomkvist said. "There, there," and wrapped his arms around him.

The boy twisted and turned with astonishing strength and managed—possibly because Blomkvist did not want to hold him too tightly—to tear himself from his embrace and rush through the door and out into the corridor, barefoot over the glass shards towards the shattered window, with Blomkvist racing after him shouting, "No."

That was when he ran into the two policemen. They were standing out in the snow with expressions of total bewilderment.

# CHAPTER 11

# NOVEMBER 21

Afterwards it was said that the police had a problem with their procedures, and that nothing had been done to cordon off the area until it was too late. The man who shot Professor Balder must have had all the time in the world to make good his escape. The first policemen on the scene, Detectives Blom and Flinck, known rather scornfully at the station as "the Casanovas," had taken their time before raising the alarm, or at least had not done so with the necessary urgency or authority.

The forensic technicians and investigators from the Violent Crimes Division arrived only at 3:40, at the same time as a young woman who introduced herself as Gabriella Grane and who was assumed to be a relative because she was so upset, but who they later came to understand was an analyst from Säpo, sent by the head of the agency herself. That did not help Grane; thanks to the collective misogyny within the force, or possibly to underline the fact that she was regarded as an outsider, she was given the task of taking care of the child.

"You look as if you know how to handle this sort of thing," Erik Zetterlund said. He was the leader of the duty investigating team that night. He had watched Grane bending to examine the cuts on the boy's feet, and even though she snapped at him and declared that she had other priorities, she gave in when she looked into the boy's eyes.

August—as he was called—was paralyzed by fear and for a long time he sat on the floor at the top of the house, wrapped in a duvet, mechanically moving his hand across a red Persian carpet. Blom, who in other respects had not proved to be especially enterprising, managed to find a pair of socks and put sticking plasters on the boy's feet. They noticed too that he had bruises all over his body and a split lip. According to the journalist Mikael Blomkvist—whose presence created a palpable nervousness in the house—the boy had been throwing himself against the bed and the wall downstairs and had run in bare feet across the broken glass on the ground floor.

Grane, who for some reason was reluctant to introduce herself to Blomkvist, realized at once that August was a witness, but she was not able to establish any sort of rapport with him, nor was she able to give him comfort. Hugs and tenderness of the usual kind were clearly not the right approach. August was at his calmest when Grane simply sat beside him, a little way away, doing her own thing, and only once did he appear to be paying attention. This was when she was speaking on her mobile with Kraft and mentioned the house number, 79. She did not give it much thought at the time, and soon after that she reached an agitated Hanna Balder.

Hanna wanted to have her son back at once and told Grane, to her surprise, that she should get out some jigsaw puzzles, particularly the one of the warship *Vasa*, which she said the boy's father would have had lying around somewhere. She did not describe her ex-husband as having taken the boy unlawfully, but she had no answer when asked why Westman had been out at the house demanding to have the boy back. It certainly did not seem to be concern for the child that had brought him here.

The fact of the boy's presence did, however, shed light on some of Grane's earlier questions. She now understood why Balder had been evasive about certain things, and why he had not wanted to have a guard dog. In the early morning Grane arranged for a psychologist and a doctor to take August to his mother in Vasastan, unless it turned out that he needed more urgent medical attention.

Then she was struck by a different thought. It occurred to her that the motive for murder might not have been to silence Balder. The killer could as easily have been wanting to rob him—not of something as obvious as money, but of his research. Grane had no idea what Balder had been working on during the last year of his life. Perhaps no-one knew. But it was not difficult to imagine what it might have been: in all likelihood a development of his AI programme, which was already regarded as revolutionary when it was stolen the first time.

His colleagues at Solifon had done everything they could to get a look at it and according to what Balder had once let slip he guarded it as a mother guards her baby, which must mean, Grane thought, that he kept it next to him while he was asleep. So she told Blom to keep an eye on August and went down to the bedroom on the ground floor where the forensic team were working.

"Was there a computer in here?" she said.

The technicians shook their heads and Grane got out her mobile and called Kraft again.

It was soon established that Westman had disappeared. He must have left the scene amid the general turmoil, and that made Zetterlund swear and shout, the more so when it transpired that Westman was not to be found at his home either.

Zetterlund considered putting out a search bulletin, which prompted his young colleague Axel Andersson to enquire whether Westman should be treated as dangerous. Maybe Andersson was unable to tell Westman himself apart from the characters he played on screen. But to give the investigator his due, the situation was looking increasingly messy.

The murder was evidently no ordinary settling of scores within the family, no booze-up gone wrong, no crime committed in a fit of passion, but a cold-blooded, well-planned assault. Matters did not improve when the chief of provincial police, Jan-Henrik Rolf, weighed in with his assessment that the killing must be treated as an attack on Swedish industrial interests. Zetterlund was finding himself at the heart of an incident of major domestic political importance and even if he were not the brightest mind in the force he realized that what he did now would have a significant long-term impact.

Zetterlund, who had turned forty-one two days earlier and was still suffering some of the after-effects of his birthday party, had never been close to taking charge of an investigation of this importance. The reason he had now been detailed to do it, if only for a matter of hours, was that there had not been very many competent people on duty during the night and his superior had chosen not to wake the National Murder Squad or any of the more experienced investigators in the Stockholm police.

Accordingly Zetterlund found himself in the midst of this confusion, feeling less and less sure of himself, and was soon shouting out his orders. In the first place he was trying to set in motion an effective door-to-door enquiry. He wanted quickly to gather as much testimony as possible, even if he was not expecting to get very much out of it. It was night-time and dark and there was a storm blowing. The people living nearby had presumably not seen anything at all. But you never knew.

So he had himself questioned Blomkvist, though God only knows what he was doing there. The presence of one of Sweden's best-known journalists did not make matters any easier and for a while Zetterlund imagined that Blomkvist was examining him critically with a view to writing a tell-all. Probably that was just his insecurity. Blomkvist himself was shaken and throughout the interview he was unfailingly polite and keen to help. But he was not able to provide much in the way of information. It had all happened so quickly and that in itself was significant, the journalist told him.

There had been something brutal and efficient about the way in which the suspect moved, and Blomkvist said it would not be too far-fetched to speculate that the man either was or had been a soldier, possibly even special forces. His way of spinning around to aim and fire his weapon had seemed practised. He had a lamp strapped to his tight-fitting black cap, but Blomkvist had not been able to make out any of his features.

He had been too far away, he said, and had thrown himself to the ground the instant the figure had turned around. He should thank his lucky stars that he was still alive. He could only describe the body and the clothes, and that he did very well. According to the journalist, the man did not seem all that young, he could have been over forty. He was fit and taller than average, over six feet tall, powerfully built with a slim waist and broad shoulders, wearing boots and black, military-style clothes. He was carrying a backpack and looked to have a knife strapped to his right leg.

Blomkvist thought that the man had vanished down along the water's edge, past the neighbouring houses, and that also matched Blom and Flinck's account. The policemen had admittedly not seen the man at all. But they had heard his footsteps and set off in vain pursuit, or so they claimed. Zetterlund had his doubts about that.

Blom and Flinck had chickened out, he presumed, and had stood there in the darkness, fearful and doing nothing. In any event, that was the moment when the big mistake was made. Instead of identifying escape routes from the area and trying to cordon them off, nothing much seems to have happened. At that point Flinck and Blom were not yet aware that someone had been killed and as soon as they knew, they had had their hands full coping with a barefoot boy running hysterically out of the house. Certainly it could not have been easy to keep a cool head. Yet they had lost precious time and, though Blomkvist exercised restraint when describing the events, it was plain to see that even he was critical. He had twice asked the policemen if they had sounded the alarm and got a nod for an answer.

Later on, when Blomkvist overheard a conversation between Flinck and the operations centre, he realized that the nod was most likely a no, or at best some sort of bewildered failure to grasp the enormity of what had happened. It had taken a long time for the alarm to be raised and even then things had not proceeded as they should have, probably because Flinck's account of the situation had not been clear.

The paralysis had spread to other levels. Zetterlund was infinitely glad he could not be blamed for that—at that point he had not yet become involved in the investigation. On the other hand he was here, and he should at least avoid making a mess of things. His personal record had not been so impressive recently and this was an opportunity to put his best foot forward.

He was at the door to the living room and had just finished a call to Milton Security about the character who had been seen on camera earlier that night. He did not at all fit the description Mikael Blomkvist had given of the presumed murderer. He looked like a skinny old junkie, albeit one who must have possessed a high level of technical skill. Milton Security believed that the man had hacked the alarm system and put all the cameras and sensors out of action.

That did not exactly make matters any easier. It was not only the professional planning. It was the idea of committing a murder in spite of police protection and a sophisticated alarm system. How arrogant is that? Zetterlund had been about to go down to the forensic team on the ground floor, but he stayed upstairs, deeply troubled, staring into space until his gaze fastened on Balder's son. He was their key witness but incapable of speech, nor did he understand a word they said. In other words pretty much what one might expect in this shambles.

The boy was holding a small, single piece of an extremely complex puzzle. Zetterlund started towards the curved staircase leading to the ground floor—then he stopped dead. He thought back to his initial impression of the child. When he arrived on the scene, not knowing very much about what had happened, the boy had seemed the same as any other child. Zetterlund would have described him as an unusually pretty but normal-looking boy with curly hair and a shocked look in his eyes. Only later did he learn that the boy was autistic and severely handicapped. That, he thought, meant that the murderer either knew him from before or else was aware of his condition. Otherwise he would hardly have let him live and risk being identified in a witness parade, would he? Although Zetterlund did not give himself time to think this through in full, the hunch excited him and he took a few hurried paces towards the boy.

"We must question him at once," he said, in a voice that came out louder and more urgent than he had intended.

"For heaven's sake, take it easy with him," Blomkvist said.

"Don't you interfere," Zetterlund snapped. "He may have known the killer. We have to get out some pictures and show them to him. Somehow we must . . ."

The boy interrupted him by slamming the puzzle with his hand in a sudden sweeping movement. Zetterlund muttered an apology and went downstairs to join his forensic team.


Blomkvist remained there, looking at the boy. It felt as if something else was about to happen with him, perhaps a new outburst, and the last thing he wanted was for the child to hurt himself again. The boy stiffened and began to make furiously rapid circular movements over the rug with his right hand.

Then he stopped and looked up pleadingly. Though Blomkvist asked himself what that might mean, he dropped the thought when the policeman whose name he now knew to be Blom sat down with the boy and tried to get him to do the puzzle again. Blomkvist went into the kitchen to get some peace and quiet. He was exhausted and wanted to go home. But apparently he first had to look at some pictures from a surveillance camera. He had no idea when that was going to happen. It was all taking a long time and seemed disorganized and Blomkvist was longing for his bed.

He had spoken to Berger twice by then and told her what had happened. They agreed that Blomkvist should write a longer piece about the murder for the next issue. Not just because the crime itself was obviously major and Professor Balder's life was worth describing, but Blomkvist had a personal connection to the story and that would raise its quality and give him an advantage over the competition. The dramatic telephone call alone, in the middle of the night, which had gotten him here in the first place, would give his article an edge.

The Serner situation and the crisis at the magazine were implicit in their conversation. Berger had already planned for their temp Andrei Zander to do the preliminary research while Blomkvist got some sleep. She had said rather firmly—like someone halfway between a loving mother and an authoritative editor-in-chief—that she refused to have her star reporter dead from exhaustion before the work had even begun.

Blomkvist accepted without protest. Zander was ambitious and pleasant and it would be nice to wake up and find all the spadework done, ideally also with lists of people close to Balder whom he should be interviewing. For a little while Blomkvist welcomed the distraction of reflecting on Zander's persistent problems with women, which had been confided to him during evening sessions at the Kvarnen beer hall. Zander was young, intelligent, and handsome. He ought to be a catch. But because there was something soft and needy in his character, he was time and again being dropped, and that was painful for him. Zander was an incorrigible romantic, forever dreaming about love with a capital L and the big scoop.

Blomkvist sat down at Balder's kitchen table and looked out at the darkness. In front of him, next to a matchbox, a copy of *New Scientist,* and a pad of paper with some incomprehensible equations on it, lay a beautiful but slightly ominous drawing of a street crossing. A man with watery, squinting eyes and thin lips was standing next to a traffic light. He was caught in a fleeting moment and yet you could see every wrinkle in his face and the folds in his quilted jacket and trousers. He did not look pleasant. He had a heart-shaped mole on his chin.

But the striking thing about the drawing was the traffic light. It shone with an eloquent, troubling glow, and was skilfully executed according to some sort of mathematical technique. You could almost see the underlying geometrical lines. Balder must have enjoyed doing drawings on the side. Blomkvist wondered, though, about the unconventional choice of subject. On the other hand, why would a person like Balder draw sunsets and ships? A traffic light was probably just as interesting to him as anything else. Blomkvist was intrigued by the fact that the drawing looked like a snapshot. Even if Balder had sat and studied the traffic light, he could hardly have asked the man to cross the street over and over again. Maybe he was imagined, or Balder had a photographic memory, just like . . . Blomkvist grew thoughtful. He picked up his mobile and for the third time called Berger.

"Are you on your way home?" she asked.

"Not yet, unfortunately. There are couple of things I still need to look at. But I'd like you to do me a favour."

"What else am I here for?"

"Could you go to my computer and log in. You know my password, don't you?"

"I know everything about you."

"Then go into Documents and open a file called [*Lisbeth stuff*]."

"I think I have an idea where this is going."

"Oh? Here's what I'd like you to write . . ."

"Wait a second, I have to open it first. OK, now . . . Hold on, there are already a few things here."

"Ignore them. This is what I want, right at the top. Are you with me?"

"Yes, I'm with you."

"Write: 'Lisbeth, maybe you already know, but Frans Balder is dead, shot in the head. Can you find out why someone wanted to kill him?'"

"Is that all?"

"Well, it's rather a lot considering that we haven't been in touch for ages. She'll probably think it's cheeky of me to ask. But I don't think it would hurt to have her help."

"A little illegal hacking wouldn't go amiss, you mean?"

"I didn't hear that. I'll see you soon I hope."

"I hope so."

Salander had managed to go back to sleep, and woke again at 7:30. She was not in top form—she had a headache and she felt nauseated. Yet she felt better than she had during the night. She bandaged her hand, had a quick breakfast of two microwaved meat piroshki and a large glass of Coca-Cola, then she stuffed some workout clothes into a sports bag and left the apartment. The storm had subsided, leaving trash and newspapers lying all over the city. She walked down from Mosebacke torg and along Götgatan, muttering to herself.

She looked angry and at least two people were alarmed enough to get out of her way. But Salander was merely determined. She was not looking forward to working out, she just wanted to stick to her routine and drive the toxins out of her body. So she continued down to Hornsgatan, and right before Hornsgatspuckeln she turned into Zero boxing club, which was in the basement down one flight of stairs. It seemed more run-down than ever that morning.

The place could have used a coat of paint and some general freshening up. It seemed as if no improvements had been made since the '70s. Posters of Ali and Foreman were still on the walls. It still looked like the day after that legendary bout in Kinshasa, possibly due to the fact that Obinze, the man in charge of the premises, had seen the fight live as a small boy and had afterwards run around in the liberating monsoon rain shouting "Ali Bomaye!" That double-time canter was not just his happiest memory, it also marked what he called the last moment of "the days of innocence."

Not long after that he and his family had been forced to flee Mobutu's terror and nothing had ever been the same again. Maybe it was not so strange that he wanted to preserve that moment in history, carry it with him to this godforsaken boxing hall in the Södermalm district of Stockholm. Obinze was still constantly talking about the fight. But then he was always constantly talking about something or other.

He was tall and mighty and bald-headed, a chatterbox of epic proportions and one of many in the gym who quite fancied Salander, even if like many others he thought she was more or less crazy. Periodically she would train harder than anyone else in there and go at the punch-balls, punch-bags, and her sparring partners like a madwoman. She possessed a kind of primitive, furious energy which Obinze had seldom come across.

Once, before he got to know her, he had suggested that she take up competitive boxing. The derisive snort he got in response stopped him from asking again, though he had never understood why she trained so hard. Not that he really needed to know—one could train hard for no reason at all. It was better than drinking hard. It was better than lots of things.

Maybe it was true, as she said to him late one evening about a year ago, that she wanted to be physically prepared in case she ever ended up in difficulties again. He knew that there had been trouble before. He had read every single word about her online and understood what it meant to be prepared in case some evil shadow from the past turned up. Both his parents had been murdered by Mobutu's thugs.

What he did not understand was why, at regular intervals, Salander gave up training altogether, not exercising at all, eating nothing but junk food. When she came into the gym that morning—as demonstratively dressed in black and pierced as ever—he had not seen her for two weeks.

"Hello, gorgeous. Where have you been?"

"Doing something highly illegal."

"I can only imagine. Beating the crap out of some motorbike gang or something."

But she did not even rise to the jest. She just marched angrily in towards the changing room and he did something he knew she would hate: he stepped in front of her and looked her straight in the face.

"Your eyes are bright red."

"I've got the mother of all hangovers. Out of my way!"

"In that case I don't want to see you in here, you know that."

"Skip the crap. I want you to drive the shit out of me," she spat, and ducked past him to get changed. When she emerged wearing her outsized boxing shorts and white T-shirt with the black skull on the chest, he saw nothing for it but to go ahead and let her have it.

He pushed her until she threw up three times in his wastepaper bin. He gave her as much grief as he could. She gave him plenty of lip back. Then she went off and changed and left the gym without even a goodbye. As so often at such moments Obinze was overcome by a feeling of emptiness.

Maybe he was even a little in love. He was certainly stirred—how could one not be by a girl who boxed like that?

The last he saw of her was her calves disappearing up the stairs, so he could not know that the ground swayed beneath her feet as she came out onto Hornsgatan. Salander braced herself against the wall of the building and breathed heavily. Then she set off in the direction of her apartment on Fiskargatan. Once home she drank another large glass of Coca-Cola and half a litre of juice, then she crashed onto her bed and looked at the ceiling for ten, fifteen minutes, thinking about this and that, about singularities and event horizons and certain special aspects of Schrödinger's equation, and Ed Needham.

She waited for the world to regain its usual colours before she got up and went to her computer. However reluctant she might be, she was drawn to it by a force which had not grown weaker since her childhood. But this morning she was not in the mood for any wild escapades. She hacked into Mikael Blomkvist's computer. In the next moment she froze. They had been joking about Balder and now Blomkvist wrote that he had been murdered, shot in the head.

"Jesus," she muttered, and had a look at the online evening papers.

There was no explicit mention of Balder, but it was not difficult to work out that he was the "Swedish academic shot at his home in Saltsjöbaden." For the time being, the police were being tight-lipped and journalists had not managed to turn up a great deal, no doubt because they had not yet cottoned on to how big the story was. Other events from the night took precedence: the storm and the power outage right across the country and the scandalous delays on the railways. There was also the odd celebrity news item which Salander could not be bothered to try to understand.

The only facts reported on the murder were that it had taken place around 3:00 in the morning and that the police were seeking witnesses in the neighbourhood, for reports of anything untoward. So far, there were no suspects, but apparently witnesses had spotted unknown and suspicious persons on the property. The police were looking for more information on them. At the end of the articles it said that a press conference was going to be held later that day, led by Chief Inspector Jan Bublanski. Salander gave a wistful smile. She had a fair bit of history with Bublanski—or Officer

Bubble, as he was sometimes called—and she thought that so long as they didn't put any idiots onto his team the investigation would turn out to be reasonably effective.

Then she read Blomkvist's message again. He needed help and without thinking twice she wrote "OK." Not only because he was asking her. It was personal. She did not do grief, not in the conventional way at least. Anger, on the other hand, yes, a cold ticking rage. And though she had a certain respect for Jan Bublanski she was not usually inclined to trust the forces of law and order.

She was used to taking matters into her own hands and she had all sorts of reasons to find out why Frans Balder had been murdered. Because it was no coincidence that she had sought him out and taken an interest in his situation. His enemies were most likely her enemies too.

It had begun with the old question of whether in some sense her father lived on. Alexander Zalachenko—Zala—had not only killed her mother and destroyed her childhood, he had also established and controlled a criminal network, sold drugs and arms, and made a living exploiting and humiliating women. She was convinced that that sort of evil never goes away. It merely migrates into other forms.

Ever since that day just over a year ago when she had woken up at dawn at Hotel Schloss Elmau in the Bavarian Alps, Salander had been pursuing her own investigation into what had become of his legacy.

For the most part his old comrades seemed to have turned into losers, depraved bandits, revolting pimps, or small-time crooks. Not one of them was a villain on her father's level, and for a long time Salander remained convinced that the organization had changed and dissolved after Zalachenko's death. Yet she did not give up, and eventually she stumbled onto something which pointed in a wholly unexpected direction. It was a reference to one of Zala's young acolytes, a certain Sigfrid Gruber.

Already during Zala's lifetime, Gruber was one of the more intelligent people in the network, and unlike his colleagues he had earned himself degrees in both computer science and business administration, which had apparently given him access to more exclusive circles. These days he cropped up in a couple of alleged crimes against high-tech companies: thefts of new technology, extortion, insider trading, hacker attacks.

Normally, Salander would have followed the lead no further. Nothing could worry her less than a couple of rich business groups being fleeced of some of their innovations. But then everything had changed.

In a classified report from Government Communications Headquarters in Cheltenham, England, which she had gotten her hands on, she had come across some codenames associated with a gang Gruber seemed now to belong to. The names had set some bells ringing, and after that she had not been able to let go of the story. She assembled all the information she could find about the group and kept coming across a rumour that the organization had stolen Balder's AI technology and then sold it to the Russian-American games company Truegames. Her source was unreliable—a half-open hacker site—but it was for this reason that she had turned up at the professor's lecture at the Royal Institute of Technology and given him a hard time about singularities deep within black holes. Or that was part of the reason.

# PART 2

# THE LABYRINTHS OF MEMORY

NOVEMBER 21–23

People with a photographic memory are also said to have an eidetic memory, an ability to recall images, sounds, or objects after only a few instants of exposure.

Research shows that people with eidetic memories are more likely to be nervous and stressed than others.

Most, though not all, people with eidetic memories are autistic. There is also a connection between photographic memory and synaesthesia—the condition where two or more senses are connected, for example when numbers are seen in colour and every series of numbers forms an image in the mind.

# CHAPTER 12

# NOVEMBER 21

Jan Bublanski had been looking forward to a day off and a long conversation with Rabbi Goldman in the Söder congregation about certain questions which had been troubling him recently, chiefly concerning the existence of God.

It would be going too far to say that he was becoming an atheist. But the very notion of a God had become increasingly problematic for him and he wanted to discuss his persistent feelings of the meaninglessness of it all, often accompanied by dreams of handing in his notice.

Bublanski certainly considered himself to be a good investigator. His record of clearing up cases was on the whole outstanding and occasionally he was still stimulated by the job. But he was not sure he wanted to go on investigating murders. He could learn some new skill while there was time. He dreamed about teaching, helping young people to find their path and believe in themselves, maybe because he himself suffered from bouts of the deepest self-doubt—but he did not know which subject he would choose. He had never specialized in one particular field, aside from that which had become his lot in life: sudden, evil death, and morbid human perversions. That was definitely not something he wanted to teach.

It was 8:10 in the morning and he was at his bathroom mirror. He felt puffy, worn out, and bald. Absentmindedly he picked up I. B. Singer's novel *The Magician of Lublin,* which he had loved with such a passion that for many years he had kept it next to the lavatory in case he felt like reading it at times when his stomach was playing up. But now he managed only a few lines. The telephone rang and his mood did not improve when he recognized the number: Chief Prosecutor Richard Ekström. A call from Ekström meant not just work, but probably work with a political and media element to it. Ekström would otherwise have wriggled out of it like a snake.

"Hi, Richard, nice to hear from you," Bublanski lied. "But I'm afraid I'm busy."

"What . . . no, no, not too busy for this, Jan. You can't miss out on this one. I heard that you'd taken the day off."

"That's right, and I'm just off to"—he did not want to say his synagogue. His Jewishness was not popular in the force—"see my doctor," he went on.

"Are you sick?"

"Not really."

"What's that supposed to mean? Nearly sick?"

"Something like that."

"Well, in that case there's no problem. We're all nearly sick, aren't we? This is an important case, Jan. The Minister of Enterprise has been in touch, and she agrees that you should handle the investigation."

"I find it very hard to believe the minister even knows who I am."

"Well, maybe not by name, and she's not supposed to be interfering anyway. But we're all agreed that we need a big player."

"Flattery no longer works with me, Richard. What's it about?" he said, and immediately regretted it. Just asking was halfway to saying yes and he could tell that Ekström accepted it as such.

"Last night Professor Frans Balder was murdered at his home in Saltsjöbaden."

"Who?"

"One of our best-known scientists, of international renown. He's a world authority on AI technology."

"On *what*?"

"He was working on neural networks and digital quantum processes, that sort of thing."

"I have no idea what you're talking about."

"He was trying to get computers to think, to replicate the human brain."

*Replicate the human brain?* Bublanski wondered what Rabbi Goldman would make of that.

"They say he's been a victim of industrial espionage in the past," Ekström said. "And that's why the murder is attracting the attention of the Ministry of Enterprise. No doubt you're aware of the solemn declarations the minister has made about the absolute requirement to protect Swedish research and new technology."

"Maybe."

"It would seem that this Balder was under some sort of threat. He had police protection."

"Are you saying he was killed while under police protection?"

"Well, it wasn't the most effective protection in the world. It was Flinck and Blom from the regular force."

"The Casanovas?"

"Yes. They were assigned late last night at the height of the storm and the general confusion. But in their defence it has to be said that the whole situation was a shambles. Balder was shot while our men were dealing with a drunk who had turned up at the house, out of nowhere. Unsurprisingly, the killer took advantage of that moment of inattention."

"Doesn't sound good."

"No, it looks very professional, and on top of it all the burglar alarm seems to have been hacked."

"So there were several of them?"

"We believe so. Furthermore, there are some tricky details."

"Which the media are going to like?"

"Which the media are going to love," Ekström said. "The lush who turned up, for example, was none other than Lasse Westman."

"The actor?"

"The same. And that's a real problem."

"Because it'll be all over the front pages?"

"Partly that, yes, but also because there's a risk we'll end up with a load of sticky divorce issues on our hands. Westman claimed he was there to bring home the eight-year-old son of his partner. Balder had the boy with him, even though . . . hang on a moment . . . I want to get this right . . . according to a custody ruling, Balder is not competent to look after him."

"Why wouldn't a professor who can get computers to behave like people be capable of looking after his own child?"

"Because previously he had shown a shocking lack of responsibility. He was a completely hopeless father, if I've understood it right. It's all rather sensitive. This little boy, who wasn't even supposed to have been at Balder's, probably witnessed the killing."

"Jesus! And what does he say?"

"Nothing."

"Is he in shock?"

"He must be, but he never says anything anyway. He's mute and apparently disabled, so he's not going to be much good to us."

"I see. So there's no suspect."

"Unless there was a reason why Westman appeared at precisely the same time as the killer entered the ground floor. You should get Westman in for questioning."

"If I decide to take on the investigation."

"As you will."

"Are you so sure of that?"

"You have no choice, in my view. Besides, I've saved the best for last."

"And that is?"

"Mikael Blomkvist."

"What about him?"

"For some reason he was out there too. I think Balder had asked to see him to tell him something."

"In the middle of the night?"

"So it would seem."

"And then he was shot?"

"Just before Blomkvist rang the bell—and it seems that the journalist caught a glimpse of the killer."

Bublanski snorted. It was an inappropriate reaction in every conceivable way and he could not have explained it even to himself. Perhaps it was a nervous reaction, or a feeling that life was repeating itself.

"I'm sorry?" Ekström said.

"Just got a bit of a cough. So you're worried that you'll end up with an investigative reporter on your back, one who'll show you all up in a bad light."

"Hmm, yes, maybe. We're assuming that *Millennium* has already gotten going with the story and right now I'm trying to find some legal justification for stopping them, or at least see to it that they're restricted in some way. I won't rule out that this case is a matter affecting national security."

"So we're saddled with Säpo as well?"

"No comment."

*Go to hell,* Bublanski thought.

"Are Olofsson and the others at Industry Protection working on this?"

"No comment, as I said. When can you start?" Ekström said.

"I have some conditions," Bublanski said. "I want my usual team, Modig, Svensson, Holmberg, and Flod."

"Of course, OK, but you get Hans Faste as well."

"No way!"

"Sorry, Jan, that's not negotiable. You should be grateful you get to choose all the others."

"You're the bitter end, you know that?"

"I've heard it said."

"So Faste's going to be our own little mole from Säpo?"

"Nonsense. I happen to think that all teams benefit from someone who thinks differently."

"Meaning that when the rest of us have got rid of all our prejudices and preconceived notions, we're stuck with somebody who will take us back to square one?"

"Don't be absurd."

"Faste is an idiot."

"No, Jan, he isn't. He's just . . ."

"What?"

"Conservative. He's not someone who falls for the latest feminist fads."

"Or for the earliest ones, either. He may have just got his head around all that stuff about votes for women."

"Come on, Jan, pull yourself together. Faste is an extremely reliable and loyal detective, and I won't listen to any more of this. Any other requests?"

*How about you go take a running jump,* Bublanski thought.

"I need to go to my doctor's appointment, and in the meantime I want Modig to lead the investigation," he said.

"Is that really such a wise idea?"

"It's a damned wise idea," he growled.

"OK, OK, I'll see to it that Zetterlund hands it over to her," Ekström said with a wince.

Ekström was far from sure he should have agreed to take on this investigation.

Alona Casales rarely worked nights. She had managed to avoid them for a decade and justified her stance on the grounds that her rheumatism forced her from time to time to take strong cortisone tablets, which not only turned her face into the shape of a moon, but also raised her blood pressure. She needed her sleep and her routine. Yet here she was, 3:10 in the morning.

She had driven from her home in Laurel, Maryland, in a light rain, past the sign that read NSA NEXT RIGHT—STAFF ONLY, past the barriers and the electric fence, towards the black, cube-like main building in Fort Meade. She left her car in the sprawling parking area alongside the pale-blue golf-ball-like radome with its myriad dish aerials, and made her way through the security gates up to her workstation on the twelfth floor. She was surprised by the feverish atmosphere there and soon realized that it was Ed Needham and his young hacker team who were responsible for the heightened concentration hanging over the department.

Needham looked like a man possessed and was standing there bawling out a young man whose face shone with an icy pallor. A pretty weird guy, Casales thought, just like all those young genius hackers Needham had surrounded himself with. The kid was skinny, anaemic-looking, with a hairstyle from hell and strangely rounded shoulders which shook with some sort of spasm. Maybe he was frightened. He shuddered every now and then, and it did not help matters that Needham was kicking at his chair leg. The young man looked as if he were waiting for a slap, a clip across the ear. But then something unexpected happened.

Needham calmed down and ruffled the boy's hair like a loving father. That was not like him. He did not go in for demonstrative affection. He was a cowboy who would never do anything as dubious as hug another man. But perhaps he was so desperate that he was prepared to give normal humanity a go. Ed's zip was undone and he had spilled coffee or Coca-Cola on his shirt. His face was an unhealthy flushed colour, his voice hoarse and rough from shouting. Casales thought that no-one of his age and weight should be pushing himself so hard.

Although only half a day had gone by, it looked as if Needham and his boys had been living there for a week. There were coffee cups and fast-food remnants and discarded caps and sweatshirts everywhere, and a rank stench of sweat and tension in the air. The team was clearly in the process of turning the whole world upside down in their efforts to trace the hacker. She called out to them in a hearty tone:

"Go for it, guys! . . . Get the bastard!"

She did not really mean it. Secretly she thought the breach was amusing. Many of these programmers seemed to think they could do whatever they liked, as if they had *carte blanche,* and it might actually do them some good to see that the other side could hit back. Here in the Puzzle Palace their shortcomings showed only when they were confronted with something dire, as was happening now. She had been woken by a call saying that the Swedish professor had been murdered at his home outside Stockholm, and even though that in itself was not a big deal for the NSA—not yet at any rate—it did mean something to Casales.

The killing showed that she had read the signs right, and now she had to see if she could move forward one more step. She logged in and opened the diagrammatic overview of the organization she had been tracking. The evasive Thanos sat right at the top, but there were also names of real people like the member of the Russian Duma, Ivan Gribanov, and the German, Gruber, a highly educated former crook from a large and complex trafficking operation.

She did not understand why the NSA gave such low priority to the matter, and why her superiors kept suggesting that other, more mainstream law-enforcement agencies should be taking care of it. They could not rule out the possibility that the network had state backing, or links to Russian state intelligence, and that it was all to do with the trade war between East and West. Even though the evidence was sparse and ambiguous, there were indications that Western technology was being stolen and ending up in Russian hands.

But it was difficult to get a clear view of this tangled web, to know whether any crime had been committed or whether purely by chance a similar technology had been developed somewhere else. These days, industrial theft was an altogether nebulous concept. Assets were borrowed all the time, sometimes as a part of creative exchanges, sometimes just dressed up to seem legitimate.

Large businesses, bolstered by threatening lawyers, regularly scared the living daylights out of small companies, and nobody seemed to find it odd that individual innovators had almost no legal rights. Besides which, industrial espionage and hacker attacks were often regarded as little more than routine research in a competitive environment. You could hardly claim that the NSA crowd was helping to raise ethical standards in the field.

On the other hand, it was not so easy to view murder in relative terms, and Casales took a solemn vow to leave no stone unturned in trying to unseat Thanos.

She did not get far. In fact she managed only to stretch her arms and massage her neck before she heard puffing and panting behind her.

Needham looked dreadful. His back must have given out on him too. Her own neck felt better just looking at him.

"Ed, to what do I owe this honour?"

"I'm thinking you and I are working on the same problem."

"Park your butt, old man."

"You know, from my limited perspective . . ."

"Don't knock yourself, Ed."

"I'm not knocking myself. It's no secret, I couldn't care less who's high or low, who thinks this and who thinks that. I focus on my own stuff. I protect our systems, and the only thing that really impresses me is when people are good at their jobs."

"You'd hire the Devil himself if he was any good in IT."

"I can respect just about any enemy, if he knows what he's doing. Does that make sense to you?"

"It does."

"As I'm sure you've heard, a root kit has been used to access our server and install a RAT. And that programme, Alona, is like pure music. So compact and beautifully written."

"You've met a worthy opponent."

"Without a doubt, and my guys feel the same way. They're putting on this outraged patriotic act or whatever the hell it is we're supposed to do. But actually they want nothing more than to meet that hacker and pit their skills against his. For a while I thought: OK, get over it! Maybe the damage isn't so great after all. This is just one genius hacker who wants to show off, and maybe there's a silver lining. I mean, we've already learned a lot about our vulnerability chasing after this clown. But then I began to wonder if maybe I was conned—maybe the whole performance on my mail server was just a smoke screen, hiding something altogether different."

"Such as?"

"Such as a search for certain pieces of information."

"Now I'm curious."

"You should be. We identified which areas the hacker was checking out and basically it's all related to the same thing: the network you've been working on, Alona. They call themselves the Spiders, don't they?"

"The Spider Society, to be precise. But I think it's some kind of joke."

"The hacker was looking for information on that group and their connections to Solifon, and that made me think maybe he's with them and wants to find out how much we know about them."

"That sounds possible. They know how to hack."

"But then I changed my mind."

"Why?"

"Because it looks like the hacker also wanted to show us something. You know, he got himself superuser status which gave him access to documents maybe even you haven't seen, highly classified stuff. But actually the file he uploaded is so heavily encrypted that we don't have the slightest chance of reading it unless the fucker who wrote it gives us the private keys. Anyway . . ."

"What?"

"The hacker revealed through our own system that we cooperate with Solifon, too, the same way the Spiders do. Did you know that?"

"No, my God, I did not."

"I didn't think so. But unfortunately what Solifon does for the Spiders, it also does for us. It's part of our own industrial espionage efforts. That must be why your project is such low priority. They're worried your investigation will drop us in the shit."

"Idiots."

"I'd have to agree with you there. Probably now you'll be taken off the job completely."

"That would be outrageous."

"Relax, there's a loophole. And that's why I dragged my sorry ass all the way over to your desk. Start working for me instead."

"What do you mean?"

"This goddamn hacker knows things about the Spiders, and if we can crack his identity we'll both get a break and then you'll be able to see your investigation through."

"I see what you're saying."

"So it's a yes?"

"It's a sort of," she said. "I want to focus on finding out who shot Frans Balder."

"And you'll keep me informed?"

"OK."

"Good."

"Tell me," she said, "if this hacker is so clever, won't he have covered his tracks?"

"No need to worry about that. No matter how smart he's been, we'll find him and we'll flay him alive."

"What happened to all that respect for your opponent?"

"It's still there, my friend. But we'll crush him all the same and lock him up for life. No fucker breaks into my system."

CHAPTER 13

# NOVEMBER 21

Blomkvist did not get much sleep. He could not get the events of the night out of his head and at 11:15 he sat up in bed and gave up.

He went into the kitchen where he made himself two sandwiches with cheddar and prosciutto and a bowl of yoghurt and muesli. But he did not eat much of it. Instead he opted for coffee and water and some headache pills. He drank five glasses of Ramlösa, swallowed two Alvedon, took out a notebook and tried to write a summary of what had happened. He did not get far before the telephone started ringing.

The news was out: "Star reporter Mikael Blomkvist and TV star Lasse Westman" had found themselves at the centre of a "mysterious" murder drama, mysterious because no-one was able to work out why Westman and Blomkvist of all people, together or separately, had been on the scene when a Swedish professor was shot in the head. The questions seemed to be insinuating something sinister and that was why Blomkvist quite candidly said that he had gone there, despite the lateness of the hour, because Balder had asked to speak to him urgently.

"I was there because of my job."

He was being more defensive than he needed to be. He wanted to provide an explanation for the accusations out there, although that might prompt more reporters to dig into the story. Apart from that he said "No comment" and if that was not the ideal response it was at least straightforward and unambiguous. After that he turned off his mobile, put his father's old fur coat back on and set out in the direction of Götgatan.

So much was going on at the office that it reminded him of the old days. All over the place, in every corner, there were colleagues sitting and working with concentration. Berger was bound to have made one or two impassioned speeches and everybody must have been aware of the significance of the moment. The deadline was just ten days away. There was also the threat from Ove Levin and Serner hanging over them and the whole team seemed up for the fight. They all jumped to their feet when they saw him and asked to hear about Balder and the night, and his reaction to the Norwegians' proposal. But he wanted to follow their good example.

"Later, later," he said, and went to Andrei Zander's desk.

Zander was twenty-six years old, the youngest person in the office. He had done his time as an intern at the magazine and had stayed on, sometimes as a temp, as now, and sometimes as a freelancer. It pained Blomkvist that they had not been able to give him a permanent job, especially since they had hired Emil Grandén and Sofie Melker. He would have preferred to take on Zander. But Zander had not yet made a name for himself, and still had a lot to learn.

He was a superb team player, and that was good for the magazine, but not necessarily good for him. Not in this cynical business. The boy was not conceited enough, although he had every reason to be. He looked like a young Antonio Banderas, and was quicker on the uptake than most. But he did not go to any lengths to promote himself. He just wanted to be a part of it all and produce good journalism and he thought the world of *Millennium*. Blomkvist suddenly felt that he loved everyone who loved *Millennium*. One fine day he would do something big for young Zander.

"Hi, Andrei," he said. "How are things?"

"Not bad. Busy."

"I expected nothing less. What have you managed to dig up?"

"Quite a bit. It's on your desk, and I've also written a summary. But can I give you some advice?"

"Good advice is exactly what I need."

"In that case go straight to Zinkens väg, to see Farah Sharif."

"Who?"

"A seriously gorgeous professor of computer science. She's taken the whole day off."

"Are you saying that what I really need right now is an attractive, intelligent woman?"

"Not exactly that, no. Professor Sharif just called and was under the impression that Balder had wanted to tell you something. She thinks she knows what it may have been all about, and she's keen to talk to you. Maybe to carry out his wishes. I think it sounds like an ideal place to start."

"Have you checked her out otherwise?"

"Sure, and we can't altogether rule out the possibility that she has an agenda of her own. But she was close to Balder. They were at university together and have co-authored a couple of scientific papers. There are also a few society-page photos which show the two of them together. She's a big name in her field."

"OK, I'll go. Will you let her know I'm on my way?"

"I will," Zander said, and gave Blomkvist the address.

So Blomkvist left the office almost immediately, just as he had the previous day, and began to leaf through the research material as he was walking down towards Hornsgatan. Two or three times he bumped into people, but he was concentrating so hard that he scarcely apologized and when at last he raised his head his feet had not taken him as far as Farah Sharif's.

So he stopped off at Mellqvist's coffee bar and drank two double espressos standing up. Not just to get rid of his tiredness. He thought a jolt of caffeine might help with his headache but afterwards he wondered if it had been the right cure. As he left the coffee shop he felt worse than he had when he'd arrived because of all the morons who had read about the night's dramatic events and were making idiotic remarks. They say that young people want nothing more than to become celebrities. He ought to explain to them that it is not worth aspiring to. It just drives you nuts, especially if you have not slept and have seen things that no human being should have to see.

Blomkvist went up Hornsgatan, past McDonald's and the Co-op, cut across to Ringvägen, and as he glanced to the right he stiffened, as if he had seen something significant. But what? It was just a street crossing with a high traffic accident rate and vast volumes of exhaust fumes, nothing more. Then it came to him.

It was the very traffic light Balder had drawn with his mathematical precision, and so once again Blomkvist puzzled over the choice of subject matter. It was not an especially interesting crossing; it was run-down and banal. Maybe that was the point.

The work of art is in the eye of the beholder, and even that tells us no more than that Balder had been here, and had maybe sat on a bench somewhere studying the traffic light. Blomkvist went on past Zinkensdamm sports centre and turned right onto Zinkens väg.


Detective Sergeant Sonja Modig had been running around all morning. Now she was in her office and looked briefly at a framed photograph on her desk. It showed her six-year-old son Axel on the football field after scoring a goal. Modig was a single parent and had a hell of a time organizing her life. She was expecting to have a hell of a time at work the next few days too. There was a knock on the door. It was Bublanski at last, and she was supposed to be handing over responsibility for the investigation. Not that Officer Bubble looked as if he wanted to take responsibility for anything at all.

He was looking unusually dashing in a jacket and tie and a freshly ironed blue shirt. He had combed his hair over his bald patch. There was a dreamy and absent look on his face, as if murder investigations were the last thing on his mind.

"What did the doctor say?" she asked.

"The doctor said that what matters is not that we believe in God. God is not small-minded. What matters is for us to understand that life is serious and rich. We should appreciate it and also try to make the world a better place. Whoever finds a balance between the two is close to God."

"So you were with your rabbi?"

"Yes."

"OK, Jan, I'm not sure whether I can help with the bit about appreciating life, apart from offering you a piece of Swiss orange chocolate which I happen to have in my desk drawer. But if we nail the guy who shot Professor Balder then we'll definitely make the world a little better."

"Swiss orange chocolate and a solution to this murder sound like a decent start."

Modig broke off a piece of chocolate and gave it to Bublanski, who chewed it with a certain reverence.

"Exquisite," he said.

"Isn't it?"

"Just think if life could be like that sometimes," he said, pointing at the photograph of the jubilant Axel on her desk.

"What do you mean?"

"If joy could express itself with the same force as pain," he said.

"Yes, just imagine."

"How are things with Balder's son?" he said.

"Hard to tell," she said. "He's with his mother now. A psychologist has assessed him."

"And what have we got to go on?"

"Not much yet, unfortunately. We've found out what the murder weapon was. A Remington 1911 R1 Carry, bought recently. We're going to follow it up, but I feel sure we're not going to be able to trace it. We have the images from the surveillance cameras, which we are analyzing. But whatever angle we look at we still can't see the man's face, and we can't spot any distinguishing features either—no birthmarks, nothing, only a wristwatch which is just about visible in one sequence. It looks expensive. The guy's clothes are black. His cap is grey without any branding. Jerker tells me he moves like an old junkie. In one picture he's holding a small black box, presumably some kind of computer or GSM station. He probably used it to hack the alarm system."

"I'd heard that. How do you hack a burglar alarm?"

"Jerker has looked into that too and it isn't easy, especially not an alarm of this specification, but it can be done. The system was connected to the Net and to the mobile network and sent a feed of information to Milton Security over at Slussen. It's not impossible that the guy recorded a frequency from the alarm with his box and managed to hack it that way. Or else he'd bumped into Balder when he was out walking and stolen some information electronically from the professor's NFC."

"What's an NFC?"

"Near Field Communication, a function on Balder's mobile which he used to activate the alarm."

"It was simpler in the days when burglars had crowbars," Bublanski said. "Any cars in the area?"

"A dark-coloured vehicle was parked a hundred yards away by the side of the road with the engine running on and off, but the only person to have seen it is an old lady by the name of Birgitta Roos; she has no idea what make it was. Maybe a Volvo, according to her. Or like the one her son has. Her son has a BMW."

"Oh, wonderful."

"Yes, the investigation is looking a bit bleak," Modig said. "The killers had the advantage of the night and the weather. They could move around the area undisturbed, and apart from what Mikael Blomkvist told us we've only got one sighting. It's from a thirteen-year-old, Ivan Grede. A slightly odd, skinny figure who had leukaemia when he was small and who has decorated his room entirely in a Japanese style. He has a precocious way of expressing himself. Young Ivan went for a pee in the middle of the night and from the bathroom window he saw a tall man by the water's edge. The man was looking out over the water and making the sign of the cross with his fists. It looked both aggressive and religious at the same time, Ivan said."

"Not a good combination."

"No, religion and violence combined don't as a rule bode well. But Ivan wasn't sure that it really was the sign of the cross. It looked like it, but there was something else too, he says. Maybe it was a military oath. For a while he was afraid that the man was going to walk into the water and drown himself. There was something ceremonial about the situation, he said."

"But there was no suicide."

"No, the man jogged on in the direction of Balder's house. He had a backpack, and dark clothes, possibly camouflage trousers. He was powerful and athletic and reminded Ivan of his old toys, he said, his ninja warriors."

"That doesn't sound good either."

"Not good at all. Presumably this was the man who shot at Blomkvist."

"And Blomkvist didn't see his face?"

"No, he threw himself to the ground when the man turned and shot at him. It all happened very quickly. But according to Blomkvist the man looked as if he had military training and that fits with Ivan Grede's observations. I have to agree: the speed and efficiency of the operation point in that direction."

"Have you got to the bottom of why Blomkvist was there?"

"Oh, definitely. If anything was done properly last night, it was the interviews with him. Have a look at this." Modig handed over a transcript. "Blomkvist had been in touch with one of Balder's former assistants who claimed that the professor had been targeted by a data breach and had his technology stolen. The story interested Blomkvist. But Balder had been living as a recluse and had virtually no contact with the outside world. All the shopping and errands were done by a housekeeper called . . . just a second . . . Fru Rask, Lottie Rask, who incidentally had strict instructions not to say a word about the son living in the house. I'll come to that in a moment. Then last night, I'm guessing that Balder was worried and wanted to get some anxiety off his chest. Don't forget, he had just been told that he was subject to a serious threat. His burglar alarm had gone off and two policemen were guarding the house. Perhaps he suspected that his days were numbered. No way of knowing. In any case he called Mikael Blomkvist in the middle of the night and said he wanted to tell him something."

"In the olden days in situations like that you would call a priest."

"So now you call a journalist. Well, it's pure speculation. We only know what Balder said on Blomkvist's voicemail. Apart from that we have no idea what he was planning to tell him. Blomkvist says he doesn't know either, and I believe him. But I seem to be pretty much the only one who does. Ekström, who's being a massive nuisance by the way, is convinced Blomkvist is holding back things which he plans to publish in his magazine. I find that very hard to believe. Blomkvist is a tricky bugger, we all know that. But he isn't someone who will knowingly, deliberately sabotage a police investigation."

"Definitely not."

"Ekström is coming on strong and saying that Blomkvist should be arrested for perjury and obstruction and God knows what else."

"That's not going to do any good."

"No, and bearing in mind what Blomkvist is capable of I think we're better off staying on good terms with him."

"I suppose we'll have to talk to him again."

"I agree."

"And this thing with Lasse Westman?"

"We've just spoken to him, and it's not an edifying story. Westman had been to the Artists' Bar and the Theatre Grill and the Opera Bar and Riche, you get the idea, and was ranting and raving about Balder and the boy for hours on end. He drove his friends crazy. The more Westman drank and the more money he blew, the more fixated he became."

"Why was this important to him?"

"Partly it was a hang-up. You get that with alcoholics. I remember it from an old uncle. Every time he got loaded, he got something fixed in his mind. But obviously there's more to it than that. At first Westman went on about the custody ruling, and if he had been a different person one might believe that he really was concerned for the boy. But in this case . . . I suppose you know that Westman has a conviction for assault."

"No, I didn't."

"He had a relationship some years ago with some fashion blogger, Renata Kapusinski. He beat the crap out of her. I think he even bit her rather badly in the cheek. Also, Balder had intended to report him. He never sent in the paperwork—perhaps because of the legal position he found himself in—but it clearly suggests that he suspected Westman of being violent towards his son as well."

"What are you saying?"

"Balder had noticed unexplained bruises on the boy's body—and in this he's backed up by a psychologist from the Centre for Autism. So it was . . ."

". . . probably not love and concern which drove Westman out to Saltsjö-baden."

"More likely it was money. After Balder took back his son, he had stopped or at least reduced the child support he had agreed to pay."

"Westman didn't try to report him for that?"

"He probably didn't dare to, in the circumstances."

"What else does the custody ruling say?" Bublanski said after a pause.

"That Balder was a useless father."

"Was he?"

"He certainly wasn't evil, like Westman. But there'd been an incident. After the divorce, Balder had his son every other weekend, and at that time he was living in an apartment in Östermalm with books from floor to ceiling. One of those weekends, when August was six, he was in the sitting room—with Balder glued to his computer in the next room as usual. We don't know exactly what happened. But there was a small stepladder propped against one of the bookshelves. August climbed it and probably took hold of some of the books higher up and fell and broke his elbow. He knocked himself unconscious, but Balder didn't hear anything. He just kept working and only after several hours did he discover August lying on the floor next to those books, moaning. At that he became hysterical and drove the boy to the emergency room."

"And he lost custody altogether?"

"Not only that. He was declared emotionally immature and incapable of taking care of his child. He was not allowed to be alone with August. But frankly I don't think much of that ruling."

"Why not?"

"Because it was an uncontested hearing. The ex-wife's lawyer went at it hammer and tongs, while Balder grovelled and said he was useless and irresponsible and unfit to live and God knows what. What the tribunal wrote was malicious and tendentious, to my mind: to the effect that Balder had never been able to connect with other people and had always sought refuge with machines. Now that I've had time to look into his life a little, I'm not that impressed by how it was dealt with. His guilt-laden tirades and self-criticism were taken as gospel by the tribunal. At any rate Balder was extremely cooperative. As I said, he agreed to pay a large amount of child support, forty thousand a month, I believe, plus a one-off payment of nine hundred thousand kronor for unforeseen expenses. Not long after that he took himself off to America."

"But then he came back."

"Yes, and there were a number of reasons for that. He'd had his technology stolen, and maybe he identified who had done it. He found himself in a serious dispute with his employer. But I think it had also to do with his son. The woman from the Centre for Autism I mentioned, she'd been very optimistic about the boy's development at an early stage. But then nothing turned out as she'd hoped. She also received reports that Hanna Balder and Westman had failed to live up to their responsibilities when it came to his schooling. It had been agreed that August would be taught at home, but the special-needs teachers seem to have been played off against each other. Probably the money for his education was misappropriated and fake teachers' names used, all sorts of crap like that. But that's an altogether different story which somebody will have to look into at some point."

"You were talking about the woman from the Centre for Autism."

"That's right. She smelled a rat and called Hanna and Westman and was informed that everything was fine. But she had a feeling that wasn't true. So against normal practice she made an unannounced home visit and, when they finally let her in, she could tell that the boy was not doing well, that his development had stagnated. She also saw those bruises. She rang Balder in San Francisco, had a long conversation with him, and soon after that he moved back and took his son with him to his new house in Saltsjöbaden, disregarding the custody order."

"How did he manage that, seeing how keen Westman was to get the child support?"

"Good question. According to Westman, Balder more or less kidnapped the boy. But Hanna has a different version of the story. She says that Frans turned up and seemed to have changed, so she let him take August. She even thought that the boy would be better off with his father."

"And Westman?"

"According to her, Westman was drunk and had just landed a big part in a new TV production, and was feeling cocky and over-confident. So he agreed to it. However much he may have gone on about the boy's welfare, I think he was glad to be rid of him."

"But then?"

"Then he regretted it, and on top of everything else he was sacked from the series because he couldn't stay sober. He suddenly wanted to have August back, or not so much him, of course . . ."

"The child support."

"Exactly, and that was confirmed by his drinking pals. When Westman's credit card was rejected during the course of the evening, he really started ranting and raving about the boy. He bummed five hundred kronor off a young woman in the bar to pay for a taxi to Saltsjöbaden in the middle of the night."

Bublanski was lost in his thoughts for a while and gazed once again at the photograph of Modig's son.

"What a mess," he said.

"Right."

"Under normal circumstances we would be close to solving this one. We'd find our motive somewhere in that custody battle. But these guys who hack alarm systems and look like ninja warriors, they don't fit the picture."

"No."

"There's something else I'm wondering about."

"What's that?"

"If August can't read, then what was he doing trying to reach those books?"


Blomkvist was sitting opposite Farah Sharif at her kitchen table with a cup of tea, looking out at Tantolunden. Even though he knew it was a sign of weakness, he wished he did not have a story to write. He wished he could just sit there without having to press her for information.

She did not look as if talking would do her much good. Her whole face had collapsed and the intense dark eyes, which had looked straight through him at the front door, now seemed disoriented. Sometimes she muttered Balder's name like a mantra or an incantation. Maybe she had loved him. Farah was fifty-two years old and a very attractive woman, not beautiful in a conventional way but with a regal bearing. He had definitely loved *her*.

"Tell me, what was he like," Blomkvist said.

"Frans?"

"Yes."

"A paradox."

"In what way?"

"In all sorts of ways. But mainly because he worked so hard on the one thing which worried him more than anything else. Maybe a bit like Oppenheimer at Los Alamos. He was engrossed in something he believed could be our ruin."

"Now you've lost me."

"Frans wanted to replicate biological evolution on a digital level. He was working on self-teaching algorithms—the idea is they can enhance themselves through trial and error. He also contributed to the development of quantum computers, as people call them, which Google, Solifon, and the NSA are working on. His objective was to achieve AGI, or Artificial General Intelligence."

"And what is that?"

"Something with the intelligence of a human being, but the speed and precision of a computer. If a thing like that could be created, it would give us enormous advantages within numerous fields."

"I'm sure."

"There is an extraordinary amount of research going on in this area, and even though most scientists aren't specifically aiming for AGI, competition is driving us in that direction. Nobody can afford *not* to create applications which are as intelligent as possible. Nobody can afford to put the brake on development. Just think of what we have achieved so far. Just think back to what you had in your mobile five years ago compared to what's in there today."

"True."

"Before he became so secretive, Frans told me he estimated that we could get to AGI within thirty or forty years. That may sound ambitious, but for my part I wonder if he wasn't being too conservative. The capacity of computers doubles every eighteen months, and the human brain is bad at grasping that kind of exponential growth. It's like the grain of rice on the chessboard, you know? You put one grain of rice on the first square, two on the second, four on the third, eight on the fourth."

"And soon the grains of rice have flooded the world."

"The pace of growth goes on increasing and in the end it escapes our control. The interesting thing isn't actually when we reach AGI, but what happens after that. Just a few days after we've reached AGI, we'll have ASI— Artificial Super Intelligence—used to describe something more intelligent than we are. After that it'll just get quicker and quicker. Computers will start enhancing themselves at an accelerating pace, perhaps by a factor of ten, and become a hundred, a thousand, ten thousand times cleverer than we are. What happens then?"

"I dread to think."

"Quite. Intelligence in itself is not predictable. We don't know where human intelligence will take us. We know even less what will happen with a superintelligence."

"In the worst case we'll be no more interesting to the computer than little white mice," Blomkvist said, thinking of what he had written to Salander.

"In the worst case? We share 90 percent of our DNA with mice, and we're assumed to be about one hundred times as intelligent. Only one hundred times. Here's something completely new, not subject to these kinds of limitations, according to mathematical models. And it can become perhaps a million times more intelligent. Can you imagine?"

"I'm certainly trying to," Blomkvist said with a careful smile.

"I mean, how do you think a computer would feel when it wakes up to find itself captured and controlled by primitive little creatures like us. Why would it put up with that?" she said. "Why on earth should it show us any consideration, still less let us dig around in its entrails in order to shut down the process? We risk being confronted by an explosion of intelligence, a technological singularity, as Vernor Vinge put it. Everything that happens after that lies beyond our event horizon."

"So the very instant we create a superintelligence we lose control, is that right?"

"The risk is that everything we know about the world will cease to be relevant, and it'll be the end of human existence."

"You *are* joking."

"I know it sounds crazy, but it's a very real question. There are thousands of people all over the world working to prevent a development like this. Many are optimists, or even foresee some kind of utopia. There's talk of friendly ASI, superintelligences which are programmed from the start to do nothing but help us. The idea is something along the lines of what Asimov envisioned in his book *I, Robot:* built-in laws which forbid the machines to harm us. Innovator and author Ray Kurzweil has visions of a wonderful world in which nanotechnology allows us to integrate ourselves with computers, and share our future with them. But there are no guarantees. Laws can be repealed. The intent of initial programming can be changed and it's fatally easy to make anthropomorphic mistakes: to ascribe human characteristics to machines and misunderstand what drives them, inherently. Frans was obsessed with these questions and, as I said, he was of two minds. He both longed for intelligent computers and he also worried about them."

"He couldn't help but build his monsters."

"A bit like that, though that's putting it drastically."

"How far had he got?"

"Further, I think, than anyone could imagine, and that may have been yet another reason why he was so secretive about his work at Solifon. He was afraid his programme would end up in the wrong hands. He was even afraid the programme would come into contact with the Internet and merge with it. He called it August, after his son."

"And where is it now?"

"He never went anywhere without it. It must have been right by the bed when he was shot. But the terrible thing is that the police say there was no computer there."

"I didn't see one either. But then my focus was elsewhere."

"It must have been dreadful."

"Perhaps you heard that I also saw the man who killed him," Blomkvist said. "He was carrying a backpack."

"That doesn't sound good. But with a bit of luck the computer will turn up somewhere in the house."

"Let's hope so. Do you have any idea who stole his technology the first time around?"

"Yes, I do, as a matter of fact."

"I'm very interested."

"I can see that. But the sad thing is that I have some personal responsibility for this mess. Frans was working himself to death, you see, and I was worried he would burn out. That was about the time he had lost custody of August."

"When was that?"

"Two years ago. He was utterly worn out. He wasn't sleeping, and he went around blaming himself, yet he was incapable of dropping his research. He threw himself into it as if it were all he had left in life, and so I arranged for him to get some assistants who could take some of the load. I let him have my best students. I knew that none of them was a model of probity, but they were ambitious and gifted, and their admiration for Frans was boundless. Everything looked promising. But then . . ."

"His technology was stolen."

"He had clear proof of that when the application from Truegames was submitted to the U.S. Patent Office in August last year. Every unique aspect of his technology had been duplicated and written down there. It was obvious. At first they all suspected their computers had been hacked, but I was sceptical from the start—I knew how sophisticated Frans's encryption was. But since there was no other plausible explanation, that was the initial assumption, and for a while maybe Frans believed it himself. That was nonsense, of course."

"What are you saying?" Blomkvist burst out. "Surely the data breach was confirmed by experts."

"Yes, by some idiot show-off at the NDRE. But that was just Frans's way of protecting his boys, or it could have been more than that. I suspect he also wanted to play detective, although heaven knows how he could be so stupid. You see . . ." Farah took a deep breath. "I learned all this only a few weeks ago. Frans and little August were here for dinner and I sensed at once that he had something important to tell me. It was hanging in the air. After a couple of glasses he asked me to put away my mobile and began to speak in a whisper. I have to admit that at first I was irritated. He was going on again about his young hacker genius."

"Hacker genius?" Blomkvist said, trying to sound neutral.

"A girl he spoke about so much that it was doing my head in. I won't bore you with the full story, but she'd turned up out of the blue at one of his lectures and practically lectured *him* on the concept of singularity. She impressed Frans, and he started to open up to her, it's understandable. A mega-nerd like Frans can't have found all that many people he could talk to on his own level, and when he realized that the girl was also a hacker he asked her to take a look at their computers. At the time they had all the equipment at the home of one of the assistants."

All Blomkvist said was "Linus Brandell."

"Yes," Farah said. "The girl came round to his place in Östermalm and threw him out. Then she got to work on the computers. She couldn't find any sign of a breach, but she didn't leave it at that. She had a list of Frans's assistants and hacked them all from Linus's computer. It didn't take long for her to realize that one of them had sold him out to none other than Solifon."

"And who was it?"

"Frans didn't want to tell me, even though I pressed him. But the girl apparently called him directly from Linus's apartment. Frans was in San Francisco at the time, and you can imagine: betrayed by one of his own! I was expecting him to report the guy right away and raise hell. But he had a better idea. He asked the girl to pretend they really had been hacked."

"Why would he do that?"

"He didn't want any traces of evidence to be tidied away. He wanted to understand more about what had happened. I suppose it makes sense—for one of the world's leading software businesses to steal and exploit his technology was obviously far more serious than if some good-for-nothing, unprincipled shit of a student had done the same. Because Solifon isn't just one of the most respected research groups in the States, they had also been trying to recruit Frans for years. He was livid. 'Those bastards were trying to seduce me and stealing from me at the same time,' he growled."

"Let me be sure I've got this right." Blomkvist said. "You're saying he took a job at Solifon in order to find out why and how they'd stolen from him?"

"If there's one thing I've learned over the years, it's just how difficult it can be to understand a person's motivation. The salary and the freedom and the resources obviously came into it. But apart from that: yes, I imagine you're right. He'd worked out that Solifon was involved in the theft even before this hacker girl examined his computers. She gave him the specific information and that enabled him to dig into the mess. In the end it turned out to be much more difficult than he expected, and people started getting suspicious. It wasn't long before he became fantastically unpopular, so he kept more and more to himself. But he did find something."

"What?"

"This is where it all gets sensitive. I shouldn't really be telling you."

"Yet here we are."

"Yet here we are. Not only because I've always had the utmost respect for your journalism. It occurred to me this morning that it may not have been a coincidence that Frans rang you last night rather than Säpo's Industry Protection Group, who he had also been in touch with. I think he was beginning to suspect a leak there. It may have been no more than paranoia—Frans displayed a variety of symptoms of persecution mania. But it was you he called, and now I hope that I can fulfil his wish."

"I understand."

"At Solifon there's a department called 'Y,' " Farah said. "Google X is the model, the department where they work on 'moonshots,' as they call them, wild and far-fetched ideas like looking for eternal life or connecting search engines to brain neurons. If any place will achieve AGI or ASI, that's probably it. Frans was assigned to 'Y.' But that wasn't as smart as it may have sounded."

"And why not?"

"Because he had found out from his hacker girl that there was a secret group of business intelligence analysts at 'Y,' headed up by a character called Zigmund Eckerwald, also known as Zeke."

"And who is that?"

"The very person who had been communicating with Frans's treacherous assistant."

"So Eckerwald was the thief."

"A thief of the highest order. On the face of it, the work carried out by Eckerwald's group was perfectly legitimate. They compiled information on leading scientists and promising research projects. Every large high-tech firm has a similar operation. They want to know what's going on and who they should be recruiting. But Frans understood that the group went beyond that. They stole—through hacker attacks, espionage, moles, and bribery."

"But then why didn't he report them?"

"It was tricky to prove. They were careful, of course. But in the end Frans went to the owner, Nicolas Grant. Grant was horrified and apparently organized an internal investigation. But the investigation found nothing, either because Eckerwald had gotten rid of the evidence or because the investigation was just for show. It left Frans in a tight spot. Everyone turned on him. Eckerwald must have been behind it, and I'm sure he had no trouble getting the others to join in. Frans was already perceived as paranoid and became progressively isolated and frozen out. I can picture it. How he would sit there and become more and more awkward and contrary, and refuse to say a word to anyone."

"So he had no concrete evidence, you think?"

"Well, he did at least have the proof the hacker girl had given him: that Eckerwald had stolen Frans's technology and sold it on."

"And he knew that for sure?"

"Without a shadow of a doubt. Besides, he had realized that Eckerwald's group was not working alone. It had backing from outside, in all likelihood from the American intelligence services and also . . ."

Farah hesitated.

"Yes?"

"This is where he was a bit more cryptic, and it may be that he didn't know all that much. But he had come across an alias, he said, for the person who was the real leader outside Solifon. 'Thanos.'"

"Thanos?"

"That's right. He said that this individual was greatly feared. But he didn't want to say more than that. He needed life insurance, he claimed, for when the lawyers came after him."

"You said you didn't know which of his assistants sold him out. But you must have given it a great deal of thought," said Blomkvist.

"I have, and sometimes, I don't know . . . I wondered if it wasn't all of them."

"Why do you say that?"

"When they started working for Frans, they were young, ambitious, and gifted. By the time they finished, they were fed up with life and full of anxieties. Maybe Frans worked them too hard. Or maybe there's something else tormenting them."

"Do you have all their names?"

"I do. They're my boys—unfortunately, I'd have to say. First there's Linus Brandell, I've already mentioned him. He's twenty-four now, and just drifts around playing computer games and drinking too much. For a while he had a good job as a games developer at Crossfire. But he lost it when he started calling in sick and accusing his colleagues of spying on him. Then there's Arvid Wrange, maybe you've heard of him. He was a promising chess player, once upon a time. His father pushed him in a pretty inhuman way and in the end Arvid had enough and came to study with me. I'd hoped that he would have completed his PhD long ago. But instead he props up the bars around Stureplan and seems rootless. He came into his own for a while when he was with Frans. But there was also a lot of silly competition among the boys. Arvid and Basim, the third guy, came to hate each other—at least Arvid hated Basim. Basim Malik probably doesn't do hate. He's a sensitive, gifted boy who was taken on by Solifon Nordic a year ago. But he ran out of steam pretty quickly. Right now he's being treated for depression at Ersta hospital and it so happens that his mother, whom I know vaguely, rang me this morning to tell me that he's under sedation. When he found out what had happened to Frans, he tried to slash his wrists. It's devastating, but at the same time I do wonder: Was it just grief? Or was it also guilt?"

"How is he now?"

"He's not in any danger from a physical point of view. And then there's Niklas Lagerstedt, and he ... well, what can I say about him? He's not like the others, at least not on the surface. He wouldn't drink himself into oblivion or even think of harming himself. He's a young man with moral objections to most things, including violent computer games and porn. He's a member of the Mission Covenant Church. His wife is a paediatrician and they have a young son called Jesper. On top of all that he's a consultant with the National Criminal Police, responsible for the computer system coming into service in the new year; which means he's had to go through security clearance. But who knows how thorough it was."

"Why do you say that?"

"Because behind that respectable façade he's a nasty piece of work. I happen to know that he's embezzled parts of his in-laws' fortune. He's a hypocrite."

"Have these guys been questioned?"

"Säpo talked to them, but nothing came of it. At that time it was thought that Frans was the victim of a data breach."

"I imagine the police will want to question them again now."

"I assume so."

"Do you happen to know if Balder did much sketching in his free time?"

"Sketching?"

"Really detailed drawings of scenes."

"No, I haven't heard anything about that," she said. "Why do you ask?"

"I saw a fantastic drawing at his home, of a traffic light up here on the intersection of Hornsgatan and Ringvägen. It was flawless, a sort of snapshot in the dark."

"How strange. Frans wasn't usually in this part of town."

"There's something about that drawing that won't let go of me," Blomkvist said, and he realized to his surprise that Farah had taken hold of his hand. He stroked her hair. Then he stood up with a feeling that he was on the scent. He said goodbye and went out onto the street.

On the way back up Zinkens väg he called Berger and asked her to type another question in [Lisbeth stuff].

# CHAPTER 14

# NOVEMBER 21

Ove Levin was sitting in his office with a view over Slussen and Riddarfjärden and not doing much at all except Googling himself in the hope of coming across something to cheer him up. What he read instead was that he was sleazy and flabby and that he had betrayed his ideals. All that in a blog written by a slip of a girl at the Institute for Media Studies at Stockholm University. It made him so furious that he could not bring himself to write her name in the little black book he kept, of people who would never get a job in the Serner Group.

He could not be bothered to burden his brain with idiots who had no idea what it takes, and would only ever write underpaid articles in obscure cultural magazines. Rather than wallow in destructive thoughts he went into his online account and checked his portfolio. That helped a bit, at least to begin with. It was a good day in the markets. The Nasdaq and the Dow Jones had both gone up last night and the Stockholm index was 1.1 percent up too. The dollar, to which he was rather too exposed, had risen, and according to the update of a few seconds ago his portfolio was worth 12,161,389 kronor.

Not bad for a man who had once covered house fires and knife fights for the morning edition of *Expressen*. Twelve million, plus the apartment in Villastaden and the villa in Cannes. They could post whatever they wanted on their blogs. He was well provided for, and he checked the value of his portfolio again. 12,149,101. Jesus Christ, was it falling? 12,131,737. He grimaced. There was no reason why the market should be falling, was there? The employment figures had been good, after all. He took the tumble in value almost personally and could not help thinking about *Millennium*, however insignificant it might be in the bigger picture. He found himself getting worked up again as he kept remembering the openly hostile look on Erika Berger's beautiful face yesterday afternoon. Things had not improved this morning.

He had just about had a fit. Blomkvist had cropped up on every site, and that hurt. Not only because Levin had so gleefully registered that the younger generation hardly knew who Blomkvist was. He also hated the media logic which said that you became a star—a star journalist or a star actor or whatever the hell it might be—simply because you found yourself in some sort of trouble. He would have been happier to read about has-been Blomkvist who wasn't even going to keep his job at his own magazine, not if Ove Levin and Serner Media had anything to do with it. Instead they said: Why Frans Balder, of all people?

Why on earth did he have to be murdered right under Blomkvist's nose? Wasn't that just typical? So infuriating. Even if those useless journalists out there hadn't realized it yet, Levin knew that Balder was a big name. Not long ago Serner's own newspaper, *Business Daily,* had produced a special supplement on Swedish scientific research which had given him a price tag: four billion kronor, though God knows how they got to that figure. Balder was a star, no doubt about it. Most important, he was a Garbo. He never gave interviews, which made him all the more sought-after.

How many requests had Balder received from Serner's own journalists? As many as he had refused or, for that matter, simply not bothered to answer. Many of Levin's colleagues out there thought Balder was sitting on a fantastic story. He couldn't bear the idea that, so the newspaper reports said, Balder had wanted to talk to Blomkvist in the middle of the night. Could Blomkvist really have a scoop on top of everything else? That would be disastrous. Once more, almost obsessively, Levin went onto the *Afton-bladet* site and was met with the headline:

## WHAT DID TOP SWEDISH SCIENTIST HAVE TO SAY TO MIKAEL BLOMKVIST?

### MYSTERY CALL JUST BEFORE THE MURDER

The article was illustrated by a double-column photograph of Mikael Blomkvist which did not show any flab at all. Those bastard editors had of course chosen the most flattering photograph they could find, and that made Levin angrier still. I have to do something about this, he thought. But what? How could he put a stop to Blomkvist without barging in like some old East German censor and making everything worse? He looked out towards Riddarfjärden and an idea came to him. Borg, he thought. My enemy's enemy can be my best friend.

"Sanna," he shouted.

"Yes, Ove?"

Sanna Lind was his young secretary.

"Book a lunch at once with William Borg at Sturehof. If he says he has something else on, tell him this is more important. He can even have a raise," he said, and thought, *Why not?* If he's prepared to help me in this mess then it's only fair he gets something out of it.

Hanna Balder was standing in the living room at Torsgatan looking in despair at August, who had yet again dug out paper and crayons. She had been told that she had to discourage him, and she did not like doing it. Not that she questioned the psychologist's advice and expertise, but she had her doubts. August had seen his father murdered and if he wanted to draw, why stop him? Even if it did not seem to be doing him much good.

His body trembled when he started drawing and his eyes shone with an intense, tormented light. The pattern of squares spreading out and multiplying in mirrors was a strange theme, given what had happened. But what did she know? Maybe it was the same as with his series of numbers. Even though she did not understand, it presumably meant something to him, and perhaps—who knows?—those squares were his own way of coming to terms with events. Shouldn't she just ignore the instructions? After all, who would find out? She had read somewhere that a mother should rely on her intuition. Gut feeling is often a better tool than all the psychological theories in the world. She decided to let August draw.

But suddenly the boy's back stiffened like a bow, and Hanna could not help thinking back to what the psychologist had said. She took a hesitant step forward and looked down at the paper. She gave a start, and felt very uncomfortable. At first she could not make sense of it.

She saw the same pattern of squares repeating themselves in two surrounding mirrors and it was extremely skilfully done. But there was something else there as well, a shadow which grew out of the squares, like a demon, a phantom, and it frightened the living daylights out of her. She started to think of films about children who become possessed. She snatched the drawing from the boy and crumpled it up without fully understanding why. Then she shut her eyes and expected to hear that heart-rending toneless cry again.

But she heard no cry, just a muttering which sounded almost like words—impossible because the boy did not speak. Instead Hanna prepared herself for a violent outburst with August thrashing back and forth over the living-room floor. But there was no attack either, only a calm and composed determination as August took hold of a new piece of paper and started to draw the same squares again. Hanna had no choice but to carry him to his room. Afterwards she would describe what happened as pure horror.

August kicked and screamed and lashed out, and Hanna barely managed to keep hold of him. For a long time she lay in the bed with her arms knotted around him wishing that she could go to pieces herself. She briefly considered waking Lasse and asking him to give August one of those tranquilizing suppositories they now had, but then discarded that idea. Lasse was bound to be in a foul mood and she hated to give a child tranquilizers, however much Valium she herself took. There had to be some other way.

She was falling apart, desperately considering one option after the next. She thought of her mother in Katrineholm, of her agent Mia, of the nice woman who rang last night, Gabriella Grane, and then of the psychologist again, Einar Fors-something, who had brought August to her. She had not particularly liked him. On the other hand he had offered to look after August for a while. He was the one who said August should not draw, so he should be sorting out this mess.

In the end she let go of her son and dug out the psychologist's card to call him. August immediately made a break for the living room to start drawing his damn squares again.

·  ·  ·

Einar Forsberg did not have a great deal of experience. He was forty-eight years old and with his deep-set blue eyes, brand-new Dior glasses, and brown corduroy jacket he could easily be taken for an intellectual. But anyone who had ever disagreed with him would know that there was something stiff and dogmatic about his way of thinking and he often concealed his lack of knowledge behind dogma and cocksure pronouncements.

It had only been two years since he qualified as a psychologist. Before that he was a gym teacher from Tyresö, and if you had asked his old pupils about him they would all have roared: "Silence, cattle! Be quiet, oh my beasts!" Forsberg had loved to shout those words, only half joking, when he wanted order in the classroom and even though he had hardly been anyone's favourite teacher he had kept his boys in line. It was this ability which persuaded him that he could put his skills to better use elsewhere.

He had been working at Oden's Medical Centre for Children and Adolescents for one year. Oden's was an emergency service which took in children and young people whose parents could not cope. Not even Forsberg—who had always been a staunch defender of whatever workplace he was in—believed that the centre functioned especially well. It was all crisis management and not enough long-term work. Children would come in after traumatic experiences at home and the psychologists were far too busy trying to manage breakdowns and aggressive behaviour to be able to devote themselves to resolving underlying causes. Even so, Forsberg thought he was doing some good, especially when he used his old classroom authority to calm hysterical children, or when he handled crisis situations out in the field.

He liked to work with policemen and he loved the tension in the air after dramatic events. He had been excited and expectant as he drove out to the house in Saltsjöbaden in the course of his night duty. There was a touch of Hollywood about the situation, he thought. A Swedish scientist had been murdered, his eight-year-old son was a witness, and none other than Forsberg had been sent to try to get the boy to open up. He straightened his hair and his glasses several times in the rearview mirror.

He wanted to make a stylish impression, but once he arrived he was not exactly a success. He could not make the boy out. Still, he felt acknowledged and important. The detectives asked him how they should go about questioning the child and—even though he did not have a clue—his answer was received with respect. That gave his ego a little boost and he did his best to be helpful. He found out that the boy suffered from infantile autism and had never spoken or been receptive to the world around him.

"There's nothing we can do for the time being," he said. "His mental faculties are too weak. As a psychologist I have to put his need for care first." The policemen listened to him with serious expressions and let him drive the boy home to his mother—who was another little bonus in the whole story.

She was the actress Hanna Balder. He had had the hots for her ever since he saw her in *The Mutineers* and he remembered her hips and her long legs—and even though she was now a bit older she was still attractive. Besides, her current partner was clearly a bastard. Forsberg did his best to appear knowledgeable and charming in a low-key way; within moments he got an opportunity to be authoritative, and that made him proud.

With a wild expression on his face the son began to draw black and white blocks, or squares, and Forsberg pronounced that this was unhealthy. It was precisely the kind of destructive compulsive behaviour that autistic children slip into, and he insisted that August stop at once. This was not received with as much gratitude as he had hoped for. Still, it had made him feel decisive and manly, and while he was at it he almost paid Hanna a compliment for her performance in *The Mutineers*. But then he decided that it was probably not the right time. Maybe that had been a mistake.

Now it was 1:00 in the afternoon and he was back home at his terraced house in Vällingby. He was in the bathroom with his electric toothbrush, feeling totally exhausted, when his mobile rang. At first he was irritated—but then he smiled. It was none other than Hanna Balder.

"Forsberg," he answered in an urbane voice.

"Hello," she said. "August, August . . ."

She sounded desperate and angry. But he could not understand why.

"Tell me, what's the problem?"

"All he wants to do is draw his chessboard squares. But you're saying he isn't allowed to."

"No, no, it's compulsive. But please, just stay calm."

"How the hell am I supposed to stay calm?"

"The boy needs you to be composed."

"But I can't be. He's yelling and lashing out at everything. You said you could help."

"Well, yes," he said, hesitant at first. Then he brightened, as if he had won some sort of victory. "Absolutely, of course. I'll see to it that he gets a place with us at Oden's."

"Wouldn't that be letting him down?"

"On the contrary, you're just taking account of his needs. I'll see to it personally that you can visit us as often as you like."

"Maybe that's the best solution."

"I'm sure of it."

"Will you come right away?"

"I'll be with you as soon as I can," he said. First he had to smarten himself up a bit. Then he added: "Did I tell you that I loved you in *The Mutineers?*"


It was no surprise to Levin that William Borg was already at the table at Sturehof, nor that he ordered the most expensive items on the menu, sole meunière and a glass of Pouilly Fumé. Journalists generally made the most of it when he invited them to lunch. But it did surprise—and annoy—him that Borg had taken the initiative, as if he were the one with the money and the power. Why did he have to mention that raise? He should have kept Borg on tenterhooks, let him sit there and sweat instead.

"A little bird whispered in my ear that you're having difficulties with *Millennium,*" Borg said, and Levin thought: I'd give my right arm to wipe that self-righteous smirk off his face.

"You've been misinformed," he said stiffly.

"Really?"

"We have the situation under control."

"How so, if you don't mind my asking?"

"If the editorial team is disposed to accept change and is ready to recognize the problems it has, we'll back them."

"And if not . . ."

"We'll pull out, and *Millennium* will be unlikely to stay afloat for more than a few months, which would of course be a great shame. But that's what the market looks like at the moment. Better magazines than *Millennium* have gone under. It's been only a modest investment for us and we can manage without it."

"Skip the bullshit, Ove. I know that this is a matter of pride for you."

"It's just business."

"I'd heard that you wanted to get Mikael Blomkvist off the editorial team."

"We've been thinking of transferring him to London."

"Isn't that a bit harsh, considering what he's done for the magazine?"

"We've made him a very generous offer," Levin said, feeling that he was being unnecessarily defensive and predictable.

He had almost forgotten the purpose of the lunch.

"Personally I don't blame you," Borg said. "You can ship him off to China, for all I care. I'm just wondering if it isn't going to be a bit tricky for you if Blomkvist makes a grand comeback with this Frans Balder story."

"Why would that happen? He's lost his sting. You of all people have pointed that out—and with considerable success, if I may say so," Levin said with an attempt at sarcasm.

"Well, yes, but I did get a little help."

"Not from me, you didn't, of that you can be sure. I hated that column. Thought it was badly written and tendentious. The one who kicked off the campaign against him was Thorvald Serner, you know that."

"But you can't be altogether unhappy about the way things are going right now?"

"Listen to me, William. I have the greatest respect for Mikael Blomkvist."

"You don't have to put on your politician act with me, Ove."

Levin felt like ramming something down Borg's throat.

"I'm just being open and honest," he said. "And I've always thought Blomkvist a fantastic reporter, of a different calibre from you and everyone else of his generation."

"Is that so?" Borg said, suddenly looking meek, and that made Levin feel better right away.

"That's how it is. We should be grateful to Blomkvist for the revelations he's given us, and I wish him all the best, I really do. But unfortunately it's not my job to get nostalgic and look back to the good old days. I have to concede that you have a point in suggesting that the man has gotten out of step with the times and that he could get in the way of your plans to relaunch *Millennium*."

"True, true."

"So for that reason it would be good if there weren't too many headlines about him right now."

"Positive headlines, you mean?"

"Maybe so, yes," Levin said. "That's another reason I invited you to lunch."

"Grateful for that, of course. And I do think I have something to offer. I had a call this morning from my old squash buddy," Borg said, clearly trying to regain his earlier self-confidence.

"And who's that?"

"Richard Ekström, the chief prosecutor. He's in charge of the preliminary investigation into the Balder killing. And he's not a member of the Blomkvist fan club."

"After that Zalachenko business, right?"

"Exactly. Blomkvist scuppered Ekström's entire strategy on that case and now he's worried that he's sabotaging this investigation as well."

"In what way?"

"Blomkvist isn't saying everything that he knows. He spoke to Balder just before the murder and came face-to-face with the killer. Even so he had surprisingly little to say for himself during the interviews. Ekström suspects he's saving the juiciest bits for his article."

"Interesting."

"Isn't it? We're talking about a man who was ridiculed in the media and is now so desperate for a scoop that he's prepared to let someone get away with murder. An old star reporter willing to cast social responsibility to the winds when his magazine finds itself in a financial crisis. And who has just learned that Serner Media wants to kick him off the editorial team. Hardly surprising that he's gone a step or two too far."

"I see your point. Is it anything you'd like to write about?"

"I don't think that would be productive, to be honest. Too many people know that Blomkvist and I have it in for each other. You'd be better off leaking to a news reporter and then supporting the story on your editorial pages. You'll get some good quotes from Ekström."

Levin was looking out onto Stureplan, where he spotted a beautiful woman in a bright red coat, with long strawberry-blond hair. For the first time that day he gave a big smile.

"Maybe that isn't such a bad idea," he added, ordering some more wine.


Blomkvist came walking down Hornsgatan towards Mariatorget. Further away, by Maria Magdalena kyrka, there was a white van with an ugly dent in its front wing, and next to it two men were waving their arms around and shouting at each other. But although the scene had attracted a crowd of onlookers, Blomkvist hardly noticed it.

He was thinking about how Balder's son had sat on the floor of the large house in Saltsjöbaden, reaching out over the Persian rug. The boy's hand had stains on the back of it and on the fingers, as if from crayons or pens, and that movement he was making looked as if he were drawing something complicated in midair, didn't it? Blomkvist was starting to see the whole scene in a new light.

Maybe it was not Frans Balder who had drawn the traffic light after all. Perhaps the boy had a gift. For some reason that did not surprise him as much as he might have expected. The first time he had met August Balder, sitting by his dead father, and seen him throwing himself against the head-board, he had already understood there was something exceptional about him. Now, as he cut across Mariatorget, a strange thought occurred to him and would not let him go. Up by Götgatsbacken he came to a stop.

He must at the very least follow it up, so he got out his mobile and looked up Hanna Balder. The number was unlisted, and unlikely to be one which he would find in *Millennium's* contacts. He thought of Freja Granliden, a society reporter at *Expressen* whose columns did not do much to enhance the prestige of the profession. She wrote about divorces and romances and royalty. But she had a quick brain and a sharp wit, and whenever they met they had a good time together. He rang her number but it was engaged, of course.

These days, reporters on the evening papers were forever on the telephone, under such deadline pressure that they never left their desks to take a look at what real life was like. But he got her in the end and was not in the least surprised that she let out a yelp of delight.

"Mikael," she said. "What an honour. Are you finally going to give me a scoop? I've been waiting for so long."

"Sorry. This time *you* have to help *me*. I need an address and a phone number."

"What do I get in return? Maybe a wicked little quote about what you got up to last night."

"I could give you some career advice."

"And what might that be?"

"Stop writing crap."

"Right, then who's going to keep track of all the telephone numbers the classy reporters need? Who are you looking for?"

"Hanna Balder."

"I can imagine why. Did you meet her drunken boyfriend out there?"

"Don't you start fishing, now. Do you know where she lives?"

"Torsgatan 40."

"You know it just like that?"

"I have a brilliant memory for trivia. If you hang on, I'll give you the front-door code and the phone number as well."

"That's really kind."

"But you know . . ."

"Yes?"

"You're not the only one looking for her. Our own bloodhounds are on the hunt too, and from what I hear she hasn't answered her telephone all day."

"Wise woman."

Afterwards Blomkvist stood in the street, unsure what to do. Chasing down unhappy mothers in competition with crime reporters from the evening papers was not quite what he had hoped his day would bring. But he hailed a taxi and was driven off in the direction of Vasastan.

Hanna Balder had accompanied August and Forsberg to Oden's Medical Centre for Children and Adolescents, opposite Observatorielunden on

Sveavägen. The medical centre consisted of two apartments which had been knocked together, but even though the furnishings and the courtyard had a private and sheltered feel to them, there was nonetheless something institutional about it all. Probably that had less to do with the long corridors and closed doors than the grim and watchful expressions on the faces of the staff. They seemed to have developed a certain distrust of the children for whom they were responsible.

The director, Torkel Lindén, was a vain little man who claimed to have a wide experience of children with autism. But Hanna did not like the way he looked at August. It was also troubling that there seemed to be no separation between teenagers and small children. But it felt too late to be having doubts now so on the way home she consoled herself with the thought that it would only be for a short time. Maybe she would pick August up as soon as this evening?

Then she thought about Lasse and his bouts of drunkenness and she told herself yet again that she needed to leave him and get a grip on her life. As she stepped out of the lift at her apartment she gave a start. An attractive man was sitting there on the landing, writing in a notebook. As he got to his feet and greeted her she saw that it was Mikael Blomkvist. She was terrified, so guilt-ridden that she supposed he was going to write some kind of exposé. That was absurd. He just gave an embarrassed smile and twice apologized for disturbing her. She could not help but feel a huge sense of relief. She had admired him for a long time.

"I have no comment to make," she said, in a voice which actually suggested the opposite.

"I'm not after a quote, either," he said. She remembered hearing that he and Lasse had arrived together—or at least at the same time—at Frans's the previous night, although she could not imagine what the two of them might have in common.

"Are you looking for Lasse?" she said.

"I'd like to hear about August's drawings," he replied, and at that she felt a stab of panic.

Yet she allowed him in. It was probably careless of her. Lasse had gone off to cure his hangover in some local dive and could be back at any time. He would go crazy if he found a journalist in their home. But Blomkvist had not only worried Hanna, he had also made her curious. How on earth did he know about the drawings? She invited him to sit on the grey sofa in the living room while she went to the kitchen to get some tea and biscuits. When she came back with a tray he said:

"I wouldn't be bothering you if it wasn't absolutely necessary."

"You're not bothering me," she said.

"You see, I met August last night, and I haven't been able to stop thinking about him."

"Oh?"

"I didn't understand it then," he said. "But I had the feeling he was trying to tell us something. Now I'm convinced he wanted to draw. He was making these determined movements with his hand over the floor."

"He's become obsessed with drawing."

"So he continued here at home?"

"And how! He started the minute we got here. He was manic and what he drew was amazing, but his face became flushed and he was breathing heavily, so the psychologist said he had to stop. It was compulsive and destructive, was his opinion."

"What did he draw?"

"Nothing special, really, I'd guess it was inspired by his puzzles. But it was very cleverly done, with shadows and perspective and everything."

"But what was it?"

"Squares."

"What kind of squares?"

"Chessboard squares, I think you would call them," she said. Maybe she was imagining things, but she detected a trace of excitement in Blomkvist's eyes.

"Only chess squares?" he said. "Nothing more?"

"Mirrors too," she said. "Chessboard squares reflected in mirrors."

"Have you been to Frans's place?" he said, a new sharpness in his voice.

"Why do you ask?"

"Because the design of the floor in the bedroom—where he was killed—looks just like chessboard squares, and they're reflected in the mirrors of the wardrobe."

"Oh my God!"

"What's the matter?"

"Because . . ."

A wave of shame washed over her.

"Because the last thing I saw before I snatched the drawing away from him was a menacing shadow emerging out of those squares," she continued.

"Do you have the drawing here?"

"No, or rather yes."

"Yes?"

"I'm afraid I threw it away. But maybe it's still in the bin."

Blomkvist had coffee grounds and yoghurt all over his hands as he pulled a crumpled piece of paper out of the trash can and smoothed it out on the draining board. He brushed it with the back of his hand and looked at it in the glare of the kitchen lights. The drawing was not finished, not by any means, and it consisted mostly of chessboard squares, just as Hanna had said, seen from above or from the side. Without having been in Balder's bedroom, it would not be obvious that the squares represented a floor, but Blomkvist immediately recognized the mirrors on the wardrobe to the right of the bed. He also recognized the darkness, that special darkness that had met him during the night.

He felt transported back to the moment when he had walked in through the broken window—apart from one small important detail. The room he had entered had been almost dark, whereas the drawing showed a thin source of light falling diagonally from above, extending out over the squares. It gave contours to a shadow which was not distinct or meaningful, but which felt eerie, perhaps for that very reason.

The shadow was stretching out an arm and Blomkvist, who saw the drawing in a different light from Hanna, had no trouble interpreting what that signified. The figure meant to kill. Above the chessboard squares and the shadow there was a face which had not yet materialized.

"Where is August now?" he said. "Is he sleeping?"

"No. He . . . I've left him with someone else for a while. I couldn't handle him, to be honest."

"Where is he?"

"At Oden's Medical Centre for Children and Adolescents. On Svea-vägen."

"Who knows that he's there?"

"No-one."

"Just you and the staff?"

Hanna nodded.

"Then it has to stay that way. Will you excuse me for a moment?"

Blomkvist took out his mobile and called Bublanski. In his mind he had already drafted yet another question for [*Lisbeth stuff*].

Bublanski felt frustrated—the investigation was going nowhere. Neither Balder's Blackphone nor his laptop had been found, so they had not been able to map his contacts with the outside world despite having had detailed discussions with the service provider.

For the time being they had little more than smoke screens and clichés to go on, Bublanski thought: a ninja warrior had materialized swiftly and effectively and then vanished into the darkness. In fact the attack had something far too perfect about it, as if it had been carried out by a person free of all the usual human failings and contradictions which as a rule feature in a murder. This was too clean, too clinical, and Bublanski could not help thinking that it had been just another day at the office for the killer. He was pondering this and more besides when Blomkvist rang.

"Oh, it's you," Bublanski said. "We were just talking about you. We'd like to have another word with you as soon as possible."

"Of course, not a problem. But right now I've got something much more important to tell you. The witness, August Balder, is a savant," Blomkvist said.

"A what?"

"A boy who may be severely handicapped but nonetheless has a special gift. He draws like a master, with a remarkable, mathematical sharpness. Did you see the drawings of the traffic light which were lying on the kitchen table in Saltsjöbaden?"

"Yes, briefly. Are you saying it wasn't Balder who drew them?"

"It was the boy."

"They looked like astonishingly mature pieces of work."

"But they were drawn by August. This morning he sat down and drew the chessboard squares on the floor in his father's bedroom, and he didn't stop at that. He sketched a shaft of light and a shadow. My theory is that it's the killer's shadow and the light from his headlamp, but of course we can't yet say for certain. The boy was interrupted in his work."

"Are you pulling my leg?"

"This is hardly the moment."

"How do you know all this?"

"I'm at the home of the boy's mother, Hanna Balder, and I'm looking at the drawing. The boy is no longer here. He's at . . ." The journalist hesitated. "I don't want to say more than that over the phone."

"You say that the boy was interrupted in the middle of his drawing?"

"A psychologist stopped him."

"How could one do something like that?"

"He probably didn't realize what the drawings represented, he just saw them as something compulsive. I suggest you send some people over right away. You've got your witness."

"We'll be there as soon as we can."

Jan Bublanski ended the call and went to share Blomkvist's news with the team, though soon after he wondered whether this had been wise.

CHAPTER 15

# NOVEMBER 21

Salander was at the Raucher Chess Club on Hälsingegatan. She did not really feel like playing. Her head was aching—she had been on the hunt all day long. But the hunt had taken her here. When she realized that Frans Balder had been betrayed by one of his own, she had promised him she would leave the traitor alone. She had not approved of the strategy, but she had kept her word, and only when Balder had been killed did she feel absolved of her promise.

Now she was going to proceed on her own terms. But it was not all that easy. Arvid Wrange had not been at home, and instead of calling him she wanted to strike down on his life like a bolt of lightning and had therefore been out searching for him, her hoodie pulled over her head. Wrange lived the life of a drone. But as with so many other drones, he had a routine, and Salander had been able to find a number of signposts through the trail of pictures he posted on Instagram and Facebook: Riche on Birger Jarlsgatan and the Theatre Grill on Nybrogatan, the Raucher Chess Club and Café Ritorno on Odengatan, and a number of others, including a shooting club on Fridhelmsgatan, plus the addresses of two girlfriends.

Wrange had changed since the last time she had him on her radar. Not only had he gotten rid of his nerdy look. His morals were also at an ebb. Salander was not big on psychological theory, but she could see for herself that his first major transgression had led to a succession of others. Wrange was no longer an ambitious student, eager to learn. Now he was addicted to porn and bought sex online, violent sex. Two of the women had afterwards threatened to report him.

The man had a fair amount of money. He also had a load of problems.

As recently as that morning he had Googled "witness protection Sweden," which was careless of him. Even though he was no longer in contact with Solifon, at least not from his computer, *they* were probably still keeping an eye on *him*. It would be unprofessional not to. Maybe he was beginning to crack up beneath the new urbane exterior, which served her purpose. When she once again rang the chess club—chess being the only connection with his former life—she was pleasantly surprised to hear that Wrange had just arrived there.

So now she walked down the small flight of steps on Hälsingegatan and along a corridor to some shabby premises where a motley crowd of mostly older men were sitting hunched over their chessboards. The atmosphere was somnolent, and nobody seemed to even notice her, let alone question her presence. They were all busy with what they were doing, and the only sound was the click of the chess clocks and the occasional swear word. There were framed photographs of Kasparov, Magnus Carlsen, and Bobby Fischer on the walls and even one of a pimply, teenaged Arvid Wrange playing the chess star Judit Polgár.

A different, older version of him was sitting at a table further in and to the right, and he seemed to be trying out some new opening. Next to him were a couple of shopping bags. He was wearing a yellow lambswool sweater with a freshly ironed white shirt and a pair of shiny English shoes, a little too stylish for the surroundings. Salander approached him with careful, hesitant steps and asked if he would like a game. He responded by looking her up and down, then he said: "OK."

"Nice of you," she replied, like a well-mannered young girl, and sat down. She opened with e4, he answered with b5, the Polish gambit, and then she closed her eyes and let him play on.

Wrange tried to concentrate on the game, but he was not managing too well. Fortunately this punk girl was going to be easy pickings. She wasn't bad, as it turned out—she probably spent a lot of time playing—but what good was that? He toyed with her a little, and she was bound to be impressed. Who knows, maybe he could even get her to come home with him afterwards. True, she looked stroppy, and Wrange did not go in for stroppy girls, but she had nice tits and he might be able to take out his frustrations on her. It had been a disaster of a morning. The news that Balder had been murdered had floored him.

It wasn't grief that he felt: it was fear. Wrange really did try hard to convince himself that he had done the right thing. What did the goddamn professor expect when he treated him as if he didn't exist? But of course it wouldn't look good that Wrange had sold him down the river. He consoled himself with the thought that an idiot like Balder must have made thousands of enemies, but deep down he knew: the one event was linked to the other, and that scared him to death.

Ever since Balder had started working at Solifon, Wrange had been afraid that the drama would take a frightening new turn, and here he was now, wishing that it would all go away. That must have been why he went into town this morning on a compulsive spree to buy a load of designer clothes, and had ended up here at the chess club. Chess still managed to distract him, and the fact was that he was feeling better already. He felt like he was in control and smart enough to keep on fooling them all. Look at how he was playing.

This girl was not half bad. In fact there was something unorthodox and creative in her play, and she would probably be able to teach most people in here a thing or two. It was just that he, Arvid Wrange, was crushing her. His play was so brilliant and sophisticated that she had not even noticed he was on the brink of trapping her queen. Stealthily he moved his positions forward and snapped it up without sacrificing more than a knight. In a flirty, casual tone bound to impress her he said, "Sorry, baby. Your queen is down."

But he got nothing in return, no smile, not a word, nothing. The girl upped the tempo, as if she wanted to put a quick end to her humiliation, and why not? He'd be happy to keep the process short and take her out for two or three drinks before he pulled her. Maybe he would not be very nice to her in bed. The chances were that she would still thank him afterwards. A miserable cunt like her would be unlikely to have had a fuck for a long time and would be totally unused to guys like him, cool guys who played at this level. He decided to show off a bit and explain some higher chess theory. But he never got the chance. Something on the board did not feel quite right. His game began to run into some sort of resistance he could not understand. For a while he persuaded himself that it was only his imagination, perhaps the result of a few careless moves. If only he concentrated he would be able to put things right, and so he mobilized his killer instinct.

But the situation just got worse.

He felt trapped—however hard he tried to regain the initiative she hit back—and in the end he had no choice but to acknowledge that the balance of power had shifted, and shifted irreversibly. How crazy was that? He had taken her queen, but instead of building on that advantage he had landed in a fatally weak position. Surely she had not deliberately sacrificed her queen so early in the game? That would be impossible—the sort of thing you read about in books, it doesn't happen in your local chess club in Vasastan, and it's definitely not something that pierced punk chicks with attitude problems do, especially not to great players like him. Yet there was no escape.

In four or five moves he would be beaten and so he saw no alternative but to knock over his king with his index finger and mumble congratulations. Even though he would have liked to serve up some excuses, something told him that that would make matters worse. He had a sneaking feeling that his defeat was not just down to bad luck, and almost against his will he began to feel frightened again. Who the hell was she?

Cautiously he looked her in the eye and now she no longer looked like a stroppy, insecure nobody. Now she seemed cold—like a predator eyeing its prey. He felt deeply ill at ease, as if the defeat on the chessboard were but a prelude to something much, much worse. He glanced towards the door.

"You're not going anywhere," she said.

"Who are you?" he said.

"Nobody special."

"So we haven't met before?"

"Not exactly."

"But nearly, is that it?"

"We've met in your nightmares, Arvid."

"Is this some kind of joke?"

"Not really."

"What do you mean?"

"What do you think I mean?"

"How should I know?"

He could not understand why he was so scared.

"Frans Balder was murdered last night," she said in a monotone.

"Well . . . yes . . . I read that," he stammered.

"Terrible, isn't it?"

"Awful."

"Especially for you, right?"

"Why especially for me?"

"Because you betrayed him, Arvid. Because you gave him the kiss of Judas."

His body froze.

"That's bullshit," he spat out.

"As a matter of fact it's not. I hacked your computer, cracked your encryption, and saw very clearly that you sold his technology to Solifon. And you know what?"

He was finding it hard to breathe.

"I'm sure you woke up this morning and wondered if his death was your fault. I can help you there: it *was* your fault. If you hadn't been so greedy and bitter and pathetic, Frans Balder would be alive now. I should warn you that's making me pretty fucking angry, Arvid. I'm going to hurt you badly. First of all by making you suffer the same sort of treatment you inflict on the women you find online."

"Are you insane?"

"Probably, yes," she said. "Empathy deficit disorder. Excessive violence. Something along those lines."

She gripped his hand with a force which scared him out of his wits.

"Arvid, do you know what I'm doing right now?"

"No."

"I'm sitting here trying to decide what to do with you. I'm thinking in terms of suffering of biblical proportions. That's why I might seem a bit distracted."

"What do you want?"

"I want revenge—haven't I made that clear?"

"You're talking crap."

"Definitely not, and I think you know it too. But there is a way out."

"What do I have to do?"

He could not understand why he said it. *What do I have to do?* It was an admission, a capitulation, and he considered taking it back, putting pressure on her instead, to see if she had any proof or if she was bluffing. But he could not bring himself to do it.

Only later did he realize that it was not just the threats she tossed out or the uncanny strength of her hands. It was the game of chess, the queen sacrifice. He was in shock, and something in his subconscious told him that a woman who plays like that must also know his secrets.

"What do I have to do?" he said again.

"You're going to follow me out of here and you're going to tell me everything, Arvid. You're going to tell me exactly what happened when you sold out Frans Balder."

"It's a miracle," Bublanski said as he stood in Hanna Balder's kitchen looking at the crumpled drawing which Blomkvist had plucked out of the rubbish.

"Let's not exaggerate," said Modig, who was standing right next to him. She was right. It was not much more than some chess squares on a piece of paper, after all, and as Mikael Blomkvist had pointed out over the telephone there was something strangely mathematical about the work, as if the boy were more interested in the geometry than in the threatening shadow above. But Bublanski was excited all the same. He had been told over and over how mentally impaired the Balder boy was, and how little he would be able to help them. Now the boy had produced a drawing which gave Bublanski more hope than anything else in the investigation. It strengthened his long-held conviction that one must never underestimate anyone or cling to preconceived ideas.

They could not be certain that what August was illustrating was the moment of the murder. The shadow could, at least in theory, be associated with some other occasion, and there was no guarantee that the boy had seen the killer's face or that he would be able to draw it. And yet deep down that is what Bublanski believed. Not just because the drawing, even in its present state, was masterful. He had studied the other drawings too, in which you could see, beyond the street crossing and the traffic light, a shabby man with thin lips who had been caught red-handed jaywalking, if you looked at it purely from a law-enforcement point of view. He was crossing the street on a red, and Amanda Flod, another officer on the team, had recognized him straightaway as the out-of-work actor Roger Winter, who had convictions for drunk driving and assault.

The photographic precision of August's eye ought to be a dream for any murder investigator. But Bublanski did realize that it would be unprofessional to set his hopes too high. Maybe the murderer had been masked at the time of the killing or his face had already faded from the child's memory. There were many possible scenarios and Bublanski cast a glum look in the direction of Modig.

"You think it's wishful thinking on my part," he said.

"For a man who's beginning to doubt the existence of God, you are surprisingly willing to hope for a miracle."

"Well, maybe."

"But it's worth getting to the bottom of. I agree with that," Modig said.

"Good, in that case let's see the boy."

Bublanski went out of the kitchen and nodded at Hanna Balder, who was sunk in the living-room sofa, fumbling with some tablets.


Lisbeth Salander and Arvid Wrange came out into Vasaparken arm in arm, like a pair of old friends out for a stroll. Appearances can be deceptive: Wrange was terrified as Salander steered them towards a park bench. The wind was getting up again and the temperature creeping down—it was hardly a day for feeding the pigeons—and Wrange was cold. But Salander decided that the bench would do and forced him to sit down, holding his arm in a vise-like grip.

"Right," she said. "Let's make this quick."

"Will you keep my name out of it?"

"I'm promising nothing, Arvid. But your chances of being able to go back to your miserable life will increase significantly if you tell me every detail of what happened."

"OK," he said. "Do you know Darknet?"

"I know it," she said.

No-one knew Darknet like Lisbeth Salander. Darknet was the lawless undergrowth of the Internet. The only way to access it was with especially encrypted software and the user's anonymity was guaranteed. No-one could Google your details or trace your activities online. So Darknet was full of drug dealers, terrorists, con men, gangsters, illegal arms dealers, pimps, and black hats. If there was an Internet hell, then this was it.

But Darknet was not in itself evil. Salander understood that better than anyone. These days, when spy agencies and the big software companies follow every step we take online, even honest people need a hiding place. Darknet was also a hub for dissidents, whistle-blowers, and informants. Opposition forces could protest on Darknet out of reach of their government, and Salander had used it for her own more discreet investigations and attacks. She knew its sites and search engines and its old-fashioned workings far away from the known, visible Net.

"Did you put Balder's technology up for sale on Darknet?" she said.

"No, I was just casting about. I was pissed off. You know, Frans hardly even said hello to me. He treated me like dirt, and he didn't care about that technology of his, either. It has the potential to make all of us rich, but he only wanted to play and experiment with it like a little kid. One evening when I'd had a few drinks I just chucked out a question on a geek site: 'Who can pay good money for some revolutionary AI technology?'"

"And did you get an answer?"

"It took a while. I had time to forget that I'd even asked. But in the end someone calling himself Bogey wrote back with some well-informed questions. At first my answers were ridiculously unguarded, but soon I realized what a mess I'd gotten myself into, and I became terrified that Bogey would steal the technology."

"Without you getting anything for it."

"It was a dangerous game. To be able to sell Frans's technology I had to tell people about it. But if I said too much then I would already have lost it. Bogey flattered me rotten—in the end he knew exactly where we were and what sort of software we were working on."

"He meant to hack you."

"Presumably. He somehow managed to get hold of my name, and that floored me. I became totally paranoid and announced that I wanted to pull out. But by then it was too late. Not that Bogey threatened me, at least not directly. He just went on and on about how he and I were going to do great things together and earn masses of money. In the end I agreed to meet him in Stockholm at a Chinese boat restaurant on Söder Mälarstrand. It was a windy day, I remember, and I stood there freezing. I waited more than half an hour, and afterwards I wondered if he had been checking me out in some way."

"But then he showed up?"

"Yes. At first I didn't believe it was him. He looked like a junkie, or a beggar, and if I hadn't seen that Patek Philippe watch on his wrist I probably would have tossed him twenty kronor. He had amateur tattoos and dodgy-looking scars on his arms, which he waved about as he walked. He was carrying this awful-looking trench coat and he seemed to have been more or less living on the streets. The strangest thing of all was that he was proud of it. It was only the watch and the handmade shoes which showed that he had at some point managed to raise himself out of the gutter. Other than that, he seemed keen to stick to his roots. Later on, when I'd given him everything and we were celebrating our deal over a few bottles of wine, I asked about his background."

"I hope for your sake that he gave you some details."

"If you want to track him down, I have to warn you . . ."

"I don't want advice, Arvid. I want facts."

"Fine. He was careful," he said. "But I still got a few things. He probably couldn't help himself. He grew up in a big city in Russia, though he didn't name it. He'd had everything stacked against him, he said. His mother was a whore and a heroin addict and his father could have been anybody. As a small boy he had ended up in the orphanage from hell. There was some lunatic there, he told me, who used to make him lie on a butcher's slab in the kitchen and whipped him with a broken cane. When he was eleven he ran away and lived on the street. He stole, broke into cellars and stairwells to get a little warmth, got drunk on cheap vodka, sniffed glue, and was abused and beaten. But he also discovered one thing."

"What?"

"That he had talent. He was an expert at breaking and entering, which became his first source of pride, his first identity. He was capable of doing in just a few seconds what took others hours. Before that he had been a homeless brat, everyone had despised him and spat at him. Now he was the boy who could get himself in wherever he wanted. It became an obsession. All day long he dreamed of being some sort of Houdini in reverse: he didn't want to break out, he wanted to break in. He practised for ten, twelve, fourteen hours a day, and in the end he was a legend on the streets—or so he said. He started to carry out bigger operations, using computers he stole and reconfigured to hack in everywhere. He made a heap of money which he blew on drugs and often he was robbed or taken advantage of. He could be clear as a bell when he was on one of his jobs but afterwards he would lie around in a narcotic haze and someone would walk all over him. He was a genius and a total idiot at the same time, he said. But one day everything changed. He was saved, raised up out of his hell."

"How?"

"He had been asleep in some dump of a place that was due to be pulled down and when he opened his eyes and looked around in the yellowish light there was an angel standing before him."

"An angel?"

"That's what he said, an angel, and maybe it was partly the contrast with everything else in there, the syringes, the leftover food, the cockroaches. He said she was the most beautiful woman he had ever seen. He could scarcely look at her, and he got this idea that he was going to die. It was an ominous, solemn feeling. But the woman explained, as if it were the most natural thing in the world, that she would make him rich and happy. If I've understood it right, she kept her promise. She gave him new teeth, got him into rehab. She arranged for him to train as a computer engineer."

"So ever since he's been hacking computers and stealing for this woman and her network."

"That's right. He became a new person, or maybe not completely new—in many ways he's still the same old thief and bum. But he no longer takes drugs, he says, and he spends all his free time keeping up to date with new technology. He finds a lot on Darknet and he claims to be stinking rich."

"And the woman—did he say anything more about her?"

"No, he was extremely careful about that. He spoke in such evasive and respectful terms that I wondered for a while if she wasn't a fantasy or hallucination. But I reckon she really does exist. I could sense sheer physical fear when he was talking about her—he said that he would rather die than let her down, and then he showed me a Russian patriarchal cross made of gold, which she had given him. One of those crosses, you know, which has a slanted beam down by the foot, one end pointing up and the other down. He told me this was a reference to the Gospel according to St. Luke and the two thieves who were hanged next to Jesus on the cross. The one thief believes in Jesus and goes to heaven. The other mocks him and is thrust down into hell."

"That's what awaits you if you fail her."

"That's about it, yes."

"So she sees herself as Jesus?"

"In this context the cross probably has nothing to do with Christianity. It's the message she wants to pass on."

"Loyalty or the torments of hell."

"Something along those lines."

"Yet you're sitting here, Arvid, spilling the beans."

"I didn't see an alternative."

"I hope you got paid a lot."

"Well, yes . . ."

"And then Balder's technology was sold to Solifon and Truegames."

"Yes, but I don't get it . . . not when I think of it now."

"What don't you get?"

"How could you know all this?"

"Because you were dumb enough to send an e-mail to Eckerwald at Solifon, don't you remember?"

"But I wrote nothing to suggest that I'd sold the technology. I was very careful about that."

"What you said was enough for me," she said. She got to her feet, and it was as if his entire being collapsed.

"Wait, what's going to happen now? Will you keep me out of it?"

"You can always hope," she said, and walked off towards Odenplan with purposeful steps.

. . .

Bublanski's mobile rang as he was on his way down to the front entrance on Torsgatan. It was Professor Edelman. Bublanski had been trying to reach him ever since he realized that the boy was a savant. Bublanski had found out online that two Swedish authorities were regularly quoted on this subject: Lena Ek at Lund University and Charles Edelman at the Karolinska Institute. But he had not been able to get hold of either, so he had postponed the search and gone off to see Hanna Balder. Now Edelman was ringing back, and he sounded shaken. He was in Budapest, he said, at a conference on heightened memory capacity. He had just arrived there and seen the news about the murder a moment ago, on CNN.

"Otherwise I would have gotten in touch right away," he said.

"What do you mean?"

"Professor Balder rang me yesterday evening."

That made Bublanski jump. "What did he want?"

"He wanted to talk about his son and his son's talent."

"Did you know each other?"

"Not in the slightest. He contacted me because he was worried about his boy and I was stunned to hear from him."

"Why?"

"Because it was Frans Balder. He's a household name to us neurologists. We tend to say he's just like us in wanting to understand the brain. The only difference is that he also wants to build one."

"I've heard something about that."

"I'd been told that he was an introverted and difficult man. A bit like a machine himself, people sometimes used to joke: nothing but logic circuits. But with me he was incredibly emotional, and it shocked me, to be honest. It was . . . I don't know, as if you were to hear your toughest policeman cry. I remember thinking that something must have happened, something other than what we were talking about."

"That sounds right. He had finally accepted that he was under a serious threat," Bublanski said.

"But he also had reason to be excited. His son's drawings were apparently exceptionally good, and that's not common at all at that age, not even with savants, and especially not in combination with proficiency in mathematics."

"Mathematics?"

"Yes. According to Balder his son had mathematical skills too. I could spend a long time talking about that."

"What do you mean?"

"Because I was utterly amazed, and at the same time maybe not so amazed after all. We now know that there's a hereditary factor in savants, and here we have a father who is a legend, thanks to his advanced algorithms. But still ... artistic and numerical talents do not usually present themselves together in these children."

"Surely the great thing about life is that every now and then it springs a surprise on us," Bublanski said.

"True, Chief Inspector. So what can I do for you?"

Bublanski thought through everything that had happened in Saltsjöbaden and it struck him that it would do no harm to be cautious.

"All I can say is that we need your help and expert knowledge as a matter of urgency."

"The boy was a witness to the murder, was he not?"

"Yes."

"And you want me to try to get him to draw what he saw?"

"I'd prefer not to comment."


Charles Edelman was standing in the lobby of the Hotel Boscolo in Budapest, a conference centre not far from the glittering Danube. The place looked like an opera house, with magnificent high ceilings, old-fashioned cupolas and pillars. He had been looking forward to the week here, the dinners and the presentations. Yet he was agitated and ran his fingers through his hair.

"Unfortunately I'm not in a position to help you. I have to give an important lecture tomorrow morning," he had said to Bublanski, and that was true. He had been preparing the talk for some weeks and he was going to take a controversial line with several eminent memory experts. He recommended a young associate professor, Martin Wolgers, to Bublanski.

But as soon as he hung up and exchanged looks with a colleague who had paused next to him, holding a sandwich—he began to have regrets. He even began to envy young Martin Wolgers, who was not yet thirty-five, always looked far too good in photographs, and on top of it all was beginning to make a name for himself.

It was true that Edelman did not fully understand what had happened. The police inspector had been cryptic and was probably worried that someone might be listening in on the call. Yet the professor still managed to grasp the bigger picture. The boy was good at drawing and was a witness to a murder. That could mean only one thing, and the longer Edelman thought about it, the more he fretted. He would be giving many more important lectures in his life, but he would never get another chance to play a part in a murder investigation at this level. However he looked at the assignment he had so casually passed on to Wolgers, it was bound to be much more interesting than anything he might be involved in here in Budapest. Who knows, it could even make him some sort of celebrity.

He visualized the headline: PROMINENT NEUROLOGIST HELPS POLICE SOLVE MURDER, or better still: EDELMAN'S RESEARCH LEADS TO BREAKTHROUGH IN MURDER HUNT. How could he be so stupid as to turn it down? He picked up his mobile and called Chief Inspector Bublanski again.


Bublanski hung up. He and Modig had managed to park not far from the Stockholm Public Library and had just crossed the street. Once again the weather was dreadful, and Bublanski's hands were freezing.

"Did he change his mind?" Modig said.

"Yes. He's going to shelve his lecture."

"When can he be here?"

"He's looking into it. Tomorrow morning at the latest."

They were on their way to Oden's Medical Centre on Sveavägen to meet the director, Torkel Lindén. The meeting was only meant to settle the practical arrangements for August Balder's testimony—at least as far as Bublanski was concerned. But even though Torkel Lindén did not yet know the true purpose of their visit, he had been strangely discouraging over the telephone and said that right now the boy was not to be disturbed "in any way." Bublanski had sensed an instinctive hostility and was not particularly pleasant in return. It had not been a promising start.

Lindén turned out not to be the hefty figure Bublanski had expected. He was hardly more than five feet tall and had short, possibly dyed black hair and pinched lips. He wore black jeans, a black polo sweater, and a small cross on a ribbon around his neck. There was something ecclesiastical about him, and his hostility was genuine.

He had a haughty look and Bublanski became aware of his own Jewishness—which happened whenever he encountered this sort of malevolence and air of moral superiority. Lindén wanted to show that he was better, because he put the boy's physical well-being first rather than offering him up for police purposes. Bublanski saw no choice but to be as amiable as possible.

"Pleased to meet you," he said.

"Is that so?" Lindén said.

"Oh yes, and it's kind of you to see us at such short notice. We really wouldn't come barging in like this if we didn't think this matter was of the utmost importance."

"I imagine you want to interview the boy in some way."

"Not exactly," Bublanski said, not quite so amiably. "I have to emphasize first of all that what I'm saying now must remain between us. It's a question of security."

"Confidentiality is a given for us. We have no loose lips here," Lindén said, in such a way as to suggest that it was the opposite with the police.

"My only concern is for the boy's safety," Bublanski said sharply.

"So that's your priority?"

"As a matter of fact, yes," the policeman said with even greater severity, "and that is why none of what I'm about to tell you must be passed on in any way—least of all by e-mail or by telephone. Can we sit somewhere private?"


Sonja Modig did not think much of the place. But then she was probably affected by the crying. Somewhere nearby a little girl was sobbing relentlessly. They were sitting in a room which smelled of detergent and also of something else, maybe a lingering trace of incense. A cross hung on the wall and there was a worn teddy bear lying on the floor. Not much else made the place cozy or attractive and since Bublanski, usually so good-natured, was about to lose his temper, she took matters into her own hands and gave a calm, factual account of what had happened.

"We are given to understand," she said, "that your colleague Einar Forsberg said that August should not be allowed to draw."

"That was his professional judgment and I agree with it. It doesn't do the boy any good," Lindén said.

"Well, I don't see how anything could do him much good under these circumstances. He saw his father being killed."

"We don't want to make things any worse, do we?"

"True. But this drawing August was not allowed to finish could lead to a breakthrough in the investigation and therefore I'm afraid we must insist. We'll make sure there are people present with the necessary expertise."

"I still have to say no."

Modig could hardly believe her ears.

"With all due respect for your work," Lindén went on, doggedly, "here at Oden's we help vulnerable children. That's our job and our calling. We're not an extension of the police force. That's how it is, and we're proud of it. For as long as the children are here, they should feel confident that we put their interests first."

Modig laid a restraining hand on Bublanski's thigh.

"We can easily get a court order," she said. "But we'd prefer not to go that route."

"Wise of you."

"Let me ask you something," she said. "Are you and Forsberg so absolutely sure what's best for August, or for the girl crying over there, for that matter? Couldn't it be that we all need to express ourselves? You and I can talk or write, or even go out and get a lawyer. August doesn't have those means of expression. But he can draw, and he seems to want to tell us something. Shouldn't we let August give form to something which must be tormenting him?"

"In our judgment . . ."

"No," she cut him off. "Don't tell us about your judgment. We're in contact with the person who knows more than anyone else in this country about this particular condition. His name is Charles Edelman, he's a professor of neurology, and he's on his way here from Hungary to meet the boy."

"We can of course listen to him," Lindén said reluctantly.

"Not just listen. We let him decide."

"I promise to engage in a constructive dialogue, between experts."

"Fine. What's August doing now?"

"He's sleeping. He was exhausted when he came to us."

Modig could tell that nothing good would come of it were she to suggest that the boy be woken up.

"In that case we'll come back tomorrow morning with Professor Edelman, and I hope that we can all work together on this matter."

# CHAPTER 16

# NOVEMBER 21–22

Gabriella Grane buried her face in her hands. She had not been to bed for forty hours and she was racked by a deep sense of guilt, only made worse by the lack of sleep. Yet she had been working hard all day long. Since this morning she had been part of a team at Säpo—a sort of shadow unit—which was investigating in secret every detail of the Frans Balder murder under cover of looking into broader domestic policy implications.

Superintendent Mårten Nielsen was formally leading the team and had recently returned from a year of study at the University of Maryland in the United States. He was undoubtedly intelligent and well informed, but too right-wing for Grane's tastes. It was rare to find a well-educated Swede who was also a wholehearted supporter of the American Republican Party—he even expressed some sympathy for the Tea Party movement. He was passionate about military history and lectured at the Military Academy Karlberg. Although still young—thirty-nine—he was believed to have extensive international contacts.

He often had trouble, however, asserting himself in the group and in practice the real leader was Ragnar Olofsson, who was older and cockier and could silence Nielsen with one peevish little sigh or a displeased wrinkle above his bushy eyebrows. Nor was Nielsen's life made any easier by the fact that Detective Inspector Lars Åke Grankvist was also on the team.

Before joining the Security Police, Grankvist had been a semi-legendary investigator in the Swedish police's National Murder Squad, at least in the sense that he was said to be able to drink anybody else under the table and to manage, with a sort of boisterous charm, to keep a lover in every town. It was not an easy group in which to hold one's own, and Grane kept an ever lower profile as the afternoon wore on. But this was due less to the men and their macho rivalry than to a growing sense of uncertainty.

Sometimes she wondered if she knew even less now than before. She realized, for example, that there was little or no proof to support the theory of the suspected data breach. All they had was a statement from Stefan Molde at the NDRE, and not even he had been sure of what he was saying. In her view his analysis was more or less rubbish. Balder seems to have relied primarily on the female hacker he had turned to for help, the woman not even named in the investigation, but whom his assistant, Linus Brandell, had described in such vivid terms. It was likely that Balder had been withholding a lot from Grane before he left for America.

For example, was it a coincidence that he had found a job at Solifon?

The uncertainty gnawed at her and she was indignant that no help was coming from Fort Meade. She could not get hold of Alona Casales, and the NSA was once again a closed door, so she in turn no longer passed on any news. Just like Nielsen and Grankvist, she found herself overshadowed by Olofsson. He kept getting information from his source at the Violent Crimes Division and immediately passing it on to the head of Säpo, Helena Kraft.

Grane did not like it, and in vain she had pointed out that this traffic not only increased the risk of a leak but also seemed to be costing them their independence. Instead of searching their own channels, they were slavishly relying on the information which flowed in from Bublanski's team.

"We're like people cheating on an exam, waiting for someone to whisper the answer instead of thinking for ourselves," she had said to the team, and this had not made her popular.

Now she was alone in her office, determined to move ahead on her own, trying to see the bigger picture. It might get her nowhere, but on the other hand it would do no harm. She heard steps outside in the corridor, the click-clack of determined high heels which Grane by now recognized only too well. It was Kraft, who came in wearing a grey Armani jacket, her hair pulled into a tight bun. Kraft gave her an affectionate look. But there were times when Grane resented this favouritism.

"How's it going?" Kraft asked. "Are you surviving?"

"Just about."

"I'm going to send you home after this conversation. You have to get some sleep. We need an analyst with a clear head."

"Sounds sensible."

"Do you know what Erich Maria Remarque said?"

"That it's not much fun in the trenches, or something."

"Ha, no, that it's always the wrong people who have the guilty conscience. Those who are really responsible for suffering in the world couldn't care less. It's the ones fighting for good who are consumed by remorse. You've got nothing to be ashamed of, Gabriella. You did what you could."

"I'm not so sure about that. But thanks anyway."

"Have you heard about Balder's son?"

"Just very quickly from Ragnar."

"At 10:00 tomorrow morning Chief Inspector Bublanski, Detective Sergeant Modig, and a Professor Edelman will be seeing the boy at Oden's Medical Centre for Children and Adolescents, on Sveavägen. They're going to try and get him to draw some more."

"I'll keep my fingers crossed. But I'm not too happy to know about it."

"Relax, leave the paranoia to me. The only ones who know about this are people who can keep their traps shut."

"I suppose you're right."

"I want to show you something: photographs of the man who hacked Balder's burglar alarm."

"I've seen them already. I've even studied them in detail."

"Have you?" Kraft said, handing over an enlarged and blurred picture of a wrist.

"What about it?"

"Take another look. What do you see?"

Grane looked and saw two things: the luxury watch she had noted before and, beneath it, barely distinguishable between the glove and the jacket cuff, a couple of lines which looked like amateur tattoos.

"Contrasts," she said. "Some cheap tattoos and a very expensive watch."

"More than that," Kraft said. "That's a 1951 Patek Philippe, model 2499, first series, or just possibly second series."

"Means nothing to me."

"It's one of the finest wristwatches in the world. A few years ago a watch like this sold at auction at Christie's in Geneva for more than two million dollars."

"Are you kidding?"

"No, and it wasn't just anyone who bought it. It was Jan van der Waal, a lawyer at Dackstone & Partner. He bid for it on behalf of a client."

"Dackstone & Partner, don't they represent Solifon?"

"Correct. We don't know whether the watch on the surveillance photo is the one that was sold in Geneva, and we haven't been able to find out who that client was. But it's a start, Gabriella. A scrawny type who looks like a junkie and who wears a watch of this calibre—that should narrow the field."

"Does Bublanski know this?"

"It was his technical expert Jerker Holmberg who discovered it. Now I want you and your analytical brain to take it further. Go home, get some sleep, and get started on it in the morning."

The man who called himself Jan Holtser was sitting at home in his apartment on Högbergsgatan in Helsinki, not far from Esplanaden park, looking through an album of photographs of his daughter Olga, who was now twenty-two and studying medicine in Gdansk.

Olga was tall and dark and intense and, as he had a habit of saying, the best thing that ever happened to him. Not just because it sounded good—he believed it. But now Olga had come to suspect what he was actually doing.

"Are you protecting evil people?" she had asked him one day, before embarking on a manic pursuit of what she called her commitment to the "weak and vulnerable."

It was pure pinko left-wing lunacy, in Holtser's opinion, not at all in keeping with Olga's character. He saw it as her attempt to stake out her independence. Behind all the talk about beggars, he thought she was still quite like him. Once upon a time Olga had been a promising 100-metre runner. She was six feet tall, muscular, and explosive, and in the old days she had loved watching action films and listening to him reminisce about the war in Chechnya. Everyone at school had known better than to pick a fight with her. She hit back, like a warrior. Olga was definitely not cut out to minister to the sick and degenerate.

Yet she claimed to want to work for Médecins Sans Frontières or go off to Calcutta like some Mother Teresa. Holtser could not bear the thought. The world belongs to the strong, he felt. But he loved his daughter, however daft some of her ideas, and tomorrow she was coming home for the first time in six months for a few days' leave. He solemnly resolved that he would be a better listener this time, and not pontificate about Stalin and great leaders and everything that she hated.

He would instead try to bring them closer again. He was certain that she needed him. At least he was pretty sure that he needed her. It was 8:00 in the evening and he went into the kitchen and pressed three oranges and poured Smirnoff into a glass. It was his third screwdriver of the day. Once he had finished a job he could put away six or seven of them, and maybe he would do that now. He was tired, weighed down by all the responsibility on his shoulders, and he needed to relax. For a few minutes he stood with his drink in his hand and dreamed about a different sort of life. But the man who called himself Jan Holtser had set his hopes too high.

The tranquility came to an abrupt end as Bogdanov rang on his secure mobile. At first Holtser hoped that Bogdanov just wanted to chat, to release some of the excitement that came with every assignment. But his colleague was calling about a very specific matter and sounded less than happy.

"I've spoken to T.," he said. Holtser felt a number of things all at once, perhaps jealousy most of all.

Why did Kira ring Bogdanov and not him? Even if it was Bogdanov who brought in the big money, and was rewarded accordingly, Holtser had always been convinced that he was the one closer to Kira. But Holtser was also worried. Had something gone wrong, after all?

"Is there a problem?" he said.

"The job isn't finished."

"Where are you?"

"In town."

"Come on up in that case and explain what the hell you mean."

"I've booked a table at Postres."

"I don't feel like going to some posh restaurant. Get yourself over here."

"I haven't eaten."

"I'll fry something up."

"Sounds good. We've got a long night ahead of us."

Holtser did not want another long night. Still less did he feel like telling his daughter that he would not be at home the next day. But he had no choice. He knew as surely as he knew that he loved Olga: You could not say no to Kira.

She wielded some invisible power and, however hard he tried, he could never be as dignified in her presence as he wanted. She reduced him to a little boy and often he turned himself inside out just to see her smile.

Kira was staggeringly beautiful and knew how to make the most of it like no other beauty before her. She was unmatched when it came to power games. She knew all the moves. She could be weak and needy when it suited, but also indomitable, hard and cold as ice, and sometimes plain evil. Nobody brought out the sadist in him like she did.

She may not have been intelligent in the conventional sense, and many pointed that out to try to take her down a peg or two. But the same people were still stupefied in her presence. Kira played them like a violin and could reduce even the toughest of men to blushing and giggling schoolchildren.

It was 9:00 p.m. and Bogdanov was sitting next to him shovelling in the lamb chop Holtser had prepared. Oddly enough his table manners were almost passable. That may have been Kira's influence. In many ways Bogdanov had become quite civilized—and then again not. However he tried to put on airs, he could never entirely rid himself of the appearance of the petty thief and speed addict. He had been off drugs for ages and was a computer engineer with university qualifications, but still looked ravaged by street life.

"Where's your bling watch?" Holtser said. "Are you in the doghouse?"

"We both are."

"It's that bad?"

"Maybe not."

"The job isn't finished, you said?"

"No, it's that boy."

"Which boy?" Holtser pretended not to understand.

"The one you so nobly spared."

"What about him? He's a retard, you know."

"Maybe so, but he can draw."

"What do you mean, draw?"

"He's a savant."

"A *what?*"

"You should try reading something other than your fucking gun magazines for once."

"What are you talking about?"

"It's someone who's autistic or handicapped in some other way, but who has a special gift. This boy may not be able to talk or think like a normal person, but he has a photographic memory. The police think the little bastard is going to be able to draw your face, and then they're going to run it through their facial-recognition software, and then you're screwed, aren't you? You must be there somewhere in Interpol's records?"

"Yes, but Kira can't expect us to . . ."

"That's exactly what she expects. We have to fix the boy."

A wave of emotion and confusion washed over Holtser and once again he saw before him that empty, glassy look from the double bed which had made him so uncomfortable.

"The hell I will," he said, without really believing it.

"I know you've got problems with children. I don't like it either. But we can't avoid this one. Besides, you should be grateful. Kira could just as easily have sacrificed you."

"I suppose so."

"Then it's settled. I've got the plane tickets in my pocket. We'll take the first flight in the morning to Arlanda, at 6:30, and then we're going to some place on Sveavägen called Oden's Medical Centre for Children and Adolescents."

"So the boy's in a clinic."

"Yes, and that's why we need to do some planning. Let me just finish eating."

The man who called himself Jan Holtser closed his eyes and tried to figure out what he was going to say to Olga.

·  ·  ·

Salander was up at 5:00 the next morning and hacked into the NSF Major Research Instrumentation supercomputer at the New Jersey Institute of Technology—she needed all the mathematical skills she could muster. Then she got out her own programme for elliptic curve factorization and set about cracking the file she had downloaded from the NSA.

But however hard she tried, she could not manage it. She had not really been expecting to do so. It was a sophisticated RSA encryption, named after the originators Rivest, Shamir, and Adleman. RSA has two keys—one public, one secret—and is based on Euler's phi function and Fermat's little theorem, but above all on the simple fact that it is easy to multiply two large prime numbers. A calculator will give you the answer in the blink of an eye. Yet it is all but impossible to work backwards and, on the basis of the answer, calculate the prime numbers you started out with. Computers are not yet efficient at prime number factorization, something which had exasperated Lisbeth Salander and the world's intelligence organizations many times in the past.

For about a year now Salander had been thinking that ECM, the Elliptic Curve Method, would be more promising than previous algorithms, and she had spent long nights writing her own factorization programme. But now, in the early hours of the morning, she realized it would need more refinement to have even the slightest chance of success. After three hours of work, she took a break and went to the kitchen, drank some orange juice straight from the carton, and ate two microwaved piroshki.

Back at her desk she hacked into Blomkvist's computer to see if he had come up with anything new. He had posted two more questions for her and she realized he wasn't so hopeless after all.

<Which of Frans Balder's assistants betrayed him?>, he wrote, which was a reasonable question.

She did not answer. She could not care less about Arvid Wrange. But she had made progress and worked out who the hollow-eyed junkie was, the man Wrange had been in touch with, who had called himself Bogey. Trinity in Hacker Republic remembered somebody with that same handle from a number of hacker sites some years previously. That did not necessarily mean anything—Bogey was not the most original alias. But Salander had traced the posts and thought she could be onto something, especially when he carelessly dropped that he was a computer engineer from Moscow University.

Salander was unable to find out when he graduated, or any other dates for that matter, but she got hold of a couple of nerdy details about how Bogey was hooked on fine watches and crazy for the Arsène Lupin films from the '70s, about the gentleman thief of that name.

Then Salander posted questions on every conceivable website for former and current students at Moscow University, asking if anybody knew a scrawny, hollow-eyed ex-junkie who had been a street urchin and master thief and loved Arsène Lupin films. It was not long before she got a reply.

"That sounds like Jurij Bogdanov," wrote someone who introduced herself as Galina.

According to this Galina, Bogdanov was a legend at the university. Not just because he had hacked into all the lecturers' computers and had dirt on every one of them. He liked to ask people: Will you bet me one hundred roubles I can't break into that house over there?

Many who did not know him thought this was easy money. But Jurij could pick any door lock, and if for some reason he failed then he would shin up the façade or the walls. He was known for his daring, and for his evil. He was said once to have kicked a dog to death when it disturbed him in his work and he was always stealing things, just for the hell of it. Galina thought he might have been a kleptomaniac. But he was also a genius hacker and a talented analyst, and after he graduated the world was his oyster. He did not want a job, he wanted to go his own way, he said, and it did not take Salander long to work out what he got up to after university—at least according to the official version.

Jurij Bogdanov was now thirty-four years old. He had left Russia and lived in Berlin at Budapester Strasse 8, not far from the Michelin-starred restaurant Hugo's. He ran a white hat computer security business, Outcast Security, with seven employees and a turnover in the last financial year of twenty-two million euros. It was ironic yet somehow entirely logical that his front was a company which protected industrial groups from people like himself. He had not had any criminal convictions since he took his exams and managed a wide network of contacts—one of the members of his board of directors was Ivan Gribanov, member of the Russian Duma and a major shareholder in the oil company Gazprom—but she could find nothing to get her further.

Blomkvist's second question was:

```
<Oden's Medical Centre on Sveavägen: Is it safe?
(Delete this as soon as you read it)>
```

He did not explain why he was interested in the place. But she knew that Blomkvist was not someone who threw questions out at random. Nor did he make a habit of being unclear.

If he was being cryptic, then he had a reason to be, and the information must be sensitive. There was evidently something significant about this medical centre. Salander soon discovered that it had attracted a number of complaints—children had been forgotten or ignored and had been able to self-harm. Oden's was managed privately by its director, Torkel Lindén, and his company Care Me and, if one was to believe past employees, Lindén's word was law. The profit margin was always high because nothing was bought unless absolutely necessary.

Lindén himself was a former star gymnast, among other things a one-time Swedish horizontal bar champion. Nowadays he was a passionate hunter and member of a Christian congregation that took an uncompromising line on homosexuality. Salander went onto the websites of the Swedish Association for Hunting and Wildlife Management and the Friends of Christ to see what kinds of tempting activities were going on there. Then she sent Lindén two fake but enticing e-mails which looked as if they had come from the organizations. Attached were PDF files with sophisticated malware which would open automatically if Lindén clicked on the messages.

By 8:23 she had gotten onto the server and immediately confirmed her suspicions. August Balder had been admitted to the clinic the previous afternoon. In the medical file, underneath a description of the circumstances which had resulted in his admittance, it said:

Infantile autism, severe mental impairment. Restless. Severely traumatized by death of father. Constant observation required. Difficult to handle.

Brought jigsaw puzzles. Not allowed to draw! Observed to be compulsive and destructive. Diagnosis by psychologist Forsberg, confirmed by T.L.

And the following had been added underneath, clearly somewhat later:

Professor Charles Edelman, Chief Inspector Bublanski, and Detective Sergeant Modig will visit A. Balder at 10:00 a.m. on Wednesday, November 22. T.L. will be present. Drawing under supervision.

Further down still it said:

Change of venue. A. Balder to be taken by T.L. and Professor Edelman to his mother Hanna Balder on Torsgatan, Bublanski and Modig will join. A.B. is thought likely to draw better in his home environment.

Salander quickly checked who Edelman was, and when she saw that his specialism was savant skills she understood straightaway what was going on. They seemed to be working towards some sort of testimony in the form of a sketch. Why else would Bublanski and Sonja Modig be interested in the boy's drawing, and why else would Blomkvist have been so cautious in framing his question?

None of this must be allowed to get out. No killer must be able to find out that the boy might draw a picture of him. Salander decided to see for herself how careful Lindén had been in his correspondence. Luckily he had not written anything more about the boy's drawing ability. He had on the other hand received an e-mail from Edelman at 11:10 last night, copied to Modig and Bublanski. That e-mail was clearly the reason why the meeting place had been changed. Edelman wrote:

```
<Hi Torkel, How good of you to see me at your
medical centre. I really appreciate it. But I'm
afraid I have to be a bit awkward. I think we
stand the best chance of getting a good result if
we arrange for the boy to draw in an environment
where he feels secure. That's not in any way to
```

```
criticize your medical centre. I've heard a lot of
good things about it.>
```

The hell you have, Salander thought, and read on:

```
<Therefore I'd like us to move the boy to his
mother Hanna Balder on Torsgatan, tomorrow
morning. The reason being that it is recognized
in literature on the subject that the presence of
the mother has a positive effect on children with
savant skills. If you and the boy can wait outside
the entrance on Sveavägen at 9:15 a.m., then I can
pick you up as I go by. That would give us the
opportunity for a bit of a chat between colleagues.
Best regards
Charles Edelman>
```

Bublanski and Modig had replied at 7:01 and 7:14 a.m. respectively. There was good reason, they wrote, to rely on Edelman's expertise and follow his advice. Lindén had, at 7:57, confirmed that he and the boy would await Charles Edelman outside the entrance on Sveavägen. Salander sat for a while, lost in thought. Then she went to the kitchen and picked up a few old biscuits from the larder while she looked out towards Slussen and Riddarfjärden. *So,* she thought, *the venue for the meeting has been changed.* Instead of doing his drawing at the medical centre, the boy would be driven home to his mother.

The presence of the mother has a positive effect, Edelman wrote. There was something about that phrase Salander did not like. It felt old-fashioned, didn't it? And the introduction itself was not much better: "The reason being that it is recognized in literature on the subject ..." It was stilted. Although it was true that many academics could not write to save their lives, and she knew nothing about the way in which this professor normally expressed himself, would one of the world's leading neurologists really feel the need to lean on what is recognized in the literature? Wouldn't he be more self-assured?

Salander went to her computer and skimmed through some of Edelman's papers online; she may have found the odd little touch of vanity, even in the most factual passages, but there was nothing clumsy or psychologically naïve in what he had written. On the contrary, the man was sharp. So she went back to the e-mails and checked to find out which SMTP server it had been transmitted through, and that made her jump right away. The server, Birdino, was not familiar, which it should have been, so she sent it a series of commands to see exactly what it was. In a matter of seconds she had the evidence in black and white: the server supported open mail relay, and the sender could therefore transmit messages from any address he wanted.

In other words, the e-mail from Edelman was a fake, and the copies to Bublanski and Modig were a smoke screen. She hardly even needed to check, she already knew what had happened: the police replies and the approval of the altered arrangements were also a bluff. It didn't just mean that someone was pretending to be Edelman. There also had to be a leak, and above all, somebody wanted the boy outside on Sveavägen.

Somebody wanted him defenceless in the street so that ... what? They could kidnap or get rid of him? Salander looked at her watch, it was already 8:55. In just twenty minutes Torkel Lindén and August Balder would be outside waiting for someone who was not Professor Edelman, and who had anything but good intentions towards them.

What should she do? Call the police? That was never her first choice. She was especially reluctant when there was a risk of leaks. Instead, she went onto Oden's website and got hold of Lindén's office number. But she only made it as far as the switchboard. Lindén was in a meeting. So she found his mobile. After ending up in his voicemail, she swore out loud, and sent him both a text and an e-mail telling him on no account to go out into the street with the boy, not under any circumstances. She signed herself "Wasp" for lack of a better idea.

Then she threw on her leather jacket and rushed out. After a second, she turned, ran back into the apartment, and packed her laptop with the encrypted file and her pistol, a Beretta 92, into a black sports bag. Then she hurried out again. She wondered if she should take her car, the BMW M6 Convertible gathering dust in the garage. But she decided a taxi would be quicker. She soon regretted it.

When a taxi finally appeared, it was clear that rush hour had not subsided. Traffic inched forward and Centralbron was almost at a standstill. Had there been an accident? Everything went slowly, everything but the time, which flew. Soon it was 9:05, then 9:10. She was in a tearing hurry and in the worst case it was already too late. Most likely Lindén and the boy went out onto the street ahead of time and the killer, or whoever it was, had already struck.

She dialled Lindén's number again. This time the call went through, but there was no answer, so she swore again and thought of Mikael Blomkvist. She had not actually spoken to him in ages. But now she called him and he answered, sounding irritated. Only when he realized who it was did he brighten up:

"Lisbeth, is that you?"

"Shut up and listen," she said.


Blomkvist was in the *Millennium* offices on Götgatan, in a foul mood. It was not just because he had had another bad night. It was TT. Usually a serious and decent news agency, TT had put out a bulletin claiming that Mikael Blomkvist was sabotaging the murder enquiry by withholding crucial information, which he intended to publish first in *Millennium*.

Allegedly his aim was to save the magazine from financial disaster and rebuild his own "ruined reputation." Blomkvist had known that the story was in the offing. He had had a long conversation with its author, Harald Wallin, the evening before. But he could not have imagined such a devastating result.

It was made up of idiotic insinuations and unsubstantiated accusations, but Wallin had nonetheless managed to produce something which sounded almost objective, almost credible. The man obviously had good sources both within the Serner Group and the police. Admittedly the headline was innocuous—PROSECUTOR CRITICAL OF MIKAEL BLOMKVIST—and there was plenty of room in the story for Blomkvist to defend himself. But whichever one of his enemies was responsible understood media logic: if a news bureau as serious as TT publishes a story like this one, not only does that make it legitimate for everybody else to jump on the bandwagon, it just about requires them to take a tougher line. It explains why Blomkvist woke up to the online papers saying BLOMKVIST SABOTAGES MURDER INVESTI-

GATION and BLOMKVIST ATTEMPTS TO SAVE MAGAZINE. MURDERER RUNS FREE. The print media were good enough to put quotation marks around the headlines. But the overall impression was nevertheless that a new truth was being served up with the breakfast coffee. A columnist by the name of Gustav Lund, who claimed to be fed up with all the hypocrisy, began his piece by writing: "Mikael Blomkvist, who has always thought of himself as a cut above the rest, has now been unmasked as the biggest cynic of us all."

"Let's hope they don't start waving subpoenas at us," said Malm, designer and part owner of the magazine, as he stood next to Blomkvist, nervously chewing gum.

"Let's hope they don't call in the Marines," Blomkvist said.

"What?"

"It was meant to be a joke."

"I get it. I don't like the tone," Malm said.

"Nobody likes it. But the best we can do is grit our teeth and keep working as usual."

"Your phone's buzzing."

"It's always buzzing."

"How about answering it, before they come up with anything worse?"

"Yes, yes," Blomkvist muttered, and answered gruffly.

It was a girl. He thought he recognized the voice but, caught off guard, he could not at first place it.

"Who's that?" he said.

"Salander," said the voice, and at that he gave a big smile.

"Lisbeth, is that you?"

"Shut up and listen," she said. And so he did.


The traffic had eased and Salander and the taxi driver, a young man from Iraq named Ahmed who had lost his mother and two brothers in terrorist attacks, had emerged onto Sveavägen and passed the Stockholm Konserthuset on their left. Salander, who was a terrible passenger, sent off yet another text message to Lindén and tried to call some other member of the staff at Oden's, anybody who could run out and warn him. No reply. She swore aloud, hoping that Blomkvist would do better.

"Is it an emergency?" Ahmed said from the driver's seat.

When Salander replied "Yes," Ahmed shot the light and got a fleeting smile out of her.

After that she focused on every foot they covered. Away to the left she caught a glimpse of the School of Economics and the Public Library—it was not far to go now. She scanned for the street numbers on the right-hand side, and at last saw the address. Thankfully there was no-one lying dead on the sidewalk. Salander pulled out some hundred-kronor notes for Ahmed. It was an ordinary, dreary November day, no more than that, and people were on their way to work. But wait . . . She looked over towards the low, green-speckled wall on the other side of the street.

A powerfully built man in a woollen hat and dark glasses was standing there, staring intently at the entrance on Sveavägen. There was something about his body language—his right hand was not visible but the arm was tensed and ready. Salander looked again at the entrance to Oden's, to the extent that she could see anything from her oblique angle, and she noticed the door opening.

It opened slowly, as if the person about to come out were hesitant or finding the door heavy, and all of a sudden Salander shouted to Ahmed to stop. She jumped out of the moving car, just as the man across the street raised his right hand and aimed a pistol with a telescopic sight at the door as it slid open.

# CHAPTER 17

# NOVEMBER 22

The man who called himself Jan Holtser was not happy with the situation. The place was wide open and it was the wrong time of day. The street was too busy, and although he had done his best to cover his face, he was uncomfortable in daylight, and so near the park. More than ever he felt that he hated killing children.

But that's the way it was and he had to accept that the situation was of his own making.

He had underestimated the boy and now he had to correct his mistake. He must not let wishful thinking or his own demons get in the way. He would keep his mind on the job, be the professional he always was, and above all not think about Olga, still less recall that glassy stare which had confronted him in Balder's bedroom.

He had to concentrate now on the doorway across the street and on his Remington pistol, which he was keeping under his windbreaker. But why wasn't anything happening? His mouth felt dry. The wind was biting. There was snow lying in the street and on the sidewalk and people were hurrying back and forth to work. He tightened his grip on the pistol and glanced at his watch.

It was 9:16, and then 9:17. But still no-one emerged from the doorway across the road and he cursed: Was something wrong? All he had to go by was Bogdanov's word, but that was assurance enough. The man was a wizard with computers and last night he had sat engrossed in his work, sending off fake e-mails and getting the language right with the help of his contacts in Sweden. Holtser had taken care of the rest: studying pictures of the place, selecting the weapon, and above all organizing the getaway car—a rental which Dennis Wilton of the Svavelsjö Motorcycle Club had fixed for them under a false name, and which was now standing ready three blocks away, with Bogdanov at the wheel.

Holtser sensed a movement immediately behind him and jumped. But it was just two young men walking past a little too close to him. The street seemed to be getting busier and he did not like that. In the distance a dog was barking and there was a smell, maybe food frying at McDonald's, then . . . at long last . . . a short man in a grey overcoat and a curly-haired boy in a red quilted jacket could be seen through the glass door on the other side of the street. Holtser crossed himself with his left hand as he always did and started to squeeze the trigger on his weapon. But what was happening?

The door did not open. The man hesitated and looked down at his mobile. *Get a move on,* Holtser thought. *Here we go . . .* Slowly, slowly the door was pushed open and they were on their way out, and Holtser raised his pistol, aiming at the boy's face through the telescopic sight, and saw once more those glassy eyes. Suddenly he felt an unexpected, violent rush of excitement. Suddenly he did want to kill the boy. Suddenly he wanted to snuff out that frightening look, once and for all. But then something happened.

A young woman came running out of nowhere and threw herself over the boy as Holtser fired and hit on his target. He hit something, and shot again and again. But the boy and the woman had rolled behind a car, quick as lightning. Holtser caught his breath and looked right and left. Then he raced across the street, commando-style.

This time he was not going to fail.

Lindén had never been on satisfactory terms with telephones. His wife Saga leaped with anticipation at every call, hoping that it would bring a new job or a new offer; he felt uncomfortable whenever his mobile rang.

It was because of all the complaints. He and the medical centre were always taking abuse. In his view that was part of their business—Oden's was an emergency centre and so inevitably emotions tended to run high. But he also knew on some level that the complaints were justified. He may have driven his cost cutting too far. Occasionally he just ran away, went out to the woods and let the others get on with it. On the other hand, he did from time to time get recognition, most recently from no less a person than Professor Edelman.

The professor had irritated him at first. He did not like it when outsiders meddled in the way the clinic managed their procedures. But he felt more conciliatory since he had been praised in that e-mail. Who knows, he might even get the professor to support the idea of the boy staying on at Oden's for a while. That would add some spark to his life, although he could not quite understand why. As a rule he tended to keep himself apart from the children.

There was something enigmatic about this August Balder which intrigued him. From the very first he had been irritated by the police and their demands. He wanted August to himself and hoped perhaps to capture some of the mystique surrounding the boy—or at least to be able to understand what those endless rows of numbers meant, the ones he had written on that comic in the playroom. But it was far from easy. The boy seemed to dislike any form of contact and now he was refusing to come out to the street. He was being hopelessly contrary, and Lindén was forced to drag him along.

"Come on, come *on*," he muttered.

Then his mobile buzzed. Somebody was determined to get hold of him.

He did not answer. Probably it was some trivial nonsense, yet another complaint. But as he reached the door, he decided to check his messages. There were several texts from a withheld number, and they were saying something strange, presumably some kind of a joke: they told him not to go outside. He was under no circumstances to go into the street.

Incomprehensible, and at that moment August seemed to want to run for it. Lindén took a firm grip on his arm, opened the door hesitantly, and pulled the boy out. Everything was normal. People walked by as they did every day and he wondered again about the text messages, but before he had time to complete the thought, a figure came rushing in from the left and threw itself over the boy. In that instant he heard a shot.

Obviously he was in danger. He looked around wildly and saw a tall, powerful man running towards him across Sveavägen. What the hell did he have in his hand? Was that a pistol?

Without a thought for August, Lindén turned to go back through the door and for a second or two he thought he was going to make it to safety. But he never did.

Salander's reaction had been instinctive as she launched herself on top of the boy. She had hurt herself when she hit the sidewalk, or at least there was pain in her shoulder and chest. But she had no time to take stock. She took hold of the child and hid behind a car and they lay there breathing heavily while shots were fired. After that it became disturbingly quiet, and when Salander peered under the car she could see the sturdy legs of their attacker racing across the street. It crossed her mind to grab the Beretta from her sports bag and return fire, but she realized she would not have time. On the other hand . . . a large Volvo came crawling past, so she jumped to her feet and in one confused rush lifted the boy and ran towards the car. She wrenched open the back door and threw herself in with him.

"Drive!" she yelled, as she saw blood spreading onto the seat.

Jacob Charro was twenty-two and the proud owner of a Volvo XC60, which he had bought on credit with his father as guarantor. He was on his way to Uppsala to have lunch with his uncle and aunt and cousins, and he was looking forward to it. He was dying to tell them that he'd gotten a place on Syrian FC's first team.

The radio was playing "Wake Me Up" by Avicii and he was drumming his fingers on the steering wheel as he drove past the Concert Hall and the Stockholm School of Economics. Something was going on further down the street. People were running in all directions. A man was shouting, and the cars in front of the Volvo were driving erratically, so Charro slowed down. If there had been an accident, he might be able to help. Charro was always dreaming of being a hero.

But this time he got a fright. The man to the left of him across the road ran into the traffic, looking like a soldier on an offensive. There was something brutal in his movements and Charro was about to floor the accelerator when he heard his rear door being yanked open. Someone had thrown themselves in. Charro started shouting, had no idea what. Maybe it was not even in Swedish. But the person—it was a girl with a child—yelled back.

"Drive!"

He hesitated for a second. Who *were* these people? Maybe they meant to rob him, or steal the car. He could not think straight, the whole situation was crazy. Then he had no choice but to act. His rear window was shattered because someone was shooting at them, so he accelerated wildly and with a pounding heart drove through a red light at the intersection with Odengatan.

"What's all this about?" he shouted. "What's going on?"

"Shut it!" the girl snapped back. In the rearview mirror he could see her examining the small boy with large terrified eyes, checking him over with practised movements, like a hospital nurse. Then he noticed for the first time that there was not just broken glass all over the backseat. There was blood too.

"Has he been shot?"

"I don't know. Just keep driving. Go left there . . . Now!"

"OK, OK," he said, terrified, and he took a hard left up along Vanadisvägen and drove at high speed towards Vasastan, wondering if they were being followed and if anyone would shoot at them again.

He lowered his head towards the steering wheel and felt the draft through the broken rear window. What the hell had he been dragged into, and who *was* this girl? He looked at her again in the mirror. Black hair and piercings and a glowering look, and for a moment he felt that as far as she was concerned he simply did not exist. But then she muttered something which sounded almost cheerful.

"Good news?" he asked.

She did not answer. Instead she pulled off her leather jacket, took hold of her white T-shirt, and then . . . Jesus! She ripped it apart with a sudden jerk and was sitting there naked from the waist up, not wearing a bra or anything, and he glanced in bewilderment at her breasts, which stood straight out, and above all at the blood that ran over them like a rivulet, down towards her stomach and the waistband of her jeans.

The girl had been hit somewhere below the shoulder, not far above her heart, and was bleeding heavily. Using the T-shirt for a bandage, she wound it tightly to staunch the flow of blood and put her leather jacket back on. She looked ridiculously pleased with herself, especially since some of the blood had splashed onto her cheek and forehead, like war paint.

"So the good news is that you got shot and not the boy," he said.

"Something like that," she said.

"Should I take you to the Karolinska hospital?"

"No."

Salander had found both the entry and exit holes. The bullet must have gone straight through the front of her shoulder, which was bleeding profusely—she could feel her heart pounding all the way up to her temples. But she did not think any artery had been severed, or at least so she hoped. She looked back. The attacker must have had a getaway car somewhere close by but nobody seemed to be following them. With any luck they had managed to escape fast enough.

She quickly looked down at the boy—August—who was sitting with his hands crossed over his chest, rocking backwards and forwards. It struck Salander that she ought to do something, so she brushed the glass fragments from the boy's hair and legs, and that made him sit still for a moment. Salander was not sure that was a good sign. The look in his eyes was rigid and blank. She nodded at him and tried to look as if she had the situation under control. She was feeling sick and dizzy and the T-shirt she had wound around her shoulder was by now soaked in blood. She was afraid that she might be losing consciousness and tried to come up with some sort of plan. One thing was crystal clear: the police were not an option. They had led the boy right into the path of the assailant and were plainly not on top of the situation. So what should she do?

She could not stay in this car. It had been seen at the shooting and the shattered rear window was bound to attract attention. She should get the man to drive her home to Fiskargatan. Then she could take her BMW, registered to Irene Nesser, if only she had the strength to drive it.

"Head towards Västerbron!" she ordered.

"OK, OK," said the man driving.

"Do you have anything to drink?"

"A bottle of whisky; I was going to give it to my uncle."

"Pass it back here," she said, and was handed a bottle of Grant's, which she opened with difficulty.

She tore off her makeshift bandage and poured whisky onto the bullet wound. She took one, two, three big mouthfuls, and was just offering some to August when it dawned on her that that was perhaps not such a good idea. Children don't drink whisky. Not even children in shock. Her thoughts were getting confused, was that what was happening?

"You'll have to give me your shirt," she said to the man up front.

"What?"

"I need something else to bandage my shoulder with."

"OK, but—"

"No buts."

"If you want me to help you, you could at least tell me why you were being shot at. Are you criminals?"

"I'm trying to protect the boy, it's that simple. Those bastards were after him."

"Why?"

"None of your business."

"So he's not your son."

"I don't even know him."

"So why are you helping him?"

Salander hesitated.

"We have the same enemies," she said. At that the young man pulled off his V-necked pullover—with a certain amount of reluctance and difficulty—as he steered the car with his other hand. Then he unbuttoned his shirt, took it off, and handed it back to Salander, who wound it gingerly around her shoulder. August, who was worryingly immobile now, looked down at his skinny legs with a frozen expression, and once again Salander asked herself what she ought to do.

They could hide out at her place on Fiskargatan. Blomkvist was the only person who knew the address, and the apartment could not be traced through her name on any public register. But it was still a risk. There had been a time when she was known up and down the country as a complete lunatic, and this enemy was certainly skilled at digging up information.

Someone on Sveavägen might have recognized her, the police might already be turning everything upside down to find her. She needed a new hiding place, not linked to any of her identities, and so she needed help. But from whom? Holger?

Her former guardian Holger Palmgren had almost recovered from his stroke and was living in a two-room apartment on Liljeholmstorget. Holger was the only person who really knew her. He was loyal to a fault and would do everything in his power to help. But he was elderly and anxious and she did not want to drag him into this if she could help it.

There was Blomkvist, of course, and in fact there was nothing wrong with him. Still, she was reluctant to contact him again—perhaps *precisely* because there was nothing wrong with him. He was such a damn good person. But what the hell . . . you could hardly hold that against him, or at least not too much. She called his mobile. He picked up after just one ring, sounding alarmed.

"It's such a relief to hear your voice! What the hell happened?"

"I can't tell you now."

"It looks like one of you's been shot. There's blood here."

"The boy's OK."

"And you?"

"I'm OK."

"You've been shot."

"You'll have to wait, Blomkvist."

She looked out at the town and saw that they were close to Västerbron already. She turned to the driver:

"Pull up there, by the bus stop."

"Are you getting out?"

"*You're* getting out. You're going to give me your mobile and wait outside while I talk. Is that clear?"

He glanced at her, terrified, then passed back his mobile, stopped the car, and got out. Salander continued her conversation.

"What's going on?" Blomkvist said.

"Don't you worry about that," she said. "From now on I want you to carry an Android phone with you, a Samsung or something. You must have one at the office?"

"Yes, I think there are a couple."

"Good. So go straight into Google Play and download the RedPhone app and also the Threema app for text messaging. We need a secure line of communication."

"Right."

"If you're as much of an idiot as I think you are, whoever helps you do it has to remain anonymous. I don't want any weak points."

"Of course."

"And then . . ."

"Yes?"

"Only use it in an emergency. All other communication should be through a special link on your computer. You or the person who isn't an idiot needs to go into www.pgpi.org and download an encryption programme for your e-mails. I want you to do that right now, then I want you to find a safe hiding place for the boy and me—somewhere not connected to you or *Millennium*, and let me have the address in an encrypted e-mail."

"It's not your job to keep the boy safe, Lisbeth."

"I don't trust the police."

"Then we'll have to find someone else you *do* trust. The boy is autistic, he has special needs, I don't think you should be responsible for him, especially not if you're wounded . . ."

"Are you going to keep talking crap or do you want to help me?"

"Help you, of course."

"Good. Check [*Lisbeth stuff*] in five minutes. I'll give you more information there. Then delete it."

"Lisbeth, listen to me, you need to get to a hospital. You need to be fixed up. I can tell by your voice . . ."

She hung up, waved the young man back in from the bus stop, got out her laptop, and through her mobile hacked into Blomkvist's computer. She wrote out instructions on how to download and install the encryption programme.

She then told the man to drive her to Mosebacke torg. It was a risk, but she had no choice. The city was beginning to look more and more blurred.

.   .   .

Blomkvist swore under his breath. He was standing on Sveavägen, not far from the body of Torkel Lindén and the cordon which the police who had been first on the scene were putting in place. Ever since Salander's original call he had been engaged in a frenzy of activity. He had thrown himself into a taxi to get here and had done everything he could during the trip to stop the boy and the director from stepping out onto the street.

The only other member of the staff he had managed to get hold of at Oden's Medical Centre was Birgitta Lindgren, who had rushed into the hallway only to see her colleague fall against the door with a fatal bullet wound to his head. When Blomkvist arrived ten minutes later she was beside herself, but she and another woman by the name of Ulrika Franzén, who had been on her way to the offices of Albert Bonniers, the publishers further up the street, had still been able to give Blomkvist a pretty coherent account of what had happened.

Which was why Blomkvist knew, even before his mobile rang again, that Salander had saved August Balder's life. She and the boy were now in some car with a driver who had no reason to be enthusiastic about helping them after getting shot at. Blomkvist had seen the blood on the sidewalk and on the street and, even though the call reassured him somewhat, he was still extremely concerned. Salander had sounded in a bad way and yet—not that it surprised him—she had been as pig-headed as ever.

She had a gunshot wound, but she was determined to hide the boy herself. That was understandable, given her history, but should he and the magazine get involved? However heroic her actions on Sveavägen, what she had done might from a legal point of view be seen as kidnapping. He could not help her with that. He was already in trouble with the media as well as the public prosecutor.

But this was Salander, after all, and he had given his word. He would damn well help her, even if Berger threw a fit. He took a deep breath and pulled out his mobile. But a familiar voice was calling out behind him. It was Jan Bublanski. Bublanski came running along the sidewalk close to physical collapse, and with him were Detective Sergeant Modig and a tall, athletic man in his fifties, presumably the professor Salander had mentioned.

"Where's the boy?" Bublanski panted.

"He was whisked away in a big red Volvo, somebody rescued him."

"Who?"

"I'll tell you what I know," Blomkvist said, not sure what he would or should say. "But first I have to make a call."

"Oh no, first you're going to talk to us. We have to send out a nationwide alert."

"Talk to that lady over there. Her name is Ulrika Franzén. She knows more than I do. She saw it happen; she's even got some sort of description of the assailant. I arrived after it happened."

"And the man who saved the boy?"

"The *woman* who saved him. Fru Franzén has a description of her as well. But just give me a minute here . . ."

"How did you know something was going to happen in the first place?" Modig spat, with unexpected anger. "They said on the radio that you had called the emergency services before any shots were fired."

"I had a tip-off."

"From whom?"

Blomkvist took another deep breath and looked Modig straight in the eye, unmoveable as ever.

"Whatever may have been written in today's papers, I hope you realize that I want to cooperate with you in every way I can."

"I've always trusted you, Mikael. But I'm beginning to have my doubts," Modig said.

"OK, I understand that. But you have to understand that *I* don't trust *you* either. There's been a serious leak; you've grasped that much, haven't you? Otherwise this wouldn't have happened," he said, pointing at the prone body inside the cordon.

"That's true, and it's absolutely terrible," Bublanski said.

"I'm going to make my call now," Blomkvist said, and he walked up the street so he could talk undisturbed.

But he never made the call. He realized that the time had come to get serious about security, so he walked back and informed Bublanski and Modig that he had to go to his office immediately, but he was at their disposal whenever they needed him. At that moment, to her own surprise, Modig took hold of his arm.

"First you have to tell us how you knew that something was going to happen," she said sharply.

"I'm afraid I have to invoke my right to protect my sources," Blomkvist answered, with a pained smile.

Then he waved down a taxi and took off for the office, deep in thought. *Millennium* used Tech Source, a consultancy firm with a team of young women who gave the magazine quick and efficient help, whenever they had more complex IT issues. But he did not want to bring them in. Nor did he feel like turning to Christer Malm, even though he knew more about IT than anyone on the editorial team. Instead he thought of Zander, who was already involved in the story and was also great with computers. Blomkvist decided to ask for his help, and promised himself that he would fight to get the boy a permanent job—provided that he and Berger managed to sort out this mess.

Berger's morning had been a nightmare even before shots were fired on Sveavägen, and that was due to the sickening TT bulletin. To some extent it was a continuation of the old campaign against Blomkvist—all the jealous, twisted souls came crawling out of the woodwork again, spewing their bile on Twitter and online forums and in e-mails. This time the racist mob joined in, because *Millennium* had been in the forefront of the battles against xenophobia and racism for many years.

The worst part was surely that this hate campaign made it so much more difficult for everyone to do their jobs. All of a sudden people were less inclined to share information with the magazine. On top of that there was a rumour that Chief Prosecutor Ekström was planning to issue a search warrant for the magazine's offices. Berger did not really believe it. That kind of warrant was a serious matter, given the right to source protection.

But she did agree with Christer Malm that the toxic atmosphere would even give lawyers ludicrous ideas about how they should act. She was standing there thinking about how to retaliate when Blomkvist stepped into the offices. To her surprise, he did not want to talk to her. Instead he went straight to Zander and ushered him into her room.

After a while she followed. She found the young man looking tense. She heard Blomkvist mention "PGP." She had taken an IT security course so she knew what that meant, and she saw Zander making notes before; without so much as a glance in her direction, he made a beeline for Blomkvist's laptop in the open-plan office.

"What was all that about?" she said.

Blomkvist told her in a whisper. She could barely take it in, and he had to repeat himself.

"So you want me to find a hiding place for them?"

"Sorry to drag you into this, Erika," he said. "But I don't know anyone who has as many friends with summer houses as you do."

"I don't know, Mikael. I really don't know."

"We can't let them down. Salander has been shot. The situation is desperate."

"If she's been shot, she should go to a hospital."

"She won't. She wants to protect the boy at all costs."

"To give him the calm he needs to draw the murderer."

"Yes."

"It's too great a responsibility, Mikael, too great a risk. If something happens, the fallout would destroy the magazine. Witness protection is not our job. This is something for the police—just think of all the questions that will be thrown up by those drawings, both for the investigation and on a psychological level. There has to be another solution."

"Maybe—if we were dealing with someone other than Lisbeth Salander."

"You know what? I get really pissed off with the way you always defend her."

"I'm only trying to be realistic. The authorities have let the Balder boy down and put his life in danger—I know that infuriates Salander."

"So we just have to go along with it, is that it?"

"We don't have a choice. She's out there somewhere, hopping mad, and has nowhere to go."

"Take them to Sandhamn, then."

"There's too much of a connection between Lisbeth and me. If it comes out that it's her, they would search my addresses straightaway."

"OK then."

"OK then, what?"

"OK, I'll find something."

She could hardly believe she was saying it. That is how it was with Blomkvist—she was incapable of saying no—but there was no limit to what he would do for her either.

"Great, Ricky. Where?"

She tried to think, but her mind was a blank. She could not come up with a single name.

"I'm racking my brains," she said.

"Well, do it quickly, then give the address and directions to Andrei. He knows what to do."

Berger needed some air and so she went down onto Götgatan and walked in the direction of Medborgarplatsen, running through one name after another in her mind. But not one of them felt right. There was too much at stake. Everyone she thought of had some drawback or, even if not, she was reluctant to expose them to the risk or put them to the trouble by asking, perhaps because she herself was so upset by the situation. On the other hand . . . here was a small boy and people were trying to kill him and she had promised. She had to come up with something.

A police siren wailed in the distance and she looked over towards the park and the tunnelbana station and at the mosque on the hill. A young man went by, surreptitiously shuffling some papers, and then suddenly—Gabriella Grane. At first the name surprised her. Grane was not a close friend and she worked at a place where it was unwise to flout any laws. Grane would risk losing her job if she so much as got near this, and yet . . . Berger could not get the idea out of her head.

It was not just that Grane was an exceptionally good and responsible person. A memory also kept intruding. It was from the summer, in the early hours of the morning or maybe even at daybreak after a crayfish party out at Grane's summer house on Ingarö island, when the two had been sitting in a garden swing on the terrace looking down at the water through a gap in the trees.

"This is where I'd run to if the hyenas were after me," Berger had said without really knowing what she meant. She had been feeling tired and vulnerable at work, and there was something about that house which she thought would make it an ideal place of refuge.

It stood on a rock promontory with steep, smooth sides, and was shielded from onlookers by the surrounding trees and elevation. She remembered Grane replying, "If the hyenas come after you, you're welcome to hide here, Erika."

Maybe it was asking too much, but she decided to give it a try. She went back to the office to call from the encrypted RedPhone app, which Zander had by then installed for her too.

# CHAPTER 18

# NOVEMBER 22

Gabriella Grane was on her way to a meeting at Säpo when her personal mobile buzzed. The meeting had been called at very short notice to discuss the incident at Sveavägen. She answered tersely:

"Yes?"

"It's Erika."

"Hi there. Can't talk now. We'll speak later."

"I have a . . ." Berger said.

But Grane had already hung up—this was no time for personal calls. She walked into the meeting room wearing an expression that suggested she meant to start a minor war. Crucial information had been leaked and now a second person was dead and one more apparently seriously wounded. She had never felt more like telling the whole lot of them to go to hell. They had been so eager to get hold of new information that they had lost their heads. For half a minute she did not hear one word her colleagues were saying. She just sat there, seething. But then she pricked up her ears.

Someone was saying that Mikael Blomkvist, the journalist, had called the emergency services before shots were fired on Sveavägen. That was strange, and now Erika Berger had called, and she was not the type to make casual calls, certainly not during working hours. She may have had something important or even critical to say. Grane got up and made an excuse.

"Gabriella, you need to listen to this," Kraft said in an unusually sharp tone.

"I have to take a call," she replied, and suddenly she was not in the least interested in what the head of the Security Police thought of her.

"What sort of call?"

"A call," she said, and left them to go into her office.

Berger at once asked Grane to call her instead on the Samsung. The minute she had her friend on the line again, she could tell that something was going on. There was none of the usual warm enthusiasm in her voice. On the contrary, Grane sounded worried and tense, as if she knew from the start that the conversation was important.

"Hi," she said simply. "I'm still really pushed. But is it about August Balder?"

Berger felt acutely uncomfortable.

"How did you know?"

"I'm on the investigation and I've just heard that Mikael Blomkvist was tipped off about what was going to happen on Sveavägen."

"You've already heard that?"

"Yes, and now of course we're eager to know how that came about."

"Sorry. I can't tell you."

"OK. Understood. But why did you call?"

Berger closed her eyes. How could she have been such an idiot?

"I'm so sorry. I'll have to ask somebody else," she said. "You have a conflict of interest."

"I'm happy to take on almost any conflict of interest, Erika. But I can't stand your withholding information. This investigation means more to me than you can imagine."

"Really?"

"Yes, it does. I knew that Balder was under serious threat, yet I still couldn't prevent the murder, and I'm going to have to live with that for the rest of my life. So please, don't hide anything from me."

"I'm going to have to, Gabriella. I'm sorry. I don't want you to get into trouble because of us."

"I saw Mikael in Saltsjöbaden the night before last, the night of the murder."

"He didn't mention that."

"It wouldn't have made sense to identify myself."

"I understand."

"We could help each other out in this mess."

"That sounds like a good idea. I can ask Mikael to call you later. But now I have to get on with this."

"I know just as well as you do that there's a leak in the police team. At this stage we could benefit from unlikely alliances."

"Absolutely. But I'm sorry, I have to press on."

"OK," Grane said, obviously disappointed. "I'll pretend this call never happened. Good luck now."

"Thanks," Berger said, and went back to searching through her contacts.


Grane went back to the meeting room, her mind whirling. What was it that Erika had wanted? She did not fully understand and yet she had a vague idea. As she came back into the room the conversation died and everyone looked at her.

"What was that about?" Kraft said.

"Something private."

"That you had to deal with now?"

"That I had to deal with. How far have you gotten?"

"We were talking about what happened on Sveavägen," said Ragnar Olofsson, the head of the division. "But as I was saying, we don't yet have enough information. The situation is chaotic, and it looks as if we're losing our source in Bublanski's group. The detective inspector has become paranoid."

"You can't blame him," Grane said.

"Well . . . perhaps not. We've talked about that too. We'll leave no stone unturned until we know how the attacker figured out that the boy was at the medical centre and that he was going to go out by the front door when he did. No effort will be spared, I need hardly say. But I must emphasize that the leak did not necessarily come from within the police. The information was quite widely known—at the medical centre of course, by the mother and her unreliable partner, Lasse Westman, and in the offices of *Millennium*. And we can't rule out hacker attacks. I'll come back to that. If I might continue with my report?"

"Please."

"We've been discussing how Mikael Blomkvist comes into all this, and this is where we're worried. How could he know about a shooting before it happens? In my opinion, he's got some source close to the criminals themselves, and I see no reason for us to tiptoe around his efforts to protect those sources. We have to find out where he got his information from."

"The more so since he seems desperate and will do anything for a scoop," Superintendent Mårten Nielsen added.

"It would appear that Mårten has some excellent sources too. He reads the evening papers," Grane said acidly.

"Not the evening papers, sweetie. TT—a source which even we at Säpo regard as fairly reliable."

"That was defamatory, and you know it as well as I do," Grane hissed.

"I had no idea you were so besotted with Blomkvist."

"Idiot!"

"Stop it at once," Kraft said. "This is ridiculous behaviour! Carry on, Ragnar. What do we know about what happened?"

"The first people on the scene were two regular police officers, Erik Sandström and Tord Landgren," Olofsson said. "My information comes from them. They were there on the dot of 9:24, and by then it was all over. Torkel Lindén was dead, shot in the back of the head, and the boy, well, we don't know. According to witnesses, he was hit too. We have blood in the street. But nothing is confirmed. The boy was driven away in a red Volvo—we do at least have parts of the registration number plus the model of the vehicle. I anticipate that we'll get the name of its owner pretty soon."

Grane noticed that Kraft was writing everything down, just as she had done at their earlier meetings.

"But what actually happened?" she asked.

"According to two students from the School of Economics who were standing on the opposite side of Sveavägen, it looked like a settling of scores between two criminal gangs who were both after the boy."

"Sounds far-fetched."

"I'm not so sure," Olofsson said.

"What makes you say that?" Kraft said.

"There were professionals on both sides. The assailant seems to have been standing and watching the door from a low green wall on the other side of Sveavägen, in front of the park. There's a lot to suggest that he's the man who shot Frans Balder. Not that anyone has seen his face; it's possible he was wearing some sort of mask. But he seems to have moved with the same remarkable efficiency and speed. And in the opposite camp there was this woman."

"What do we know about her?"

"Not much. She was wearing a black leather jacket, we think, and dark jeans. She was young with black hair and piercings, a punk according to one witness, also short, but fierce. She appeared out of nowhere and shielded the boy with her body. The witnesses all agree that she was not some ordinary member of the public. She seemed to have training, or had at least found herself in similar situations before. Then there's the car—we have conflicting reports. One witness says it just happened to be driving by, and the woman and the boy threw themselves in more or less while it was moving. Others—especially those guys from the School of Economics—think the car was part of the operation. Either way, I'm afraid we have a kidnapping on our hands."

"It doesn't make sense. This woman saved the boy only to abscond with him?" Grane said.

"That's what it looks like. Otherwise we would have heard from her by now, wouldn't we?"

"How did she get to Sveavägen?"

"We don't know yet. But a witness, a former editor-in-chief of a trade union paper, says the woman looked somehow familiar," Olofsson said.

He went on to say something else, but by then Grane had stopped listening. She was thinking: "Zalachenko's daughter, it has to be Zalachenko's daughter," knowing full well how unfair it was to call her that. The daughter had nothing to do with the father. On the contrary, she had hated him. But Grane had known her by that name ever since, years earlier, she had read everything she could lay her hands on about the Zalachenko affair.

While Olofsson continued speculating she began to feel the pieces falling into place. Already the day before she had identified some commonalities between Zalachenko's old network and the group which called itself the Spiders, but had dismissed them. She had believed there was a limit to how far thuggish criminals could develop their skills; it seemed entirely unreasonable to suppose that they could go from seedy-looking biker types in leather vests to cutting-edge hackers. Yet the thought had occurred to her. Grane had even wondered if the girl who helped Linus Brandell trace the break-in on Balder's computers might have been Zalachenko's daughter. There was a Säpo file on the woman, with a note that said "Hacker? Computer savvy?," and even though it seemed prompted by the surprisingly favourable reference she had received for her work at Milton Security, it was clear from the document that she had devoted a great deal of time to research into her father's criminal organization.

Most striking of all was that there was a known connection between the woman and Mikael Blomkvist. It was unclear what exactly that connection was—Grane did not for one moment believe the malicious rumours that it was sado-masochistic sex—but the connection was there. Both Blomkvist and the woman who matched the description of Zalachenko's daughter appeared to have known something about the shooting on Sveavägen beforehand, and afterwards Erika Berger had rung to discuss something important. Wasn't it all pointing in the same direction?

"I was wondering," Grane said, perhaps too loudly, interrupting Olofsson.

"Yes?" he said testily.

She was about to present her theory when she noticed something which made her hesitate.

It was nothing remarkable, just that Kraft was once again meticulously writing down what Olofsson had said. It was probably good to have a senior boss who was so committed, but there was something rather too zealous about that scratching pen, and it made Grane wonder why that senior boss, whose job it was to see the bigger picture, should be preoccupied with every tiny detail.

Without really knowing why, Grane began to feel very uneasy. It may have been because she was formulating suspicion on flimsy grounds. Then Kraft realized that she was being observed and looked away in embarrassment. It looked like she was blushing. Grane decided not to finish the sentence she had begun. "Or rather . . ."

"Yes, Gabriella?" Olofsson prompted.

"Oh, nothing," she said, feeling a sudden need to get away. Even though she knew it would not look good, she left the meeting room once more and went to the toilet.

Later she would remember how she stared at herself in the mirror and tried to understand what she had seen. Had Kraft blushed, and if so what did that mean? Maybe nothing, she decided, absolutely nothing, and even if it really was shame or guilt that Grane had read in her face it could have been about almost anything. It occurred to her that she did not know her boss all that well. But she knew enough to realize that Kraft would not send a child to his death for financial or any other gain, no, that was out of the question.

Grane had simply become paranoid, a typically suspicious spy who saw moles everywhere, even in her own reflection. "Idiot," she muttered, and smiled at herself despondently, as if to dismiss the idea and come back down to earth. But that didn't solve anything. In that instant she thought she saw a new kind of truth in her own eyes.

She suspected that she was quite like Helena Kraft in that she was capable and ambitious and wanted to get a pat on the back from her superiors. That was not necessarily always a good thing. With that tendency, if you operate in an unhealthy culture you risk becoming just as unhealthy yourself. Who knows, perhaps the will to please leads people to crime as often as evil or greed does. People want to fit in and do well, and they do indescribably stupid things because of it. Is that what happened here?

Hans Faste—because surely he was their source in Bublanski's group—had been leaking to them because that was what he was expected to do and because he wanted to score points with Säpo. Olofsson had seen to it that Kraft was kept informed of every little detail; she was his boss and he wanted to be in her good books. And then—well, maybe Kraft in turn had passed on some information because she wanted to be seen as doing a good job. But, if so, by whom? The head of the national police, the government, foreign intelligence, in that case most likely American or English, who perhaps then . . .

Grane did not take this thought any further. She asked herself again if she was letting her imagination run away with her. Even if she was, she still could not trust her team. She wanted to be good at her job, but not necessarily by doing her duty to Säpo. She just wanted the Balder boy to be all right. Instead of Kraft's face she now saw Berger's, so she went to her office and got out her Blackphone, the same one she had been using to call Frans Balder.

Berger had left the office to have an undisturbed conversation and was now standing in front of Söderbokhandeln, the bookstore on Götgatan, wondering if she had done something stupid. Grane had argued her case in such a way that Berger could not defend herself. That is no doubt the disadvantage of having intelligent friends. They see straight through you.

Not only had Grane worked out what Berger wanted to talk to her about, she had also persuaded her that she felt a moral responsibility and would never reveal the hiding place, however much that might appear to conflict with her professional ethics. She said she had a debt to repay and insisted on helping. She was going to courier over the keys to her summer house on Ingarö and arrange for directions to be sent via the encrypted link which Andrei Zander had set up.

Further up Götgatan a beggar collapsed, scattering two carrier bags full of plastic bottles across the sidewalk. Berger hurried over, but the man, who was soon on his feet again, declined her help so she gave him a sad smile and went back up to the *Millennium* offices.

Blomkvist was looking upset and exhausted. His hair stood on end and his shirt hung outside his trousers. She had not seen him looking so worn out in a long time. Yet when his eyes shone like that, there was no stopping him. It meant he had entered into that absolute concentration from which he would not emerge until he had gotten to the heart of the story.

"Have you found a hiding place?" he said.

She nodded.

"It might be best if you say nothing more. We have to keep this to as small a circle of people as possible."

"That sounds sensible. But let's hope it's a short-term solution. I don't like the idea of Lisbeth Salander being responsible for the boy."

"Who knows, maybe they're good for each other."

"What did you tell the police?"

"Almost nothing."

"Not a good time to be keeping things under wraps."

"Not really, no."

"Maybe Salander is prepared to make a statement, so you can get some peace and quiet."

"I don't want to put any pressure on her. She's in bad shape. Can you get Zander to ask her if we can send a doctor out there?"

"I will. But you know . . ."

"What?"

"I'm actually coming round to the idea that she's doing the right thing," Berger said.

"Why do you say that, all of a sudden?"

"Because I too have my sources. Police headquarters isn't a secure place right now," she said, and walked over to Andrei Zander with a determined stride.

# CHAPTER 19

# NOVEMBER 22—EVENING

Bublanski was standing alone in his office. In the end Hans Faste had admitted to keeping Säpo informed, and without even listening to his justification Bublanski removed him from the investigation. But even if that had provided further evidence that Faste was an unscrupulous opportunist, he could not bring himself to believe that the man had also been leaking to criminals.

Inevitably there were corrupt and depraved people in the force. But to deliver a small, mentally disabled boy into the hands of a cold-blooded murderer was beyond the pale, and he refused to believe that any policeman would be capable of that. Perhaps the information had seeped out by some other route. Their phones might be tapped or they could have been hacked, though he could not remember notes about August's abilities being entered in any police computer. He had been trying to reach the Säpo head, Helena Kraft, to discuss the matter. He had stressed that it was important, but she had not returned his call.

The Swedish Trade Council and the Ministry of Enterprise had called him, which was worrisome. Even if it was not said in so many words, their main concern was not for the boy or the shooting on Sveavägen, but rather for the research programme which Frans Balder had been working on, which appeared to have been stolen on the night of his murder.

Several of the most skilled computer technicians in the force and three IT experts from Linköping University and the Royal Institute of Technology had been to the house in Saltsjöbaden, but they had found no trace of this research, either on his computers or among the papers which he had left behind.

"So now, on top of everything else, we have an Artificial Intelligence on the loose," Bublanski muttered to himself. He was reminded of an old riddle his mischievous cousin Samuel liked to put to his friends in synagogue. It was a paradox: If God is indeed omnipotent, is he then capable of creating something more intelligent than himself? The riddle was considered disrespectful, he recalled, even blasphemous. It had that evasive quality which meant that, however you answered, you were wrong. There was a knock at the door, and Bublanski was brought back to the questions at hand. It was Modig, ceremoniously handing over another piece of Swiss orange chocolate.

"Thank you," he said. "Have you got anything new?"

"We think we know how the killers got Lindén and the boy out of the building. They sent fake e-mails from our and Professor Edelman's addresses and arranged a pickup on the street."

"Is that possible?"

"Sure, it's not even very difficult."

"Terrifying."

"True, but that still doesn't explain how they knew to access the Oden's Medical Centre computer, or how they found out that Edelman was involved."

"I suppose we'd better have our own computers checked out," Bublanski said gloomily.

"Already in hand."

"Is this how it was meant to be, that we won't dare to write or say anything for fear of being overheard?"

"I don't know. I hope not. Meanwhile we have a Jacob Charro out there waiting to be interviewed."

"Who's he?"

"A footballer, plays for Syrian F.C. He's the one who drove the woman and August Balder away from Sveavägen."


A muscular young man with short dark hair and high cheekbones was sitting in the interview room. He was wearing a mustard-coloured V-necked pullover without a shirt and seemed at once agitated and a little proud.

Modig opened with "6:35 p.m. on November 22. Interview with witness

Jacob Charro, twenty-two years old, resident in Norborg. Tell us what happened this morning."

"Well . . ." Charro said. "I was driving along Sveavägen and noticed some commotion in the street ahead of me. I thought there'd been an accident, so I slowed down. But then I saw a man come from the left and run across the road. He ran out without even looking at the traffic and I remember thinking he must be a terrorist."

"Why is that?"

"He seemed to be bursting with this sacred fury."

"Were you able to see what he looked like?"

"Not really, but since then it's struck me that there was something unnatural about his face."

"What do you mean?"

"Like it wasn't his real face. He was wearing sunglasses, which must have been secured around his ears, but his cheeks, it looked as if he had something in his mouth, I don't know. Then there was his moustache and eyebrows, and the colour of his skin."

"Do you think he was wearing a mask?"

"Something like that. But I didn't have time to think too much about it. Before I knew it the rear door of the car was yanked open and then . . . what can I say? It was one of those moments when everything happens all at once, the whole world comes down on your head. Suddenly there were strangers in my car and the rear windscreen shattered. I was in shock."

"What did you do?"

"I accelerated like crazy. The girl who jumped in was shouting at me to drive, and I was so scared I hardly knew what I was doing. I just followed orders."

"Orders?"

"That's how it seemed. I reckoned we were being chased, and I didn't see any other way out. I kept swerving just like the girl told me to, and besides . . ."

"Go on."

"There was something about her voice. It was so cold and intense, I found myself hanging on to it, as if it were the only thing that was under control in the mayhem."

"You said you thought you recognized the woman?"

"Yes, but not at the time, definitely not. I was scared to death and was busy concentrating on all the weird things that were happening. There was blood all over the place."

"Coming from the boy or the woman?"

"I wasn't sure at first, and neither of them seemed to know. But then I heard her say 'Yes!,' like something good had happened."

"What was that about?"

"The girl realized she was the one bleeding and not the boy, and that really struck me. It was like, 'Hurray, I've been shot,' and I tell you, it wasn't some little graze. However she tried to bandage it, she couldn't staunch the blood. It just kept oozing out, and the girl kept getting paler and paler. She must have felt like shit."

"And still she was happy that it wasn't the boy who'd been hit."

"Exactly. Like a mother."

"But she wasn't the child's mother."

"No. They didn't even know each other, she said, and that became more and more obvious. She didn't have a clue about children."

"On the whole," Modig said, "how did you think she treated the boy?"

"Not sure how to answer that, to be honest. I wouldn't say she had the world's best social skills. She treated me like a damn servant, but even so . . ."

"Yes?"

"I reckon she was a good person. I wouldn't have liked her to babysit, if you see what I mean. But she was OK."

"So you think the child is safe with her?"

"She's obviously fucking crazy. But the little boy . . . he's called August, right?"

"That's right."

"She'll guard August with her life, if it came to it. That was my impression."

"How did you part company?"

"She asked me to drive them to Mosebacke torg."

"Is that where she lives, on the square?"

"I have no idea. She gave me no explanation whatsoever. I got the feeling she had some other kind of transport from there, but she didn't say more than was necessary. She just asked me to write down my details. She was going to pay for the damage to the car, she said, plus a little extra."

"Did she look as though she had money?"

"Going by her appearance alone, I'd say she lived in a dump. But the way she behaved . . . I don't know. It wouldn't surprise me if she was loaded. You could tell she was used to getting her own way."

"What happened then?"

"She told the boy to get out of the car."

"And did he?"

"He just rocked backwards and forwards and didn't move. But then her tone hardened. She said it was a matter of life and death or something like that, and he tottered out of the car with his arms stiff, as if he was sleep-walking."

"Did you see where they went?"

"Only that it was to the left—towards Slussen. But the girl . . ."

"Yes?"

"Well, she was obviously still feeling like shit. She was weaving about and seemed on the point of collapse."

"Doesn't sound good. And the boy?"

"Probably wasn't in great shape either. He was looking really odd. The whole time in the car I worried he was going to have some sort of fit. But when he got out he seemed to have come to terms with the situation. In any case he kept asking 'Where?' over and over, 'Where?'"

Modig and Bublanski looked at each other.

"Are you sure about that?" Modig said.

"Why shouldn't I be?"

"Well, you might have thought you heard him saying that because he had a questioning look on his face."

"Why would I have thought that?"

"Because the boy's mother says he doesn't speak at all, never has," Modig continued.

"Are you joking?"

"No, and it would be odd for him to suddenly start speaking under these very circumstances."

"I heard what I heard."

"OK, and what did the woman answer?"

"'Away,' I think. 'Away from here.' Something like that. Then she almost collapsed, like I said. And she told me to drive off."

"And you did?"

"Like a bat out of hell."

"And then you realized who you'd had in your car?"

"I'd already worked out that the boy was the son of that genius who'd been murdered. But the girl . . . She vaguely reminded me of someone. I was shaking like a leaf and in the end I couldn't drive anymore. I stopped on Ringvägen, by Skanstull, got myself a beer at the Clarion Hotel and tried to calm down. And that's when it hit me. It was the girl who was wanted for murder a few years ago but then the charges were dropped, and it came out that she'd been through some terrible things in a mental hospital when she was a child. I remember it well; the father of a friend of mine had been tortured in Syria, and he was having more or less the same stuff done to him at the time, electroshock therapy and that sort of shit, because he couldn't deal with his memories. It was like he was being tortured all over again."

"Are you sure about that?"

"That he was tortured?"

"No, that it was her, Lisbeth Salander."

"I looked at all the pictures online and there's no doubt about it. There were other things that fit too, you know . . ."

Charro hesitated, as if embarrassed.

"She took off her T-shirt because she needed to use it as a bandage and when she turned to wrap it around her shoulder I saw that she had a large tattoo of a dragon all the way up her back. That same tattoo was mentioned in one of the old newspaper articles."


Berger arrived at Grane's summer house with several shopping bags filled with food, crayons and paper, a couple of difficult puzzles, and a few other things. But there was no sign of August or Salander. Salander had not responded, either on her RedPhone app or on the encrypted link. Berger was sick with anxiety.

Whichever way she looked at it, this did not bode well. Admittedly Salander was not known for unnecessary communication or reassurance, but it was she who had asked for a safe house. Also she had responsibility for a child, and if she was not answering their calls under those circumstances, she must be in a bad way.

Berger swore and walked out onto the terrace, to where she and Grane had been sitting and talking about escaping from the world. That was only a few months ago, but it felt like an age. There was no table now, no chairs, no bottles, no hubbub behind them, only snow, branches, and debris flung there by the storm. It was as if life itself had abandoned the place. Somehow the memory of that crayfish party increased the sense of desolation, as if the festivities were draped like a ghost over its walls.

Berger went back into the kitchen and put some microwaveable food into the refrigerator: meatballs, packets of spaghetti with meat sauce, sausage stroganoff, fish pie, potato cakes, and a whole lot of even worse junk food Blomkvist had advised her to buy: Billy's Pan Pizza, piroshki, chips, Coca-Cola, a bottle of Tullamore D.E.W., a carton of cigarettes, three bags of crisps, three bars of chocolate, and some sticks of fresh liquorice. She set out drawing paper, crayons, pencils, an eraser, and a ruler and compass on the large round table. On the top sheet of paper she drew a sun and a flower and wrote the word *WELCOME* in four warm colours.

The house was near Ingarö beach, but you could not see it from there. It lay high up on the rock promontory, concealed behind pine trees, and consisted of four rooms. The kitchen with glass doors onto the terrace was the largest and also the heart of the house. In addition to the round table there was an old rocking chair and two worn, sagging sofas which nonetheless managed to look inviting thanks to a pair of red tartan rugs. It was a cozy home.

It was also a good safe house. Berger left the door open, put the keys in the top drawer of the hall closet, as agreed, and wandered down the long flight of wooden stairs flanking the steep, smooth rock slope—the only way to the house for anyone arriving by car.

The sky was dark and turbulent, the wind blowing hard again. Her spirits were low and did not improve during the drive home. Her thoughts turned to Hanna Balder. Berger had not exactly been a member of the fan club—Hanna often played the parts of women who were both sexy and dim-witted, whom all men thought they could seduce, and Berger was disgusted by the film industry's devotion to that type of character. But none of that was true any longer and Berger regretted that she had been so ungracious at the time. She had been too hard on the woman; it was only too easy to criticize a pretty girl who gets a big break early in her career.

Nowadays, on the rare occasions Hanna Balder appeared in a major production, her eyes tended to reflect a restrained sorrow, which gave depth to the parts she played, and—what did Berger know?—that may have been genuine. She had been through some difficult times, not least the past twenty-four hours.

Since morning Berger had been insisting that Hanna be taken to August. This was surely a situation in which a child needed his mother more than ever. But Salander, who was still communicating with them at the time, had been against the idea. No-one yet knew where the leak had come from, she had written, and they could not rule out the mother's immediate circle. Lasse Westman for one, whom nobody trusted, seemed to be staying in the house all day to avoid the journalists camped outside.

They were in a bind, and Berger did not like it. She hoped *Millennium* would still be able to tell the story with dignity and depth, without the magazine or anyone else coming to harm. She had no doubt that Blomkvist would be up to it, given the way he looked right now. Besides, he had Zander to help him.

Berger had a soft spot for Zander. Not long ago, over dinner at her and Greger's home in Saltsjöbaden, he had told them his life story, which had only increased her sympathy.

When Zander was eleven he lost both his parents in a bomb blast in Sarajevo. After that he came to live in Tensta outside Stockholm with an aunt who altogether failed to notice either his intellectual disposition or the psychological wounds he bore. He had not been there when his parents were killed, but his body reacted as if he were suffering from post-traumatic stress. To this day he detested loud noises and sudden movements. He hated seeing unattended bags in public places, and loathed violence with a passion Berger had never encountered before.

As a child he sought refuge in his own worlds. He immersed himself in fantasy literature, read poetry and biographies, adored Sylvia Plath, Borges and Tolkien, and learned everything there was to know about computers. He dreamed of writing heart-rending novels about love and human tragedy, and was an incurable romantic who hoped that great passion would heal his wounds. He was not in the least bit interested in the outside world. One evening in his late teens, however, he attended a public lecture given by Mikael Blomkvist at the Institute for Media Studies at Stockholm University, and it changed his life.

Blomkvist's fervour inspired him to bear witness to a world which was bleeding with injustice and intolerance and petty corruption. He started to imagine himself writing articles critical of society instead of tear-jerking romances. Not long after that he knocked on *Millennium*'s door and asked if there was anything they would let him do—make coffee, proofread, run errands. Berger, who had seen the fire in his eyes right from the start, assigned him some minor editorial tasks: public notices, research, and brief portraits. But most of all she told him to study, and he did so with the same energy he put into everything else. He read political science, mass media communications, finance, and international conflict resolution, and at the same time he helped out on temporary assignments at *Millennium*.

He wanted to become a heavyweight investigative journalist, like Blomkvist. But unlike so many other investigative journalists he was no tough guy. He remained a romantic. Blomkvist and Berger had both spent time trying to sort out his relationship problems. He was too open and transparent. Too good, as Blomkvist would say.

But Berger believed that Zander was in the process of shedding that youthful vulnerability. She had been seeing the change in his journalism. That ferocious ambition to reach out and touch people, which had made his writing heavy-handed at first, had been replaced by a more effective, matter-of-fact style. She knew he would pull out all the stops now that he had been given the chance to help Blomkvist with the Balder story. The plan was for Blomkvist to write the big, central narrative, and for Zander to help with the research as well as writing some explanatory sidebars. Berger thought they made a great team.

After parking on Hökens gata she walked into the offices and found Blomkvist and Zander sitting there, deep in concentration, just as she expected. Every now and then, Blomkvist muttered to himself and she saw that sense of purpose in his eyes, but there was also suffering. He had hardly slept all night. The media campaign against him had not let up and in his police interviews he had to do the very thing the press accused him of— withhold information. Blomkvist did not like it one bit.

He was in many ways a model, law-abiding citizen. But if there was anyone who could get him to cross the line, it was Lisbeth Salander. Blom-kvist would rather dishonour himself than betray her, which is why he kept repeating to the police: "I assert my right to protect my sources." No wonder he was unhappy and worried about the consequences. But, like Berger, he had far greater fears for Salander and the boy than for their own situation.

"How's it going?" she asked, after watching him for a while.

"What? . . . Well . . . OK. How was it out there?"

"I made up the beds and put food in the fridge."

"Good. And the neighbours didn't see you?"

"There wasn't a soul out."

"Why are they taking so long?" he said.

"I don't know, but I'm worried sick."

"Let's hope they're resting at Lisbeth's."

"Let's hope so. What else did you find out?"

"Quite a bit. But . . ." Blomkvist trailed off.

"Yes?"

"It's just that . . . it feels as if I'm being thrown back in time, or going back to places I've been to before."

"You'll have to explain better," she said.

"I will . . ."

Blomkvist glanced at his computer screen.

"But first I have to keep on digging. Let's speak later," he said, and so she left him and got her things to drive home, although she would be ready to join him at a second's notice.

# CHAPTER 20

# NOVEMBER 23

The night had turned out to be calm, alarmingly calm, and at eight in the morning a brooding Bublanski stood facing his team in the meeting room. Having kicked out Faste, he felt reasonably sure that he could talk freely again. At least he felt safer in here with his colleagues than at his computer, or with his mobile.

"You all appreciate how serious the situation is," he said. "Confidential information has been leaked. One person is dead as a result. A small boy's life is in danger. In spite of immense efforts we still don't know how this happened. The leak could have been at our end, or at Säpo, or at Oden's Medical Centre, or in the group around Professor Edelman, or from the boy's mother and her partner, Lasse Westman. We know nothing for certain, and therefore we have to be *extremely* circumspect, paranoid even."

"We may also have been hacked or phone tapped," Modig said. "We seem to be dealing with criminals whose command of new technologies is far beyond anything we've seen before."

"Very true," Bublanski said. "We need to take precautions at every level, not say anything significant relating to this investigation—or to any other—over the telephone, no matter how highly our superiors rate our new mobile phone system."

"They think it's great because it cost so much to install," Holmberg said.

"Maybe we should also be reflecting a little on our own role," Bublanski said, ignoring him. "I was just talking to a gifted young analyst at Säpo, Gabriella Grane—you may have heard of her. She pointed out that the concept of loyalty is not as straightforward as one might think for us policemen. We have many different loyalties, don't we? There's the obvious one, to the law. There's a loyalty to the public, and to one's colleagues, but also to our bosses, and to ourselves and our careers. Sometimes, as you all know, these interests end up competing with each other. We might choose to protect a colleague at work and thereby fail in our duty to the public, or we might be given orders from higher up, like Hans Faste was, and then that conflicts with the loyalty he should have had to us. But from now on—and I'm deadly serious—there's only one loyalty I want to hear of, and that is to the investigation itself. We're going to catch the murderers and we're going to make sure that no-one else falls victim to them. Agreed? Even if the prime minister himself or the head of the CIA calls and goes on about patriotism and huge career opportunities, you still won't utter a peep, will you?"

"No," they all said in unison.

"Excellent. As we all know, the person who intervened on Sveavägen was none other than Lisbeth Salander, and we're doing everything in our power to locate her."

"Which is why we've got to release her name to the media!" Svensson called out, somewhat heatedly. "We need help from the public."

"We don't all agree on this, I know, so I'd like to raise the question again. Let's remember that in the past Lisbeth Salander has had some very shabby treatment, from us and from the media."

"At this point that doesn't matter," Svensson said.

"And it's conceivable that people recognized her on Sveavägen and her name will come out at any moment anyway. In which case this would no longer be an issue. But before that happens, keep in mind she saved the boy's life."

"No doubt about that," Svensson said. "But then she more or less kidnapped him."

"Our information suggests that she was determined to protect the boy at all costs," Modig said. "Salander's experience of public institutions has been anything but positive—her entire childhood was marred by the injustices inflicted on her by Swedish officialdom. If she suspects, as we do, that there's a leak inside the police force then there's no chance she's going to contact us. Fact."

"That's irrelevant," Svensson insisted.

"Maybe," Modig said. "Jan and I share your view that the most important thing here is whether it's in the interests of the investigation to release her name. And as to the investigation, our priority is the boy's safety, and that's where we have a big element of uncertainty."

"I follow your reasoning," Holmberg said in a low, thoughtful tone which immediately commanded everyone's attention. "If people know of Salander's involvement then the boy will be at risk. But that still leaves a number of questions—first: What's the ethical thing to do? And I have to say, even if there's been a leak here we cannot accept that Salander should keep the boy hidden away. He's a crucial part of the investigation and, leak or no leak, we're better at protecting a child than an emotionally disturbed young woman could ever be."

"Absolutely. Of course," Bublanski muttered.

"And even if this isn't a kidnapping in the ordinary sense—yes, even if it's been carried out with the best of intentions—the potential harm to the child could be just as great. Psychologically it must be hugely damaging for him to be, as it were, on the run after everything he's been through."

"True," Bublanski said. "But the question still remains: How do we handle the information we have?"

"There I agree with Curt. We have to release her name and photo right away. It could produce invaluable leads."

"Probably," Bublanski said. "But it could at the same time give the killers invaluable leads. We have to assume that they haven't given up looking for the boy—quite the opposite, in fact—and since we have no idea what the connection is between the boy and Salander, we don't know what sort of clues her name would provide them with. I'm not persuaded that we would be protecting the boy by giving the media these details."

"But neither do we know if we're protecting him by holding them back," Holmberg said. "There are too many pieces of the puzzle missing for us to draw any conclusions. Is Salander doing this for someone else, for example? Does she have her own agenda for the child, other than to protect him?"

"And how could she have known that the boy and Torkel Lindén would come out onto Sveavägen at that exact moment?" Svensson said.

"Maybe she just happened to be there."

"Doesn't seem likely."

"The truth is often unlikely," Bublanski said. "That's the nature of truth. But I agree, it doesn't feel like a coincidence, not under the circumstances."

"What about the fact that Mikael Blomkvist also knew something was going to happen?" Amanda Flod said.

"There's some sort of connection between Blomkvist and Salander," Holmberg said.

"True."

"Blomkvist knew that the boy was at Oden's Medical Centre, didn't he?"

"The mother told him," Bublanski said. "As you might imagine, she's feeling desperate right now. I've just had a long conversation with her. But there was no reason on earth why Blomkvist should have known that the boy and Lindén would be tricked into going out onto the street."

"Could he have had access to a computer at Oden's?" Flod said pensively.

"I can't imagine Mikael Blomkvist getting involved in hacking," Modig said.

"But what about Salander?" Holmberg said. "What do we actually know about her? We have a massive file on the girl. Yet the last time we had anything to do with her, she surprised us on every count. Maybe appearances are just as deceptive this time around."

"I agree," Svensson said. "We have far too many question marks."

"Question marks are about all we have. And that's exactly why we ought to stick to the rules," Holmberg said.

"I didn't realize the rule book covered quite so much," Bublanski said, with a sarcasm even he did not like.

"I only mean that we should take this for what it is—the kidnapping of a child. They disappeared almost twenty-four hours ago. We haven't heard a word from them. We should put out Salander's name and picture and then look carefully at all the tip-offs that come in," Holmberg said with authority. He seemed to have the backing of the whole group, and at that Bublanski closed his eyes and reflected that he loved them all. He felt a greater affinity with his team than he did for his own brothers and sisters, or even his parents. But right now he felt compelled to disagree with them.

"We'll do everything we can to try to find them. But for the time being we will not release the name and picture. That would only make the situation more fraught, and I don't want to risk giving the killers any leads at all."

"And you feel guilty," Holmberg said, without warmth.

"I feel very guilty," Bublanski said, thinking again of his rabbi.

Blomkvist was so worried about the boy and Salander that he had hardly slept. Time and again he had tried to reach Salander on her RedPhone app, but she had not answered. He had not heard a word from her since yesterday afternoon. Now he was sitting in the office, trying to immerse himself in his work and figure out what it was that had escaped him. For some time already he had had a sense—impossible to put his finger on—that there was a key piece missing, something which could shed light on the whole story. Perhaps he was fooling himself. Maybe it was just wishful thinking, a need to see a grand design. The last message from Salander on the encrypted link was:

```
<Jurij Bogdanov. Check him out. He's the one who
sold Balder's technology to Eckerwald at Solifon.>
```

There were some images of Bogdanov online. They showed him wearing pin-striped suits which fit perfectly but still managed to look wrong on him, as if he had stolen them on the way to the photographer's. Bogdanov had long, lank hair, a pockmarked face, and large rings under his eyes, and you could just about make out some amateurish tattoos beneath his shirt cuffs. His look was dark, intense, and piercing. He was tall but cannot have weighed more than 130 pounds.

He looked like an old jailbird, but most striking: there was something about his body language which Blomkvist recognized from the images on the surveillance cameras at Balder's place. The man gave the same tattered, rough-edged impression.

There were also interviews he had given as a businessman in Berlin in which he vouchsafed that he had been born more or less on the streets. "I was doomed to end up dead in an alleyway with a needle stuck in my arm. But I managed to pull myself out of the muck. I'm intelligent and I'm one hell of a fighter," he said. There was nothing in the details of his life to contradict these claims, save for the suspicion that he may not have been raised exclusively through his own efforts. There were clues to suggest he had been given a helping hand by powerful people who had spotted his talent. In a German technology magazine, a security chief at the Horst credit institution was quoted as saying, "Bogdanov has magic in his eyes. He can detect vulnerabilities in security systems like no-one else. He's a genius."

So Bogdanov was a star hacker, although the official version had him acting only as a "white hat," someone who served the good, legal side, who helped companies identify flaws in their IT security in exchange for decent compensation. There was nothing in the least suspicious about his company, Outcast Security. The board members were all respectable, well-educated people. But Blomkvist did not leave it at that. He and Zander scrutinized every individual who had had any contact with the company, even partners of partners, and they noticed that somebody called Orlov had been a deputy board member only for a short time, which seemed strange. Vladimir Orlov was no IT man, but a minor player in the construction sector. He had once been a promising heavyweight boxer in the Crimea and, judging by the few pictures Blomkvist found online, he looked ravaged and brutal.

There were rumours that he had been convicted of assault and procuring. He had been married twice—both wives were dead, and Blomkvist had not been able to find a cause of death in either case. But the most interesting discovery he made was that the man had served as a substitute board member of a company—minor and long since defunct—by the name of Bodin Construction & Export, which had dealt in "sales of construction materials."

The owner of the company had been Karl Axel Bodin, the alias of Alexander Zalachenko, a name that revived memories of the evil conspiracy which became the subject of *Millennium*'s greatest scoop. Zalachenko who was Salander's father, and her dark shadow, the black heart behind her throbbing determination to exact revenge.

Was it a coincidence that his name cropped up? Blomkvist knew better than anyone that if you dig deep enough into a story, you will always find links. Life is constantly treating us to illusory connections. It was just that when it came to Lisbeth Salander, he stopped believing in coincidence.

If she broke a surgeon's fingers or delved into the theft of some advanced

AI technology, you could be sure that she had not only thought it through to the last particle, she would also have a reason. Salander was not one to forget an injustice. She retaliated and she righted wrongs. Could her involvement in this story be connected to her own background? It was by no means inconceivable.

Blomkvist looked up from his computer and glanced at Zander. Zander nodded back at him. The faint smell of something cooking was coming from the kitchen. Thudding rock music could be heard from Götgatan. Outside the storm was howling, and the sky was still dark and wild. Blomkvist went into the encrypted link out of habit, not expecting to find anything. But then his face lit up. He even let out a small whoop of joy.

It said:

```
<OK now. We'll be going to the safe house shortly.>
```

He wrote:

```
<Great news. Drive carefully.>
```

Then he could not resist adding:

```
<Who are we actually after?>
```

She answered at once:

```
<You'll soon work it out, smartarse!>
```

OK was an exaggeration. Salander was better, but still in bad shape. For half of yesterday, in her apartment, she had been barely conscious and only managed with the greatest difficulty to drag herself out of bed to see that August had something to eat and drink and make sure he had pencils, crayons, and paper. But as she approached him now she could see even from a distance that he had drawn nothing.

There was paper scattered all over the coffee table in front of him, but no drawings. Instead she saw rows of scribbles. More absentmindedly than out of curiosity she tried to make out what they were—he had written numbers, endless series of numbers, and even if at first they made no sense to her, she was intrigued. Suddenly she gave a whistle.

"Oh my God," she muttered.

They were staggeringly large numbers, which formed a familiar pattern alongside the numbers next to them. As she looked through the papers and came across the simple sequence 641, 647, 653, and 659, there was no longer any doubt: they were sexy prime quadruplets, sexy in the sense that they differed from each other by six.

There were also twin primes, and every other imaginable combination of prime numbers. She could not help but smile. "Wicked."

But August neither responded nor looked up at her. He just kept kneeling by the coffee table, as if he wanted nothing more than to go on writing his numbers. It occurred to her that she had read something about savants and prime numbers, but she put it out of her mind. She was far too unwell for any kind of advanced thinking. Instead she went into the bathroom and took two more Vibramycin antibiotics which had been lying around in her apartment for years.

She packed her pistol and her computer, a few changes of clothes, and to be on the safe side she put on a wig and a pair of dark glasses. When she was ready she asked the boy to get up. He did not respond, just held his pencil in a tight grip. For a moment she stood in front of him, stumped. Then she said sternly, "Get up!," and he did.

They put on their outer layers, took the lift down to the garage, and set off in her BMW for the safe house on Ingarö. Her left shoulder was tightly strapped and it ached, so she steered with her right hand. The top of her chest was hurting, she had a fever and had to stop a couple of times at the side of the road to rest. When finally they got to the beach and the jetty by Stora Barnvik on Ingarö, and followed the directions to climb the wooden stairs alongside the slope to the house, she collapsed exhausted on the first bed she saw. She was shivering and freezing cold.

Soon after, breathing laboriously, she got up and sat at the kitchen table with her laptop, trying once more to crack the file she had downloaded from the NSA. But she did not even come close. August sat next to her, looking stiffly at the pile of paper and crayons Berger had left for him, no longer interested in prime numbers, still less in drawing pictures. Perhaps he was in shock.

The man who called himself Jan Holtser was sitting in a room at the Clarion Hotel Arlanda talking on the telephone with his daughter. As he had expected, she did not believe him.

"Are you scared of me?" she said. "Are you afraid I'm going to cross-examine you?"

"No, Olga, absolutely not," he said. "It's just that . . ."

He could not find the words. He knew Olga could tell he was hiding something, and ended the conversation sooner than he wanted to. Bogdanov was sitting next to him on the hotel bed, swearing. He had been through Balder's computer at least a hundred times and found "fuck all," as he put it. "Not a single fucking thing!"

"I stole a computer with nothing on it," Holtser said.

"Right."

"So what was the professor using it for?"

"For something very important, clearly. I can see that a large file, presumably connected to other computers, was deleted recently. But I can't recover it. He knew his stuff, that guy."

"Useless," Holtser said.

"Completely fucking useless."

"And the Blackphone?"

"There are a couple of calls I haven't been able to trace, presumably from the Swedish security services or the NDRE. But there's something bothering me much more."

"What?"

"A long conversation the professor had just before you stormed in—he was talking to someone at the MIRI, Machine Intelligence Research Institute."

"What's the problem with that?"

"The timing. I get the feeling he was having some sort of crisis. Also this Institute works to ensure that intelligent computers don't become a threat to mankind—it doesn't look good. Balder could have given the MIRI his research or . . ."

"Or what?"

"Or he could have spilled the beans on us, at least what he knew."

"That would be bad."

Bogdanov nodded and Holtser swore quietly. Nothing had gone as planned and neither of them was used to failing. But here were two major mistakes in a row, and all because of a child, a retarded child.

That was bad enough. But the worst of it was that Kira was on her way, unhinged on top of everything else. Neither of them was used to that either. On the contrary, they had grown accustomed to her cool elegance, the air of invincibility it gave their operations. Now she was furious, completely off the wall, screaming at them that they were useless, incompetent cretins. It was not so much that those shots may have missed Balder's son. It was because of the woman who had appeared out of nowhere and rescued the boy. That woman sent Kira around the bend.

When Holtser had begun to describe her—the little he had seen—Kira bombarded him with questions. Every answer he gave was wrong, according to Kira. She went berserk, yelling that they should have killed her and that this was typical of them, brainless, useless. Neither of them could make sense of her violent reaction. They had never heard her yell like that before.

In fact there was a lot they did not know about her. Holtser would never forget his evening with her in a suite at the Hotel d'Angleterre in Copenhagen—they had had sex for the third or fourth time, and afterwards had been lying in bed drinking champagne and chatting about his wars and his murders, as they so often did. While stroking her arm he had discovered three scars side by side on her wrist.

"How did you get those, gorgeous?" he had said, and got a look of pure loathing in return.

He had never been allowed to sleep with her again. He took it to be a punishment for having asked. Kira looked after the group and gave them a lot of money. But neither he nor Bogdanov, nor anyone else, was allowed to ask about her past. That was one of the unspoken rules and none of them would even dream of trying. For better or for worse she was their benefactress, mostly for better, they thought, and they went along with her whims, living in constant uncertainty as to whether she would be affectionate or cold, or even give them a brutal, stinging slap.

Bogdanov closed the computer and took a swallow of his drink. They were trying to limit their drinking, so that Kira would not use that against them. But it was nearly impossible. The frustration and adrenalin drove them to it. Holtser fingered his mobile nervously.

"Didn't Olga believe you?" Bogdanov said.

"Not a word. Soon she'll see a child's drawing of me on every billboard."

"I don't buy that drawing thing. Probably wishful thinking on the part of the police."

"So we're supposed to kill a child for no reason?"

"It wouldn't surprise me. Shouldn't Kira be here by now?"

"Any minute."

"Who do you think it was?"

"Who?"

"The girl who appeared from nowhere."

"No idea," Holtser said. "Not sure Kira knows either. But she's worried about something."

"We'll probably end up having to kill them both."

"That might be the least of it."


August was not feeling well. That was obvious. Red patches flared on his throat and he was clenching his fists. Salander, sitting next to him at the round table, working on her RSA encryption, was afraid he was on the verge of some sort of fit. But August only picked up a crayon, a black one.

At the same moment a gust of wind shook the large windowpanes in front of them. August hesitated and moved his hand back and forth across the table. But then he started to draw, a line here, a line there, followed by some small circles, buttons, Salander thought, then a hand, details of a chin, an unbuttoned shirt front. It began to go more quickly and the tension in the boy's back and shoulders subsided—as if a wound had burst open and begun to heal.

There was a searing, tortured look in his eyes, and every now and then he shivered. But there was no doubt that something within him had eased.

He picked up some new crayons and started to draw an oak-coloured floor, on which appeared pieces of a puzzle that seemed to represent a glittering town at night-time. It was clear at this stage that the drawing would be anything but a pleasant one.

The hand and the unbuttoned shirt front became part of a large man with a protruding belly. The man was standing, bent like a jackknife, beating a small person on the floor, a person who was not in the drawing for the simple reason that he was observing the scene, and on the receiving end of the blows.

It was an ugly scene, no doubt about that. But even though the picture revealed an assailant, it did not seem to have anything to do with the murder. Right in the middle, at the epicentre of the drawing, a furious, sweaty face appeared, every foul and bitter furrow captured with precision. Salander recognized it. She rarely watched TV or went to the cinema, but she knew it was the face of the actor Lasse Westman, August's mother's partner. She leaned forward to the boy and said, with a holy, quivering rage:

"We'll never let him do that to you again. Never."

# CHAPTER 21

# NOVEMBER 23

Casales knew at once that something was wrong when she saw Commander Ingram's lanky figure approach Needham's desk. You could tell from his hesitant manner that the news was not good.

Ingram usually had a malicious grin on his face when he stuck a knife in someone's back, but with Needham it was different. Even the most senior bosses were scared of Needham—he would raise all hell if anyone tried to mess with him. Ingram did not like scenes, still less humiliation, and that was what awaited him if he picked a fight with Needham.

While Needham was brash and explosive, Ingram was a refined upper-class type with spindly legs and an affected manner. Ingram was a serious power player and had influence where it mattered, be it in Washington or in the world of business. As a member of the NSA management, he ranked just below Admiral Charles O'Connor. He might be quick to smile and adept at handing out compliments, but his smile never reached his eyes.

He had leverage over people and was, among other things, in charge of "monitoring strategic technologies"—more cynically known as industrial espionage, that part of the NSA which gives the American tech industry a helping hand in global competition. He was feared as few others were.

But now as he stood in front of Needham in his fancy suit, his body seemed to shrink even from one hundred feet away. Casales knew exactly what was about to happen: Needham was on the brink of exploding. His pale, exhausted face was going red. Without waiting he got to his feet, his back crooked and bent, his belly sticking out, and roared in a furious voice.

"You sleazy bastard!"

No-one but Needham would call Jonny Ingram a "sleazy bastard," and Casales loved him for it.

· · ·

August started on a new drawing.

He sketched a few lines. He was pressing so hard on the paper that the black crayon broke and, just like the last time, he drew rapidly, one detail here and another one there, disparate bits which ultimately came together and formed a whole. It was the same room, but there was a different puzzle on the floor, easier to make out: it represented a red sports car racing by a sea of shouting spectators in a stand. Above the puzzle not one but two men could be seen standing.

One of them was Westman again. This time he was wearing a T-shirt and shorts and he had bloodshot, squinting eyes. He looked unsteady and drunk, but no less furious. He was drooling. Yet he was not the most frightening figure in the drawing. That was the other man, whose watery eyes shone with pure sadism. He too was unshaven and drunk, and he had thin, almost nonexistent lips. He seemed to be kicking August, although again the boy could not be seen in the picture, his very absence making him extremely present.

"Who's the other one?" Salander said.

August said nothing. But his shoulders shook, and his legs twisted into a knot under the table.

"Who's the other one?" Salander said again, in a more forceful tone, and August wrote on the drawing in a shaky, childish hand:

## R O G E R

Roger—the name meant nothing to Salander.

A couple of hours later in Fort Meade, once his hacker boys had cleaned up after themselves and shuffled off, Needham walked over to Casales. The odd thing was, he no longer looked at all angry or upset. He was radiant with defiance and carrying a notebook. His shirt was disheveled.

"Hey, bud," she said. "Tell me, what's going on?"

"I got some vacation time," he said. "I'm off to Stockholm."

"Of all places. Isn't it cold this time of year?"

"Freezing, by all accounts."

"So you're not really going there on vacation."

"Strictly between us?"

"Go on."

"Ingram ordered us to halt our investigation. The hacker goes free, and we're supposed to be satisfied with stopping up a few leaks. Then the whole thing gets swept under the carpet."

"How the hell can he lay down something like that?"

"They don't want to awaken any sleeping dogs, he says, and run the risk of anyone finding out about the attack. It would be devastating if it ever got out. Just think of all the malicious glee, and all the people whose heads would roll, starting with yours truly."

"He threatened *you*?"

"Did he ever! Went on about how I would be publicly humiliated, even sued."

"You don't seem worried."

"I'm going to break him."

"How? Our glamour boy has powerful connections everywhere, you know that."

"I have a few of my own. Besides, Ingram isn't the only one with dirt on people. That damn hacker was gracious enough to link and match our computer files and show us some of our own dirty laundry."

"That's ironic, isn't it?"

"It takes a crook to know one. At first the data didn't look all that spectacular, not compared to the other stuff we're doing. But when we started to really get into it . . ."

"Yes?"

"It turned out to be dynamite."

"In what way?"

"Ingram's closest colleagues not only *collect* trade secrets to help our own major companies. Sometimes they also *sell* the information for a lot of money. And that money, Alona, doesn't always find its way into the coffers of the organization . . ."

"But into their own pockets."

"Ex*actly*. I already have enough evidence on that to put two of our top industrial espionage executives behind bars."

"Jesus."

"Unfortunately it's less straightforward with Ingram. I'm convinced he's the brains behind the whole thing. Otherwise all of this doesn't add up. But I don't have a smoking gun, not yet, which makes the whole operation risky. There's always a chance—though I wouldn't bet on it—that the file the hacker downloaded has something specific on him. But it's impossible to crack—a goddamn RSA encryption."

"So what are you going to do?"

"Tighten the net. Show the world that our own co-workers are in cahoots with criminal organizations."

"Like the Spiders."

"Like the Spiders. And plenty of other bad guys. It wouldn't surprise me if they were involved in the killing of your professor in Stockholm. They had a clear interest in seeing him dead."

"You've got to be joking."

"I'm completely serious. Your professor knew things that could have blown up in their faces."

"Holy shit. And you're off to Stockholm like some private detective to investigate?"

"Not like a private detective, Alona. I'm going to be official, and while I'm there I'm going to give our hacker such a pummelling she won't be able to stand."

"Wait, Ed. Did you say she?"

"You better believe it. Our hacker's a she!"


August's drawings took Salander back in time. She thought of that fist beating rhythmically and relentlessly on the mattress. She remembered the thuds and the grunting and the crying from inside the bedroom next door. She remembered the times at Lundagatan when her comics and fantasies of revenge were her only refuge.

But she shook off the memories. She changed the dressing on her shoulder. Then she checked her pistol, made sure that it was loaded. She went onto the PGP link. Andrei Zander was asking how they were, and she gave a short reply.

Outside, the storm was shaking the trees and bushes. She helped herself to some whiskey and a piece of chocolate, then went out onto the terrace and from there to the rock slope where she carefully reconnoitred the terrain, noticing a small cleft some way down. She counted her steps and memorized the lay of the land.

By the time she got back, August had made another drawing of Westman and the Roger person. She supposed he needed to get it out of his system. But still he had not drawn anything from the night of the murder. Perhaps the experience was blocked in his mind.

Salander was overcome by a feeling of time running away from them and she cast a worried look at August. For a minute or so she focused on the mind-boggling numbers he had put down on paper. She studied their structure until suddenly she spotted a sequence which did not fit in with the others.

It was relatively short: 2305843008139952128. She got it immediately. It was not a prime number, it was—and here her spirits lifted—a number which, according to a perfect harmony, is made up of the sum of all its positive divisors. It was, in other words, a perfect number, just as 6 is because it can be divided evenly by 3, 2, and 1, and 3 + 2 + 1 happen to add up to 6. She smiled. And then she had an exhilarating thought.


"Now you're going to have to explain yourself," Casales said.

"I will," Needham said. "But first, even though I trust you, I need you to give me a solemn promise that you won't say any of this to anybody."

"I promise, you jerk."

"Good. Here's the story: After I yelled at Ingram, mostly for the sake of appearances, I told him he was right. I even pretended to be grateful to him for putting a stop to our investigation. We wouldn't have gotten any further anyway, I said, and it was partly true. From a purely technical point of view we were out of options. We'd done everything and then some, but it was pointless. The hacker put red herrings all over the place and kept leading us into new mazes and labyrinths. One of my guys said that even if we got to the end, against all odds, we wouldn't believe we'd made it. We'd kid ourselves that it was a new trap. We were prepared for just about anything from this hacker, anything but flaws and weaknesses. So if we kept going the usual way, we'd had it."

"You don't tend to go the usual way."

"No, I prefer the roundabout way. The truth is, we hadn't given up at all. We'd been talking to our hacker contacts out there and our friends in the software companies. We did advanced searches, surveillance, and our own computer breaches. You see, when an attack is as complex as this one, you can always be sure there's been some research up front. Certain specific questions have been asked. Certain specific sites have been visited and inevitably some of that becomes known to us. But there was one factor above all that played into our hands, Alona: the hacker's skill. It was so incredible that it limited the number of suspects. Like a criminal suddenly running a hundred metres in 9.7 seconds at a crime scene—you'd be pretty sure the guy is a certain Mr. Bolt or one of his close rivals, right?"

"So it's at that level?"

"Well, there are parts of this attack that just made my jaw drop, and I've seen a fair amount in my day. That's why we spent a hell of a lot of time talking to hackers and insiders in this industry and asking them: Who is capable of something really, really big? Who are the *seriously* big players these days? We had to be pretty smart about how we framed our questions, so that nobody would guess what actually happened. For a long time we got nowhere. It was like shooting in the dark—like calling out into the dead of night. Nobody knew anything, or they claimed they didn't. A few names were mentioned, but none of them felt right. For a while we chased down some Russian, a Jurij Bogdanov—an ex-druggie and thief who apparently can hack into anything he damn well likes. The security companies were already trying to recruit him when he was living on the street in St. Petersburg, hot-wiring cars, weighing in at 90 pounds of skin and bone. Even the people from the police and intelligence services wanted him on their side. They lost that battle, needless to say. These days Bogdanov looks clean and successful and has ballooned to 130 pounds of skin and bone, but we're pretty sure he's one of the crooks in your organization, Alona. That was another reason he interested us. There had to be a connection to the Spiders, because of the searches that got carried out, but then . . ."

"You couldn't understand why one of their own would be giving us new leads and associations?"

"Exactly, and so we looked further. After a while another outfit cropped up in the conversations."

"Which one?"

"They call themselves Hacker Republic. They have a big reputation out there. A bunch of talents at the top of their game and rigorous about their encryptions. And for good reason. We're constantly trying to infiltrate these groups, and we're not the only ones. We don't just want to find out what they're up to, we also want to recruit people. These days there's big competition for the sharpest hackers."

"Now that we've all become criminals."

"Ha, yes, maybe. Whatever, Hacker Republic has major talent. Lots of the guys we talked to backed that up. And it wasn't just that. There were also rumours that they had something big going on, and then a hacker with the handle Bob the Dog, who we think is linked to the gang, was running searches and asking questions about one of our guys, Richard Fuller. Do you know him?"

"No."

"A manic-depressive, self-righteous prick who's been bugging me for a while. The archetypal security risk who gets arrogant and sloppy when he's in a manic phase. He's just the kind of person a bunch of hackers *should* be targeting, and you'd need classified information to know that. His mental health issues aren't exactly common knowledge, his own mother hardly knows. But I'm pretty confident that in the end they didn't get in via Fuller. We've examined every file he's received recently and there's nothing there. We've scrutinized him from top to bottom. But I bet Fuller was part of Hacker Republic's original plan and then they changed strategies. I can't claim to have any hard evidence against them, not at all, but my gut feeling is still that these guys are behind the break-in."

"You said the hacker was a girl."

"Right. Once we'd homed in on this group we found out as much as possible about them. It wasn't easy to separate rumour from myth and from fact. But one thing came up so often that in the end I saw no reason to question it."

"And what's that?"

"Hacker Republic's big star is someone who uses the alias Wasp."

"Wasp?"

"I won't bore you with technical details, but Wasp is something of a legend in certain circles, one of the reasons being her ability to turn accepted methods on their heads. Someone said you can sense Wasp's involvement in a hacker attack the same way you can recognize Mozart in a melodic loop. Wasp has her own unmistakable style and that was the first thing one of my guys said after he'd studied the breach: this is different from anything we've come across, it's got a completely new threshold of originality."

"A genius, in short."

"Without a doubt. So we started to search everything we could find about this Wasp, to try to crack the handle. No-one was particularly surprised when that didn't work. This person wouldn't leave openings. But you know what I did then?" Needham said proudly.

"Tell me."

"I looked up what the word stood for."

"Beyond its literal meaning, you mean?"

"Right, but not because I or anyone else thought it would get us anywhere. Like I said, if you can't get there on the main road, you take the side roads; you never know what you might find. It turns out Wasp could mean all sorts of things. Wasp is a British fighter plane from World War Two, a comedy by Aristophanes, a famous short film from 1915, a satirical magazine from nineteenth-century San Francisco, and there's also of course White Anglo-Saxon Protestant, plus a whole lot more. But those references are all a little too sophisticated for a hacker genius; they don't go with the culture. You know what did fit? The superhero in Marvel Comics: Wasp is one of the founding members of the Avengers."

"Like the movie?"

"Exactly, with Thor, Iron Man, Captain America. In the original comics she was even their leader for a while. I have to say, Wasp is a pretty badass superhero, kind of rock-and-roll, a rebel who wears black and yellow with insect's wings and short black hair. She's got attitude, the underdog who hits back and can grow or shrink. All the sources we've been talking to think that's the Wasp we're looking for. It doesn't necessarily mean the person behind the handle is some Marvel Comics geek. That handle has been around for a while, so maybe it's a childhood thing that stuck, or an attempt at irony. Like the fact that I named my cat Peter Pan even though I never liked that self-righteous asshole who doesn't want to grow up. Anyway . . ."

"Yes?"

"I couldn't help noticing that this criminal network Wasp was looking into also uses names from Marvel Comics. They sometimes call themselves the Spider Society, right?"

"Yes, but I think that's just a game, as I see it, sticking it to those of us who monitor them."

"Sure, I get that, but even jokes can give you leads, or cover up something serious. Do you know what the Spider Society in Marvel Comics does?"

"No."

"They wage war against the 'Sisterhood of the Wasp.'"

"OK, fine, it's an interesting detail, but I don't understand how that could be your lead."

"Just wait. Will you come downstairs with me? I have to head to the airport soon."


It was not late, but Blomkvist knew that he could not keep going much longer. He had to go home and get a few hours' sleep and then start working again tonight or tomorrow morning. It might help too if he had a few beers on the way. The lack of sleep was pounding in his forehead and he needed to chase away a few memories and fears. Perhaps he could get Zander to join him. He looked over at his colleague.

Zander had youth and energy to spare. He was banging away at his keyboard as if he had just started work for the day and every now and then he flicked excitedly through his notes. Yet he had been in the office since five o'clock in the morning. It was now a quarter to six in the evening and he had hardly taken a break.

"What do you say, Andrei? How about we get a beer and a bite to eat and discuss the story?"

At first Zander did not seem to understand. Then he raised his head and suddenly no longer looked quite so energetic. He gave a little grimace as he massaged his shoulder.

"What . . . well . . . maybe," he said hesitantly.

"I'll take that as a yes," said Blomkvist. "How about Folksoperan?"

Folksoperan was a bar and restaurant on Hornsgatan, not far away, which attracted journalists and the arty crowd.

"It's just that . . ." Zander said.

"Just that what?"

"I've got this portrait to do, of an art dealer working at Bukowski's who got onto a train at Malmö Central and was never seen again. Erika thought it would fit into the mix."

"Jesus, the things she makes you do, that woman."

"I honestly don't mind. But I'm having trouble pulling it together. It feels so messy and contrived."

"Do you want me to have a look at it?"

"I'd love that, but let me do some more work on it first. I would die of embarrassment if you saw it in its present state."

"In that case deal with it later. But come on now, Andrei, let's go and at least get something to eat. You can come back and work afterwards if you must," Blomkvist said. He looked over at Zander.

That memory would stay with him for a long time. Zander was wearing a brown checked jacket and a white shirt buttoned up all the way. He looked like a film star, at any rate even more like a young Antonio Banderas than usual.

"I think I'd better stay and keep plugging away," he said. "I have something in the fridge which I can microwave."

Blomkvist wondered if he should pull rank, order him to come out and have a beer. Instead he said:

"OK, we'll see each other in the morning. How are they doing out there meanwhile? No drawing of the murderer yet?"

"Seems not."

"We'll have to find another solution tomorrow. Take care," Blomkvist said, getting up and putting on his overcoat.


Salander remembered something she had read about savants a long time ago in *Science* magazine. It was an article by Enrico Bombieri, an expert in number theory, referring to an episode in Oliver Sacks's *The Man Who Mistook His Wife for a Hat* in which a pair of autistic and mentally disabled twins recite staggeringly high prime numbers to each other, as if they could see them before their eyes in some sort of inner mathematical landscape.

What these twins were able to do and what Salander now wanted to achieve were two different things. But there was still a similarity, she thought, and decided to try, however sceptical she might be. So she brought up the encrypted NSA file and her programme for elliptic curve factorization. Then she turned to August. He responded by rocking back and forth.

"Prime numbers. You like prime numbers," she said.

August did not look at her, or stop his rocking.

"I like them too. And there's one thing I'm particularly interested in just now. It's called factorization. Do you know what that is?"

August stared at the table as he continued rocking and did not look as if he understood anything at all.

"Prime number factorization is when we rewrite a number as the product of prime numbers. By product in this context I mean the result of a multiplication. Do you follow me?"

August's expression did not change, and Salander wondered if she should just shut up.

"According to the fundamental principles of arithmetic, every whole number has a unique prime number factorization. It's pretty cool. We can produce a number as simple as 24 in all sorts of ways, for example by multiplying 12 by 2 or 3 by 8, or 4 by 6. Yet there's only one way to factorize it with prime numbers and that's $2 \times 2 \times 2 \times 3$. Are you with me? The problem is even though it's easy to multiply prime numbers to produce large numbers, it's often impossible to go the other way, from the answer back to the prime numbers. A really bad person has used this to code a secret message. Do you understand? It's a bit like mixing a drink: easy to do but harder to unmix again."

August neither nodded nor said a word. But at least his body was no longer rocking.

"Shall we see if you're any good at prime number factorization, August? Shall we?"

August did not budge.

"I'll take that as a yes. Let's start with the number 456."

August's eyes were bright but distant, and Salander had the feeling that this idea of hers really was absurd.

It was cold and windy and there were few people out. But Blomkvist thought the cold was doing him good—he was perking up a bit. He thought of his daughter Pernilla and what she said about writing "for real," and of Salander of course, and the boy. What were they doing right now?

On the way up towards Hornsgatspuckeln he stared for a while at a painting hanging in a gallery window which showed cheerful, carefree people at a cocktail party. At that moment it felt, perhaps wrongly, as if it had been ages since he had last stood like that, drink in hand and without a care in the world. Briefly he longed to be somewhere far away. Then he shivered, struck by the feeling that he was being followed. Perhaps it was a consequence of everything he had been through in the last few days. He turned round, but the only person near him was an enchantingly beautiful woman in a bright red coat with flowing dark-blond hair. She smiled at him a little uncertainly. He gave her a tentative smile back and was about to continue on his way. Yet his gaze lingered, as if he were expecting the woman to turn into something more run-of-the-mill at any moment.

Instead she became more dazzling with each passing second, almost like royalty, a star who had accidentally wandered in among ordinary people, a gorgeous spread in a fashion magazine. The fact was that right then, in that first moment of astonishment, Blomkvist would not have been able to describe her, or provide even one single detail about her appearance.

"Can I help you?" he said.

"No, no," she said, apparently shy, and there was no getting away from it: her hesitancy was beguiling. She was not a woman you would have thought to be shy. She looked as if she might own the world.

"Well then, have a nice evening," he said, and turned again, but he heard her nervously clear her throat.

"Aren't you Mikael Blomkvist?" she said, even more uncertain now, looking down at the cobbles in the street.

"Yes, I am," he said, and smiled politely, as he would have done for anybody.

"Well, I just want to say that I've always admired you," she said, raising her head and gazing into his eyes with a long look.

"I'm flattered. But it's been a long time since I wrote anything decent. Who are you?"

"My name is Rebecka Mattson," she said. "I've been living in Switzerland."

"And now you're home for a visit?"

"Only for a short time, unfortunately. I miss Sweden. I even miss November in Stockholm. But I guess that's how it is when you're homesick, isn't it?"

"What do you mean?"

"That you miss even the bad bits."

"True."

"Do you know how I cure it all? I follow the Swedish press. I don't think I've missed a single issue of *Millennium* in the last few years," she said.

He looked at her again, and noticed that every piece of clothing, from the black high-heeled shoes to the checked blue cashmere shawl, was expensive and elegant. Rebecka Mattson did not look like your typical *Millennium* reader. But there was no reason to be prejudiced, even against rich expatriate Swedes.

"Do you work there?" he said.

"I'm a widow."

"I see."

"Sometimes I get so bored. Were you going somewhere?"

"I was thinking of having a drink and a bite to eat," he said, at once regretting his reply. It was too inviting, too predictable. But it was at least true.

"May I keep you company?" she asked.

"That would be nice," he said, sounding unsure. Then she touched his hand—unintentionally, at least that is what he wanted to believe. She still seemed bashful. They walked slowly up Hornsgatspuckeln, past a row of galleries.

"How nice to be strolling here with you," she said.

"It's a bit unexpected."

"So true. It's not what I was thinking when I woke up this morning."

"What were you thinking?"

"That the day would be as dreary as ever."

"I don't know if I'll be such good company," he said. "I'm pretty much immersed in a story."

"Are you working too hard?"

"Maybe so."

"Then you need a little break," she said, giving him a bewitching smile, filled with longing or some sort of promise. At that moment he thought she seemed familiar, as if he had seen that smile before, but in another form, distorted somehow.

"Have we met before?" he said.

"I don't think so. Except that I've seen you a thousand times in pictures, and on TV."

"So you've never lived in Stockholm?"

"When I was a little girl."

"Where did you live then?"

She pointed vaguely up Hornsgatan.

"Those were good times," she said. "Our father took care of us. I often think about him. I miss him."

"Is he no longer alive?"

"He died much too young."

"I'm sorry."

"Thank you. Where are we headed?"

"Well," he said. "There's a pub just up Bellmansgatan, the Bishops Arms. I know the owner. It's quite a nice place."

"I'm sure . . ."

Once again she had that diffident, shy look on her face, and once again her hand happened to brush against his fingers—this time he wasn't so sure it was accidental.

"Perhaps it isn't fancy enough?"

"Oh, I'm sure it's fine," she said apologetically. "It's just that people tend to stare at me. I've come across so many bastards in pubs."

"I can believe it."

"Wouldn't you . . . ?"

"What?"

She looked down at the ground again and blushed. At first he thought he was seeing things. Surely adults don't blush that way? But Rebecka Mattson from Switzerland, who looked like seven million dollars, went red like a little schoolgirl.

"Wouldn't you like to invite me to your place instead, for a glass of wine or two?" she said. "That would be nicer."

"Well . . ."

He hesitated.

He badly needed some sleep, to be in good shape tomorrow. Yet he said:

"Of course. I've got a bottle of Barolo in the wine rack," and for a second he thought something exciting might be about to happen after all, as if he were about to embark on an adventure.

But his doubt would not subside. At first he could not understand why. He did not normally have a problem with this kind of situation—he had more success than most when it came to women flirting with him. This particular encounter had developed very quickly, but he was not unused to that either. So it was something about the woman herself, wasn't it?

Not only was she young and exceptionally beautiful and should have had better things to do than chase after burned-out middle-aged journalists. It was something in her expression, the way she switched between bold and shy, and the physical contact. Everything he had at first found spontaneous increasingly seemed to him to be contrived.

"How lovely. I won't stay long; I don't want to spoil your story," she said.

"I'll take full responsibility for any spoiled stories," he said, and tried to smile back.

It was a forced smile and in that instant he caught a strange twitch in her eyes, a sudden icy chill which in a second turned into its very opposite, full of affection and warmth, like an acting exercise. He became more convinced that there was something wrong. But he had no idea what, and did not want his suspicions to show, at least not yet. What was going on? He wanted to understand.

They continued on up Bellmansgatan. He was not thinking of taking her back to his place any longer, but he needed time to figure her out. He looked at her again. She really was gorgeous. Yet it occurred to him that it was not her beauty which had first captivated him. It was something else, something more elusive. Just then he saw Rebecka Mattson as a riddle to which he ought to have the answer.

"A nice part of town, this," she said.

"It's not bad." He looked up towards the Bishops Arms.

Diagonally across from the pub, just a bit higher up by the intersection with Tavastgatan, a scrawny, lanky man in a black cap was standing studying a map. He looked like a tourist. He had a brown suitcase in his other hand and white sneakers and a black leather jacket with its fur collar turned up, and under normal circumstances Blomkvist would not have given him a second glance.

But now he observed that the man's movements were nervous and unnatural. Perhaps Blomkvist was suspicious to begin with, but the distracted way he was handling the map seemed more and more put on. Now he raised his head and stared straight at Blomkvist and the woman, studying them for a brief second. Then he looked down at his map again, seeming ill at ease, almost trying to hide his face under the cap. The bowed, almost timid head reminded Blomkvist of something, and again he looked into his companion's dark eyes.

His look was persistent and intense. She gazed at him with affection, but he did not reciprocate; instead he scrutinized her. Then her expression froze. Only in that moment did Blomkvist smile back at her.

He smiled because suddenly the penny had dropped.

# CHAPTER 22

# NOVEMBER 23—EVENING

Salander got up from the table. She did not want to pester August any longer. The boy was under enough pressure as it was and her idea had been crazy from the start.

One always expects too much of these poor savants, and what August had done was already impressive. She went out onto the terrace again and gingerly felt the area around the bullet wound, which was still aching. She heard a sound behind her, a hasty scratching on paper, so she turned and went back inside. When she saw what August had written, she smiled:

$2^3 \times 3 \times 19$

She sat down and said, without looking at him this time, "OK. I'm impressed. But let's make this a little harder. Have a go at 18,206,927."

August was hunched over the table and Salander thought it might have been unkind to throw an eight-digit figure at him right away. But if they were to stand any chance of getting what she needed they would need to go much higher than that. She was not surprised to see August begin to sway nervously back and forth. After a few seconds he leaned forward and wrote on his paper: $9419 \times 1933$.

"Good. How about 971,230,541?"

August wrote, $983 \times 991 \times 997$.

"That's great," Salander said, and on they went.

Outside the black, cube-like office building in Fort Meade with its reflective glass walls, not far from the big radome with its dish aerials, Casales and Needham were standing in the packed parking lot. Needham was twirling his car keys and looking beyond the electric fence in the direction of the surrounding woods. He should be on his way to the airport, he said, he was late already. But Casales did not want to let him leave. She had her hand on his shoulder and was shaking her head.

"That's twisted."

"It's out there," he said.

"So every one of the handles we've picked up for people in the Spider Society—Thanos, Enchantress, Zemo, Alkhema, Cyclone, and the rest—what they have in common is that they're all . . ."

"Enemies of Wasp in the original comic book series, yes."

"That's insane."

"A psychologist would have fun with it."

"This kind of fixation must run deep."

"I get the feeling it's real hate," he said.

"You will be careful over there, won't you?"

"Don't forget I used to be in a gang."

"That was a long time ago, Ed, and many pounds too."

"It's not a question of weight. What is it they say? You can take the boy out of the ghetto . . ."

"Yes, yes."

"You can never get rid of it. Besides, I'll have help from the NDRE in Stockholm. They're itching as much as I am to put that hacker out of action once and for all."

"What if Ingram finds out?"

"That wouldn't be good. But as you can imagine, I've been laying the groundwork. Even exchanged a word or two with O'Connor."

"I figured as much. Is there anything I can do for you?"

"Yep."

"Shoot."

"Ingram's crew seems to have had full insight into the Swedish police investigation."

"They've been eavesdropping on the police?"

"Either that or they have a source, maybe an ambitious soul at Säpo. If I put you together with two of my best hackers, you could do some digging."

"Sounds risky."

"OK, forget it."

"That wasn't a no."

"Thanks, Alona. I'll send info."

"Have a good trip," she said, and Needham smiled defiantly and got into his car.

Looking back, Blomkvist could not explain how he had worked it out. It may have been something in the Mattson woman's expression, something unknown and yet familiar. The perfect harmony of that face may have reminded him of its opposite, and that, together with other hunches and misgivings, gave him the answer. True, he was not yet certain. But he had no doubt that something was very wrong.

The man now walking off with his map and brown suitcase was the same figure he had seen on the security camera in Saltsjöbaden, and that coincidence was too improbable not to be of some significance, so Blomkvist stood there for a few seconds and thought. Then he turned to the woman who called herself Rebecka Mattson and tried to sound confident:

"Your friend is heading off."

"My friend?" she said, genuinely surprised. "What friend?"

"Him up there," he said, pointing at the man's skeletal back as he sauntered gawkily down Tavastgatan.

"Are you joking? I don't know anyone in Stockholm."

"What do you want from me?"

"I just want to get to know you, Mikael," she said, fingering her blouse, as if she might undo a button.

"Stop that!" he said sharply, and was about to lose his temper when she looked at him with such vulnerable, piteous eyes that he was thrown. For a moment he thought he had made a mistake.

"Are you cross with me?" she said, hurt.

"No, but . . ."

"What?"

"I don't trust you," he said, more bluntly than he intended.

She smiled sadly and said: "I can't help feeling that you're not quite yourself today, are you, Mikael? We'll have to meet some other time instead."

She moved to kiss his cheek so discreetly and quickly that he had no time to stop her. She gave a flirtatious wave of her fingers and walked away up the hill on high heels, so resolutely self-assured that he wondered if he should stop her and fire some probing questions. But he could not imagine that anything would come of it. Instead he decided to follow her.

It was crazy, but he saw no alternative, so he let her disappear over the brow of the hill and then set off in pursuit. He hurried up to the intersection, sure that she could not have gone far. But there was no sign of her, or of the man either. It was as if the city had swallowed them up. The street was empty, apart from a black BMW backing into a parking space some way down the block, and a man with a goatee wearing an old-fashioned Afghan coat who came walking in his direction on the opposite sidewalk.

Where had they gone? There were no side streets for them to slip into, no alleys. Had they ducked into a doorway? He walked on down towards Torkel Knutssonsgatan, looking left and right. Nothing. He passed what had been Samir's Cauldron, once a favourite locale of his and Berger's; now called Tabbouli, it served Lebanese food. They might have stepped inside.

But he could not see how she would have had time to get there, he had been hot on her heels. Where the hell was she? Were she and the man standing somewhere nearby, watching him? Twice he spun around, certain that they were right behind him, and once he gave a start because of an icy feeling that someone was looking at him through a telescopic sight.

When eventually he gave up and wandered home it felt as though he had escaped a great danger. He had no idea how close to the truth that feeling was, yet his heart was beating fiercely and his throat was dry. He was not easily scared, but tonight he had been frightened by an empty street.

The only thing he did understand was who he needed to speak to. He had to get hold of Holger Palmgren, Salander's old guardian. But first he would do his civic duty. If the man he had seen was the person from Balder's security camera, and there was even a minimal chance that he could be found, the police had to be informed. So he rang Bublanski.

It was by no means easy to convince the chief inspector. It had not been easy to convince himself. But he still had some residual credibility to fall back on, however many liberties he had taken with the truth of late. Bublanski said that he would send out a unit.

"Why would he be in your part of town?"

"I have no idea, but it wouldn't hurt to see if you could find him, would it?"

"I suppose not."

"The best of luck to you in that case."

"It's damn unsatisfactory that the Balder boy is still out there some-where," Bublanski said reproachfully.

"And it's damn unsatisfactory that there was a leak in your unit," Blom-kvist said.

"I can tell you, we've identified *our* leak."

"You have? That's fantastic."

"It's not all that fantastic, I'm afraid. We believe there may have been several leaks, most of which did minimal damage except maybe for the last."

"Then you'll have to make sure you put a stop to it."

"We're doing everything we can, but we're beginning to suspect . . ." And then he paused.

"What?"

"Nothing."

"OK, you don't have to tell me."

"We live in a sick world, Mikael."

"We do?"

"A world in which paranoia is a requirement."

"You could be right about that. Good night, Chief Inspector."

"Good night, Mikael. Don't do anything silly now."

"I'll do my best."


Blomkvist crossed over Ringvägen and went down into the tunnelbana. He took the red line towards Norsborg and got off at Liljeholmen, where for about a year Holger Palmgren had been living in a small, modern apart-ment. Palmgren had sounded alarmed when he heard Blomkvist's voice on the telephone. But as soon as he had been assured that Salander was in one piece—Blomkvist hoped he wasn't wrong about this—he made him feel welcome.

Palmgren was a lawyer, long retired, who had been Salander's guardian for many years, ever since the girl was thirteen and had been locked up in St. Stefan's psychiatric clinic in Uppsala. He was elderly and not in the best of health, having suffered two strokes. For some time now he had been using a walker, and had trouble getting around even so. The left side of his face drooped and his left hand no longer functioned. But his mind was clear and his long-term memory was outstanding—especially on Salander.

No-one knew Lisbeth Salander as he did. Palmgren had succeeded where all the psychiatrists and psychologists had failed, or perhaps had not wanted to succeed. After a childhood from hell, when the girl had lost faith in all adults and in all authority, Palmgren had won her confidence and persuaded her to open up. Blomkvist saw it as a minor miracle. Salander was every therapist's nightmare, but she had told Palmgren about the most painful parts of her past. That was why Blomkvist now keyed in the front-door code at Liljeholmstorget 96, took the lift to the fifth floor, and rang the doorbell.

"My dear old friend," Holger said in the doorway. "It's so wonderful to see you. But you're looking pale."

"I haven't been sleeping well."

"Not surprising, when people are shooting at you. I read about it in the paper. A dreadful story."

"Appalling."

"Have there been any developments?"

"I'll tell you all about it," Blomkvist said, sitting on a yellow sofa near the balcony, waiting for Palmgren to settle with difficulty into a wheelchair next to him.

Blomkvist ran through the story in broad outline. When he came to the point of his sudden inspiration, or suspicion, on the cobblestones in Bell-mansgatan, he was interrupted:

"What are you saying?"

"I think it was Camilla."

Palmgren looked stunned.

"*That* Camilla?"

"The very same."

"Jesus," Palmgren said. "What happened?"

"She vanished. But afterwards I felt as if my brain were on fire."

"I can well understand. I was sure Camilla had disappeared off the face of the earth."

"And I had almost forgotten that there were two of them."

"There were two of them all right, very much so, twin sisters who loathed each other."

"I remember that," Blomkvist said. "But I need to be reminded of as much as you can tell me, to fill in the gaps. I've been asking myself why on earth Salander got involved in this story. Why would she, the superhacker, take an interest in a simple data breach?"

"Well, you know the background, don't you? The mother, Agneta Salander, was a cashier at Konsum Zinken and lived with her two daughters on Lundagatan. They might have had quite a nice life together. There wasn't much money and Agneta was very young and had had no opportunity to get an education. But she was loving and caring. She wanted to give her girls a good upbringing. It was just . . ."

"That the father came to visit."

"Yes, the father, Alexander Zalachenko. He came from time to time and his visits nearly always ended in the same way. He assaulted and raped Agneta while the girls sat in the next room and heard everything. One day Lisbeth found her mother unconscious on the floor."

"And that was the first time she took revenge?"

"The second time. The first was when she stabbed Zalachenko repeatedly in the shoulder."

"But now she firebombed his car."

"Yes. Zalachenko burned like a torch. Lisbeth was committed to St. Stefan's psychiatric clinic."

"And her mother was admitted to Äppelviken Nursing Home."

"For Lisbeth that was the most painful part. Her mother was just twenty-nine, and she was never herself again. She survived at the nursing home for fourteen years, with severe brain injuries and suffering a great deal of pain. Often she could not communicate at all. Lisbeth went to see her as frequently as she could, and I know she dreamed that her mother would one day recover so they could talk again and look after each other. But it never happened. That if anything is the darkest corner of Lisbeth's life. She saw her mother wither away and eventually die."

"It's terrible. But I've never understood Camilla's role in the story."

"That's more complicated, and in some ways I think one has to forgive the girl. After all, she too was only a child, and before she was even aware of it she became a pawn in the game."

"In what way?"

"They chose opposite camps in the battle, you could say. It's true that the girls are fraternal twins and not alike in appearance, but they also have completely different temperaments. Lisbeth was born first. Camilla came twenty minutes later and was apparently a joy to behold, even when she was tiny. While Lisbeth was an angry creature, Camilla had everyone exclaiming 'Oh, what a sweet girl,' and it can't have been a coincidence that Zalachenko showed more forbearance towards her from the start. I say forbearance because it was never a question of anything kinder in those first years. Since Agneta was no more than a whore to him, it followed that her children were bastards with no claim on his affections, little wretches who just got in the way. And yet . . ."

"Yes?"

"And yet even Zalachenko noticed that one of the children was beautiful. Sometimes Lisbeth would say there was a genetic defect in her family and, though it's doubtful that her claim would stand up to medical scrutiny, it cannot be denied that Zala fathered some exceptional children. You came across their half-brother, Ronald Niedermann, didn't you? He was blond, enormous, and had congenital analgesia, the inability to feel pain, so was therefore an ideal hit man and murderer, while Camilla . . . well, in her case the genetic abnormality was quite simply that she was astoundingly, ridiculously lovely to look at, and that just got worse as she grew older. I say worse because I'm pretty sure it was a misfortune. The effect may have been exaggerated by the fact that her twin sister always looked sour. Grown-ups were liable to frown when they saw her. But then they would notice Camilla, and go soft in the head. Can you imagine how that must have impacted her?"

"It must have been hard to get passed over."

"I wasn't thinking of Lisbeth, and I don't remember seeing any evidence that she resented the situation. If it was just a question of beauty, she probably would have felt her sister was welcome to it. No, I'm talking about Camilla. What must it do to a child who doesn't have much in the way of empathy to be told all the time how divine she is?"

"It goes to her head."

"It gives her a sense of power. When she smiles, we melt. When she doesn't, we feel excluded, and do absolutely anything to see her beam again. Camilla learned early on to exploit that. She became a master manipulator. She had large, expressive doe eyes."

"She still does."

"Lisbeth told me how Camilla would sit for hours in front of the mirror, practising her look. Her eyes were a fantastic weapon. They could both bewitch you and freeze you out, make children and adults alike feel special one day and rejected the next. It was an evil gift and, as you could guess, she soon became very popular at school. Everyone wanted to be with her and she took advantage in every conceivable way. She made sure that her classmates gave her presents daily: marbles, sweets, small change, pearls, brooches. And those who didn't, or generally didn't behave as she wanted, she wouldn't even look at the next day. Anyone who had ever found themselves basking in her radiance knew how painful that was. Her classmates did everything they could to be in her good graces. They fawned over her. With one exception, of course."

"Her sister."

"That's right, and so Camilla turned them against Lisbeth. She got some fierce bullying going—they pushed Lisbeth's head into the toilet and called her a freak and a weirdo and all sorts of names. This went on until one day they found out who they were picking on. But that's another story, and you're familiar with."

"Lisbeth doesn't turn the other cheek."

"No indeed. But the interesting thing in this story from a psychological point of view is that Camilla learned how to dominate her surroundings from an early age. She worked out how to control everybody, apart from two significant people in her life, Lisbeth and her father, and that annoyed her. She put a vast amount of energy into winning those fights as well, and she needed totally different strategies for each of them. She could never win Lisbeth over, and pretty soon I think she gave up. In her eyes, Lisbeth was simply strange, a surly, stroppy girl. Her father, on the other hand . . ."

"He was evil through and through."

"He was evil, but he was also the family's centre of gravity. He was the one around whom everything revolved, even if he was rarely there. He was the absent father. In a normal family such a figure can take on a quasi-mystical status for a child, but in this case it was much more than that."

"In what way?"

"I suppose I mean that Camilla and Zalachenko were an unfortunate combination. Although Camilla hardly understood it herself, she was only interested in one thing, even then: power. And her father, well, you can say many things about him, but he was not short of power. Plenty of people can testify to that, not least that wretched lot at Säpo. No matter how firmly they tried to put their foot down, they still ended up huddled like a flock of frightened sheep when they came eyeball to eyeball with him. There was an ugly, imposing self-assurance about Zalachenko which was merely amplified by the fact that he was untouchable. It made no difference how many times he was reported to the social welfare agency—the Security Police always protected him. This is what persuaded Lisbeth to take matters into her own hands. But for Camilla, things were different."

"She wanted to be like him."

"Yes, I think so. Her father was her ideal—she wanted the same aura of immunity and strength. But most of all, perhaps, she wanted to be acknowledged by him. To be seen as a worthy daughter."

"She must have known how terribly he mistreated her mother."

"Of course she knew. Yet still she took her father's side. One could say she chose to side with strength and power. Apparently even as a little girl she often said that she despised weak people."

"She despised her mother, do you think?"

"Unfortunately I think you're right. Lisbeth once told me something which I've never been able to forget."

"What's that?"

"I've never told anyone."

"Isn't it about time, then?"

"Well, maybe, but in that case I need a strong drink. How about a good brandy?"

"That wouldn't be such a bad idea. But you stay right where you are, I'll get some glasses and the bottle," Blomkvist said, going to the mahogany drinks cabinet in the corner by the kitchen door.

He was digging around among the bottles when his iPhone rang. It was Zander, or at least his name was on the display. But when Blomkvist answered no-one was there, it must have been a pocket call, he thought. He poured out two glasses of Rémy Martin and sat down again next to Palmgren.

"So tell me," he said.

"I don't know where to begin. But one fine summer's day, as I understood it, Camilla and Lisbeth were both sitting in their bedroom. The door was locked."

# CHAPTER 23

# NOVEMBER 23—EVENING

August's body stiffened again. He could no longer find the answers, the numbers were too big. Instead of picking up his pencil he clenched his fists so that the backs of his hands whitened. He banged his head against the tabletop.

Salander should have tried to comfort him, or at least prevent him from hurting himself. But she was not entirely conscious of what was happening. Her mind was on her encrypted file. She realized she was not going to get any further by this route either. It was hardly surprising—how could August succeed where supercomputers had failed? Her expectations had been absurdly high from the start. But still she felt disappointed.

She went out into the darkness to survey the barren, untamed landscape before her. Below the steep rock slope lay the beach and a snow-covered field with a deserted dance pavilion.

The place probably teemed with people on a lovely summer's day. Now it was empty. The boats had been pulled up on land and not a soul could be seen, no lights were shining in the houses on the other side of the water. Salander liked it. At least she liked it as a hiding place at the end of November.

If someone arrived by car she was unlikely to pick up the sound of the engine. The only conceivable place to park was down by the beach, and to get to the house you had to climb up the wooden stairs along the steep rock slope. Under the cover of darkness, someone might be able to sneak up on them. But she would sleep tonight. She needed it. Her wound was still giving her pain—maybe that was why she had gotten her hopes up about August, against the odds. But when she went back into the house, she realized that there was something else besides.

"Normally Lisbeth isn't someone who bothers about the weather or what's going on beyond her immediate focus," Palmgren said. "She blocks out everything she considers unimportant. But on this occasion she did mention that the sun was shining on Lundagatan and in Skinnarviksparken. She could hear children laughing. On the other side of the windowpane, people were happy. Perhaps that is what she was trying to say—she wanted to point out the contrast. Ordinary people were having ice cream and playing with kites and balls. Camilla and Lisbeth sat locked in their bedroom and could hear their father assaulting their mother.

"I believe this was just before Lisbeth took her revenge on Zalachenko, but I'm not sure about the sequence of events. There were many rapes, and they followed the same pattern. Zala would appear in the afternoon or evening, very drunk. Sometimes he would ruffle Camilla's hair and say things like: 'How can such a pretty girl have such a loathsome sister?' Then he would lock his daughters in their room and settle down in the kitchen to have more to drink. He drank his vodka neat, and often he would sit quietly at first, smacking his lips like a hungry animal. Then he would mumble something like: 'And how's my little whore today?,' sounding almost affectionate. But Agneta would do something wrong, or rather, Zalachenko would decide that she had done something wrong, and then the first blow came, usually a slap followed by: 'I thought my little whore was going to behave herself today.' Then he would shove her into the bedroom and beat her. After a while slaps would turn to punches. Lisbeth could tell from the sounds. She could tell exactly what sort of blows they were, and where they landed. She felt it as clearly as if she herself were the victim of this savagery. After the punches came the kicks. Zala kicked and shoved her mother against the wall and shouted 'bitch' and 'tramp' and 'whore,' and that aroused him. He was turned on by her suffering. Only once Agneta was black-and-blue and bleeding did he rape her, and when he climaxed he would yell even fouler insults. Then it would be quiet for a while. All that could be heard was Agneta's choked sobbing and Zala's own heavy breathing. Then he would get up and have another drink and mutter and swear and spit on the floor. Sometimes he unlocked the door to the children's room, with something like 'Mummy's behaving herself again now.' And he would leave, slamming the door behind him. That was the usual pattern. But on this particular day something new happened."

"What?"

"The girls' bedroom was quite small. However hard they tried to get away from each other, the beds were still close and, while the abuse went on, each one sat on her own mattress, facing the other. They hardly ever said anything, and usually avoided eye contact. On this day Lisbeth was staring through the window at Lundagatan, that's probably why she talked about the sunlight and the children out there. But then she looked at her sister, and that's when she saw it."

"She saw what?"

"Camilla's right hand, beating against her mattress. It could have been a sign of nervous or compulsive behaviour. That's what Lisbeth thought at first. But then she noticed that the hand was beating in time with the blows from the bedroom, and at that she looked up at Camilla's face. Her sister's eyes were glowing with excitement, and the eeriest thing was: Camilla looked just like Zala himself and she was smiling. She was suppressing a smirk, and in that instant Lisbeth realized that Camilla was not only trying to ingratiate herself with her father. She was also right behind his violence. She was cheering him on."

"That's sick."

"But that's how it was. Do you know what Lisbeth did? She remained perfectly calm. She sat down next to Camilla and took her hand almost tenderly. Perhaps Camilla thought her sister was looking for some comfort or closeness. Stranger things have happened. Lisbeth rolled up her sister's shirt sleeve and dug her fingernails into Camilla's wrist—down to the bone—ripping open a terrible wound. Blood streamed onto the bed. Lisbeth dragged Camilla to the floor and swore she would kill both her and her father if the beatings and the rapes did not stop."

"Jesus!"

"You can imagine the hatred between the sisters. Both Agneta and the social services were so worried that something even more serious would happen that they were kept apart. For a while they arranged a home elsewhere for Camilla. Sooner or later they probably would have clashed again, but in the end, as you know, things did not turn out like that. I believe the sisters only saw each other once after Lisbeth was locked up—several years later—when a disaster was narrowly averted, but I know none of the details. I haven't heard anything of Camilla for a long time now. The last people to have had contact with her are the foster family with whom she lived in Uppsala, people called Dahlgren. I can get you the number. But ever since Camilla was eighteen or nineteen and she packed a bag and left the country she hasn't been heard from. That's why I was astonished when you said that you had met her. Not even Lisbeth, with her famous ability to track people down, has been able to find her."

"So she *has* tried?"

"Oh yes. As far as I know, the last time was when her father's estate was to be apportioned."

"I didn't realize."

"Lisbeth mentioned it in passing. She didn't want a single penny from that will—to her it was blood money—but she could tell that there was something strange about it. There were assets of four million kronor: the farm in Gosseberga, some securities, a run-down industrial site in Norrtälje, a cottage somewhere, and various other bits and pieces. Not insignificant by any means, and yet . . ."

"He should have been worth much more."

"Yes, Lisbeth was aware that he ran a vast criminal empire. Four million would have been small change in that context."

"So you're saying she wondered if Camilla inherited the lion's share."

"I think that's what she's been trying to find out. The mere thought that her father's fortune was going on doing harm after his death was torture to her. But for a long time she got nowhere."

"Camilla concealed her identity well."

"I assume so."

"Do you have any reason to think Camilla might have taken over her father's trafficking business?"

"Maybe, maybe not. She may have struck out into something altogether different."

"Such as?"

Palmgren closed his eyes and took a large sip of his brandy.

"I can't be sure of this, Mikael. But when you told me about Professor

Balder, I had a thought. Do you have any idea why Lisbeth is so good with computers? Do you know how it all started?"

"I have no idea."

"Then I'll tell you. I wonder if the key to your story doesn't lie there."

When Salander came in from the terrace and saw August huddled in a stiff and unnatural position by the round table, she realized that the boy reminded her of herself as a child.

That is exactly how she had felt at Lundagatan, until one day it became clear to her that she had to grow up far too soon, to take revenge on her father. It was a burden no child should have to bear. But it had been the beginning of a real life, a more dignified life. No bastard should be allowed to do what Zalachenko or Balder's murderer had done with impunity. She went to August and said solemnly, as if giving an important order, "You're going to go to bed now. When you wake up I want you to do the drawing that will nail your father's killer. Do you get that?" The boy nodded and shuffled into his bedroom while Salander opened her laptop and started to look for information about Lasse Westman and his circle of friends.

"I don't think Zalachenko himself was much use with computers," Palmgren said. "He wasn't of that generation. But perhaps his dirty business grew to such a scale that he had to use a computer programme to keep his accounts, and to keep them away from his accomplices. One day he came to Lundagatan with an IBM machine which he installed on the desk next to the window. Nobody in the family had seen a computer before. Zalachenko promised that if anyone so much as touched the machine he would flay them alive. From a purely psychological point of view, that was telling. It increased the temptation."

"Forbidden fruit."

"Lisbeth was around eleven at the time. It was before she tore into Camilla's right arm, and before she went for her father with knives and petrol bombs. You could say it was just before she became the Lisbeth we know today. She lacked stimulation. She had no friends to speak of, partly because Camilla had made sure that nobody came anywhere near her at school, but partly because she was different. I don't know if she realized it herself yet. Her teachers and those around her didn't. But she was an extremely gifted child. Her talent alone set her apart. School was deadly boring for her. Everything was obvious and easy. She needed only to take a quick look at things to understand them, and during lessons she sat there daydreaming. I do believe, however, that by then she had managed to find some things in her free time which interested her—advanced maths books, that sort of thing. But basically she was bored stiff. She spent a lot of time reading her Marvel comics, which were way below her intellectual level but perhaps fulfilled another, therapeutic function."

"In what sense?"

"To be honest I'm reluctant to try to play the shrink with Lisbeth. She would hate it if she could hear me. But those comics are full of superheroes fighting against supervillains, taking matters into their own hands to exact revenge and see to it that justice is done. For all I know, that may have been the perfect sort of reading material. Perhaps those stories with their black-and-white view of the world helped her to gain some clarity."

"You mean she understood she had to grow up and become a superhero herself."

"In some way, maybe, in her own little world. At the time she didn't know that Zalachenko had been a Soviet spy, and that his secrets had given him a unique position in Swedish society. She wouldn't have had any idea either that there was a special section within Säpo which protected him. But like Camilla, she sensed that her father had some sort of immunity. One day a man in a grey overcoat appeared at the apartment and hinted that their father must come to no harm. Lisbeth realized early on that there was no point in reporting Zalachenko to the police or the social services. That would only result in yet another man in a grey overcoat turning up on their doorstep.

"Powerlessness, Mikael, can be a devastating force, and before Lisbeth was old enough to do something about it she needed a place of strength, a refuge. She found that in the world of superheroes. I know better than most how important literature can be, whether it's comic books or fine old novels, and I know that Lisbeth grew particularly attached to a young heroine called Janet van Dyne."

"Van Dyne?"

"That's right, a girl whose father was a rich scientist. The father is murdered—by aliens, if I remember right—and in order to take revenge Janet van Dyne gets in touch with one of her father's old colleagues, and in his laboratory acquires superpowers. She becomes the Wasp, someone you can't push around, either literally or figuratively."

"I didn't know that. So that's where she gets her handle from?"

"Not just the handle. I knew nothing about all that sort of stuff—I was an old dinosaur who got the Phantom mixed up with Mandrake the Magician. But the first time I saw a picture of the Wasp, it gave me a start. There was so much of Lisbeth in her. There still is, in a way. I think she picked up a lot of her style from that character. I don't want to make too much of it. But I do know she thought a great deal about the transformation Janet van Dyne underwent when she became the Wasp. Somehow she understood that she herself had to undergo the same drastic metamorphosis: from child and victim to someone who could fight back against a highly trained and ruthless intelligence agent.

"Thoughts like these occupied her day and night and so the Wasp became an important figure for her during her period of transition, a source of inspiration. And Camilla found out about it. That girl had an uncanny ability to nose out other people's weaknesses—she used her tentacles to feel for their sensitive points and would then strike exactly there. So she came to make fun of the Wasp in whichever way she could. She even found out who Wasp's Marvel enemies were and began to call herself by their names, Thanos and all the others."

"Did you say Thanos?" said Blomkvist, suddenly alert.

"I think that's what he was called, a destroyer who once fell in love with Death itself. Death had appeared to him in the shape of a woman, and after that he wanted to prove himself worthy of her, or something like that. Camilla became a fan of his so as to provoke Lisbeth. She even called her gang of friends the Spider Society—in one of the comics that group are the sworn enemies of the Sisterhood of the Wasp."

"Really?" Blomkvist said, his mind racing.

"Yes, I suppose it was childish, but that didn't make it innocent. There was such hostility between the sisters even then that those names took on a nasty significance."

"Do you think that's still relevant?"

"The names, you mean?"

"Yes, I suppose so."

Blomkvist was not sure what he meant, but he had a vague feeling that he had lit upon something important.

"I don't know," Palmgren said. "They're grown women now, but we mustn't forget that those were decisive times in their lives. Looking back, it's perfectly possible that small details could turn out to be of fateful significance. It wasn't just that Lisbeth lost a mother and was then locked up. Camilla's existence too was smashed to pieces. She lost her home, and the father she admired suffered severe burns. As you know, after the petrol bomb, Zalachenko was never himself again. Camilla was put in a foster home miles from the world whose undisputed leading light she had been. It must have been bitterly hurtful for her too. I don't doubt for one second that she's hated Lisbeth with a murderous fury ever since."

"It certainly looks like it," Blomkvist said.

Palmgren took another sip of brandy.

"The sisters were in a state of out-and-out war during this period, and somehow I think they both knew that everything was about to blow up. I think they were even preparing for it."

"But in different ways."

"Oh yes. Lisbeth had a brilliant mind, and infernal plans and strategies were constantly ticking away in her head. But she was alone. Camilla was not so bright, not in the conventional sense—she never had a head for studies, and was incapable of understanding abstract reasoning. But she knew how to manipulate people to do her bidding, so unlike Lisbeth she was never alone. If Camilla discovered that Lisbeth was good at something which could be a threat to her, she never tried to acquire the same skill, for the simple reason she knew she couldn't compete with her sister."

"So what did she do instead?"

"Instead she would track down somebody—or better still, more than one person—who could do whatever it was, and strike back with their help. She always had minions. But forgive me, I'm getting ahead of myself."

"Yes, tell me, what happened with Zalachenko's computer?"

"Lisbeth was short of stimulation, as I said. And she would lie awake at night, worrying about her mother. Agneta bled badly after the rapes but wouldn't go to a doctor. She probably felt ashamed. Periodically she sank into deep depressions and no longer had the strength to go to work or look after the girls. Camilla despised her even more. Mamma is weak, she'd say. As I told you, in her world, to be weak was worse than anything else. Lisbeth, on the other hand, saw a person she loved—the only person she had ever loved—fall victim to a dreadful injustice. She was a child in so many ways, but she was also becoming convinced that she was the only person in the world who could save her mother from being beaten to death. She got up in the middle of the night—quietly, so as not to wake Camilla—and saw the computer, on the desk by the window overlooking Lundagatan.

"At that time she didn't even know how to switch on a computer. But she figured it out. The computer seemed to be whispering to her: 'Unlock my secrets.' She didn't get far, not at first. A password was needed. Since her father was known as Zala, she tried that, and Zala666 and similar combinations, and everything else she could think of. But nothing worked. I believe this went on for two or three nights, and if she slept at all then it was at school or at home in the afternoon.

"Then one night she remembered something her father had written in German on a piece of paper in the kitchen: *Was mich nicht umbringt, macht mich stärker.* What doesn't kill me makes me stronger. At the time it meant nothing to her, but she realized that the phrase was important to her father, so she tried it. That didn't work either. There were too many letters. So she tried Nietzsche, the source of the quote, and there she was, suddenly she was in. A whole world opened up to her. Later she would describe it as a moment which changed her forever. She thrived when she overcame that barrier. She explored what was meant to stay hidden."

"And Zalachenko never knew of this?"

"It seems not. She understood nothing at first—it was all in Russian. There were various lists, and some numbers, accounts of the revenues from his trafficking operations. To this day I have no idea how much she worked out then and how much she found out later. She came to understand that her mother was not the only one made to suffer by her father. He was destroying other women's lives too, and that made her wild with rage. That is what turned her into the Lisbeth we know today, the one who hates men who . . ."

"... hate women."

"Precisely. But it also made her stronger. She saw that there was no turning back—she had to stop her father. She went on with her searches on other computers, including at school, where she would sneak into the staff room. Sometimes she pretended to be sleeping over with the friends she didn't have while in fact she stayed overnight at school and sat at the computers until morning. She started to learn everything about hacking and programming, and I imagine that it was the same as when other child prodigies discover their niche: she was in thrall. She felt that she was born for this. Many of her contacts in the digital world began to take an interest in her even then, the way the older generation has always engaged with younger talents, whether to encourage or crush them. Many people out there were irritated by her unorthodox ways, her completely new approach. But others were impressed, and she made friends, including Plague—you know about him. She got her first real friends by way of the computer and above all, for the first time in her life, she felt free. She could fly through cyberspace, just like the Wasp. There was nothing to tie her down."

"Did Camilla realize how skilled she'd become?"

"She must have had her suspicions. I don't know, I shouldn't speculate, but sometimes I think of Camilla as Lisbeth's dark side, her shadow figure."

"The evil twin."

"A bit, though I don't like to call people evil, especially not young women. If you want to dig into it yourself I suggest you get in touch with Margareta Dahlgren, Camilla's foster mother after the havoc at Lundagatan. Margareta lives in Stockholm now, in Solna, I think. She's a widow and has had a desperately sad life."

"In what way?"

"Well, that may also be of interest. Her husband Kjell, a computer programmer at Ericsson, hanged himself a short time before Camilla left them. A year later their nineteen-year-old daughter also committed suicide, by jumping from a Finland ferry—at least that's what the inquest concluded. The girl had emotional problems, she struggled with her self-esteem. But Margareta never believed that version, and she even hired a private detective. Margareta is obsessed by Camilla, and to be honest I've always had a bit of a problem with her. I'm embarrassed to say, Margareta got in touch with me straight after you published your Zalachenko story. As you know that's when I had just been discharged from the rehabilitation clinic and I was mentally and physically at the end of my tether. Margareta talked endlessly, she was fixated. The sight of her number on my telephone display would exhaust me, and I went to some efforts to avoid her. But now when I think about it I understand her more. I think she would be happy to talk to you, Mikael."

"Can you let me have her details?"

"I'll get them for you. Just wait a moment."

When Palmgren came back he said: "So you're sure that Lisbeth and the boy are safely tucked away somewhere?"

"I'm sure," Blomkvist said. *At least I hope I am,* he thought. He stood up and embraced Palmgren.

Out on Liljeholmstorget the storm tore into him again. He pulled his coat close and thought of Salander and her sister, and for some reason also of Andrei Zander.

He decided to call him to find out how he was getting on with his story on the art dealer. But Zander never picked up.

# CHAPTER 24

# NOVEMBER 23—EVENING

Zander had called Blomkvist because he had changed his mind. Of course he wanted to go out for a beer. How could he not have taken him up on the offer? Blomkvist was his idol and the very reason he had gone in for journalism. But once he dialled the number he felt embarrassed and hung up. Maybe Blomkvist had found something better to do. Zander did not like disturbing people unnecessarily, least of all Blomkvist.

Instead he worked on. But however hard he tried, he got nowhere. The words just would not come out right. After about an hour he decided to take a walk, and so he tidied his desk and checked once again that he had deleted every word on the encrypted link. Then he said goodbye to Emil Grandén, the only other person left in the office.

Grandén was thirty-six and had worked at both TV4's *Cold Facts* and *Svenska Morgon-Posten*. Last year he had been awarded the Stora Journalist prize for Investigative Reporter of the Year. But Zander thought—even though he tried not to—that Grandén was conceited and overbearing, at least towards a young temp like him.

"Going out for a bit," Zander said.

Grandén looked at him as if there was something he had forgotten to say. Then he uttered in a bored tone:

"OK."

Zander felt miserable. It may only have been Grandén's arrogant attitude, but it was more likely because of the article about the art dealer. Why was he finding it so difficult? Presumably because all he wanted to do was help Blomkvist with the Balder story. Everything else felt secondary.

But he was also spineless, wasn't he? Why had he not let Blomkvist take a look at what he had written? No-one could raise the level of a story like Blomkvist could, with just a few light pen strokes or deletions. Never mind. Tomorrow he would see the story with fresh eyes and then Blomkvist could read it, however bad it might be.

Zander closed the door to the office and walked out towards the lift. Further down the stairs a drama was unfolding. At first he could not make out what was going on, but there was a scrawny, hollow-eyed figure molesting a beautiful young woman. Zander froze—he had always loathed violence, ever since his parents had been killed in Sarajevo. He hated fights. But his self-respect was at stake. It was one thing to run away for your own sake, but quite another to leave a fellow human being in danger, and so he rushed down the stairs yelling: "Stop, let her go!"

At first that seemed like a fatal mistake. The hollow-eyed man pulled out a knife and muttered some threat in English. Zander's legs nearly gave way, yet he managed to muster the last remnants of his courage and spat back, like something from a B movie, "Hey, get lost! If you don't, you'll regret it." After a few seconds of posturing, the man took off. Zander and the woman were left alone in the stairwell, and that too was like a scene from a film.

The woman was shaken and shy. She spoke so softly that Zander had to lean in close to hear what she was saying, and it took a while before he understood what had happened. The woman had been in a marriage from hell, she said, and even though she was now divorced and living with a protected identity her ex-husband had managed to track her down and send some stooge to harass her.

"That's the second time that foul man has thrown himself at me today," she said.

"Why were you up here?"

"I tried to get away and ran in, but it didn't help. I can't thank you enough."

"It was nothing."

"I'm so fed up with nasty men," she said.

"I'm a nice man," he said, perhaps a little too quickly and that made him feel pathetic. He was not in the least bit surprised that the woman did not answer, but looked down at the stairs in embarrassment. He felt ashamed of such a cheap reply.

But then, just as he thought he had been rejected, she raised her head and gave him a careful smile.

"I think you really might be. My name's Linda."

"I'm Andrei."

"Nice to meet you, Andrei, and thank you again."

"Thank you too."

"What for?"

"For . . ."

He didn't finish his sentence. He could feel his heart beating, his mouth was dry. He looked down the staircase.

"Yes, Andrei?" she said.

"Would you like me to walk you home?"

He regretted saying that too.

He was afraid it would be misinterpreted. But instead she gave him another of her enchanting, hesitant smiles, and said that she would feel safe with him by her side, so they went out into the street and down towards Slussen. She told him how she had been living more or less locked up in a big house in Djursholm. He said that he understood—he had written a series of articles on violence against women.

"Are you a journalist?" she said.

"I work at *Millennium.*"

"Wow," she said. "Seriously? I'm a huge fan of that magazine."

"It's done a lot of good things," he said shyly.

"It really has," she said. "A while ago I read a wonderful article about an Iraqi who had been wounded in the war and got sacked from his job as a cleaner at some restaurant in the city. He was left destitute. Today he's the owner of a whole chain of restaurants. I cried when I read it; it was so beautifully written and inspiring."

"I wrote that," he said.

"Are you joking?" she said. "It was fantastic."

Zander was not exactly spoiled when it came to praise for his journalistic efforts, especially from unknown women. Whenever *Millennium* was mentioned, people wanted to talk about Mikael Blomkvist, and Zander did not object to that. But secretly he dreamed of recognition for himself too, and now this beautiful Linda had praised him without even meaning to.

It made him so happy and proud that he plucked up the courage to suggest a drink at Papagallo, since they were just passing. To his delight she said: "What a good idea!," so they went into the restaurant, Zander's heart pounding.

He tried to avoid looking into her eyes. Those eyes had knocked him off his feet and he could not believe this was really happening. They sat down at a table not far from the bar and Linda tentatively put out her hand. As he took it he smiled and mumbled something, hardly aware of what he was saying.

He looked down at his phone—Grandén was calling. To his own surprise he ignored it and turned off his ringer. For once the magazine would have to wait. He just wanted to gaze into Linda's face, to drown in it. She was so beautiful that it felt like a punch to the stomach, yet she seemed fragile, like a wounded bird.

"I can't imagine why anyone would want to hurt you," he said.

"It happens all the time."

Perhaps he could understand it after all. A woman like her probably attracted psychopaths. No-one else would dare ask her out. Most men would just shrivel up and feel inferior.

"It's so nice to be sitting here with you," he said.

"It's so nice to be sitting here with *you*," she repeated, gently stroking his hand. They each ordered a glass of red wine and started to talk; they had so much to say, and he didn't notice his mobile vibrating in his pocket, not once but twice, which is how he came to ignore a call from Mikael Blomkvist for the first time in his life.

Soon afterwards she took his hand and led him out into the night. He did not ask where they were going. He was prepared to follow her anywhere. She was the most wonderful creature he had ever met, and from time to time she gave him a smile that made every paving stone, every breath, sound out a promise that something wonderful and overwhelming was happening. You live an entire life for the sake of a walk like this, he thought, barely noticing the cold and the city around him.

He was intoxicated by her presence and what might await him. But maybe—he wasn't sure—there was a hint of suspicion too. At first he dismissed these thoughts, his usual scepticism at any form of happiness. And yet he could not help asking himself: Is this too good to be true?

He studied Linda with a new focus, and noticed that not everything about her was attractive. As they walked past Katarinahissen he even thought he noticed something hard in her eyes. He looked anxiously down at the choppy waters. "Where are we going?"

"I have a friend with a small apartment in Mårten Trotzigs gränd," she said. "She lets me use it sometimes. We could have another drink there." That made him smile as if it were the most wonderful idea he had ever heard.

Yet he felt more and more confused. Not long ago he had been looking after her, and now she had taken the initiative. When a quick glance at his mobile told him that Blomkvist had rung twice, he felt he had to call back immediately. Come what may, he could not let the magazine down.

"I'd like that," he said. "But first I have to make a call. I'm in the middle of a story."

"No, Andrei," she said, in a surprisingly firm tone. "You're not calling anyone. Tonight it's just you and me."

They got to Järntorget. In spite of the storm there were quite a few people around and Linda stared at the ground, as if she did not want to be noticed. He looked over to the right at Österlånggatan and the statue of Evert Taube. The troubadour was standing there immobile, holding a sheet of music in his right hand, looking up at the sky in dark glasses. Should he suggest that they meet the following day?

"Maybe . . ." he started.

He got no further, because she pulled him to her and kissed him with a force which emptied his mind. Then she stepped up the pace again. She held his hand and pulled him to the left into Västerlånggatan, then right into a dark alley. Was that someone behind them? No, no, the footsteps and voices he could hear came from further away. It was just him and Linda, wasn't it? They passed a window with a red frame and black shutters and came to a grey door which Linda had some trouble opening. The key was shaking in her hand and he wondered at that. Was she still afraid of her ex-husband and his goon?

They climbed a dark stone stairway. Their footsteps echoed and there was a faint smell of something rotten. On one of the steps past the third floor he saw a playing card, the queen of spades, and he did not like that, he could not understand why, it was probably some silly superstition. He tried to ignore it, and think about how great it was that they had met. Linda was breathing heavily. Her right hand was clenched. A man's laughter could be heard in the alley. Not laughing at him, surely? He was just agitated. But it felt as if they were climbing and climbing and not getting anywhere. Could the house really be so tall? No, here they were. The friend lived in the attic apartment.

The name on the door was Orlov and again Linda took out her bunch of keys. This time her hand was not shaking.

Blomkvist was sitting in an apartment with old-fashioned furniture on Prostvägen in Solna, next to a large churchyard. Just as Palmgren had anticipated, Margareta Dahlgren agreed to see him at once, and even though she had sounded manic over the telephone she turned out to be an elegant lady in her sixties. She was wearing a fashionable yellow sweater and neatly pressed black trousers. Perhaps she had had time to dress up for him. She was in high-heeled shoes and had it not been for her restless eyes he would have thought her to be a woman at peace with herself, despite everything.

"You want to hear about Camilla," she said.

"Especially about her life more recently—if you know anything about it," he said.

"I remember when she came to us," she said, as if she had not been listening. "My husband Kjell thought we could make a contribution to society at the same time as adding to our little family. We had only one child, you see, our poor Moa. She was fourteen then, and quite lonely. We thought it would do her good if we took in a foster daughter of roughly the same age."

"Did you know what had happened in the Salander family?"

"We didn't have all the details, but we knew that it had been awful and traumatic and the mother was ill and the father had suffered serious burns. We were deeply moved and were expecting to meet a girl who had fallen apart, someone who would need an incredible amount of care and affection. But do you know what arrived?"

"Tell me."

"The most adorable girl we'd ever seen. It wasn't just that she was pretty. My goodness, you should have heard her talk. She was so wise and mature, and she told such heart-rending stories about how her mentally ill sister had terrorized the family. Yes, of course I now know how far from the truth that was. But how could we have doubted her then? Her eyes were bright with conviction, and when we said, 'How dreadful, poor you,' she answered, 'It wasn't easy, but I still love my sister, she's just sick and now she's getting treatment.' It sounded so grown up and full of empathy, and for a while it almost felt like she was the one taking care of us. Our whole family lit up, as if something glamorous had come into our lives and made everything bigger and more beautiful, and we blossomed. Moa blossomed most of all. She began to take care of her appearance, and quite soon she became more popular at school. There was nothing I wouldn't have done for Camilla right then. And Kjell, my husband, what can I say? He was a new person. He was smiling and laughing all the time, and we began to make love again, if you'll forgive my being so frank. Perhaps I should have started to worry even then. But it felt like everything had finally fallen into place for our family. For a while we were all happy, as everybody is who meets Camilla. They're happy to start with. Then . . . after some time with her you don't want to live anymore.

"Is it that bad?"

"It's horrific."

"So what happened?"

"A poison began to spread among us. Camilla slowly took control of our family. Looking back, it's impossible to tell when the party ended and the nightmare began. It had happened so gradually and imperceptibly that we woke up one day and realized everything was ruined: our trust, our sense of security, the very foundations of our life together. Moa's self-confidence plummeted. She lay awake at night weeping, saying she was ugly and horrible and didn't deserve to live. Only later did we find out that her savings account had been cleaned out. I still don't know how that happened, but I'm convinced Camilla blackmailed her. Blackmail came as naturally to her as breathing. She collected compromising information on people. For a long time I thought she was keeping a diary, but instead it was a catalogue of all the dirt she had on people close to her. And Kjell . . . the bastard . . . you know, I believed him when he said that he'd started having problems sleeping and needed to use the bed in the basement guest room. But that was an excuse to be with Camilla. Starting when she was sixteen, she would sneak in there at night and have perverted sex with him. I say perverted because I got wind of what was going on when I asked about the cuts on Kjell's chest. He didn't say anything then, of course. Just gave me some unconvincing explanation and somehow I managed to suppress my suspicions. But do you know what they did? In the end Kjell came clean: Camilla tied him up and cut him with a knife. He said she enjoyed it. Sometimes I even hoped it was true, strange though that may sound—I hoped she got something out of it and didn't only want to torture him, to destroy his life."

"Did she blackmail him too?"

"Oh yes, but I don't have the full story. He was so humiliated by Camilla that he wasn't willing to tell me the truth, even when all was lost. Kjell had been the rock in our family. If we lost our way while out driving, if there was a flood, if any of us fell ill, he was the calm, sensible one. It'll all be all right, he would say in his wonderful voice—I still fantasize about it. But after a few years with Camilla in the house he was a wreck. Hardly dared to cross the road, looked a hundred times to make sure it was safe. And he lost all motivation at work, just sat with his head hanging. One of his closest colleagues, Mats Hedlund, rang and told me in confidence that an enquiry had been set up to investigate whether Kjell had been selling company secrets. It sounded crazy. Kjell was the most honest man I've ever known. Plus if he'd sold anything, where was the money? We had less than ever. His bank account was stripped bare, same with our joint account."

"Forgive me for asking, but how did he die?"

"He hanged himself—without a word of explanation. I came home from work one day and found him swinging from the ceiling in the guest room, yes, the same room in which Camilla had had her fun with him. I was a well-paid CFO at the time, and chances are I would have had a great career to look forward to. But after that, Moa's and my world collapsed. I won't go into it any further. You want to know what happened to Camilla. But there was no end to the misery. Moa started cutting herself and practically stopped eating. One day she asked me if I thought she was scum. 'My God, darling,' I replied. 'How can you say something like that?' Then she told me it was Camilla. That Camilla had claimed every single person who had ever met Moa thought she was repulsive. I sought all the help I could: psycholo-

gists, doctors, wise friends, Prozac. But to no avail. One gloriously beautiful spring day, when the rest of Sweden was celebrating some ridiculous
triumph in the Eurovision Song Contest, Moa jumped from a ferry, and
my life ended with hers—that's how it felt. I no longer had the will to live
and spent a long time in hospital being treated for depression. But then . . .
I don't know . . . somehow the paralysis and grief turned to rage, and I felt
that I needed to understand. What had actually happened to our family?
What sort of evil had seeped in? I started to make enquiries about Camilla,
not because I wanted to see her again, not under any circumstances. But I
wanted to understand her, the same way a parent of a murder victim wants
to understand the murderer."

"What did you discover?"

"Nothing to begin with. She had covered her tracks—it was like chasing
a shadow, a phantom. I don't know how many tens of thousands of kronor
I spent on private detectives and other unreliable people who promised
to help me. I was getting nowhere, and it was driving me crazy. I became
fixated. I hardly slept, and none of my friends could bear to be with me
anymore. It was a terrible time. People thought I was being obsessive and
stubborn, maybe they still do, I don't know what Holger Palmgren told you.
But then . . ."

"Go on?"

"Your story on Zalachenko was published. Naturally the name meant
nothing to me, but I started to put two and two together. I read about his
Swedish identity, Karl Axel Bodin, and about his connection with Svavelsjö
Motorcycle Club, and then I remembered all the dreadful evenings towards
the end, after Camilla had turned her back on us. At the time I was often
woken up by the noise of motorbikes, and I could see those leather vests
with that awful emblem from my bedroom window. It didn't surprise me
that she mixed with those sorts of people. I no longer had any illusions
about her. But I had no idea that this was the world she came from—and
that she was expecting to take over her father's business interests."

"And did she?"

"Oh yes. In her own dirty world she fought for the rights of women—at
least for her own rights—and I know that it meant a lot to many of the girls
in the club, most of all to Kajsa Falk."

"Who is she?"

"A lovely looking sassy girl; her boyfriend was one of the leaders. She spent a lot of time at our home during that last year, and I remember liking her. She had big blue eyes with a slight squint, and a compassionate, vulnerable side behind her tough exterior. After reading your story I looked her up again. She didn't say a word about Camilla, though she was by no means unpleasant. I noticed that her style had changed: the biker girl had become a business woman. But she didn't talk about it. I thought I'd hit another dead end."

"But it wasn't?"

"No. About a year ago Kajsa looked me up of her own accord, and by then she had changed again. There was nothing reserved or cool about her. This time she was hounded and nervous. Not long after that she was found dead, shot at Stora Mossens sports centre in Bromma. When we met she told me there had been a dispute over the inheritance after Zalachenko's death. Camilla's twin sister, Lisbeth, came away more or less empty-handed—apparently she didn't even want the little that she got—while the majority of the assets fell to Zalachenko's two surviving sons in Berlin, and some to Camilla. She inherited part of the trafficking business you wrote about in your report, and that made my heart bleed. I doubt Camilla cared about those women, or felt any compassion for them. But still, she didn't want to have anything to do with those activities. She said to Kajsa that only losers bother with that sort of filth. She had a completely different, modern vision of what the organization should be doing, and after hard negotiation she got one of her half-brothers to buy her out. Then she disappeared to Moscow with her capital and some of the employees who wanted to follow her, Kajsa Falk among them."

"Do you know what sort of business she was setting up?"

"Kajsa never got enough of an insight to understand it, but we had our suspicions. I think it was to do with those trade secrets at Ericsson. By now I'm almost certain Camilla got Kjell to steal and sell something valuable, presumably by blackmailing him. I've also found out that in her first years with us she asked some computer geeks at school to hack into my computer. According to Kajsa, she was more or less obsessed with hacking. Not that she learned anything about it herself, not at all, but she was forever talking about the money one could make by accessing bank accounts and hacking servers and stealing information. She must have developed a business along those lines."

"That sounds possible."

"It was probably at a very high level. Camilla would never settle for anything less. According to Kajsa, she soon found her way into influential circles in Moscow, and among other things became the mistress of some rich, powerful member of the Duma—with him she began to forge connections with a strange crew of top engineers and criminals. Because she wound them round her little finger, she knew exactly where the weak point in the domestic economy was."

"And that was?"

"The fact that Russia is little more than a petrol station with a flag on top. They export oil and natural gas, but manufacture nothing worth mentioning. Russia needs advanced technology."

"She wanted to give them that?"

"At least that's what she pretended. But obviously she had her own agenda. I know that Kajsa was impressed by the way she built alliances and got herself political protection. She probably would have been loyal to Camilla forever if she hadn't become scared."

"What was she scared of?"

"Kajsa got to know a former elite soldier, a major I believe, and just lost her bearings. According to confidential information that Camilla had access to via her lover, the man had carried out a few shady operations for the Russian government. Among other things he had killed a well-known journalist, I presume you've heard of her, Irina Azarova. She'd taken a line against the government in various reports and books."

"Oh yes, truly a heroine. A horrible story."

"Absolutely. Something went wrong in the planning. Azarova was supposed to meet a critic of the regime in an apartment on a backstreet in a suburb southeast of Moscow, and according to the plan the major was supposed to shoot her as she came out. But no-one knew that the journalist's sister had developed pneumonia, and Irina had to look after two nieces aged eight and ten. As she and the girls walked out of the front entrance the major shot all three of them in the face. After that he fell into disgrace—

not that anybody was particularly bothered about the children, but public opinion was getting out of hand and there was a risk that the whole operation would be uncovered and turned against the government. I think the major was afraid he'd be made a scapegoat. He was also dealing with a load of personal problems at the same time. His wife took off, he was left alone with a teenage daughter, and I believe there was even a possibility of his being evicted from his apartment. From Camilla's perspective that was a perfect setup: a ruthless person whom she could use, and who found himself in a vulnerable situation."

"So she got him on board."

"Yes, they met. Kajsa was there too, and the strange thing was that she immediately took a liking to this man. He wasn't at all what she'd been expecting, nothing like the people she knew at Svavelsjö M.C., who were killers. He was very fit and had a brutal look about him, but he was also cultivated and polite, she said, somehow vulnerable and sensitive. Kajsa could tell that he felt terrible about shooting those children. He was a murderer, a man whose speciality had been torture during the war in Chechnya, but he still had his moral boundaries, and that's why she was so upset when Camilla got her claws into him—almost literally. She dragged her nails across his chest and hissed like a cat, 'I want you to kill for me.' Her words were charged with sexual tension and with the skill of the devil she awakened the man's sadism. The more gruesome his descriptions of his murders, the more excited she became. I'm not sure I understood it, but it scared Kajsa to death. Not the murderer himself—Camilla. Her beauty and allure managed to bring out the predator in him."

"You never reported this to the police?"

"I asked Kajsa over and over. I told her she needed protection. She said she already had it and she forbade me to talk to the police. I was stupid enough to listen to her. After her death I told the investigators what I'd heard, but I doubt they believed me. It was nothing but hearsay about a man without a name in another country. Camilla was nowhere to be found in any records, and I never discovered anything about her new identity. At any rate Kajsa's murder is still unsolved."

"I understand how painful this all must be for you," Blomkvist said.

"You do?"

"I think so," he said, and was about to rest a sympathetic hand on her arm.

He was brought up short by his mobile buzzing in his pocket. He hoped it was Zander. But it was Stefan Molde. It took Blomkvist a few seconds to identify him as the person at the NDRE who had been in touch with Linus Brandell.

"What's this about?" he said.

"A meeting with a senior civil servant, an American who's on his way to Sweden. He wants to see you as early as possible tomorrow morning at the Grand Hôtel."

Blomkvist made an apologetic gesture in Fru Dahlgren's direction.

"I have a tight schedule," he said, "and if I'm to meet anybody at the very least I want a name and an explanation."

"The man is Edwin Needham, and it's about someone using the handle Wasp, who is suspected of serious crimes."

Blomkvist felt a wave of panic.

"OK," he said. "What time?"

"Five o'clock tomorrow morning would work."

"You've got to be joking!"

"Regrettably there's nothing to joke about in all this. I suggest you be punctual. Mr. Needham will see you in his room. You'll have to leave your mobile at reception, and you'll be searched."

Blomkvist got to his feet and took his leave of Margareta Dahlgren.

# PART 3

# ASYMMETRIC PROBLEMS

NOVEMBER 23—DECEMBER 3

Sometimes it is easier to put together than to put asunder.

Nowadays computers can easily multiply prime numbers with millions of digits. Yet it is extremely complicated to reverse the process. Numbers with only a few hundred digits present huge problems.

Encryption algorithms like RSA take advantage of the difficulties involved in prime number factorization. Prime numbers have become secrecy's best friends.

# CHAPTER 25

# NOVEMBER 23–24

It had not taken long for Salander to identify the Roger whom August had been drawing. She had seen a younger version of the man on a website showing former actors from Revolutionsteatern in Vasastan. He was called Roger Winter. He had had a couple of major film roles at the beginning of his career, but lately had ended up in a backwater, and was now less well known than his wheelchair-bound brother Tobias, an outspoken professor of biology who was said to have distanced himself altogether from Roger these days.

Salander wrote down Roger Winter's address and then hacked into the supercomputer NSF MRI. She also opened the programme with which she was trying to construct a dynamic system for finding the elliptic curves which were most likely to do the job, and with as few iterations as possible. But whatever she tried, she was unable to get any closer to a solution. The NSA file remained impenetrable. In the end she went and looked in on August. She swore. The boy was awake, sitting up in bed writing something on a piece of paper, and as she came closer she could see that he was doing more prime number factorizations.

"It's no good. It's not getting us anywhere," she muttered, and when August began to rock back and forth hysterically once again she told him to pull himself together and go back to sleep.

It was late and she decided that she should rest for a while too. She took the bed next to his, but it was impossible to sleep. August tossed and turned and whimpered and in the end Salander decided to say something, to try to settle him. The best she could think of was, "Do you know about elliptic curves?"

Of course she got no answer. That did not deter her from giving as simple and clear an explanation as she could.

"Do you get it?" she said.

Still August did not reply.

"OK, then," she went on. "Take the number 3,034,267, for example. I know you can easily find its prime number factors. But it can also be done using elliptic curves. Let's take curve $y = x^3 - x + 4$ and point $P = (1:2)$ on that curve, for example."

She wrote the equation on a piece of paper on the bedside table. But August did not seem to be following at all. She thought about those autistic twins she had read up on. They had some mysterious way of identifying large prime numbers, yet could not solve the simplest equations. Perhaps August was like that too. Perhaps he was more of a calculating machine than a genuine mathematical talent, and in any case it didn't matter right now. Her bullet wound was aching again and she needed some sleep. She needed to drive out all her old childhood demons which had come to life again because of the boy.

It was past midnight by the time Blomkvist got home, and even though he was exhausted and had to get up at the crack of dawn he sat down at his computer and Googled Edwin Needham.

There were quite a few Edwin Needhams in the world, including a successful rugby player who had made an extraordinary comeback having had leukaemia. There was one Edwin Needham who seemed to be an expert on water purification, and another who was good at getting himself into society photographs and looking daft. But none of them seemed right for someone who could have been involved in cracking Wasp's identity and accusing her of criminal activity. There was an Edwin Needham who was a computer engineer with a PhD from MIT, and that was at least the right line of business, but not even he seemed to fit. He was now a senior executive at Safeline, a leading business in computer virus protection, and that company would certainly have an interest in hackers. But the statements made by this Ed, as he was known, were all about market share and new products. Nothing he said rated higher than the usual clichéd sales talk, not even when he got the chance to talk about his leisure pursuits: bowling and fly fishing. He loved nature, he said, he loved the competitive aspect . . . The most threatening thing he seemed capable of doing was boring people to death.

There was a picture of him, grinning and bare-chested, holding up a large salmon, the sort of snap which is a dime a dozen in fishing circles. It was as dull as everything else, and yet, gradually Blomkvist began to wonder whether the dullness might be the whole point. He read through the material again and this time it struck him as something concocted, a façade. Slowly but surely he came to the opposite conclusion: this was the man. You could smell the intelligence service a mile off, couldn't you? It felt like NSA or CIA.

Once again he looked at the photograph with the salmon, and this time he thought he saw something very different. He saw a tough guy putting on an act. There was something unwavering about the way he stood and grinned mockingly into the camera, at least that is what Blomkvist imagined, and again he thought of Salander. He wondered if he ought to tell her about this meeting. But there was no reason to worry her now, especially since he did not actually know anything, so instead he decided to go to bed. He needed to sleep for a few hours and have a clear head when he met Needham in the morning.

Pensively he brushed his teeth and undressed and climbed into bed. He realized he was more tired than he could have imagined and fell asleep in no time. He dreamed that he was being dragged under and almost drowned in the river Needham had been standing in. Afterwards he had a vague image of himself crawling along the riverbed surrounded by flopping, thrashing salmon. But he cannot have slept for long. He woke with a start and the growing conviction that he had overlooked something. His mobile was lying on the bedside table and his thoughts turned to Zander. The young man must have been on his mind all along.

Linda had double-locked the door. There was nothing odd about that—a woman in her situation had to take security precautions. It still made Zander feel uncomfortable, but he put that down to the apartment, or so he tried to convince himself. It was not at all what he had been expecting. Could this really be the home of one of her girlfriends?

The bed was broad but not especially long, and both the headboard and the footboard were made of shiny steel latticework. The bedspread was black, which made him think of a bier and he disliked the pictures on the walls—mostly framed photographs of men with weapons. There was a sterile, chilly feel to the whole place.

On the other hand he was probably just nervous and exaggerating everything, or looking for an excuse to get away. A man always wants to kill the thing he loves—hadn't Oscar Wilde said something like that? He looked at Linda. Never before had he seen such an extraordinarily beautiful woman, and now she was coming towards him in her tight blue dress which accentuated her figure. As if she had been reading his mind she said, "Would you rather go home, Andrei?"

"I do have quite a lot on my plate."

"I understand," she said, kissing him. "Then you must of course go and get on with your work."

"Maybe that would be best," he muttered as she pressed herself against him, kissing him with such force that he had no defence.

He responded to her kiss and put his hands on her hips, and she gave him a shove. She pushed him so hard that he staggered and fell backwards onto the bed, and for a moment he was scared. But then he looked at her. She was smiling as tenderly now as before and he thought: This was nothing more than a bit of rough play. She really wanted him, didn't she? She wanted to make love with him there and then, and he let her straddle his body, unbutton his shirt, and draw her fingernails over his stomach while her eyes shone with an intense glow and her large breasts heaved beneath her dress. Her mouth was open. A trickle of saliva ran down her chin and she whispered something he could not at first hear. "Now, Andrei," she whispered again. "Now!"

"Now?" he repeated uncertainly, and felt her tearing off his trousers. She was more brazen than he had expected, more accomplished and wildly lascivious than anybody he had met.

"Close your eyes and lie absolutely still," she said.

He obeyed and could hear her fiddling with something, he was not sure what. Then he heard a click and felt metal around his wrists, and realized he had been handcuffed. He was about to protest, he did not really go in for that sort of thing, but it all happened so fast. With lightning speed, as if she had experience, she locked his hands to the headboard. Then she bound his feet with rope and pulled tight.

"Gently," he said.

"Don't worry," but then she gave him a look he did not like and said something in a solemn voice. He must have misheard. "*What?*" he said.

"I'm going to cut you with a knife, Andrei," she said, and fixed a large piece of tape across his mouth.


Blomkvist was trying to tell himself not to worry. Why would anything have happened to Zander? No-one—apart from Berger and himself—knew that he was involved in protecting the whereabouts of Salander and the boy. They had been extremely careful with that piece of information, more careful than with any other part of the story. And yet . . . why had there been no word from him?

Zander was not someone who ignored his phone. On the contrary, he normally picked up on the first ring whenever Blomkvist called. But now there was no way of getting hold of him, and that was strange, wasn't it? Or maybe . . . again Blomkvist tried to convince himself that Zander was busy working and had lost track of time, or in the worst case had dropped his mobile. That was probably all it was. But still . . . after all these years Camilla had appeared out of nowhere. Something must be going on, and what was it Bublanski had said?

"*We live in a world in which paranoia is a requirement.*"

Blomkvist reached for the telephone on the bedside table and called Zander again. He got no answer this time either, so decided to wake their new staff member, Emil Grandén, who lived near Zander in Röda bergen in Vasastan. Grandén sounded less than enthusiastic but promised to go over to Zander's right away to see if he was there. Twenty minutes later he rang back. He had been banging on Zander's door for a while, he said, and he definitely wasn't at home.

Blomkvist got dressed and left his apartment, hurrying through a deserted and storm-lashed Södermalm district up to the magazine offices on Götgatan. With any luck, he thought, Zander would be lying asleep on the sofa. It would not be the first time he had nodded off at work and not heard the telephone. That would be the simple explanation. But Blomkvist felt more and more uneasy. When he opened the door and turned off the alarm he shivered, as if expecting to find a scene of devastation, but after a search of the premises he found no trace of anything untoward. All the information on his encrypted e-mail programme had been carefully deleted, just as they had agreed. It all looked as it should, but there was no Zander lying asleep on the office sofa, which was as shabby and empty as ever. For a short while Blomkvist sat there, lost in thought. Then he rang Grandén again.

"Emil," he said, "I'm sorry to harass you like this in the middle of the night. But this whole story has made me paranoid."

"I can understand that."

"I couldn't help hearing that you sounded a bit stressed when I was talking about Andrei. Is there anything you haven't told me?"

"Nothing you don't already know," Grandén said.

"What do you mean?"

"I mean that I've spoken to the Data Inspection Authority too."

"What do you mean, you too?"

"You mean you haven't—"

"No!" Blomkvist cut him short and heard Grandén's breathing at the other end of the line become laboured. There had been a terrible mistake.

"Out with it, Emil, and fast," he said.

"So . . ."

"Yes?"

"I had a call from a Lina Robertsson at the Data Inspection Authority. She said that you'd spoken and she agreed to raise the level of security on your computer, given the circumstances. Apparently the recommendations she'd given you were wrong and she was worried the protection would be insufficient. She said she wanted to get hold of the person who'd arranged the encryption for you ASAP."

"And what did you say?"

"That I knew nothing about it, except that I'd seen Andrei doing something at your computer."

"So you said she should get in touch with Andrei."

"I happened to be out at the time and told her that Andrei was probably still in the office. She could ring him there, I said. That was all."

"Jesus, Emil."

"She sounded really—"

"I don't care how she sounded. I just hope you told Andrei about the call."

"Maybe not right away. I'm pretty snowed under at the moment, like all of us."

"But you told him later."

"Well, he left the office before I got a chance to say anything."

"So you called him instead."

"Absolutely, several times. But . . ."

"Yes?"

"He didn't answer."

"OK," Blomkvist said, his voice ice-cold.

He hung up and dialled Bublanski's number. He had to try twice before the chief inspector came to the telephone. Blomkvist had no choice but to tell him the whole story—except for Salander and August's location.

Then he called Berger.


Salander had fallen asleep, but she was still ready for action. She was in her clothes, with her leather jacket and her boots on. She kept waking up, either because of the howling storm or because August was moaning in his sleep. But each time she dozed off, she had short, strangely realistic dreams.

Now she was dreaming about her father beating her mother, and she could feel that fierce old rage from her childhood. She felt it so keenly that it woke her up again. It was 3:45 a.m. and those scraps of paper on which she and August had written their numbers were still lying on the bedside table. Outside, snow was falling. But the storm seemed to have calmed and nothing unusual could be heard, just the wind rustling through the trees.

She felt uneasy, and at first she thought it was the dream lying like a fine mesh over the room. Then she shuddered. The bed next to her was empty—August was gone. She shot out of bed without making a sound, grabbed her Beretta from the bag on the floor, and crept into the large room next to the terrace.

The next moment she breathed a sigh of relief. August was sitting at the table busy with something. Without wanting to disturb him she leaned over his shoulder and saw that he was not writing new prime number factorizations, or drawing fresh scenes of abuse. He was sketching chess squares reflected in the mirrors of a wardrobe, and above them could be made out a threatening figure with his hand outstretched. The killer was taking shape. Salander smiled, and then she withdrew.

Back in the bedroom she sat on the bed, removed her pullover and the bandage, and inspected the bullet wound. It didn't look good, and she still felt weak. She swallowed another couple of antibiotic pills and tried to rest. She may even have gone back to sleep for a few moments. She was aware of a vague sensation that she had seen both Zala and Camilla in her dream, and the next second she became aware of a presence, though she had no idea what. A bird flapped its wings outside. She could hear August's laboured breathing in the kitchen. She was just about to get up when a scream pierced the air.

By the time Blomkvist left the office in the early morning hours to take a taxi to the Grand Hôtel, he still had no news of Zander. He tried again to persuade himself that he had been over-reacting, that any moment now his colleague would call from some friend's place. But the worry would not go away. He was vaguely aware that it had started snowing again, and that a woman's shoe had been left lying on the sidewalk. He took out his Samsung and called Salander on the RedPhone app.

Salander did not pick up, and that did not make him any calmer. He tried once more and sent a text from his Threema app: <Camilla's after you. Leave now!> Then he caught sight of a taxi coming down from Hökens gata. The driver gave a start when he saw him—at that moment Blomkvist looked dangerously determined. It did not help that he failed to respond to the driver's attempts to chat. He just sat back there in the darkness, his eyes bright with worry.

Stockholm was more or less deserted. The storm had abated but there were still white-crested waves on the water. Blomkvist looked across to the Grand Hôtel on the other side and wondered if he should forget about the meeting with Mr. Needham and drive straight out to Salander instead, or at least arrange for a police car to swing by. No, he couldn't do that without warning her. Another leak would be disastrous. He opened the Threema app again and tapped in:

```
<Shall I get help?>
```

No answer. Of course there was no answer. He paid the fare and climbed out of the taxi lost in thought. By the time he was pushing through the revolving doors of the hotel it was 4:20 in the morning—he was forty minutes early. He had never been forty minutes early for anything. But he was burning up inside and, before going to the reception desk to hand in his mobiles, he called Berger. He told her to try to get hold of Salander and to keep in touch with the police.

"If you hear anything, call the Grand Hôtel and ask for Mr. Needham's room."

"And who's he?"

"Someone who wants to meet me."

"At this time of day?"

Needham was in room 654. The door opened and there stood a man reeking of sweat and rage. There was about as much resemblance to the figure in the fishing photograph as there would be between a hungover dictator and his stylized statue. Needham had a drink in his hand and looked grim, unkempt, and a little bit like a bulldog.

"Mr. Needham," Blomkvist said.

"Ed," Needham said. "I'm sorry to haul you over here at this ungodly hour, but it's urgent."

"So it would seem," Blomkvist said drily.

"Do you have any idea what I want to talk to you about?"

Blomkvist shook his head and sat down on a sofa. There was a bottle of gin and some small bottles of Schweppes tonic on the desk next to it.

"No, why would you?" Needham said. "On the other hand it's impossible to know with guys like you. I've checked you out. You should know that I hate to flatter people—it leaves a bad taste in my mouth—but you're pretty outstanding in your profession, aren't you?"

Blomkvist gave a forced smile.

"Can we just get to the point?" he said.

"Just relax, I'll be crystal clear. I assume you know where I work."

"Not exactly," he answered truthfully.

"In Puzzle Palace, SIGINT City. I work for the world's spittoon."

"The NSA."

"Damn right. Do you have any idea how fucking insane you have to be to mess with us, Mikael Blomkvist, do you?"

"I have a pretty good idea," he said.

"And do you know where I think your girlfriend really belongs?"

"No."

"She belongs behind bars. For life!"

Blomkvist gave what he hoped was a calm, composed little smile. But in fact his mind was spinning. Did Salander hack the NSA? The mere thought terrified him. Not only was she in hiding, with killers on the hunt for her. Was she also going to have the entire U.S. intelligence services descend on her? It sounded . . . well, how did it sound? It sounded totally off the wall.

One of Salander's abiding characteristics was that she never did anything without first carefully analyzing the potential consequences. She did not follow impulses or whims and therefore he could not imagine she would take such an idiotic risk if there was the slightest chance of being found out. Sometimes she put herself in harm's way, that was true, but there was always a balance between costs and benefits. He refused to believe that she had gotten herself in to the NSA, only to allow herself to be outwitted by the splenetic bulldog standing in front of him.

"I think you're jumping to conclusions," he said.

"Dream on, dude. But you might be able to save your girlfriend's skin if you promise to help me with one or two things."

"I'm listening," he said.

"Peachy. Let me begin by asking for a guarantee that you won't quote me as your source."

Blomkvist looked at him in surprise. He had not expected that.

"Are you some kind of whistle blower?"

"God help me, no. I'm a loyal old bloodhound."

"But you're not acting officially on behalf of the NSA."

"You could say that right now I have my own agenda. Sort of doing my own thing. Well, how about it?"

"I won't quote you."

"Great. I also want to make sure we agree that what I'm going to tell you now will stay between us. You might be wondering why the hell I'm telling a fantastic story to an investigative journalist, only to have him keep his trap shut."

"Good question."

"I have my reasons. And I trust you, don't ask me why. I'm betting that you want to protect your girlfriend, and you think the real story is else-where. Maybe I'll even help you with that, if you're prepared to cooperate."

"That remains to be seen," Blomkvist said stiffly.

"Well, a few days ago we had a data breach on our intranet, our NSANet. You know about that, don't you?"

"More or less."

"NSANet was created after 9/11, to improve coordination between our own intelligence services and those in other English-speaking countries—known as the Five Eyes. It's a closed system, with its own routers, portals, and bridges, and it's completely separate from the rest of the Internet. We administer our signals intelligence from there via satellite and fibre optic cables and that's also where we have our big databases and store classified analyses and reports: from Moray-rated documents, the least sensitive, all the way up to Umbra Ultra Top Secret, which even the President of the United States isn't allowed to see. The system is run out of Texas, which by the way is idiotic. But it's still my baby. Let me tell you, Mikael Blom-kvist, I worked my ass off. Hammered away at it day and night so that no fucker could misuse it, never mind hack it. Every single little anomaly sets my alarm bells ringing, plus there's a whole staff of independent experts monitoring the system. These days you can't do a goddamn thing online without leaving footprints. At least that's the theory. Everything is logged and analyzed. You shouldn't be able to touch a single key without triggering a notification. But . . ."

"Someone did."

"Yes, and maybe I could have made my peace with it. There are always weak spots; we can always do better. Weak spots keep us on our toes. But it wasn't just the fact that she managed to get in. It was how she did it. She forced our server and created an advanced bridge, and got into the intranet via one of our systems administrators. That alone was a damn masterpiece. But that wasn't all: then the bitch turned herself into a ghost user."

"A what?"

"A ghost. She flew around in there without anyone noticing."

"Your alarm bells didn't go off?"

"That damn genius introduced a Trojan unlike anything else we knew, because otherwise our system would have identified it right away. The malware then kept upgrading her status. She got more and more access and soaked up highly classified passwords and codes and started to link and match records and databases, and suddenly—bingo!"

"Bingo what?"

"She found what she was looking for, and then she stopped wanting to be invisible. She wanted to show us what she'd found, and only then did my alarm bells go off: exactly when she wanted them to."

"And what did she find?"

"She found our hypocrisy, Mikael, our double-dealing, and that's why I'm sitting here with you and not on my fat ass in Maryland, sending the Marines after her. She was like a thief breaking into a house just to point out that it was already full of stolen goods, and the minute we found that out she became truly dangerous—so dangerous that some of our senior people wanted to let her off."

"But not you."

"Not me. I wanted to tie her to a lamppost and flay her alive. But I had no choice except to give up my pursuit and that, Mikael, seriously pissed me off. I may look calm now, but you should have seen me . . . Jesus!"

"You were hopping mad."

"Damn right. And that's why I had you come here at this godforsaken hour. I need to get hold of Wasp before she flees the country."

"Why would she run?"

"Because she went from one crazy thing to the next, didn't she?"

"I don't know."

"I think you do."

"What makes you so sure she's your hacker in the first place?"

"That, Mikael, is what I'm going to lay on you now."

But he got no further.

The room telephone rang and Needham picked up right away. It was reception looking for Mikael Blomkvist, and Needham handed him the receiver. He soon gathered that the journalist had been given some alarming news, so it was no surprise when the Swede muttered a confused apology and ran out of the room. But Needham would not let him get away that easily. He grabbed his coat and chased after him.

Blomkvist was racing down the corridor like a sprinter. Needham did not know what was going on, but if it had something to do with the Wasp/Balder story, he wanted to be there. He had some trouble keeping up—the journalist was in too much of a hurry to wait for the lift and instead hurtled down the stairs. By the time Needham reached the ground floor, panting, Blomkvist had already retrieved his mobiles and was engrossed in another conversation while he ran on towards the revolving doors and out into the street.

"What's happening?" Needham said as the journalist ended his call and tried to hail a taxi further down the street.

"Problems!" Blomkvist said.

"I can drive you."

"Like hell you can. You've been drinking."

"At least we can take my car."

Blomkvist slowed his pace and turned to Needham.

"What is it you want?"

"I want us to help each other."

"You'll have to catch your hacker on your own."

"I no longer have the authority to catch anybody."

"OK, so where's the car?"

As they ran to Needham's rental car parked over by the Nationalmuseum, Blomkvist hurriedly explained that they were heading out to the Stockholm archipelago, towards Ingarö. He would get directions on the way and was not planning to observe any speed limits.

# CHAPTER 26

# NOVEMBER 24—MORNING

August screamed, and in the same instant Salander heard rapid footsteps along the side of the house. She grabbed her pistol and jumped to her feet. She felt terrible but ignored it.

As she rushed over to the doorway she saw a large man appear on the terrace. She thought she had a split-second advantage, but the figure did not stop to open the glass doors. He charged straight through them with his weapon drawn and shot at the boy.

Salander returned fire, or perhaps she had already done so, she did not know. She was not even conscious of the moment in which she started running towards the man. She only knew that she had crashed into him with a numbing force and now lay on top of him right by the round table where the boy had been sitting moments before. Without hesitation she headbutted the man.

The contact was so violent that her skull rang, and she swayed as she got to her feet. The room was spinning and there was blood on her shirt. Had she been hit again? She had no time to think. Where was August? No-one at the table, only pencils and drawings, crayons, prime number calculations. Where the hell was he? She heard a whimpering by the refrigerator and yes, there he was, sitting and shaking, his knees drawn up to his chest. He must have had time to throw himself to the floor.

Salander was about to rush over to him when she heard new, worrying sounds from outside, voices and branches snapping. Others were approaching, there was no time to lose. In a blinding flash she visualized the surrounding terrain and raced over to August. "Come on!" she said. August did not budge. Salander picked him up, her face twisted in pain.

Every movement hurt. But they had to get away and August must have understood that too because he wriggled out of her grasp and ran alongside her. She sprang over to the table, grabbed her computer, and made for the terrace, past the man on the floor who raised himself groggily and tried to catch hold of August's leg.

Salander considered killing him. Instead she kicked him hard in the throat and stomach and threw away his weapon. Then she ran across the terrace with August and down towards the steep rocky slope. But suddenly she thought of the drawing. She had not seen how much progress August had made. Should she turn around? No, the others would be here any moment. They had to get away. But still . . . the drawing was also a weapon, and the cause of all this madness. She left August with her computer on the rock ledge she had identified the night before. She then launched herself back up the slope and into the house and looked on the table, and at first she could not see it. Drawings of that bastard Westman were everywhere, and rows of prime numbers.

But there—there it was, and above the chess squares and the mirrors there was now a pale figure with a sharply defined scar on his forehead, which Salander by now recognized only too well. It was the same man who was lying on the floor in front of her, moaning. She whipped out her mobile, took a photo and sent it to Bublanski and Modig. She had even scribbled a line at the top of the paper. But a second later she realized that was a mistake.

They were surrounded.

Salander had sent the same word to Blomkvist's Samsung as she had to Berger: CRISIS. It hardly left room for misunderstanding, not coming from Salander. However he looked at it, it could only mean that she and August had been discovered, and at worst they were under attack even now. He floored the accelerator as he passed Stadsgårdskajen and emerged onto the Värmdö road.

He was driving a new silver Audi A8, with Needham sitting next to him. Needham looked grim, and every now and then tapped something into his mobile. Blomkvist was not sure why he had allowed him to come along. Maybe he wanted to discover what the man had on Salander, or no, there was something else as well. Maybe Needham could even be useful. In any case he could hardly make the situation worse. The police had by now been alerted, but he doubted they would be able to assemble a unit quickly enough—especially as they were sceptical about the lack of information. Berger had been the focal point, trying to keep them all in contact with each other, and she was the only one who knew the way. He needed all the help he could get.

He was approaching Danviksbron. Needham said something, he did not hear what. His thoughts were elsewhere. He thought of Zander—what had they done to him? Why the hell had he not come along for a beer? Blomkvist tried his number again. He tried calling Salander too. But nobody answered.

"Do you want me to tell you what we have on your hacker?" Needham said.

"Yes . . . why not."

But they did not get anywhere this time either. Blomkvist's mobile rang. Bublanski.

"I hope you realize that you and I are going to have a lot to talk about later, and you can count on there being legal consequences."

"I understand."

"But for now I'm calling to give you some information. We know that Lisbeth Salander was alive at 4:22. Was that before or after she texted you?"

"Before, just before."

"OK."

"How can you be so specific about the time?"

"She sent us something extremely interesting. A drawing. I have to say, Mikael, it exceeded our hopes."

"So she was able to get the boy to draw."

"Oh yes. I have no idea what technical issues, if any, might arise in terms of admissibility of evidence or what objections a clever defence lawyer might raise. But as far as I'm concerned there's no doubt this is the murderer. The drawing is incredibly vivid, with that extraordinary mathematical precision again. In fact there's also an equation written at the bottom of the page, I have no idea if it's relevant to the case. But I sent the drawing to Interpol. If the man is anywhere in their database, he's toast."

"Are you going to send it to the press as well?"

"We're debating that."

"When will you be at the scene?"

"As soon as possible . . . hold on a second."

Blomkvist could hear another telephone ringing in the background, and for a minute or so Bublanski was gone on another call. When he returned he said briefly:

"We've had reports of gunfire out there. It doesn't sound good."

Blomkvist took a deep breath.

"Any news on Andrei?" he said.

"We've traced his mobile signal to a base station in Gamla Stan, but no further. We've had no signal at all for a while now, as if the mobile had been smashed or just stopped working."

Blomkvist drove even faster. Fortunately the reads were empty at that hour. At first he said very little to Needham, just a brief account of what was going on, but in the end he could not hold back. He needed something else to think about.

"Will you tell me what you've found out?"

"About Wasp? For a long time, zip. We were convinced we'd reached the end of the line," Needham said. "We'd left no stone unturned, and still got nowhere. In a way it made sense."

"How so?"

"A hacker capable of a breach like that should also be able to cover all tracks. I realized we wouldn't get anywhere by conventional means. So I skipped the forensic bullshit and went straight for the big question: Who had the chops to pull this off? That question was our best hope. There's hardly anyone out there with that level of ability. In that sense, you could say that the hacker's skill worked against them. Plus, we had analyzed the rootkit itself, and . . ."

Needham looked down at his mobile.

"Yes?"

"It had artistic qualities. Personal style, you might say. Now we just had to find its author, and so we started to send posts to the hacker community. There was one name, one handle, which came up time after time. Can you guess which one?"

"Maybe."

"It was Wasp. Sure, there were other names, but Wasp stood out. I ended up hearing so much mythical bullshit about this person that I was dying to crack their identity. We read every word Wasp had written online, studied every operation that had Wasp's signature on it. Soon we were certain that Wasp was a woman, and we guessed that she was Swedish. Several of the early posts were written in Swedish, which isn't much to go on, but since there was a Swedish connection in the organization she was tracking, and Frans Balder was Swedish, it was at least a place to start. I got in touch with the NDRE, and they searched their records, and then in fact . . ."

"What?"

"They had a breakthrough. Many years earlier they investigated a hacker operation that used that very handle, Wasp. It was so long ago that Wasp wasn't even particularly good at encryption yet."

"What happened?"

"Wasp had been looking for data on individuals who'd defected from other countries' intelligence services, and that was enough to trigger the NDRE's warning system. Their investigation led them to a psychiatric clinic for children in Uppsala, to a computer belonging to the head physician there, a man named Teleborian. Apparently he'd done some work for the Swedish Security Police, so he was above suspicion. Instead the NDRE concentrated on some mental health nurses who were targeted because they were . . . well, to be blunt about it, immigrants. It was such a stupid strategy. Anyway, nothing came of it."

"I can imagine."

"So I asked a guy at the NDRE to send over all the old material, and we sifted through it with a different mindset. You know, you don't have to be big and fat and shave in the mornings to be a good hacker. I've met twelve- and thirteen-year-olds who are crazy good. It was obvious to me that we should look at every child in the clinic at the time. I had three of my guys investigate each one of them, inside and out, and do you know what we found? One of the children was the daughter of former spy and arch-villain Zalachenko, who was known to our colleagues at the CIA. Then everything got really interesting. As you probably know there are some overlaps between the network the hacker was investigating and Zalachenko's old crime syndicate."

"That doesn't necessarily mean it was Wasp who hacked you."

"Of course not. But we took a closer look at this girl, and what can I say? She has an interesting background, doesn't she? A lot of information about her in the public record has been mysteriously deleted, but we still found more than enough and ... I don't know, I could be wrong, but I get the feeling we're on the right track. Mikael, you don't know shit about me. But I know what it's like for a kid to see extreme violence at close quarters. And I know what it's like when society doesn't lift a finger to punish the guilty. It hurts like hell, and I'm not at all surprised that most children who experience it go under. They turn into destructive bastards themselves."

"Yes, unfortunately."

"But just a few grow to be as strong as bears, Mikael, and they stand up and fight back. Wasp was one of those, wasn't she?"

Blomkvist nodded pensively and pressed down on the accelerator a little more.

"They locked her up and kept trying to break her. But she kept coming back, and do you know what I think?"

"No."

"She got stronger each time. She became positively lethal. I bet she hasn't forgotten a single thing that happened. It's all etched into her, isn't it? And maybe that's at the bottom of this whole goddamn mess."

"You still haven't told me what you want," Blomkvist said bluntly.

"I want what Wasp wants. I want to set some things right."

"And get your hands on the hacker."

"I want to meet her and give her a piece of my mind and plug every last damn hole in our security. But above all I want to retaliate against certain people who wouldn't let me finish my job because Wasp exposed them. I have reason to believe you're going to help me with that."

"Why?"

"Because you're a good reporter. Good reporters don't want dirty secrets to go on being dirty secrets."

"And Wasp?"

"Wasp is going to get a chance to do her worst. You're going to help me with that too."

"Or else?"

"Or else I'll find a way of putting her inside, and making her life hell again, I swear."

"But for now all you want to do is talk to her?"

"No fucker is going to be allowed to hack into my system again, so I need to understand exactly how she did it. I want you to give her that message. I'm prepared to let your girlfriend go free if she'll sit down with me and explain."

"I'll tell her. Let's just hope . . ."

"That she's still alive," Needham said. They turned left at high speed in the direction of Ingaröstrand.


It was rare for Holtser to get things so wrong.

He had this romantic delusion that you could tell from a distance if a man was likely to succeed in close combat. That was why he had not been surprised when Kira's attempted seduction of Blomkvist had failed. Orlov and Bogdanov had been completely confident. But Holtser had had his doubts having seen the journalist for only one giddy second in Saltsjöbaden. Blomkvist looked like a problem. He looked like a man who could not be fooled or broken so easily.

With the younger journalist it was different. He looked like the archetypal weakling, yet nothing could have been further from the truth. Zander had resisted for longer than anyone Holtser had ever tortured. Despite excruciating pain he had refused to break. His eyes shone with a grim determination which seemed buttressed by a higher principle, and at one point Holtser thought they would have to give up, that Zander would rather endure any suffering than talk. It was not until Kira solemnly promised that both Berger and Blomkvist from *Millennium* would be made to suffer the same that Zander finally caved.

By then it was 3:30 in the morning. Holtser knew that he would always remember the moment. Snow was falling over the skylights. The young man's face was dried out and hollow-eyed. Blood had splashed up from his chest and flecked his mouth and cheeks. His lips, which for a long time had been covered with tape, were split and oozing. He was a wreck, but still you could tell that he was a beautiful young man.

Holtser thought of Olga—how would she have felt about him? Wasn't this journalist just the kind of educated man she liked, someone who fights injustice, takes the side of beggars and outcasts? He thought about that, and about other things in his own life. After that he made the sign of the cross, the Russian cross, where one way leads to heaven and the other to hell, and then he glanced over at Kira.

She was lovelier than ever. Her eyes burned with light. She was sitting on a stool by the bed wearing an elegant blue dress—which had largely escaped the bloodstains—and said something in Swedish to Zander, something which sounded soft and tender. Then she took him by the hand. He gripped hers in return. He had nowhere else to turn for comfort. The wind howled outside in the alley. Kira nodded and smiled at Holtser. Snowflakes fell on the window ledge.

Afterwards they were sitting together in a Land Rover on the way out to Ingarö. Holtser felt empty, and was not happy with the way things were going. But there was no getting away from the fact that his own mistake had led them there, so he sat quietly, listening to Kira. She was strangely excited and spoke with searing hatred of the woman they were about to confront. Holtser did not think it was a good sign, and if he could have brought himself to do so he would have urged her to turn back and get the hell out of the country.

But he said nothing as they drove on in the darkness. Kira's sparkling, cold eyes frightened him, but he pushed away the thought.

He had to at least give her credit: she had been amazingly quick to put two and two together. Not only had she worked out who had hurtled in to save the boy on Sveavägen. She had also guessed who would know where the boy and the woman had disappeared to, and the person she came up with was none other than Mikael Blomkvist. They were baffled by her reasoning. Why would a reputable Swedish journalist harbour a person who appeared from nowhere and abducted a child from a crime scene? But the more they examined the theory, the more it held together. Not only did the woman—whose name was Lisbeth Salander—have close ties to the reporter, but something also happened at the *Millennium* offices.

After the murder in Saltsjöbaden, Bogdanov had hacked into Blomkvist's computer to try to find out why Balder had summoned him to his home in the middle of the night. Getting access to his e-mail had been easy enough. But that now stopped. When was the last time it had been impossible for Bogdanov to read someone's e-mails? Never, so far as Holtser was aware. Blomkvist had suddenly become much more careful—right after the woman and the boy disappeared from Sveavägen.

That in itself was no guarantee that the journalist knew where they now were. But as time went on there were more indications that the theory might be right, and in any case Kira did not seem to need ironclad evidence. She wanted to go for Blomkvist. Or, if not him, then someone else at the magazine. More than anything she was obsessive in her determination to track down the woman and the child.

Maybe Holtser could not understand the subtleties of Kira's motives. But it was for his benefit that they were going to do away with the boy. Kira chose to take significant risks for Holtser, and he was grateful, he really was, even though now in the car he felt uneasy.

He tried to draw strength from thinking about Olga. Whatever happened, she must not wake up and see a drawing of her father on all the front pages. He tried to reassure himself that the hardest part was behind them. Assuming Zander had given them the right address, the job should be straightforward.

They were three heavily armed men, four if you counted Bogdanov, who spent most of the time staring at his computer as usual. The team consisted of Holtser, Bogdanov, Orlov, and Dennis Wilton, a gangster who had been a member of Svavelsjö M.C. but now worked for Kira. Four men against one woman who was probably asleep, and was also protecting a child. It shouldn't be a problem, not at all. But Kira was almost manic:

"Don't underestimate Salander!"

She said it so many times that even Bogdanov, who always agreed with everything she said, began to get irritated. Of course Holtser had seen how fit and fast and fearless the woman had been on Sveavägen. But the way Kira described her, she must be some kind of superwoman. It was ridiculous. Holtser had never met a woman who could remotely match him—or even Orlov—in combat. Still, he promised to be careful. First he would go up and check out the terrain and prepare a strategy. They would not be drawn into a trap. He stressed this many times over, and when finally they arrived at an inlet next to a rocky slope and a jetty he took command. He told the others to get ready in the shelter of the car while he went ahead to locate the house.

Holtser liked early mornings. He liked the silence and the feeling of transition in the air. Now he was walking along, leaning forward and listening. It was reassuringly dark—no lights were on. He left the jetty behind him and came to a wooden fence with a rickety gate, next to an overgrown prickly bush. He opened the gate and started to climb steep wooden stairs holding the handrail on the right.

Soon he was able to make out the house above. It lay hidden behind pine trees and aspens and was only a dark outline, with a terrace on the south side. On the terrace were some glass doors which they would have no trouble breaking through. At first he saw no major difficulties. He was moving almost soundlessly and for a moment he considered finishing off the job himself. Maybe it was even his moral responsibility. It should be no more difficult than other jobs he had done, on the contrary. There were no policemen this time, no guards, nor any sign of an alarm system. True, he did not have his assault rifle with him, but then there was no need for it. The rifle was excessive, the result of Kira's heated imagination. He had his pistol, his Remington, and that was more than enough.

Suddenly—without his usual careful planning—he started moving along the side of the house, up to the terrace and the glass doors. Then he stiffened, without at first knowing why—it could have been a sound, a movement, a danger he had only half sensed. He looked up at the rectangular window above him, but from his position he could not see into it. He kept still, now less and less sure of himself. Could it be the wrong house?

He resolved to get closer and peer in, and then . . . he was transfixed in the darkness. He was being observed. Those eyes which once before had looked at him were now staring glassily in his direction. That is when he should have reacted. He should have sprinted around to the terrace, gone straight in, and shot the boy. But again he hesitated. He could not bring himself to draw his weapon. Faced with that look, he was lost.

The boy let out a shrill scream which seemed to set the window vibrating, and only then did Holtser tear himself out of his paralysis and race up to the terrace. Without a moment's reflection he hurtled straight through the glass doors and fired with what he thought was great precision, but he never found out whether he hit his target.

An explosive shadowlike figure came at him with such speed that he hardly had time to brace himself. He knew that he fired another shot and that someone shot back. In the next instant he slammed onto the floor with his full weight, a young woman tumbling over him with a rage in her eyes that was beyond anything he had ever seen. He reacted instinctively and tried to shoot again. But the woman was like a wild animal. She threw her head back and . . . Crack!

When he came to he had a taste of blood in his mouth and his pullover was sticky and wet. He must have been hit. Just then the boy and the woman passed him, and he tried to grab hold of the boy's leg. At least he thought he did. But suddenly he was gasping for breath.

He no longer understood what was going on. Except that he was beaten, and by whom? By a woman. That insight became a part of his pain as he lay on the floor amid broken glass and his own blood, breathing heavily, his eyes shut. He hoped it would be over soon. When he opened his eyes again he was surprised to see the woman still there. Had she not just left? No, she was standing by the table, he could see her thin boyish legs. He tried his utmost to get up. He looked for his weapon, and at the same time caught a glimpse of Orlov through the window. He moved once more to attack the woman.

But before he could do anything the woman grabbed some papers and stormed out. From the terrace she threw herself headlong into the trees. Shots resounded in the dark and he muttered to himself, "Kill the bastards." But it was all he could do to get to his feet, and he cast a dull glance at the table in front of him.

There was a mass of crayons and paper which he looked at without really focusing. Then it was as if a claw took hold of his heart. He saw an evil demon with a pale face raising his hand to kill. It took a second or so for him to realize that the demon was himself, and he shuddered. Yet he could not take his eyes off the image.

Only then did he notice something scribbled at the top:

*Mailed to police 4:22.*

# CHAPTER 27

# NOVEMBER 24—MORNING

When Aram Barzani of the Rapid Response Unit made his way into Gabri-ella Grane's house at 4:52 he saw a large man dressed in black spread-eagled on the floor next to the round table.

He approached cautiously. The house seemed to have been abandoned, but he was not taking any risks. There were recent reports of a fierce gun-fight up at the house and he could hear the excited voices of his colleagues outside on the steep rock slope.

"Here!" they shouted. "Here!"

Barzani did not understand what was going on, and for a moment he hesitated. Should he go to them? He decided to first see what condition the man on the floor was in. Broken glass and blood lay all around, and the table was strewn with torn-up pieces of paper and crushed crayons. The man on the ground was crossing himself feebly. He was mumbling some-thing. Probably a prayer. It sounded Russian, Barzani caught the word "Olga." He told the man that a medical team was on its way.

"They were sisters," the man said in English.

But it sounded so confused that Barzani attached no importance to it. Instead he searched through the man's clothes, made sure that he was unarmed, and thought he had probably been shot in the stomach. His pull-over was soaked in blood, and he looked alarmingly pale. Barzani asked what had happened. He got no reply, not at first. Then the man gasped out another strange sentence.

"My soul was captured in a drawing," he said, and seemed to be about to lose consciousness.

Barzani stayed for a few minutes to watch him, but when he heard from the ambulance crew he left the man and went down to the rocky slope. He wanted to discover what his colleagues had been shouting about. The snow was still falling and it was icy underfoot. Down by the water voices could be heard and the sound of more cars arriving. It was still dark and hard to see and there were many uneven rocks and straggly pines. The landscape was dramatic and steep. It could not have been easy to fight in this terrain and Barzani was gripped with foreboding. He noticed that it had become strangely quiet.

But his team members were not far away behind an overgrown aspen. He felt afraid—a rare occurrence for him—when he saw them staring down at the ground. What had they seen? Was the autistic boy dead?

He walked over slowly, thinking about his own boys, six and nine now. They were crazy about football—did nothing else, talked about nothing else. Björn and Anders. He and Dilvan had given them Swedish names because they had thought it would make their lives easier. What kind of people come out here to kill a child? He was gripped by a sudden fury. But in the next moment he breathed a sigh of relief.

There was no boy there, but two men lying on the ground, apparently both shot in the stomach. One of them—a brutal-looking type with pock-marked skin and a stubby boxer's nose—tried to get up but was pushed down again. His face betrayed his humiliation and his right hand was shaking with pain or rage. The other man, who was wearing a leather jacket and had his hair in a ponytail, seemed in worse shape. He lay still and stared in shock at the dark sky.

"No evidence of the child?" Barzani said.

"Nothing," his colleague Klas Lang answered.

"And the woman?"

"No sign of her."

Barzani was not sure if this was good news and he asked a few more questions. But no-one knew what had happened. The only certainty was that two automatic weapons, Barrett REC7s, had been found thirty or forty yards away, towards the jetty. They were assumed to belong to the men, but when asked how they had ended up there, the man with the pock-marked face spat out an incomprehensible answer.

Barzani and his colleagues spent the next fifteen minutes combing the terrain. All they could find were further signs of combat. More and more people began to arrive on the scene: ambulance crew, Detective Sergeant Modig, two or three crime scene technicians, a succession of regular policemen, and the journalist Mikael Blomkvist, who was accompanied by a massive American with a crew cut who immediately commanded everyone's respect. At 5:25 they were informed that a witness was waiting to be interviewed down by the seashore and parking area. The man wanted to be addressed as K.G. He was actually called Karl-Gustav Matzon. He had recently bought a new-build on the other side of the water. According to Lang, he needed to be taken with a grain of salt: "The old boy has a very vivid imagination."

Modig and Holmberg were standing in the parking area, trying to make sense of what had happened. The picture so far was fragmented and they were hoping that the witness K.G. Matzon would bring a measure of clarity to the night.

But when they saw him coming towards them along the shoreline, that seemed less and less likely. K.G. Matzon was resplendent in a Tyrolean hat, green checked trousers, and a red Canada Goose jacket and he was sporting an absurd twirly moustache. He looked as if he were trying to be funny.

"K.G. Matzon?" Modig asked.

"The very same," he said, and without any prompting—maybe he realized that his credibility needed a boost—he explained that he ran True Crimes, a publishing house which produced books on notable crimes.

"Excellent. But right now we'd like a factual account, not some sales pitch for a forthcoming book," Modig said, to be on the safe side.

Matzon said of course he understood. He was after all a "respectable person." He had woken up at a ridiculous hour, he said, and lain there listening to "the silence and the calm." But just before 4:30 he heard something which he immediately recognized as a pistol shot, so he quickly got dressed and went onto his terrace—which had a view of the beach, the rock promontory, and the parking area where they were now standing.

"What did you see?"

"Nothing. It was eerily quiet. Then the air exploded. It sounded as if a war had broken out."

"You heard more shots?"

"There were cracks of gunfire from the promontory on the other side of the inlet and I stared across, stunned, and then . . . did I mention I was a birdwatcher?"

"No, you didn't."

"Well, it's made my eyesight very good, you see. I've got eagle eyes. I'm used to pinpointing tiny details far off, and I'm sure that's why I noticed a small dot on the rock ledge up there, do you see it? The edge of it sort of cuts into the slope like a pocket."

Modig looked up at the slope and nodded.

"At first I couldn't tell what it was," Matzon continued. "But then I realized it was a child, a boy I think. He was sitting up there in a crouch and trembling, at least that's how it seemed to me, and then suddenly . . . my God, I'll never forget it."

"What?"

"Someone came racing down from above, a woman, and she leaped into the air and landed so violently on the rock ledge that she all but fell off it. After that they sat there together, she and the boy, and just waited, waited for the inevitable. And then . . ."

"Yes?"

"Two men appeared holding assault rifles and shot and shot. As I'm sure you can imagine, I threw myself to the ground. I was scared I'd get hit. But I couldn't help looking up at them all the same. You see, from where I was the boy and the girl were clearly visible, but they were invisible to the men standing at the top, at least for the moment. It was obvious to me that it was only a matter of time before they were discovered and there was no escape. As soon as they left the rock ledge the men would see them and kill them. It was a hopeless situation."

"But we've found neither the boy nor the woman up there," Modig said.

"That's just it! The men got closer and closer—they only needed to lean forward to see the woman and the child. In the end they could probably have heard them breathing. But then . . ."

"Yes?"

"You're not going to believe this. That man from the Rapid Response Unit definitely didn't."

"Well, go ahead and tell me, and we can worry later about whether it's believable."

"When the men stopped to listen, maybe they sensed they were very close, the woman leaped to her feet and shot them. Bang, bang! Then she rushed forward and threw their weapons away. It was like an action film, and after that she ran, or rather rolled, almost fell down the slope with the boy to a BMW standing here in the parking area. Just before they got into the car I saw that the woman was holding something, it looked like a computer bag."

"Did they drive off in the BMW?"

"At a fearful speed. I have no idea where they went."

"OK."

"But that's not all."

"What do you mean?"

"There was another car there, a Range Rover, I think, black, a new model."

"And what happened to that one?"

"I was busy ringing the emergency services, but just as I was about to hang up I saw two more people coming down from the wooden stairs over there, a tall skinny man and a woman. I didn't get a good look at them from that distance. But I can tell you two things about that woman."

"Yes?"

"She was a twelve-pointer, and she was angry."

"Twelve-pointer meaning beautiful?"

"Or at least glamorous, classy. You could see it a mile off. But, boy, was she furious. Just before they got into the Range Rover she slapped the man, and the weird thing is: he hardly reacted. He just nodded as if he thought he deserved it. Then he got behind the wheel and they were gone."

Modig noted everything down, realizing that she had to get out a nation-wide search bulletin for both the Range Rover and the BMW without delay.


Gabriella Grane was drinking a cappuccino in her kitchen on Villagatan and thinking that she was holding it together, all things considered. But she was probably in shock.

Helena Kraft wanted to see her at 8:00 a.m. in her office at Säpo. Grane guessed that she wouldn't just get the sack. There would be judicial consequences too, which would pretty much ruin her prospects of finding another job. At thirty-three, her career was over.

And that was by no means the worst of it. She had known that she was flouting the law and had taken a conscious risk. But she had done it because she believed it was the best way to protect Frans Balder's son. Now, after the shoot-out at her summer place, no-one seemed to know where the boy was. He might be injured, or even dead. Grane was racked by the most devastating feelings of guilt: first the father and then the son.

She got up and looked at the clock. It was 7:15 and she needed to get going to give herself time to clean out her desk before the meeting with Kraft. She made up her mind to behave with dignity, to not make any excuses or beg to be allowed to stay. Her Blackphone rang, but she couldn't be bothered to answer. Instead she put on her boots and her Prada coat and an extravagant red scarf. If she was going under, she might as well go with a bit of panache. She stood in front of the hall mirror and touched up her makeup, wryly giving herself the victory sign, as Nixon had when he resigned. Then her Blackphone rang again. This time she picked up reluctantly. It was Casales at the NSA.

"I just heard," she said.

Of course she had.

"How are you feeling?"

"How do you think?"

"Like the worst person in the whole world?"

"Pretty much."

"Who'll never get another job?"

"Spot on, Alona."

"In that case let me tell you, you have nothing to be ashamed of. You did the right thing."

"Are you trying to be funny?"

"This isn't the time for jokes, sweetheart. You have a mole on your team."

Gabriella took a deep breath. "Who is it?"

"Nielsen."

Gabriella froze. "Do you have proof?"

"Oh yes, I'll send it all over in a few minutes."

"Why would Nielsen betray us?"

"I guess he didn't see it as a betrayal."

"What on earth did he see it as, if not betrayal?"

"Collaborating with Big Brother maybe, doing his duty by the leading nation in the free world, what do I know?"

"So he gave you information."

"He helped us to help ourselves, actually. He gave us information about your server and your encryption. It's not as outrageous as it sounds. Let's face it, we listen in on everything from the neighbours' gossip to the prime ministers' phone calls."

"But this time the information was leaked a stage further."

"In this case it seeped out like we were a funnel. I know, Gabriella, that you didn't exactly stick to the rule book. But I'm absolutely convinced that you were in the right, and I'll make sure your superiors get to hear it. You could see that there was something rotten in your organization, so you couldn't act within it, yet you were determined not to shirk your responsibility."

"But it went wrong."

"Sometimes things go wrong, no matter how careful you are."

"Thanks, Alona, it's nice of you to say so. But if anything has happened to August Balder, I will never forgive myself."

"Gabriella, the boy is OK. He's cruising around in a car somewhere with Miss Salander, in case someone's still chasing them."

Grane could not take it in. "What do you mean?"

"That he's unhurt, babe, and thanks to him his father's murderer has been caught and identified."

"You're saying August is alive?"

"That's right."

"How do you know?"

"Let's just say I have a very well-placed source."

"Alona . . ."

"Yes?"

"If what you say is true, you've given me back my life."

After hanging up, Grane rang Kraft and insisted that Mårten Nielsen be present at their meeting. Reluctantly, Kraft agreed.

It was 7:30 in the morning when Needham and Blomkvist made their way down the steps from Grane's summer house to the Audi in the parking area by the beach. Snow lay over the landscape and neither of them said a word. At 5:30 Blomkvist had gotten a text message from Salander, as brisk and to the point as ever.

```
<August unhurt. We'll keep our heads down awhile
longer.>
```

Again Salander had not mentioned her own state of health. But it was an incredible relief to hear about the boy. Afterwards Blomkvist had been questioned at length by Modig and Holmberg and he told them every detail of what he and the magazine had been doing over the past few days. They were not particularly well disposed towards him, yet he got the feeling that somehow they understood. Now, an hour later, he was walking past the jetty. Up the slope a deer scampered into the forest. Blomkvist settled into the driver's seat and waited for Needham, who came loping along in his wake. The American's back was giving him trouble.

On the way towards Brunn they found themselves in traffic. For several minutes no cars were moving and Blomkvist thought of Zander, who was constantly on his mind. They had still not had any sign of life.

"Can you get something noisy on the radio?" Needham said.

Blomkvist tuned into 107.1 and got James Brown belting out what a sex machine he was.

"Give me your phones," Needham said.

He stacked them next to the speakers at the back of the car. He clearly meant to talk about something sensitive, and Blomkvist had nothing against that—he had to write his story and needed all the facts he could get. But he also knew better than most that there's no such thing as a leak without an agenda. Although Blomkvist felt a certain affinity with Needham and even appreciated his grumpy charm, he did not trust him for one second.

"Let's hear it," he said.

"You could put it this way," Needham began. "We know that in business and industry there's always someone taking advantage of inside information."

"Agreed."

"For a while we were pretty much spared that in the world of intelligence, for the simple reason that we guarded different kinds of secrets. The dynamite was elsewhere. But since the end of the Cold War, that's changed. Surveillance in general has become more widespread. These days we control huge amounts of valuable material."

"And there are people taking advantage of this, you say."

"Well, that's basically the whole point. Corporate espionage helps keep companies informed about the strengths and weaknesses of the competition. It's a grey area. Something that was seen as criminal or unethical decades ago is now standard operating procedure. We're not much better than the NSA, in fact maybe we're even . . ."

"The worst?"

"Just take it easy, let me finish," Needham said. "I'd say we have a certain moral code. But we're a large organization with tens of thousands of employees and inevitably there are rotten apples—one or two very highly placed rotten apples I was thinking of handing you."

"Out of the kindness of your heart, of course," said Blomkvist with a touch of sarcasm.

"OK, maybe not entirely. But listen. When senior management at our place crosses the line and gets into criminal activities, what do you think happens?"

"Nothing very nice."

"As you know, there's a corrupt unit at Solifon, headed up by a man called Zigmund Eckerwald, whose job it is to find out what the competing tech companies are up to. They not only steal the technology but also sell what they steal. That's bad for Solifon and maybe even for the whole Nasdaq."

"And for you too."

"That's right. It turns out that our two most senior executives in industrial espionage—their names are Jacob Barclay and Brian Abbot—get help from Eckerwald and his gang. In exchange the NSA helps Eckerwald with large-scale communications monitoring. Solifon identifies where the big innovations are happening, and our idiots pluck out the drawings and the technical details."

"I assume the money this brings in doesn't always end up in the state coffers."

"It's worse than that, buddy. If you do this sort of thing as a state employee, you make yourself very vulnerable, especially because Eckerwald and his gang are also helping major criminals. To be fair, at first they probably didn't know their clients were major criminals."

"But that's what they were?"

"Damn right. And they took advantage too. I could only dream of recruiting hackers at their level of expertise. The essence of this illegal business is to exploit information, so you can imagine: once they realized what our guys at the NSA were up to, these criminals knew they were sitting on a goldmine."

"So they were in a position to blackmail."

"Talk about having the upper hand. Our guys haven't just been stealing from large corporations. They've also plundered small family businesses and solo entrepreneurs who are struggling to survive. It wouldn't look too good if everything came out. So as a result the NSA is forced to help not just Eckerwald and Solifon, but also the criminals."

"You mean the Spiders?"

"You got it. Maybe for a while everyone stays happy. It's big business and the money's rolling in. But then a little genius pops up in the middle of the action, a certain Professor Balder, and he's just as good at ferreting around as he is at doing everything else. So he finds out about this scheme, or at least part of it. Then of course everyone's scared shitless and decides that something has to be done. I'm not entirely clear on how these decisions got made. I'm guessing our guys hoped legal threats would be enough. But when you're in bed with a bunch of criminals . . . The Spiders prefer violence. They probably drew our guys into the plan at a late stage, just to bind them in even more tightly."

"Jesus."

"I would never have gotten to know any of this if we hadn't been hacked," said Needham.

"Another reason to leave the hacker in peace."

"Which is exactly what I'm going to do, so long as she tells me how she did it."

"I don't know how much your promises are worth. But there's another thing I've been wondering about," Blomkvist went on.

"Shoot."

"You mentioned two guys, Barclay and Abbot. Are you sure it stops with them? Who's their boss?"

"I can't give you his name, unfortunately. It's classified."

"I suppose I'll have to live with that."

"You will," Needham said inflexibly. At that moment Blomkvist noticed that traffic was starting to flow again.

# CHAPTER 28

# NOVEMBER 24—AFTERNOON

Professor Edelman was standing in the parking lot at the Karolinska Institute wondering what in heaven's name he had let himself in for. He was embarking on an arrangement which would mean his having to cancel a whole series of meetings, lectures, and conferences.

Even so he felt strangely elated. He had been entranced not just by the boy but also by the young woman, who looked as if she had come straight from a street brawl but who drove a brand-new BMW and spoke with chilling authority. He had barely been aware of what he was doing when he said, "Yes, sure, why not," to her questions, although it was obviously rash.

The only grain of independence he had shown was to have declined all offers of compensation. He was going to pay his own travel and hotel expenses, he said. He must have felt guilty. But he was moved to take the boy under his wing, and his scientific curiosity was piqued. A savant who both drew with photographic exactitude and could perform prime number factorization—how absolutely riveting. To his own surprise he even decided to skip the Nobel Prize dinner. The young woman had made him take leave of his senses.

Hanna Balder was sitting in the kitchen on Torsgatan, smoking. It felt as if she had done little else aside from sit there and puff away with a pit in her stomach. She had been given an unusual amount of support, but she had also been getting an unusual amount of physical abuse.

Lasse Westman could not handle her anxiety. It detracted from his own martyrdom. He was always flying into a rage and yelling, "Can't you even keep track of your own brat?" Often he lashed out with his fists or threw her across the apartment like a rag doll. Now he would probably go crazy. She had spilled coffee all over the *Dagens Nyheter* culture section, and Lasse was already worked up because of a theatre review he found too sympathetic to actors he did not like.

"What the hell have you done?"

"I'm sorry," she said quickly. "I'll wipe it up."

She could tell from the set of his mouth even before he even knew it himself that he would hit her, and she was so well prepared for his slap that she did not say one word or even move her head. She could feel the tears welling up and her heart pounding. But actually that had nothing to do with the blow.

That morning she had received a call which was so perplexing that she hardly understood it: August had been found, had disappeared again, and was "probably" unharmed—"probably." It was impossible for Hanna to know if she should be more worried, or less. Hours had gone by without further news.

Suddenly she got to her feet, no longer caring whether she would get another beating or not. She went into the living room and heard Lasse panting behind her. August's drawing paper was still lying on the floor and an ambulance was wailing outside. She heard footsteps in the stairwell. Was someone on their way here? The doorbell rang.

"Don't open. It'll be some bloody journalist," Lasse snapped.

Hanna did not want to open either. Still, she could not very well ignore it, could she? Perhaps the police wanted to interview her again, or maybe, maybe they had more information now, good news or bad news.

As she went to the door she thought of Frans. She remembered how he had stood there saying that he had come for August. She remembered his eyes and the fact that he had shaved off his beard, and her own longing for her old life, before Lasse Westman—a time when the telephone rang and the job offers came flooding in, and fear had not yet set its claws into her. She opened the door with the safety chain on and at first she saw nothing; just the lift door, and the reddish-brown walls. Then a shock ran through her, and for a moment she could not believe it. But it really was August! His hair was a tangled mess and his clothes were filthy. He was wearing a pair of sneakers much too big for him, and yet: he looked at her with the same serious, impenetrable expression as ever. She would not have expected him to turn up on his own. But when she undid the safety chain she gave a start. Next to August stood a cool young woman in a leather jacket, with scratch marks on her face and earth in her hair, glaring down at the floor. She had a large suitcase in her hand.

"I've come to give you back your son," she said without looking up.

"Oh my God," Hanna said. "My God!"

That was all she managed to say. For a few seconds she was completely at a loss as she stood there in the doorway. Then her shoulders began to shake. She sank to her knees and, forgetting that August hated to be hugged, she threw her arms around him, murmuring, "My boy, my boy," until the tears came. The odd thing was: August not only let her do it, he also seemed on the verge of saying something, as if he had learned to talk on top of everything. But before he had the chance, Lasse was standing behind her.

"What the hell . . . well, look who's here!" he growled, as if he wanted to carry on with their fight.

But then he got a grip on himself. It was an impressive piece of acting, in a way. In the space of a second he began to radiate the presence which used to make women swoon.

"We get the kid delivered to our front doorstep," he said to the woman on the landing. "How convenient. Is he OK?"

"He's OK," the woman said in a strange monotone, and she walked into the apartment with her suitcase and her muddy boots.

"Just come right on in," Lasse said in an acid tone.

"I'm here to help you pack, Lasse."

This was such a strange reply that Hanna was convinced she had misheard. Lasse did not seem to understand either. He just stood there looking stupid, his mouth wide open.

"What did you say?"

"You're moving out."

"Is this some kind of joke?"

"Not at all. You're leaving this house, right now, and you're not coming anywhere near August ever again. You've seen him for the last time."

"You must be insane!"

"Actually I'm being unusually generous. I was planning on throwing you down the stairs, but instead I brought a suitcase, thought I'd let you pack some shirts and pants."

"What kind of a freak are you?" Lasse shouted, both bewildered and beside himself with rage. He bore down on the woman with the full weight of his hostility, and Hanna wondered if he was going to take a swipe at her as well.

But something stopped him. Maybe it was the woman's eyes, or possibly the fact that she did not react like anyone else would have done. Instead of backing off or looking frightened she only smiled at him, and handed him a few crumpled pieces of paper from an inside pocket.

"If ever you and your friend Roger should find yourselves missing August, you can always look at this and remember," she said.

Lasse turned over the papers, confused. Then he screwed up his face in horror and Hanna took a quick look herself. They were drawings and the top one was of . . . Lasse. Lasse swinging his fists and looking profoundly evil. Later she would hardly be able to explain it. It was not just that she now understood what had been going on when August had been alone at home with Lasse and Roger. She also saw her own life more clearly and soberly than she had in years.

Lasse had looked at her with exactly that twisted, livid face hundreds of times, most recently a minute ago. She knew this was something no-one should have to endure, neither she nor August, and she shrank back. At least she thought she did, because the woman looked at her with a new focus. Hanna eyed her uneasily. They seemed on some level to understand each other.

"Am I right, Hanna, he's got to go?" the woman asked.

The question was potentially lethal, and Hanna looked down at August's oversize shoes.

"What are those shoes he's wearing?"

"Mine."

"Why?"

"We left in a hurry this morning."

"And what have you been doing?"

"Hiding."

"I don't understand—" she began, but got no further.

Lasse grabbed hold of her violently.

"Why don't you tell this psychopath that the only one who's leaving is her!" he roared.

Hanna cowered, but then . . . It may have been something to do with the expression on Lasse's face, or the sense of something implacable in the young woman's bearing. Hanna heard herself say, "You're leaving, Lasse! And don't ever come back!"

It was as if someone else were speaking in her place. After that things moved quickly. Lasse raised his hand to strike her, but no blow came, not from him. The young woman reacted with lightning speed, and hit him in the face two, three times like a trained boxer, felling him with a kick to the leg.

"What the hell!" was all he was able to say.

He crashed to the floor, and the young woman stood over him. Hanna realized how long and how desperately she had wished Lasse Westman out of her life.

Bublanski longed to see Rabbi Goldman.

He also longed for some of Modig's orange chocolate, for his new Dux bed, and for springtime. But right now it was his job to get some order into this investigation. It was true that, on one level, he was satisfied. August Balder was said to be unharmed and on his way home to his mother.

Thanks to the boy himself and to Lisbeth Salander, his father's killer had been arrested, even though it was far from certain that he would survive his injuries. He was in intensive care at Danderyd Hospital. He was called Boris Latvinov but had for some time been using the name Jan Holtser. He was a former elite soldier from the Soviet army, a major, and his name had cropped up in the past in several murder investigations, but he had never been convicted. He had his own business in the security industry, and was both a Finnish and Russian citizen, and a resident of Helsinki; no doubt someone had doctored his government records.

The other two people who had been found at the summer house on Ingarö had been identified by their fingerprints: Dennis Wilton, an old gangster from Svavelsjö MC who had done time for both aggravated robbery and assault; and Vladimir Orlov, a Russian with a criminal record in Germany for procuring, whose two wives had died in unexplained circumstances. None of the men had yet said a word about what happened, or about anything at all. Nor did Bublanski hold out much hope that this would change. Men like that tend to hold their tongues in police interviews. But then those were the rules of the game.

What Bublanski was unhappy about, though, was the feeling that these three men were no more than foot soldiers and that there was a leadership above them linked to the upper echelons of society in both Russia and in the United States. He had no problem with a journalist knowing more about his investigation than he did. In that respect he was not proud. He just wanted to move ahead, and was grateful for all information, whatever its source. But Blomkvist's discerning approach to the case had pointed up their own shortcomings and reminded Bublanski of the leak and the dangers to which the boy had been exposed because of them. On this score his anger would never subside, and perhaps that explains why he was so irritated at Helena Kraft's eager efforts to get hold of him—and the head of Säpo was not the only one. The IT people at the National Criminal Police were also after him, as were Chief Prosecutor Richard Ekström and a Stanford professor by the name of Steven Warburton from the Machine Intelligence Research Institute, who wanted to talk about "a significant risk," as Amanda Flod put it.

That bothered Bublanski, along with a thousand other things. And there was someone knocking at his door. It was Modig, who looked tired and was wearing no makeup, revealing something different about her face.

"All three prisoners are having surgery," she said. "It'll be a while before we can question them again."

"Try to question them, you mean."

"I did manage to have a brief word with Latvinov. He was conscious for a while before his operation."

"Did he say anything?"

"Just that he wanted to talk to a priest."

"How come all lunatics and murderers are religious these days?"

"While all sensible old chief inspectors doubt the existence of their God, you mean?"

"Now, now."

"Latvinov also seemed dejected, and that's a good sign, I think," Modig said. "When I showed him the drawing he waved it away with a resigned expression."

"So he didn't try to claim it was a fabrication?"

"He just closed his eyes and started to talk about his priest."

"Have you discovered what this American professor wants, the one who keeps calling?"

"What . . . no . . . he'll only talk to you. I think it's about Balder's research."

"And Zander, the young journalist?"

"That's what I came to talk about. It doesn't look good."

"What do we know?"

"That he worked late and was spotted disappearing down past Katari-nahissen accompanied by a beautiful woman with strawberry- or dark-blond hair and expensive clothes."

"I'd not heard that."

"They were seen by a man called Ken Eklund, a baker at Skansen. He lives in the *Millennium* building. He said they looked as if they were in love, or at least Zander did."

"You think it could have been some sort of honey trap?"

"It's possible."

"And this woman, might she be the same one who was seen at Ingarö?"

"We're looking into that. But I don't like the idea that they seemed to be heading towards Gamla Stan. Not only because we picked up Zander's mobile phone signals there. That revolting specimen Orlov, who just spits at me whenever I try to question him, has an apartment on Mårten Trotzigs gränd."

"Have we been there?"

"Not yet. We've only just located it. The apartment was registered in the name of one of his companies."

"Let's hope there's nothing unpleasant waiting for us there."


Westman was lying on the floor in the entrance hall on Torsgatan, wondering how he could be so terrified. She was just a chick, a pierced punk chick who hardly came up to his chest. He should be able to throw her out like some little rat. Yet he was as if paralyzed and it had nothing to do with the way the girl fought, he thought, still less with the fact that her foot was planted on his stomach. It was something about her look or her whole being that he could not put his finger on. For a few minutes he lay there like an idiot and listened.

"I'm reminded of the fact," she said, "that there's something really wrong in my family. We seem to be capable of the most unimaginable cruelties. It may be a genetic defect. Personally, I've got this thing against men who harm children and women, and that makes me dangerous. When I saw August's drawings of you and your friend Roger, I wanted to hurt you, badly. But I think August has been through enough, so there's a slight chance that you and your friend might get off more lightly."

"I'm—" Westman began.

"Quiet," she said. "This isn't a negotiation, it's not even a conversation. I'm just setting out the terms, that's all. Legally, there are no problems. Frans was wise enough to register the apartment in August's name. This is how it's going to be: You have precisely four minutes to pack your things and get out. If you or Roger ever come back here or contact August in any way, I'll make you suffer so much that you'll be incapable of doing anything nice again, for the rest of your lives. In the meantime, I'll be preparing to report you to the police with full details of the abuse you've subjected August to. As you know we have more than the drawings to go on. We have testimonies from psychologists and experts. I'll also be contacting the evening papers to tell them that I have material which substantiates the image of you that emerged in connection with your assault on Renata Kapusinski. Remind me, Lasse, what was it that you did? Bite through her cheek and kick her in the head?"

"So you're going to go to the press."

"I'm going to go to the press. I'm going to cause you and your friend every conceivable disgrace. But maybe—I'm saying maybe—you can hope to escape the worst of the humiliation so long as you're never again seen near Hanna and August, and if you never again harm a woman. As a matter of fact I couldn't give a shit about you. Once you leave, and if you live like a shy and timid little monk, you may be all right. I have my doubts—as we all know, the rate of re-offending for violence against women is high, and basically you're a bastard, but with a bit of luck, who knows . . . Got it?"

"I've got it," he said, hating himself for saying so.

He saw no way out, he could only agree and do as he was told, so he got up and went into the bedroom and quickly packed some clothes. Then he took his coat and his mobile and left.

He had nowhere to go. He had never felt more pathetic in his life. Outside an unpleasant sleety rain lashed into him.


Salander heard the front door slam and footsteps receding down the stone stairs. She looked at August. He was standing still with his arms straight down by his sides, staring at her intently. That troubled her. A moment ago she had been in control, but now she was uncertain, and what on earth was the matter with Hanna Balder?

Hanna seemed about to burst into tears, and August . . . on top of everything else he started shaking his head and muttering. Salander just wanted to get out of there, but she stayed. Her work was not yet complete. Out of her pocket she took two plane tickets, a hotel voucher, and a thick bundle of notes, both kronor and euros.

"I'd just like, from the bottom of my heart—" Hanna began.

"Quiet," Salander cut in. "Here are some plane tickets to Munich. Departure is at 7:15 this evening so you've got to hurry. I've organized transport to take you directly to Schloss Elmau. It's a nice hotel not far from Garmisch-Partenkirchen. You'll be staying in a large room on the top floor, in the name of Müller, and you'll be there for three months to start with. I've been in touch with Professor Edelman and explained to him the importance of absolute confidentiality. He'll be making regular visits and seeing to it that August gets good care. Edelman will also arrange for suitable schooling."

"Are you serious?"

"I'm deadly serious. The police now have August's drawing and the murderer has been arrested. But the people behind the attacks are still at large; it's impossible to know what they might be planning. You have to leave this apartment at once. I'm busy with a few other things, so I've arranged for a driver to take you to Arlanda. He's a bit weird looking, maybe. But he's OK. You can call him Plague. Have you got all that?"

"Yes, but . . ."

"Forget the buts. Just listen: You mustn't use your credit card or your own mobile, Hanna. I've fixed an encrypted mobile for you, a Blackphone, in case there's an emergency. My number is already programmed in. I'll pick up all the costs of the hotel. You'll get a hundred thousand kronor in cash, for unforeseen expenses. Any questions?"

"It sounds crazy."

"Not to me."

"But how can you afford this?"

"I can afford it."

"How can we . . ."

Hanna looked completely bewildered, as if she were not sure what to believe. Then she began to cry.

"How can we ever thank you?" she struggled to say.

"*Thank* me?"

Salander said the words as if they were incomprehensible. When Hanna came towards her with outstretched arms she backed away, and with her eyes fixed on the hallway floor she said:

"Pull yourself together! Get a grip and get off whatever stuff you're on, pills or anything else. That's how you can thank me."

"I will . . ."

"And if anyone gets it into their head that August needs to be put in some home or institution, I want you to fight back as hard and as ruthlessly as you can. Aim for their weakest point. Be a warrior."

"A warrior?"

"Exactly. Don't let anyone—"

Salander stopped herself. They were not perhaps the greatest words of farewell, but they would have to do. She turned and walked towards the front door. She did not get far. August started to mutter again, and this time they could make out what the boy was saying.

"Not go, not go . . ."

Salander had no good answer to that either. She just said: "You'll be OK," and then added, as if talking to herself, "Thanks for the scream this morning." There was silence for a moment, and Salander wondered if she should say more. But instead she slipped out.

Hanna called after her: "I can't tell you what this means to me!"

But Salander heard nothing. She was already running down the steps to her car. When she reached Västerbron, Blomkvist called on the RedPhone app to say that the NSA had tracked her down.

"Tell them hi and that I'm on their tracks too," she said.

Then she drove to Roger Winter's house and scared him half to death. After that she drove back to her place and set to work with the encrypted NSA file, without coming any closer to a solution.

Needham and Blomkvist had worked a long day in the hotel room at the Grand. Needham's story was fantastic and Blomkvist would be able to write the scoop *Millennium* so badly needed, but his feeling of unease did not abate. It was not just because Zander was still missing. There was something about Needham that did not add up. Why had he turned up in the first place, and why was he putting so much energy into helping a small Swedish magazine, far from all the centres of power in the United States? Blomkvist had undertaken not to disclose the hacker breach, and had half promised to persuade Salander to talk to Needham. But that hardly seemed enough.

Needham behaved as if he were taking enormous risks. The curtains were drawn and their mobiles were lying at a safe distance. There was a feeling of paranoia in the room. Confidential documents were laid out on the bed. Blomkvist was permitted to read them, but not to quote from or copy them. And every now and then Needham interrupted his account to discuss various aspects of the right to protect journalistic sources. He was obsessive about ensuring that the leak could not be traced back to him, and sometimes he listened nervously for footsteps in the corridor or looked out through a gap in the curtains to check that no-one was out there watching the hotel, and yet . . . Blomkvist could not help feeling that most of it was play-acting.

He became more and more convinced that Needham knew exactly what he was doing, and was not even especially worried about someone listening in. It occurred to Blomkvist that Needham was playing a part with the backing of his superiors. Maybe he himself had also been given a role in this play which he did not yet understand.

Therefore he paid close attention not just to what Needham said, but also to what he did not. He considered what Needham might be trying to achieve by going public. There was undoubtedly a certain amount of anger in the mix. Some "bastards" in a department called Protection of Strategic Technologies had prevented Needham from nailing the hacker who had gotten into his system, because they didn't want to be exposed with their pants round their ankles, and that infuriated him, he said. Blomkvist had no reason not to believe him, still less to doubt that Needham genuinely did want to exterminate these people, to "crush them, grind them to pulp under my boots." But there were other aspects of the story he was not quite so comfortable with. It felt as if Needham were wrestling with some kind of self-censorship.

From time to time Blomkvist went down to the lobby just to think, or to call Berger or Salander. Berger always answered on the first ring and, even though they were both enthusiastic about the story, Zander's disappearance haunted their conversations.

Salander did not pick up all day, until eventually he got hold of her at 5:20. She sounded distracted, and informed him that the boy was now safe with his mother.

"And how are *you*?" he said.

"OK."

"Not hurt?"

"Nothing new at least."

Blomkvist took a deep breath.

"Have you hacked into the NSA's intranet, Lisbeth?"

"Have you been talking to Ed the Ned?"

"No comment."

He would say nothing, even to Salander. Protection of sources was even more important to him than loyalty to her.

"Ed isn't so dumb after all," she said.

"So you have."

"Possibly."

Blomkvist felt the urge to ask her what the hell she thought she was doing. Instead, as calmly as he could, he said:

"They're prepared to let you off if you'll agree to meet them and tell them how you did it."

"Tell them that I've got more than they think."

"OK. But would you consider meeting . . ."

"Ed?"

How the hell did she know, Blomkvist thought. Needham had wanted to be the one to reveal himself to her.

"Ed," he repeated.

"A cocky bugger."

"Pretty cocky. But would you consider meeting him if we provide guarantees that you won't be arrested?"

"There are no such guarantees."

"I could get in touch with my sister Annika and ask her to represent you."

"I've got better things to do," she said, as if she did not want to talk about it anymore.

He could not stop himself from saying, "This story we're working on . . . I'm not sure I understand all of it."

"What's the problem?" Salander said.

"First of all, I don't understand why Camilla has surfaced after all these years."

"I suppose she'd just been biding her time."

"How do you mean?"

"She probably always knew she would be back to get revenge for what I did to her and Zala. But she wanted to wait until she had built up her strength on every level. Nothing is more important to Camilla than to be strong, and she must have seen an opportunity, a chance to kill two birds with one stone. At least that's my guess. Why don't you ask her next time you have a drink together?"

"Have you spoken to Holger?"

"I've been busy."

"Thank God you got away," Blomkvist went on.

"I made it."

"But aren't you worried that she could be back at any moment?"

"It has occurred to me."

"OK, good. You do know that Camilla and I did nothing more than walk a short way down Hornsgatan?"

Salander did not answer.

"I know you, Mikael" was all she said. "And now that you've met Ed, I guess I'll have to protect myself from him too."

Blomkvist smiled to himself.

"Yes," he said. "You're probably right. Let's not trust him any more than we absolutely have to. I don't want to become his useful idiot."

"Doesn't sound like a role for you, Mikael."

"No, and that's why I'd love to know what you discovered when you accessed the NSA intranet."

"A whole load of compromising shit."

"About Eckerwald and the Spiders' relationship with the NSA?"

"That and a bit more besides."

"Which you were planning to tell me about."

"I might do, if you behave yourself," she said with a teasing tone, and that only made him feel happy.

Then he chuckled, because at that moment he realized what Ed Needham was trying to do. It hit him so forcefully that he had a hard time keeping up his act when he returned to the hotel room, but he went on working with the American until ten that night.

# CHAPTER 29

# NOVEMBER 25—MORNING

Vladimir Orlov's apartment on Mårten Trotzigs gränd was neat and tidy. The bed was freshly made with clean sheets and the laundry basket in the bathroom was empty. Yet there were signs that something was not quite right. Neighbours reported that some moving men had been there the morning before and a close inspection revealed blood stains on the floor and on the wall above the headboard. The blood was compared to traces of saliva in Zander's apartment and the match confirmed.

But the men now in custody—the two still capable of communicating— claimed to have no knowledge of blood stains or of Zander, so Bublanski and his team concentrated on getting more information on the woman who had been seen with him. By now the media had published columns and columns about not only the drama on Ingarö but also about Andrei Zander's disappearance. Both evening newspapers and *Svenska Morgon-Posten* and *Metro* had carried prominent photographs of the journalist, and there was already speculation that he might have been murdered. Usually that would jog people's memories and prompt them to remember anything suspicious, but now it was almost the exact opposite.

Such witness accounts as came in and were thought to be credible were peculiarly vague, and everyone who came forward—except for Mikael Blomkvist and the baker from Skansen—took it upon themselves to remark that they could not imagine the woman guilty of any crime. She had apparently made an overwhelmingly good impression on everyone who had encountered her. A bartender called Sören Karlsten, who had served the woman and Zander in Papagallo on Götgatan, went on and on boasting that he was a good judge of character and claimed to be absolutely certain that this woman "would never hurt a soul."

"She was class personified."

She was just about everything personified, if one were to believe the witnesses, and from what Bublanski could see it would be virtually impossible to produce a police sketch of her. The witness accounts all depicted her in different terms, as if they were projecting their ideal image of a woman onto her, and so far they had no photographs from any surveillance camera. It was almost laughable. Blomkvist said that the woman was without a shadow of a doubt Camilla Salander, twin sister of Lisbeth. But going back in the records for many years, there was no trace of her. It was as if she had ceased to exist. If Camilla Salander were still alive, then it would be under a new identity.

Bublanski especially did not like that there had been two unexplained deaths in the foster family she left behind. The police investigations at the time were deficient, full of loose threads and question marks which had never been followed up.

Bublanski read the reports, ashamed that out of some bizarre respect for the family's tragedy his colleagues had failed to get to the bottom of the glaring problem that both the father and the daughter had emptied their bank accounts just before their deaths, or that in the very week he had been found hanged the father had started writing a letter which began:

"Camilla, why is it so important to you to destroy my life?"

This person who seemed to have enchanted all the witnesses was shrouded in ominous darkness.


It was now 8:00 in the morning and there were a hundred other things Bublanski should have been attending to, so he reacted with both irritation and guilt when he heard that he had a visitor. She was a woman who had been interviewed by Modig but who now insisted on meeting him. Afterwards he wondered if he had been exceptionally brusque, maybe because all he was expecting was further problems.

The woman in the doorway had a regal bearing but was not tall. She had dark, intense eyes which gave her a melancholy look. She was dressed in a grey coat and a red dress that looked a bit like a sari.

"My name is Farah Sharif," she said. "I'm a professor of computer sciences and was a close friend of Frans Balder's."

"Yes, of course," said Bublanski, suddenly embarrassed. "Take a seat, please. My apologies for the mess."

"I've seen worse."

"Is that so. Well. To what do I owe this honour?"

"I was far too naïve when I spoke to your colleague."

"Why do you say that?"

"Because I have more information now. I've had a long conversation with Professor Warburton."

"He's been looking for me too, but it's been so chaotic, I haven't had time to call him back."

"Steven is a professor of cybernetics at Stanford and a leading researcher in the field of technological singularity. These days he works at the Machine Intelligence Research Institute, whose aim is to ensure that artificial intelligence is a positive help to mankind rather than the opposite."

"Well, that sounds good," said Bublanski, who felt uncomfortable whenever this topic came up.

"Steven lives somewhat in a world of his own. He found out what happened to Frans only yesterday, and that's why he didn't call sooner. But he told me that he had spoken to Frans as recently as Monday."

"What did they discuss?"

"His research. You know, Frans had been so secretive ever since he went off to the States. I was close to him, but not even I knew anything about what he was doing. I was arrogant enough to think I understood some of it at least, but now it turns out I was wrong."

"In what way?"

"Frans had not only taken his old AI programme a step further, he had also developed fresh algorithms and new topographical material for quantum computers."

"I'm not sure I follow."

"Quantum computers are computers based on quantum mechanics. They are many thousand times faster in certain areas than conventional computers. The great advantage with quantum computers is that the fundamental constituent quantum bits—qubits—can superposition themselves."

"They can *what*?"

"Not only can they take the binary positions one or zero as do traditional computers, they can also be both zero and one at the same time. For the time being quantum computers are much too specialized and cumbersome. But—how can I best explain this to you?—Frans appeared to have found ways to make them easier, more flexible and self-learning. He was onto something great, at least potentially. But as well as feeling proud of his breakthrough, he was also worried—and that was the reason he called Steven Warburton."

"Why was he worried?"

"In the long term, because he suspected his creation could become a threat to the world, I imagine. But more immediately because he knew things about the NSA."

"What sort of things?"

"I don't know anything about that aspect of his discoveries. He somehow stumbled upon the messier side of their industrial espionage. But I do know this: It's no secret that the organization is working hard specifically to develop quantum computers. For the NSA that would be paradise, pure and simple. An effective quantum machine would actually enable them to crack all encryptions, all digital security systems. Then no-one would be safe from that organization's watchful eye."

"A hideous thought," said Bublanski with surprising feeling.

"But there is an even more frightening scenario: if such a thing were to fall into the hands of major criminals," Farah Sharif said.

"I see what you're getting at."

"So I'm keen to know what you've managed to get hold of from the men now under arrest."

"Unfortunately nothing like that," he said. "But these men are not exactly outstanding intellects. I doubt they would even pass secondary school maths."

"The real computer genius got away?"

"I'm afraid so. He and a female suspect have disappeared without a trace. They probably have a number of identities."

"Worrying."

Bublanski nodded and gazed into Farah Sharif's dark eyes, which looked beseechingly at him. A hopeful thought stopped him from sinking back into despair.

"I'm not sure what it means," he said.

"What?"

"We've had IT guys go through Balder's computers. Given how security-conscious he was, it wasn't easy. You can imagine. But we had a spot of luck, you might say, and what we soon realized was that one computer must have been stolen."

"I suspected as much," she said. "Damn it!"

"Wait, I haven't finished. We also understood that a number of machines had been connected to each other, and that occasionally these had been connected to a supercomputer in Tokyo."

"That sounds feasible."

"We can confirm that a large file, or at least something big, had recently been deleted, although we haven't been able to restore it."

"Are you suggesting Frans might have destroyed his own research?"

"I don't want to jump to any conclusions. But it occurred to me while you were telling me all this."

"Don't you think the perpetrator might have deleted it?"

"You mean that he first copied it, and then removed it from Balder's computers?"

"Yes."

"I find that hard to believe. The killer was only in the house for a very short while, he would never have had time—let alone the ability—to do anything like that."

"OK, that sounds reassuring, despite everything," Sharif said doubtfully. "It's just that . . ."

"Yes?"

"I don't think it fits with Frans's character. Would he really destroy the greatest thing he'd ever done? That would be like . . . I don't know . . . chopping off his own arm, or even worse, killing a friend, destroying a life."

"Sometimes one has to make a big sacrifice," Bublanski said thoughtfully. "Destroy what one loves."

"Or else there's a copy somewhere."

"Or else there's a copy somewhere," he repeated. Suddenly he did something strange: he reached out his hand.

Farah Sharif did not understand. She looked at the hand as if she were expecting him to give her something. But Bublanski decided not to let himself be discouraged.

"Do you know what my rabbi says? That the mark of a man is his contradictions. We can long to be away and at home, both at the same time. I never knew Professor Balder, and he might have thought that I was just an old fool. But I do know one thing: we can both love and fear our work, just as Balder seems to have both loved and run away from his son. To be alive, Professor Sharif, means not being completely consistent. It means venturing out in many directions all at the same time, and I wonder if your friend didn't find himself in the throes of some sort of upheaval. Maybe he really did destroy his life's work. Maybe he revealed himself with all his inherent contradictions towards the end, and became a true human being in the best sense of the word."

"Do you think so?"

"We may never know. But he had changed, hadn't he? The custody hearing declared him unfit to look after his own son, yet that's precisely what he did. He even got the boy to blossom and begin to draw."

"That's true, Chief Inspector."

"Call me Jan. People sometimes even call me Officer Bubble."

"Is that because you're so bubbly?"

"No, I don't think so somehow. But I do know one thing for sure."

"And what's that?"

"That you're . . ."

He got no further, but he did not need to. Farah Sharif gave him a smile which in all its simplicity restored Bublanski's belief in life and in God.


At 8:00 a.m. Salander got out of her bed on Fiskargatan. Once again she had not managed to get much sleep, not only because she had been working on the encrypted NSA file without getting anywhere at all. She had also been listening for the sound of footsteps on the stairs and every now and then she checked her alarm and the surveillance camera on the landing.

She was no wiser than anyone else as to whether her sister had left the country. After her humiliation on Ingarö, it was by no means impossible that Camilla was preparing a new attack, with even greater force. The NSA could also, at any moment, march into the apartment. Salander was under no illusions on either point. But this morning she dismissed all that. She went to the bathroom with resolute steps and took off her top to check her bullet wound. She thought it was finally beginning to look better, and in a mad moment she decided to take herself off to the boxing club on Horns-gatan for a session.

To drive out pain with pain.

Afterwards she was sitting exhausted in the changing room, with hardly the energy to think. Her mobile buzzed. She ignored it. She went into the shower and let the warm water sprinkle over her. Gradually her thoughts cleared, and August's drawing reappeared in her mind. But this time it wasn't the illustration of the murderer which caught her attention—it was something at the bottom of the paper.

Salander had only a very brief glimpse of the finished work at the summer house on Ingarö; at the time she had been concentrating on sending it to Bublanski and Modig. If she had given it any thought at all, then like everyone else she would have been fascinated by the detailed rendering. But now her photographic memory focused on the equation August had written at the bottom of the page, and she stepped out of the shower deep in thought. The only thing was, she could hardly hear herself think. Obinze was raising hell outside the changing room.

"Shut up," she shouted back. "I'm thinking!"

But that did not help much. Obinze was absolutely furious, and anyone other than Salander would understand why. Obinze had been shocked at how weak and half-hearted her effort at the punchbag was, and had worried when she began to hang her head and grimace in pain. In the end he had surprised her by rushing over and rolling up the sleeve of her T-shirt, only to discover the bullet wound. He had gone crazy, and evidently hadn't calmed down yet.

"You're an idiot, do you know that? A lunatic!" he shouted.

She was too tired to answer. Her strength deserted her completely, and what she had remembered from the drawing now faded from her mind. She sank down on the bench in the changing room next to Jamila Achebe. She used to both box and sleep with Jamila, usually in that order. When they fought their toughest bouts it often seemed like one long, wild foreplay. On a few occasions their behaviour in the shower had not been entirely decent. Neither of them set much store by etiquette.

"I actually agree with that noisy bastard out there. You're not right in the head," said Jamila.

"Maybe," Salander answered.

"That wound looks nasty."

"It's healing."

"But you needed to box?"

"Apparently."

"Shall we go back to my place?"

Salander did not answer. Her phone was buzzing again in her black bag. Three text messages with the same content from a withheld number. As she read them she balled up her fists and looked lethal. Jamila decided it might be better to have sex with Salander another day instead.

Blomkvist had woken at 6:00 with some great ideas for the article, and on his way to the office the draft came together in his mind with no effort at all. He worked in deep concentration at the magazine and barely noticed what was going on around him, although sometimes he surfaced with thoughts of Zander.

He refused to give up hope, but he feared that Zander had given his life for the story, and he did what he could to honour his colleague with every sentence he wrote. On one level he intended the report to be a murder story about Frans and August Balder—an account of an eight-year-old autistic boy who sees his father shot, and who despite his disability finds a way of striking back. But on another level Blomkvist wanted it to be an instructive narrative about a new world of surveillance and espionage, where the boundaries between the legal and the criminal have been erased. The words came pouring out, but still it was not without its difficulties.

Through an old police contact he had gotten hold of the paperwork on the unsolved murder of Kajsa Falk, the girlfriend of one of the leading figures in Svavelsjö MC. The killer had never been identified and none of the people questioned during the investigation had been willing to contribute anything of value, but Blomkvist nevertheless gathered that a violent rift had torn apart the motorcycle club and that there was an insidious fear among the gang members of a "Lady Zala," as one of the witnesses put it.

Despite considerable efforts, the police had not managed to discover who or what the name referred to. But there was not the slightest doubt in Blomkvist's mind that "Lady Zala" was Camilla and that she was behind a whole series of other crimes, both in Sweden and abroad. It was not easy to find any evidence, though, and that exasperated him. For the time being he referred to her in the article by her codename Thanos.

Yet the biggest challenge was not Camilla or her shadowy connections to the Russian Duma. What bothered Blomkvist most was that he knew Needham would never have come all the way to Sweden and leaked top secret information if he were not bent on hiding something even bigger. Needham was no fool, and he knew that Blomkvist was not stupid either. He had therefore avoided making any part of his account too pretty.

On the contrary, he painted a fairly dreadful picture of the NSA. And yet ... a closer inspection of the information told Blomkvist that, all in all, Needham was describing an intelligence agency which both func-tioned well and behaved reasonably decently, if you ignored the revolting bunch of criminals in the department known as Protection of Strategic Technologies—as it happens the self-same department which had pre-vented Needham from nailing his hacker.

The American must have wanted to do serious harm to a few specific colleagues, but rather than sink the whole of his organization, he preferred to give it a softer landing in an already inevitable crash. So Blomkvist was not especially surprised or angry when Berger appeared behind him and handed him a TT telegram with a worried expression.

"Does this scupper our story?" she said.

The telegram read:

TWO SENIOR EXECUTIVES AT THE NSA, JACOB BARCLAY AND BRIAN ABBOT, HAVE BEEN ARRESTED ON SUSPICION OF SERIOUS FINAN-CIAL MISCONDUCT AND ARE ON INDEFINITE LEAVE AWAITING TRIAL.

"THIS IS A BLOT ON THE REPUTATION OF OUR ORGANIZATION AND WE HAVE SPARED NO EFFORT IN TACKLING THE ISSUES AND

HOLDING THOSE GUILTY TO ACCOUNT. ANYONE WORKING FOR THE NSA MUST HAVE THE HIGHEST ETHICAL STANDARDS AND WE UNDERTAKE TO BE AS TRANSPARENT DURING THE JUDICIAL PROCESS AS WE CAN, WHILE REMAINING SENSITIVE TO OUR NATIONAL SECURITY INTERESTS," NSA CHIEF ADMIRAL CHARLES O'CONNOR HAS TOLD AP.

The telegram did not contain very much apart from the long quote; it said nothing about Balder's murder and nothing that could be linked to the events in Stockholm. But Blomkvist understood what Berger meant. Now that the news was out, the *Washington Post* and the *New York Times* and a whole pack of serious American journalists would descend on the story, and it would be impossible to anticipate what they might dig up.

"Not good," he said calmly. "But not a surprise."

"Really?"

"It's part of the same strategy that led the NSA to seek me out: damage control. They want to take back the initiative."

"How do you mean?"

"There's a reason why they leaked this to me. I could tell right away that there was something odd about it. Why did Needham insist on coming to talk to me here in Stockholm, and at five in the morning?"

"You think his actions were sanctioned higher up?"

"I suspected it, but at first I didn't get what he was doing. It just felt off. Then I talked to Salander."

"And that clarified things?"

"I realized that Needham knew exactly what she'd dug up during her hacker attack, and he had every reason to fear that I would learn all about it. He wanted to limit the damage. I suspect he gave me just enough to keep me happy and let me have my scoop and to prevent me from digging any deeper."

"He's in for a disappointment, then."

"Let's at least hope so. But I can't see how to break through. The NSA is a closed door."

"Even for an old bloodhound like Mikael Blomkvist?"

"Even for him."

# CHAPTER 30

# NOVEMBER 25

The text message had said <Until next time, sister!> Salander could not work out if it had been sent three times in error or if it was an absurd attempt to be overexplicit. It made no difference now anyway.

The message was evidently from Camilla, but it added nothing to what Salander already knew. The events on Ingarö had only deepened the old hatred—she was certain Camilla would come after her again, after having gotten so close.

It was not the wording of the texts that upset Salander so much as the thoughts it brought to mind, the memory of what she had seen on the steep rock slope in the early-morning light when she and August had crouched on the narrow ledge, gunfire rattling above them. August had not been wearing a jacket or shoes and was shivering violently in the falling snow as the seconds went by. Salander realized how desperately compromised their situation was. She had a child to take care of and a pathetic pistol for a weapon, while the bastards up there had assault rifles. She had to take them by surprise, otherwise she and August would be slaughtered like lambs. She listened to the men's footsteps and the direction they were shooting in, even their breathing and the rustle of their clothes.

But the strange thing was, when she finally saw her chance, she hesitated. Crucial moments went by as she broke a small twig into pieces on the rock ledge in front of them. Only then did she spring to her feet right in front of the men and, taking advantage of that brief millisecond of surprise, she fired two, three times. From experience she knew that moments like these burn an indelible impression on your mind, as if not only your body and muscles are sharpened, but also your perception.

Every detail shone with a strange precision and she saw each ripple in the landscape in front of her, as if through a camera zoom. She noted the surprise and fear in the men's eyes, the wrinkles and irregularities in their faces and clothes, and the weapons which they were waving and firing off at random, narrowly missing their targets.

But her strongest impression did not come from any of that. It came from a silhouette further up the slope which she caught out of the corner of her eye. Not menacing in itself, it still made more of an impact on her than the men she had shot: it was her sister. Salander would have recognized her half a mile away, even though they had not seen each other in years. The air itself was poisoned by her presence and afterwards Salander wondered if she should have shot her too.

Camilla stood there a moment too long. It was careless of her to be out on the rock slope in the first place, but presumably she could not resist the temptation of seeing her sister executed. Salander recalled how she half squeezed the trigger and felt a holy rage beating in her chest. Yet she hesitated for a split second, and that was enough. Camilla threw herself behind a rock and a scrawny figure appeared on the terrace and started shooting. Salander jumped back onto the ledge and tumbled down the slope with August.

Now, walking away from the boxing club, thinking back to it all, Salander's body tightened in readiness for a new battle. It struck her that perhaps she should not go home, but leave the country for a while. Something else drove her back to her desk, though: what she had seen in her mind's eye in the shower, before reading Camilla's texts, which was now occupying her thoughts more and more. August's equation:

$N = 3034267$

$E : y^2 = x^3 - x - 20; P = (3.2)$

From a mathematical point of view, there was nothing unique or outstanding about it. But what was so remarkable was that August had started with the random number she had given him at Ingarö and taken that further to develop a considerably better elliptic curve than the one she herself had made. When the boy had not wanted to go to sleep, she had left it on the bedside table. She had not gotten any answer then, nor even the slightest reaction, and she had gone to bed convinced that August understood nothing about mathematical abstractions, that he was only a kind of human calculator of prime number factorizations.

But, my God . . . she had been wrong. August had stayed up in the night not just drawing; he had also perfected her own mathematics.

She did not even take off her boots or leather jacket, she just stomped into her apartment and opened the encrypted NSA file along with her programme for elliptic curves.

Then she rang Hanna Balder.


Hanna had scarcely slept because she had not brought any of her pills with her. Yet the hotel and its surroundings still cheered her. The breathtaking mountain scenery reminded her of how cramped her own existence had become. Slowly she began to unwind, and even the deep-seated fear in her body was beginning to let go. But that could have been wishful thinking. She also felt slightly at sea in such extravagant surroundings.

There had been a time when she would sail into rooms like these with perfect self-assurance: *Look at me, here I come.* Now she was timid and trembling and had difficulty eating anything even though the breakfast was lavish. August sat beside her, compulsively writing out his series of numbers, and he was not eating either, but he drank unbelievable volumes of freshly pressed orange juice.

Her new mobile rang, startling her. It had to be the woman who had sent them here. Nobody else had the number so far as she knew. No doubt she just wanted to know if they had arrived safely so Hanna answered cheerfully and launched into an effusive description of how wonderful everything at the hotel was. She was brusquely interrupted:

"Where are you?"

"We're having breakfast."

"In that case stop now and go up to your room. August and I have work to do."

"Work?"

"I'm going to send over some equations I want him to take a look at. Is that clear?"

"I don't understand."

"Just show them to August, and then call me and tell me what he's written."

"OK," said Hanna, nonplussed.

She grabbed a couple of croissants and a cinnamon bun and walked with August to the lifts.


It was only at the outset that August helped her. But it was enough. Later she could see her mistakes more clearly and make new improvements to her programme. Deep in concentration she worked on for hour after hour, until the sky darkened outside and the snow began to fall again. Then suddenly—in one of those moments she would remember forever—something strange happened to the file. It fell apart. A shock ran through her. She punched the air.

She had found the secret keys and cracked the document, and for a little while she was so overcome by this that she hardly managed to read. Then she began to examine the contents, and her amazement grew with every passing moment. Could this even be possible? It was more explosive than anything she had imagined and the reason it had all been written down could only have been that someone believed the RSA algorithm was impenetrable. But here it was, all that filth in black and white. The text was full of internal jargon and strange abbreviations and cryptic references, but that was not a problem for Salander since she was familiar with the subject. She got through about four-fifths of the text before the doorbell rang.

She chose to ignore it, probably only the postman. But then she remembered Camilla's text message and checked the camera on the landing via her computer. She stiffened.

It was not Camilla but her other nemesis, the one she had almost forgotten with everything else that was going on. Ed the fucking Ned. He looked nothing like his pictures online, but he was unmistakable all the same: grumpy and determined. Salander's brain started ticking. How had he managed to track her down? What should she do? The best she could come up with was to send the NSA file off to Blomkvist on their PGP link.

Then she shut down her computer and hauled herself to her feet to open the door.

What had happened to Bublanski? Sonja Modig was at a loss to understand it. The pained expression he had been wearing in recent weeks had vanished and now he smiled and hummed to himself. It's true that there was plenty to be pleased about. The murderer had been caught, August Balder had survived, despite two attempts on his life, and Frans Balder's conflict and connection with the research company Solifon were becoming clearer.

But many questions remained, and the Bublanski she knew was not one to rejoice without good reason. He was more inclined to self-doubt, even in moments of triumph. She could not understand what had gotten into him. He walked around the corridors beaming. Even now, as he sat in his office reading the dull report on the questioning of Zigmund Eckerwald by the San Francisco police, there was a smile on his lips.

"Sonja, my dear, there you are!"

She decided not to comment on the unwonted enthusiasm of his greeting and went straight to the point.

"Jan Holtser is dead."

"Oh no."

"And with him went our last hope of learning more about the Spiders."

"So you think he was about to open up?"

"There was a chance, at least."

"Why do you say that?"

"He broke down completely when his daughter showed up."

"I didn't know. What happened?"

"He has a daughter called Olga," Modig said. "She came from Helsinki when she heard that her father had been injured. But when I talked to her and she realized that Holtser had tried to kill a child, she went berserk."

"In what way?"

"She stormed into him and said something incredibly aggressive in Russian."

"Could you understand what she was saying?"

"Something like he could die alone and she hated him."

"Strong words, then."

"Yes, and afterwards she told me that she would do everything in her power to help us with the investigation."

"How did Holtser react?"

"That's what I was saying. For a moment I thought we had him. He was totally destroyed, had tears in his eyes. I'm not big on that Catholic teaching which says that our moral worth is determined just before we die, but it was almost touching to see. This man, who had done so much evil, was crushed."

"My rabbi . . ." Bublanski began.

"Please, Jan, don't start with your rabbi now. Let me continue. Holtser started saying what a terrible person he had been, so I told him that he should as a Christian take the opportunity to confess, and tell us who he was working for. At that moment I'm convinced he came close. He hesitated and his eyes flitted from side to side. But instead of confessing he began to talk about Stalin."

"Stalin?"

"About how Stalin didn't only punish the guilty but also their children and grandchildren and the entire family. I think he was trying to say that his boss was the same."

"So he was worried about his daughter."

"However much she may have hated him, he was. I tried to tell him that we could get the girl into a witness protection programme, but Holtser had started to drift away. He fell unconscious and died an hour later."

"Anything else?"

"Only that someone we're beginning to think may be a superintelligence has vanished and that we still have no trace of Andrei Zander."

"I know, I know."

"We've made progress on one front at least," Modig said. "You remember the man identified by Amanda on August's drawing of the traffic light?"

"The former actor?"

"That's right, he's called Roger Winter. Amanda interviewed him for background information, to find out whether there was any relationship between him and the boy or Balder, and I don't think she expected to get much out of it. But Winter seemed badly shaken and before Amanda had even started to put pressure on him he confessed to a whole catalogue of sins."

"Really?"

"And we're not talking innocent stories. You know, Westman and Winter have been friends since they were young men at Revolutionsteatern and they used to get together to drink in the afternoons at the apartment in Torsgatan when Hanna was out. August would sit in the next room doing his puzzles, and neither of the men paid him much attention. But on one of these occasions the boy had been given a thick maths book by his mother—it was clearly way above his level, but he still leafed through it frantically, making excited noises. Lasse became irritated and grabbed the book from the boy and threw it in the bin. It seems August went completely crazy. He had some sort of fit, and Lasse kicked him several times."

"That's appalling."

"That was just the beginning. After that August became very odd, said Roger, and took to glaring at them with this weird look. One day Roger found that his jeans jacket had been cut into tiny pieces, and another day someone had emptied out all the beer in the fridge and smashed the bottles of spirits. It turned into some kind of trench warfare. I suspect that Roger and Lasse in their alcoholic delirium began to imagine all sorts of strange things about the boy, and even became scared of him. The psychological aspect of this isn't easy to understand. Roger said it made him feel like shit, and he never talked about it with Lasse afterwards. He didn't want to beat the boy, but he couldn't stop himself. It was as if he got his own childhood back, he said."

"What on earth did he mean by that?"

"It's not altogether clear. Apparently Roger Winter has a disabled younger brother. Throughout their childhood Roger was a constant disappointment, while his brother was showered with praise and distinctions and appreciated in every possible way. I guess that bred some bitterness. Maybe Roger was subconsciously getting his own back on his brother. Or else . . ."

"What?"

"He put it in an odd way. He said it felt as if he were trying to beat the shame out of himself."

"That's sick."

"Yes. Strangest of all is the way he suddenly confessed everything. It was almost as if he wanted to be arrested. Amanda said he was limping and had two black eyes."

"Peculiar."

"Isn't it? But there's one other thing which surprises me even more," Modig said.

"And what's that?"

"That my boss, that brooding old grouch, has become a little ray of sunshine."

Bublanski looked embarrassed.

"So it shows."

"It shows."

"Well, yes," he stammered. "It's just that a woman has agreed to come out to dinner with me."

"You haven't gone and fallen in love, have you?"

"It's just dinner," Bublanski said, blushing.

Needham knew the rules of the game even if he did not enjoy it. It was like being back in Dorchester. Whatever you did, you could not back down. If Salander wanted to play hardball, he would show her hardball. He glared at her. But it did not get him very far.

She glared back and did not say a word. It felt like a duel, and in the end Needham looked away. The whole thing was ridiculous. The girl had been unmasked and crushed, after all. He had cracked her secret identity and tracked her down, and she should be grateful that he wasn't marching in with the Marines to arrest her.

"You think you're pretty tough, don't you?" he said.

"I don't like surprise visits."

"I don't like people who break into my system, so we're square. Maybe you'd like to know how I found you?"

"I couldn't care less."

"It was via your company in Gibraltar. Not too smart to call it Wasp Enterprises."

"Apparently not."

"For a smart girl, you make a lot of mistakes."

"For a clever boy, you work for a pretty rotten organization."

"You got me there. But we're a necessary evil in this wicked world."

"Especially with guys like Jonny Ingram around."

He was not expecting that. He really was not expecting that. But he would not let it show.

"You have a good sense of humour," he said.

"It's hilarious. To have people murdered and to work together with villains in the Russian Duma making megabucks and saving your own skin; that's comical, isn't it?" she said.

For a moment he could barely breathe. He could no longer keep up the pretence. Where the hell had she gotten that from? He felt dizzy. But then he realized—and it slowed his pulse a little—that she was bluffing. If he believed her even for one second it was only because in his worst moments he too had imagined that Ingram might be guilty of something like that. But Needham knew better than anyone that there was not a shred of evidence of such a thing.

"Don't try to bullshit me," he growled. "I have the same material you do and a lot more besides."

"I wouldn't be so sure of that, Ed, unless you too have the private keys to Ingram's RSA algorithm?"

Needham looked at her and told himself that this could not be true. Surely she could not have cracked the encryption? Not even he, with all the resources and experts at his disposal, had thought it was worth trying.

But now she was suggesting . . . Impossible. Maybe she had a mole in Ingram's inner circle? No, that was just as far-fetched.

"This is how it is, Ed," she said in a new authoritative tone. "You told Blomkvist that you would leave me in peace if I told you how I carried out my data breach. It's possible you're telling the truth there. It's equally possible that you're lying, or that you won't have any say in the matter anyway. You could get the sack. I don't see any case for trusting you or the people you work for."

Needham took a deep breath.

"I respect your attitude," he said. "But I'm a man of my word. Not because I'm a decent person. I'm a vengeful maniac, just like you, young lady. But I wouldn't have survived as long as I have if I let people down when it mattered. You can either believe that or not. I swear to you, though, I will make your life hell if you don't open up."

"You're a tough guy," she said. "But you're also a proud bugger, aren't you? You need to make absolutely sure that no-one ever gets wind of my breach, whatever the cost. As to that, I'm ridiculously well prepared. Every detail could be made public before you even have time to blink. I don't in fact want to do it, but I *will* humiliate you if I have to."

"You're full of shit."

"I wouldn't have survived either if I was full of shit," she said. "I hate this society where we're watched over all the time. I've had enough of Big Brother and authorities in my life. But I'm prepared to do something for you, Ed. If you can keep your trap shut, I can give you information that will put you in a stronger position, and help you clear out the corruption in Fort Meade. I'm not telling you anything about my breach—only because it's a matter of principle for me. But I can help you get your own back on the bastards."

Ed stared at the strange woman in front of him. Then he did something which would surprise him for a long time.

He burst out laughing. He laughted until he cried.

# CHAPTER 31

# DECEMBER 2–3

Levin woke up in a good mood at Häringe castle after a long conference about the digitalization of the media, which had ended with a big party where the champagne and hard liquor had flowed. A failure of a trade union representative from the Norwegian newspaper *Kveldsbladet* had remarked spitefully that Serner's parties "grow more lavish the more people you sack," and made a bit of a scene, which resulted in Levin getting red wine on his tailor-made jacket. But he was happy to let him have that. Especially since it had enabled him to get Natalie Foss up to his hotel room in the small hours. Natalie was twenty-seven and sexy as hell, and despite the fact that he was drunk, Levin had managed to have sex with her both last night and this morning.

Now it was already 9:00 and his mobile was pinging and he had more of a hangover than he could afford, bearing in mind all the things he had to do. On the other hand he was a champion in this discipline. "Work hard, play hard" was his motto. And Natalie—how many fifty-year-olds could pull a bird like that? But now he had to get up. He was dizzy as he lurched to the bathroom for a pee. Then he checked his share portfolio. It was a good way to start hungover mornings. He picked up his mobile and went into Internet banking.

Something must have gone wrong, some technical mishap he could not understand. His portfolio had crashed, and as he sat there shaking and skimming through his assets he noticed something peculiar. His large holding in Solifon had as good as evaporated. He was beside himself as he went into the stock exchange sites and saw the same headline everywhere:

## THE NSA AND SOLIFON CONTRACTED FOR THE MURDER OF PROFESSOR FRANS BALDER. *MILLENNIUM* MAGAZINE REVELATIONS SHOCK THE WORLD

What he did next is unclear. He probably yelled and swore and banged his fists on the table. He vaguely remembered Natalie waking up, asking what was going on. But the only thing he knew for sure was that he kneeled for a long time over the toilet bowl, vomiting as if there were no end to it.

Grane's desk at Säpo had been tidied. She would not be coming back. Now she sat there for a little while, leaning back in her chair and reading *Millennium*. The first page was not what she had expected from a magazine serving up the scoop of the century. It was black, elegant, sombre. There were no pictures. At the top it said:

### IN MEMORY OF ANDREI ZANDER

And further down:

### THE MURDER OF FRANS BALDER AND THE STORY OF HOW THE RUSSIAN MAFIA GOT TOGETHER WITH THE NSA AND AMERICA'S LEADING TECHNOLOGY COMPANY

Page two consisted of a close-up of Zander. Even though Grane had never met him, she was moved. Zander looked beautiful and a little vulnerable. His smile was searching, tentative. There was something at once intense and unsure about him. In an accompanying text Erika Berger wrote about how Zander's parents had been killed by a bomb in Sarajevo. She went on to say that he had loved *Millennium* magazine, the poet Leonard Cohen, and Antonio Tabucchi's novel *Sostiene Pereira*. He dreamed of a great love and a great scoop. His favourite films were *Dark Eyes* by Nikita Mikhalkov and *Love Actually* by Richard Curtis. Berger regarded his report on Stockholm's homeless as a classic piece of journalism. And even though Zander hated people who offended others he himself refused to speak ill of anyone. The piece went on:

As I write this, my hands are shaking. Yesterday our friend and colleague Andrei Zander was found dead on a freighter in Hammarbyhamnen. He had been tortured, and had suffered terribly. I will live with that pain for the rest of my life.

But I am also proud to have had the privilege of working with him. I have never met such a dedicated journalist and genuinely good person. Andrei was twenty-six years old. He loved life and he loved journalism. He wanted to expose injustices and help the vulnerable and displaced. He was murdered because he tried to protect a small boy called August Balder and, as we reveal in this issue, one of the biggest scandals in modern times, we honour Andrei in every sentence. In his report, Mikael Blomkvist writes:

"Andrei believed in love. He believed in a better world and a more just society. He was the best of us."

The report ran to more than thirty pages of the magazine and was perhaps the best piece of journalistic prose Grane had ever read. She sometimes had tears in her eyes but still smiled when she came to the words:

Säpo's star analyst Gabriella Grane demonstrated outstanding civic courage.

The basic story was simple. A group of individuals under Commander Jonny Ingram—who ranked just below the NSA head, Admiral Charles O'Connor, and had close contacts with the White House and Congress—had begun to exploit the vast numbers of trade secrets in the hands of the organization for their own gain. He had been assisted by a group of business intelligence analysts at Solifon's research department "Y."

If the matter had stopped there, it would have been a scandal which was in some way comprehensible. But the course of events followed its own evil logic when a criminal group—the Spiders—entered the drama. Mikael Blomkvist had evidence to show how Jonny Ingram had gotten together with the notorious Russian Duma member Ivan Gribanov and "Thanos," the mysterious leader of the Spiders, to plunder tech companies of ideas and new technology worth astronomical sums of money, and to sell it all. But they really plumbed the depths of moral depravity when Professor Frans Balder picked up their tracks and it was decided to eliminate him. That was the most astonishing part of the story. One of the most senior executives at the NSA had known that a leading Swedish researcher was going to be murdered and did not lift a finger to prevent it.

It was not the account of the political quagmire that most engaged Grane, but rather the human drama. There Blomkvist's gifts as a writer were on full display. She shuddered at the creeping realization that we live in a twisted world where everything, both big and small, is subject to surveillance, and where anything worth money will always be exploited.

Just as she finished reading she noticed someone standing in the doorway. It was Helena Kraft, beautifully dressed as always.

Grane could not help remembering how she had suspected Kraft of being the leak in the investigation. What she had taken to be guilty shame had been Kraft's regret at the unprofessional way in which the investigation was being conducted—at least that is what she had been told during their long conversation after Mårten Nielsen confessed and was arrested.

"I can't begin to say how sorry I am to see you go," Kraft said.

"Everything has its time."

"Do you have any idea what you're going to do?"

"I'm moving to New York. I want to work in human rights, and as you know I've had an offer on the table from the U.N. for some time."

"It's a loss for us, Gabriella. But you deserve it."

"So my betrayal's been forgiven?"

"Not by all of us, I can assure you. But I see it as a sign of your good character."

"Thanks, Helena. Will I see you later at the Pressklubben's memorial for Andrei Zander?"

"First I have to do a presentation for the government on this whole mess. But later this evening I'll raise a glass to young Zander, and to you, Gabriella."


Alona Casales was sitting at a distance, contemplating the panic with an inward smile. She observed Admiral O'Connor crossing the floor, looking like a bullied schoolboy rather than the head of the world's most powerful intelligence organization. But then all the powerful figures at the NSA were feeling pathetic today, all except Needham.

Needham was not in a good mood either. He waved his arms around and was sweaty and bilious. But he exuded all his usual authority. It was obvious that even O'Connor was afraid of him. Needham had come back from Stockholm with real dynamite, had caused a huge argument and insisted on a complete shake-up throughout the organization. The head of the NSA was not going to thank him for that; he probably felt like sending Needham to Siberia immediately and forever.

But there was nothing he could do. He looked small as he approached Needham, who did not even bother to turn in his direction. Needham ignored the head of the NSA in the same way he ignored all the other poor bastards he had no time for, and plainly nothing improved for O'Connor once the conversation got going.

For the most part Needham seemed dismissive and, even though Casales could not overhear, she could imagine what was being said, or rather, what was not being said. Over the course of her own long conversations with Needham he refused to say one word about the way he got hold of the information. He was not going to compromise on a single point, and she respected that.

Needham seemed determined to milk the situation for all it was worth, and Casales solemnly swore that she would stand up for integrity in the agency and give Needham as much backing as she could if he ran into any problems. She also swore to herself that she would call Gabriella Grane in a final bid to ask her out, if rumours were true that she was on her way over here.

Needham was not in fact deliberately ignoring the NSA head. But neither was he going to interrupt what he was doing—yelling at two of his controllers—just because the admiral was standing at his desk. Only after about a minute did he address him and then in fact he said something friendly, not to ingratiate himself or compensate for his nonchalance, but because he really meant it.

"You did a good job at the press conference."

"Did I?" said the admiral. "It was hell."

"Well, you can thank me, then, for giving you time to prepare."

"Thank *you*? Are you kidding? Every news site around the world is posting pictures of Ingram and me together. I'm guilty by association."

"In that case for Christ's sake keep your own people in line from now on."

"How dare you talk to me like that."

"I'll talk however the hell I want. We're in the middle of a crisis and I'm responsible for security. I don't get paid for being polite."

"Watch what you say . . ." O'Connor began.

But he was thrown when Needham suddenly stood up, big as a bear, either to stretch his back or assert his authority.

"I sent you to Sweden to clean all this up," the admiral went on. "Instead when you came back everything was a complete disaster."

"The disaster had already happened," Needham snapped. "You know it as well as I do."

"So how do you explain all the shit that ended up in that Swedish magazine?"

"I explained it to you a thousand times."

"Right, your hacker. Guesswork and bullshit."

Needham had promised to keep Wasp out of this mess, and it was a promise he meant to keep.

"Top-quality bullshit, don't you think?" he said. "That damn hacker, whoever he may be, must have cracked Ingram's files and leaked them to *Millennium*. That's bad, I agree. But do you know what's worse? What's worse is that we had the chance to cut the hacker's balls off and put an end to the leaking. Instead we were ordered to shut down our investigation. Let's not pretend you went out of your way to stand up for me then."

"I sent you to Stockholm."

"But you called off my guys and our entire investigation came to a grinding halt. Now the rail is cold. And how much good would it do us if it came out that some lousy little hacker had taken us for a ride?"

"Not much, probably. But we can still make trouble for *Millennium* and that reporter Blomström, believe you me."

"It's Blomkvist, actually. Mikael Blomkvist. Be my guest. You'd win a lot of popularity contests if you marched in on Swedish territory and arrested the world's most celebrated journalist right about now," Needham said. The admiral muttered something inaudible and stormed off.

Needham knew as well as anyone that O'Connor was fighting for political survival and could not afford to make any reckless moves. He himself was fed up with working his fingers to the bone, and he loped over to Casales to chat with her instead. He was in the mood for something irresponsible.

"Let's go get hammered and forget this whole fucking mess."

Hanna Balder was standing on the little hill outside Hotel Schloss Elmau in her snow boots. She gave August a push and watched him whizz down the slope on the old-fashioned wooden toboggan the hotel had lent them. He came to a stop near a brown barn. Even though there was a glimmer of sunshine, a light snow was falling. There was hardly any wind. In the distance the mountain peaks touched the sky and wide-open spaces stretched out before her.

Hanna had never stayed in such a wonderful place, and August was recovering well, not least thanks to Charles Edelman's efforts. But none of it was easy. She felt terrible. Even here on the slope she had stopped twice and felt her chest. Withdrawal from her pills—benzodiazepines—was worse than she could have imagined. At night she would lie in bed curled up like a shrimp and examine her life in the most unsparing light, sometimes banging her fist against the wall and crying. She cursed Lasse Westman, and she cursed herself.

And yet . . . there were times when she felt strangely purified and occasionally she came close to being happy. There were moments when August would work quietly on his equations and his number series and would even answer her questions—albeit in monosyllables and somewhat odd terms.

The boy was still an enigma to her. Sometimes he spoke in numbers, in high numbers to the power of even higher numbers, and seemed to think that she would understand. But something had changed. She would never forget how she had seen August sitting at the desk in their hotel room that first day, writing out long winding equations which poured from him with amazing fluency, and which she photographed and sent on to the woman in Stockholm. Late that evening a text message had come in on Hanna's Blackphone:

```
<Tell August we've cracked the code!>
```

She had never seen her son so happy and proud. Even though she had no idea what it was all about and never mentioned it, even to Charles Edelman, it meant the world to her. She began to feel proud too, immeasurably proud.

She developed a passionate interest in savant syndrome, and when Charles was staying at the hotel they often sat up after August had gone to bed and talked into the small hours about her son's abilities, and about everything else too.

She was not sure it had been such a good idea to jump into bed with Charles. Yet she was not sure it had been a bad idea either. Charles reminded her of Frans. They formed a little family of sorts: she; August; Charles; the rather strict but kind teacher, Charlotte Greber; and the Danish mathematician Jens Nyrup who visited them. Their whole stay was a voyage of discovery into her son's remarkable universe. As she now sauntered down the snowy hill and August got up from the toboggan, she felt, for the first time in ages: She would become a better mother, and she would sort out her life.


Blomkvist could not understand why his body felt so heavy. It was as if he were trying to move through water. And yet there was a commotion going on out there, a victory celebration. Nearly every newspaper, website, radio station, and TV channel wanted to interview him. He did not accept any of the requests. When *Millennium* had published big news stories in the past, he and Berger had not been sure whether other media companies would latch onto them. They had needed to think strategically, make sure they were syndicated in the right places and sometimes even share their scoop. Now none of that was necessary.

The news broke with a bang all by itself. When NSA head Charles O'Connor and U.S. Secretary of Commerce Stella Parker appeared at a joint press conference to apologize publicly for what had happened, the last lingering doubts about the story's credibility were dispelled. Now a heated debate was raging on editorial pages around the world about the consequences and implications of the disclosures.

But in spite of all the fuss and the telephones which never stopped ringing, Berger had decided to arrange a last-minute party at the office. She felt they deserved to escape from the hullaballoo for a little while and raise a glass or two. A first print run of fifty thousand copies had sold out the previous morning and the number of hits on their website, which also had an English version, had reached several million. Offers of book contracts poured in, their subscription base was growing by the minute, and advertisers were lining up.

They had also bought out Serner Media. Berger had managed to push the deal through a few days earlier, though it had been anything but easy. Serner's representatives had sensed her desperation and taken full advantage, and for a while she and Blomkvist had thought that it would prove impossible. Only at the eleventh hour, when a substantial contribution came in from an unknown company in Gibraltar, bringing a smile to Blomkvist's face, had they been able to buy out the Norwegians. The price had been outrageously high, given the situation, but it was still a minor coup when a day later the magazine's scoop was published and the market value of the *Millennium* brand rocketed. They were free and independent again, though they had hardly had time to enjoy it.

Journalists and photographers had even hounded them during Zander's memorial at Pressklubben. Without exception they had wanted to offer congratulations, but Blomkvist felt smothered, and his responses had not been as gracious as he would have liked them to be. The sleepless nights and headaches continued to plague him.

Now in the late afternoon of the following day, the furniture in the office had been hurriedly rearranged. Champagne, wine, beer, and catered Japanese food had been set out on the desks. And people started to stream in, first the staff and freelancers, then a number of friends of the magazine, not least Holger Palmgren. Mikael helped him out of the lift and the two embraced.

"Our girl made it," said Palmgren, with tears in his eyes.

"She generally does," Blomkvist replied with a smile. He installed Palmgren in the place of honour on the sofa and gave orders that his glass was to be kept filled.

It was good to see him there. It was good to see all sorts of old and new friends. Gabriella Grane was there too, and Chief Inspector Bublanski, who should probably not have been invited, in view of their professional relationship and *Millennium*'s status as independent watchdog over the police force, but Blomkvist had wanted to include him. Officer Bubble spent the whole evening talking to Professor Farah Sharif.

Blomkvist drank a toast with them and the others. He was wearing jeans and his best jacket, and unusual for him he had quite a lot to drink. But he could not shake off that empty, leaden feeling and that was because of Zander, of course. Andrei was constantly in his thoughts. The moment in the office when his colleague had so nearly taken up his offer of a beer was etched in his mind, a moment both humdrum and life-determining. Memories of the young man flashed up all the time, and Blomkvist had difficulty concentrating on conversations.

He had had enough praise and flattery—the only tribute that did affect him was Pernilla's text: <you do write for real, Pappa>—and occasionally he glanced over towards the door. Naturally Lisbeth Salander had been invited, and would have been the guest of honour had she turned up. Blomkvist had wanted to thank her for the handsome contribution during the Serner dispute. But there was no sign of her. What did he expect?

Her sensational decrypted document had allowed him to unravel the whole story, and had even persuaded Needham and the head of Solifon, Nicolas Grant, to give him more details. But he had heard from Salander only once since then: when he had interviewed her—to the extent that was possible—over the RedPhone app about what had happened out at the summer house on Ingarö.

That was a week ago now and Blomkvist had no idea what she thought of his article. Maybe she was angry that he had dramatized it. He had no choice but to fill in the blanks around the meagre answers she gave. Or perhaps she was furious because he had not mentioned Camilla by name but had simply referred to her as a Swedish-Russian woman known as Thanos. Or else she was disappointed that he had not taken a harder line across the board. It was impossible to know.

The situation was not improved by the fact that Chief Prosecutor Ekström really did appear to be considering a case against Salander: unlawful deprivation of liberty and seizure of property were the charges he had cooked up.

Eventually Blomkvist got fed up with it all and left the party without saying goodbye. The weather was awful and for lack of anything better to do he scrolled through his text messages. There were congratulations and requests for interviews and a couple of indecent proposals. But nothing from Salander. He switched off his mobile and trudged home with surprisingly heavy steps for a man who had just pulled off the scoop of the century.

Salander was sitting on her red sofa on Fiskargatan, gazing emptily out at Gamla Stan and Riddarfjärden. It was a little over a year since she had started the hunt for her sister and her father's criminal legacy, and there was no denying her success on many counts.

She had tracked down Camilla and dealt the Spiders a serious blow. The connections with Solifon and the NSA had been severed. Ivan Gribanov, the Duma member, was coming under tremendous pressure in Moscow, Camilla's hit man was dead and her closest henchman, Jurij Bogdanov, and several other computer engineers were wanted by the police, forced to go underground. But Camilla was alive somewhere out there. Nothing was over. Salander had only winged her quarry and that was not enough. Grimly she looked down at the coffee table, where a packet of cigarettes and her unread copy of *Millennium* lay. She picked up the magazine and put it down again. Then she picked it up once more and read Blomkvist's report. When she reached the last sentence she stared for a while at the new photograph next to his byline. Then she jumped to her feet and went to the bathroom to put on some makeup. She pulled on a tight black T-shirt and a leather jacket and went out into the December evening.

She was freezing. It was crazy to be wearing so little, but she did not care. She cut down towards Mariatorget with quick steps, turned left into Swedenborgsgatan, and walked into a restaurant called Süd, where she sat down at the bar and alternated between whisky and beer. Since much of the clientele came from the world of culture and journalism, it was hardly surprising that many of them recognized her. Guitarist Johan Norberg, for example, who wrote a regular column for *We* and was known for picking up on small yet significant details, observed that Salander was not drinking as if she enjoyed it, but rather as if she had to get it out of the way.

There was something determined about her body language, and a cognitive behavioral therapist who happened to be sitting at a table nearby wondered if Salander was even aware of anyone else in the restaurant. She hardly looked around the room and seemed to be preparing herself for some kind of operation or action.

At 9:15 she paid in cash and stepped into the night without a word or gesture.


Despite the cold, Blomkvist walked home slowly, deep in gloom. A smile only crossed his lips when he ran into some of the regulars outside the Bishops Arms.

"So you weren't washed up after all!" Arne, or whatever his name was, bellowed.

"Maybe not quite yet," Blomkvist replied. For a moment he considered having a last beer inside and chatting with Amir.

But he felt too miserable. He wanted to be alone, so he continued to the entrance door of his building. On the way up the stairs he was overcome by a vague sense of unease, maybe as a result of all he had been through. He tried to dismiss it, but it would not go away, especially when he realized that a light had blown on the top floor. It was pitch-black up there.

He slowed his steps and sensed a movement. There was a flicker, a weak sliver of light as if from a mobile, and a figure like a ghost, a slight person with dark flashing eyes, could be made out.

"Who's that?" he said, frightened.

Then he saw it was Salander.

He brightened at first and opened his arms, but she looked furious. Her eyes were rimmed with black and her body seemed coiled, as if prepared for an attack.

"Are you angry with me?" he said.

"Quite."

"Why is that?"

Salander took a step forward, her face shining and pale, and he remembered her gunshot wound.

"Because I come to visit, and there's no-one at home," she said. He walked towards her.

"That's a bit of a scandal, isn't it?" he said.

"I'd say so."

"What if I ask you in now?"

"Then I suppose I'll have to accept."

"In that case, welcome," he said, and for the first time in ages a broad smile spread across his face.

A star fell outside in the night sky.

## ACKNOWLEDGMENTS

My sincere thanks to my agent, Magdalena Hedlund; Stieg Larsson's father and brother, Erland and Joakim Larsson; my publishers, Eva Gedin and Susanna Romanus; my editor Ingemar Karlsson; and Linda Altrov Berg and Catherine Mörk at Norstedts Agency.

I also owe thanks to David Jacoby, senior security researcher at Kaspersky Lab, and Andreas Strömbergsson, professor of mathematics at Uppsala University, as well as to Fredrik Laurin, digger-in-chief at Ekot, Mikael Lagström, V.P. services at Outpost 24, the authors Daniel Goldberg and Linus Larsson, and Menachem Harari.

And of course to my Anne.

## A NOTE ABOUT THE AUTHOR

David Lagercrantz is an acclaimed Swedish writer and crime journalist. He is the author of *Fall of Man in Wilmslow*, a novel inspired by the life and death of Alan Turing, and coauthor of the best-selling autobiography by international soccer star Zlatan Ibrahimović, *I Am Zlatan Ibrahimović*, which was short-listed for the William Hill Sports Book of the Year award and nominated for the August Prize in Sweden.

## A NOTE ABOUT THE TRANSLATOR

George Goulding was born in Stockholm, educated in England, and spent his legal career working for a London-based law firm. Since his retirement in 2011 he has worked as a translator of Swedish fiction.

## A NOTE ON THE TYPE

This book was set in Minion, a typeface produced by the Adobe Corporation specifically for the Macintosh personal computer, and released in 1990. Designed by Robert Slimbach, Minion combines the classic characteristics of old-style faces with the full complement of weights required for modern typesetting.

Composed by North Market Street Graphics,
Lancaster, Pennsylvania

Printed and bound by Berryville Graphics,
Berryville, Virginia